Acclaim for John Casey's

THE HALF-LIFE OF HAPPINESS

"Funny and fun . . . fast and ferocious. . . . John Casey is marvelous at conjuring up the excitement of a campaign meeting or a boxing match or the repartee of a domestic row. But the precision with which everything is described lets in fear, anxiety, pity, contingency—and that world outside, where you can still smell the earth."

—*The New York Times Book Review*

"Marvelously insightful. . . . It never slackens as it draws us steadily deeper into the psyches of Casey's delightfully and excruciatingly recognizable men and women." —*People*

"I love and admire completely John Casey's *The Half-life of Happiness*. His is the perfect ear for conversation, the perfect pen for exploring the great, painful comedy of American life. As a portrait of a family and of a community, this may be his best book yet; certainly it is impossible to put down."

—Lorrie Moore

"Generous and indelible." —*The New Yorker*

"*The Half-life of Happiness* is riveting: a richly exciting exploration of that turbulent frontier where the personal intersects with the political. Casey is the Trollope of postmodern America." —Amitav Ghosh

"Moving. . . . Few write so believably about truly bright people, or about the dense particulars of family life."

—*Kirkus Reviews*

"Casey's prose shuttles smoothly between American colloquialism, lyrical exactitude, and the lightning wit of the Reardons at home." —*The New York Observer*

"One of the wisest and most prescient novels about the stumblers and survivors of American life I have ever read. A compassionate, funny, ominous story of the breakup of a marriage, seen over the shoulders of a husband and wife, and watched, commented on, and remembered by two wonderful, clear-eyed, no-nonsense children."

—Mary Lee Settle

"Casey's rich novel offers many pleasures—witty dialogue, numerous literary references, brainy characters—but it is most notable for its generous vision." —*Booklist*

John Casey

THE HALF-LIFE OF HAPPINESS

John Casey was born in 1939 in Worcester, Massachusetts, and educated at Harvard College, Harvard Law School, and the University of Iowa. His previous novel *Spartina* won the 1989 National Book Award for fiction. He lives with his wife in Charlottesville, Virginia, where he is Professor of English Literature at the University of Virginia.

ALSO BY JOHN CASEY

Spartina

Supper at the Black Pearl

An American Romance

Testimony and Demeanor

THE HALF-LIFE OF HAPPINESS

THE HALF-LIFE OF HAPPINESS

JOHN CASEY

VINTAGE CONTEMPORARIES

Vintage Books

A Division of Random House, Inc.

New York

FIRST VINTAGE CONTEMPORARIES EDITION, AUGUST 1999

 Published in the United States by Vintage Books, a division of Random House, Inc., New York, and simultaneously in Canada by Random House of Canada Limited, Toronto. Originally published in hardcover in the United States by Alfred A. Knopf, Inc., New York, in 1998.

Owing to limitations of space, acknowledgments for permission to reprint previously published material may be found on paged 517.

Vintage Books, Vintage Contemporaries, and colophon are trademarks of Random House, Inc.

The Library of Congress has cataloged the Knopf edition as follows:
Casey, John.
The half-life of happiness / John Casey.—1st ed.
p. cm.
ISBN 0-679-40978-5 (hc)
I. Title.
PS3553.A79334H35 1998
813'.54—dc21 97-49450
CIP

Vintage ISBN: 0-375-70608-9

Author photograph © Lynne Brubaker

www.vintagebooks.com

Printed in the United States of America
10 9 8 7 6 5 4 3

THE HALF-LIFE OF HAPPINESS

§ 1

For no reason he could think of Mike felt terrific. What had seemed a smaller life in a smaller town now seemed as large as the clear spring sky. He took an extra turn around Courthouse Square and was happy to see faces opened up, even the faces of fellow lawyers, even the faces of those who did not necessarily bargain in good faith.

The pretty tax specialist rang her bicycle bell at him and pedaled by in her slit skirt. He felt no base stirring, nothing but benign sympathy for how good she must feel coasting home with a breeze lifting her hair. During the winter on his walks home he'd often felt peppery grains of lust falling on the plain boiled meat of his day. Now he was full of serene benedictions. Here was another for the tap-dance teacher on her way to class, her springy ringlets crushed under a wool watch cap. (He'd once been unable to resist putting his hands on her hair at a party, and she'd said, "I wish I had a nickel for every guy who does that." Mike's wife had laughed and put her hand in. The tap teacher had said, "Maybe I could get into this." Later Mike had claimed she'd said this looking at him, and his wife had said, "Dream on, buster.") Now the tap teacher saw him and waved. As usual she looked a mess in her street clothes, even a little squat and dumpy in her oversize sweater and leg-warmers. But the first time Mike dropped his daughter Nora off at class, he'd watched the teacher warm up, peeling off layer after layer down to her red leotard and silver tights. She wasn't thin, but trim and compact and, when she moved, as bouncy as a rubber ball. Her leotard was dark red around her short small waist but stretched to pale rose over her hips and cannonball bottom. Now she smiled across the street and yelled, "Nora's doing great!" Mike waved back and dipped his head, a well-behaved, pleased dad.

He dropped by the secondhand bookstore to say hello to the clerk who worked the evening shift, a graduate student from the deep South whose mouth was so wide and full that when she drawled, "Hey there, Mike," and broke into a smile, Mike imagined exquisitely slow hydraulic pressures moving her cheeks and lips.

On his way past Martha Jefferson Hospital, he saw the family doctor, Mary Ames. She looked up and said, "Hi, M-M-Mike." She only stuttered when speaking to grown-ups. With Edith and Nora she was fluent. Mike had a crush on her, but it was high-minded, based mostly on gratitude for how kind and precise she'd been when she'd diagnosed Nora's idiopathic thrombocytopenic purpura. Mike had been wildly alarmed, and Dr. Ames had calmed him, holding his hand and explaining every word. Purpura—bruising. Thrombocytes—blood platelets. Penic—deficiency. Idiopathic—of unknown origin. "There's an old joke," she'd said. "Idiopathic means that the patient's got the p-p-pain, and the doctor's an idiot."

Mike had a theory about his little crushes. Like all lawyers, he formulated lots of theories to justify his clients. His off-the-job theories were to justify his off-the-job habits. This particular theory depended on a distinction between dangerous crushes and harmless ones. Dangerous crushes he compared to aerobic bacteria. They thrived on exposure to the oxygen of possibility: signs of response, opportunity, reported inclination of the crush-object. Harmless crushes he compared to anaerobic bacteria. They thrived in a sealed fantasy but died on being exposed to the open air: a further conversation that placed the crush-object in a taboo zone (family friend, girlfriend of a friend, professional relationship to the family, etc.) or—even more deadly to the fantasy bacteria—a conversation in which the crush-object said something patently stupid, snorted unpleasantly when she laughed, or didn't get the joke.

If he sensed that a crush might contain dangerous aerobic bacteria, there were two solutions. He could invite her home, and the crush would become friendly with his wife, Joss. Mike had used this as an extra prevention with his law associate Ganny, who was now friends with Joss and on his roster of safely adored women. Or he could introduce the crush to his single male friends. He had recently tried this solution for the graduate student with the hydraulic smile. He had yet to hear from his friend Bundy how their date had gone.

Had he carved out an arguable qualification to the Sermon on the Mount? "But I say unto you, that whosoever looketh on a woman to lust after her hath committed adultery with her already in his heart." Matthew 5:28.

For someone who was no longer a practicing Catholic, Mike spent a lot of time spinning Jesuit spiderwebs. But this spring day was too bright to spend niggling and spinning. He looked with affection at the muddy little Rivanna River eddying under the Free Bridge. He quickened his pace on the city-maintained road, past the last store, past Ezra's gym, where the paved street turned away from the river and where a little spur of dirt road led to his own one-lane wooden bridge. He crossed it and caught sight of his house up on the wooded ridge. A ramshackle house, as cluttered as a pharaoh's tomb with things Joss or he might need in middle life. Garden tools, canoe paddles and fishing gear, their daughters' toys and sports equipment, Joss' movie gear sprawled on the industrial shelving in her studio, mismatched furniture. The girls' wardrobes were filled with four versions of clothing: Joss' mother's gifts of *jeune-fille-de-bonne-famille* dresses, Mike's notions of outfits for the great outdoors, and Joss' indulgence of their wish to look like the other kids at school and her own wish that they be the prettiest girls at the peace march. All these things spilled from closets and racks and chests so that the whole house was a series of partly assembled kits for family happiness.

The house, like their marriage, was a place for storing years that weren't ever quite what was planned but which he believed might still be made whole by someone turning up with the missing piece.

◇

Mike was early picking up Nora at her tap class. It was on the top floor of the McGuffey Art Center, an old red-brick public school which the city had given over to an association of artists who paid nominal rent and provided classes and exhibits for the students and citizens of Charlottesville. Mike was the lawyer for the association, whose legal difficulties were minor but whose intramural disputes often needed a disinterested patient audience.

Mike went to Bundy's studio to ask him how his date with the graduate student had gone.

"'Slow hydraulic smile,'" Bundy said. "You got the slow part right. Maybe I'll go for slow when I get to be your age."

Mike said, "I'll bet you got into one of your let's-stir-things-up moods. I'll bet you told her about how to gut a deer. I'll bet you—"

"Nope," Bundy said. "I was as nice as you please. She was—what was that other thing you said?—languorous. She was so languorous when she danced it was like there was a sandbag in one hip and she'd move some and all that sand would pour over into the other hip. And then she'd try again and sag back the other way. I could have boiled an egg."

"Well, maybe you shouldn't have—"

"Slow's not so bad if it's on the beat. She couldn't keep time to a bass drum."

"Okay, okay."

"She did say one good thing. When I took her home she said, 'I suppose you'd like to hear I had a wonderful time.' She waited a second and then she said, 'I had a good time.'" Bundy laughed.

"Okay, okay," Mike said. "I've got a better idea. Come with me to pick up Nora at her tap class. You want someone to dance with, take a look at the dance teacher."

"I've seen her. She comes dragging in looking like a dust ball someone swept out from under the bed."

"Wait'll you see her in her dance outfit."

Bundy came up the stairs, grumbling the whole way. He brightened up at the sight of the color photo on the studio door—the dance teacher in midair wearing silver shoes, red short shorts, an American flag vest, and a top hat. A toothpaste-ad smile.

The title under the photo said: Polly Trueheart. Tap, Jazz, Modern.

Mike opened the door a crack.

From inside there came a screech as harsh as a crow's caw. Then the shrill scramble of a tape rewind.

Polly shouted, "No, don't stop! I don't care how bad it is, don't stop!"

Bundy said to Mike, "Yeah. I'd sure love to go dancing with her."

Mike opened the door wider and caught sight of Nora. The tape hissed and then played the vamp for "Singin' in the Rain." There was a clatter of taps as the line of kids marched forward unevenly.

"You're supposed to be in *two* rows," Polly shouted. *"Don't stop!* Raymond, you're in the back row!"

The kids were carrying furled umbrellas, whose tips they now hit on the floor, blurring the rhythm further.

"Dah DUM du di dum," Polly shouted. "Now turn and . . ."

The girl next to Nora struggled to open her umbrella and got bumped by the boy next to her. The girl turned toward him as her umbrella popped open. Nora let out a high-pitched sliver of a sound.

Nora was sitting on the floor holding her eye. Mike shoved his way to her. He knelt beside her. She wasn't crying but she was whining and panting. He said, "Let me take a look, honey."

She yelled, "No!"

He started to coax her, but she lowered her hand to look at it.

Mike said, "Jesus Christ!"

Nora put both hands over her eye and said, "Dad?"

Mike scooped her up.

In the hall Bundy said, "I've got my truck here. Out back."

Bundy drove them to the emergency room at Martha Jefferson. Nora stayed curled up in Mike's lap, making little noises, but not crying. Bundy jumped out and opened Mike's door and stormed in ahead of him. By the time Mike got inside, Bundy was at the front desk saying, "I'll move my pickup as soon as we see an eye doctor."

Mike managed to get his wallet out of his suit coat and give the Blue Cross card to the receptionist.

When a nurse tried to take Nora, she kicked her hand. Mike was somehow encouraged by this. He said, "Dr. Ames is her doctor. Dr. Mary Ames. But if you can get an eye doctor faster . . ."

Mike turned to Bundy. "It'll be okay, you might as well park it."

Bundy looked all around the room as if deciding who to start with.

An intern arrived and said to Nora, "What's your name, honey?"

Mike said, "Tell her your name, honey."

Nora whispered her name.

Mike said, "Nora."

The intern said, "My name's Sue. I'm a doctor. You want to let me take a peek, Nora?"

Nora didn't say anything. The intern said, "You're her father? Well, let's go right in here, away from all these people, and take a look." She started to lead them to a room but stopped to look at Mike.

Mike said, "It was an umbrella. I don't know if it was the tip or a spoke."

"Uh-huh." She touched Nora's forehead and then touched Mike's. "I think your daddy needs to sit down, Nora."

"In there," Mike said. "It'll be easier for you if I hold her. I did a lot of this in the Navy." He was about to lie wildly and say he'd been a medic, but the intern put an arm across his back and guided him into an examining room.

"Okay, babe," he said to Nora. "The doctor's on the right track here, so we can ease up." His voice was strange to him, floating uselessly in the small room. He sat Nora on the gurney and held her free hand.

He closed his eyes when the intern started to take Nora's other hand away. He tried to make himself look. When he opened his eyes, Nora's good eye was shut and the intern's gloved hands were cupped around the other eye.

A nurse came in and took Nora's other hand, squeezing in against her.

The intern said, "Don't move, Nora. I'll be right back."

Mike said, "This is the hospital where you were born, babe. They'll make sure you're okay."

He touched Nora's back. It was hard as a turtle's.

All this nonsense he was saying was as useless as Bundy's stomping around the lobby.

Mary Ames came in followed by a male doctor who Mike supposed was the eye specialist. When Mike started to ask her what was going on she held up her hand and tipped her head toward the male doctor—it must be the eye specialist, Mike thought, we're all deferring. The thing that the eye doctor had around his head wasn't a reflector, as Mike had taken it to be, but a sort of magnifying glass. The eye doctor swiveled it down and hovered over Nora's eye.

A bony man with a bony face. He hardly moved. He didn't even say "Mmm." Mike had a feeling this guy would say the worst in the same monotone he'd say the not-so-bad.

Mary Ames moved next to Mike, and put an arm around his back and a hand on his arm.

Mike couldn't see anything except the eye doctor's magnifying glass. The eye doctor dabbed around Nora's eye and then hovered some more.

He told a nurse to hold another light to one side. "Up. Now left. Good. Right there."

Mike began to have confidence in the guy's monosyllables.

Nora, who'd been amazingly still, wiggled her feet. The eye doctor said, "Don't."

He didn't even say "Mmm" when he clicked off his light. He said to the nurse, "Prep her. Use my OR. I'll need you and Dr. Akerblad. Page me when Dr. Akerblad gets there."

And he was gone.

Mike looked at Mary Ames. He said, "Isn't he going to explain anything?"

She said, "Mmm, maybe later. I don't think it's *that* serious. If it was really serious I don't think he'd go away. What I saw looked like not a whole lot more than a scratch, but I just got a glimpse. He's very very good."

The nurse had stretched Nora out on another gurney. Mary Ames said to her, "You're not supposed to talk. And don't put your hands near your face. If you'd like me to stay with you, give my hand a little squeeze."

Mike took Nora's other hand and said, "You'll be all right, babe. One thing about eyes is they don't do anything that hurts."

"Uh-huh. We don't want you twitching or blinking, so we make you real comfy. You won't be all the way asleep, but we'll give you something that makes you feel all relaxed and snug. What I saw was a little tear in the skin right near the corner of your eye, and that's the thing you probably feel. Then there's this tiny tiny little scratch that the eye doctor probably wants to just take a look at."

The nurse, Mary Ames, and Nora all swept away together.

Mike still felt the alert nerve that ran through him that had been receiving the staticky rush of Nora's wordless broadcast. Now he'd lost contact. He was in one of Joss' movie clichés now—"Alameida calling *China Clipper,* Alameida calling *China Clipper* . . . Come in, *China Clipper.*"

Joss loved to juggle them for fun. She wished life to be that simple; she wouldn't allow life to be that simple. Now it was that simple—here he was nothing but attention—an attention that was as anxious and helpless as Nora, as precariously flying through clouds. "Alameida calling *China Clipper.*" He thought he should call Joss. Then he thought he should wait to call Joss until he could say, "Look, first off, everything's okay now, but we had a little scare."

And he should see if Bundy was still waiting—of course he would be.

As though he'd been in a bathroom he checked his tie, cuffs, fly, shoes. That reminded him he was a lawyer: was Polly Trueheart negligent in having a room full of seven-to-nine-year-olds tap-dance with umbrellas? Now, there was a cutie-pie who wouldn't be darkening the door of his fantasy. . . .

Bundy was filling the waiting room with his pacing, making everyone nervous with his menacing energy. Bundy said he'd stay and keep Mike company. Mike had to come out and say he'd rather be alone.

Mike called home. Nobody there. Joss might reproach him anyway, say in an iron-hard voice, "Thanks for letting me know." Joss and Bundy had that in common—their reproaches were never gentle. They had only two gears—reproachful high-speed forward or self-lacerating apologetic reverse.

He stood in a corner where he could look out two windows at once. He thought with gratitude of Mary Ames' cooing at Nora.

He wondered if Mary Ames liked treating children because she didn't stutter when she spoke to them. Or had it worked the other way—by caring for children, she'd stopped stuttering with them? Would her gentleness be boring in the long run? When she was giving medical explanations the mix of hard and soft was just right, but what if she never stopped being nice, never showed a tooth?

His occasional fantasy—which even now flickered briefly through his mind—had her saying, "I don't know what's come over me—I feel like a completely different person," so some revision was necessary. But his Mary Ames fantasy was based on the one time he'd said something funny to her and she'd become helpless with laughter, squeezing tears out of the corners of her eyes and choking herself pink. He'd taken her hand and said with mock severity, "Doctor, control yourself," and she'd clung to his hand and laughed some more.

Could this man be alone for five minutes without dreaming about women? Can we forgive him for having a fantasy about his daughter's doctor at the very moment his daughter is going under the knife? It's not a rhetorical question. I know lots of men afflicted in this way who nevertheless lead normal productive lives. I'm joking. I guess I'm joking. But it makes it hard to take men seriously, if they just drift off into fantasy land when things get a little tough. One *problem is that they then want some of their fairy tale acted out for them. And if you do, you can end up one of their thousand-and-one fantasies, as shelvable as all their other videocassettes.*

It's true, the man was genuinely in distress, and because there was nothing he could do, he slipped into a little displacement activity. Would I be criticizing him if he fantasized about, say, boats? Is the problem that our parents wanted us to be perfect, and the flip side (not even a conscious reverie, just a reflex) is we want them to have been perfect at the time they were the potent perfectionists in our lives? Is this just an American middle-class problem? Let's let the boy get on with it.

It occurred to Mike that Joss and Edith might be at Edmond and Evelyn's. He tried that number. No answer. He got a little cross. Where the hell was everyone?

He had one spasm of terrible worry—Nora losing her eye. All right, then, take one of mine. I'm halfway through my life, done all the stuff you need to look good for—college, gone around the world, got married. Now all there is to do is write a few briefs, putter around the house.

He was relieved when the receptionist brought him his Blue Cross card and had some more forms to fill out and sign.

Maybe this was just another trip to the hospital. With the four of them plus the dog there wasn't a month that went by without a trip to some doctor. Just family life—a little wait, a little anxiety, and then you got to go home. A comforting superstition: if enough goes wrong in small ways, it wards off disaster. Just sit here and be dumb for a little while. He picked up a *Ladies' Home Journal* and read it, including the twenty-day shape-up program.

That's what he was doing when Joss came in. She looked like a whirling dervish just standing in the doorway—her swept-back eyes flicking from side to side, her nose jutting, her collar with one cocked wing, the weight of her solid body unsettled. It was his job to calm her down. He tried jauntiness. He waved the magazine toward the corridor leading into the hospital maze and said, "No news yet. Probably everything's okay. Mary Ames is with her, but some eye doc is doing the work."

"What work? What happened? What are they doing?"

It took him a moment to think of where to begin, which made Joss frantic.

He said, "How'd you get here? When I called there was no answer."

"Never mind. Bundy drove by. But what's going on?"

"Okay. Mary Ames thinks there's a little tear in the skin. The skin, right? Not the eye. Maybe a scratch on the eye."

"Thinks? Doesn't she know?"

"The eye doctor did the examination. She was just looking over his shoulder. He didn't say anything."

"Didn't you ask?"

Mike felt dumb. He sighed. He thought of explaining that he was being slow because he'd already gone through the frantic part and now . . . he wanted to be as calm as sleep. He also was trying to think of just why it was he hadn't asked the eye doctor. It seemed to him now that he should have. He finally said, "Mary Ames said that, if it was really serious, he would have said. We didn't really go into it in front of Nora."

Joss looked around the room.

Mike said, "So we have to wait. Want to sit down?"

Joss went off to the front desk.

Sometimes they danced well together, sometimes they didn't.

Joss was talking a blue streak to the receptionist, who was listening amiably.

Mike believed in the essences of things. He had no specific belief, such as Neoplatonism, but he liked the idea of things having deep cores inside which they could retreat to cure themselves of disorder.

Joss looked around the room again, as the receptionist pointed out someone. Joss trotted down the hall, unignorably energetic.

Mike, in spite of his Jesuit schooling, had a Franciscan notion of souls, which is that pretty much everything has a soul.

Joss came back up the corridor, walking briskly but apparently somewhat calmed by whoever it was she'd chased down.

Because Mike had this Franciscan tendency (animism, really, in Catholic robes) he believed that marriage too had an invisible soul that existed independent of Joss and him. He thought that most problems could be solved by waiting, that there was a natural stabilizing grace which would sooner or later reach *them*.

Joss came back and sat down. She crossed her legs and wiggled her foot. She twirled her wedding ring with her thumb.

On a practical level Mike knew that Joss didn't like to be stared at when she was fidgeting. He also knew that she didn't like him to be completely still, because that too implied disapproval. She preferred sympathetic but noncompeting nerves.

In her own calm moods she was very acute about the subtle tyrannies of marriage—the ones she was subject to and, to an extent, the ones she inflicted. In her calm moods she laughed at both of them. She had other moods, however, in which she was a hypochondriac of marriage. She could take what Mike took to be a normal short conversation and, putting it under her microscope, find dangerous bacilli crawling on every word.

For the first ten years of marriage Mike had been able to kid or coax her out of it. Lately he seemed to have lost the knack. Or perhaps the energy.

Once, at a very long French movie which Mike was liking but which was driving Joss nuts, she couldn't help crossing and recrossing her legs. She did this as carefully as she could, but still there was the sound of the upper regions of her panty hose slithering mesh against mesh. Mike finally whispered to her, "You're either trying to get me to leave or you're trying to arouse the man on the other side of you."

She'd laughed. Then she'd said, "Eros wanes." But then she'd laughed again. Nothing like that now. He was too precarious himself. He couldn't get himself to go back to the first stage of anxiety, which Joss was still in.

But just then—out of God knows what secondhand lore—no, it was out of an old *Reader's Digest* in his dentist's waiting room, he saw the double-column page, the pathetic drawing, and—out of his magpie memory—the title, "Doctor, Will My Child See Again?" The crucial fact of that case was that loss of vision in one eye had somehow resulted in loss of vision in the other eye.

He strained to remember the rest of the story. Surely some hope, maybe even a happy ending? But then his memory switched from visual to audio and he heard the dental hygienist call his name, the sound of the *Reader's Digest* plopping on the coffee table with exasperating nonchalance. Then even the audio went blank in the mint-mouthwash smell of the dentist's office.

He grunted a sort of snarl-moan, a noise Joss usually couldn't stand because he could never explain what he meant. Joss took his hand in both her hands, put her forehead on his shoulder. She said, "I'm sorry. You did a great job getting her here, kiddo."

You just couldn't ever tell. He said, "Well, look. I think it'll be okay. Except, boy, are you going to hate the way this eye doctor talks. Mr.

Monotone." Joss lifted her head. She was on the edge of crying but laughed a little. She thought a second, then opened the fingers of one hand and rippled them closed again, which in Naples would have meant "stolen goods" but for Joss just now meant "so long as he does the job."

Mike said, "Yeah."

Leaning their shoulders against each other over the plastic arms of their chairs, for the moment they were as companionably exhausted as if they were dancing at the tag end of a daughter's wedding. What did they know about this guy? They didn't know beans really. So they shuffled gently once more around the floor, dazed but aware of each other, each feeling just how much the other hoped everything would be all right.

◇

It was mostly good news. Nora would have to stay completely still for a couple of days. She'd have to wear an eye patch for a while after that. The "slight laceration" would in all likelihood heal nicely. The tear in the skin might result in a little droop to the corner of her eye, but that could be taken care of later with a little cosmetic surgery. Maybe it wouldn't even be necessary.

Joss wanted to go see her. Mike wanted to sit quietly for a bit. The eye doctor said to Joss, "You can look in, but she's still out. We had to give her a general anesthetic after all." And then he was off. Joss ran him down in ten steps with a clatter of her stacked-heel sandals. "What's her room number?"

"Ask the nurse."

"And I'd like to thank you," Joss said, with irritated correctness.

Mary Ames smiled at Mike and said, "She'll be just fine." She looked at him more closely and said, "Are you all r-r-r-right?"

"Yeah. What's the deal? That intern thought I was about to keel over too."

She took his hand, which pleased him, but it was to take his pulse. She said, "Mmm. You have this far-off l-luh-look."

"Just a long day." He took her hand. "It was very nice of you to stay." Joss was off wandering the hospital; he was filled with dizzy relief. He said, "Have I ever told you how attractive your stutter is?"

This man needs a guardian, a dog handler with a leash, someone. What is it with him? Is he lonely? Then why didn't it occur to him to come home and play with me? Okay—actually I can see he might have burned off a lot of high-octane child-worry. But there's an arrogance here—I remember Dr. Ames and she wasn't all that *great-looking, so did he figure she would be flattered by any sort of attention from the big-suit lawyer? Dad's father was the same way, apparently, flirted his head off around Washington. But that was back in the days of the complete double-standard, when the women wore little capes made of a single fox pelt and they fastened it around their shoulders by clipping the little fox mouth to the tail. The fox head was whole, it even had little fox eyes made of glass. What were these women saying? "I'm a little furry creature"? The actresses all had little furry voices too—Jean Arthur, June Allyson. They used to lean way over backward and lift one foot when the hero kissed them. But Dr. Ames wasn't straightening the seams of her nylons, she was doing her job and being nice, so what's this guy's excuse?*

She withdrew her hand and said, "I think someone must have given you a shot of sodium pentothal by mistake."

It took Mike a second to remember what sodium pentothal did—it made you babble. He blushed.

She patted his shoulder. He shook his head and said, "Look, I just meant . . . I'm very relieved. Thank you."

She said, "Okay. Nora will be awake in a couple of hours. She'd probably like to have you or your wife there then. It hasn't been, mmm, a real painful procedure for her, but she was a scared little g-girl."

Mike said, "It was really good of you to go with her."

"But don't let her talk too much. You do most of the talking, okay? That shouldn't be too hard for you."

All right. Dr. Ames, it turns out, can look out for herself. And handle him. Always a good move with him was to give him a job to do. So now this compulsive lawyer takes out his pocket appointment book and writes himself a memo. I still have a stack of his little leather appointment books—his billable hours to clients and in the same writing "Edith's birthday," "Nora's lacrosse game," "do times-tables with Edith." His client children.

Mike wrote: "Call: (1) Bundy (2) Polly Trueheart (3) Edith—where's Edith? Call Edmond and Evelyn to see—feed Edith."

It also crossed his mind to get some flowers for Mary Ames. He began to laugh at himself and tumbled into visions of his Mary Ames behavior run amok, the finishing touch a note with the flowers that said "S-s-sorry."

Joss showed up and plopped into a chair. "Poor little Ora-Nora. I just got a glimpse of her there breathing like a little fish. They have her hands tied down." Joss blew out her breath, stamped her feet in a short tattoo, and sat jiggling one leg. "I can't stand hospitals."

"Look," Mike said. "She won't wake up for a couple of hours. You want to go home and eat supper? Is Edith at Edmond and Evelyn's?"

"No. She's with Tyler."

Arrangements felt like rain to Mike—even sounded like rain—unsettling if you were out in the open, soothing if you were under your own roof. Back to the house? Edith's supper, Edith would like you to check her arithmetic, and exactly what do we tell her about Nora?—She gets a peculiar anguish when Nora gets hurt. And she has this eye fear—remember how she was about the prince in "Rapunzel" when he gets his eyes poked out in the thornbush? Wait'll she reads *Oedipus*. . . . But then maybe you should be the one to come back here, a little continuity for Nora. Though I don't like to be alone out there without a car. Tyler's going out and he's taking Evelyn's car. Edmond and Evelyn are already gone in Edmond's truck, they're out owl watching.

"Let's just go," Mike said. "We can figure it out when we get home."

An hour at home was an hour at home. He said to Edith, "If it's two miles to the hospital, and I go ten miles an hour on Edmond's bicycle, how long will it take me?"

"Wait," Edith said and began writing with her pencil.

Nora would have told him to get lost. He'd already drilled Edith on her regular homework, but Edith liked to go for extra credit.

"It's . . . five," Edith said.

Mike looked at her paper. She'd conscientiously written "R = T/D." "Look, slugger," he said. "Didn't they tell you Teddy Roosevelt is Dead? TR equals D. Now, the R multiplies on this side, so it has to do the opposite on the other side. So T = D/R. And that's 2/10 . . ."

"That's a fifth," Edith said.

Nora would have said, I got it *part* right when I said five.

"Okay," Mike said. "We're dealing with miles per hour and hours, so it's a fifth of an hour. So, now, how many minutes is a fifth of an hour?"

Edith squinted and then said, "Twelve?"

"Good. That's good. So just remember Teddy Roosevelt is Dead."

"Why are you such a traditionalist?" Joss said. "Why not True Rapture is Delightful? Thelma Ritter is Dowdy? Why not Total Recall is Dumb?"

What? *What?* Eight hours at the office, go to pick up Nora, two hours at the hospital, let's not forget a little math, about to ride a goddamn bicycle back to the hospital . . . and Joss is finding something to criticize? Can't fucking believe it. Can *not* . . .

He held still, except for grinding his molars, until the spurt of anger passed.

"Okay, Edith, get everything squared away. Don't forget to feed Miss Dudley. I'm off."

He's right, right? He could file a motion for summary judgment, case closed, right? But let's enlarge the context. I saw his jaw working, even though Mom was just hacking around. He got all huffy because she tweaked two things he was crazily proud of—his astounding memory and his Dad's-in-charge-when-things-are-really-tough, cool-under-fire, iron-man, I-wouldn't-ask-my-men-to-do-anything-I-wouldn't-do, anchors-aweigh act. He was sometimes funny, but not about that. I see now it was more fragile than it looked. Inside there was a fat little boy who quit his Boy Scout hike because his thighs chafed. A college freshman who quit crew because the coach said, "You're too short for any seat but bow and you're too fat for that." At the time he was only just under six feet and a few pounds overweight at one ninety. The coach figured he'd sting Dad and make him lean and mean. Typical macho-jock mentality. Coach didn't know he was talking to a ten-year-old fat boy. So Dad quit. That would have been great if Dad had let it go for a laugh. But he joined a canoe club and went crazy. It was crazy revenge but also crazy self-humiliation, because canoeing compared to crew was a no-status sport, sort of like learning to ride a donkey because you weren't good on a horse. This wasn't white-water thrills. It was flat-water racing. It's an Olympic sport that no one watches, sort of like archery or badminton. Poor Dad. I call him Dad, but I've got to remember he was nineteen. Two hours a day for two years. He still has his little trophies. And then he saw that he wasn't really going to get any better. I don't know how you know those things, but it came to him. And it came to him too that he just didn't like it that much. The part I love, though, is when he got on a four-man team and they were practicing two hours a day up and down the Potomac, paddling like mad in their genuflect position. Dad was hoping the rowing coach would go by and say, "Hey you—you're just what we're looking for." No. The person who said, "You're just what we're looking for," was a crazy sports doctor who was trying to find a way to measure the body temperature of endurance athletes. For reasons that will soon be apparent he couldn't get rowers or bicycle racers or even runners to volunteer. It shows you what these canoeists were like: The doctor fitted all four of Dad's canoe team with rectal thermometers. They were wired to a machine in the stern that recorded their temperatures and also gave a readout on a screen. So they paddled up and down the river with thermometers up their butts and wires down their legs and the doctor in a motorboat—I somehow imagine him with a German accent—saying things like, "Now ve vill stop and you vill drink a liter of vater."

I wish Dad had told me this much sooner.

Joining the canoe club because the rowing coach was mean to him—that's what he was doing when he rode a bicycle back to the hospital and spent the night on the floor beside Nora's bed.

But the rowing coach didn't ever notice him. Mom had to. If Dad could've had the gift of being right without . . . inflicting it . . .

So where was I in all this? I was being his dutiful daughter (An extra math problem? Let me at it!) who was nevertheless beginning to get angry, not because he was a demanding coach (I loved that), but angry with an anger that started out as self-loathing. Teddy Roosevelt is Dead, the names of the stars, how a pump works. I thought he knew everything, that he remembered everything. And I thought he wanted me to know everything and remember everything too. In a way, that second part is true: if he could have given me what he knew as a painless gift he would have. He didn't mean to inflict pain. He just had no idea about the panic of inadequacy I felt. No—that's not true—when I was eleven I told him how mad I was that he knew everything and I wouldn't ever. He laughed—he was pleased and flattered—and then he said that I was really very smart and that I'd know everything that he knew—and, hey, kid, it isn't everything—when I got to be as old as he was. "Even more," he added, waxing reflective. "Honey, you'll see things in the next century that I haven't dreamed of." So how come none of this made any difference? Leaving aside his implicit little boo-hoo about his being an old geezer on his way to the grave, he gave the correct answer to my kiddie complaint.

Is it that there are some curses that can't be lifted?—Not by common sense, not by love?

The only way to lift them is by another curse. Once, when I came home from college, I got in very late at night, and there he was waiting up, watching TV in his plaid bathrobe. Tired, gray-skinned, some white beard stubble. All alone in the house. He was watching National Velvet—I think he'd been crying. Dirty dishes in the sink.

All squared away, Dad? Everything shipshape?

He was as glad to see me as I'd ever been to see him when I was little. But his lighting up with pleasure didn't light me up.

He said, "Hey, babe, am I glad to see you." Then he said, "I didn't hear you come in."

I'd wondered before if he was a little deaf.

I said, "Where is everyone?"

He looked surprised, as if he couldn't think who I meant. "I don't know," he said. "Oh yeah. Nora's . . . in Washington, I guess."

I was his joy his sweetness his mercy and his hope. And I just hoped he wouldn't start a long conversation. Teddy Roosevelt is Dead, Dad.

I'd been loving a rival (it's not true that only sons compete with their fathers), and it was a long time before that victory, that disappointment, that distaste, and that miserable taunting glee released me. The first curse of being his awed pupil had been less painful. Under that curse we both supposed that I was getting somewhere as he recited to me his instruction manual to the world page by page, while I struggled not to resist, struggled to make my mind a worthy receptacle for his lore.

He wanted to make me more sure of myself and I became more anxious, to enlarge me and I felt dwarfed. So then I wanted him to be less outfitted and armed, to be—as we all used to say—more vulnerable. But when he was, I couldn't help saying to myself, "Boy, is that *not what I had in mind."*

That's the bitter side of that little saying that otherwise seems so sweet—the heart has its reasons that reason does not know. TR = D.

§ 2

Mike and Joss had both grown up in Washington in what at long range would have appeared to be identical circumstances. Joss' father had been a Navy hero in World War II and then, after further service in Naval Intelligence, what the French call a *haut fonctionnaire* in the CIA. Mike's father had been a New Deal politico, not as visible as certain members of the Brain Trust, but an industrious Roosevelt aide, and then a senior member of the Democratic National Committee up through the Kennedy administration. Both fathers had been known for their good looks and charm, and each of them had made an enemy or two by not being able to resist a witty remark at someone's expense.

Viewed at middle range—through a lens of general knowledgeability—enough to qualify a journalist to write a political column, or for someone at a New York cocktail party to qualify as sophisticated about Washington—the two men and their families were distinguishable. Joss' father was a WASP patrician, adored by both Alsop brothers, elegant without effort, and democratic—both middle-range admirers and enviers would have said—out of *noblesse oblige.* When as a young man Mr. Rogers had supported Roosevelt, he too was called a traitor to his class.

Mike's father was Boston Irish Catholic. He went to public high school, served briefly in the Army, skipped college, and became a lawyer. When he supported Roosevelt he was considered a traitor to Irish-Catholic interests. For some Irish-Catholic politicians who had only achieved local power within living memory, the New Deal was a giant rival to their cozy patronage systems.

From 1939 through 1941, up until Pearl Harbor, a great many Irish-Catholic voters were pleased to see England get what was coming to her. Once, when Mr. Reardon was making a speech as a Democratic congressional candidate—pro-Roosevelt and pro–Lend-Lease—a man called out in a jeering brogue, "Are you running for Congress, Mr. Reardon? Or are you standing for Parliament?"

But by the Eisenhower administration (when Mike was a teenager and

Joss in grade school), the two families had friends and acquaintances in common, partly because they shared real interests, and partly because Admiral and Mrs. Rogers had no further use for social aspiration, whereas Mr. and Mrs. Reardon (particularly Mrs. Reardon) did.

By the time Joss and Mike met and fell in love both fathers had retired and, as it turned out, had only a few years to live, the Admiral dying in his sixties, Mr. Reardon at eighty. Both men had a year or two of quiet happiness that took them and their families by surprise. It was much more than being released from work, more even than being released from the combined feeling of responsibility, alarm, and helplessness (the emotion that distinguishes high functionaries from most journalists). They both were given the gift of dissolving their disappointments and mistakes, of distilling their combative energies, as if by alchemy, into serenity.

The Admiral spent his time sailing the shallow waters around the Northern Neck in a very small boat. Alone, and then, after a mild stroke, with Mike. He bought expensive binoculars to watch birds and an even more expensive telescope to look at the stars.

Mr. Reardon became more and more Irish in his old age, a cultural and sentimental atavism rather than political or religious. He read Frank O'Connor and Joyce (except *Finnegans Wake*), and memorized a lot of Yeats.

His dying was as long as the Admiral's had been abrupt, and he had a series of pleasurably argumentative conversations with the young priest who came to attend him. At the funeral mass the priest quoted Mr. Reardon quoting Yeats—"Strong sinew and soft flesh / Are foliage round the shaft / Before the arrowsmith has stripped it. / And I pray that I, all foliage gone, / May shoot into my joy."

Mike and Joss became close in their mourning. Mike had freely loved the Admiral and painfully loved his father. Joss had liked Mr. Reardon and would have loved him if they'd had more time before Mr. Reardon began his outward drift. She had loved her father a lot when she was little; then, for a long time, she quarreled with him, both face to face and possibly more bitterly in his absence. In his last year she was puzzled and tender.

The evening she heard of her father's death she and Mike went to bed early. He woke up in the middle of the night. Joss was sitting upright in bed saying, "Tommy Rogers, little Tommy Rogers." He'd never heard her say her father's name—only "Daddy." "Little Tommy Rogers, sailing out onto the ocean."

It took Mike a while to figure out that she was remembering a story from her father's childhood—at the age of seven he'd taken a boat out all by himself past the breakwater onto Long Island Sound.

Joss began to sob. Mike held her.

Mike's mother died. He in his turn woke Joss up when he saw his mother in the doorway of their bedroom. She was wearing her hospital gown. He called out, "Mommy, Mommy, Mommy!" in a high little-boy voice. He was sure he was awake. He heard his own voice, he felt it in his throat. It also seemed to come from thirty years before, as if it had been wrapped up and put in a trunk in the attic, rediscovered by accident while he was looking for something else.

Joss grabbed his arm, at first in fright, and then to calm him.

For a while these deaths made them old together. Then, when Edith was two, they went to live for a year with Joss' mother in her big house on the Northern Neck. By then each of them had absorbed the other's family life and they had visited and revisited their parents' pasts. Joss and Mike also heard the anthology of stories told by family friends lingering late at the dinner table and addressing Joss and Mike in a way that assumed they were a nice young couple who were not only junior members of the liberal establishment but also junior friends, qualified for intimacy because they carried their parents' scent. This was the close-range view, a blend of detailed perception, projection, and blind feeling, the same view of the young by the old as in any family orbit, the only difference being that the old family friend, in addition to hoping that the young couple preserve the characters of the parents, also hoped that the promising young man would serve a civic purpose. It was an old-fashioned liberal, patriotic, and patriarchal hope.

But after the deaths of the fathers and Mike's mother, sometime during the year Joss and Mike spent with Joss' mother, Mike's sense of things changed. Mike and Joss, having spent a while in shadow, began to feel young again. Mike spent most weeknights on the houseboat they rented—a converted barge. Every so often he would arrive unexpectedly at the house on the Northern Neck. He loved finding Joss, her mother, and Edith together, three distinct flavors of affection.

At the same time he became bored with his job as a congressional aide. It also became clear that the congressman he worked for had a limited future. Among the young people who worked for congressmen, the Legislative Reference Service, and various departments and commissions, the fervors of the sixties became tepid. Some of his acquaintances became cynical. Mike heard himself becoming caustic. Watergate was a triumph of journalism, a corrective victory, but not part of the legislative agenda Mike worked on—admittedly duller stuff by any narrative standard.

When Mike was first working for his congressman, another Democratic congressman from New Jersey came into the inner office. Without waiting for Mike to leave, he said, "There's this professor teaching at a state university. Right in my district. I'm reading this newspaper and I see where this professor says . . ." He held up the newspaper and hit it with the back of his hand. "This professor says he would welcome a Viet Cong victory. I want to get on top of this. I can get to the regents, I got some credit with some people. I can be the one to nail this guy. Get him fired. What do you say?"

Mike's congressman said, "Yeah, you should nail him. But you know what? Academic freedom." He said it as if it were a sour and unfamiliar taste in his mouth. "They call it academic freedom and they'll clobber you with it. What you do is you enter some remarks in the record and get someone else to get after the professor."

A few years later the congressman from New Jersey was presiding over the Judiciary Committee's hearings to impeach Nixon.

In the meantime Mike's congressman, in the common phrase of the other aides with whom Mike ate lunch, had managed to step on his own dick. Mike's congressman had got into a squabble over committee staff appointments with Emanuel Celler, an ancient Jewish Democrat from Brooklyn who'd been in the House since the Hoover administration. Celler won hands down. Mike's congressman, speaking on the floor of the House, said, "The merchant of Brooklyn has taken his pound of flesh."

At the damage-control meeting the senior administrative aide had the idea that they should counterattack, that the charges of anti-Semitism could be rebutted if they could come up with some remark by Celler that was anti-Catholic. "The guy's been talking for forty years. He must've said something. Dumped on some priest, maybe the Holy Father. Mike, get over to the library, go through *The New York Times*. Don't palm this off on your pals at the LRS, you know who I mean."

Mike shook his head.

The senior aide said, "What? This job too big for you? You got a better idea? We're in this together, Mikey." He said "Mikey" when he wanted to needle Mike, which was whenever there was a problem he couldn't solve himself.

Mike said, "Maybe we shouldn't get into a pissing contest." Mike felt greasy—his tough-guy cliché was a lame substitute for saying that the congressman should apologize. "By the way," Mike said, "in the play, the merchant of Venice isn't Shylock. The merchant of Venice is an Italian guy named Antonio."

The senior AA and the congressman said simultaneously: "Nobody likes a smart-ass, Mikey."

So Mike spent the rest of that day and night peering through the microfilm scanner at *The New York Times* and the *Congressional Record*, skimming every speech and interview old Mannie Celler had ever given. At 2:00 a.m., still nothing useful. Mike twirled the knob on the scanner faster and faster, drinking more and more coffee, washing his face with cold water every half-hour.

His congressman had a favorable rating from Americans for Democratic Action and from organized labor, he'd voted for all of Johnson's Great Society programs. He was also childishly petulant, irrational, disorganized, vain, and vindictive. Mike told himself to think of the congressman as a client.

At 3:00 a.m. Mike found Celler's argument against a bill that would require congressmen to disclose all their outside financial interests. Celler, who was still a partner in a Brooklyn law firm, said that this was an unrealistic, puritanical bill. "If this bill passes we might as well say to ourselves, as Hamlet said to Ophelia, 'Get thee to a nunnery.'"

Mike made a note on his blank page. He twirled for another hour and was done. Nothing really. And how had any sane person thought there would be anything? Celler's constituency was Brooklyn, for years a classic three-I district—Ireland, Italy, and Israel.

Mike let himself into the congressman's inner office, took off his shoes, took three belts of whiskey from the congressman's bottle, lay down on the couch with his suit coat over his shoulders. He fell asleep trying to remember the lyrics to Cole Porter's song "Brush Up Your Shakespeare." Joss' favorite line was "If she says your behavior is heinous / Kick her right in the 'Coriolanus.'"

The congressman woke Mike up. He said, "At it all night, Mike? Good boy. So what've you got for us?"

"Nothing."

The senior AA said, "Wake up, Mike." He was holding Mike's notepad. "What's this? What's this about a nunnery?"

"That's all there is. He's not really insulting anyone. The only connection is he's quoting Shakespeare in a half-assed way."

"We'll take it from here, Mikey. You go wash up."

The senior AA drafted a statement—"There was no intent to insult the honorable member from Brooklyn by comparing him to Antonio, an Italian merchant of Venice. His taking offense would be as oversensitive as our taking offense at the remarks the gentleman from New York made referring to nuns in a disparaging way."

But when Mike's congressman called in the congressman from New Jersey to try it out, it didn't fly.

"Nah. No good. Just say you meant no offense, you're sorry you were misinterpreted. Then ride it out. If the press tries to string it out, you stick with misinterpreted, taken out of context. All this fancy footwork, you'll end up on your ass again. And, if it was me, I'd go see Mannie in private and get down on my knees."

After that, whenever the senior AA was criticizing an idea of Mike's, he would say things like, "Watch out for that fancy footwork," or "That sounds like more of your Shakespearean research, Mikey." After a while the senior AA seemed to have convinced himself that Mike had been the chief screw-up.

However, it wasn't the little abrasions of office life that made Mike leave. It was the congressman's suggestion that he could have a job as a staff member of the Judiciary Committee. By then Emanuel Celler had been knocked off in a primary. Mike's congressman had been redistricted, and it looked as if he wouldn't survive. On the face of it the congressman's offer was selfless and generous. Mike said he was grateful and that he'd think about it.

It was when he found that he spent a lot of time trying to figure out the congressman's underlying motive that he became fed up with himself, with what he feared he was becoming. Once that brick came loose, a number of others began to tumble.

Joss had a short film accepted at the Charlottesville Film Festival. Joss, her mother, and Mike drove over from the Northern Neck. An old classmate and canoeing buddy of Mike's took him for a paddle. He kept his canoe on the Rivanna River, downhill from an old warehouse that had been crudely remodeled into a three-bedroom house. It was for sale. The warehouse, two outbuildings, and seven acres of land. Mike took Joss and Mrs. Rogers to see it. Joss was so enchanted with the people she'd met at the film festival that she was blithely ready for everything. Her mother's skepticism made her even more eager. Mrs. Rogers finally said, "Well, at least it's on dry land. That barge of yours is no place to raise a child."

"Or two," Joss said. "And we can't go on using your house as a nursery."

"But of course you may," Mrs. Rogers said, but among the notes in her voice was one of relief.

Mike got hooked up with a couple of lawyers who hired him, Mike thought, rather casually. At the initial interview, after some polite chat, Mike said, "You'd probably like to know why I'm moving to Charlottesville." They looked mildly puzzled. Mike thought at first he'd offended them, that he wasn't the proper one to end the chat phase. He figured he might as well let them know he wouldn't waste time in the office. But he didn't mind being slightly oblique, so he said, "A friend of mine moved from Washington to Pittsburgh. Became general counsel for an aluminum company. I asked him how he liked Pittsburgh after Washington. He said, 'In Pittsburgh they make things.'" Mike paused and then said, "The parallel is only this—I'm eager to deal with clients who have real problems. In Washington I've been working for people who manipulate other people's problems. I'd like a more direct connection to problems."

Both partners smiled and nodded. The younger one—he was only a bit older than Mike—said, "Pittsburgh," and smiled some more.

Mike went to work with a will, and was happy when it became clear that they relied on him to deal with matters that required the firm to go to court. Otherwise they let him paddle his own canoe. Mike thought this was a generous and effective way to keep him hard at it.

It was some time before it dawned on him that (A) they were simply competent lawyers content to graze, (B) they didn't have an overall plan, and (C) they had as cloudy a notion of him as he'd had of them.

The reason they'd looked puzzled when he'd said he should explain why he was moving to Charlottesville was that they thought it didn't need any explanation. They simply knew that Charlottesville was the great good place.

This was not an idiotically smug notion, but it was smug.

They also had a notion that Mike shared their values. This was a companionable view which let things move along for some time without much discussion. What made this companionability easier for them was Mike's notion that he was a guest worker in a land of temporary exile. And of course he was also well trained in the institutional habit of keeping his judgments and doubts to himself.

It took Mike a while to feel that he was no longer being supervised by Jesuit teachers or Naval officers or senior administrative aides.

But his partners did have some expectations. When the younger partner came to the warehouse for supper, he was at first taken aback by the raw oddity of it. He perked up when he saw some of the photos in an album on the kitchen bookshelf. There was one of Mike's father on the rear platform of a train beside an orating FDR. A portrait photograph of Truman inscribed to Mike's mother—"To Polly Reardon—a pretty, intelligent lady"—with a scrawled signature. Mike said, "My father used to joke that my mother put the comma in between 'pretty' and 'intelligent.'"

Jack Ritter laughed politely and turned the page to Eisenhower and

Mike's father playing golf. Mike started to tell the story about his father being one of a series of Democratic officials sent to ask Eisenhower to run as a Democrat, but Jack was scanning the others. He recognized Jack and Jacqueline Kennedy, didn't recognize Allen Dulles with Joss' father, both of them smoking pipes that were exactly like Stalin's curved-stem briar.

Joss said, "The point of that is that Mr. Dulles had a sense of humor, sort of."

"That's John Foster Dulles?"

"No, Allen Dulles. Allen Dulles was CIA, his brother was secretary of state. John Dulles is the one the Democrats made the wisecrack about—dull, duller, Dulles."

"You should get some of these framed," Jack said. "We could hang them in a corner of our waiting room. No Nixon? No Ford? No Carter?"

Joss said, "There's one of Mike with J. Edgar Hoover, and Mike is practically naked."

For a second Jack looked alarmed. Mike said, "I was three years old. At some beach. Look, we're not running for office—we're running a law firm."

Jack shrugged. "We don't mind clients' knowing we've been around the block somewhere besides Charlottesville."

But for Mike the point was to go around the block in Charlottesville.

Joss said, "I'm glad to see you're getting over your Excalibur complex."

"What's that?"

"Have you ever considered that all the older men in your life held public office? Not just your father and my father, but almost all the fathers of your childhood friends. You thought you wouldn't really be a man until you pulled the sword from the stone."

"Well, now I can say what Sam Ervin used to say at the Watergate hearings—I'm just a simple country lawyer."

"Puh-lease."

Joss also teased Mike about how pious he was on the subject of civil rights. "The way you go solemn all over—you furrow your brow, you talk in your slow-motion basso. If I were black all that goody-goody goodness would make me itch." She was delighted when one of Mike's black clients turned out to be Emmanuel Pritchett, known to the carriage trade as a dealer in black-market pheasant and venison. Emmanuel Pritchett was Ezra Pritchett's uncle. Ezra, whom Mike already represented, was a boxer who ran the gym near Mike's house. Mike counseled Ezra on the legal aspects of his business, but had also successfully defended him on a criminal charge. Emmanuel Pritchett was an old fox with easy wicked charm. He showed up at the house one evening with a brace of pheasant. Joss was pleased. Mike said, "Mr. Pritchett, I'm sorry, but you know I can't take these."

"What you talking about?"

"If I take these, knowing how you came by them—"

"I went shooting. What else you think you know?"

Joss said, "Well, *there,*" and took the birds. "Thank you, Mr. Pritchett. Should I hang them a while or are they ready now?"

"I hung 'em a few days. They're ready to roast. Now, don't you go letting 'em dry out in the oven."

They all went into the kitchen, Joss and Mr. Pritchett discussing larding, basting, and stuffing. Mr. Pritchett turned to Mike. "Don't you know your partners been buying from me for years? Everybody in town that likes to eat fine food knows Uncle Manuel's poultry and meat."

"When they come to your place do they ask for chicken?"

"Mostly they do. Some of the new ones, they ask for pheasant, and I tell 'em they must have in mind one of my special free-range roasting chickens. Or they ask for quail and I tell 'em they'll have to make do with my free-range Cornish game hens. Now, if I'm bringing someone a present, then that's a different thing, then I go out and shoot a regular cock pheasant. There's lots of pheasant stray onto that little piece of land I own out in the country."

"And that's what you'll say," Mike said. "I mean if you get nailed one day, and I have to defend you—you'll say that stuff about free-range chicken?"

"What makes you think you'll be defending me? You're just my business lawyer." He laughed and Joss did too. "But don't go on talking about something that's never going to happen. Everybody knows me. Sometimes they call me Deacon Pritchett 'cause I'm a deacon in my church. Sometimes they call me Uncle Manuel on account of how they respect my age."

Joss said, "What would you say if I asked you for venison?"

"You must mean my free-range goat. I raise a lot of goats."

Joss was enchanted. She had a weakness for cheerful scoundrels. Mike's partners were coolly neutral about his eccentric client-list, considered his billable hours passably satisfactory. Mike was pretty sure they were expecting him to bring in bigger game.

The most senior partner, Dickie Mosby, did a lot of estate planning. He was in his fifties, with white hair, but still was called Dickie. One or two Monday mornings a month he asked if Mike had an interest in golf or tennis or riding or bird-shooting. And then he'd describe his own weekend activities at the Farmington Country Club, the Boar's Head Sports Club, or the Keswick Hunt. At first Mike took this as a kindly interest in his health and well-being.

After a year Jack Ritter was clearer, if not more direct. First Jack laid out the sociology of Charlottesville. "There's still a small old Southern town here, the courthouse, the statue of Lee on Traveller, a couple of hotels near the railroad station. Used to be the town was separate from the university, there were cow pastures in between. Used to be the professors of the university were mostly nice old Virginia gentlemen. Then everything began to grow. The university got a whole lot bigger. Admitted blacks during the sixties, women just a couple of years ago. The university bought a lot of famous professors from up north, from all over. The county grew. A while back a lot of rich Southerners came. After them there were rich Yankees, people who owned things like newspapers or radio stations or part of downtown Cincinnati. Anytime you get a community of rich people you get more rich people. And you get real-estate agents, stockbrokers, architects, accountants and psychiatrists, and the like to take care of them."

"And lawyers."

"Didn't I mention lawyers? I thought I mentioned lawyers. I should have mentioned lawyers."

Mike said, "There's a play by George Bernard Shaw called *The Doctor's Dilemma*. Maybe you've seen it."

"I don't believe I have."

"In the play someone asks one of the doctors what his specialty is. The doctor says, 'Diseases of the rich.'"

Jack said, "I admire how widely read you are." He said this slowly, with just enough bitter taste to have it come out as the saccharine equivalent of "Nobody likes a smart-ass, Mikey."

Mike said, "I'm sorry, maybe you weren't through with—"

"That's the most of it. There's more social layers of course. There's a lot of cultural activities of one kind and the other. Your wife knows some of those people. By the way—the kind of movie she's involved with—is that like the movies at regular movie theaters? Or—"

"Not first-run movie theaters, no."

"So she wouldn't know any of those movie people that've been moving into the county?"

"Well, I imagine that, when they're here, they're here to get away from business. But I get the idea. You and Dickie think I could get out and around more."

Jack cocked his head. "That's not *exactly* my thought. Dickie and I have been here all our lives, we're pretty much part of the wallpaper. Some of the bigger firms, it just naturally happens that they have a variety of lawyers. Of us three, you're the one with the difference. Georgetown Law, Washington . . . Another dimension." Jack said "Another dimension" again, lingering as if it were the last chord of his slow movement. He shifted in his chair and said more briskly, "Now, we're just crazy about the way you handle yourself in court. Of course we knew you'd tried cases as a Navy lawyer—before a panel of officers. But you seem to have got the knack of how to talk to a jury."

Mike was annoyed by the word "knack"—an accidental and easy little quirk like being able to tell jokes. Forget the preparation, interviewing witnesses, the discipline of composing a story largely through other people's voices. But equally annoying was Jack's implication that a jury was a single, unchanging, and necessarily inferior entity. An invariable bunch of clucks to be talked down to, unlike a board of officers and gentlemen. Mike's own attitude, if not an unrippled belief in the wisdom of the common people, was at least one of wariness. You just couldn't tell. Even Mike's reading of law-journal studies and mock-trial juries' deliberations and post-trial interviews of real jurors didn't add much clarification. But what Mike had seen of courts-martial (or congressional-committee hearings, for that matter) hadn't shown him that rank or office either improved or diminished the quality of judgment. He occasionally thought he should go into it all in greater depth, a pious resolution that remained as unimproved as his *faute-de-mieux* belief in juries. He certainly knew Churchill's parallel idea—"Democracy is the worst form of government—until you consider the others"—and was embarrassed at how often he'd written it into the speeches his congressman gave. It was a staple of any speech to a graduating class or Rotary Club—along with Santayana's "Those who cannot remember the past are condemned to repeat it."

In the years that followed, Mike thought he might have made a mistake in not having it out with Jack Ritter then and there. His reason for not having it out was that he was still the new kid on the block. What he did instead was to make sure he kept up his share of the business by working a bit longer and harder. He then went his own way of silent semi-compliance, discussing what he was up to as briefly as possible, fulfilling his partners' wishes only in the ways that cost him the least time. One way he was useful was that Jack, and to a lesser extent Dickie, both of whom had been shy about going to court, could now point to Mike as their bulldog litigator, straining at the leash. Mike figured this was enough help that he didn't have to spend as much time courting clients. In some ways his relation to his partners was like that of a husband who's always too busy to talk.

Over several years he served on the Charlottesville School Board, a regional watershed commission, as voluntary counsel for community-action groups, and as a member of the local Democratic committee.

Joss noticed the size of this annex to Mike's life when she read in the Charlottesville paper that Mike was named counsel to a state task force studying the taxation of government pensions. The article listed his other activities. She said, "I see you're still grappling with your Excalibur complex."

"You don't have to worry. If this is Excalibur, it's only the size of a butter knife."

Joss became more sympathetic, as she usually did if he answered by batting back her own figure of speech. She brought him another cup of coffee. She put it down and said, "Is it any fun at all? Or is it like Carter's energy policy?" "Carter's energy policy" was Joss' code phrase for virtuous tedium. Her other code word was "tofu." Joss herself did good deeds—she'd tutored Edith's classmates who didn't read very well and she volunteered at the hospital. But she preferred that good deeds have redeeming narrative value—or at least take place where there were faces.

What Joss and Mike did share by that time was supper at a communal table: Edmond and Evelyn had moved into the cottage and Tyler into the bungalow; Mike hired Ganny and met Ezra at the gym, and Ezra introduced Bundy. At least three nights a week most of the gang showed up, and both Joss and Mike felt these gatherings were the best part of their life. They felt tumbled and squeezed, exhilarated and comforted. There were of course some snarls and yips, minor jealousies and sharpnesses. And there were times when what someone said seemed to pass by without being understood, but much less often than if there were only the two of them.

A misgiving that Mike sometimes had was that all the others were contemplating enlarging their lives. He knew Ganny would move on, ought to move on. Bundy, for all his talk about the impossibility of making a living as an artist, wanted to get better, had days when he knew he was getting better. Ezra was in training for a fight. Tyler had literary visions, academic plans. Edmond was using his Fish and Wildlife Service job to gather material so that he could eventually say something about the nature of nature. (*The Nature of Nature* was Joss' suggested title for Edmond's *magnum opus.*) Mike didn't know what Joss was up to. She didn't like to talk about her work with him, but she came out of her studio with such varieties of expression—one day grim, another day hopeful—that he imagined that she was like the others. Mike felt that his work was more like Evelyn's veterinary practice, but she was like the others in her sense that little by little she was changing people's attitude toward animals. Mike's notion that he had taken a step back in order to move forward, that an ordinary law practice was a preparation for a place in the larger world, seemed to be dissolving. Some days he thought that his dispersed attention to lots of little problems was a healthy dissolution of vain ambition. Other days he thought it was the first sign of middle-aged subsidence and resignation. About once a month, just as he laid his head on his pillow, he had to fight off the thought—Another day nearer to death.

◇

Should I give Dad credit that he didn't mention the dark side of his thoughts to Nora and me when we were kids?

I remember Nora asking him about death. She must have been about six, and she'd furrowed her little brow and was working out the first-grade version of the classic syllogism: "All men are mortal; Socrates is a man; therefore Socrates . . ."

Nora said to Dad, "Your mother is dead."

"Yes."

"So Mom's mother is going to die."

"Yes, but not for a long time."

"So everybody dies."

"Yes."

"So I'm going to die?"

"Yes, but—"

"So I'm going to *not be here*?"

"Well, nobody knows what happens, honey. Lots of people think there's heaven, that your soul—"

"Here!" Nora smacked the sofa cushion. "I mean *here*. I don't care about someplace up in the sky." Dad tried the we-turn-into-earth-and-renew-life number, which had worked for me two years before. That was when the first-grade hamster died. But Nora wasn't talking about class pets, and she wasn't sad, she was furious. She yelled, "So who thought this up? This is the worst rule of all!"

Dad was stunned. I could see in his eyes that he was undone with love for Nora.

I was jealous.

I was cured by thinking that Nora didn't realize how good she was, that she'd blazed up this way by accident. (I was partly right. It was spontaneous, but, then, Nora later played the same scene with Evelyn. To be fair, I have to say that I now know that Nora can replay an emotional scene and risk real bewilderment and pain all over again. More than her ear for imitation, that's what made her a good actress when she grew up.)

Dad recovered enough to soothe Nora in a different way. He said, "Lots of really smart people say what you're saying, Ora-Nora. You'll see. Lots of really smart people worry the way you do. There's a lot of good poems—they write them and then they feel better." Nora was distracted by the flattery. She also may have seen what I'd seen in Dad's face, and that was enough. And she could always tell, faster than I could, when Dad was about to bore her. She said, "Okay."

"There's Shakespeare," Dad said. "And Keats." He squinted, trying to remember. "'When I have fears that I may cease to be . . .' Well, no, that's more melancholy than angry. Oh, yeah. 'Rage, rage against the dying of the light. . . .'"

Nora got up.

I looked to see if Dad had hurt feelings. He didn't. He said, "Okay, then," and touched her head as she went by.

I now see that part of the reason Dad was so moved by Nora was that he was going through his own moody bafflements, which he kept to himself. And which he submerged in work. And he counted work as something that steadied the whole family. (Another of Mom's favorite movie clichés: But I did it all for you!)

I now see that he was moved by Nora because for an instant in her rage she was torn open; and in his sympathy so was he. Those moments of human sympathy were for Dad a replacement for the religious moments of his youth.

During one of the long periods when I didn't come home from California, Dad and I had long talks on the phone. After supper for me, midnight for him. One night he told me this story.

There was a six-month lag between when he got out of law school and when he got his Navy commission. He decided to spend the time as part of a volunteer task force working for one of the few black lawyers in Georgia. This was 1963. At the first conference the lawyers were deciding which of the civil-rights cases were the most important. Dad said to me, "One client wanted me to file a motion enjoining the officers of the court to stop addressing black witnesses by their first names. I said that I thought we had cases that presented more substantial issues. I said, 'On my way down here I paid for my ticket by check and the airline clerk said, "Can I see some ID, Mike?"'

"One of the other young lawyers said, 'At the Greyhound station they called me Mister.'

"One of the young black lawyers said to me, 'I suppose you won't mind if some white man calls me "boy."'

"Mr. Crawford—he was the older black lawyer—held up his hand. He said to me, 'Well, what's a case that you think has more substance?'

"I said, 'There's that jury-selection issue.'

"Mr. Crawford said, 'Yes. What do you see going on there?'

"I said, 'They write the names of prospective black jurors on yellow slips and prospective white jurors on white slips.'

"'Yes. And what'll they say about that?'

"'They'll say they pick the slips blindfolded.'

"Mr. Crawford said, 'And what'll you say to that?'

"I said, 'As long as a mechanism for discrimination is in place, any reasonable person would have to conclude it has some effect. And there's statistical evidence to show that juries are disproportionately white. We're not asking for black jurors on every jury—or even asserting that there's a crooked selection in any particular case. Just that there's this mechanism—'

"Mr. Crawford said, 'That's good.' He looked at the young black lawyer and said, 'Okay with you if we let him write that brief?'

"So I researched the cases and wrote the brief. Mr. Crawford scratched it up, and I rewrote it. Several times. Mr. Crawford filed it and argued it before the Georgia appellate court. He won. In the Georgia court. I was amazed. I thought we'd have to make a federal case out of it.

"Mr. Crawford invited me to his house for dinner. He asked us all one by one. When we sat down to eat, he and his wife said grace and crossed themselves. I did too.

"Mr. Crawford said to me, 'Am I right in assuming you're Catholic?'

"I said yes.

"'So are we. I should have thought of this earlier—we go to Saint Thomas. It's mostly a black parish, but you'd be most welcome.'

"By that time I hadn't gone to mass for a few years, but I said I'd like to.

"Mr. Crawford said, 'When I was little we used to go to Our Lady of Victory. It was almost all white. There was one priest who was famous for how fast he gave communion. He would say *"Corpus domini nostri Jesu*

Christi custodiat animam tuam in vitam aeternam" in one breath, and all the while his hand was whipping back and forth putting the wafers right into one mouth after another.'

"I laughed a little, because I thought that was the point of his story, just a little riff on the holy mutter of the mass. But then Mr. Crawford said, 'When he got to me he said it slower. He took a breath in the middle, right after *custodiat* and just before *animam tuam*. And I'd feel the wafer *drop.* Then he'd speed up again. *In vitam aeternam*. His fingers never came close to my lips. His knuckles never brushed the side of my mouth. You have some experience. Do you ever feel the priest's hand? See if you remember.'

"I knew—I thought I knew what he was getting at, but I felt hypnotized. I felt I should behave like a good witness, answer from my own experience, so I closed my eyes and opened my mouth the way we used to receive communion. And tried to remember. I said, 'I think so. I'm pretty sure. I felt something.'

"Mr. Crawford said, 'It may be hard for you to remember. It's such a small detail.'

"I got his point."

"Dad," I said. "I want to be sure that I get it. You mean he was saying the wafer thing was like calling black people by their first name."

"Yes, but that's not . . . Yes. But what happened to me then was much more than just being shown that one thing. You're right, he was being a sly old Jesuit teacher. But it was more. There we were, we'd won a case together, and then we discovered that we were both Catholics, both part of that historical glacier the church—*unam sanctam catholicam apostolicam ecclesiam.*"

"Dad," I said. "I don't speak Latin."

"One holy Catholic apostolic church," Dad said in his fast footnote voice. "It's part of the Credo, the Nicene Creed." I could picture him moving the phone away from his ear, looking at it impatiently. He said, "Three twenty-five A.D." and got cross with himself. "Never mind about that. The point is that just as I began to think how much Mr. Crawford and I had in common—all the law and all those sacraments, all those Catholic phrases and gestures . . . that kneeling at the communion rail, lifting our faces, closing our eyes, and opening our mouths—I felt as if Mr. Crawford pointed a finger at the ground we were standing on and the ground cracked open between us."

Dad didn't say anything for a while. He gave a little grunt, one of his conversational punctuation marks.

I said, "But, Dad . . . you understood his story."

Dad said, "I did and I didn't. I mean I took it in. It came in and broke loose something I hadn't thought of for years. I saw myself taking communion as a boy. I was eight. I took communion in my blue wool suit and afterward I was standing outside the church and I looked up into the sky and thought I would like to die. I wished to die. If I died right then I'd go straight to heaven. I'd go right into the bliss I felt when I swallowed the wafer, but it would go on and on without all the little things going wrong like my wool pants itching or looking at Mary Hanrahan's curly hair and wondering if Mary Hanrahan liked me. I saw myself, I saw that pious little boy, that little favorite of the nuns. . . . Wanted to die. What an asshole. Little pink flesh in a wool suit. Flesh and no bones. Just flesh and words."

Another pause. Another little grunt. Then Dad said, "And I saw Mr. Crawford as a little boy taking communion. Not so clearly, just a blur until I saw his mouth. I saw him open his mouth wide and squeeze his tongue down to make a big hole for the body of Christ. And being shamed by the priest's fingers avoiding his lips. I say 'shamed,' but what do I know? I understood and I didn't. Shamed? Insulted? Angered? All those words are too crude, they're too awkward to pick out that sliver."

Dad stopped again for a bit. I didn't say anything.

Dad said, "So I sat there. I was twenty-five years old. I had a law degree. I was about to be commissioned in the Navy. I felt insufficient. No, that's wrong. I felt the insufficiency of words, not just my words to pick out this man's exact feeling. . . . I mean, here was this phrase—*Corpus domini nostri Jesu Christi custodiat animam tuam in vitam aeternam*—"

"Dad," I said. "Latin."

"'May the body of our Lord Jesus Christ keep your soul in eternal life.' It didn't matter that I didn't go to mass anymore, I still had all the words, I still loved that sentence. I loved the word *corpus,* I loved the subjunctive verb, I loved *animam tuam.* And now I was learning that they could be degraded by this priest holding back his fingers an inch." Dad made another noise, and I could see the expression on his face—his lips pulled to the right as he gave a little puff out of the corner of his mouth. "And here's the queer thing," he said. "Part of my law-and-dogma brain was coming up with this—'The transmission of grace through a sacrament is not affected by whether or not the priest is in a state of grace.' But that was like some bit of wreckage pulled in by the whirlpool. The other thing I thought . . . the last thing I thought . . . I looked at Mr. Crawford. He must have been nearly fifty. I knew he was a good man. He was certainly the most patient and calm man I'd known. And I thought how terrible it was that for forty years he'd carried this hurt. I'm pretty sure it wasn't hate. But it was a hurt, and it had been preserved in him without decay. I thought that. Preserved without decay, as if it were the body of a saint."

He stopped.

He said, "Look. I'm sorry, babe. I'm keeping you up."

I said, "No, it's okay, Dad. The time difference."

I was about to say that that was one of his better stories, but he might have started another one. Or he might have been encouraged to ask me when I was coming home, and I would have to say, "I *am* home."

Afterward I wished he'd told me all this much sooner. And I thought of him as a little boy in his itchy wool suit, with what he thought was a taste of God in his mouth, wanting to die and go to heaven. And in a strange way it made sense to me why he'd been so moved by Nora's baby rage at death. And I thought of him now, alone in the house, feeling readier to go to bed for having told us both a bedtime story, feeling better because he'd included a mistake of his youth (not understanding the importance of the first-name issue), feeling as if he'd made a good confession. I wondered when he would bring his confessions up to date, up to a time that included me. Dad, you don't have to say I'm good, as serene as Mr. Crawford. You might not even have to accuse yourself of sins. You might only need to acknowledge a few things. You might only need to see what you were like for Nora and me. Even that priest might not have seen himself holding back his fingers.

◇

The eye doctor took off Nora's bandage, said the eye looked good, gave her an eye patch, and sent her home. She had to stay in bed for two more days.

After Mike drove her back, in one of those unspoken family trade-offs, Joss took over fussing over Nora. Mike switched to Edith—got up a little earlier than normal to have breakfast with her—"Get us two working stiffs fueled up and on the job." He went to work a little early and stayed a little late to catch up. He was finishing work when Ganny came into his office wearing a nun's habit.

Before Mike got around to saying anything Bundy came in wearing his old Air Force uniform. Bundy said to Ganny, "Aw no. That's not right."

Ganny said, "What do you think, Mike? I look all right to you?"

"Yeah, you look—"

"You look gorgeous, Sheba. That ain't the problem."

Mike was often put on edge by the way Bundy kidded with Ganny.

When he'd first met her he had said, "Mercy! 'She is black but she is comely.' You are too pretty to be in the same room with."

"That's funny," Ganny had said. "Ezra swore to me you weren't a fool." But she'd seen something interesting behind Bundy's first awkward lurch—perhaps she'd liked his paintings.

Now Ganny said, "What *is* the problem, Bundy?"

"Let's forget the sacrilege for a minute and just think who's going to dance with you, huh? The very disturbed, that's who."

It came back to Mike that tonight was a McGuffey Art Center benefit, a masquerade. He looked at his appointment book and saw that he was supposed to go. The next day the McGuffey board, for whom he was general counsel, met with the city manager. He couldn't remember if he'd told Joss about the benefit. He called her up.

Joss said, "Did it *occur* to you to tell me you'd ordered a wrecking crew this morning?"

"What?"

"Some rednecks with a bulldozer and chain saws." She said "redneck" because another of his pieties was that he didn't like the word.

It took him a second to remember. "Oh yeah. They're there to put in some dead-men to keep the yard from sliding into the river."

"What's this dead-men shit?"

Mike thought he'd gain some time by explaining. "You bury these cross-ties—that's the dead-men—and then run a long piece of pipe out to the bulkhead—that's the front of the retaining wall—"

"Never mind. Why today of all days?"

"I didn't know it would be today. I got the price down by telling them they could come whenever it was convenient for them. It's a small job, so they're fitting it in."

"Well, when *they're* here, *I* can't work."

"Why didn't you go to the library?"

"It's a small detail in your busy life, but Nora is still home from school."

"Oh yeah. Look, I'm sorry about the chain saws and the backhoe—"

"Thank you. Thank you for pointing out it's a backhoe."

"Well, that's what they'd use. Did they finish?"

"No."

"But Nora goes back to school tomorrow, right?"

"Yes."

"Look, there's an empty studio at McGuffey. I'll ask if you can use it. I've got to stop by there now." That was pretty neat. He took a deep breath. "I told you about the benefit, right? I can't remember if—"

"The masquerade party. I thought we decided—"

"That's what I can't remember."

"We were going to skip it. Too hard to get a babysitter on a weeknight and all that fuss about a costume."

"I'm supposed to make an appearance. One of the board members wants to see me about something."

"Well, have a ton of fun."

He said, "I'll just be an hour or so," but Joss had hung up.

Now he *wanted* to go to a party. He'd feel like a fool in his business suit, but what the hell. Then he remembered that his senior partner, who'd thought a few years back that he was going to be made a judge, had hung his premature judicial robes in the back of the coat closet.

Ganny disapproved. Bundy thought it was fine. "That's the son of a bitch who wouldn't let you hang my painting in the conference room. I'm going to get a six-pack. They never have anything but white wine at these damn things."

He caught up with them on the McGuffey steps. He'd bought Mike a toy mallet made of pink foam rubber. He said, "Here come da judge, here come da judge," and bopped Mike on the bean.

A plump city councilman whom Mike had never liked said, "You three going as the Mod Squad?" and hiked up the steps.

"What's that?" Mike asked.

"It's an old TV cop show," Ganny said. "With a cute integrated threesome."

"That fat Republican."

"Never mind, Mike. I'll tell you what the women at the massage parlor said about him." One of Ganny's clients was a massage parlor on Route 29 North. They had an industrial-size washer-drier for all the towels they went through and they'd invited Ganny to do her laundry with them. As they folded and ironed their towels they chatted about their clients—no names, but not hard to figure out. There had been four masseuses, but three of them got together and fired the fourth because she wouldn't follow the rules.

Ganny had been amazed at their elaborate code of conduct. "It's pretty much of a geisha operation. The men park in garage slots with these fluffy-string curtains so you can see there's a car inside but you can't read the license plate. The clients get real attached to a particular woman, bring her presents. Most of the time they just get a rubdown and get to talk and flirt. And if they get something else, the rule is hands only. That's why they fired the fourth one. They said she used to get carried away and 'do things' and they couldn't have that. Among other things, it might get back to their boyfriends—who apparently don't mind as long as they follow the code."

At first Mike didn't want to hear about the clients. Then he was willing to hear a story or two with no names. Then he retrenched to just not hearing about his brothers at the bar. He said he had trouble enough keeping a straight face with some of them as it was.

Bundy popped one of his cans of beer and took a long pull. Mike remembered another reason he'd come. Bundy hated these benefits. Since he was one of the artists with a McGuffey studio, he said it felt no better than begging. He sometimes got a little surly. At the Christmas benefit he'd got a snootful and stood by the door saying, "Gawd bless you, Gawd bless you. We 'preciate it. Hit's a act of mercy for us poor artists."

Now Mike said, "Bundy—don't do anything to . . ."

Bundy put on his wide-eyed look and Mike gave up. Maybe Ganny could take care of him.

There were buffet tables in the hall, and one of the big first-floor studios was cleared out for dancing. Mike found one of the board members. He was trying to eat peanuts, but his Groucho nose kept hitting his hand. Mike asked what he was supposed to take a look at. It turned out Polly Trueheart wanted a speed bump on the driveway to the parking lot. "She has a point," the board member said. "But we thought maybe you could, you know, review what the traffic regulations are now and talk to the city manager and keep her apprised."

"Yeah. You don't want to pay for a speed bump, so you'd like me to bury her under some paper."

"That would be a great help."

"Okay. Is she around? Is she wearing a mask?"

"She's in her Uncle Sam costume."

Mike took a step away and then turned back. "Oh. Is that third-floor studio still empty? If I could borrow the key just for the day . . . I can pick it up in the office. In fact, I'll come by here around ten and I can pick up whatever memo you've got. One-stop shopping . . ."

Now everybody ought to be happy. Mike sidestepped through the crowd in the huge hall. No Polly.

He tried the studio where there was dancing. It was dark except for a black-light strobe that made all the dancers look like they were in a jerky old-time movie. He thought he saw Ganny—just the light hitting her coif, which blazed a purplish white. He made his way around the edge of the room. Most of the studios were divided in two, but this one and Polly's were undivided, enormous spaces with high ceilings. You had to use a pole with a hook to lower the top window sashes. Two walls were mirrored and gave another version of the kaleidoscope of faces, white collars, shiny buttons, white cuffs. Mike had to keep one hand on the dancers' barre to make his way, peering for the white stripes of Polly's red-and-white vest. The speakers for the music were so big and the volume was turned up so high Mike could hold his hand up and feel the bass throb in the middle of his palm. In this artificial deafness and occulting half-blindness he was about to give up when he bumped into her. She was sitting in a corner with her knees to her chest. He'd bumped into her shoulder with his shin, looked down, and recognized her silvery shoes in a couple of flashes. He had to kneel so she could hear him. She took his hand and got up. He led her back the way he'd come. When they got to the hall she kept on going to the end, through the swinging doors to the stair landing. She picked up the hem of his robe and dabbed her eyes.

"Well, I got your message on my answering machine about Nora being okay," she said. "That was nice of you. I mean, for you to remember that I'd be worried too. So she's all right."

"Yeah. She's home now. She goes back to school tomorrow."

"I wasn't going to come to this party, but I was just miserable sitting home. I was just sick about it. I've been in a weird way the last couple of days." She looked up at him for the first time. "I canceled class," she added.

"Yeah, well, look, about this speed bump—"

"This accident has been an eye-opener for me." She clutched Mike's forearm. "Oh my God. I can't say anything right." She laughed. "I'm just still so nervous."

She held on to his forearm as though it were a banister and she was having a hard time getting down the stairs.

Mike said, "The board and I are taking up the whole traffic-safety question with the city. But look. Are you sure you want a speed bump?"

"Well, I like speed bumps. I hate cars. I only drove here tonight because I'd look funny walking down the street."

"You look great, Polly."

"I want to *do* something, I want to make McGuffey safe for children."

"Yeah, but it's going to—"

"Maybe I want a big wooden bar that goes up and down. With stripes and a yellow light."

He suspected that this was more than her usual ditziness, which he liked. He began to think she was drunk. Ever since Joss had begun to have crazy reactions to liquor he'd become nervously prim about drinking. He said, "The problem with a speed bump—"

"Or those strips that make your tires sound funny when—"

"Maybe you said 'speed bump' when you really just want an umbrella stand."

Polly laughed for about two seconds, then she looked stunned. "Oh," she said, "You do think it was my fault."

Mike felt terrible now. He said, "No. Look. Polly. I was just trying to kid you out of the speed bump. It was dumb of me."

"I wouldn't blame you for hating me."

"Polly, I certainly don't," Mike said, but Polly began to cry. "Polly, kids have accidents. Even when everything's perfect, kids just have accidents. We should be glad this wasn't anything terrible."

"Oh, you don't under*stand*. You're just being . . . reasonable." She took a handful of his robe and wiped her eyes.

"What else can I say?"

"You could say something that doesn't sound like a scary lawyer."

Mike said, "I'm not a scary lawyer. I'm—"

Polly began to cry again. She took another handful of his robe. "Can you forgive me? Or am I just hateful?"

He patted her back and said, "Polly, Polly. It's okay."

"Don't pat," she said. "Just hug."

She rolled her cheeks dry on his chest. Mike held on to her back and she stopped crying. He thought he'd have to send the robe to the cleaners.

Polly said, "Good," and put her face up to be kissed. Maybe she meant it to be her cheek, but her mouth was the closest part. It was a short kiss, a little plump push.

The second was much bigger and even plumper.

Polly smoothed his cheek and moved away. One side of his brain thought this was just as well, the other moved him forward. She stepped backward up onto the first step of the stairs. "There," she said. "Now I'm so tall you'd better watch out."

She laughed and grabbed the lapels of his robe.

This was a new mood, but she was still giving the robe a workout.

"Hey," she said, "watch this."

She ran almost halfway up the flight of stairs toward the landing, threw her arms in the air, and launched herself down. Her trailing foot hit each step with the Bell-tone tap of her silver shoe.

She skidded on the floor but kept her feet. "Whoa!" she said and plucked his hand out of midair. She sank slowly into a split and beamed up at him. She held up her other hand for Mike to lift her. Halfway up she said, "There's a nun there." Mike was looking at the top of her bosom squeezing up from her red-and-white vest. By the time he turned, he only saw the door settling shut.

"It's Ganny," he said. "She's my associate."

This made Polly laugh. She was still laughing when he got her all the way up.

"I feel so much better," she said. "Want to dance?"

"I can't really dance," he said. "Not to keep up with you. I have this bad knee."

"Aww, poor little kitten."

She patted his chest and tugged his robe straight. He hoped she would say "poor little kitten" again, because then there might be a third kiss. He didn't know what had happened to the good-sense side of his brain—it had stopped transmitting.

Polly looked around with a suddenly puzzled expression—What the hell am I doing here?

She said, "Oh my. Someone left a little lipstick on you." She lifted a fold of his robe, licked it, and scrubbed his mouth.

This was such sudden good sense from another station it made him laugh. "Well, you're a fun couple," he said, "but now it's time to play *You Bet Your Life*."

"What?"

"I guess you're too young to remember *You Bet Your Life*."

"Mmm," she said, and opened the swinging door. She pinned it against the wall with her butt. If he'd thought of it earlier, he could have found out if it felt as good as it looked.

"So," he said, "I'll be in touch about the speed bump."

"You sure you don't want to dance?"

"Yes."

The board member with the Groucho Marx half-mask caught Mike's eye and gave a little approving nod. So that was where *You Bet Your Life* came from. But kissing Polly Trueheart?

Polly went into the dance studio. Mike thought he'd have a bite to eat. A venial sin. That's all we have here, a little venial sin. A funny little venial sin that a little white wine would wash down. But who would have thought Polly Trueheart was such a great kisser?

In the bright big hall, elbow to elbow with the patrons of the arts, Mike ate raw vegetables for health (though he slathered them in some kind of sweet dip), then went for the egg rolls. There were only four left or he would've gone on and on.

"Any more of these?"

"I'll go check for you, sir."

He looked around to see if Ganny or Bundy was free to give him a ride home. He was about to give up and walk—he could use the walk—when he thought he saw the swirl of Ganny's black habit through the door to the dance floor. Maybe Bundy was still with her. Now that he knew where everyone was, time for another glass of wine. It seemed better than usual, or maybe just colder.

He plunged in again to the dance studio. Polly was in the middle, dipping and turning, visible as a barber's pole in her red-and-white glitter-striped vest. She really was a nifty dancer, showy but right on the beat.

He got stuck in the corner, hemmed in by a guy in a bathing suit and clay-white body paint and a girl in a Playboy Bunny costume (I'm cute enough to be a Bunny, but I'm an artist, so I'm not a Bunny, I'm making a statement). They were wildly athletic dancers who nevertheless were being gradually squeezed toward his corner. He saw a flash of nun coif on the far side. He put one arm over his head and hunched around the edge. He tapped Ganny on the back. She turned and he saw she wasn't Ganny. Whoever she was, she must have thought he wanted to dance, because she took his hand. He leaned close to her face. "I'm . . . sorry. I thought you were . . . the other nun."

"I *am* the other nun."

Mike laughed and nodded. He realized she might have missed his nod in the oscillating light, so he leaned forward again to say "I meant Ganny," but she put her mouth to his ear and said, "And Sister knows you've been a bad boy."

Mike pulled back. He saw three or four flashes of her white domino and pale-white cheeks and receding chin.

He said, "That's what all the sisters used to say. They also used to say they had eyes in the back of their head."

"Think I'm bluffing? Dance with Sister and she'll tell you how bad you've been. She might even absolve you."

"Nuns don't hear confession."

"Maybe I'm a priest. Maybe you'll find out if we slow-dance."

They were almost slow-dancing already—a kind of whooping-crane courting dance—sticking their heads side by side each time one of them said something. He put an arm around her waist, which was far inside the unbelted fall of her habit. Her coif touched his cheek and she danced into him lightly. She seemed made of small loose bones. She didn't snuggle up to slow-dance, but kept close enough so that they kept touching here and there. She swayed away with her upper body, pushing away with her hand on his shoulder but brushing the inside of his knee with her leg.

She moved back and said, "Maybe we should get Polly Trueheart to dance with us."

"There wouldn't be room."

She laughed a dry laugh in his ear. "We could squeeze her in."

Mike said, "Actually I'm looking for the other nun."

"You *are* a bad boy."

Mike shook his head. "She's my ride home."

The nun moved away into the crowd, but she kept Mike's hand in hers, trailing him in her wake. He looked around for Ganny, realized she might not be there, the other nun might be the only nun he'd seen, and therefore the nun that Polly had seen at the door.

She moved back toward him, and he moved back to the edge of the floor until he reached the barre. He thought it might be time to find Ganny and Bundy. This nun gave off some slithery little thrills, maybe he could fox-trot her around once more, and then walk it all off on the way home.

"This is my friend Polly Trueheart," the nun said. "Maybe you all know each other already."

There was Polly, clutching a half-full plastic cup that was amazingly unspilled.

"Drink your wine, Polly," the nun said. "We want to dance with you."

Polly took a sip and said, "Mike doesn't dance. He's got a knee." She laughed and tried again. "He's got a bad knee."

"We'll hold him up. But you have to dance real slow."

Polly looked undecided, but perhaps she was just thinking what to do with her drink. She drank it and dropped the empty cup.

Mike said, "Polly, you have a ride home?"

"That's sweet, Mike," the nun said. "But don't you worry, after Polly's had a little more fun someone'll drive her home."

Polly said, "I'm not going home. I'm going to dance till I drop."

"You look great, Polly," the nun said. "I love your hair. You have exuberant hair." She ran her fingers through the back of Polly's hair. She said to Mike, "Have you ever felt exuberant hair?"

Mike said, "She wishes she had a nickel for every guy that did that."

"But you're not very exuberant, Mike," the nun said. She trailed her other hand through Mike's hair. "Does this hair feel exuberant to you, Polly?" Polly put her hand up and brushed Mike's hair over his ear. The nun said, "Any exuberance?"

The nun's hand trailed down Mike's cheek and paused in midair in front of their faces, flashing in the light, particularly the silvery nails. It touched her own cheek, then Polly's.

"If we all just put our fingertips on Polly's cheeks we could lift her right up. It's like magic." Her hand picked up Mike's lightly, like a woman guiding the hand of a man lighting her cigarette. "You've got to get closer," she said.

Mike put his other hand on Polly's cheek. He thought of an excuse—it's just a parlor game.

"Very lightly," the nun said. "Just the fingertips. And you have to close your eyes, Polly."

The nun was now in back of Polly, her face to one side of Polly's face. "Lift your arms, Polly," she said, putting her fingertips on Polly's upper arms and brushing upward. She said, "Are you feeling lighter, Polly? Lighter and lighter?"

Polly said, "Uh-huh. I could get into this."

The nun put her fingers in between Mike's. She put her mouth close to Polly's ear. Mike put his head closer to hear. Polly put her hands on his neck. The nun said, "You can't tell which fingers are which, can you, Polly?" She slid her fingers out from between Mike's and then down to Polly's throat, back up to Polly's chin, then around Polly's mouth, brushing past Mike's fingers to Polly's forehead. "Mmm," she said into Polly's ear, "I wish I were you. You feel . . . pretty exuberant." She reached over Polly's head and took Mike's cheeks in the palms of her hands. "Now you should give her a little kiss on her forehead. Just one." She kept her hands on his cheeks as Mike's lips touched Polly's forehead.

"She's getting lighter," she said. "Do you feel lighter, Polly? Way inside you feel light as air."

She turned Polly slowly around once and then another half-turn so that Polly ended up with her back to Mike.

Polly said, "Whoa—I don't feel as light now."

The nun said, "That's because you thought about it." She slid Mike's hand under Polly's left breast. "I can feel your heart beat when you think. Now we've got to make you light again."

Then she was gone.

Polly stretched her arms up in the air. She said, "I don't know. . . . Maybe you should do some more face tickles."

Mike couldn't tell if Polly was still drunk, half hypnotized, or going along with a good time. But what was his excuse?

Polly leaned back against him and lifted his hand to her cheek. She said, "Lighter, lighter, lighter."

But the exuberance was gone with the nun. He was about to put his arm around Polly's shoulder and tell her the nun had gone but she was a good sport and they should go see if there were more egg rolls. Then the nun was back with a swarm of people. Some of them stooped, some of them came round beside Mike. The nun said, "Keep your eyes shut, Polly. You're going . . . up."

Up she went, with hands all over her, at least four to each leg and two to each arm and some guy one-handing her butt like a waiter with a tray.

Polly didn't make a sound as they carried her away across the floor.

Mike stood there. So that's all it was, not much harm in it after all.

The nun took his index finger in her hand. "Who had fun?" she said. "Was it pretty Polly?"

Mike didn't say anything.

She took his forefinger in her hand and said, "Didn't you get a little exuberant there, Mike?"

Mike was still too off balance to say anything, but he felt himself inwardly pulling back from her tone, though it still had its feathery teasing, its seductive ripple.

"Shall we get Polly back?" she said. "I'll bet she's still got some exuberance in her."

"I don't think so," Mike said.

"Polly's plump and pretty but I know what you mean." She'd been speaking into one of his ears and then the other, pausing to look at his face, as she went from side to side. Now she hovered in front. He tried to see her eyes, but her mask cast a shadow.

"Are we dancing?" she said, sliding her fingers off his finger. "Or are you being a scary lawyer?"

Mike said, "You must have listened in for the whole show."

"I thought when a girl says you're a scary lawyer you're supposed to kiss her. Or do I have to cry too?"

She was a gobbly kisser, or at least this kiss was a gobbly kiss. He liked it, he even liked the way she made up for her thin lips by gobbling.

The nun said, "Let's go see what they're up to with Polly."

But then there was a commotion in the hall. Mike went to the door and heard Ganny's voice calling "Bundy!"

Bundy had squared off with some guy. Bundy had his Air Force belt cinched around one hand with the buckle across his knuckles. The guy was backing away, but not giving up. The guy said, "We should get this drunk out of here," with a confidence that probably meant he had a couple of buddies.

Mike got in between them, said, "Hey, Bundy." Then he turned to the other guy, held both hands up, and said, "Give us a little room here, we don't want—"

"Just so long as you get this crazy redneck out of here."

Mike heard Bundy start and turned toward him, but Bundy was already chest to chest with him and moving. Mike toppled backward. He saw Ganny coming down toward him, and then his head hit the floor.

The next thing was a ring of faces that made him dizzy, for a second he thought he was being lifted into the air like Polly Trueheart.

Bundy was lying belly-down beside him. Ganny was sitting on Bundy's back. Bundy said to him, "Blessed are the peacemakers, for they shall end up on their ass—"

Ganny said, "Shut up, Bundy."

Bundy said, "We could have had a good time if you'd come in on my side."

Ganny said to Mike, "How's your head feel?"

Mike said, "Let's get out of here."

"You lie still." She held up a finger and told him to look at it while she moved it back and forth. "Keep your head still," she said sharply. "Just move your eyes. Now open them real wide. . . . I guess it's just a bump." She said to Bundy, "Your truck out back?" Bundy nodded. "Then give me the keys."

"If you'll get your ton of meat off of me."

"You're asking for me to put you to sleep, sugar."

Ganny, Mike thought. I should have hung out with Ganny.

Ganny led them both out, one on each arm. When they got outside he looked up at the steeple clock and saw with dismay what time it was. But as the clockworks began to strain and clink just before chiming, he thought with relief that the Bundy incident covered him. That was what he could report to Joss. He thought of Francis Parkman—"It is the nature of great events to obscure those great events that preceded them." Parkman was talking about the American Revolution eclipsing the French and Indian War, but, hey, it could work for a small-town lawyer obscuring his venial sins. True—Polly Trueheart had tap-danced her way out of harmless fantasy into an actual stairwell for an actual kiss. Or two. All right—over time a little spark built up, then suddenly the poor girl was in distress, there was some confusion of real feelings with boozy masquerade-party foolishness. And Polly Trueheart shuffled off to Buffalo, not part of a consequential plot.

Now, the nun—the other nun—was a different matter. She produced a lot of plot at short notice. Or was it just a lot of stage effects in search of a plot?

Was that it? She was too edgy in her searching? Or was she edgy in the sense of going over the edge of his limits, even his fantasy limits? Or was she too edgy in the sense of having the edge, staying one step ahead, having the last word? That thought made him wince. Was he guilty of scripting his fantasies so that the woman's last word had to be a joyful cry of submission?

He gave that a quick no. Then wondered a minute. No. All an ordinary guy wants is a little shared enthusiasm. Dancing in step. ". . . Our lips are blending in a magic kiss—or two or three." Okay. So he liked his fantasy as operetta, not a Pinter play. Save perplexity for real life. Plenty of perplexity in his daily rounds.

The steeple bell stopped chiming. Ganny unlocked her car door. Bundy resisted when Ganny said she'd drive him home. He finally said, "Okay, okay. If you say so, Sister."

The *other* nun, it occurred to Mike, unsettled him because she infiltrated his little scene with Polly, absorbed their energy. This was disquieting not so much because of her petty larceny but because she jiggled the frame of what was really going on. She must have had her eye on Polly in her glittering costume and visible moodiness. Must have tailed Mike and Polly off the dance floor, down the hall. Peeked through the little safety-glass window in the door to the stairwell. Would she then have been content to savor what she'd seen? Or would she have latched on to Polly or him even if he hadn't mistaken her for Ganny? Very likely—he floated into her, but then she got her hands on Polly. And after that it was as though Polly and he were subjects in her fantasy.

He wasn't sure whether to admire her bold stagecraft, or to be irritated at the intrusion, or to be alarmed by the teasing hint of blackmail ("Sister knows you've been a bad boy"), or to feel sympathy for her neediness, her craving for other people's "exuberances."

Mike got into the back seat of Ganny's car and rolled down the window.

He hadn't solved the other nun, but he knew that his own order of fantasy was knocked out of kilter. All that stuff about the anaerobic bacteria of harmless fantasy was flimsy nonsense. Not a barrier between fantasy and flesh.

So. Take a breath of night air. Go home and be private. Go to the office and be public. Roll up the window.

Mike had the house to himself for a while. Joss and the girls and Joss' mother went on a trip to Baltimore to get a little cosmetic surgery for the sagging corner of Nora's eye. (Joss' mother knew just the doctor.) Then they went to the Northern Neck.

Mike was supposed to join them there for the weekend, but he began to think he should stay home, because Miss Dudley wasn't up to the car ride. She was acting a bit more addled than usual. She'd bark to be let out, forget why she'd gone out, bark to be let in, and then piss on the floor.

Miss Dudley was a delicately balanced issue between Mike and Joss. Earlier Joss had raised the question of whether Miss Dudley should be put down. Mike had sighed and said, "I don't know."

Joss had said, "She has more and more days when she just doesn't have anything going on. Even her good eye isn't so good anymore, it hurts her to move, and her breathing is getting worse."

"I know, I know," Mike had said. "But I just don't know."

Joss had put her hand on his arm and dropped the subject. It was one about which they were their most companionable. Mike had got Miss Dudley before they were married. Miss Dudley had lived on the barge with them. She'd moved to Charlottesville with them in her prime, been a matronly dog with the girls when they were crawling and learning to walk, and grown old as they grew up. Joss was grateful for her attention to the girls. Now Miss Dudley's only pleasure as far as anyone could tell was lying near Mike and thumping her tail when he said her name.

The evening before he was due to go to the Northern Neck, Miss Dudley came down toward the river, where he was cutting saplings with a brush hook. When he started back she couldn't get up the slope. She whined when he picked her up, but then settled over his shoulder, her forepaws pressed on his back—helpfully and affectionately, he thought. He asked Evelyn to look at her. Evelyn had become Miss Dudley's second-favorite person, an attachment that had given Joss a grain of jealousy, which soon dissolved, chiefly because Evelyn's relationship to animals was just the sort of pure eccentric passion that Joss admired.

Evelyn was a very good vet, but she lost a few clients when she turned out to be blunter than they expected, lulled as they'd been by her South Carolina voice.

One owner said to Evelyn that his dog was incontinent and it was time to "put him to sleep."

"It's not sleep," Evelyn said. "And he looks pretty healthy to me. Maybe you should walk him more often before you ask me to kill him."

Now Evelyn said to Mike, "She's just worn out. I think what she'd like best is to sleep on your side porch when there's a little breeze. And just listen to you talk. If you want to read to me, I'll come over. I'll bring our yellow bug-light."

Evelyn didn't like to read books by herself, but she loved to be read to. Edmond read professional journals to her, Tyler read poetry, and she sometimes came over to listen to Mike read to Edith or Nora. They refused to be read to together, but they liked it when Evelyn sat in.

Mike liked her a lot. She was severely and finely pretty, but since Mike had known and liked Edmond for an even longer time, he had a solid taboo he didn't even have to think about. "Chastity based on male-bonding," as Joss pointed out.

Mike was one of those who were pleased to find out how difficult Evelyn could be. She was a blend of Southern politeness and abruptness. She was particularly abrupt about animals of course, though she never used the phrase "animal rights," because she disliked the dulling of feelings by legal language. She also was an early antismoking activist, and had several other rectitudes that would have made her a puritan except that she liked her pleasures, which were very specific, and she was free about demanding them. For Mike, her vegetarianism was offset by her delicious nine-vegetable stews, and she was always happy to bring over a kettle-full. She also loved parties, wine, pie, and ice cream (she made better ice cream than Mike). From time to time she declared a rest day for herself if there was nothing urgent at the animal clinic. Joss thought Evelyn had a retrograde view of the relations between men and women, but she admired the way Evelyn made a good thing of it. Evelyn's view of her husband's duties, for example, included his warming her cold feet against his stomach in bed, and carrying anything that weighed more than ten pounds.

Evelyn had the same queenly relationship to Tyler, who, being single and an academic, would sometimes be available to read to her on a rest day.

This was all too gallant for Joss, who, early on, said to Mike that Evelyn's rest days (which Joss referred to as "the vapors") corresponded to Evelyn's periods. Mike furrowed his brow. Joss looked at his face and said, "Oh, you're right—Saint Evelyn doesn't have periods."

And at first Joss also blamed the men for conspiring to indulge Evelyn, for mounting this elaborate buffoonery that Joss suspected was somehow to the men's advantage. Then Joss herself became very fond of Evelyn, and Evelyn's feeling for Joss turned out to have a sharp electric current that suited their friendship very well.

If there was any disloyalty to Joss in Mike's affection for Evelyn it was that he once thought that Evelyn, of all the people living on the property, had the best array of feelings for everyone else, and that her capacity for unselfish affection, for delight in the others as they were, was steadier than anyone's. As this thought came to him it seemed innocent, but as he thought about it more he realized that it was also a lament for Joss' increasingly unpredictable explosions of anger. Mike reminded himself that Joss' explosiveness also made her funnier and wilder in ways that he sometimes liked. If she lashed out at him (and sometimes at Tyler), if she withdrew from Edith and Nora to avoid lashing out at them . . . he could stand it. He gave himself credit for stoic endurance, for waiting Joss out. He sometimes worried that this was a deadening tactic in the long run (though it worked very well in his business life), that some elasticity in him was being compressed beyond its ability to bounce back. He also worried that Joss wanted something from fighting that he couldn't provide, some rhythm of hurting and getting hurt that would have left her feeling better than one-sided out-of-control rage. Maybe it was the verbal equivalent of Bundy's monthly bar-brawling, something that Mike found just as puzzling and alien.

Now Mike called Joss at her mother's house. Joss was in a good mood. Nora's little plastic surgery had been easy, they were all having a good time. If Evelyn thought Mike should stay with Miss Dudley, then he'd better obey. Joss even laughed a little at this. Mike asked if Joss and the girls might drive back Saturday so they could all spend Sunday in a peaceful way at home.

"You think you could make it by nine or ten?" Mike asked. This was code, since for some time Joss had been refusing sexual advances after 10:00 p.m. The girls went to bed at nine, so there was a narrow window of opportunity.

"That could be," Joss said. "But don't get your hopes up. You know how hard it is to get the girls to bed when it's not a school night."

Mike knew he could improve his chances if he said "I love you" or even "I miss you," or anything approaching what Joss called "poochy affection."

"Well, give it a shot," he said. "I still know how to show a girl a good time." He was warming up to something a little less jaunty when Evelyn came in with a book and the bug light.

Evelyn said, "Is that Joss?" and got on the phone. "We *miss* you," she said. "We miss you something terrible. And I can't wait to see the girls. And give my love to your mother. Mike's about to read me the end of *Tarka the Otter* and I know it's going to make me real sad, so you all get back just as soon as you can and cheer me up."

When Mike got back on all he could say was, "It's me again, your tongue-tied middle-aged American male."

Joss snorted, which meant "Don't I know it."

Mike was about to take another stab at it but Tyler came in singing "'When the moon hits your eye like a big pizza pie, that's *amore*!'"

Joss said, "Sounds like quite a party."

"Must be," Mike said. "Tyler can't carry a tune in a bucket. See you soon."

"So long, kiddo," Joss said.

After Mike hung up, Tyler held up his hands and said, "News flash. I've found love. I have kept a green bough in my heart and at last the singing bird has lit upon it."

"Well that's real nice," Evelyn said. "But you'll just have to wait to tell us more, 'cause Mike has to start reading to Miss Dudley and me. You're welcome to sit with us."

"Where's Edmond?" Tyler asked.

"Watching some ball game on TV." Evelyn didn't like professional sports on TV.

"See you all later," Tyler said, and went to join Edmond.

Halfway through the last chapter Evelyn began to cry. Mike offered to stop, but Evelyn said, "Go on, go on." Tyler and Edmond came up, and Edmond got in the hammock with her and held her hand. "This *is* real sad," Evelyn said.

When it was over, Evelyn ran off to her house and came back with a quart of her plum ice cream. She served everyone and encouraged Tyler to tell them about his new girlfriend, but she was still having sniffles for Tarka the otter.

"There's a real otter in the Rivanna," Edmond said to Evelyn. "Three miles above the dam. We can go see him."

"You all can meet her Sunday morning," Tyler said. "I'll make brunch."

Mike had been planning to dig in his garden Sunday, put in some more azaleas. Maybe he could bag his usual Saturday morning at the office, get some green boughs in before Joss got back. Maybe the singing bird would light on them.

Joss and the girls rolled in Saturday night at half past nine. Miss Dudley even got up and made her way down to the car. Nora wanted to take her new bandage off to look. Edith was a little withdrawn, but too tense to go to bed, so Mike decided to show Joss the new azaleas by flashlight, but on the way he caught a whiff of beer. He stiffened but caught himself. He said, "I guess you stopped for supper on the way."

"Yeah, and I had a beer. One goddamn beer."

Mike shone the flashlight around the bushes, but his heart wasn't in it.

Joss said, "Pretty. Very pretty. I see you've been a busy boy."

When she was in bed, Edith wanted to hear the end of *Tarka the Otter.* Mike said it was too sad, it had made Evelyn cry, but he promised to read it the next day. Edith said, "But Evelyn cried at the end of *Charlotte's Web* and I didn't."

"This even made Miss Dudley cry."

Edith said, "Do dogs really cry?" and Mike sat down on her bed. The kid wanted to have a conversation.

When he got to their bedroom Joss was in the bathroom. He heard the click of her diaphragm case.

"Hark!" he said.

"Hark yourself," Joss said. "But you better hark fast because . . ."

Mike used one of Joss' favorite grade-B movie lines, from a World War II cheapie with a Boston private eye. "'Come outta theah, you smaht Japs. We've got you surrounded.'" He added, "I'll give you a back rub. You don't have to pay me back."

"My. You are a victim of fluid backup."

So it was one of their ironic fucks. That was okay just so long as everyone was happy. Afterward Mike told her about Tyler's new girlfriend. "You'll meet her tomorrow," Mike said. "Tyler's making us all brunch." But Joss was asleep.

The next morning the girls came in and woke Mike up. They said, "Miss Dudley's lying down and there's a fly walking on her eye."

Mike put on his pants and went out barefoot, the girls trailing shyly after him as though there was a strange visitor in the yard. Mike felt Miss Dudley's shoulder, and then closed her eyes. He put his hand in her mouth. The girls asked if she was dead. Mike said, "Yes. She wanted to see you and so she waited until you got back." Then he began to cry. He leaned over her, running his hands over her fur, cleaning away the dust.

The girls were astonished. Joss was alarmed for them. But then they tentatively put their hands on Mike's shoulders, made grown-up soothing noises, and said exactly what their grandmother would have said, "It's just not fair, is it. It's just too unfair."

Mike seemed to ignore them, which annoyed Joss. He went and got his Navy bridge-coat and wrapped Miss Dudley up in it, with just her muzzle sticking out. She weighed nearly seventy pounds, so Mike had to struggle to his feet after he scooped her up. The girls followed him into the woods. Joss stayed on the porch, her mouth pursed, sad herself but mainly worrying about the girls.

Mike reappeared. Joss said, "Are they all right?"

"I need a mattock—you seen the mattock?" She looked puzzled. He said, "It's got a mattock on one side, a pick on the other." He held up his hands in a vague way, and, after concentrating a bit, dove them together to form a point. Then he said, "It's over at Tyler's." He started off for it, but came back to put on his sneakers.

She asked, "What are the girls doing?"

"They're out there," he said. "They're finding a big rock."

She waited for him to ask her to come. He got the mattock and came by the porch again to pick up the spade. She wasn't annoyed with him anymore—he looked too far off—but she was still worried about the girls. She said, "They've always known her. It's the end of an era," and this startled her. Mike was too remote to have a conversation.

After a half-hour the girls came back. Nora said, "I think it'll be a while. He's digging a humongous hole."

Joss went to the edge of the woods and listened to the noise—she could picture how absorbed Mike was from the regular rhythm. Mike liked doing things like digging holes until he hurt. He could stand a lot of self-inflicted pain, but was a baby about surprising pain. Once he got his finger caught in the hole of a baby-wipes container. It had pointed plastic bits sticking inward around the hole out of which you pulled the baby wipes. The points were to snag the second one apart from the top one, whose tuft was poking out. There hadn't been a loose one, so Mike had stuck his finger in. The plastic points bent in, but when he tried to pull his finger out they stuck into the flesh. By the time he woke Joss up with his yells and she'd come trotting through the dark, he'd unscrewed the top and was dancing around the bathroom with a big blue ring on his pointer finger. He pushed his finger in deeper in the same direction the plastic points were bent. Of course it just made it worse when they got to the fattest part of his finger. He said, "Ah! Ah! Ah!" and banged his free hand on the wall.

She said, "What?"

He said, "Get the scissors. No, the wire-cutters, the pliers with the wire-cutters. They're in my jacket, the jean jacket. Ow, shit, ow! I'm going to sue these bastards!"

She couldn't find his jean jacket, so she came back with the kitchen scissors. When he yelled at her, she yelled back, "I'm trying to help!" He held out his finger and she began to hack at the blue plastic. He snatched his hand away. "You're making it worse. Give 'em to me."

With a lot more crying out, he cut the ring. They both examined his finger. It was puffed up and reddish. He smoothed it with the fingertips of his other hand. It went back almost to normal.

Joss said, "Is it bleeding?"

"No, it's not bleeding," he said ferociously. He added, "These things are worse when they don't bleed." Then he became embarrassed.

Joss tried to keep on being sympathetic. "Does it still hurt? Does it hurt as much as a gorilla biting you?" This was the family formula for measuring pain.

He threw the sliced plastic ring on the floor and jumped up and down on it. She stepped back. He said, "I'm being funny now. I'm making light of it."

She said, "I'm going to see if the girls woke up."

"If you ever tell anyone about this . . ."

She laughed.

"I'll deny it," he said. He laughed a little.

She said, "I wonder. If Tyler or Bundy or Edmond had been here, would you have made such a fuss?"

Later she thought that he hadn't ever pondered a remark of hers with such seriousness, with such stopped-in-his-tracks consideration.

Finally he grunted and said, "Maybe not." He grunted again and said, "No. I only yell for you."

So, when she listened to him burying his dog, she thought of him just after he got his finger free from the baby-wipe top. Had it been love she felt then? She'd certainly known him then. She'd liked him then. For a while now she hadn't known him or liked him. She didn't know if she loved him.

She listened to him grunting to himself as he dug a hole for his dog, and couldn't rid herself of the oppression of having to say the right thing, of making an effort at sympathy that he would deal with too quickly, either brushing it aside or gulping it down whole.

It was at that moment that Tyler drove up, blew his horn, and came striding up to the house saying, "Everybody up! Banquet! Banquet breakfast!"

Pell-mell, she thought. It's Mike who likes it all pell-mell.

Tyler had a young woman with him. When she got out Joss saw with irritation that she had a ribbed knit dress that was tight but didn't look tight. Or maybe it looked tight but wasn't. In either case she had a wavy-noodle figure, and was wearing very narrow Italian shoes.

"So where's Mike?" Tyler said. "Joss—this is Bonnie."

"How do you do," Joss said. "Mike is burying Miss Dudley."

Tyler genuinely slumped. He said, "That's terrible. Oh, that's terrible! Does Evelyn know?" He turned to Bonnie. "Miss Dudley is Mike's dog. Oh my! She was old, but this . . ."

Bonnie said, "Ohh . . . Mike's . . . dog. I thought . . ." She spoke with what Joss thought was affected slowness even for a Southerner.

Tyler said, "Evelyn is going to be just heartbroken." Joss realized how irritated she'd been the first time he asked about Evelyn.

She said, "So much for the banquet breakfast."

Bonnie came over and put her fingers on Joss' arm. "Mmm, I'm real sorry. I don't want to . . . intrude. Maybe it'd be better if Tyler and I just slipped away."

Joss realized she was being wheedled, but since not even the girls had made an effort over her, she thought she could do with a little sugary wheedling.

Evelyn and Edmond came up. Edmond was all smiles. He shook Bonnie's hand. "Well, this is a real pleasure. Tyler's been bubbling over. I mean even more than usual."

Meanwhile Tyler told Evelyn about Miss Dudley, and she began to cry. She cried without a sound, without moving, and with her usual perfect posture—her head high and still, as if there was a thread from her crown to the sky, her fine hair straight down the middle of her back and tears running straight down her cheeks.

Joss thought she herself was having either an anxiety attack or a vision. She looked at all these people who appeared so perfectly themselves, but they seemed strange to her. But perhaps *she* had changed, become heartless. Edmond, who'd been in one of his depressed periods, looked suddenly wide awake, sensitive, alert to his wife and feeling a concoction of emotions that Joss knew would be delicious if she could taste it. Tyler's ball of cheerful energy had bounced once in the yard and not come down—it hung in the air, a cherub over the scene. Evelyn was a Pre-Raphaelite picture of her beautiful feelings. Then Mike appeared at the edge of the woods, pick-ax over his shoulder, his chest smeared with red clay and sweat, his own red handprint on his baggy white shorts. His muscles were pumped up from digging. He would have seemed attractive to Joss if he weren't so alien. His eyes squinted as he came out of his cave. He looked like a Neanderthal in an American Museum of Natural History diorama of the Stone Age. He too was turned to a statue of his feelings in this garden of monsters.

Joss felt she was the only one who saw it all. But *all* she could do was see. This cold clarity scared her by its lack of normal feelings, but of course there was a thrill, a scary thrill to her 3-D frozen vision.

Bonnie whispered to her, so close she felt the breath, "You look a little desperate. Why don't we just go inside and make ourselves some coffee?"

Joss touched her own ear, the only part of her that felt real since the rest of her had turned to glass.

Bonnie said, "Mmm? Just let them . . ."

The girls ran out. Nora yelled, "Dad! Is it ready? Did you move the rock? Should we change?"

They grew quieter as they got closer to him. Joss barely heard Edith say to Nora, "We should just wear normal clothes."

Bonnie said, "So these are your wonderful girls! Tyler's told me about them." She wasn't touching Joss, but Joss felt touched in a cozy way. Bonnie said, "Maybe you can tell me what's really going on here," and steered her inside.

§ 3

I taught for a while in a California high school for the gifted. The students were gifted, all right, but they weren't curious. They lived in a world enclosed by their own age group and between their houses and the surf. They moved easily. They figured out how to be gifted mainly because it was the least hassle.

One of the class periods was labeled Guidance and Enrichment. During the fall of their senior year it was for filling out college applications. The rest of the time it was bullshit.

One year I made them read novels and flunked the 60 percent who only saw the movie. The principal retested them and they all passed.

So the next year I just told them stories. About my family. Twenty years before and across the continent—it was like science fiction for most of them. After a bit I began to think they were right—it was science fiction. But they liked it—they didn't have to *read* it, and I brought in pictures, among them a picture of the interior of our house.

"It looks like a warehouse."

"I saw that in film history—*Diva*."

I told them it *was* an abandoned warehouse.

I showed them the picture of the McGuffey masquerade ball that had run in the alternative newspaper. It was of Dad on his back, Ganny in her nun outfit sitting on Bundy and apparently wagging her finger in Dad's face.

"I don't know . . . maybe a film noir of *Going My Way*?"

I showed them a picture of Dad and Mom, Nora and me, Edmond and Evelyn, Tyler and Bonnie, Ganny, Ezra, and Bundy in the garden plot among the other houses. No Miss Dudley. Dad had his beard and Tyler still had his beard, so I knew exactly when it was.

"That's you!" The kids said, "You grew up in a hippie commune?"

That made me laugh, but I could see what they saw.

They tried to figure out who the people "looked like," meaning which movie stars. They couldn't do it, the people didn't look enough like any of the seven ways to look.

"You know what's wrong with you guys?" I said. "You're too high-concept. You don't really see people who don't 'look like someone.' The problem with labels and clichés is they stop you from thinking any further. They're inert."

One of the girls said, "Stanislavsky said that." She was taking acting. I didn't like her.

I said, "Is he right?"

"I guess so. I don't know."

I said, "Maybe you're right. Maybe it's better not to have an opinion."

In an aside to the boy next to her, she said, "What's *her* problem?"

I wasn't being as sarcastic as she thought. My problem was that I was becoming aware that I had inherited Dad's prodigious memory (just as he was beginning to lose it)—as though it were some premature ghost of his that had blown across the country and possessed me. I found it hard to deal with. Mom found it spooky too.

Not only was I able to remember stuff from my own life, I was getting flashbacks to Dad's life . . . to his flashbacks of his father's life. I could imitate Grandpa's voice—or, rather, voices—he used to do lots of voices when he told stories. I got the stories from Dad, but I could do his father too. It came up because Mom asked me to tell her about conventions, as in Democratic National Conventions. The list started coming out of my mouth and into the phone. Nineteen twenty-four. Deadlocked. "Alabama casts its twenty-four votes for Oscar W. Underwood." Grandpa Reardon is a messenger boy to Al Smith, who is in a back room chewing a cigar with his feet on a desk and says to Grandpa, "Tell 'em they can stew in their own juice." And on through the New Deal, World War II. In 1948 Grandpa, still in a sense a messenger boy though by then a national committeeman, is sent to ask Senator Alben Barkley of Kentucky if he'd like to be Truman's vice-presidential candidate. Barkley knew the offer had gone around some. He said, drawling it out in his beautiful Kentucky voice, "Col-l-d-d biscuits. It's cold biscuits."

Grandpa loved that line. He laughed. He liked Senator Barkley. He said, "I'll tell the President that. He'll like it." But they had another cup of coffee and Grandpa said, "You know, Senator, in a month—hell, in a week—no one'll remember how cold the biscuits were."

Mom said to me, "My God. I'd forgotten cold biscuits, but you're right, pooch. This is scary, this is like DNA. This is like when you learned to talk. You learned to talk after we'd moved to Mom's, but when you began to talk it was about living on the barge."

"That's not eerie, Mom."

"It was to me."

"Mom—"

"You were so little and you'd open your mouth to talk and there'd be the barge and boats and airplanes and the river. There was this demon movie camera in you. And now it's happening again."

She was getting emphatic and cooing in a way that was going to make her cry after she hung up. To chill her out some, I said, "It's just that I've been reconstructing Dad. I just happen to be going over the material."

"But I thought—"

"No, this is okay. It's . . . relaxed. It's almost fun."

But the truth was that even the old stuff made me sad, and when I got to—not my own memories but peeling away my own to try to let in others'—it was painful all over again, not scary and crazy, but painful. Sometimes it was like going to the burn-treatment clinic center, getting in the saltwater bath and having them pull away skin—dead skin and skin that wasn't so dead.

In a way I needed the shallowness of my teenage students to offset my own unease at finding canyons and abysses in me. I liked their not caring very much about anything. One of them asked me if she should go to college.

I said, "You're bright. Why not?"

"The way you talk, college won't really, like, get me a job. It'll just make me worry about more stuff. I really don't want to worry about stuff that happened before I was born."

"If you could be sure you could spend your life shopping or laying out on the beach without getting a wrinkle in your forehead, I'd say go for it. But once you start to worry, it's better to worry about everything. You can find solace in the strangest places."

She said, "Huh?"

"Did you read the novel where the guy says, 'History is a nightmare from which I'm trying to awaken'?"

"I don't think so."

I sometimes think these guys are speaking a language that doesn't have the words "yes" or "no." Like Irish (*there's* a bit of Dad-lore).

I said, "It doesn't matter. Sometimes history is a nightmare and sometimes it's solace. At least my father said it was comforting—it replaced poetry for him. 'Emotion recollected in tranquillity.'"

"Mmm."

I put it another way. "You get to see your own life in a long shot."

"If you say so . . ."

"Look. Go to UCLA. A bunch of your friends are going. It's fifteen minutes from the beach. You'll meet some real grown-ups. With luck, something'll rub off."

I felt tender toward her, but it wouldn't have interested her to hear about it.

I liked her honesty too. When I asked some of them about college, they gave Miss America answers—I'm going to college to achieve world peace.

Praise should be hard. As hard as love. Hard to give, hard to accept. In her up moods, Mom gushed all over me. Dad filled me up with lore and advice, and then made me eat a dessert of praise. It would've been better if they were stingier. Better defined as to who they were and who I was.

I once saw a questionnaire that Mom filled out. Dad had kept a copy because he liked Mom's answer to the question, "Who were your parents?" Mom wrote, "My mother was music, my father was law."

I'm still working on my questionnaire. I'm more fearful than Mom. I've been into space sometimes. Certain distances can terrify me.

Look at that picture of the gang in the vegetable garden: Dad and Mom, Nora and me, Edmond and Evelyn, Tyler and Bonnie; Ezra, Bundy, and Ganny.

Leaving aside the dragon that is about to chomp down on some of them, even the picture of me terrifies me: there I am—here I am.

Nora thinks I obsess about all this. *She* has yes/no opinions. Maybe I'm the one who's speaking Irish. Bundy once asked Edmond if Dad was a bullshitter or if he honest-to-God knew stuff. Edmond squinched up his forehead and finally said, "You can count on around eighty percent of it." Bundy, who was a troublemaker, reported this to Dad. Dad was pleased!

Mom used to joke that having Nora and me in the bedroom on top of theirs was like living downstairs from an unhappily married couple. Now Nora is my buddy.

I rate her affections at around 80 percent. Just kidding, Nora.

Bundy said to Dad, "I'm not so pleased with myself as you are. That twenty percent can get you D-E-D dead."

A lot of those guys really loved each other—I think more intensely than most people. Maybe 80 percent. I don't know if I'm just kidding about that. I don't even know with certainty that what I said about their loving each other more intensely is true. But it floats in my mind like a truth bubble. If it is true, it's bad news for what loving people gets you.

What is certain is that it was a nervous group. Sometimes everyone left the compound and there was just Nora and me and one of our good babysitters—one who let us stay up, was happy to watch whatever we wanted to watch on TV, was pleasant, calm, even inert. (I now realize our favorite babysitters were girls *just like my students now.*) When it was just us, both Nora and I felt a stillness that was eerie—like a ship when the engines stop. Then a bliss of no intensity. (My students could identify with that. One of their ways of putting someone down is to say, "Well, he's just so *intense.*")

Nora claims everyone was more high-strung after Bonnie moved in. Maybe. Maybe at first it was just that there were *two* more people always around—when he was unattached Tyler used to be away a lot, but with Bonnie he became a homebody. Tyler and Dad made each other more extravagant, and that accounted for a lot of the surface noise.

I made my students make up the people in the photograph. They had to pick one character and then I asked them questions. Who do you love? Who loves you?

I told them that at least two of the people were incapable of lying. Really and truly. Are you one of them? All but one of the rest of them could lie but then it got to them. Is that you?

One of them could lie fluently, thought that everyone lies so you might as well get good at it. It's part of the game, and if you don't have the moves, you don't belong on the varsity. I told my students that's my sister's view of the fluent liar. I told them my view is that the fluent liar lied for the same reasons Nora and I lied when we were kids—out of fear. I told them what Edmond told me about nature: How does a little sea creature avoid being eaten? By camouflage, by inflating itself to look bigger, by squirting a cloud of ink. Isn't that lying?

My students didn't like answering these questions. The girl who took acting said, "Are you getting off on making us feel strange?" I think she meant "strange—as strange as you." They preferred that I just tell them things so they could listen at a distance. Which is just what I couldn't do when I lived with all those people in the photograph.

Edmond explained Darwin's theory of evolution to me when I was in fifth grade, and then again in sixth and seventh. He said, "Does it scare you to think of that much time?" I felt strange because it did scare me and because he saw it did.

Tyler recited poems right at me. But when he asked me questions he was quieter than usual, and I was calmer. I didn't mind when he'd put on his corny voice and say, "Miz Edith, you are the smartest thing!" When Dad taught me stuff and told me I was smart, one of us was making me nervous.

Evelyn was the greatest teacher, but Nora hogged her and got jealous when Evelyn paid attention to me.

Ezra taught Nora and me how to punch. He'd drop by the house, nod to one of us, hold up his hand, and say, "Two jabs and a straight right." We'd whack the flat of his hand with our little fists. He wouldn't say much, just reach out and set our wrists flat or move our feet farther apart with his toe. Then hold up his hand again.

Ezra was easy then. Just showing us stuff. The strange part came from somewhere else. When Nora was in second grade and I was in fourth, a third-grade girl called Nora a bitch. All the kids were in the hall after assembly. Nora stood her up with a left jab and then hit her with a right. It was perfect miniature Ezra.

The third-grader landed on her butt, too stunned to cry. Nora burst into tears, which helped when the hall monitor came running up. The janitor leaned on his dust mop and laughed.

Everyone left but him and me.

He said to me, "Where your sister learn to punch like that?"

I was surprised he knew Nora was my sister. He was black and only said hi to some of the black kids.

He said, "Where she learn that?" He was still smiling a smile left over from his laugh.

I said, "Ezra Pritchett."

"Is that right?" He laughed again. "I know Ezra Pritchett. I seen him fight on the TV. Ezra 'Mulekick' Pritchett, that's what they call him. He teach you that good punch too?"

I shook my head and looked around. Somehow this was Dad's fault, maybe Mom's too. They didn't care if people noticed them.

The janitor held up his hand the same way Ezra did. He said, "Come on, honey. Let's see." I flicked two jabs and a right. "Uh-huh," he said. "That's sweet. I guess you saving your mulekick for when you need it."

After that the janitor started saying hi to Nora and me. He sometimes said to Nora, "Hey there, mulekick."

Dad would have liked that, he would have thought it was cool to be a white kid the black janitor said hi to. For me it was something that people noticed and that eventually someone would ask about. Probably a fifth-grader, black or white—someone would say, "Hey, how come he knows you?" with their head cocked back and their eyes slitted.

Dad should have thought of that. He thought he knew about my life but it was just his life. His one civil-rights case, his being in the Navy. He always had a rank. He should have imagined life at ground level.

But we got used to Ezra. Bundy I never got used to. He was moody. That was usually okay, because he used up most of his moods on Dad. When he paid attention to us, it was to teach us Catholic stuff he thought Dad should have. Bundy converted to Catholicism. In the tiny town he came from—the hills lumbered out, then strip-mined, then abandoned except for a chemical plant that turned the river purple—there were no Catholics or communists, so he had to be one or the other. That's flip, but he certainly was looking for something bigger than him. Perhaps a religion that was high-powered enough to make him gentle? Or a church that liked art? Anyway, he believed fiercely, and was angry at Dad (even though Dad had told him, when Bundy asked Dad to be his godfather, that he was a weak reed). Bundy was particularly upset at Dad for not baptizing Nora. I was baptized but hadn't made my First Communion. Bundy's priest finally made him lay off us, though by then Bundy had got me to memorize a lot of the Baltimore Catechism: "Edith . . . why'd God make you, Edith?"—he said "Edith" as though it was a personal conversation. Answer: "God made me to love, serve, and obey Him in this world and to be happy with him in the next."

This wasn't Edmond teaching me Darwin or Mendel, opening milkweed pods in my hand and getting me to blow. Bundy made a vast invisible world hover nearby, magical and scary.

But in all this flash-card ghost-game I could feel how Bundy wanted to use me to dive into Dad's soul. And I was for Bundy doing that—go get him, Bundy. Fish him out for us, Bundy. Fish him out for me.

The first time I really looked back at my childhood from far away, I was amazed at how rich it was. What I saw was wonderfully foreshortened—grown-up attentions and kindnesses that may have been months apart stood together in a thicket.

For an instant it all seemed to me whole and coherent. Bright cherubim and seraphim, orders, dominions, powers, archangels, angels' choirs. All of God's grown-ups in a tableau of goodness and love for Nora and me.

For an instant the happiest feelings I had *then* curved in an arc to me *now.*

And then I blinked and changed them into pain and loss.

So why do I have this strange pleasure in setting them up yet again for my students?

Maybe because this time it's a dollhouse for these mild children to play with. An old thing brought down from the attic. It has a momentary puzzling charm. But it can't be the real middle of anyone's real life.

Just for a little while I don't want to think of *me* in that piece of life. I don't know which is more painful—to think of it as a story with me in the middle (an egocentric version that is its own punishment) or with Mom and Dad in the middle—struggling hard—they were both wildly strong—but so amazingly wrong. . . . If they were my children I'd have a fit. Just stop it, you two. Right now. I don't *care* who did what. Just cut it out.

But my voice is this tiny little childish whine—Mo-om, Da-ad. And they can't even hear them*selves.*

But if *they're* that fucked up in their story, why bother to start my own?

What is odd is that I can see movies with roguish characters and be charmed, I can sympathize with novel heroines and heroes who do bad or crazy things, I can even hold hands with my friends as they tell me what shameful deeds they've been up to, but I'm not at all sure I want to know my parents' real-life story.

A part of me wants to stay too young to get it.

Perhaps the old-fashioned world was organized better. Nice people told you nothing but good about your parents. If you found out stuff, it was in old sepia photos covered with dusty glass and everyone was wearing clothes that made them seem antique.

Parents should settle down into a shelvable book and gather some dust for a while. I really don't want them going from being bright rulers of my childhood directly to being lurid people at my elbow who want my sympathy as fellow humans. Not so fast. They should have got old, they should have stopped whizzing around the board. Go directly to Jail. Do not pass Go. Do not collect $200.

◇

Joss called Mike at the office to tell him he was late for their own dinner party. "It was on the kitchen calendar," she said.

He said, "I'm sorry." He knew he should stop there. He went on—"I've told you if you don't see me write it down in my appointment book—"

"Just take a look in that appointment book of yours. Switch off your total recall of things that matter only to you and just take a look. Take just one second of your busy day—"

"Okay, okay." He looked. It was there. In his own handwriting. He said, "I think Ganny's still here. I'll get her to give me a lift."

"Ganny," Joss said. "You *did* ask Ganny, didn't you?"

Mike clicked his tongue and exhaled. Joss said, "I take it that you did not. Never mind. But perhaps in the next ten minutes you'll make an effort to overcome your peculiar amnesiac response to *home*—or is it *wife*?"

"All right," Mike said, "I've got the picture."

"Oh, he's got the picture. I guess I just don't know when to stop. Here I was thinking it's hard to get through to him, sort of like using a pea-shooter on a rhinoceros, when actually he's been wounded. And wronged. An action for wrongful wounding is the defendant's counterclaim."

When Mike got home—not only with Ganny but within ten minutes—Joss was in a completely different mood.

Edmond, Evelyn, Tyler, Bonnie, and Bundy were at the table. Joss was circling behind them with an open bottle of wine. When she saw Ganny and Mike she cried out, "Oh, good!" without a trace of sarcasm. She said, "Ganny, Ganny, Ganny," in her Cary Grant voice. "I apologize. I throw myself on your bosom of mercy."

Bundy said, "I'll drink to that."

"So will I," Joss said. "I gift my lass. I mean, I lift my glass—"

"I like 'gift my lass,'" Bonnie said. "All you boys should gift your lass."

Mike looked up at the stair landing in front of Edith and Nora's bedroom. There was a blanket hanging over the rail. Mike figured the girls had put it there and were hiding behind it. He thought of going up and herding them back to bed, decided not to spoil their fun.

This stray scrap of good will had the odd effect of making him feel isolated.

He'd noticed that, whenever the gang got together like this, there was always one person who didn't have fun. He put his briefcase in the living room, behind the armchair where he hoped to get in an hour of work after the party.

Joss and Bonnie brought in the first course—brioches (Joss made them from scratch) filled with minced mushrooms.

Tyler and Edmond were sitting on either side of Joss. Tyler, addressing the table at large, said, "I hope you're not just gulping this wine."

Bonnie said, "Oh, honestly, Tyler—wine snobbery? You can't even pronounce it."

Joss said, "But he says all those things. . . . He says, 'Note the slight fruity aftertaste.'" Joss took a swig and swallowed it after a noisy gargle. She said, "Why can't you say things like, 'Ah! This wine tastes like the fall of Rome'? Or 'Note the crisp bouquet—a savor of Joan of Arc at the stake'?"

Mike heard the first faint harmonics in Joss' voice that meant she was getting a buzz on. Sometimes the heat of her manic moods seemed to burn off the alcohol. Other times the alcohol took hold. He had some hope that gaiety would win this round.

The next course was a roast of venison they'd had in the freezer since Bundy had shot it. Joss asked Mike to get it out of the oven while she served Evelyn a vegetarian main dish—white beans with carrot shreds, parsley, sage, and a trace of hot pepper.

Bonnie said, "Hey, that looks good! That's a real Italian dish. I can smell *salvia.*" Bonnie had spent a fellowship year in Rome. *"Prezzemolo e salvia!"*

Tyler said, "Next thing you'll be calling grits *polenta.*" Tyler, in spite of his own tendency to elaboration, liked to remind people to talk plain American.

Bonnie said, "You just say things like that because it took you three tries to pass your foreign-language requirement." She followed Mike into the kitchen. He pulled out the roast and moved it from the pan to a platter. Bonnie got out a fork and a carving knife. She said, "Are you going to carve it here or are you going to be the daddy and do it at the head of the table?"

"Look," he said. "I wonder—"

"What do you wonder?"

"Look. Joss hates it when I try to slow down her drinking. I wonder if you could . . . at least not keep filling her glass."

Bonnie put her hand on his. She said, "Is it really a problem? I didn't know, Mike."

"I'm all for her having fun. . . ."

"That's rıght, Mike. She is having fun."

"But . . ."

Bonnie dipped her finger in the sauce and licked it. "Of course, Mike." She dipped her finger in again. "This is delicious." She dipped her finger again and put it to his lips. "What do you think?"

"Yes."

Bonnie lowered her eyes and slid by him. The shadow of his head crossed her face, and he realized—by the shape of her eyes, by the twitch of her lips—that she was the other nun. The nun who'd called Polly Trueheart's hair "exuberant." The nun who had such casual deft fingers.

He may have made a sound or perhaps jerked his head back.

She said, "What?" and raised one eyebrow. She laughed and said, "'Curiouser and curiouser.' Isn't that what Alice says? Alice in Wonderland?"

He recognized the diction too, the tone of a knowing remark that was more elusive than clarifying, that lingered like a trace of scent.

He thought, Well, now she's with Tyler, nothing to do with me. He shrugged his shoulders. The roast rolled on the platter. He tipped it toward his belly and pinned the roast with one hand. The knife and fork clattered to the floor.

Bonnie picked them up. "I thought you were the second-string fullback who never fumbled." She dabbed at his shirtfront with a dishrag, furrowing her brow, earnestly helpful. She said, "There. That won't show at all once it's dry—not a trace—like a stolen kiss."

When they came in with the venison, Bundy said, "Now, this is going to be some sweet meat. The secret's in how careful you stalk him. If you don't spook him, and if you make a clean kill, then there's no fear. He gets fear in his blood, that'll sour the meat."

"You all go ahead and enjoy your meal," Evelyn said. "But I'd prefer not to hear talk like that."

"Well, I'm sorry," Bundy said. "I'll just talk about the wine." He held up his glass and said, "'This is my blood.'"

"You behave yourself," Ganny said. "I'll tell Father Gregory."

"And he'll be mean to me? I'm quaking."

Ganny said, "No. He'll be nice to you and you can't stand that."

Bundy laughed.

Ganny said, "The only thing that gets to you worse is when he tells you your sins aren't all that serious."

Mike and Ganny laughed, but Bundy looked reproachfully at Ganny. Ganny said, "Okay—I won't tease you. And you won't tease Evelyn."

"I was just putting her pigtail in the inkwell," Bundy said. "You're violating the seal of the confessional."

Joss said, "You'll have to explain that to us non-Catholics, Bundy." Bundy turned to her—nothing he liked better than explaining to non-Catholics. Joss said, "What does it mean—putting her pigtail in the inkwell?"

That sort of misdirection joke was always good for a laugh with the gang. And then everyone started talking at once, some of them trying to top Joss, Bundy apologizing to Evelyn, and Mike, who'd actually gone to a grade school that had still had desks with open inkwells, earnestly explaining, also to Evelyn, that you only dipped the pigtail of the girl in front of you if you really liked her.

They swirled on noisily. Mike noticed that Bonnie filled Joss' wineglass with water and that Joss didn't object—she took a sip and kept on talking. When Joss and Mike got up to clear the table for dessert, Mike noted that Joss had no trouble carrying a plate in each hand and didn't even rattle the knives and forks. He relaxed. When she slid Evelyn's pie out of the oven and cut it into even eighths, he said, "Look. I'm sorry I was late."

She gave him a quick but vacant look and handed him two plates.

He thought how odd it was that he didn't mind when Joss changed her mood in a way that was mysterious to him, but that it irritated her if he changed *his* mood without explaining. At least she used to complain about it. And he used to argue that, as long as he was *doing* what she wanted, why should she worry about his inner state? And she used to say, "That's just the point. You only care that things run right." And he used to say, "Don't overstate your case. You'll never win an argument if you overstate your case." To which she used to say, "Don't tell me how to argue."

They didn't say these things anymore. Nowadays one of them would get mad but be too tired or bored to go through the old arguments. Or else one of them would rant and the other would deflect it. Was Joss right that he didn't mind this state of affairs because things were still running all right? He heard an old echo of a Joss overstated attack: Mussolini! Mussolini made the trains run on time.

But here they were with their friends. Perhaps that was the inevitable natural step—in their middle years friends and children would be the principal source and object of their good will and tenderness. Was that a notion Joss could stand to hear? If he said it out loud it would make her shriek. Perhaps it was one of those inevitable things that were better off happening without a fuss.

He felt a slip of misgiving in his thought. How come he ended up the party of quiet resignation? The grow-old-with-me party? How come Joss got to be the one who ranted and raved? Now he wondered if he deflected too much . . . if he was conventional, if he was lazy . . . if he was afraid. Of what?

There was no answer, so he brushed the whole damn thing away. He went out each day with a will—that would have to be answer enough.

While he'd been in a brown study the others had finished their pieces of pie. He pushed his away—he'd get back to fighting weight, starting right now.

The women were talking about beards. Bonnie and Joss were eyeing Tyler's critically. "It's very rabbinical in *form*," Bonnie said. "But it's just so *blond*."

Evelyn said, "I like his beard. He's like a sweet old sheepdog."

Bonnie said, "Well, exactly." She turned toward Mike. "Now, Mike's beard is mainly brown with a bit of gray. But then the mustache is ginger. If I were on a jury I'd wonder about that."

"Oh no," Evelyn said. "Mike looks like a good old Airedale."

"Well, I'd worry about what he was really up to behind that mask," Bonnie said. She turned her attention back to Tyler. "Now, I'd like to see more of your face. I mean, so far so good, but maybe I'm missing something."

Joss got up, went to the kitchen, and came back with two pairs of scissors. Bonnie got up and tied her napkin around Tyler's neck.

Tyler liked group activity. He liked it best when he got to be the Tom Sawyer of the gang, the one who made up the rules and elaborated the meaning, but, since he prided himself on being chief enthusiast, it was now hard for him to say no. He did try to get out ahead of the pack by saying, "My handmaidens attend me," but Bonnie and Joss were snicking their scissors and fluffing Tyler's beard, their heads bobbing and nodding with such bright animation that their darting hands, snapping scissors, and Tyler's immobile head seemed like puppets in a Punch and Judy show. The first curls fell into Tyler's lap. He held one up and said, "Surely someone wants this for a keepsake." Bonnie and Joss kept snipping, one of them tilting Tyler's chin up to get at the hair on his throat.

Joss laid a dish towel across Tyler's lap, which soon filled with clippings. She said, "Hot water and plenty of it," one of her favorite movie clichés. Bonnie got a bowl of steaming water from the kitchen, and Joss brought her pink Lady Gillette, a bar of soap, and a towel from the bathroom. Joss tied the towel over the napkin around Tyler's neck.

Bundy said, "Now it looks like John the Baptist's head on a plate." Bundy seemed both pleased and suspicious that Tyler was the star victim.

Evelyn reached across the table and picked up a clump of beard that had fallen near Tyler's plate. "Well, I *am* going to put this in a locket."

Bundy said, "I don't know, Tyler—I'd make 'em stop. I've seen neater work at a sheep-shearing."

Bonnie and Joss kept on snipping. The beard was now down to uneven clumps and stubble. Bonnie and Joss soaped Tyler's face and began to work up a lather. "This feels pretty good," Tyler said.

Joss started in with the razor. Bonnie chanted, "'Shave him like *this*! Shave him like *that*! Shave his little goatee beard. . . .'"

Evelyn said, "You all be careful of his throat."

Bonnie snorted—a soft imitation of one of Joss' derisive snorts—and said, "My leg is as tender as his throat." And then, with nothing else to do for the moment, she gestured toward Joss with her hands in the stylized manner of a magician's assistant.

Tyler said, "It's pulling some. I think you've clogged the razor."

Joss said, "More lather!" and Bonnie soaped up her hands and dabbed the suds onto Tyler's cheeks. Joss shook the razor around in the bowl and shaved some more.

Bonnie dipped her napkin in the water and wiped Tyler's face. The shaving was uneven. There were a few spots of sparse stubble, some patches that were scaly white and some that were scraped pink.

Joss said, "Oh my."

Bundy shook his head. He said, "You know what you look like, Tyler? You look like *Spam*."

There was a silence. The silence was in two parts. During the first part everyone looked at Tyler's face; during the second part everyone looked away.

Tyler ran his hands over his cheeks and chin. He said gamely, "I guess I better go look." He got up and headed to the bathroom.

Bonnie took a step after him, but stopped. She said, "Nothing that a day in the sun won't take care of."

Joss looked around the room, her eyes wide and bright. She picked up the scissors, razor, soap, and towels and crammed them in the bowl, slopping a little wave of soapy hairy water onto her skirt. Mike could feel her radiating embarrassment and guilt. Joss pursed her lips. Mike knew she felt bad, bad enough so that the next thing she would radiate would be a flush of defiance. He thought he should say something to make her feel better—perhaps remind her of the doctrine of assumption of risk—"*Volenti non fit injuria*" ("No injury is done to a willing person"). But he also wished her . . . not *punished*, he rejected the word *punished*, that was a word Joss could use against him. Make that—he wouldn't mind her learning a lesson. And now his thoughts began to pick up a Joss frequency—Just what might that lesson be? The sanctity of the patriarchal beard? Was that the lesson? Or maybe it was no tipsy fun? No games that the boys lost?

He jammed Radio Free Joss, but he also lost his own impulse to make her feel better. It was Bonnie who took her hand and said, "I've been after him to shave off that beard for a week now."

Tyler came back in, looking slightly better after washing his face. He said, "The part I really don't like is that my mouth seems to have shrunk."

Evelyn said, "Just give your lips a little rub with a piece of flannel. That'll plump them up."

"That's a country-girl secret," Bonnie said. "From the frontier days, when women didn't have lipstick."

Evelyn said, "Some people *choose* not to wear lipstick."

"Or you could just talk," Bundy said. He was about to go on but Mike gave him a sharp look. Mike was alarmed by all these little antagonisms. He knew about Bundy's occasional pangs of jealousy about Tyler's easy ride (family, education, and buoyant charm). He was surprised by the slight chill between Bonnie and Evelyn. Mike had thought that Bonnie was working her way into the gang with ease, and that Evelyn paid no attention to the sort of cryptic floating comment Bonnie had made.

Ganny got up abruptly, went over to Joss, and thanked her. Joss got up and walked Ganny out to her car. Bonnie stirred in her seat as if to follow but then simply cocked her head and watched them.

After a moment Bundy leaned across the table and said, "I'll tell you what, Tyler. Let's us go set on the porch and swap lies." Bundy spread his arms. "Hell. Let's all go out under the stars."

Tyler looked surprised and pleased by this kind attention from Bundy. Mike was also surprised and pleased, but then as disoriented by it as he'd been by his earlier stray kindness to Edith and Nora.

Mike went up the stairs. As he'd guessed, they were behind the blanketed railing, but now fast asleep, Edith curled up and Nora sprawled.

From the balcony he watched his friends file out toward the side porch, Bundy leading the way, one hand on Tyler's shoulder, the other holding a wine bottle.

Mike felt a subsidence in himself. At first he thought he was just quieting down, feeling pleased with Bundy's amiable gesture. He carried the girls to bed and pulled their sheets up. The subsidence was not just a comfortable quieting. It was an ebbing of the confidence that his life was replenished daily with reliable affection.

This ebbing occurred smoothly and serenely. If it had come as an assault he could have stepped back and countered it. If it had come as an idea . . . But it was a draining of color from what he saw. It didn't disturb any of the forms of his life. They were still intact—in fact clearer and simpler for being pale and bare. And above all fragile. Why should any of these people in this house, why should anyone at all be relied on to supply affection? There were as many reasons to be cold as to be warm. Forget reasons—there were as many impulses. There were boundless impulses and no odds in favor of the good, the dutiful, the domestic.

But this recalculation of the odds wasn't the essence of the bleakness he felt—the recalculation was only a short trickle, then a seepage, then a few beads of condensation left behind.

From the balcony he saw Joss come through the front door. She looked puzzled for a second. There was the sound of a voice from the side porch. She pivoted toward it with a bounce that was comically elaborate, bending her arms like a sprinter while her skirt and hair swung wide of her turn. For all he knew her energy came from outer space, from a rock band, from the chipped edge of one of her own molecules. No alarm, not even surprise that he couldn't call to her. He opened his mouth, but it was empty. There was no motion of the word "Joss," just his untroubled breath.

She was full—her senses were absorbing energy and she was circulating it in herself as vitally as her heart circulated blood.

She opened the screen door to the porch, stepped through, and let it go. He twisted his mouth, waiting for the slam. Joss lifted her heel and caught the door. She slipped her heel away and the door bumped shut.

Mike stopped feeling incoherent. He felt simple, as if he'd been trying to put on a coat and caught his hand in the sleeve, then relaxed and slipped it through.

Odd. The phrase "it doesn't matter" could mean the last surrender to indifference, or it could mean "nothing to worry about."

◇

For most of the gang, life became very festive. In the past they'd only got together for supper once a week; now they were up to something every other night—parlor games, going out to the movies, lofty discussions. Mike thought this was the way life should be, but for some reason it was only occasionally a good time for him. He figured that it was still his turn to be the one not having fun. He figured—on a less theoretical level—that he'd get some points for skipping the movies and being the babysitter. But they all thought he was either being stingy for not paying for a babysitter or that he was a party-pooper, except for Edmond, who knew a depression when he saw one. Edmond said to Mike, "One of those times when life has lost its flavor, huh?"

Mike said, "Well, yeah. Not all the time, but once in a while. Often enough. Can you be depressed for no apparent reason and it's *not* clinical depression?"

Edmond pondered. "I think so. You could be depressed for a reason and just not know the reason. You don't seem dysfunctional, just kind of low."

Edmond was the slowest talker of the gang, and Mike found it soothing. Bonnie, having picked up a lot of Joss' speech patterns and rhythms, now talked a lot faster than she had at first, and had moved from the slowest to the fastest of the four Southerners. Tyler, who had been the fastest, was talking faster to keep up with Bonnie.

They saw a lot more of Ganny these days. She was getting a kick out of the dinner-table discussions.

Bundy had disappeared. He still dropped in at Mike's office, and occasionally showed up at the house when the gang went out to the movies and Mike was home with the girls. Mike had been worried that Bundy was nursing a resentment at being excluded. Bundy was capable of feeling slighted when he was withdrawn and no one tried to pull him out.

One night the gang was out at the movies, and Bundy came by to keep Mike company. Mike read a story to each of the girls and then sat down by the woodstove. He hadn't done much all day but felt tired. Bundy couldn't sit still.

Mike said, "You want a beer?"

"You haven't noticed, have you?"

Before Mike could say anything Bundy added, "I've given up drinking."

"So that's why you can't sit down for five minutes."

"No, that's not why, dummy. Even if I was drinking I'd burn it right off. I'm cooking with something else."

"What? You painting a lot?"

Bundy shook his head. "I've stopped painting."

"Then what?"

Bundy smiled and kept on pacing up and down the room.

Mike said, "You been reading the Bible? Or something like that? Some more of that Brother Fire and Brother Wolf Saint Francis stuff?"

Bundy stopped pacing and grinned at him. "No more reading. Given up reading words. I'm dealing with *things*. And then *things* is the next thing to go." Bundy smiled again. Mike hadn't ever seen him smile so much.

Bundy turned and went out the door. He came back with his pistol belt, holster, and revolver. He put them down on the coffee table. "You don't have a gun," he said. "You should have one."

Mike said, "In a house with two children? Joss would have a cow."

"You don't want a present, give it to Ezra, then."

"Bundy. Ezra's on probation. He shouldn't have a gun."

"Give it to Ganny. Ganny ought to have one, living all alone."

Bundy poked a cartridge out of one of the loops.

Mike said, "*You* give it to Ganny."

Bundy wasn't paying attention to him. Bundy held the bullet up and said, "I used to like big things. When I was painting. Now it's germs and Jesus. And I never seen either one. Who told me that? Was it you?" Bundy held the bullet behind his back. "Which hand?"

Mike said, "Oh brother."

"You're right," Bundy said. "No games. I used to accuse you of playing games. Putting a lot of curlicues on your talk. Keeping things behind your back. We all do it. Hell, I used to think that was the way to paint. You paint something best when you're making people guess what's behind. That's what I thought. Maybe I was wrong about that white-on-white guy. Maybe he was trying to say 'when no secrets shall be hid.' He's still hooey, 'cause he talked about it too much. He should've kept quiet. Not tried to make it something. Just let it be nothing on nothing."

Mike believed that Bundy had given up drinking. Bundy didn't lie.

He told stories with a spin but he never lied. Mike wondered, though, whether there was some flashback, some lingering toxic effect. Bundy was like Joss in his reaction to liquor. One day he could drink a six-pack and just get a buzz. Another day he'd have one beer and be poisonously drunk. Joss would sometimes get drunk and have a wicked sullen hangover; other times she'd get up cheerful but a day later, three days later, she'd have an angry ghost of a hangover. One time she gave up drinking and smoking at the same time. She was radiant for a week—chewing gum and cracking jokes—and then she woke him up in the middle of the night banging around in the kitchen. She'd been beating a piece of meat with a metal mallet until it was pulverized—just a smear of red fiber mixed with the splintered kitchen counter. She stopped when he said her name. She asked him when the guests were coming. Then she became suddenly docile. He washed her hands and forearms in the kitchen sink. He led her back to bed and she went to sleep. The next day she didn't remember anything. She looked at the mashed wooden counter with puzzlement. She didn't seem to disbelieve him, and she didn't seem to believe him.

The evidence was complicated by the fact that Miss Dudley had apparently come in later, eaten the remains of the meat, and gnawed at the wood.

Mike had pointed at the marks made by the prongs of the meat mallet. Joss wouldn't look. She didn't resist, she didn't tell him to leave her alone, but her gaze wandered indifferently around the kitchen.

She finally said, "Is it hard to fix? Can you do it or are you going to call what's-his-name?"

Mike cut out the section of counter with a saw but had to get Edmond to make a new section that fit just right.

Mike came out of this memory because Bundy was pacing again.

Mike thought it wasn't like a captain pacing the quarterdeck or even a soon-to-be father pacing outside the delivery room. Bundy's pacing had no rhythm. He didn't stop, he just didn't keep time.

Mike said, "Bundy?"

"I'm okay."

"I was wondering where you've been."

"I was worrying a lot. But I got it all set now." Bundy stopped and smiled. "It'd take too long to tell you now. I'll tell you sometime."

Mike suddenly felt a lightheaded craziness. He had the idea that Bundy was praying for the stigmata, imagined he had the stigmata. . . . Mike knew it was crazy, feared that he'd picked up some part of Bundy's mood—he knew that was a little crazy too—but he couldn't keep from trying to see Bundy's palms.

Bundy paced by him again, said he was going to maybe take a trip.

Mike said, "Like that last one? Do a little farmwork somewhere? Maybe that's not a bad idea. Are your hands hard enough?"

Bundy opened his hands to look at them. "They're okay."

Mike got a look and was relieved. Just normal Bundy hands, big and bony with some old yellow calluses.

Mike said, "Yeah."

A car came up the driveway.

Bundy said, "I'll tell you sometime," and went out to his truck. He drove off as the gang piled out of Joss' station wagon.

Mike felt a whole new set of nerves as they all came in. He wished he could tell Joss his odd notion about Bundy's hands, but his thoughts had been pinging off her lately, not amusing her.

Joss looked at the revolver, holster, and belt.

Mike said, "I guess I'm supposed to give it to Ganny. It's from Bundy."

Joss turned to the gang and said, "Anyone want anything?" with a flip of her hand that meant booze.

"Not me," Tyler said. "I'm off to bed."

Joss said to Bonnie, "Maybe a little *vino* for you, kiddo."

Bonnie said, "What I really feel like is a little walk. What do you say to a little walk, Joss?"

Maybe Bonnie was going to keep Joss on the straight and narrow.

It's like having another child, he thought, and Bonnie can babysit for a while. Why did the people he loved weigh so much? Maybe he took it all too seriously. But maybe that's why the English talked about a bit of fluff on the side. Was that what he wanted? No. Yes. No. What he wanted was someone who took steps the same length as his, who sailed at the same speed, who paddled her side as well as he paddled his, who fished her side of the river while he fished his. . . .

What nonsense was this? Was it *My Fair Lady*? "Why can't a woman be more like a man?" No. Bundy weighed a lot and he loved Bundy too.

Then Mike wondered whether he was doing something that had always pissed him off when he'd seen others do it—take on every job in sight and then make everyone else feel like shit for not doing enough.

And what was he doing anyway except *worry*.

He got a phone call at his office from a woman who had some trouble explaining who she was. He could hear another woman in the background instructing the woman on the phone. The woman in the background had a voice that would cut glass. After a bit he recognized the background voice as Bundy's landlady. She was a rich hypochondriac who was also genuinely sick. She disliked Bundy and Bundy disliked her, but she'd continued to rent a cottage to Bundy on her jewel-box farm, month to month for two years. They spoke nothing but ill of each other, with a mutually hypnotized fascination.

The woman on the phone was the housekeeper—Mike now recognized her soft whispering voice. She said, "Miz Andrews would like you to come out here. She says your boy Bundy is cutting up some."

"Would you put Mrs. Andrews on?"

"Well, she's took to her bed. She'd . . . just wants you to come out here before she calls the sheriff."

Mike said, "What's he doing? Did Mrs. Andrews and him have another spat about rent?"

"No sir. Miz Andrews and me locked ourselves in. He was walking around in the pawpaw patch with his gun and he's been firing it off."

"At what? At a deer? At the house?"

"I don't know. Miz Andrews just said—"

"Okay. I'm coming. . . ."

He told Ganny about the phone call. She got up to come with him. He said, "I've got a client in a half-hour. Maybe you should stay and deal with him."

Ganny didn't say anything, just kept coming. Her car was closer, so she drove.

When they got there a deputy's car was in the circular drive in front of the big house. The car was empty. Mike knocked on the front door. He heard women's voices inside, but no one opened. He was about to call out to them when he saw the deputy come back toward his car. Mike recognized the deputy and went toward him.

The deputy looked at him blankly.

Mike started to speak to him but found he couldn't. Something about the deputy alarmed him.

Mike found himself at the corner of the house, his hand on the white stucco. He heard the deputy's voice, Ganny's voice, but it seemed to him that there was a silence that kept him from hearing anything. He took another step to look around the corner and he saw the tree, the chair, the sky, the shotgun which seemed much too long. The silence which held everything grew denser, stopped his ears, stopped all his senses. It let in slivers of light, nothing but a few lines in the stillness. But he saw that it was Bundy and that Bundy had put his own shotgun in his mouth.

. . .

Later Ganny told him she'd guessed. That's why she'd come with him.

Mike was in the backseat, where Ganny and the deputy had taken him. They'd made him put his feet up on the tilted-back driver's seat. His feet stuck out the open door. Ganny had got in and was sitting in the front. She was holding his hand and talking to him. He understood her when she told him she'd guessed and that's why she'd come with him. Then he became clearer and she became less clear.

He said, "Let's go out and stand up."

They stood separately without speaking.

The deputy directed the other people who arrived—the two men in the ambulance, another deputy, the county coroner.

Mike finally asked Ganny to call the office. When Ganny came out of the house the landlady came out behind her, followed by the housekeeper.

The landlady said to the deputy, "What on earth was wrong with that boy?" Her voice was a screech. She had a sharp voice all the time, but this sound seemed to be tearing her throat out. She turned to Mike. "Was he on *drugs*?"

"No," Mike said.

"I knew *something* was wrong with him. Coming and going all hours. Wouldn't stop to say something nice, just drove that awful truck in and out whenever he pleased."

Mike felt her voice land on him, stick to him like June bugs on his skin.

Ganny said to her, "You've had a shock, Mrs. Andrews. You shouldn't be talking now. You should go back in and rest. And then you should call up Mr. Ritter."

Mike had forgotten for the moment that the woman was a client of his partner.

Ganny said, "I'll come with you if you'd like me to call him for you." Mrs. Andrews turned her whole body to Ganny but pointed at Mike. "*He* should be taking care of this. I don't want them putting my name in some police report, putting my name in some newspaper. . . ."

"Mr. Ritter is who you should talk to. Let's go inside. You don't want to be saying everything right here. Let's us go call Mr. Ritter."

Mrs. Andrews said to the other woman, "Get my chair, Martha." Mrs. Andrews tried to put her arm around Ganny's shoulder, but Ganny was much too tall. Ganny put an arm around her until Martha rolled out the wheelchair. It was almost too much for Mike. A layer of his own shock—too early for sorrow—then a layer of recoiling from Mrs. Andrews, a layer of anger. And then Mike got his first whiff of how Bundy would have looked at all this. That was too much. He recoiled from Bundy's ferocious energy.

It became quiet again. He heard a floater of Joss' voice, one of her movie clichés: "'It's quiet in here.'—'Yeah. Too quiet.'" And it was too beautiful—the green grass, the blue, blue sky over the pawpaw trees. The colors too bright, the lines too sharp.

Another floating voice. ". . . and for all the souls of the faithful departed."

He thought that he should call a priest. Extreme unction. The priest could still administer extreme unction if the body was warm. Where did that notion come from? What a strange, technical fragment. But he felt a relief that he was going to act on it.

Mrs. Andrews was still on the phone. Mike asked Ganny for the keys. She didn't think he should drive. "Then you drive," he said. "I need to call his priest. Before they take his body away. There must be a phone down the road."

Ganny took him. He started to explain but gave up. "I just better call."

Ganny said, "Okay. Okay, Mike."

When she pulled into the gas station her hands began to tremble. They flew off the rim of the steering wheel and fluttered up in front of her face. She made them grip the steering wheel again. She turned to him and for an instant they stared at each other angrily, as still as strange dogs. Then they became dull and clumsy again.

"I don't know," Mike said. "I had the idea. . . . Maybe I made it up."

"Call. There's the pay phone. Just tell the priest. Then . . ."

Mike couldn't get either of the priests at Bundy's church. He left a message with the housekeeper at the rectory. He felt mechanical now. When he said Bundy's name the housekeeper said, "Dear God, I know the boy." This exclamation was as familiar and distant as his school days.

Mike recited the directions to Mrs. Andrews' house. The housekeeper said, "I'll tell Father Gregory. I don't know where he is but he won't be long. I'll tell him."

Nothing would come of it, then. The heat of the body. What a strange idea. And they didn't call it extreme unction anymore. He didn't know what to call it now.

He got back in the car. Ganny lifted her forehead off the backs of her hands. She was as quiet and slow as he was now.

"It's odd," Mike said. "I couldn't say 'suicide.' I couldn't say 'He killed himself.' I said, 'There's been an accident and he's dead.' What was I doing? Trying to get a mortal sin knocked down to venial? Jesus, you can't get more mortal." He sounded like Bundy. He looked at Ganny and spoke more like himself. "I don't know what they call extreme unction. It's not last rites. It's anointing of the sick. No—sacrament of the sick. When my father was dying, that was slow. But finally certain. Anyway, the priest came into the hospital room and opened his box. My father said, 'It's the last rites, is it?' The priest said, 'No,' and started to explain. My father said, 'Never mind. We'll call it next-to-last rites.' "

Ganny looked at him, raised a hand, and then dropped it.

Mike said, "I was there but I can't remember if it was funny. I mean I can't remember whether I thought it was funny."

Ganny held his wrist. "Think of something else to do," Ganny said. "There's still things we should do. We should go back there. We shouldn't just sit here and talk."

They drove back. The deputies and ambulance were still there, hadn't done much except put the body on a gurney and cover it.

Mike wasn't sure if Ganny had meant what he took her to mean. Don't slide away. Don't think of rites or other deaths. Pay attention to this death. Open up. Don't try to make sense of it. Open up. Don't be afraid of feeling the fierceness or the emptiness. Or go ahead and be afraid.

It turned out he couldn't help taking that advice. There was no more stillness. That great stillness began to move. He was swept into the rest of the day, rolled like a rock down the Rivanna in a flood.

§ 4

Some of it is in his appointment book. "Tell Edith & Nora. Call Bundy's mother. Get Ritter to keep Mrs. A out of cottage. Call undertaker. Give undertaker's name to morgue."

And his little checkmarks.

I don't remember what he said to Nora and me or what I thought of it. I do remember him going to the phone to call Bundy's mom. We had one phone in the house and that was a wall phone. No chair near it. It was Dad's idea that we'd all talk less on the phone if we had to stand up. Dad moved like a soldier doing a parade drill. Face the phone. Plant feet. Dial each single number. Speak each word.

I don't remember what he said to her. I remember that voice, not like his ordinary voice but a true voice, as if some wind had blown through him and cleansed him so that his voice was very clear and slow. It seemed careful, but not as though he was holding back or picking his words.

I bring this up because I became aware of his voice in such a way that from then on I could tell when it was true and when it was false. True in the way he was with Bundy's mom—not necessarily telling the truth, because he said to her there'd been an accident. But true. Later in Dad's life, even later that year, I could hear what was false—not necessarily telling a lie but murky and confused or sometimes just saying the appropriate thing.

On the phone with Bundy's mom he was silent for fairly long periods. But then his voice *started* in a different way—no preparatory noise, the word was just there.

How did *I* feel about Bundy killing himself? I didn't feel much, because I didn't have much to attach it to. I was a child and everything I saw and heard about it seemed severely grown-up. When Miss Dudley died I knew why it was sad, and I knew how to be sad. I felt easy about touching Dad or speaking to him. I even felt that I was more grown-up and Dad less grown-up, so we were together.

Bundy was in another country.

Later on in life, when I read lines about death that compared it to a country, I felt a shock. "That undiscover'd country, from whose bourn no traveller returns." I thought, Shakespeare, is that all you can say? That's what *kids* think.

Nowadays thinking of Bundy still makes me shrink into my childhood, reminds me how I was reduced, of how I was about to be reduced even more. But I can also reconstruct the event and feel sympathy for all of them. Dad, of course. He moved to perform his duties as if he were an old-fashioned deep-sea diver—covered with a steel helmet, wearing lead boots—deliberate, armored, but dependent on a thread of air from far away.

Mom reconstructed is like a silent shriek. Like the scream of a tree having a limb ripped off. She felt for Dad at the very time she didn't want to feel for him. She was—is—*good*. At that time she was trying to gather her goodness to herself, to withdraw it from the marriage bank. But there was Dad, nobly wounded, and she couldn't keep herself from tearing in two.

I heard Bonnie talking to Mom one of those afternoons. It was certainly after the memorial service in Charlottesville, and probably before Dad drove with Ganny and Edmond to the actual burial, way over the mountains.

Bonnie said to Mom, "It must be hard for you having to go to a Catholic church. I mean, your sense of things is so much freer and more open. I know how you love beauty—all kinds of beauty. . . . I mean, I love to think of you seeing the churches in Rome. But the way they did that service here in that squat little fifties church . . . pretending it was all free and folksy. That guitar playing. Having people come up to testify. As if it was a real honest-to-God Southern Protestant thing. . . . It was the worst of both."

Mom said, "Mike was good."

"Of course he was," Bonnie said. "He has courtroom presence, indeed he does. And there he was in a Catholic church—you could see how . . . you could see the altar boy in him."

Mom said, "I think it was just Bundy on his mind."

"Yes, of course," Bonnie said. "I only meant the church was familiar to him, he felt at home in that church."

"I don't think he was an altar boy," Mom said. "I think he was a choirboy."

Bonnie said, "Yeh-ess. A choirboy."

"Urban choirboy," Mom said.

Bonnie laughed her chugging laugh. Then she said, "It's good you can joke. It must be so hard for you, Mike being so . . . intense. It must be so hard for you to do anything while he's so . . . Of course he's not demanding, is he? It's amazing really how he shows no need. It must be hard for you to know what in the world is going on inside him. Does he talk to you about how he feels? Does he tell you?"

Mom pursed her mouth. "He told me what happened. The details. He keeps remembering details."

"Well, yes," Bonnie said. "Physical reality. He really *believes* in facts and physical reality. If he could say more, then you could help him. He's good at seeing things, and you're so good at seeing *into* things."

I was on my bed in the loft. I could see Mom but not Bonnie. It made me itchy hearing all this. I didn't know what it meant, I didn't even know what the tone was, but it made everyone seem miles away from everyone else, flying away from each other.

And it corresponded to something spooky I'd felt when I'd listened to Dad speak in church about Bundy. I'd been nervous when Dad had stood up and gone up front. I'd heard him in court once, but that had been so slow and boring that I hadn't been nervous at all. I'd thought the courtroom was less intense than supper at home. But the church was full and hushed, and Dad seemed to be barely there in the gray light. His suit seemed to be moving by itself. When he started talking it was like someone else. His voice seemed to come from the back of the church, from the side, all around.

He was quoting the Bible, the kind of things Bundy used to quote. The only one I remember is "Because thou art neither hot nor cold I will spew thee out." It was his voice, but he sounded like Bundy, the way Bundy sounded angry—not angry at anyone in particular, angry at everything.

And then Dad stopped just the way Bundy used to stop, as though he'd come back to where he was and knew he'd been too harsh. Dad paused. He was just standing there, but it felt to me like he was sinking. Finally he said, "The sad thing is . . ." He stopped. He clenched his fists and said again, "The sad thing is . . ." He said it one more time. Each time it seemed harder, as if he had to squeeze it out of himself with his hands.

". . . that we can't know . . ." He stopped and gave up. Then he began again, easily. "We can't know if he felt the love we felt for him. We have some idea of what he thought was beautiful. Some of his paintings are beautiful, even though he wasn't ever satisfied. We have some idea of what he was angry about—all the wrong he saw. If he seemed angry at us, sometimes it was because he had a hard time accepting admiration or praise. I think that was because he was reaching for the next handhold up and didn't want to be distracted.

"Right now a lot of the memories we have are painful. After a while I think some of them will be good memories.

"Right now the one memory I have that is comforting is of his hands. I never saw him paint, but I saw him whittle things—he made toy boats and whistles, fishing plugs and wooden bowls and spoons. I saw him tie flies, cast. He knew he was good with his hands. It was one part of his life that was easy for him, that was useful to him and to his friends.

"After that small but certain memory I think it will be possible to remember more and more of what he did, of how he was. The bigger, more difficult, and dangerously inspired parts. His painting, but not just his painting. His love and anger for . . . just about everything. He was alive. He lived in so many ways . . . that it would be a mistake to remember only the ways that led to death."

Dad should have stopped there. Maybe I think that because I understood up to there, and it sounded right, as though Dad was just explaining.

But something happened then. Ezra's uncle said "Amen." Ezra looked at him to shush him.

Ezra's uncle said, "That's right, Mike," in a louder voice. Dad was startled. But then he took a breath and said, "You knew him, Emmanuel. And you know there are sorrowful mysteries."

Ezra's uncle said, "Uh-huh."

Dad said, "And you know there are joyful mysteries too."

"That's right," Ezra's uncle said, "joy in the morning."

For a second Dad looked like he was going to go on. I was afraid he was going to sing. I curled over so tight I hurt myself. Ezra shot his hand onto his uncle's arm, and looked at Dad.

Dad said "Amen" in a low voice and took a step back.

Mom let out a breath through her teeth.

There had been something spooky about the whole thing in church, about Dad talking about his dead friend. I'd seen him the day before, when he went down to the river by himself. I thought he was going out in his canoe and started after him. But he just touched it. Ran his hands along it. I understood that part. Bundy was the only person he let take it out alone. So Dad was touching a thing that he'd shared completely with Bundy.

I understood his face when he came back up the hill. His mouth was pressed tight but his eyes were wide open. He saw me and his eyes didn't change at all. He looked at me in such a way that I wasn't embarrassed he'd found me watching him. He took my hand and we climbed back up without having to say anything.

Much later I told Nora all this. About Bonnie criticizing the church service to Mom, about Dad going down to the canoe, touching it, clinging to it, and then walking back up the hill.

Nora and I talked about the church service. She laughed when I told her that I'd been afraid Dad was going to sing. When we went to ball games Dad always sang "The Star-Spangled Banner" so loud that someone would stare. He was vain about being able to hit the high notes. Nora remembered being surprised at the part about Ezra's uncle, but she was more sympathetic. "What else could Dad have done?" she said. "He was taken by surprise too. There are lots of things he did that're more embarrassing. You remember how Mom got mad at him for listening to black preachers on the radio on Sunday mornings? She said she wouldn't mind if he really believed, but he was just entertaining himself. She was wrong—not *all* wrong, but he really *admired* . . . Anyway, his talking to Ezra's uncle like that—*I* think that made a difference for what happened later. More than his having argued before judges. More than what he *said* about Bundy in church. He got better at it later. If you can forget your own weirdness about his getting up in public and think of it as something that just happened to Dad . . ."

I said, "Of course you liked that part of his life. You got to be his favorite daughter." I said this lightheartedly.

Nora laughed. "It was a dirty job," she said. "But someone had to do it."

"Oh, a movie cliché," I said. "So now you're being Mom too. You can't have everything, you know."

"Oh, come on," Nora said. "You should rejoice in your sister's good fortune." Another family joke. Dad used to write us his Christmas wishes and put them on cards in our stockings. They were beyond human possibility, or at least beyond eight- or ten-year-old possibility. He didn't want us to envy each other's presents, so he wrote on each of our cards, "Rejoice in your sister's good fortune."

I remember reading in the Bible, "Be ye therefore perfect . . . ," and laughing. Right, Dad—first thing tomorrow.

It was on that same visit that Nora said to me, "I've been angry with him but I've never been disillusioned. That's because I didn't have as many illusions about him. So you had a harder time for a while. You carried more weight inside. All I did was spoil a few Christmases and have everyone get mad at me. I hated having everyone mad at me, but in a funny way it made me free. One of Dad's evil powers was that he could go into a stonewall of reasonableness—he could block his own tantrum *and* he could block yours. I don't mean just *yours,* I mean Mom's, yours, anybody else's. But he couldn't block mine. And sometimes I could get him so mad he'd have his own tantrum."

"Weren't you ever afraid that everyone would stay mad at you? That no one would come to your room and make up?"

"No. Maybe that was because I didn't stay mad, and I was self-centered enough to think everyone else would stop being mad when I did. Or maybe because, however crazy we'd all get, none of us was ever mean. And of course I knew I could always go over to see Evelyn."

"I rejoice in your good fortune."

Nora said, "Do not."

"Do too."

"Nuh-huh."

"Uh-huh too."

"Nuh-huh either."

We both laughed.

Nora said, "Okay. I believe you. Have you ever thought what a relief it was for Mom and Dad that we finally really liked each other?"

◇

Mike was walking home. He didn't much want to get there. He was taking odd loops, trying to avoid the routes where he'd left traces. The first few times he'd walked home since the funeral had been fierce and dense. He hadn't been consciously grieving for Bundy, but he'd heard Bundy's voice several times. Not distinct words, just the sound of his twang braided into the noise of the street, then into the sound of trees and the river.

Each time it startled him.

The night before, it had seemed it was going to be easier. He'd been walking easier, dully floating along, when he suddenly found himself held still. Not just from the outside, from the inside too. It was peaceful. He wasn't aware of anything for a moment. Then he smelled gun bluing. He recognized the smell from boot camp years before. Then he tasted metal. Everything else was calm. Everything else was gone. It wasn't meant to frighten him. His mouth watered as he tasted and felt metal in his mouth.

Then he was surprised by what he felt. He felt temptation. He was pulled by it. He felt the soothing brush of a promise. But it wasn't for him.

It was for Bundy. And then he felt a sympathy he'd never felt before—clear, deep, without pity.

It left as abruptly as it had come. His next step might have been a minute after his last one, or it might have been only a second.

He'd walked easily again, not pressed by what had happened, not thinking. Whatever it was had gone into him without troubling the surface of his mind.

He'd thought about it a mile later, almost home.

He thought how Joss had caught glimpses of her father off and on for several months after he died. She thought she saw him driving a passing car, or walking ahead of her and turning into a doorway. He thought it was right that Joss' main sense was sight.

He thought that without his having been alerted by smell and taste he wouldn't ever have felt that particular force in Bundy's mind.

For a moment he was glad he had felt it. Then he was undone again, grieving for how terribly truthful Bundy was.

He sat down on the crown of the gravel driveway.

Bundy had been a border to one side of his life. For all the troubles on that border, it had been a good strong side to his life. Mike grieved consciously and selfishly. He was shaken, but he was himself again.

Now—walking home as differently as he could—zigzagging, crossing his usual route as seldom as possible—he was thinking shallowly. It was the equivalent of the shallow breathing that Joss and he had learned in Lamaze class. He thought it was odd that he didn't think it was important to wonder whether what had happened came from outside him or from inside: Bundy as a phantom or Bundy as a phantom-limb. It didn't seem to matter at all.

He thought of psychiatrists' reports he'd read in connection with law cases. "Delusional material." Was that an oxymoron? Ghostly matter.

He thought it was right that he didn't worry about his sanity. There was clinical depression and "situational" depression—so why not clinical delusional material and situational delusional material?

He recognized that his inner chatter was an effort to avoid last night, the same way he was avoiding his straight road home. Not out of fear, just out of being tired, tired from last night and tired from a day of not doing much on account of being tired.

He felt an arm around his neck, another arm around his chest. He said, "Bundy?"

A voice close behind his ear said, "Say what?"

Before Mike could speak the voice said, "Aw shit!" Then laughed. Then said, "Sorry, counselor."

The arms let go. More laughter. Mike turned. It was so dark he didn't recognize the face, but he now knew the laugh, the figure. He said, "Jesus, Ezra!"

Ezra was still laughing.

Mike said, "Ezra, you dumb son of a bitch!" Ezra stopped laughing. Mike saw that Ezra was wearing a gray sweatsuit. Mike said, "You call this roadwork?"

Ezra laughed at that. "Aw, man," he said. "You shouldn't ought to be down here in a big suit. Walking like a drunk man. Wearing a necktie."

Mike said, "What the hell is it? You don't need the money. Do you? Your uncle told me he's paying you to train. You call this training?"

Ezra said, "Hey, I'm sorry, Mike."

"What in hell were you thinking?"

"I don't know, man. I was trucking along. There you were. You didn't even hear me. I thought if I ran by you'd be scared. Then I thought you ought to be scared, wandering around. I don't know if I was going to lift your wallet or not. Old habits, man."

"Last time I got you off, you promised your uncle . . ."

"Yeah, I promised him. He wasn't supposed to tell you."

"Look. If you get caught and put in the slammer they won't let you out to train."

"Well, I guess it's lucky it was you."

Mike threw his briefcase on the sidewalk. "Goddamn it, Ezra!" He jumped up and down in a clownish rage. He said, "Jesus, Mary, and Joseph!" Then he began to laugh.

Ezra said, "I'm sorry, Mike."

Mike said, "I want ringside seats. I want *free* ringside seats. And you better promise me now. Promise *me*."

"Yeah. Okay. Yeah. Nothing like this'll come up again." Mike began to laugh again. Ezra took him by the arm. "You all right?"

"Yeah, fine. You're lucky I was thinking about something or I might've got a judo hold on you."

Ezra laughed politely. Then he said, "You called out, you know? You called out Bundy's name."

Mike picked up his briefcase. He held it, tapped his forehead with it. He looked up at Ezra. "Yeah." He looked around. "This road goes on down to the bridge, right?"

Ezra put his hand back on Mike's arm. "Yeah. You sure you feeling all right?"

"Yeah. I'm tired. I've been hearing things."

"Were you surprised? You know, surprised by Bundy shooting himself."

"Yeah. Were you?"

"Naw. I'm sad about it, I think about it, you know . . . but not surprised." Ezra rubbed his chin with the back of his hand. "He gave away all his things. We went jacklighting, he gave me a bunch of stuff. Flashlight, buck knife. Everything but his over-and-under."

Mike said, "I didn't have any idea. I should have."

"Naw. You couldn't have. That priest was right—he said you shouldn't go on second-guessing. I should've done this, I should've done that. Bundy decided to go and he's gone."

"I hear his voice."

"Yeah, I expect so. What's he saying?"

"I just hear the sound."

"Uh-huh. He had that real crackly voice."

Mike said, "Last night I got a taste in my mouth. A taste and smell. Gun bluing. For a second there I felt how . . . powerful. How someone might want to go there."

Ezra said, "You own a gun?"

"No."

"That's good."

Mike said, "It's not something I have in mind. Not in my mind."

"You should go home. Go home, go about your business. You'll be your old self soon enough. You been a little bit up in the air."

"Yeah."

"Something like this happen, everyone around him's bound to act strange. I ain't been close to doing something like I just done to you—not for a long time. Not since the time I told you about. You remember? It was a house. A house'll get in your mind same as a woman. Once it gets going in you, you either got to do it or get it clean out. You start dreaming about windows, doors. You feel what the air be like that first second you slip inside, how it's all still and warm. How it'll settle against your cheek. But I just put it out of my mind."

Mike was startled by how sympathetic he was to Ezra's description of temptation. Yet another temptation. Mike pulled back. All this adhesive sympathy was bad for a practicing lawyer; *detached* sympathy was what you needed, being able to find the bones of events, not the flesh. On the other hand, he was glad to get Ezra's slant on housebreaking—a dance of energy and sensation. Mike was pretty sure Ezra had resisted since he'd got out of the Navy. His two arrests for B&E had been as a juvenile—his one conviction, at age seventeen, had led to a suspended sentence provided he volunteer for military duty. Lucky he got the right judge. And Ezra shrewdly chose the Navy. No way he was going to *walk* into Vietnam.

And lucky again that someone in the Seventh Fleet command was a fight fan, picked up that Ezra was a Golden Gloves state finalist. Most of Ezra's four years had been in the Mediterranean, either on a carrier or on shore, as well trained as he would have been in any gym in Virginia, though not as well as if he'd gone to Philadelphia or New York.

He'd been arrested once since coming back to Charlottesville. A cop had come round a corner and seen Ezra in a parking lot. Ezra had a guy's wallet in his hand.

Ezra said that the guy had driven into the lot without looking and had brushed Ezra with the car. Ezra regained his balance and was at the car door when the guy got out. Ezra asked to see the guy's license. The guy refused, Ezra insisted, the guy took a poke at him, Ezra slipped the punch, got behind the guy, put a forearm across the guy's throat, and lifted his wallet. That was Ezra's version.

The guy's story was that he got out of his car and got mugged. Period.

On cross-examination Mike got the guy to admit that Ezra did say something to him.

"What *did* Mr. Pritchett say to you?"

"I don't know."

"The words 'Let me see your license' don't ring a bell with you?"

"I don't know. He was coming at me. I don't know what he said. He was—"

"Okay. You don't know—"

"He was threatening me."

"Threatening you? Did he say 'Give me your wallet'? Or—"

"He was in my face."

"In your face saying what?"

"I don't know."

"So he said something and you don't know what he said. Did you ask him what he said?"

"No. He was—"

"Did you say anything?"

"No. I don't know."

"So then you threw a punch at him."

"He was coming at me. I defended myself."

"And after you threw a punch, what then?"

"He mugged me."

"How did he do that?"

"I don't know. He sneaked round behind me and—"

Mike repeated slowly, "He sneaked . . . round behind you."

There was some laughter.

The guy looked up and said, "Hey, it was *dark*."

More laughter. The judge said "Order" in a mild way.

Mike said, "So you threw a punch and missed, and Mr. Pritchett sneaked around behind you and took your wallet. Is that right?"

"He mugged me."

"He put one hand on your wallet and mugged you with the other?"

"He had his arm across my throat."

"Did you struggle?"

"No."

"How come? You're a pretty big guy. Bigger than Mr. Pritchett."

"I didn't know how many of them there were."

Laughter. The witness said, "That's how they'll do."

Mike said, "They. You mean—"

"Bad guys. Muggers." But then, because he hadn't said "niggers" or "Negroes" or "black guys," the witness looked a little pleased with himself.

"But you'd thrown a punch. . . ."

"Well, that was before I thought—"

"Yes. I understand."

"Before I thought about . . . the danger."

"The danger from the other guys—"

"No."

"From the other guys you imagined."

"No. From him. From him moving so quick I figured he was a professional."

"And then you stood still?"

"Yeah, that's all I could do."

"Did you hear him say anything then?"

"I don't know."

"Mr. Pritchett was standing behind you—touching you—your head and his couldn't have been a foot apart. And yet you don't know if he said anything?"

"Well, he moved away."

"Moved away? You mean he ran off with your wallet?"

"No. He was right there. I turned around and I saw him with his fingers in my billfold."

"In the dark?"

"I could see. There was some light where he was just then. It was dark but—"

"So now Mr. Pritchett was standing in the light with your wallet. How far away?"

"I don't know. A ways. As far as me to you."

"Okay. At that point did he say anything?"

"I don't know. He may have mumbled something."

"Is your hearing good? Can you hear me all right?"

"Yes."

"Did you say anything back?"

"Yes."

"Why?"

"I said I hadn't . . . I said I was just parking my car and I was driving carefully. Which is true."

"I asked you *why* you said something."

"Why? I just said something to get him off me."

"You said he'd already moved away."

"I was saying something to calm him down so he wouldn't come at me again. . . . I was in a state of fear. I'd just been mugged."

"You said to him that you were just parking your car, that you were driving carefully. So he must have said something about your car."

"I could've said almost anything. I was—"

"But what you did say was in response to Mr. Pritchett's claim that you'd hit him with your car."

The witness said, "The thing about the car—"

"Did you think he made it up?"

The prosecutor said, "Objection. The witness can't testify as to what was in someone else's mind."

Mike said, "Your honor, I'm asking what the *witness* thought."

But now the question wouldn't work. The guy had had time to back into his shell of "I don't know." So Mike had to go on trying to get the guy to say "I don't know" so often that the jury wouldn't buy his story. But by now Mike was afraid that he seemed to be bullying the guy or that he seemed too cute.

The judge said, "Overruled. The witness may answer. . . ."

The witness said, "I don't get it. I don't know what he was saying, let alone thinking."

Mike said, "Okay. Never mind. Maybe you can tell me this—who said anything about a car?"

"Well, I said 'car.'"

"Who talked about the car first—you or Mr. Pritchett?"

"That's hard to say. I mean we weren't having a conversation, we were having a mugging."

Laughter. This time at Mike's expense. Mike forced himself to give a laugh and say, "Yeah, that's funny. But here you are—you remember every detail of light and dark, every move—and you can't remember what was said. You're a smart guy, you're a verbal guy. So who started talking about your car?"

The prosecutor said, "Objection. Asked and answered."

"Your honor," Mike said, "the witness said it would be hard for him to say. I'm just asking for him to give it a try. Squeeze that old memory a little bit harder."

"Overruled. The witness may answer."

"Who started talking about your car?"

"My car? I don't know. The car could've come up any of a dozen ways. He could've asked for the car keys."

"Oh, come on. Who started talking about the way you were driving?"

"I wasn't driving recklessly."

"I'm sorry. You're not answering my question. Here it is: Were you responding to what Mr. Pritchett said about your driving? Please answer yes or no."

The witness looked at the prosecutor and said, "I can't say. I don't want to say anything that's not exactly right. This lawyer's trying to get me to say yes or no and it's not that way."

Mike said, "Will the court direct the witness to answer the question?"

The prosecutor said, "He says he doesn't know. That's an answer."

The witness said, "I've told you what *happened*. I just can't say the exact words that the mugger said. That's—"

Mike said, "Oh, no you don't! I've had enough of your mugger bull. I've put up with your evading the truth—with your it-was-dark, it-was-light, with your imaginary muggers, with your—"

The judge gaveled. The prosecutor objected. The judge said, "Mr. Reardon, you're over the edge."

Mike said, "I'm sorry, your honor. I'll withdraw the question."

The prosecutor said, "Question! That wasn't a question. That was a speech. It's—"

The judge said, "Cut it out. Both of you, cut it out. Mr. Reardon, go on to your next question if you have one."

Mike said, "Your honor, I had asked the court to direct the witness to answer—"

The prosecutor said, "Your honor—"

"If you'll please let me finish this sentence," Mike said. "If the answer is that the witness doesn't know—strike that—that he can't say . . ." Mike shrugged. "If he won't say, he won't say, and let's not waste any more time. I have no further questions."

The prosecutor said, "Objection."

The judge said, "To what? Mr. Reardon has no further questions."

The prosecutor said, "I object to his insinuation that the witness won't answer. The witness said he *can't*."

The judge said, "Defense counsel has no further questions, so what's the point? Do you really want a ruling on *won't* and *can't*?"

Mike said, "I don't want to prolong this. Can't answer, can't say. Whatever. I'll trust the jury. I'll withdraw the last question, and I have no further questions."

At the time of the trial Mike didn't know if Ezra was guilty. Mike's lawyer acquaintances who had real experience with criminal law all told him this was pretty much par for the course. Joss had been shocked when he told her he didn't know, didn't really want to know, probably couldn't ever know exactly what Ezra had done.

Ezra himself had told Mike later that it had crossed his mind to take some folding money. He said, "Like a fine, you know. I might've got hurt. Big-ass white boy with a big-ass car."

Mike said, "And a big-ass wallet."

"That's right."

"But you just wanted to see his driver's license."

Ezra pursed his lips. "Yes sir, that's it."

Mike said, "You may not have larceny in your heart, but you're a bad-ass. Even in a big city, the police know who's a bad-ass. In a town like this, you don't want the hassle. Your uncle tells me you want to start a gym. You may want some of the city recreation budget to run some exercise programs, maybe have boxing classes. The city helps pay for karate and judo at the recreation centers, why not good old boxing, the manly art of self-defense? It makes it harder if you're a bad-ass. Harder to deal with the city, with banks."

Ezra said, "I thought that was where you and my uncle come in."

Mike said, "*I'm* not starting a gym. *You're* starting a gym. You get a name as a boxer, that helps. You get a name as a good citizen, that helps. All that boring stuff like credit rating, safety record, no weirdness. Yeah, it bores me too. It's not the fun part of life. You have lots of fun parts, for God's sakes. You're single. You go hunting. You get in the ring and—"

"That's work," Ezra said. "It ain't fun."

"Oh. I thought—"

"Roadwork, sit-ups, skip-rope, weight-training. Soon as you're through with tracking at dawn, you lay down to rest up and the alarm goes off for your noonday workout. Then you do a chore or two, sit down for a minute, and it's your sparring. If you're lucky, you don't get hit so it hurts. If you're lucky, you get a rubdown, but then you can't keep your eyes open when you got to talk about the evening workout. You know, *think* about it. So, yeah, it's just three hours, but it takes the whole damn day."

Mike had thought about it. Ezra had watched him, and then smiled. Ezra didn't smile often, but when he did it was a truly charming sideways slide. Ezra said, "I won't tell you a story, there is one part that's real good. I get working in a fight and I get that edge, just a little edge. Then it's like the other guy's in slow motion. Not all the time, you know, just when he goes to do something. There's this . . . like blank space and like extra time. Just a speck of time. And before I think about it I've done something right. You know, like hook him twice. Like jab-jab-jab and there's a right underneath. And I know it'll come again. I just keep moving, that edge be there. It's a feeling." Ezra shrugged. "It's all I can say, it's a feeling."

"That sounds good," Mike said. "That must be really good."

"It ain't frustrating."

Maybe it was that remark, maybe the whole conversation—maybe it was that Mike was flattered that Ezra trusted him enough to ask him to help with the paperwork for Ezra's gym—whatever it was, Mike had fallen for Ezra. Maybe it was because Mike knew that they wouldn't ever be friends, not friends in the sense of easy openness. There was, however, enough good will so that Ezra would appear from time to time either at Mike's office or his house, usually with a problem or a question, but once in a while just to hang out. Mike's relations with Ezra were different from those with Ezra's uncle Emmanuel. Emmanuel started out at a certain level of self-revelation and that was it. Ezra, on the other hand, was guarded and elusive at the start—understandably—and even after a couple of years, each meeting with Mike began as carefully as the first. Sometimes he'd shy off, but other times he'd let himself go. Then, for no reason Mike could see, Ezra would slip back into himself. He didn't seem nervous or tense; if anything, he became calmer—extraordinarily still—and then he'd mumble a few disconnected words and be gone.

So it seemed normal to Mike to be standing on a dark street with Ezra. It even seemed normal that Ezra, having yoked him, was now flickering into the most intimate conversation they'd ever had. Mike was touched that Ezra worried about him—"You own a gun?"—and Mike found himself hungry—starving—for Ezra's company. He said, "Can you walk a ways? You going to the gym?"

"I got to be tracking, can't cool down in this night air."

"How come you're doing roadwork at night?"

"Ten rounds, man. Ten rounds. I've never gone ten. I'll save you a couple of seats. Hey, you bring your girls." Ezra began to jog in place. "Bring me some good luck."

"Ezra—"

But Ezra was dancing around now.

"Drop by, will you, Ezra?"

"You come by the gym. Sweat it out, whatever's on your mind." Ezra jabbed him on the shoulder. "Hey. You going to tell Manuel about this?"

"Let's say this comes under the lawyer-client privilege."

Ezra smiled, then slid away, camouflaged in gray in the thick moonlight.

Mike was abruptly desolate. He wished Ezra would've walked with him. He was off-balance. Two minutes before he'd been laughing. Now he was shrunken, clumsy, at a loss in the night.

A little while later, still standing there, he felt sympathy—another sympathy—for the complaining witness in Ezra's old case. "I don't know," the guy had said, "I can't say." It was dark, it was light. The guy had been stonewalling, but he'd been genuinely baffled too, poor bastard, at a loss in the night.

He tucked his briefcase under his arm and started walking home. He felt himself floating far away, far from Ezra's moonlit disappearance, far from Bundy, far from life at home. A few more yards and he saw the cars crossing the Free Bridge. He scuttled to the other side of the bypass. He walked past the bright Safeway, past the dim cinder-block stores and warehouses, past the gym, the last city building. He walked beside the sycamores that lined the river, their white splotches hovering in dark midair, light and dark. He heard the river, a slight sound for all its mass. The night was flowing into him through all his senses. This opening of his senses was usually a joy. Now he felt alarmed. Why? Because usually he held back the flow, made a pool, made words, categories, pictures, made sense of it. Now it was pouring through and he made nothing of it.

◇

One of the bits of modern folklore that everyone swallows is that women living together—girls' dorm or prison—all get their periods at the same time. Maybe it's true, maybe it's myth-information (Hi, Mom!). In any case I've always heard it cited by men, and it strikes me as part of the ongoing male preoccupation both with menstruation (either as repugnance, cf. *mikvah*; or, more rarely, envy, cf. male subincision so that they can bleed and share the magic). It is also part of male preoccupation with female union: we're one vast witches' coven.

But men could have unions, and I don't just mean going out and killing deer or fish or getting off on vicarious violence like watching football (What a hit! That cleaned his clock!) or two boxers pounding each other's faces flat. Men could have lots of finer empathies, but they usually blow it. There was Dad feeling blue. Tyler was in his own fit of anxiety coming up for tenure. And even Edmond went into one of his depressions.

What did they do? They sealed themselves off. Dad stayed at his office twelve hours a day. Tyler did the same. Edmond stayed out in his truck counting the hawk migration, the fish in the James, the lonesome pines in the Blue Ridge Mountains of Virginny.

A boys' club of solitude is what it is. Yet in some eerie way I think that all three of them were as in touch as a dorm-full of simultaneously menstruating women. Because they were boys, of course it had to be competitive—Who's the most bloody but unbowed? Who's the most stoic? Who's the Spartan boy who steals a fox, hides it under his robe, and then stands at attention on parade not uttering a sound while the fox eats his entrails?

A question I have is whether the boys are getting off on having their souls grow hard and erect in solitary or are they getting off on an audience finally saying, "Wow! Forty days and forty nights in the desert. What a guy!" I sometimes hope Dad, Edmond, and Tyler were playing to an audience, that in an indirect shy way they were begging for sympathy from each other. I remember one story Edmond told which may have been . . . I was up late because all the grown-ups were so intent on themselves—first because all three men showed up for supper, a rarity at that time, and also Bonnie and Dad had an argument that got everyone's attention. I remember Edmond's story because Edmond, though he was the quietest of the three, told very good stories. I also remember it because Dad got it into his repertoire and told it to me several times later on. Edmond started off by saying to Dad that he knew what Dad meant when he'd said, "Life has lost its flavor."

Dad said, "Yeah. At the time I thought that was bad."

Bonnie and Mom both laughed. Bonnie sang, "'Does your chewing gum lose its flavor on the bedpost overnight?'" and Mom joined in.

Dad didn't turn his head. "But then there's life losing its *color.* I think that's the next stage."

Edmond and Tyler nodded.

Dad said, "But there's a stage after that, when you can see that life has all its flavor and all its color but it just doesn't matter."

Bonnie poured more wine for herself and Mom. Mom sang a snatch of *Pirates of Penzance.* "'No it really doesn't matter, this unintelligible patter. . . .'"

"One time," Dad said, "I had shore leave when my ship docked in Naples. Got a train to Rome. Walked to the Capitoline Hill. You can see four different ages. You can look down on the Roman Forum and across to the Palatine. You can turn around and see a Dark Ages church. You can see two Renaissance buildings by Michelangelo on either side of you. Behind the church there's the back of the Victor Emmanuel monument to celebrate the unification of Italy in 1870 or so. You can look out over Rome and see all those Renaissance domes."

"More Baroque than Renaissance," Bonnie said.

"Churches everywhere. Santa Maria of this, Santa Maria of that. I must have seen fifty of them when I was tramping around without a map."

"Rome on roller skates," Bonnie said.

"But the main point came at this one place on this one hill. I was in a vortex of everything that had thrilled me. I was one of those kids who actually liked reading Caesar's *Gallic Wars,* Cicero. And I'd been pious, I was still holding on to the idea that the Church did something wonderful during the Dark Ages, and there was this actual church, Ara Coelis—"

"Ara Coelis is a Roman temple."

"Whatever it's called, there were still pilgrims there. There was one guy going up the stairs on his knees, and there was another guy kicking a soccer ball, keeping it in the air in front of him while he climbed all those steps. He was like the guy who juggled in front of the statue of the Virgin Mary on Christmas Eve. And there was the big equestrian statue of Marcus Aurelius—"

"That was still there?" Bonnie said. "They've taken it away to be restored now."

"And I'd read about Garibaldi, so he comes into it too—the unification of Italy, Victor Emmanuel—"

"Romans call that monument 'the typewriter.' Everyone hates it."

Dad said, "I'm talking about a mood here, a sense of history, not aesthetics."

Bonnie said, "That's why you went to law school."

Mom laughed.

Dad said, "Anyway I kind of like the Victor Emmanuel monument. It's grandiose, it's noisy, but it's about something. It's like the Verdi *Requiem.*"

Mom said, "Mike has a thing about requiems."

Bonnie said, "I guess that's why he wears dead people's clothes."

It was true that Dad's best suits were ones he'd inherited from his father and from Mom's father. He also wore a sweater of Bundy's.

Dad stuck to his monument. "It's about the Risorgimento. I happen to think Garibaldi was a hell of a fellow. But the point is that there was all this stuff that had thrilled me, but when I finally *saw* it, suddenly physically in front of me, it all went blank. And I was left with this . . . dismay. It happened faster than I could think why. There were little *reasons* flitting in my brain. . . . The ancient Romans suddenly struck me as bad guys. Hard-ass army engineers. Squashed the Etruscans by persistence, not brilliance. The Romans weren't even good sailors, but they beat the Carthaginians by grappling and boarding and just turning the sea battles into land battles. And the Church suddenly repelled me. I felt like Luther. . . .

"And, yes, I get the point about the Victor Emmanuel monument being bogus. Not your aesthete's point but the historical point that Garibaldi got conned. He was a republican who got outfoxed by Count Cavour and the House of Savoy—they even gave away Garibaldi's hometown to France—and Italy got a king instead of a republic.

"But it wasn't that restatement of the facts. All that stuff went through my head in a flash, but the main thing was . . . a vision. It wasn't a vision of evil. It was just blank. The guys I'd read about were gone. Now that I finally saw the ruins and monuments and churches, all I could think was that even the good guys were gone for good. No immortal spirits. Just these termite mounds, and all the termites were dead. I'd been ready to receive this physical place where what I knew about law and justice and civilization were *made*. . . . But instead of receiving it like a sacrament, I was inert. I saw all those old stones as if they were that little sieve on top of the bathtub drain where a few hairs and dead skin get caught."

Everyone was quiet. I was scared. All of Dad's history lectures to me had always had happy endings. America became independent. The slaves were freed. Roosevelt ended the Depression. America won the war. Even the ancient stuff—the Athenians were better sailors than the Persians, and that was good, because Athens was clarity and reason and democracy. The fall of Troy led to the founding of Rome. The Norman invasion of England made the English language twice as rich, the best of Anglo-Saxon and French. Every story I'd ever heard him tell had been like the *Odyssey* or *Where the Wild Things Are.* If you're resolute and clever and a good sailor, you have adventures and get home, where somebody loves you best of all.

In this silence Evelyn was the one who noticed me. She took my hand and said to Dad, "But then what happened? You can't just stop at the scary part."

"I walked. I couldn't just turn around and go back to my ship, even though that's what I felt like doing. After a while the *anguish* stopped, but I wasn't any happier. I'd always thought that beauty was another sacrament. Another outward and visible sign of an inward and invisible grace—the sacrament of the inward and invisible splendor of everything, a sign that everything tends to organize itself. Not neatly, but beautifully. That all the best parts of everyone's lives get to be part of larger, longer pieces of time."

"But what *happened*?" Evelyn said.

"Oh. It got to be late afternoon. All the stores opened up again, so it must have been four. I was physically exhausted, I was beginning to flap around when I walked. I sat down at a café and wrote Joss' father a letter and said I wanted a real sea duty on a small ship, not just duty as a lawyer on a carrier the size of a city. I said I thought this would make me a better officer. I knew he'd take this to mean I was thinking of a career in the Navy and that he'd like that and do something. I walked to the Vatican to mail it, because everyone had said the Italian mail was slow. I could have gone back to Naples and sent it through the Navy, but I was afraid I'd change my mind on the train. I wanted to do something then and there. Some act that would get me out of all the stuff that made me. Out of Rome, out of America. It was crazy."

Edmond said, "No." Everyone was surprised. Edmond never contradicted someone directly. "It wasn't crazy. I know what you were doing. You were doing what I saw an orangutan do."

"Edmond," Evelyn said, "maybe Mike—"

"I know," Edmond said. "But this has to do with Mike, it really does. Look—if you're born a female orangutan you spend two years with your mother, she teaches you all the two hundred leaves and berries to eat, and all their poisonous look-alikes, she teaches you all the local escape routes to get away from leopards. Leopards can climb trees, but—"

"Edmond," Evelyn said.

Edmond said, "Yes. The young female orangutan. At the end of two years she moves away but not all that far, maybe a quarter-mile, just out to the border of her mother's territory, and they keep on getting together socially. But if you're a *male*, your mother drives you away after only one year, just as soon as you begin to make your first male hooting sounds." Edmond gave a little tenor hoot. "Your mama does a whole aggressive display—yelling and tearing up things and she might even hit you or bite you. The little male is terrified, he gives his little supplication cries, but this time they don't work. So he'll try to stand up to her—he gives his male hoot. That just makes her worse, and she keeps driving him out of her territory. Way, way out. So now when he gives his hoot"—Edmond gave a tenor hoot—"he's likely to hear the louder, deeper hoot of the male of the territory he's wandered into. Each female has about a quarter of a square mile of territory, but each male has a whole square mile with four adult females in it. So the young male gets driven out of his mother's patch, then gets hooted out of his father's bigger patch, though he doesn't know it's his father. And he wanders on and on. He keeps moving through more and more adult male territories until he finds a place where he's not out-hooted. Now he's *miles* from home. There's probably slightly different things to eat, maybe some new poisonous berries his mama couldn't teach him about. The trees and vines are in a different pattern, so he has to work out new escape routes if he gets chased by a leopard. The average life expectancy for a male is way, way less than a female's. Of course the survival of the orangutans only requires one male for every four females, so there's no problem if more than half the males die young. In fact it may produce better male breeding specimens. But the little wandering male doesn't know all that.

"Anyway, some time back I was in Borneo as an assistant to the man who wrote the book on orangutans, and I actually got to see a mother drive out her one-year-old son. Professor Horr and I had been watching for months and we finally got to see the . . . I was going to say *'ritual,'* but it was real—"

Bonnie said, "There speaks a fellow Protestant. Ritual just ain't real."

Edmond, without looking at Bonnie, cocked his head for a second and went on. "I mean this orangutan mother honest-to-goodness chased her little boy. Just drove him right out. When I read about this display beforehand, I took it in pretty calmly. But when I saw it, I could hardly stand it. I saw the *expressions* on his face. He was surprised, then he was scared. Then he got desperate. That's when he gave his little supplication cries—they were *like* the food-begging cry but so *sad* it would have broken your heart. Then, just the way it was supposed to happen, he hooted his grown-up male hoot. Not quite grown-up—more like a kid whose voice is changing. But his mama roared and growled and carried on even worse. And off he went. He was tottering away—you could see he was in shock—but he wasn't going off fast enough for her, and she made another dash at him, and he crabbed along right quick across the clearing. Professor Horr followed the mama to see what she'd get up to. I followed the male. It wasn't that hard, because he kept stopping—he'd go along for a bit and then he'd lean against a tree. I wasn't close enough to hear, but it looked to me like he *sighed*. Then he started moving along steadier, as if a little exercise would cheer him up. But when he got to another clearing he stopped. He looked around, and I swear I could tell what he was thinking. He was thinking that this glade looked a lot like the last one, where that terrible thing happened. He sat down with his hands hanging over his head. Then he gave a supplication cry. But *then* he turned around, backed up, and faced where he'd just been, and he acted out his mama's growling and baring her teeth. Then he played himself again, whimpering and begging. Then he turned around and did his mama's display again, and this time he made a little charge. Then he turned around again and played himself—backing away, scampering sideways. And then he gave his hoot. He turned around again to act his mama's part, but just then we both heard this other male hoot off in the trees. Now, *that* hoot was the real thing. I'd thought my little male was hooting pretty good, but that other hoot made the hair on my neck rise. I didn't get to see what my little male thought of that—he was gone."

Mom said to me, "Don't worry, pooch—I'll never bite you or drive you out."

Bonnie said, "Of course not. Women are smart enough to stick together."

"Good Lord," Evelyn said. "That's not the point."

"The reason I brought this up," Edmond said to Dad, "is that you wrote that letter to your father-in-law—"

"Father-in-law-to-be," Dad said.

"—out of the same impulse that made my orangutan make up a play. It was displacement activity. That happens when an animal has equally strong urges toward fight or flight. The classic example is a Siamese fighting fish. If you put a mirror up against his bowl he'll rush up to attack his reflection, but as he gets close he sees it's exactly his size, and exactly as fierce. If it was bigger he'd retreat, if it was smaller he'd attack. But what he sees is someone exactly his size. So what he does is back up and build a nest. This puzzled people for a long time until they figured out the fish had all this energy, and it wouldn't go into one or the other of the usual responses, so he had to do *something*—so he transfers all this built-up energy into another instinctive thing he knows to do. What I like about my little orangutan is he did something extraordinary. And he did it consciously. He had the worst day of his life, and he didn't collapse—he invented drama. So there you were—you had all these attachments to a maternal Rome, but you felt chased out. You could have just got depressed, but instead you found some displacement activity."

Dad said, "I think your orangutan handled it a lot better."

I was amazed. I'd heard Dad say a couple of modest things, but never *believably*. What was equally amazing was that this version of how he'd given up his cushy job in the Mediterranean and got transferred, as it turned out, to South Vietnam was completely different from the one he'd told me before. The earlier version had him thinking about it all, reasoning out his obligations to the country, the Navy, and coming up with an answer. He later saw that his answer had been wrong, but the moral of the story to me was that you're supposed to *ponder* what's the right thing to do and then, even if you end up wrong in some way, you're morally okay. This new version was that it was displacement activity, and not even as good as the orangutan's.

"Still and all," Edmond said. "You and that orangutan . . ."

Dad said, "I like your orangutan. And it's good you were there to see what he did. Do you think he knew you were there?"

"I think not."

Dad said, "That's too bad."

Mom said, "Not everybody needs an audience."

Dad was only paying attention to Edmond. He brightened for a second, and said, "But maybe he got to do it again for the other young males. Do they hang out in bachelor groups, like those elk—"

"No." Edmond shook his head. "No. Once his mama drives him out, he leads a completely solitary life. He keeps on hooting, but his hoot, when it gets stronger, drives away other males. And it makes the females hide from him—except for when they're in heat. But a female only comes in heat once every year or two. Longer if she has a daughter. And mating is real quick. So the male's social life is maybe two or three short dates a year."

"But then the female social life is only *one* date a year," Bonnie said. "Or one date every two years if she has a daughter."

"That's just the sexual part of her social life," Edmond said. "The females get together with each other. Two or three meet up and spend the afternoon browsing. If two of them have daughters they might even have nests in the same tree for a while. They have real friendships."

"It's just real sad for those males," Evelyn said.

"Hunh," Bonnie said. "Male territoriality. If they weren't so fixated on territory . . ."

"Well, that's what worries me," Edmond said. "It's that terrible overlap between instinct—what's programmed into them—and their conscious intelligence and feeling. There's something really beautiful about some instincts. Migration is just amazing, not just hawks or geese, but butterflies. Monarchs. They do this wonderful thing in a way that I imagine must make them feel . . . I shouldn't say *happy,* but I can't help imagining what it would feel like to have their senses become so alert to the sky, the earth—an enormous curve of the world. They don't have a choice, but still it must feel good—and huge. On the other hand, that little male orangutan was obeying *his* program, but he'd got a bigger brain too, and he could think about what was going on, and all it got him was a whole lot of perplexity and suffering. The evolution of consciousness is sometimes pretty depressing."

Evelyn said, "But if you weren't conscious, you wouldn't know all those things that animals do. I don't know anyone who knows how to see them and love them better."

Edmond shook his head. "Some days I think it's all pretty good, everything's part of a big shaping. The little I know is part of a pattern way beyond my imagination. Other days I think there's a struggle between shaping and shapelessness. And then there's a lot of days when I think . . . nothing. In the beginning there was nothing. For a little while now there's something. An accidental bubble of something—a universe, some wriggling around of life. And then nothing."

One of the things I thought then was that Edmond and Dad were taking back presents they'd given, were breaking promises they'd made to me. I'd been thrilled when Dad had said to me—just a few days before this orangutan day—"Honey, I think you have a sense of history." Paternal blessing! Better than his saying, "You're turning into a really pretty girl." And Edmond, my adjunct professor of natural history, the coziest of the communal men, had always told stories, like Dad's, with mysteries that promised for the next lesson even better, even more beautifully woven stories about the nature of things.

I was worried by the substance of what Dad and Edmond were saying now, but I also felt a slice of disappointment, because I began to suspect on my own that they were just telling themselves how sad they were. I suspected that all their lore was just their own lore, not truth, but their own consoling snack food.

So I didn't mind a bit when Mom began to bat at them. She said, "You guys are so fucking abstract! Why can't you just be in a bad mood without involving the whole world? What's the big idea? Why can't you just say"—and here Mom went into her ham-actor voice—"'And somewhere men are laughing, and somewhere children shout; / But there is no joy in Mudville—mighty Casey has struck out.' So get over it. Stop worshipping your own bad moods. They're not infinity. They're just way too long."

Bonnie laughed. Tyler laughed. Even Evelyn laughed. Edmond and Dad got hurt feelings. Edmond blinked. Dad got dignified.

"If I'm not mistaken," Dad said, "Edmond said that he has good days and bad days. We're being reflective and you start some emotional harangue."

"Order in the court," Bonnie said to Mom. "Another outburst like yours and he'll hold you in contempt."

Dad looked at Bonnie and said, "Fuck you."

Everyone sat still. Mom got red in the face. Bonnie raised one eyebrow without moving any other part of her face.

Evelyn got up and began to take out the glasses.

It wasn't as though Mom and Dad didn't both have foul mouths, Mom even more than Dad. It was some other rule Dad had broken.

Mom said, "You'd better apologize."

Dad stood up and got a cigar out of his cigar box.

Mom said, "You'd better not smoke that in here."

"Certainly not," Dad said, and went out to the porch.

They suddenly seemed childish to me but at the same time grown-up, grown-up in that alien way that men and women were in Mom's favorite black-and-white movies. I don't mean the funny ones. I mean the ones where the glossy-lipped heroine says to the man framed in the doorway, "You shouldn't have come back, Johnny." Then she kisses him, or slaps him. Close-up of her long fingernails on his shoulder pushing him away, pulling him to her. Hollywood grown-ups, perfect humanoids, their spasmodic emotional displays pulled out of them by the ratchets of the plot.

Tyler said, "Well, that was bound to happen."

I didn't get it, so I was glad again for Mom, who said, "What the hell is that supposed to mean?"

Bonnie said, "I think he means Mike's still on edge. On account of his best friend . . ."

Tyler looked at Bonnie as though to correct her.

Bonnie said, "Well, you know what I mean. He's just so pent up. Maybe we shouldn't have teased him."

Mom snorted. Bonnie stood up, smoothed her skirt, and went out to the porch.

I wished Mom would have asked more questions. I wished someone would have asked why the wrong people were doing the wrong things to the wrong people. Too many wires were crossed. Why did Dad just get mad at Bonnie and not Mom? Why was it Evelyn who noticed me? Why was it Edmond comforting Dad? Why was it Bonnie sashaying onto the porch to smooth out Dad?

I knew she could do it. About once a week she'd bicker with Dad and sting him. Then she'd wheedle him out of his bad mood while Mom laughed about it. Bonnie could even give Dad a little neck rub with her light narrow fingers and Mom would laugh.

I could feel gusts of invisible wind. I could feel things moving. I could feel all the grown-ups being blown around inside themselves.

Later—much, much later—I learned not to panic when I have sensations like that. They're not like Dad's ghosts, they're not like Mom's wiggly worms or her visions of things all being made of glass.

Maybe they're mild delusions, maybe they're a form of extrasensory perception, maybe *hypersensory* perception. And then my souped-up brain, racing like mad to make pictures or sentences, puts out these bits of 3-D film or Sensurround. Like that sensation that gusts of wind were blowing inside everyone. I felt compressed, immobile, and silent. A sentence in a slithery bubble was working its way up inside me, squeezing in between bones and organs until it hovered so I could read it. It was in wiggly writing, like notes from the Tooth Fairy or Santa Claus. It said, "You should be the one to go out to Dad."

◇

Mike was in a rage. His hands shook when he lit his cigar. He hated his rage, he hated every symptom of it. He would hate emerging from it into the hungover stage with its after-cringes. He willed it all to end. He pressed it down. Then he tried to stop up the little leakages of puzzlement—Why was he so mad? What set him off? And then he tried to stop carrying on the argument—what argument?—in his head. But even when he reached a state of calm he could hear what Joss would say and how she would sound. She would say in her taunting lilt, "Oh, I see you've reached your state of brutal calm." He pressed her voice down too.

He'd caught a glimpse of Edith's face as he'd left. She looked scared, and that thought chilled him.

That was always a stopper. That was a trump card that both Joss and he held back from playing even at their most furious: What will the children think of this? Of us? Of you? So his pressed-down anger trickled over into general father-guilt, and so to a specific father-blunder he'd made—not huge but indiminishable by any penance. Edith had asked him to get Joss to trim her bangs. Joss was working in her studio. Mike decided to do it himself. He used the kitchen scissors, a snip here, a snip there. He was puzzled by the result. Nora came into the kitchen. Edith saw Nora's face and ran to the bathroom to look in the mirror. She came out slowly, weeping silently. Nora ran to get Joss. Joss looked at Edith and said, "What happened?"

Edith said to Mike, "Did you do it on purpose?"

"No. Of course not, honey. Maybe if we wet it down—"

"No," Joss said.

Nora said, "You made her look like Tommy Fetch." Tommy Fetch was a boy at school whom Edith and Nora hated. He had a spiky crew cut.

All four of them got in the station wagon for an emergency appointment with a hairdresser who was a client of Mike's, a willowy German man with a green-card problem. The hairdresser turned Edith's head this way and that, saying, "So . . . So . . . So. You attempted to cut this hair by yourself?"

Edith, Nora, and Joss all said, "No," and looked at Mike.

The hairdresser said, "So! Your own father has done this?"

For Joss and Nora it became a comic line. Sometime later, after Edith's hair had grown out, when it was Mike's turn to cook supper, he served a watery casserole of canned mackerel, cauliflower, and sliced black olives. Joss took a bite and said, "So. Your own father has done this?" Nora laughed. Mike felt a fine wire from Edith to him transmit her still perfectly intact pain. He accepted it, but resented Joss.

Nora said to Mike, "You remember the hairdresser? The one who fixed Edith's hair?"

Mike warily said, "Yeah . . ." So why didn't he resent Nora? He said, "Yeah, of course."

Nora said, "So why did he say 'so' so many times? Was he saying, like, it was *so* awful?"

"No. He was just—"

"He didn't mean 'So what's the big deal?' He didn't mean that, did he?"

"No. He meant it like 'ah.' Or 'aha.' Germans say it a lot."

"So," Nora said. "So, so, so. If you say it a lot it doesn't mean anything."

She got up and went to her room. Mike divided the mackerel casserole between Miss Dudley and him. Joss and Edith made scrambled eggs. Nora came out an hour later with an armful of pictures. Mike said, "Can I take a look?" Nora shook her head and went out the door to Evelyn's. This was routine. Nora always took her drawings to Evelyn, who then picked out one or two and pinned them up. When Nora brought more, Evelyn put the old ones in a folder and pinned up the new ones. Evelyn had two years' worth of Nora's drawings. Once they were up on the wall or in Evelyn's folder, Nora didn't mind Mike or Joss looking at them, but she was still prickly about praise or criticism from either of them. She was annoyed by gush as much as by critical suggestions. The only safe thing was to be attentive and agree with whatever Evelyn said.

Mike liked Nora's *so* series. The first one was of Edith in the barber's chair with exaggeratedly spiked hair. The hairdresser's speech bubble was of course: "So. Your own father has done this to you." What made it all right—more than all right—was that in the background there was a dark-brown blob of a man with a beard, holding his head with both hands. Mike didn't mind that the beard was more gray than his own—if Nora hadn't used the silver crayon the beard wouldn't have been visible, he might not have known it was him, he might not have felt understood. To be understood without having to explain!

Joss preferred the second of Nora's *so* pictures. An officer with gold braid on his hat, two silver medals on his chest, and a large purple heart over his heart (or possibly it *was* his heart) said in his speech bubble, "Do you know you're the first girl in the Navy?" The girl, who was dancing, or at least standing on one toe, looked back over her shoulder. Her speech bubble said, "So? So? So?"

Mike sat back in the deck chair, put his feet up on the leg rest, no longer tense with anger or brutal calm, but not quite through with argument. Nora's brown blob of a dad feeling bad, Edmond's male orangutan . . . So, if daughters and friends could sympathize, then why couldn't Joss? Was she afraid of giving up ground?

All right, fair's fair—did he sympathize with her? Or, to be even fairer, did he show her by some token, by some brown blob or orangutan, that her understood her?

He did sympathize with her filmmaking—he was glad when she'd won her prize, the one that brought them to Charlottesville. And glad again when she'd won another a few years later. But his one attempt to be helpful hadn't worked. He talked to some of the other filmmakers in town and found out that they spent an awful lot of time trying to raise money. He said to Joss that he thought he could find someone to help her. She said, "What? What are you talking about? I work the way I work. . . . You haven't the foggiest . . ."

He said, "Not to work on your work. Just to help with the money. Someone with some business savvy." He couldn't believe he'd uttered that phrase. It came from pretending to be some other person who just happened to float by.

"Business *savvy*?" she said. "*Savvy*?"

"Strike that. Just to help with arranging financing."

"I'll tell you one thing," she said. "I'll tell you this one thing, because I don't want to talk about what I do. Whatever I'm doing, I want to be ready to throw it in the fire. For no reason. For any reason. Because it isn't good. Or because it is good. And I don't want to account for it to some accountant who has business savvy."

He believed her. At least he believed that she wished to feel independent, pure, and drastic. He also knew that she was wildly variable in her feelings, one day treasuring her two prizes, another day snorting contemptuously—puny prizes given out by puny people.

She was shrewd about regular movies, sentimentally forgiving to old movies, and wildly variable about small independent films—sometimes infatuated, sometimes bitterly scornful. However, she was equally scornful of other people's scorn.

Mike could see that at large arty parties Joss was envious of the several filmmakers who lived in Charlottesville. She was envious of many of the recognized artists of any kind—photographers, actors, painters, writers. She was envious and contemptuous of the way they greeted each other. She saw in the tilt of their heads, the peculiar half-smile they gave each other, a Masonic sign of recognition.

Mike was impatient with some of them when they talked politics. They were more or less liberal, but more fascinated by their feelings than the real difficulties. Once in a while Mike got into arguments and, as he saw it, supplied a few crucial facts. No credit from Joss; Joss wanted no alliances. The enemy of her enemy wasn't her friend. In fact she could be infuriated by someone who was contemptuous of work she herself held in contempt.

At a party recently a man had been holding forth on a historical novel by a local woman writer. Joss and Mike both thought the novel was a swashbuckler, but Mike thought that was a good thing. The man took a sip of his drink and said, "It's not *War and Peace,* but, then, it's not *Gone with the Wind* either."

Joss said, "And you're not God Almighty, but, then, you're not just a traffic cop."

The man said, "What?"

"You're not Lake Superior, but, then, you're not just a mud puddle." Joss had only drunk one glass of wine, but it seemed to be mixing with some emotional chemical. The next glass might make her incoherent, but for the moment she was surfing.

"Really," the man said. "What brought this on?"

"Something not quite as dumb as the Miss America contest but dumber than . . . Freud talking about penis envy."

"Oh, I get it," the man said. "You're—"

"No you don't."

"—a friend of the author."

"Not me. I'm just doing my civic duty. Not as big as a citizen's arrest but bigger than picking up litter."

The man said, "So what do *you* think? Do you think her book is as good as *War and Peace*? Or worse than *Gone with the Wind*?"

Joss said, "I think if you gave up trying to put someone else's house in your watch pocket with a pair of tweezers . . ." Joss stalled.

The man said, "If I stopped picking up houses with tweezers, then what?"

"You still wouldn't be happy," Joss said. "But you might have a fairly good time."

"Edith Wharton," the man said. "Edith Wharton said that."

"So?" Joss said. "You want extra credit on the weekly quiz? You want another A-plus? Actually it wasn't Edith Wharton. Actually it was Edith Wharton's cook. She said it to the upstairs maid, who was nipping at the sherry, and the cook caught her and said—"

"You know, you must be just a ton of fun at home."

Mike took a step closer to the man, but Tyler, who'd been laughing along, put his arm around the man's shoulders and said amiably, "Aw, come on, now. Keep it funny."

The man said, "Why, Tyler, I didn't—"

Joss said, "Don't interrupt, Tyler."

The man said to Tyler, "I didn't realize you were part of this merry revel."

"Yup," Tyler said. "Right here, just reveling along."

The man slipped out from under Tyler's arm and said, "Well, it must be just your sort of fun." Then he walked away.

Joss said to his back, "And Edith Wharton's cook said, 'Don't you know sherry makes you fart?'" She turned to Tyler and said, "Who the hell is that guy?"

"He's the chair of my department."

"The chair?" Joss said. "He looks more like a . . . Oh shit, Tyler. A big cheese, huh?" She called to the man, "Did I say 'fart'? I meant to say 'fat.'" She hunched her shoulders, held her fingers to her lips, and said, "Oops."

Tyler said, "Well, you know what we say in Texas."

"Maybe he didn't hear me."

Mike said, "Oh, he heard you."

Joss looked at him crossly.

Tyler said, "Well, fuck 'em if they can't take a joke."

Joss looked at Tyler brightly. "They say that in Texas? That's so sweet." Joss sat down on the floor.

"Are you all right?"

"I'm fine. It's just this gravity thing. . . ."

Mike couldn't remember how he got Joss home. Maybe Tyler and Bonnie helped. He now thought he should have told her he thought she was really funny, except for the very end. No—like Nora, Joss didn't like qualifications. Could he have just said, "Joss, you were really funny"? No, he couldn't. He tried to figure out why he couldn't. It was fear. He feared to give ground in the struggle. . . . And what struggle was that?

For a long time he'd thought the struggle was for the moral high-ground. But all that winning that struggle had got him was that he was stuck with sticking up for sobriety, order, and duty. The struggle he hadn't paid attention to was: Who gets to be the crazy one? Who gets to be the one whose temperature has to be taken, the one whose tantrums are absorbed, whose rants are registered, whose doubts are reassured? The one who gets to say, "I can't stand it," while the other one says, "It's all right, I know it's hard for you, but it's going to be all right."

Evelyn and Edmond traded off getting to be the crazy one. Had they figured it out or did they do it intuitively?

As far as he could remember, the last time he got to be the crazy one was when he got the top of the baby-wipes jar stuck on his finger. Just now, when he said "Fuck you" to Bonnie, he didn't get to be the crazy one—he got to be the bad one. Edmond had been telling him, "You're a poor little male orangutan, you're a brown-blob sad dad," and Joss said, "Get over it." All right, fair's fair—when Joss had gone too far with Tyler's department chairman, Tyler had said, "Fuck 'em if they can't take a joke." Mike had said, "Oh, he heard you." Not just the sensible one but the I-told-you-so sensible one.

How had they got stuck with Dad is law, Mom is music?

Sometime ago they'd terrified each other with worst possibilities. Joss had wondered aloud about spending a summer at a spiritual commune. Mike had conjured up a grade-B fantasy of hypnotic gurus, Kundalini yoga, and Tantric sex. He kept his mouth shut, but Joss pointed out that his face turned to stone and his eyes became cold marbles. *His* moment of wondering aloud and terrifying her was when he'd mentioned running for office. Joss said, "Working for a politician was bad enough. Painting a billboard for one of the guys is one thing—*being* the billboard is another. And what would that make me? A politician's wife. I'd rather go to jail."

Joss called this standoff their Mutually Assured Destruction missile policy. At least she used the word "mutually."

More recently she'd said, "You think you care about me, but all you are is *anxious*." He'd considered a range of responses. Joss later claimed he'd said, "The problem with that formulation is—" He might have. He doubted it. He couldn't remember. He might have said, "The problem . . ." He *did* remember her hands grabbing her hair, her snarl coming up from her throat, squeezing past her gritted teeth. *His* problem was that he'd considered a range of responses—strike that—that he'd considered. Period. That he'd stepped back instead of lunging, that he'd uttered a word instead of a noise. That he'd given up a chance to be the crazy one.

Maybe she wanted him to give her a fight on her terms, to mix it up with her snarling and snorting. It wasn't that he didn't have the energy or the angry heat. But maybe it was selfish of him to spend his heat off by himself—digging holes, splitting wood, paddling his canoe upstream until he hurt enough to feel calm—to be the sensible one again.

He tried out a Joss-like cry of exasperation. It came out as a grunt.

Behind him Bonnie laughed. He jerked around and cracked his hand on the back of the chair.

Bonnie said, "I'm sorry. I didn't mean to . . . Did you hurt your hand?"

She put the fingertips of one hand on the back of his neck, the fingertips of the other on his wrist. "We were too mean to you just now, we really were. So I'm sorry."

Mike felt himself resisting but he wasn't sure what he was resisting. He surely couldn't ask for a sweeter apology. He fanned away the cigar smoke with his hand. "Yeah, okay. I shouldn't have . . . barked at you." He sounded stuffy and awkward.

Bonnie said, "Well, good. So you'll come on back in?" She moved her hands to his shoulders.

"In a bit. I don't want to throw away a good cigar. Not just yet."

"Oho," Bonnie said. Still standing over him, she bent her head nearer his ear and recited, "'And a woman is only a woman, / but a good cigar is a Smoke.'" She poked the top of his chest twice with one finger, saying, "I just bet you're a secret Kipling-admirer."

Mike said, "Well, yeah. But that sentiment isn't Kipling's. It's what one of his old-geezer characters says to—"

"There you go again—Mike Reardon for the defense. And, oops, there *I* go again. . . . But you know why I tease you, don't you? It's because I don't want Tyler to be jealous. He has an excessively jealous nature. Well, you know how he was about you and Bundy. . . ." Bonnie took her hands from his shoulders. "You don't mind if I bring that up, do you? I mean the subject of Bundy. I'm only bringing it up in a peripheral way to point out something about Tyler. For all his bubbling-over cheerfulness, Tyler does fret a good deal about whether people really love him. It sometimes makes him childishly possessive. It's not an unbearable flaw, but it sometimes means that I have to stand aloof—that I can't just . . . mmm . . . let things go the way they want to. I can't be as free-floating as I'd wish." She touched his shoulders again. "I have to give up some of my electrons, my charmed quarks."

Mike was beguiled. He generally liked the game, but with Bonnie he felt that his reflexes were slow. Of course now there was the taboo—Bonnie was Tyler's girlfriend—but even before, when she'd been the other nun, the free-floating other nun, he'd felt a step behind.

"Charmed quarks," he said. "I've never really known what they are. I understand you're being loosely figurative." He cleared his throat and instantly felt pompous. "By the way—"

"By the way," Bonnie said. "I can tell you're about to start your cross-examination. Your scary-lawyer mode."

"Do you tell Tyler about your . . . free-floating electrons?"

"Now, why would I do that?"

"Because, as much as you enjoy your free-floating electrons, I think you also enjoy seeing what effect they have on someone else."

"Oho. I feel a little probe, indeed I do. I trust it's a friendly little probe. Or maybe it's a worried little probe. Maybe you just want to know if—let's just pick a random example—maybe you want to know if I told Joss about you at the masquerade party. About you and the masked nun. Or about you and pretty Polly Trueheart." Bonnie patted his shoulder. "You know, you shouldn't worry so much. You've got this tendency to worry about things that don't matter. Maybe it's because you went to an all-boys school, an all-boys *Catholic* school, and that's why you take kissing so seriously. You probably think kissing is like taking communion. But it can mean so many different things. . . . You should know there are times when things dissolve. When the whole context dissolves."

"Dissolves," Mike said. "I'm not sure I get—"

"Let me tell you a little nature story. It's much shorter than Edmond's orangutan story. You know about electrons, right? They go round and round the nucleus in circles. Sometimes there are four or five orbits, each with electrons in it. But some atoms, because they get loaded up with all the orbits they can stand—or for some other reason—then they have this pi ring of electrons. The electrons in the pi ring don't go in a circle. They go in a figure eight. Well, when I heard this I naturally wondered the same thing you're probably wondering. When those electrons do their figure eight, how come they don't smash into the nucleus? So this scientist who was telling me all this—this shows how good the scientist was at dissolving contexts—my scientist gave me a science-fiction story to read. The crucial setup for the story is that there are several alternate universes occupying the same space. Each one pulsates. When one is there, the others aren't. But they pulsate so fast that the people in each universe experience their universe as continuous. So I went back to my scientist and said, 'So do you mean to tell me that the nucleus pulsates? Or the pi ring pulsates? Or both?' The scientist said, 'Don't be so literal, honey. I just wanted you to loosen up so you'd stop thinking of matter as marbles.'"

Mike thought about it for a while. He was impressed. Then he said, "So did he ever tell you if the nucleus pulsates?"

Bonnie took him by the ear. At first he thought it was another caress, but then she tugged it just hard enough to cancel that idea. She said, "Sister is going to keep you after school. Teach you to dissolve contexts better. Matter isn't marbles, and my scientist is a she."

Without turning to look, he was sure Bonnie was arching one eyebrow. He said, "I like your pi-ring story. And I really like your science teacher assigning you science fiction. But one thing I've learned from arguing in front of juries—if you don't mind a bit of advice—is that you lose their sympathy if you're too clever."

"'Be good, pretty maid, and let who will be clever.' Is that it?"

"No," Mike said. "Not clever. *Too* clever."

Bonnie said, "You know, sometimes it's just uncanny the way you and Tyler are alike. For a while I thought Tyler couldn't stand to lose an argument because he's from Texas. Sort of an Alamo complex. But really it's just a boyish urge to get in the last word."

"Okay," Mike said. "It was nice of you to come out here."

Bonnie laughed. Mike heard the soles of her shoes scratch as she turned, then her footsteps as she crossed the porch. Then the door closed.

His cigar smoke rose straight up, but there was a movement of air higher up that rustled the topmost leaves. He felt his body grow light with involuntary alertness. At the edge of his hearing he heard Bundy's dry laugh. Then something less distinct than a voice, but spelled out clearly. "The last word? I got the last word, dummy."

§ 5

Because he was junior to his two partners, Mike had a back office with a view of the small parking lot. If he stood up, he also had a view of the Blue Ridge twenty miles away. His office was the quietest except when the psychologist on the fourth floor of the next building held her screaming sessions. Mike had gone over to see her to ask about the screaming. She apologized for the noise and said there would be less in the future since she was giving up primal-scream, going to be trying out something different. She studied him silently for a moment, then said, "You look like a nice sort of lawyer." She asked if he could help her with her lease. Her landlord—the law firm that occupied the bottom three floors of her building—wanted to get her out. She had two years to go on her lease. They'd offered to buy it out and she'd refused. They then said she was in violation of some section. The noise was a problem—they claimed it interfered with the conduct of their business. That's why she was cutting out the primal-scream and maybe even the therapy where her clients hit a pillow with a tennis racket, though she didn't think that made all *that* much noise.

She was small and pale with hair like straw that jutted out from under her hats. She had lots of hats. She often wore floppy pants suits that looked too big for her, with flower patterns that were also too big. She looked funny, sort of a miniature Harpo Marx. Her name, coincidentally, was Bonnie.

Mike liked the idea of annoying the law firm next door. He liked the idea of her wacky counseling business in this otherwise staid zone of lawyers.

The landlord law firm had some other objections besides the noise. She'd spent a few nights there when she'd had fights with her boyfriend, a violation of the lease, but probably not grounds for eviction if she didn't do it again.

The law firm also claimed that she wasn't a real psychologist as she didn't have a Ph.D., and the lease specified that her business was psychological counseling. She had an M.S.W. and a certificate from a six-week course in music therapy.

Mike said that he'd have to look into it more, but it sounded as though her landlords were trying to see if a little bullying would make her move.

"We'll send them a letter on my letterhead saying you're in compliance—you're giving up the scream stuff, you're not using the office as a residence—hell, I *know* one of them has slept in his office. And your business is psychological counseling—the lease doesn't specify you have to have a Ph.D."

Mike's partners had been pissed off.

They didn't like her any better than her landlords did, and of course they didn't want to cross their brother lawyers.

"She doesn't really fit in with . . ." The most senior partner gestured out his front window at the handsome row of nineteenth-century brick houses with little white-pillared porches.

Mike said, "I don't object to your clients just because I don't like them. Otherwise I'd be a real pain in the ass."

"You *were* a pain in the ass about Albemarle Land—"

"That was a potential conflict of interest with one of my clients."

"Well, what about this woman's landlord?"

"You think that's a conflict of interest?"

"Don't be obtuse. They're our neighbors, they're our—"

"—brothers at the bar. Give me a break." Mike brightened. "Of course I could always send her over to Mad Dog."

"They'd be even more pissed off if they found out it was you that—"

"They might not find out," Mike said. "But Mad Dog'd probably make a counterclaim. Their saying she's not a psychologist—that could be libelous. Mad Dog might organize a protest march."

"Why can't you just let them ease her on out? She can find an office at one of those hippie alternative deals, do all her screaming somewheres else."

"I'll ask her. But maybe she likes it where she is."

"All right. She's all yours. Do whatever you please."

Mike knew this abrupt about-face was meant to throw him into confusion, make him admit that he'd just been rattling his senior partner's chain.

So finally he'd decided to go over and just have a chat with whoever at Broome and Havermeyer was trying to chuck Bonnie Number Two out. He got to see sweet old Mr. Broome. Mike took the line that it was just as well she'd come to him because he too had an interest in peace and quiet, and Mr. Broome and he could just sit down and pat it all smooth. Mike had to concede among other things that Bonnie Two and her clients would only use the outside stairs that zigzagged up the building from the rear parking lot.

So he himself had gone up the back stairs to her office. It looked like a graduate-student apartment—posters thumbtacked to the walls, mismatched bookshelves, and pieces of stained glass hanging in the windows. Bonnie Two had thanked him and then looked shy and embarrassed in the way that Mike had seen dozens of times and that almost always meant the client was about to say he couldn't pay. Mike had been about to tell Bonnie Two to forget it when she'd said, "Maybe, instead of me paying the bill, I could give you a free counseling session." Mike didn't want to offend her. He couldn't manage to look eager, so he settled for curious.

She said, "I could make it two sessions."

He laughed. Her expression didn't change but the skin on her face tightened. "I'm sorry," he said, "I wasn't laughing at . . . I laughed because you thought I was driving a bargain. I must have kept my bargaining face from downstairs. It's an occupational hazard, I guess. A couple of people have complained about my scary-lawyer face. I was about to say to you that I only had a ten-minute talk with Mr. Broome, so I was going to just let it go. In fact I'm sort of going to chicken out on you. There was some resistance on the part of my partners to my getting involved in a dispute with our neighboring law firm. If you get into another wrangle with them, you'd probably better try another lawyer."

Her expression still didn't change. He was used to that with clients who were in big big trouble. With smaller stuff, their faces were more expressive—stern resolve, outrage—at least a normal alertness. Emmanuel Pritchett spent a lot of time laughing.

Mike sighed. He felt like a heel. For her, two years of a lease *was* a big deal. Maybe if she were more attractive he'd have stuck with it. It wasn't that she wasn't pretty—she could be pretty—but her tentative voice, her lack of expression, her being so bundled in floppy clothes that you couldn't tell if she was vital or listless—he preferred a spark of life in any client, man or woman.

She said, "Mmm. I think maybe I'd like you to take it anyway. . . ." Her voice rose on "anyway" as if it was a question. An hour of sentences as wispy as that would drive him nuts. "Thank you," he said briskly. "Three possibilities for you to consider. One: what this may be about is something as dumb as that you don't carry a briefcase. They may just be fuddy-duddy and want you to blend in with everyone else in the building. Two: it may be about their wanting more rent money. If it's more rent, they'll wait two years. Then they'll jack it up so high you won't be able to afford it.

Three: it may be they want the fourth floor for themselves. In that case you could probably get them to pay to relocate you—a good bit more than their original offer to buy up your lease. It doesn't look that crowded right now, but I could find out if they're hiring."

"Mmm. I kind of don't like moving. Right now it might be just that extra drain on my psyche."

Mike said, "A brand-new office and some money in your pocket might do wonders for your psyche."

She already looked mournful. Now, although moving her features almost imperceptibly, she managed to look pained. Mike knew he sounded crass and rough, but conversation with Bonnie Two was like having cobwebs brush his face.

After that day his view of the rear parking lot and the wooden staircase was livened up by glimpses of her clientele. He noticed with a pang that she'd bought a big shiny leather briefcase. He hadn't meant her to take his remark literally. In any case the professional effect was ruined by her boyfriend occasionally coming to get her in his pickup. He would honk the horn and then sit in the cab with the motor running. On the first really warm day, he'd rolled the window down and kept time to the music on his radio by tapping his beer can on the door handle.

He called her up. "Ms. Sproul, this is Mike Reardon."

"Oh, I know I've got to do something," she said. "It's just that today's not a really great day to bring up stuff. Randy's kind of upset. It's kind of a, mmm, bad day."

Mike was about to say something severe when he saw the boyfriend get out of his truck. He popped another beer, slammed the door, and kicked it. He yelled up toward Bonnie Two's office, "Hey, Bonnie!" He stuck his hand in through the window and leaned on the horn.

Bonnie bleated and hung up the phone.

Mike saw her come out on her fourth-floor landing. She called down to the boyfriend, "I'll come down if you stop yelling."

"Damn straight you'll come down."

She started down. The boyfriend started up. He swung his right leg straight and wide to get onto the first step. Mike remembered an odd detail from one of Bundy's bar stories—a red-headed guy with one leg who'd take his plastic leg off when he got drunk. The boyfriend had on a ball cap, so Mike couldn't be sure about the red hair—the sideburns looked sort of red.

Bonnie and the boyfriend got to the second-floor landing at the same time. Mike couldn't hear what they were saying. Bonnie pointed up, the boyfriend took her by the wrist.

An associate from Broome and Havermeyer opened the door onto the second-floor landing. The boyfriend took a step toward the door. The door closed. Mike heard Bonnie give out a long high-pitched complaint. "Raaan-dy!"

Randy. That *was* the name of the red-headed guy with one leg. What else had Bundy said about him?

Mike wafted out the back door onto his fourth-floor landing. He trotted down to the parking lot radiant with good will and a dizzy confidence. He looked up and said, "Hey, Randy!"

Randy had picked Bonnie Two up and sat her on the railing. She grabbed the corner post and hooked a foot through the banisters. Her hat fell off and fluttered down in front of Mike. He picked it up and said, "Hey, Randy."

Randy said, "Who the fuck are you?"

"I'm a friend of Bundy's. He told me—"

"Bundy's dead." Randy pointed his finger at his mouth and said, "Blam."

"Yeah, I know. He told me he used to hang out with you."

"Yeah. So?"

"Hold on a second." Mike held up a hand. "I got to come up that way anyway."

Mike trotted up the stairs. When he got to the landing, Randy turned. He was holding one of Bonnie's legs by the ankle. Mike said, "Hey. Know what? One of those assholes in there is on the phone. I think he's calling the police. Let's us get on down."

Randy mimicked him—"Let's us get on down." He dropped Bonnie's leg. She slid slowly to the floor, holding on to the corner post and the railing.

Randy said, "You must think I'm really stupid."

Mike said, "No. I—"

"Then don't condescend to me, asshole."

"Look—" Mike said.

"Are you part of her bullshit?"

Mike said, "I don't know what—"

"You disgust me," Randy said. Mike couldn't tell if he was talking to him or to Bonnie.

Bonnie said, "He's my lawyer."

"So you got a lawyer," Randy said to her. "So he *is* part of your bullshit. You got a lawyer, but you better hope you don't try to pull some legal bullshit on me."

"It was about her office lease," Mike said. "But—"

"Then you don't know what's going on. So what the fuck are you doing here? You come up here to help the little birdie with the broken wing? She ain't the bird, asshole, she's the snake."

Mike said, "Well, that's your view."

Randy turned completely toward him, suddenly breathing hard, each breath a rasping effort. Mike blocked the punch, which Randy telegraphed with an enormous roll of his shoulder. Mike caught Randy's wrist and forearm with both hands. Mike was pleased by this move—it felt complete.

While Mike was congratulating himself, Randy, now warmed up a little, got busy. He jerked his fist down, pulling Mike off balance. Then he got Mike in a headlock and twisted Mike to the floor. Mike tried to roll away and ended up on his stomach. He heard lots of breathing, then just his own as Randy pushed himself up, putting a lot of weight in the small of Mike's back. Randy peeled Mike's suit coat off his shoulders. He pulled it down so that Mike's arms were caught in the bunched sleeves at his sides.

Mike felt a shove on the back of his head that banged his forehead on the floor. He tried to pull both arms free at once. By the time he caught on that that wouldn't work, Randy was pulling on his foot. Randy lifted it and fitted it between the tops of two banisters. There was plenty of room where the spindles were slender, but then Randy pushed it down until Mike's ankle wedged in the gap between the thicker middle parts.

Mike now tried to get one arm free. He felt Randy's foot step on his arm—hard enough to hold it still.

When Randy shoved Mike's second foot between another pair of banisters it hurt more than the first.

Now when he tried to move his arms it hurt his ankles. His feet were also stuck so high and wide apart that it was impossible to roll far enough to one side to wriggle a single arm loose.

Bonnie said, "I don't feel like this is a good thing, Randy."

"Shut your fat mouth," Randy said. "Shut your fat lying dirty puking mouth."

He ran out of breath and began gasping again.

Mike said, "Maybe you should take a look and see what those guys inside are up to."

Randy said, "Maybe you should shut up." He added, "If you weren't an old guy, I'd kick the shit out of you."

As though it were an entry in his volume of legal words and phrases, Mike saw in typeface "Adding insult to injury."

Mike heard Bonnie Two cry out. She piped, "Oh! Oh! Oh!" It sounded more like alarm than pain.

Trying to see, Mike turned his head so that it lay on the other cheek. Randy's feet walked backward past his eyes. Then came Bonnie Two being pulled feet-first. She too had the jacket of her pants suit pulled down so that her arms were at her sides. Her head went by. She had her eyes closed. Then Randy turned and shuffled backward, his feet on either side of Mike. He was still pulling Bonnie Two on her back. He tugged her by the ankles until her crotch bumped into Mike's head. Randy grabbed a handful of Mike's hair and lifted his head. With his other hand he pulled down the elastic waistband of Bonnie Two's trousers. He dropped Mike's head and let go of the waistband. It caught on Mike's chin. His nose was on the midseam of Bonnie Two's panty hose.

Randy said, "Eat that and die."

Then he left. His footsteps grew fainter going down the wooden steps, an irregular beat—light, heavy, pause, light, heavy, pause.

Neither Mike nor Bonnie Two moved until they heard the pickup door slam. As the motor started, Bonnie Two wriggled backward on her elbows. Mike lifted his chin and the waistband snapped free. The door to the landing opened. Several pairs of wing-tip shoes appeared.

Bonnie Two was raised to her feet.

Someone said, "Are you all right?"

Bonnie Two said, "Sometimes America is just so violent."

Mike thought how Joss would laugh her head off at that.

When the lawyers from Broome and Havermeyer tried to pull Mike's ankles loose, Mike winced and gritted his teeth. They got the janitor to bring a saw to cut the banisters. Ganny wanted to take Mike to the emergency room for X-rays, but Mike insisted nothing was broken, so Ganny drove him home. She put his arm over her shoulder, and he hobbled in.

Mike and Ganny stopped in the middle of the main room. Mike called out, "Joss? Joss? Alameida calling *China Clipper.* Come in, *China Clipper.*" He was trying to be funny or at least lighthearted to prepare the way for telling the story as farce: frail New Age therapist with flyaway hair as Olive Oyl, Randy as a one-legged Bluto, himself as a would-be Popeye who forgot to eat his spinach.

Joss yelled back from her studio, "I'm working!"

Mike headed for the kitchen but Ganny steered him to bed. "Ice," she said. "You ought to put ice on your ankles. And stay off your feet. I'll get the ice. You all got an ice bag?"

Mike said, "Joss can take care of that. You should get back to the office and see to Bonnie Sproul. They're probably trying to kick her out again."

Ganny said, "She's going to be more trouble than Emmanuel Pritchett. And less money. If I were you, I wouldn't mess with her."

Joss appeared, followed by Bonnie One. Joss said, "Mess with who? Are you sick? What's going on?"

Ganny gave Joss the short version and left.

◇

Joss didn't know what to make of all this. Bonnie guided Joss toward the bed. They unlaced Mike's lawyer shoes. Each one pulled off a shoe, then peeled off a sock, rolling it down until it slipped off in a soft ring. His ankles were raspberried, especially on the bony knobs, and they were also beginning to show some blue bruises and swelling. Joss and Bonnie put each of his feet on a pillow and draped his ankles with plastic grocery bags filled with ice.

"Are you sure nothing's broken?" Joss said. "Shouldn't you get an X-ray?"

Mike wiggled his toes. "See? If my ankle was broken I couldn't do that."

"Is that right?" Bonnie said.

"Yes," Mike said. "Look, Joss, I'm fine now. You can go back to work."

"You rescued a damsel in distress," Bonnie said. "We should attend you, we should be your handmaidens."

"That's okay," Mike said. "You go ahead with whatever you were doing."

Joss' arm flew up chest-high, lifted by what felt like gas bubbles in the crook of her elbow. Bonnie put her fingers around Joss' bicep and smoothed the arm down.

"We really should do *something*," Bonnie said. "Bring you a drink. Tickle your feet. Something."

"No," Mike said. "The girls'll be home later. I'll take a nap. You go ahead and get some work done. Well, maybe get me an aspirin."

Bonnie said to Joss, "You go on back to work, I'll get him his aspirin." She let Joss go first and closed the bedroom door behind her.

Joss was breathing out in little puffs. Bonnie said, "You're going to hyperventilate if you blow out like that."

Joss went into her studio. She took handfuls of her own hair and said, "Jeez Louise."

Bonnie put a finger on Joss' lips and said, "Shh." She closed the studio door behind her.

Joss held out her hands and watched her fingers twitch in a fine tremor.

Bonnie pulled Joss' hands down. She said, "I'll get him his aspirin and make sure he's tucked in."

Joss laughed and then said, "This isn't funny."

Bonnie said, "You can make anything funny. I'll be right back."

Joss heard each little noise distinctly—Bonnie's soft footsteps, the click of the childproof cap, the running water. A moment of silence. The bedroom door clicked shut. Footsteps. Joss closed her eyes. The studio door opened and closed. The bolt slid across. Joss put her hands over her eyes. She saw herself as a cartoon—Krazy Kat on a cartoon raft on a cartoon wavy sea.

Joss felt Bonnie standing in front of her. Bonnie breathed on the backs of Joss' hands. Bonnie said, "I stroked his brow like this." She touched Joss' forehead with her fingers. "Shall I tell you what else?" Bonnie said. "What else do you think?" She put her hands over Joss'. "Well, maybe I didn't do this," she said. She put her thumbs on the corners of Joss' mouth, her fingers still on the backs of Joss' hands.

Joss saw the wavy sea again, this time a Japanese print with huge white crests curling above a tiny boat.

She felt Bonnie's thumbs slide on her mouth, so lightly she could imagine Bonnie's thumb whorls engaging the furrows of her lips. When she couldn't stand waiting any longer she made a noise. It came out louder than she'd meant. Bonnie said, "Shh," and kissed her very slowly, so slowly it felt as if Bonnie was pouring her breath and lips onto Joss' like a warm glaze.

Joss took her hands away from her eyes and wrapped her arms around Bonnie, pressing her hands on Bonnie's back.

"Wait," Bonnie said. "You have to promise not to make a sound."

"Promise," Joss said.

"Just as quiet as a dream," Bonnie said and began to gather up Joss' skirt inch by inch. "Just as dreamy and quiet as a little creek—even if it goes over the waterfall."

◇

Later—a good deal later—I got the job of sticking up for Mom's life. Maybe it was because of my early training in being the dutiful daughter—that would be a laugh on Dad, the trainer. Mom didn't train me for anything, let alone duty.

But there's this to be said for her: whether she was in a rage (and Dad wasn't the only one to get blasted by her blowtorch anger) or in a sentimental spill, she was right there in front of me. Whether she was nutty or making sense, she was present. Dad could be absent in lots of ways. He wasn't as bad off as what they said about Gerald Ford—couldn't chew gum and walk at the same time—but Dad couldn't *think* and be loving at the same time, he couldn't be crazy and be loving, he couldn't be hurt and be loving. He could be loving, but he had to shut down the other engines to do it. At least he thought he had to. He could be receptive to news, be fair, fulfill his duties, even do nice things, but he tried to keep his emotions in check until he saw how they would fit into the overall pattern. Unaccountable emotion, in others or in himself, threw him for a loop. Of course Mom's unaccountable emotions threw Mom for a loop too, but she didn't ever stop the flow. Maybe she couldn't. The phrase "contradictory emotions" didn't strike her as a pejorative. It might *describe* what was going on in her, but it wasn't a commandment to stop, as in "Your arguments are contradictory."

So she could yell at Nora and me in a terrifying way—really screeching with anger—but she could be simultaneously building up a charge of affection that would suddenly overwhelm her anger. I keep using anger and love as the examples of contradictory emotions—they're the ones onstage at the moment—but it was just as common for her that an urge to be funny would ambush her anger.

That was the one "contradiction" Dad could get along with. In fact, he himself could go from anger (slow, righteous, and rationalized in his case) to being funny. It was a slower, more awkward shift for him, but he could do it. In the quick-temper department, Mom could go from zero to sixty in two seconds. But she could downshift through all her gears just as fast—go through a series of blind curves and come out flying.

Let's drop the automotive stuff.

Mom's in love.

That's what's up. That's the new emotion here.

Later on various people would argue that it was part of her craziness; that she was seduced, that she could have, should have just said "no"; that it was narcissistic, adolescent. . . . There would be shrink arguments to devalue it, moral and legal commandments to oppose it, appeals to Mom's other emotions to divert it.

I remember Mom in one of her rages about dumb bad movies, even some of the ones she loved. She said, "Horror movies. What's the plot? Boo! That's it. Boo. Even my favorite line—'There are secrets of nature, doctor, that man should not tamper with.' It's just part of the boo. And all those song-and-dance movies. 'Let's put on our own show.' 'Oh, Johnny, I just know you're gonna be a star.' Who gives a flying fuck? And love stories. Boy meets girl. Boy loses girl. Boy oh boy. Love conquers all. Why can't someone make a movie about how weird everything really is? Why can't they make a movie out of *Being and Nothingness*?"

Being and Nothingness is a nine-hundred-page existentialist philosophy book that one of the big cousins—her favorite nephew—sent Mom. He wanted to talk to her about it. He read it seven times. She started it seven times.

I said, "Mom, you haven't read *Being and Nothingness*."

She said, "I'm waiting for the movie."

I nodded and said, "Oh." Nora laughed. By then she was about to be ten, but she could tell when Mom was funny just by the rhythm.

Dad came in from the porch, where he'd been listening. I now know he knew by then. Nora and I didn't.

Dad said, "Love conquers all. Is that the plot? *Amor omnia vincit*."

"Oh," Mom said, "if it's in Latin, then it can't be a bad movie."

"Anything can be a bad movie," Dad said. "The problem with bad movies isn't their plots. It's that everything has to happen so fast. Everything has to happen without anyone reflecting. In Hollywood movies love has to be either a cotton-candy sunset with violins or a car crash. In real life love is part of the architecture of people's lives. Love is duty. It's hard to make a thrilling scene out of that."

Mom snorted and shifted her weight from foot to foot like a skittish horse. She said, "I suppose your favorite movie is *The Ten Commandments*."

Nora laughed. Dad sighed, lifted a hand, and let it fall against the top of his leg. He said, "I'm going to work in the yard. You girls want to come?"

Nora said, "Okay."

Mom said, "Remember, it's your night to cook supper. You might want to get some groceries."

"I'll take the girls out."

"Suit yourself."

Nora said, "Pizza!"

I said, "We had pizza last time." I was annoyed she'd said she'd do yard work. She hated yard work.

Dad said, "I'll need the car."

"I can get a ride," Mom said.

Nora said, "Aren't you coming?"

"Tomorrow night, honeybun, I'll make shepherd's pie."

I said, "Then tonight it's my turn to pick."

"No fair," Nora said. "You like shepherd's pie too."

"Don't."

"Yuh-huh."

"Nuh-huh either."

So now there were two unhappy couples.

Of course . . . Of *course* I can't rationally expect that Nora and I could have done anything, but I still hear Nora and me bickering. Nora is louder and funnier; what I say is usually a muttered aside, but I have a gift for slyly disruptive timing.

When I feel self-pity for Nora and me, it's a tepid sloshing emotion. It makes me impatient and I can paddle through it. But when I am haunted by our *voices* I am frozen. I can't do anything to stop the perfect clarity of our recital. I hear our voices and all I can do is hold them in so that our little-girl voices can't reach the rest of me.

I don't want to argue. Let someone else say something.

◇

Everything Joss looked at seemed ready to split in two. She saw the cleavage lines in trees, boulders, roast chickens, married couples, anyone's life story. Anyone's life story: I was wild/obedient. I was lonely/one of a great gang of kids. I was a prince/a pauper. I knew what I was doing/ I didn't have a clue.

She herself wanted to lead the life her mother led/she wanted to go to extremes.

When she started making love with Bonnie she was terrified/calmed. It was reward/punishment. It was the end/beginning. It was one huge force/it was a zillion little things.

Mike was a tyrant oppressor jailer/a nice man who did his best. He deserved to be overthrown/he was about to get beaned by a meteorite out of the clear blue sky.

Being in love with Bonnie was heading into a railroad tunnel with the train coming the other way/being in love with Bonnie was a secret corner of her life that she could manage the way most people managed their secret corners.

Being in love with Bonnie made everything that was already wrong with her worse/better.

Joss spun through this series of bad/good twice a day. She got used to spinning through it. She got good at spinning through it. She thought that perhaps her spinning was a gyroscope that made her stable. That wouldn't be the strangest thing.

It didn't take long to go through the spins—in fact less and less time as she gave up word-thoughts for pictures, pictures for sensations.

The rest of the day was details. There were twice as many details, because she was leading a double life. Half of the time she had twice as much energy as usual; half of the time she had half as much. Was that enough energy for twice as many details? She'd never been good at math. To hell with math—she was better off. And she wasn't alone. Maybe about to be ostracized from the civilized world, but what the hell.

Joss believed that Bonnie was good at math. That she had an organizing and analytical mind. This talent—as sharp as any of the men's—didn't obsess her and didn't distract her from her feelings. And Bonnie didn't think it counted for more than Joss' intuitive flashes.

On a daily basis Bonnie's analytical abilities were a great help. She would calculate arrivals and departures. This was necessary not just because there were eight people living in the three houses on top of each other, but also because Tyler was on the road a lot. He'd got the word that his prospects for tenure were iffy at best, so he was arranging interviews and giving lectures at other colleges and universities. Bonnie, who came up for tenure the year after Tyler did, had learned that she was almost a shoo-in. Her book on Jesuit art and architecture (mainly about the Gesù and Sant' Ignazio) was going to be published, indeed, well published. The fine-arts department had not one tenured woman, and the pressure was on. Her chairman adored her, took her to lunch so often it made Tyler jealous.

Tyler wanted to go on living in the bungalow no matter what, and he wanted to go on living there with Bonnie. If he'd been sure of getting tenure he would have proposed. He'd received a small insured package from his family in Texas which he'd hidden away, and Bonnie was pretty sure it was a family engagement ring.

Bonnie and Joss talked freely and intimately about Tyler and Mike. At first Joss had been shocked and hesitant. Bonnie said, "Have you ever read really good science fiction? That Polish writer Lem? He has this one story about alternating universes—they occupy the same space but they pulsate in and out of existence. There are some lucky people who get to live in both." In general Joss talked more than Bonnie. One of Bonnie's entrancing characteristics was that she listened to Joss, looked at Joss while Joss spoke, touched Joss' knee to show that she was interested and couldn't wait to hear more.

One afternoon, before anyone else came home, Joss told Bonnie about getting a crush on Ganny. Joss thought it a smaller topic than her life with Mike. Joss said, "I'd always liked her, but she was standoffish with me. Then, one night, she was here for supper and she was talking to Mike about what drove her nuts about a lot of the lawyers in town. She said that they think in little tiny moves, as if their minds are graph paper. Their thoughts build up one square at a time. Ganny said she knew that was what the job *was* after all, but she missed talking to people who had more speculative minds. People who had thoughts that shot off like rockets, that just carried them off to they didn't know where. Then she turned to me and said, 'I think you're like that.'"

Bonnie said, "Well, she's right. Of course she's right. And I can see why you loved hearing that. I mean, if she was the first person to tell you. And she is just gorgeous. It's one of the items to Mike's credit that he hired her. Not because she's gorgeous." Bonnie laughed. "Though I'm sure he's aware of it." Bonnie laughed again, then added, "Do you think she likes to kiss girls?"

Joss was annoyed that the story of her compliment was getting sidetracked. The *point* was about what kind of intelligence she had, how someone had noticed it at last. She would have soon enough brought the story back around to how happy she now was to have Bonnie's appreciation.

But then Joss' annoyance was jostled offstage by two very different feelings. One was wonder that Bonnie was jealous; Joss felt a nine-year-old's naïve, pitiless curiosity at seeing a grown-up unsuccessfully camouflaging an emotion. Joss' second feeling came to her more slowly but grew larger. It was a delicious feeling of power—not of domination, but of power that was perfectly equal to Bonnie's. They were outlaws together, they needed each other more than any two people she could think of, they were magnified to each other. This feeling of being enlarged ran down her arms. It made her hands feel masterful. She put her fingertips on Bonnie's forehead and ran them into her hair, tilting Bonnie's face up. She had never felt so filled by someone else or so capable of filling someone else. She had the power in her hands to clear the opaqueness between them.

Of course there were a few eddies of unsteadiness in all this, and Joss also felt her usual thorns of self-mockery (herself as wacko faith-healer laying her hands on Bonnie's head saying, "Be healed . . . in Cheese's name!").

But Bonnie's face became bigger and bigger, a sweet creamy dish Joss was lifting in her hands, Bonnie's face had no expression of anything at all but waiting for Joss to kiss her.

◇

Time became irregular for everyone on the property. It raced and eddied, dammed up and then raced again. It was an effect of their jangled feelings, and then it was a cause of them.

For Edith and Nora it seemed a normal jostling and jamming of time. They were used to the childhood variations; as for any child in a classroom at quarter to three on a Friday afternoon, for example, time congealed until by five to three it was almost immovable sludge.

For Edith and Nora's grandmother, however, living on the Northern Neck in her white house in the middle of a lawn of perfect grass, time slipped evenly and quickly no matter what she was doing, no matter of whom she was thinking. She looked forward to Joss and Edith and Nora and Mike, to the whole rackety summer that would exhaust her and make her happy in gusts until Labor Day, when she would put on her old patchwork gardening coat and feel loneliness and relief.

She knew, without taking pride in the fact, that almost all of her grandchildren, children, and friends who came to her would feel loved. She also knew, without feeling alarmed, that a certain number—perhaps only one or two, perhaps as many as half of them—would be in one kind of misery or another. She was sure she would be of some help, but she was unsure what the matter would be, so her preparations for happiness or misery were the same practicalities: she had the windows cleaned, the floors waxed, the boathouse aired out. She culled the record-and-tape collection and phoned her three children to find out what the grandchildren's new tastes might be. She said to each child, "I'm not sure I'm altogether hep." She noticed that this year no one told her to say "hip." Perhaps "hip" had had its day.

Without consulting anyone, she booked the same old caller and string band for her Fourth of July square dance, which was also her oldest grandson's birthday.

Joss and her family would come earlier than anyone for a long weekend in May, and she'd ask Joss if she could borrow Mike. She'd have Mike see to it that the wooden rowboat and the Admiral's gig were caulked and painted and that the Boston Whaler's outboard and towing line were ready for water-skiing.

She would also find out if Joss and Mike were going to invite anyone. She quite liked their friend Ganny, but it had been difficult when Ganny had arrived—without Joss having said anything—on the day before her one big local party. The Stamples, from the place next door, whom she absolutely had to invite once a year, were out-and-out racists, rather surprising in this day and age, and although it had been unlikely that they would behave badly, she knew they weren't very bright and she didn't trust them not to stiffen, or at any rate appear startled. She couldn't very well put them off, since they would certainly hear about the party from someone else. She didn't know them or like them quite well enough to have a little chat with them. And two summers ago Mike and Mrs. Stample had crossed swords rather loudly over school prayer (Mike was sometimes very Papist, but he was vehemently against public-school prayer). And the two oldest grandchildren despised Mr. Stample, she wasn't sure why, perhaps it was just chemistry, but they'd certainly taken a scunner to him. And Joss . . . well, Joss might be in one of her quarrelsome states.

In the event it hadn't been a problem—she'd steered the Stamples to a corner with some people they liked and had one of the sweeter grandchildren bring them their plates from the buffet. But it had been one more thing to worry about on the most worrisome day of that summer. Perhaps this summer she'd get the Stamples and a few others out of the way early—not much fun, but easier. Last summer she'd had a terrific row with Joss, who had insisted on misunderstanding her. Joss had called her a kowtowing pillow plumper. In fact her only concern had been to make sure that no one made Ganny feel uncomfortable. She didn't mind the Stamples' being ruffled, just that there not be any unpleasantness. But Joss had said it again—"You're plumping pillows. You're plumping pillows for those bigots." What annoyed her was that on another occasion Joss had gone on at some length in a romantic and sentimental way about the code of hospitality of the Sioux, the Eskimos (no—Joss said they were now to be called Inuit), or the Bedouin, but Joss wouldn't acknowledge that her own mother had a code of hospitality that was every bit as important to her.

Joss had apologized the next morning, one of her disarming apologies, red-faced and very funny.

But still Joss might be touchy if asked directly who was going to visit. . . . The best way to put it would be to say positively to Joss that she looked forward to seeing her and her friends, and, as an afterthought, ask who she might expect.

Having thought out *that* detail, she went back to the more pleasant preparations. The wharf in the creek was in fine shape. All the grandchildren could swim now, no worry about that. There was the jellyfish problem—the jellyfish came right up the creek. She put Adolph's on her shopping list and laughed out loud. When Mike was still a new son-in-law—she'd liked him right off but he took some getting used to, he could be awfully abrupt—he had come charging into the kitchen with her oldest grandson in tow. The boy had huge welts across his face from having swum into a jellyfish. Mike had barked at her, "Meat tenderizer. Where's the meat tenderizer?"

She'd been puzzled, but obediently rummaged around in a drawer and pulled out a mallet with little steel teeth, her meat tenderizer.

Mike stared at her for a second, then turned away and started flinging open cabinets. He said, "Adolph's. Adolph's meat tenderizer. In a *bottle*."

She'd offered him Worcestershire sauce. Mike had grunted and led the boy to his car and driven off to the general store, where he'd grabbed a bottle of Adolph's off the shelf, stepped onto the porch, and doused his nephew's face. Two of the old-timers on the porch had been puzzled but a third had nodded and said, "Yeah, it'll draw the hurt right out. Just like juice from a dock leaf for a nettle sting."

"Is that right?" Mike said. "Dock." And, according to her grandson, Mike had then had a half-hour conversation with the old geezers, occasionally reapplying the Adolph's meat tenderizer.

From then on, every time she sent Mike to the general store she had to allow at least an extra half-hour for his lingering.

Joss didn't like Mike's habit of lingering at the general store—"Faux populism." Joss didn't like her mother sticking up for him either.

"Joss darling," she said. "He's a workaholic all year, I'm happy that he can relax a bit here."

Joss rolled her eyes. "You say 'workaholic' with admiration."

"Indeed. He's a very hard worker."

"And so am I, in case you hadn't noticed."

"Of course you are." She'd held back from explaining that nobody depended on Joss' work, neither a family nor clients, and that all those dependent people added a good deal of stress. She said again, "Of course you are. And Mike appreciates it."

Joss snorted.

She'd said, "He really would like to help you out with the financial side of some of your projects. He's quite good with money. And he completely understands your need for privacy, your artistic temperament."

"I don't want him to understand," Joss had said, "completely or any other way. I don't want anyone to understand." Joss made a face. "'Artistic temperament.' What a soggy thing to say."

Difficult. Like her father. Volatile and stubborn, but electric with good impulses, ready to be suddenly wonderful. She thought of Joss in the nursery, age three, in mid-tantrum. She and the nurse were slowly and patiently overwhelming Joss. Her father had come in and said, "Don't break her spirit."

And Joss later so completely sweet and tender with her baby brother. And now so good and funny with Edith and Nora. How happy they would have made their grandfather. Edith had known him. Hard to tell if Edith remembered any of that time—learning to speak at the same time her grandfather was relearning to speak after his stroke. They'd watched *Sesame Street* together.

It was exactly the age that he'd missed with Joss—he hadn't come back from the Pacific until Joss was almost three. Edith had been perfect for him—he'd been entranced with her in a way he hadn't ever had time to be with his own children. Joss and Mike had stayed six months, Mike commuting up to Washington, sometimes spending the night on that awful houseboat. But Edith. Edith had been the grace of that last year. Such bright life right to the end.

She felt her pleasure move toward a good cry. She took a deep breath and said out loud, "Now, that's enough of *that*."

But all of this remembering, both from long ago and not so long ago, was part of the preparation for the summer. Three children, six grandchildren, two daughters-in-law, a son-in-law. And so she went on with her list, each item like a rosary bead the contemplation of which helped her to remember and foresee all the troubles and wishes that would visit her in June.

◇

Joss' preparation for June was more fraught. She knew there would be misery, and maybe the proper preparation for misery was misery. She was driving herself nuts editing another short film by the deadline for the Virginia Filmmakers' Contest.

She was also worrying about how Mike was going to arrange his summer—he was still waiting for a judge to set a trial date. *He* hoped it would be either in June or after Labor Day, so he could spend most of the summer at the shore. Joss wasn't sure she could spend so much time away from Bonnie. On the other hand, she didn't want to plead for time in her studio if Tyler was going to be working at home, hanging around with Bonnie in the bungalow. There was a chance that Tyler would be teaching summer school in Washington for six weeks, too far to commute daily. More and more was up in the air while Bonnie and she waited for the men to settle their plans.

Joss recognized that her behavior toward Mike alternated between hostility and penance. She couldn't help it. Ill temper seemed the only form of honesty she was now capable of. But then an urge to make one of Mike's favorite meals would come on her—she wasn't penitential but she found penance stabilizing.

She and Bonnie One—now that Mike had a client named Bonnie he'd started saying Bonnie One and Bonnie Two, and Joss had taken it up. It became part of her private language in public with her Bonnie. "O where have you been, Lord Randall my son / Where have you been, my bonnie one?"

Another item of their private public language was reciting to each other fragments of what they'd done together, as if the incidents were dreams. "I was driving down a country road with someone—you know how it is in dreams—your high-school English teacher turns into Marcello Mastroianni—anyway, I was driving with someone whose presence was stirring me in some way—"

"Wait. Was this in Italy? I mean in your dream."

"No, not Italy. Someplace near here. Anyway, my hair kept blowing in my face and then whoever it was started brushing it away from my eyes. It's amazing sometimes how it's just the little touches that are so powerful in dreams."

One time Tyler, overhearing them, said, "Bonnie, honey, I think your dreams have become more ordinary. No, no—I mean that as a compliment. It's like the genius of certain American short stories. The most powerful things that people say to each other in these stories are plain everyday phrases. Just plain old five-cent pieces that have been handed around so often they're worn smooth."

Bonnie said, "I'll bet that's the big idea for your new article. I can always tell when you're quoting yourself."

Tyler said good-naturedly, "Just trying to wear my idea smooth."

Bonnie said, "Isn't it pretty smooth already? I mean it's an awful lot like Joss' idea for Cliché Canasta."

Joss said, "Well, no. I'm collecting *clichés*. I think there's a difference between plain everyday phrases and movie clichés. I mean, take one of my favorites—probably Jean Arthur—says to the guy—probably Gary

Cooper—'Aw ya big lug, can't you see I'm just crazy about you?' No one could say that in real life. It's too . . . big-screen."

"Why, Miz Jocelyn," Tyler said, putting on the cornpone, "you're just so *sma-art*."

"Why, fiddle-de-dee," Bonnie said. "You never tell me that."

Tyler said, "Aw, come on. Every other day."

"Well, what's a plain old everyday phrase, then?" Bonnie said.

" 'You're on your own,' " Tyler said. "Or 'Nobody told me.' Or 'So that's all there is to it.' You can hear them all over the place. But the trick is to arrange the drama, to set up the context so the plain phrase is recharged."

Bonnie One said, "So what's another movie cliché?"

Tyler said, " 'This town isn't big enough for the two of us.' "

Joss nodded.

Bonnie said, "Well, then, which is it when Mike is in court and says stuff like, 'She killed him just as surely as if she put a gun to his head and pulled the trigger'?"

From across the room Mike said, "Movie cliché. And I've *never* said that."

"I was speaking hypothetically," Bonnie said. "You've never tried a murder case."

"I'm not really a criminal lawyer," Mike said. "And certainly not a prosecutor. But that's a dandy movie cliché. Do you have that one, Joss? That'd make a good card."

Bonnie said, "How would you know?"

Mike tilted his head toward her.

Bonnie said, "I meant, 'How would you know?' as an example of a plain everyday phrase—"

Tyler said, "She's got it; by George, she's got it."

"—which could be recharged by the right context," Bonnie said. "But suppose Mike is cross-examining a witness and pulls out Exhibit A and says, 'Perhaps this will refresh your recollection.' "

Joss said, "Hmm."

Mike said, "Too British. Sort of like, 'Let me put it to you that your entire testimony is nothing but a tissue of lies.' " He said this in a stage hoity-toity English accent, pronouncing "tissue" as "tiss-you."

Tyler laughed.

Bonnie said, "How *do* you talk over in that courtroom of yours?"

"Just plain talk," Mike said. "Just plain old everyday phrases."

Bonnie turned back to Joss. "I wish you'd get that game of yours ready. You'd be so good at it. And I'll bet it makes you a million bucks."

"I can't figure out how to make it a *game*," Joss said. "I thought I could really have it be like canasta—draw cards until you get four clichés that make a book. In this case I had in mind a *literal* book—a story. The trouble is that almost any time you put four clichés together you get a story."

"Is that just in movies?" Bonnie said.

"Sometimes in real life."

◇

Mike felt the rage inside him again. It puzzled and alarmed him. It was small but unpredictable. When it flared it was like burning phosphorus, white hot and hard to put out.

He was puzzled and alarmed that he didn't know the reason for it. He was afraid that he wasn't trying hard enough to find the reason for it. But he was also afraid that finding the reason for it wouldn't end it. On the contrary, it might grow stronger, it might overwhelm him. So he kept on smothering it with his ordinary life.

He made a few guesses, but they were timid. Was it because Bonnie Two's boyfriend—ex-boyfriend—had beaten him up so easily? Trussed him up in front of everyone in Broome and Havermeyer. Even his two partners, after initial sympathetic utterances, made jokes.

Or was it something to do with Bundy? The wisps of phantom smell, taste, and hearing were sometimes rasping and salty, yet finally oddly gentle and reassuring. But perhaps there was some residue that was still troubled into anger.

Bonnie One pissed him off from time to time, but she almost always buttered him up afterward. And those rilings were over such small things. . . .

She drifted in one evening, as she often did when Tyler was away. Mike and Joss were playing casino. They'd played lots of games over the years, but chess, Scrabble, and Chinese checkers had been too arduously competitive. They'd started out as equals in chess—with Joss having an edge in blitz games. Then Mike read a book on chess tactics, a tactic that Joss thought violated the spirit of games. In Scrabble, Joss managed to put up with Mike's using nautical, legal, and ecclesiastical words (pyx, pax) which turned out to be in the dictionary. She even put up with his challenging her use of "scaredy," as in "scaredy-cat," which turned out not to be in the dictionary without the "cat." She appealed to his general sense of language. He said, "Rules for games—that's one of the good uses for legal formalism." But when he played all seven of his tiles for the second time in a row, she flipped the board over. He said evenly, "I take it you're conceding."

For a long time Joss was better than Mike at Chinese checkers. When it was her turn she drove him nuts by hanging her hand over the board and rubbing the tips of her fingers against her thumb. He claimed she was obscuring his view of his next move. She claimed he played too defensively. When he finally won she picked up the circular metal board and threw it at him. When she picked it up, the marbles rattled off, and then she took a huge backswing, so he had plenty of time to duck. She threw it like a Frisbee, so hard that the flimsy sheet metal buckled across the middle and made a point which gouged the wall.

She'd turned pale. Then her hands trembled and began to jump. She became so dizzy and wobbly she had to lean on the table. Mike had been more alarmed than angry. He helped her sit down and got her a glass of water.

He put this incident in the same category as the time when he'd heard an awful thumping in the bathroom. He'd run in—he was afraid she was having a seizure—and found Joss kneeling in the tub punching the wall.

"What?" he'd said. "What?"

She'd howled, "Why aren't I a genius?"

He'd said "What?" again, but then, for a second, he'd felt completely how swift and uncontrolled her wishes were, spinning and grinding against each other until they produced a thunderclap.

Then she'd laughed at herself and sat back down in the water. Her face was so red it looked unbearably hot. He wetted a washcloth with cold water and put it across her cheeks.

He'd said, "Maybe you are a genius." He'd meant it. Not so much for whatever work she was doing as for herself—her temper, her tense muscular back, her wild blue eyes over the washcloth veil.

She'd said, "Maybe you're a sex maniac," when he got in the tub with her.

"No," he'd said. "Sex maniacs don't take their shoes off."

That had certainly been before Eros waned. Even Joss' throwing the Chinese-checkers board had been, if not Eros, a spasm that had Eros in it.

Now Bonnie One hovered over their game of casino, irritating him as much as Joss' rubbing her fingers over the Chinese-checkers board. "We're almost done," Joss said. "I'm about to crush him. I've won all the aces."

They played out the game. Mike picked up his stack and counted through them once. He said, "Twenty-eight cards, seven spades, that's three. Plus the ten of diamonds and the two of spades. That makes six points."

Joss had sorted out her point cards. "Four aces. I thought I had more cards. That is disgusting. You are disgustingly lucky."

Bonnie said to Mike, "Did I just see you count your spades at the same time as you were counting your cards? I mean, I only saw you go through your cards once."

"Yes," Mike said.

"That is amazing. I mean, I can't even count my fingers without moving my lips."

Mike said, "It's not much of a knack."

"But what is the knack? How on earth do you do it?"

"You just keep count in separate rooms. You visualize different rooms. . . ."

"Ah," Bonnie said. "Like that great Jesuit Matteo Ricci. Did you read about him? About his memory palace? Did the Jesuits train your memory?"

"Matteo Ricci. He went to China."

Bonnie said, "But tell me—can you keep track of the spades while the game is going on?"

"Yeah."

"That is amazing. It really is Ricci's memory palace. A room for the number of spades, another room for . . . what? Can you keep track of all the cards?"

"Yeah, pretty much. I sometimes lose track of the little cards."

"My gracious," Bonnie said. "You've got a little adding machine tucked away in your brain."

Mike recognized a skillful, lulling cross-examination.

"Wait a second," Joss said. "Do you mean that all this time you've been counting everything? You've been counting every goddamn card?"

"Of course I've been counting. Counting is part of playing cards. What have *you* been doing? I've heard you say out loud to yourself 'three aces down, one to go.'"

"But that's nothing. That's a pathetic little nothing. So when we get near the end you know exactly what's in my hand just as surely as if you'd peeked."

"Not necessarily. Sometimes—"

"You might as well be playing with a marked deck."

Although Mike was making what was a perfectly sound argument, he felt a sliver of guilt. What surprised him even more was his dagger of rage against Bonnie One.

Joss said, "You should have told me."

"Oh, for God's sake, Joss. You can't stand it when I tell you stuff. Remember when I tried to teach you how to paddle a canoe? You had a fit. You can't have it both ways."

Bonnie said, "Now, there's a good plain everyday phrase for Tyler's collection—'You can't have it both ways.'"

"It's not the same," Joss said. "All these years I've been complaining about your dumb luck, and you were just gloating in secret."

"No," Mike said. "Only last week you said to me, 'Your luck is going to rot your brain,' and I said, 'It's not luck, it's skill,' and you snorted and said—"

"That wasn't telling me," Joss said. "You just said that to piss me off. That was just gloating."

Bonnie said, "Ah."

Mike said, "Who asked you?"

"That's another one," Bonnie said. "'Who asked you?' That should be on Tyler's list. Mike, you're a regular old gold mine for everyday phrases."

Mike said to Joss, "You want to play another hand?"

Bonnie One said, "'Never play cards with a man named Doc.' I guess that's just a saying, not a plain everyday phrase or a movie cliché."

"No," Joss said. "And it goes on too long—it goes, 'Never eat at a place called Mom's, never play cards with a man named Doc, and never sleep with someone whose problems are worse than your own.'"

"Ooo," Bonnie said. "That last one. That's a hard one. How could you *know*? I mean, until it was too late. I certainly didn't ever know about men's problems until it was too late. Of course the big problem men have is they can't tell you their real problems, because they don't even *know* what their real problems are."

Mike got a cigar. He didn't think he was angry, just annoyed, just getting out of range of the twittering. He sat on the deck chair. Then he decided he didn't want to seem to be waiting for Bonnie One to come out and soothe him. He walked down to the river—slowly, so as not to puff too hard on his cigar. He sat beside his canoe. He felt his anger—all right, he was angry—settle into depression.

He put his hand on the canoe. He missed Miss Dudley. They'd say, "Oh—movie cliché—a boy and his dog."

He said out loud, "Just suck it up, dummy." Now, there was an everyday Bundy phrase. He looked around at the trees. He wouldn't hear from Bundy tonight. He thought of Ezra willing himself to do his roadwork in the dark. Ezra's fight. Okay—take the whole family to Ezra's fight, blow some money on a hotel in Richmond. Joss loved hotels, the girls loved hotels. Let 'em have a room-service breakfast. A family outing. And then family life on the Northern Neck. Joss liked him at her mother's. Make the girls happy. Make Joss happy. Family outing, family vacation—the middle-class remedy. Why did they make fun of it in the movies? It was just the thing for real life.

◇

Tyler drove up, beep-beeped his horn, got out, and sang, "Ding dong, the witch is dead!"

Evelyn, Edmond, and Nora were on Evelyn's front porch shelling peas. Bonnie, Joss, and Edith opened the big casement window in the side of Joss' kitchen and leaned out. Mike, who'd been on all fours in a garden bed, heaved himself up.

"They nailed him," Tyler said. "Or she nailed him. Hey, Joss, remember that sleazy chairman? The one who couldn't take a joke? He's defrocked. He's decommissioned, defenestrated."

Almost everyone said, "What?"

"She taped him," Tyler said. "But, Lord, I hope you ladies never . . . She let that slimy slug . . . Well, it could have been worse."

Evelyn said, "Tyler, you never begin at the beginning. You always begin in the middle. Sit down and organize yourself."

Tyler laughed, then stopped himself. "It's not funny. I mean I haven't actually heard the tape, the dean of the faculty is sitting on it now, but she told me about it because . . . and then she gave me a transcript. She wasn't in tears but she was shaky, a little lip-tremble every so often, I don't blame her, I mean, she's been like a French Resistance heroine—"

"Tyler," Evelyn said. "You come here, sit down, and start over."

"Okay," Tyler said. He waited until his audience had gathered on Evelyn's porch. "Okay. Assistant professor, female, modernist. Like me. A rival for my job. If there's truly only one slot . . ."

Evelyn said, "Tyler."

"Okay. Our chairman has a sneaker for her. Nobody knew, but all year he's having meetings with her. At first he's careful not to say anything to her except how much he likes her work. Then he says something about how all her male students must have crushes on her. Then he says he can get her a summer grant so she'll have time to turn her thesis into a really first-rate book. Maybe he could arrange a semester off with pay. He really wants her to blossom, et cetera, et cetera. Finally he wants to meet her in his office to go over a chapter of hers that he's made some notes on. He actually is helpful—she has to give him that. The appointments get later and later. He explains that it's better if they meet after most folks have gone home, he wants to be discreet about having a mentor-protégé arrangement—after all, he is the chairman, above the fray, blah blah blah. It's all inch by inch—at some point he starts taking her by the hand and then kissing her on the cheek when she comes in. And then he offers her the use of his cottage, just out of town. He says he's done *his* best work there, he'll try to arrange a better office for her next year, but in the meantime the cottage . . . At least she could come look at it. He says he'll meet her there for lunch, show her around. He draws a map. Okay—you're thinking this is when she should back off. She *does* tell him it's too much. He laughs and says no, no. Then purses his little mouth and looks off at the corner of the ceiling. He says that her work is first-rate, at least it has all the promise of being first-rate . . . but the next step for her is to learn to accept guidance and even favors in a mature way. He says that pointedly. 'In a mature way.' So far he's been careful to be ambiguous, but his tone is now clear. She went numb for a second, then felt furious and helpless. She said, 'I think I know what you mean.' He said, 'Of course you do. And now you have the map . . . to the cottage.'

"She says she'll call him. He says, 'Not at home, dear. I never answer the phone at home.'

"So, the next day, she bought herself a voice-activated mini–tape recorder. Then she left a note in his box saying it was on. When she got to his cottage he was already there. He'd prepared a seduction lunch—her phrase—flowers on the table, white wine in a cooler. She said to me that it really is a beautiful little cottage—one side is all windows looking toward the mountains. A flagstone terrace, beds of tulips and irises. It gave her pause. It was all suddenly more scary. Since the place was more than she'd imagined—more polished, more perfected—maybe *he* was more than she'd imagined—more adroit, more powerful.

"She could barely eat anything. After lunch she raised the subject of my work. She said she liked it, and that some other people in the department liked it too.

"He said, 'Oh, Tyler's not a problem for you, my dear. When you assistant professors come up at the tenure meeting most of us only read the committee report. And so the crucial job for the chairman is to select the appropriate people for the committee.'

"Well, that got the goods on him in one way. But she wasn't sure but that he mightn't still be able to slither out of it.

"She said, 'I had no idea it would all be so competitive. I've never felt so tense.'

"She didn't have to fake being nervous. She says her hand was so shaky she couldn't pick up her wineglass.

"She figured that would be his cue to do some more hand-patting and what not. What she was worrying about now was how far she was going to go, especially if he didn't say anything recordable to go along with it. But he suddenly scooped her out of her chair, got his arms around her, and said, 'I've been reassuring you. But I need reassurance too.'

"She managed to untangle herself, pick up her handbag—with the tape recorder in it—and go to the bathroom. When she came back she laid the bag on the table by the sofa, where he was now sitting. He got right down to it, not even a kiss, just ran his hands up under her skirt while she was standing there. He had a hand on the back of each of her thighs. She stood there, I guess kind of dazed. She'd lost track of whatever game plan she had, but she had to say *some*thing. So she asked him what he'd meant when he said he needed reassurance too. He said, 'I was *going* to say that at my age one might worry whether one will be equal to the occasion.' He was still groping around, mind you. He said, 'And how awkward it can be to explain one's needs. But right now I feel completely reassured. I feel like a roebuck springing on the mountain.'

"So now she's got enough, and besides she's coming out of her daze and is getting outraged that he's quoting the Bible—Song of Songs. She says, 'Stop that,' and pulls at his arms. He says, 'Spring—how I love spring—flowers and bare legs.'

"He moves his hands still higher and leans forward to kiss her knee or maybe just burrow into her. . . . But she steps back and he falls forward off the sofa. She can't remember planning it, but the next thing she knows she's kneed him on the chin. At this point in the transcript the transcriber has typed, 'Ow, ow, ow, ow!' Her line is—I love this—'You should have been a pair of ragged claws / Scuttling across the floors of silent seas.'"

Tyler laughed again. Nobody else laughed. "She quoted 'Prufrock,'" Tyler said. "She should get tenure just for that."

Bonnie One said, "Is she going through with it? She won't get talked out of it? She's really going to ask for his head on a platter?"

"She gave the tape to the dean of the faculty," Tyler said.

Evelyn said, "Is this man married? I think you said he is. I just feel real sorry for his wife."

"If you knew her, you wouldn't."

"Tyler," Evelyn said. "Don't get like them."

"Well, hell," Tyler said. "It's just not that often that the bad guys lose."

When Tyler was bouncing it was hard to smother him, but he wanted more of a party. He said, "Come on, you all!"

Mike pinched back his first reaction, which was to ask a lot of questions, raise a lot of issues. Query: Was an academic-committee investigation bound by the rules of evidence? Was there entrapment? Did the woman realize—did Tyler realize—that, if there was only one job for the two of them, she had improved Tyler's chances more than her own?

Mike didn't want to be the wet blanket. One of Joss' complaints was that he could ruin a good time just by squinting his eyes and looking like he was about to cross-examine.

It was Joss who said, "Okay—all together now! 'The Eyes of Texas Are Upon You'!"

Everyone sang. Halfway through Tyler yelled, "Good! I love it! I don't even care if you're being sarcastic!"

That was the beginning of another manic mood. They had a big rollicking supper on the porch. Evelyn's nine-vegetable stew in a cauldron, mulberries and various winged seeds falling onto the table. And every other night a big supper. Mike made super-garlic lentils with red peppers. Tyler made green beans covered with spicy peanut sauce.

Outdoor kids' games like Kick the Can, Capture the Flag. One night they closed the shutters in the big house, turned out the lights and played Murder in the Dark. Joss fixed the draw so that the girls got to be either the detective or the murderer.

The grown-ups had an ongoing game of Murder. The rules for that were that the murderer had to get the victim to pick up and read a note that said, "You're dead." There was a twenty-four-hour time limit. The first day, Mike drew the murderer card, Bonnie One was the victim. Mike left a note wrapped up in a 50-percent-off-your-next-purchase coupon in the open box of corn flakes in the bungalow. Tyler got it.

Mike also put a note in their morning newspaper, inside the first page. It fell out when Tyler opened the paper. Now he had only until after supper. During his lunch hour he borrowed Ganny's car and put a note in an envelope attached to a bouquet of flowers on the porch of the bungalow. That was a red herring. He went to their bathroom and unrolled the toilet-paper roll four sheets and printed "You're dead" on the next four sheets. Then he rerolled the toilet paper, making sure the edges were aligned.

He went back to his office.

Mike was worried by how seriously he was taking the game. Joss—of all people—had told him he was getting too competitive. He couldn't stop worrying: suppose Bonnie One only used two sheets of toilet paper. No—

she must use more than that. The girls and Joss went through vast amounts of toilet paper. He had to change the roll daily. Whenever Joss and the girls went to Joss' mother's house for five days and left him behind, he noticed he didn't have to put toilet paper on his grocery list or even change the roll.

Then he felt uneasy for a completely different reason. He'd thought of the idea of toilet paper in a purely analytical way—he'd asked himself, "What paper does Bonnie One have to handle during a day?" But now he imagined Joss imagining him imagining Bonnie One. . . . He could hear Joss say, "You *creep.* You *lurker.* You're as bad as Tommy Fetch." Poor Tommy Fetch wasn't just famously fat and ugly—Nora's teacher had also caught him peeking into the girls' bathroom.

It was odd. They were all playing kids' games these days, laughing like crazy over kid stuff. There was something wonderful about the mood—no High Romantic reaction to the full flower of late spring, no lofty poetry, no more melancholy. Even Edmond was laughing himself silly and making the girls laugh. Edith had to learn the Gettysburg Address by heart for school and Edmond said he'd help her. He recited the whole thing talking like Donald Duck. Edith, serious Edith, got the giggles.

Every supper that week, someone showed up with some silly thing—a wig, a fake nose, a whoopee cushion, a buttonhole flower that squirted water. Everyone was being a kid—not the kid he or she had actually been but some zany Katzenjammer version. Edith and Nora had always liked hearing stories from the grown-ups about when the grown-ups had misbehaved as children. This acting out was even better. Edith and Nora couldn't get enough of it, wouldn't go to bed without an encore of some piece of silliness or scariness or grossness. Edmond had a trick they particularly adored since it was silly, scary, and gross all at once. He lay down on the table and hung his head off the end upside down. He covered his forehead, eyes, and nose with his napkin and perched his eyeglasses on his chin. The effect was of a noseless blob of a face with a mouth that was human but very strange. The upper teeth—now the lower teeth—were especially disconcerting. When Edmond talked the girls writhed with a giggly revulsion. They asked him to talk more. When he said their names they shrank back and curled up as if he was tickling them too much. Then they asked him to do it again.

They also liked the act that Joss and Bonnie One put on. Joss got behind Bonnie and stuck her arms under Bonnie's armpits so that it looked as if Joss' hands were Bonnie's. Bonnie gave a serious talk about table manners while Joss' hands gestured at odds with what Bonnie was saying. The hands scratched Bonnie's chin, twirled a strand of hair and put it in

Bonnie's mouth, itched her ear, and, as a finale, a finger started creeping toward her nostril. Nora said, "Oh, gross!" as the finger actually slithered into the nose hole.

Tyler's moment was when he showed up for supper on all fours wearing a bear suit with a rubber Pluto mask over his head. He barked and whined and sniffed the girls' feet—all that played okay, but—best for last—he'd rigged the squirting daisy so that the daisy was his pee-pee, revealed when he lifted his hind leg and squirted on Edith's foot. Edith said "Ick" but finally laughed. Tyler said in a growly voice, "Real dog pee-pee." Nora said, "Gross!" And then "Do it to me!"

So Mike figured that all week there'd been enough pee-pee and poo-poo jokes that his toilet paper had some precedents. Thinking about the week had cheered him up in general. The girls were having a barrel of fun, they would like his toilet-paper trick, toilet paper was always good for a laugh with them. He hoped Bonnie One would bring the sheets to supper. It then crossed his mind that Bonnie One might cheat. Just flush them away and claim she didn't see them. Was that a plausible defense?

Mike went to the partners' bathroom, sat on the lid of the can, and pulled off some sheets. No—you had to look, if only to see where to tear them off.

He felt ridiculous.

When Mike got home Edith was waiting outside the bathroom door for Nora to finish a bath. "Make her get out, Dad. She said she wouldn't wash her hair and I can hear her washing her hair."

He said, "You can come with me. I'm going to the bungalow. You can use their shower."

Joss said, "Tyler's not there. His car's there but he took Bonnie's. He was afraid his wouldn't make it—he's giving another lecture somewhere."

Mike said, "I thought he didn't have to now that—"

"He scheduled it before the chairman self-destructed."

Mike said to Edith, "Come on."

Joss said, "So why are you going to the bungalow?"

"My deadline is coming up," Mike said. "I've got to check on Bonnie One, see if my Murder device worked."

For a second Joss looked horrified. Then she said, "Oh, that."

On the way across the yard Mike said to Edith, "When we get there, you go in first and ask her if she's been murdered yet."

Edith said, "Why do you need me to ask? Why can't *you* ask?"

Mike said, "It's better if you ask. She's . . ." Then he felt how small

Edith was, her head bobbing along beside his elbow. "It's okay," he said. "I'll ask."

"I'll ask if you want," Edith said. "It's just that it's kind of . . . It's not embarrassing exactly, but it's . . ."

"You're right," Mike said. "You're one of the players and it's every man for himself." He turned toward her and said, "Have you thought of what you're going to do when it's your turn?"

"Are Nora and me going to have a turn?"

"Sure."

"Oh." Edith started walking again and said, "Would you be mad if I didn't? I mean, I've got a ton of homework."

"No," Mike said. "Not at all." He worried again that she worried too much. "You know, something that would make you happier is if you just let things tumble along. You're good at school. You can handle it easier than you think. You make it harder for yourself by imagining how hard—"

"Dad, I know what you're going to say—'be blithe, be carefree.' Or that thing Bundy used to say all the time—'Consider the lilies of the field.' "

She stopped walking. Mike turned and saw that she looked stricken. He said, "You're right. You've heard all that."

She said, "I didn't mean to sound mean about Bundy. I just remembered how he used to say that."

Mike looked away. He looked up at the crowns of the trees. The leaves were stirring, though there was no wind where he was. What could he say? She was too smart for kid stuff, too small and tender to help bear his unsteady weight. He said, "No, it's good that you remember. He knew a lot of the Bible by heart. I'd forgotten that one. I'm glad you remember." He pointed at the treetop. "See how there's wind up there and not down here. It's usually that way. You'll see when we go sailing at your grandma's. In light air you want a tall mast to catch some of that."

◇

I do remember that.

I remember being as light as a helium balloon that whole week of funny games. They were funny, but it wasn't fun. No—it was fun but too light, too fast. When Dad and I stopped in the middle of the yard I was glad. I was nervous when he wanted me to ask Bonnie if she was murdered, and I was afraid that he really wanted me to take a turn, and then I was horrified that I'd said something wrong about Bundy. I couldn't explain that I'd been sassy about Dad's advice because I was too light. . . . The whole week I'd been more and more nervous and giddy, and that was why the Bundy remark popped out of me. But I was truly truly happy just after that, when Dad said it was okay. I wanted us to sit down right there under the trees for a long time. I wouldn't even have minded if he'd gone on with his lecture about wind and sailing. No—I would have minded, but I had the feeling that if we'd sat down I could have changed the subject, that I could have made him be still. I didn't have the words to say, "I know why you want to instruct me, I know you hope that somehow I'll recognize that it's your awkward way of paying attention to me. But all you have to do is sit down and shut up. Then it'll be okay. I'll be blithe. You'll be blithe. We'll consider the lilies of the field."

But I had the feeling just then that I wouldn't have had to explain—that if I'd just sat down on the grass he would have read my mind. That we could have mumbled and murmured in a dumb way about going to Grandma's, we could have skipped the seamanship and navigation and just talked about what I liked—how clean and light our rooms were, how nice it was when Grandma sent the big cousins away to have fun somewhere else and made tea for just Nora and me, how calm it was on a summer afternoon when the sun got behind the big trees and they made shadows on the terrace, and how it was even nicer when, after tea, we got our pails and walked as slowly as grazing cows along the fence with the blackberry bushes, and for a while at first the bottoms of our pails chimed a note for each berry, and then there was only the sound of the three of us stepping on dry summer grass and Grandma saying things to Nora and me, to herself, it sounded the same—"There's mint. *That* wasn't here last year. Go ahead and pick a few leaves. And look at that! All those daylilies! I remember when they were taller than you. Don't pick them, dear. Just look at them."

◇

Bonnie One came out on her porch. She said, "Hey, darlin'," to Edith. To Mike she said, " 'Thou hast conquered, pale Galilean.' "

Mike laughed. "You got my message, I guess."

"Your daddy is diabolically clever," Bonnie said to Edith. "He is just a shark at games."

"Can I take a shower here?" Edith said. "Nora's hogging our bathroom."

"May I," Bonnie said. "You certainly may, honey."

Mike said, "Is my message still in there? Dangling from the roll like a hangman's noose?" He felt roly-poly with winning.

Bonnie waited until Edith was inside. She arched one eyebrow. "You're asking an awfully intimate detail about a lady's toilette, don't you think?"

Mike laughed, but he was abashed. He figured that Bonnie and Joss would pull on that loose thread if he gloated—the naughty, nasty Tommy Fetch thread.

Bonnie said, "You want a drink? A glass of wine?"

Mike said, "Sure, thanks." He started toward the door.

Bonnie said, "You just sit yourself there in the winner's chair."

This good sportsmanship seemed genuinely cheerful, with a pinch of teasing to keep it from being too sweet. Bonnie came back out and handed him a glass of wine. She held on to it when he reached for it, clinking her ring on the stem. She let go, laughed, and said, "And you're supposed to be the eagle-eyed observer."

He looked at the glass, looked around the porch, looked at her. He said, "You've done something to your hair?"

Bonnie laughed, held up her left hand, and waggled her fingers. "This is Tyler's Texas heirloom."

"So you're engaged."

"I guess that's right. He just slipped it on me this morning and drove off. In my car, I might add."

"Well, congratulations."

Bonnie said, "You may kiss the bride," and pecked him on the mouth. She picked up her wineglass, sat down, crossed her legs, and took a sip. "Then I got murdered."

"When does Tyler get back? We should have a party."

"*Another* party? Wouldn't you say we're about partied out around here? Tyler won't be back till late tomorrow night, though, so we can rest up for a couple of days."

"Good," Mike said. "I mean you're right. I just noticed Edith's pretty tuckered out. This week has been too many treats. And the girls still have school. We'll have to put off a party anyway—Joss' mother wants me to come down to fix the boats up. Joss says she has too much to do here, but she should take a break too."

"If you want my opinion, Joss'll get more of a break if you leave her alone in her studio. It won't be that hard for you, minding the girls for a weekend. From what I hear, Joss' mother pampers them. And carries you around on a feather pillow too."

Mike was struck by the phrase, especially since it came out very

Southern—"feathah pillar." He said, "There's a fair amount to be done on the boats. But in the evening it's an old-fashioned household."

Bonnie laughed. "By old-fashioned you mean you get spoiled."

He had a counterargument in mind, but didn't want to interrupt a surprisingly agreeable conversation.

Bonnie said, "Tyler's thinking of asking you to add a room to the bungalow."

Mike nodded. "We could probably work something out. It would mean the rent going up some. What do you have in mind? A nursery?"

Bonnie laughed. "I was thinking of a study. Or two. One at each end."

"Oh. We'd have to pick a time when the construction wouldn't interfere with Joss' work. Edmond and Evelyn and I are away all day, but Joss . . ."

"Well, Joss has been thinking of renting a studio somewhere away from home. I think it distracts her, having to work right alongside all her household chores. You know, on her way to her studio there's a pile of laundry, and then a sink full of dishes, or she has to answer the door for the plumber or the electrician. And on Saturday and Sunday, there you are banging away with your pick and shovel."

He said, "I don't make that much noise. And there aren't that many interruptions—how many times do we have the plumber or the electrician? It's not that often."

"I don't only mean the plumber or the electrician. There's always something. You just don't realize how many interruptions there are. . . ."

Mike wondered why he was having this conversation with Bonnie One. But he said, "Well, for the sake of argument, let's suppose someone does come, let's say, twice a week. (A) that's not that much of a burden and (B) who's going to let them in? It's not—"

Bonnie laughed. "I'll tell you who—the gorgeous Swedish au-pair girl you hire. Or maybe French. Imagine coming home after a hard day's work, there's the smell of fresh-baked bread and *pot-au-feu*, there's Yvette or Françoise trilling a little *chanson*. You enter. She stops her song. She stares wide-eyed across the pantry counter, her pretty bare skin turning pink. She drapes herself with a dish towel. She recovers and says merrily, 'Oh, Monsieur Reardon, you 'ave surprise me. I don't embarrass you, I 'ope. It's that I have the habitude to bake the bread when I am all nude.'"

Mike laughed. He said, "Leaving aside your fantasy—"

"*Your* fantasy—"

Mike said, "Your fantasy of my fantasy. Which strikes me as more like an Englishman's fantasy of Paris circa 1950 . . . Leaving all that aside, things are getting pretty expensive around here. An addition to the bungalow, an au-pair girl, rent for Joss' studio."

"Oh, you know you just love it. You get to be an old-fashioned patriarch. Besides, the bungalow rent will pay for the addition. Joss has enough money of her own to pay for the studio—if she operates at a loss *you* get a deduction on your joint return. . . . So all you have to do is pay for Yvette."

Why did all this make him so uneasy? Bonnie One was being pushy, but that shouldn't ruffle him—all he had to do was sit tight if he didn't want to do anything. One of the few things he'd learned from his partner Ritter about bargaining was to sit tight and keep still. (Ritter was known to the local bar as Catfish because he said to his clients, "Even a catfish don't get caught if he keeps his mouth shut.") But around home it wasn't supposed to take arm's-length bargaining, there was supposed to be a communal spirit, even if he was the official landlord. With Edmond and Evelyn he'd set a low rent, and once in a while they'd insisted on raising it. When Edmond and Evelyn brought Tyler along, Edmond, Mike, and Tyler had a boy's-club spurt of enthusiasm fixing up the bungalow. The most expensive project had been a tin roof for Evelyn and Edmond's cottage. Evelyn had spoken nostalgically of the sound of rain on a tin roof, and Mike had a roofer put one on. But then Edmond had put in hours of carpentry on Joss' studio, not by explicit contract but sneaking his work in bit by bit.

The group arrangements worked a lot better than the arrangements between Joss and Mike. Joss and Mike were at a stalemate when it came to interior decoration. Bundy's paintings had ended up in Mike's office. Joss wanted to get rid of the wallpaper in the front hall. It was originally blue and covered with lots of sailboats, but over the years the pale sea had darkened and the dark boats had paled until, as Joss pointed out, they might as well be in a greenish fog. Mike insisted on them as sacred relics. Joss in turn had padded the stairs to the girls' sleeping loft with remnants of brown and orange carpeting. She became as talismanically attached to her carpeting as he was to his wallpaper. And so on, until the battle lines were as entrenched as the Western Front in 1916.

They did have a few handsome things—wedding presents, hand-me-downs from Joss' mother, and a painting and a rug they'd once agreed on—but they couldn't agree where to put them.

Both Joss and he had cooperated happily in the group projects. Now that Bonnie One was individually and expressly proposing changes, part of Mike's uneasiness was that Joss would take her side. Another part of his uneasiness was that he'd stiffened at the prospect in some way that he hadn't ever in the past. He asked himself what he would have done if Tyler alone had come to him wanting another room. He would have jumped at it, treated it as a communal benefit, a boys'-club adventure. Rejoiced in his friend's good fortune. Now he felt a stirring of petty power and spite, and he felt as afflicted by it as if he'd discovered he had a tapeworm.

Edith came out in her bathrobe, her clothes bundled in her arms, her wet hair a tangle over her collar. Bonnie One lifted Edith's hair with a finger. "Did you use conditioner? Let me just comb a little in for you, darlin'."

Mike remembered when Edith hadn't liked showers. Was it five, six years ago? She'd been afraid of something—not just water getting in her eyes, but the feeling—as far as Mike had been able to piece it together—of being at the mercy of all that water shooting at her. It must have been at her grandmother's—he remembered the tiled shower stall with a clear glass door. He bought Edith a little umbrella with ducks on it. Step by step—just a little trickle of water, then more. They sang "Singin' in the Rain." She finally got so brave she caught water in her mouth and spat it at him as he stood on the other side of the glass door. She coaxed him close and did it again. He jumped back each time, and she laughed each time, master of the water.

A pleasure to be master to the girls' masteries. Swimming, reading, bicycle riding . . . Now both girls could do things he couldn't: ride horseback, tap-dance, read music. And he was certainly disqualified from having anything to do with their hair. But he felt a pang of being excluded when Edith followed Bonnie One back inside for this female attention.

◇

He was sinking again. He sat with his legs stretched on the deck chair and let Joss put the girls to bed. Bonnie One had eaten with them. Evelyn and Edmond came over for dessert. Edmond asked him if he wanted to watch the NBA playoffs—a Lakers home game, so it would be West Coast time, very late. Evelyn said, "Isn't this foolishness over yet?"

Bonnie uncorked another bottle of wine. Mike disapproved, but didn't say anything. Besides, with five of them sharing it . . . and Joss seemed okay. In fact lately she'd been stopping at two or three glasses and not having more of a buzz than anyone else.

Joss and Bonnie were all for the boys' watching the game. Evelyn said, "I don't see why you can't tape it instead of staying up till all hours."

Edmond said, "I can tell the difference."

"Well, of course you can—you're putting a tape in."

"No. Even without that. I can feel the difference. There's a feeling when it's live."

Edmond sounded so much like Tyler that Mike laughed.

Edmond said, "Like birds feeling a change in the weather, I have glands that can pick up that live action."

Evelyn said, "That is just nonsense."

"Maybe not," Joss said. "The last acting exercise in that Stanislavsky book is about that. Stanislavsky ties the actor up, blindfolds him, and gags him, and the actor is supposed to act the scene, to emanate the main emotion of the scene."

"It sounds a lot more interesting than Edmond watching TV," Bonnie One said. "Onstage bondage."

"Miss Dudley could tell all sorts of things," Mike said. "She could tell who was on the other side of the front door. She couldn't see them or smell—all she could do was hear the knocker."

"She could hear the footsteps," Evelyn said. "Dogs can tell footsteps. But how could *you* tell she knew who it was?"

"She had a different bark for each person she knew. If she didn't know, she gave her I-don't-know bark."

Joss snorted.

Evelyn said, "All this is a long way from a dumb old TV set."

"What can *you* tell from behind a door?" Bonnie One said to Mike. "I wonder, if we trussed you up like one of Stanislavsky's actors, what you could tell. I wonder if you could even tell who's touching you."

Mike said, "Am I allowed to sniff? Miss Dudley bequeathed me her sense of smell."

"We'll see," Bonnie said. She twirled her napkin up into a band and tied it over Mike's eyes. "Everybody, take off your shoes," Bonnie said. "No noise. The only clue should be touching your palm to his cheek. Now, everyone mill around so he can't tell who's coming from where."

"Do we put our hands on the beard part of his cheek or the bare part?" Evelyn said.

"We could all kiss him," Bonnie said.

Edmond said, "Not by the hair of your chinny-chin-chin. I'm going to go watch the game."

Evelyn called after him, "I'll be right along. I just want to kiss Mike through his cute little beard."

"Well, just once," Edmond said. "And it better not be a special delivery."

Bonnie said, "This isn't Post Office, it's science."

"Well, I'm going to kiss him," Evelyn said. "At least if he hasn't been smoking one of his smelly old cigars."

"All right," Bonnie said. "But you have to be quiet now."

Mike heard them padding around in their bare feet, their skirts brushing the chairs. He felt a puff of breath on his face, a soft nuzzle of a kiss.

"Evelyn," Mike said. "But I'm not sure. You'd better do it again for science."

Evelyn laughed. Then it sounded as if all three of them were saying, "Shh." Then bare feet going round and round his deck chair. But from farther away, along the path to the cottage, he heard Evelyn say, "Ow!" More shushing. Then the neck of a wine bottle touching the lip of a glass.

He suddenly felt vacant. Not depressed or elated, not warm or cold, not heavy or light. Just a shell of skin. Nothing but skin waiting to be written on. He thought of Ezra's description of first setting foot in a house, reading the air on his face.

They were trying to tease him by making him wait. They didn't know he was vacant. Not patient or impatient, just floating in his own vacancy.

Did all Ezra's training make him more tactile? Or did it dull his senses? Maybe it dulled them temporarily, so that when he got in the ring he was fresh, and raw, every patch of his skin alert—the soles of his feet on the canvas, his taped hands curled inside the gloves, his whole body tuned to the other fighter so that he felt the man's movements as acutely as if he were touching him—as if there were an invisible spiderweb between their bodies. Was that what Ezra felt when he felt his edge? That he could read the spiderweb faster, sense the other guy's move beforehand?

Nothing here. Wind in the trees far far away. He was still vacant. Not receiving Stanislavsky emanations, not giving any. It was comfortable being blank. This state of mind was so odd it didn't feel as if it was his.

It ended abruptly. He was sure they were looking at him, he felt them looking—maybe one and then the other. Maybe one was whispering right into the other's ear while the other looked. Maybe they were nervous that he hadn't stirred for so long. Maybe it had been a minute, maybe five or ten.

It wasn't that he was himself again. It was only that he'd slipped from his vacancy into their nervousness.

He felt fingers in his beard. A hand on each side—definitely two hands. One set of fingers was twirling the near hairs, the other combing them straight. But no kissing. He put his hands behind his back. Maybe they were nervous that he would reach out or that he would take off his blindfold. When he moved his arms, the fingers in his beard drew away. But putting his hands behind his back was the thing to do. When he lay still again the fingers came back, stroking his mustache. And then there was a comb combing his mustache. First straight down, then out to each side.

He had no urge to guess. He didn't care who these people were. He liked having his mustache combed. And now they were combing his beard. Maybe they were going to cut his beard, shave it all off.

What was happening to his mouth now might not be kissing. Half-kissing. It was disembodied and hypnotic. At first it was no more than having his lips brushed very lightly—probably by other lips, but perhaps by something else as soft as lips. Perhaps fingertips, perhaps the edge of a finger. Perhaps they were putting lipstick on him, finger-painting it lightly across his lips.

Now someone was putting things in his mouth. A grape, easy to guess. He used to play that game with Edith and Nora to get them to eat their vegetables. Close your eyes and guess what this is. Carrot? Broccoli? A Brussels sprout?

Another grape, this time slithered in by a tongue that had an aftertaste of dry white wine. But he was supposed to guess who. It was Bonnie One—thin quick lips. He didn't say anything. It was both erotic and irritating, as though Joss had mixed him up with the man on the other side of her at the movie theater. He began to feel as if he *was* the man on the other side of her. As if Bonnie One was the woman on the other side of the man.

They both pressed their faces on his, trailed their fingers around his neck, his ears, under the hair on his head, through his beard. They drew away and came back. He felt duller and duller at his center. He heard their breathing now, distinct from the air in the treetops. Less distinct than their breathing, less distinct than the air in the treetops, he heard something like Bundy's voice, perhaps an echo of Bundy's voice. It said, or had just finished saying, "Monkey sex . . ."

He slumped back in the deck chair. If he was the Stanislavsky actor emanating his part in the play, he was only dullness. They were the monkeys, and he was too dull to tease them, too dull even to say who they were. He took off his blindfold and opened his eyes. They looked lively standing at the foot of the deck chair. *They* could speak, they could laugh or dance across the porch.

They'd made him duller than himself. Other days he could sing, he could be funny—he could make Joss laugh. But here he was drugged with dullness. For this game they'd changed him into a nearsighted blundering animal—a bull in a bullring—less, a dancing bear on a short chain.

Joss walked into the house. Bonnie One watched her, then turned to look at him. He moved his head and shoulders in an incomplete gesture.

Bonnie One said brightly, "Now, where did my shoes get to? If I don't find my shoes, you'll have to carry me back to the bungalow—that yard is just full of prickly things. See if they got under that cushion you're sitting on. My shoes, I mean."

Mike got up and looked.

"There they are," Bonnie One said. "Right under your old deck chair." She pulled them out. She put a hand on Mike's shoulder to steady herself as she lifted one foot to put her shoe on. Then the other hand and the other shoe. Then she faced him squarely but didn't say anything. She stood so close to him he could feel her breath.

It made him nervous. He said, "When is Tyler getting back?"

"Is that your question?" she said. "You don't think of me, do you? You don't *consider* me."

"I didn't mean—"

"You're very attentive to everyone else. You know them—but you must have decided not to know me."

She wasn't touching him and she was speaking softly, but her face was so close to his that he felt strapped down for interrogation. He said, "Is this another lesson in dissolving contexts?"

"Do you think everyone has to stay the same all the time?"

"If they don't, how does anyone get to know anyone else?"

Bonnie One sighed. "By not being difficult. By not being rule-oriented all the time." She sighed again. "You probably think you have to do the same things over and over or you'll go to pieces. But look—you love water—you love the river, you love the sea. Water changes but it's always water." She put a hand on his chest as if to push him away, but she didn't push. She said, "I can tell by your eyes you're getting set to argue. Getting set to just *crush* me. Maybe it's because you can't think of what else to do. You say, 'When is Tyler getting back?' so you can relegate me. So everyone stays in place all the time. That's such a one-context frame of mind. So totalitarian." She gave his chest a little push. "You couldn't see, you were hiding behind your blindfold, but Joss didn't mind. Joss didn't mind our little floating back and forth just now. There's no harm in a little floating if you find the right context. There's no harm in emanating some little shred of feeling. You don't have to fall from grace."

Across the yard a phone started ringing. It was in the bungalow.

"Too bad," Bonnie One said. "If I run I can just catch it." She gathered her skirt with one hand. He reached for her other hand, which was moving across his chest. He held her wrist. She said, "I have to run." She slipped away and started across the lawn, holding her skirt just above her knees. She stopped and turned around. "Did I just get an emanation?" She spun and ran on, her pale bare legs trotting away into the dark.

She was right—he did stay away from knowing her. And now he made an effort to seal off the effects of her warm-breathed hovering, her touches like froth, her kissing with pulses and nibbles. Hard not to imagine what he would feel in the wrap of her limbs.

Tyler's girlfriend, Tyler's fiancée, Joss' friend. His taboos weren't good enough. No, let the blame come closer. He was letting things happen—doing no more than hoping, relying on old habits, on inertia.

He went inside. Joss had turned off all the lights. Probably gone to bed. Gone to bed mad? Gone to bed because some wine had snuck up on her? Gone to bed because she did mind after all?

To be sure where he was in the room, he reached out for the end of the sofa. He jumped when Joss stood up. For a moment he didn't know what she meant as she moved toward him, touched him with her hand, then let herself collide with him. Both their skins felt hot. Too hot and rough for light-fingered touching. Their bodies felt solid, as solid and heavy as the sofa, as bulky as the cushions. They tugged and opened their clothes, pulled a cushion onto the floor, and jostled themselves onto it.

◇

At that time I'd already begun to collect Grandma sayings the same way Mom collected her favorite movie clichés, the same way Tyler collected plain everyday phrases. Not *exactly* the same way—I didn't have a project in mind. I'd just hear them in my head and sometimes I'd write them down, because writing helped me listen more carefully to the wonderful buzz of Grandma's voice. At that time I didn't understand the implications of her old-fashioned upper-class accent—I just loved the things she said, the way she said them—the swoop of emphasis, the vibration in her lower register that was close to laughter.

Of course, sometimes she was prim. I can hear her voice saying, "Now, *that* is not a suitable topic for the dinner table." Her two sons (Uncle Jonathan, her older son, especially) might keep on. Jonathan could be very funny, and Grandma sometimes couldn't help laughing. But soon then she'd say, "Your *nieces,* dear boy." The final warning came when she'd pick up her knife with her fingertips and drop it flat. In the moment of silence that followed, Mom and Dad and the uncles would still be bubbling inside, on the verge of trying one more variation on the theme. Then Grandma would launch a new topic in her addressing-a-child flute-voice, usually calling on Nora or me. "Now, Edith, dear girl, tell me about *your* day." For me this was an exercise in wanting two things at once: I wanted to obey

Grandma—more than obey, I wanted to please her—and at the same time I wished to be one of the boisterous ones. No, I knew that was beyond me. I could only wish to be allied to the boisterous ones, to be their gun-bearer, their water-boy, to tag along somehow, anyhow, on their border raid.

This sounds like such an insignificant thing that it's hard for me to believe it became the first unit of my understanding Mom. Later on, when I sort of knew what was going on with Mom and Bonnie and when Mom and Dad were arguing and Mom was comparing herself to the Viet Cong and Dad to LBJ, I knew what she meant. She adored her mother, she wanted a life like hers, a husband like hers, a household like hers, and at the same time she wanted a way to be completely different, to have an alternate universe of her very own. Dad and Grandma were really pretty good specimens of Western Civ. In fact, in one of Mom's diary entries during the divorce she wrote, "Maybe something *is* wrong with me—Ma and even Mike are good. And I'm rejecting both of them. OK. So I'm wrong. Big deal." Mom didn't want to ride the Western Civ monorail. She wanted to hop a freight.

Grandma had a hard time with the divorce, but she tried to be on Mom's side, though of course she couldn't try quite hard enough for Mom. Grandma couldn't stop liking Dad. She'd say to him that she was sticking up for Mom, that she was completely loyal to Mom, and Dad would say, "Right. That's right. Of course you are." And then, when Mom went off for a weekend and left us with Dad, Grandma would invite us all to come stay with her. It may have been because she believed that a single man couldn't care properly for two daughters, or that she didn't want Mom's hometown to see the spectacle of Dad, forsaken but gallant, escorting Nora and me to a restaurant, to a movie, to the Dogwood Festival Fair. (As it turned out, Dad discovered that there is nothing so appealing to free-range women as a single man out on the town with his small daughters—but that's a later chapter.) In any case, Mom took it hard that Grandma invited Dad along with us. Mom didn't want Grandma to dislike Dad, but she wanted Grandma to hold him at arm's length. And unfortunately, no matter how Grandma tried, she couldn't bring herself to say to Mom that she liked Bonnie One. (Years later—I was in college—Grandma took me out for supper. She suddenly held my hand and said, "Edith, dear girl—men are where it's at." I blushed at the time, but now I love the way she blurted it out.) If Grandma couldn't warm to Bonnie One, the next-best sign of loyalty would have been for Grandma to make Dad drive back home alone on Friday, then come back on Sunday to pick us up. Of course it doesn't make sense, of course it seems spiteful—and of course deep down Mom liked it that Grandma and Dad kept on liking each other. But Mom was struggling to keep both her worlds equal, and at that time Western Civ seemed to have all the power. I can see how Grandma and Dad looked like NATO to Mom when she felt as if she was taking out citizenship papers in the third world.

But to get to Bonnie and Mom playing kissing games with Dad, blindfolded and psychically tied up—how to deal with that?

Nora doesn't want to talk about it.

Maybe that's a good reaction, maybe that's the right reaction. But I've come too far to stop.

One thing to bear in mind is that Bonnie One thought it was okay to use her flirty skills as a smoke screen, *and* that Dad was a sucker for them. Ganny once asked Dad if he'd read Jean-Jacques Rousseau's *Confessions.* Dad said no. Ganny said, "You really ought to. You have something in common with him. He frequently finds himself in compromising situations—for example, in a room with an Italian chambermaid with his pants around his ankles—and he writes that he really can't imagine how this could happen to a simple lad like himself." Dad said that he'd never been in a room with an Italian chambermaid with his pants around his ankles. Ganny laughed and said that he was being either too literal or too forgetful.

Ganny was right. Dad had at least this much of a double standard: a good earnest boy like him could get so flustered his moral right hand didn't know what his naughty left hand was up to, whereas women—in Dad's view—always know what they're doing. At least all the women that he had anything to do with. There were of course innocent naïve women who were preyed upon by wicked knowing men, but that was a completely different play with a completely different cast of characters.

Maybe his left hand hoodwinked his right hand into thinking the left hand was just being blithe. Blithe is okay, blithe is one of the good things to be, blithe is the third son of the king setting out on the same quest as the overserious first and second sons, but the third son is singing as he rides through the forest, stops to chat with anyone who says hi, gives his loaf of bread to a beggar-woman, is in tune with the sunlight dappling the path through fluttering leaves. . . .

Sometimes when Dad was preaching to me to be more blithe and carefree, he would quote the French translation of the Sermon on the Mount; in that version, "Blessed are the pure of heart" comes out "*Heureux sont les débonnairs.*" Happy are the debonair, Dad? You old Parisian *boulevardier*. Meanwhile, your other half is picturing yourself as a choirboy, light-years away in fact but right inside your dream version of your self. Perfume . . . incense. "Thank Heaven for Little Girls" . . . *"Nunc dimittis servum tuum, Domine."*

Here's a plain everyday phrase: "I just didn't know what I was doing." But it takes a lot of willful blindness to be blithe, to keep seeing yourself as the happy-go-lucky third son of the king, to keep on being the perpetually taken-by-surprise Jean-Jacques Rousseau.

So let's figure that bit of complicity into the picture of the blindfolded cuckold on the deck chair.

And then there's Mom. Let's not use the excuse that she's had too much wine. And let's not use the I-didn't-know-what-I-was-doing line. In fact let's not try to justify her at all. Just imagine some notion that might have flashed through her Captain Midnight starburst-kaleidoscope mind. Here's one I'm sympathetic to: A tiresome trait in men is that their physical affection is so restless. They *say* that they want the woman to take the initiative, but what they mean is they want the woman to nibble their earlobe or play with their hair for about five seconds until they get their boiler full of steam. Then they're chugging away, all pistons, drive shafts, and wheels, clickety-clacking down those familiar rails.

Let's drop the locomotive-phallic metaphor. Let's just think of how nice it is to be expecting something nice and not have to rush. Stepping outside into the sun, slowly getting warm, feeling it on the backs of your hands, your shoulders, little by little. Sitting down and stretching now that you're warmer and looser and more peaceful. Just when it begins to get too hot, a puff of cool air slips along your cheek and into your collar. Then you hike your skirt up, lean back on your hands, close your eyes, and tilt your face up.

It would be nice if you could have a lover like the sun. It would be even nicer if men could sometimes let women be the sun.

It's not surprising that one of Mom's favorite movie clichés—this one strictly visual—is the starched but pretty nurse wheeling the convalescent soldier out into the garden, turning him so he's looking at the sea, so he can close his eyes and tilt his face to the sun. He sighs with gratitude.

So do we want men to be wounded? There's something to be said for it if that's what it takes to make them be still. Immobile but attentive, peaceful, and grateful. Unfortunately, there are other states of mind that go along with being wounded—e.g., self-pity, either stoical, sullen, or whining. You don't really want a guy to be *vulnerable*. When they just roll over and show you their soft white underbelly, it's hard not to feel like a shark. So get it right, guys—you've been wounded, but you've got it together now and you're bravely and cheerfully convalescent, more aware of the subtle slow aspects of physical affection, and, while generally robust, aware of what it's like to feel fragile. Got it?

Maybe Dad got it right later. Certainly Mom did. Just not with each other. I've never brought it up with either of them. It's squirmy enough just imagining it. Maybe Nora is right that I shouldn't have started. But until I get to some conclusion, I'm afraid I won't be able to stop obsessing, be able to unbraid their lives from mine. Every time I have a wish, I remember when they had it too. I can't help imagining my wishes in them, their wishes in me.

Cast them out like devils? No, I want all of us to be free, happy, and equal.

Nora and I both went through the standard thing that most divorced kids go through of wanting them to get back together. Both Nora and I outgrew it. I'm thinking of that year when I was suddenly coming into my own imagination, into my hyperimagination, just in time to feel the radiation of their upheavals, to receive all the energy of their seismic shifts, just in time to receive all that energy without a language of my own, without any distancing abstractions of my own, without any astronomy or zoology that wasn't part of the extravagant nursery we all lived in then.

Perhaps I go back there now to make the little girl I was then who I am now. Or perhaps to make her better than I am now, so that who I am now will be better.

Nora did it. Nora got better. I used to think she did it by not having sensed what I sensed. Now I think she did, but she countered what was going on with immediate instinctive rage, both in real life and in her dreams. She countered what she sensed before she understood it, and that may have been the good thing to do.

I'm not jealous. I rejoice in her good fortune. I'm not being ironic. She comes to see me and makes me laugh.

§ 6

Mike drove to his mother-in-law's with the girls. On the way there the girls announced that they weren't going to help him with the boats. On Saturday morning, however, the fifteen-year-old son of the tenant farmer showed up. He'd been hired by their grandmother to help Mike. In the time since they'd last seen him the boy had become handsome. And now his new lean face was already tanned, his dark-brown hair already lightened with streaks of copper from the spring sun. When Mike shook hands with him, he clapped the boy on the shoulder and said, "You sure put on a lot of muscle there." The boy blushed. The girls rolled their eyes away from their embarrassing father. They volunteered to help scrape and paint. The boy called Mike "sir" and the girls Miz Edith and Miz Nora.

Their grandmother took Mike and the girls out for supper—the girls in the new dresses their grandmother had bought them, Mike in an old suit of the Admiral's because he'd forgotten to pack one for the weekend. Over dessert Nora said to Edith, "I think he looks like Donny."

Their grandmother said, "Who? And who is Donny? I can't abide pronouns without antecedents."

Edith said, "The farmer's son, Walter. Donny is Donny of Donny and Marie. But Walter looks more like Sean Cassidy."

Mike laughed, because he knew Edith once made a scrapbook of Sean Cassidy pictures. His mother-in-law hit his arm with her napkin and said, "You girls are quite right. Walter is a very good-looking boy, and what's more he's very nice."

The girls, who'd been embarrassed at having blurted out that they'd even noticed Walter and had been irritated by Mike's laughing, began to be smoothed. Their grandmother went on a bit about how she'd admired young men who reminded her of Leslie Howard or Fred Astaire (so sophisticated, but obviously terribly sweet), but then having come round to Gary Cooper (at first you felt uneasy at his awkwardness, but then you just ached for it).

Nora said, "Who was Grandpa like?" Edith looked worried.

Their grandmother said, "He was just himself. I knew right away that he'd be an almost impossible man, but that I was going to marry him. And he *was* a very difficult man. But I was very fortunate."

Mike saw Edith look surprised and then contented. He looked at Nora, who looked pleased but still curious. Her grandmother said to her, "I'll tell you a lot more another time. He would certainly have liked you."

On the ride back to the house Mike felt relaxed in a way he hadn't felt for a long time. Mrs. Rogers was driving, the girls were quiet, perhaps asleep, in the backseat. He was tired from a day in the sun, pleased that the boats were going to be ready ahead of schedule, that the girls were so buoyed by their grandmother. One thing he liked was that so much of life here was tacit—that the way he was called on to be in charge of the boats and the boathouse, for example, was much less a contractual duty than Mrs. Rogers' giving him a sense of place in the family household. Odd—Anglo-American law was mostly about contracts; Roman law had concepts of status as well—in some cases offensive to a modern liberal lawyer, especially regarding slaves . . . although the *status* of slave, now that he thought of it, had made the Roman slave better off than the American slave, who'd had no status and was therefore unprotected against any contractual transfer.

Mike came back from his mental drift and didn't recognize the road. He said, "Have we passed the turn?"

Mrs. Rogers said, "What are you talking about?"

Mike said, "This isn't the road—"

"Until you've lived here, dear boy, all the roads look alike. Especially at night."

In twelve years of being son-in-law and mother-in-law, they'd never had a cross word. Well, hardly ever. He looked into the backseat. The girls were asleep. He looked at the fuel gauge—plenty of gas.

Mrs. Rogers said, "I'm driving at a perfectly safe speed."

"I was just checking the fuel."

"Well, don't be such a mother hen."

Without leaning over, Mike stole a look at the odometer. After another five minutes and three miles they crossed a bridge over a creek. It was a much more deeply cut creek than the one near the house.

He said, "I don't think that was the bridge."

"What bridge? A bridge without an antecedent is as bad as a pronoun without an antecedent."

Mike rolled down his window and looked at the stars. He saw the Big Dipper ahead, Orion behind.

Mrs. Rogers said, "Do you feel all right?"

"Yes, I'm fine. I was just looking at the stars. Lots of stars."

"Well, calm down. You're making me nervous."

The road was a pretty country road, gently curving this way and that, going up and down in easy little swoops. The Neck wasn't that big. They were bound to hit a main road soon. But Mike felt on edge. At first he was pondering this first little frailty in his mother-in-law: he was reminded of going sailing with the Admiral after his stroke. At times, especially when they were trying to get home at dusk, the Admiral had had trouble reading the compass, had mistrusted it, and Mike had been caught between shyness and alarm.

But perhaps now the trouble was more in him. Lately he'd been too alarmed by little things being out of place, he'd been startled by small disorder into fearing larger disorder. Even now, with no reason to worry about anything but Mrs. Rogers' missing a turn, he felt that this was signaling him as obliquely as Bundy's voice, pointing to some frailty in the nature of things, to how quickly even the most familiar happiness could change shape, to how little it took for the familiar to become strange.

Mrs. Rogers stopped the car. She said crossly, "Now, what's *that* doing there?" They'd come to a T. She looked at Mike and said, "Well, you *appear* to be as surprised as I am, which is terribly polite of you." Then she laughed, either at herself or at her joke, and Mike was dumbly happy again. Maybe all that the frailty of the nature of things meant was that you spiraled down for a while, then you caught a puff of air and went up.

Mike got out the map of Westmoreland County. It didn't take long to find where they were—it was the only T north of a creek in their neck of the woods. "If we go left, we'll come back around to the road that goes to the general store."

Nora mumbled something, but she was just talking in her sleep. They went up a dark slope and then down, rattling across a planked one-lane bridge, the sky and black creek open and shining, then back into the tunnel of trees and brambles and roadside daylilies. He didn't regret the passing of spring; dark summer stillness settled him, would settle them all.

They left late on Sunday. The girls helped with the final coat of paint even though Walter didn't show up. "His family observes the Sabbath," their grandmother explained with remote approval, "except for haying, of course." The girls nodded sagely. Mike was about to explain about making hay while the sun shines but decided they would enjoy the flavor better if he shut up.

When they got home the girls were asleep, Edith slumped in the front seat, Nora sprawled in the back. Mike went in to get Joss to help carry them in. Joss was in her studio watching a videotape, pedaling her exercise bike, and chewing gum. She was listening to the sound through earphones. The joined wires ran down the back of her black tank top, then looped around to the machine like a prehensile tail. All that Mike could hear was the whirring of the wheel, the rustling of her black nylon sweat pants, and an occasional snap of gum.

The sight of her so engrossed, so totally plugged in, startled and puzzled him. He thought he should be pleased. It could be worse—she was there waiting for them after all. And yet she seemed not there, as if she were a simulacrum she'd left behind, something more elaborate than pillows under a blanket to fool the nighttime assassin with the dagger, more elaborate than Sherlock Holmes putting his pipe-smoking cardboard in the window of his Baker Street lodgings.

He left Joss as she was and carried the girls in one by one. He tucked them in bed in their underwear, came back down, and flicked the light in the main room several times. He thought if he made a noise Joss would be scared. She finally noticed the light blinking and was scared anyway. She said, "Oh my God!" and tore off the earphones.

He said, "It's just me."

"What is this? You putting on your own production of *Gaslight*?"

"I thought . . . Never mind. Can you put that machine on pause? Come sit with me for a second? I'm going out on the porch."

"I'll go look at the girls first."

He got a beer and a cigar and sat on the deck chair, ready to narrate the weekend. But when Joss sat down in a chair by the picnic table, he felt strangely awkward. He couldn't start talking.

Joss was fidgety in a new way—not twirling her wedding ring or jiggling her foot but turning her head to one side and then the other, looking into the night as if she were a nervous sentry. She finally said, "So what's new down on the Neck?"

He started in, but then stopped. "I'm not just boring you," he said. "I'm boring myself."

Joss laughed.

He noticed that the lights were out in Evelyn and Edmond's cottage—that wasn't strange, they usually went to bed early—but the bungalow was dark too.

"It's quiet in here," he said. "Too quiet."

She laughed, but still didn't say anything.

"So where is everyone? I mean Tyler and Bonnie."

"I don't know. It's very odd. They haven't been here all day."

"Tyler got back, did he? When was he coming back? Friday? Saturday?"

"Something like that. I didn't see him. But then Bonnie's been gone too. Very odd."

"Is anything wrong?"

"No," Joss said. "I don't know. Maybe. Just odd. I'm really tired."

"Been working hard? Get much done?"

"Mmm. Some."

"Good for you."

Joss got up and went into the house. The artificial good cheer of his "Good for you" hung in the air. His body became abruptly inert, sunk in this hog-wallow of a deck chair, his flesh all unfeeling bristles and thick hide. How had this happened? His mind was nimble, ready to dance. In fact he couldn't get it to be still, it kept prancing around, flinging up bits of conversation, items of interest, polite inquiries, things they could do.

But for Joss it was just the opposite. Her body felt weightless as she moved through the main room. Everything seemed weightless. She'd put off speculation about what it meant that Bonnie and Tyler had been away for two days, but now that Mike was back, she got stuck in a single thought, an unmoving mental block, although it came in variations of her grade-B movie clichés. "The jig's up." "We've got you surrounded, come out with your hands up."

She couldn't think; her body floated into the kitchen, her hollow arms and hands pulling knives and forks out of the drying rack. They dropped into the drawer as if by themselves.

She flitted through the house, switching off lights, fixing the sofa cushions, fishing out nickels, bobby pins, paper clips. Out to the car for the girls' suitcases, dirty clothes into the laundry hamper outside their bedroom door. She felt her own clothes against her skin, the air in the house breathing on her face, hands, and ankles. She couldn't get any other thought going, she couldn't coax any feelings into motion. She knew their names—fear, relief, guilt, defiance—but not one broke loose inside her.

At last her body wound down. She laid her head on her pillow. As she fell toward sleep she saw herself moving around and around her studio, stopping at her corkboard, her blackboard, her notebook—her mother's dressing table on the Neck with its triptych of vanity mirrors. At each station she was making a plan, plan after plan after plan, each plan incomplete. When this whirl-away vision stopped, she opened her eyes, and, still without feeling—at least without any feeling she could name—she saw that she had more energy of her own than she had fear.

◇

Mike's day filled up with oddities. The first thing was that the chairman of Tyler's department asked Ganny to be his counsel for the internal proceedings at the university. Mike saw the sense in this. Ganny was a good trial lawyer, knew a lot of the university administrators from her undergraduate and law-school years, when she'd been on student-council committees, she was still a popular figure from having been on the women's basketball team and then one of the assistant coaches when she was working her way through law school. For the chairman to choose a black single woman as his lawyer might counter the appearance that he was just another male-chauvinist pig relying on the old-boy network, might de-demonize him as a despoiler/despiser of women. It was a crudely transparent tactic, but if his attackers pointed out that it was a crudely transparent tactic, they would be seen to be disparaging Ganny's ability, demoting her from lawyer to symbol.

From Ganny's point of view, there were some advantages. The proceedings would give her a chance to show her ability to the university bigwigs, and there would likely be a discussion of the case at the next Board of Visitors meeting, etc., etc. It might very well lead to more university business for Ganny; the university would love to take on a black woman as a visible legal adviser.

A problem was of course that Ganny worked for Mike, and Mike was one of Tyler's best friends, and Tyler, although not a party to the case, was involved.

Ganny, in her preliminary discussions with the chairman, had told him that she knew Tyler socially, but he'd brushed that aside.

Ganny asked Mike if he thought Tyler would be called as a witness.

Mike said, "He doesn't have any direct knowledge of the incident, but it's hard to tell where these things can go. It's not a courtroom, and these *ad-hoc* investigations can go rambling all over the place. There are at least two issues—one is the seduction-for-favors issue, which has a subissue of the girl's entrapping—"

Ganny cleared her throat.

Mike said, "The woman's entrapping him. Issue number two is the chairman's saying in effect that he can rig Tyler's tenure committee. Jeez, Ganny, I don't know. . . . Tyler's going to come up. Maybe even that weird thing at that cocktail party where Joss got after the chairman and Tyler said, 'Fuck 'em if they can't take a joke.' If you take it on, you and I can't get into it together."

Ganny said, "He didn't ask you, big boy."

Mike laughed. "I mean even get together to chat, like we're doing now, big girl. Big woman. You'll have to be behind a Chinese Wall. Because here's another part of the problem—you told the chairman that you know Tyler and he brushed it aside. But the guy's probably under stress—I mean his whole career may be about to derail. Down the line he may decide you're not doing a good job and blame it on your being part of our gang. Of course he'd look bad if he fired you halfway through. But if he loses big, he might come back at you, claim he didn't know how tight the connection was. It'd be feeble, but messy for you. At heart you'd better run it by him again. Spell it out so he really gets it. Make sure you have a good memo.

"Then there may be some questions about what you yourself can stomach. For instance, would you mind digging up the woman's past sex life? Even if you yourself think it's inadmissible, but your client wants her to know you're digging? Wants to scare her . . . I'd sure want to let the client know what some of the boundaries are." Mike leaned back in his chair and eyed the corner of the ceiling. He hadn't felt so wise for weeks. "I imagine you're already looking to get some agreement with him about lines of defense. What do you have in mind? Worthy career, years of service to the university versus one brief moment of middle-aged infatuation. The poor man was a fool for love, his tender feelings only smoldering until this woman fanned them into flame with her apparent eagerness. . . ."

Ganny laughed. "Hey. You're getting into it pretty good. Maybe I should call you as an expert witness. An authority on middle-aged male foolishness." She got up and put her hand on his shoulder. She said, "Aw, Mike." Then she squeezed the back of his neck and rocked him a little side to side. Not a flirtatious gesture, but he became hollow with tenderness.

After she left he thought that maybe the chairman wasn't just a scumbag, maybe he'd started out genuinely liking the woman. Maybe that would be a line to take. . . .

He cringed at how fast he could get dumb. Maybe it had been happening a lot lately—he wasn't sure he'd been noticing each time.

. . .

Tyler called Mike up and asked if he could stop by. Mike said, "Sure. Come at the end of the day, we can go home together."

There was a pause, then Tyler said, "At five o'clock?"

"Fine."

Then Emmanuel Pritchett called to ask if Mike could come to a meeting with Ezra's manager. Mike asked what the matter was. Emmanuel said there were just a couple of things that the manager hadn't been tough enough about concerning the fight arrangements. Mike said, "You want to meet with him here in my office?"

"That would be the most convenient thing."

"Look, I don't want to upset Ezra, or Ezra's relationship with his manager. If you want to lean on the manager, you'd better come in and talk to me first so we can talk it over."

"You're my lawyer, and I need you to talk some sense into that—"

"I am your lawyer. But I also don't want to screw anything up for Ezra. It's getting close to the fight. If Ezra gets worried about things, he's not as resilient as you are. So let's the two of us talk before we do anything else."

"Resilient," Emmanuel said, and laughed. "I bet you're a sweet talker with the girls."

"That's right. So come on in. I'll buy you lunch."

"If your meter's running, you'll still come out ahead."

"That's right. Tomorrow suit you?"

"You go ahead and write me down for tomorrow. You're just lucky my real lawyer's out of town."

Emmanuel's saltiness cheered Mike up so much that he forgot about how strange Tyler had sounded. When the secretary announced Tyler near the end of the day, Mike bounced up ready for the boisterous Tyler. But Tyler looked like hell. His face was puffy, his eyes were red, and he looked like he'd slept in his suit. He sat heavily and wearily in the armchair on the other side of Mike's desk. Tyler said, "I may not be around for a while. Or I may be coming and going at odd times. I'm telling you 'cause I don't want you to worry. Everything's in a turmoil and I don't know what in hell I'm going to do. But it's nothing life-threatening. Nobody's sick or hurt." He stopped and leaned his forearms on the briefcase across his knees.

Mike said, "I'm sorry, Tyler. That's terrible. But I don't understand yet. . . ."

"I wasn't going to go into any of this, but what the hell. . . . For one thing, Bonnie and I aren't engaged."

Mike's first thought was that life at home would be better, would be the way it was before. Then he looked at Tyler, and felt guilty. Mike said, "I hope . . . I mean I know that Bonnie and I have had some quarrels, and I hope that didn't make things worse."

Tyler shook his head without looking up. Then Mike was alarmed that the strange interlude of the deck-chair kissing game had somehow come up. Tyler opened his briefcase and handed Mike a page of handwriting. It was a rough draft with a lot of crossed-out and rewritten phrases.

"My present to you has finite dimensions but will hold an infinite amount. In itself it is nothing, but in it is everything. You can't keep it forever, but what it will give you is for all time. It is small, but I can't wrap it up. I can only tell you where to find it and how to get it to give you its secret treasures."

Mike read it. He said, "I don't get it. I mean I guess it's a kind of love letter, but I don't get the riddle."

"It took me a while," Tyler said. "It's Bonnie's handwriting."

"How do you know it wasn't meant for you?"

" 'Cause I never got it. There's some other reasons too, but I don't want to get into all this."

"How do you know it's not old? For some old boyfriend years ago?"

"There's a date on the back."

Mike turned the sheet over and saw the current year in elaborate calligraphy and a drawing of a naked woman stooping to fill a water jug in a stone-rimmed pool.

Tyler said, "I really don't mean to go into all this. I just wanted to tell you enough so as you won't worry unnecessarily. I don't want to hire you as my riddle-solving lawyer."

Mike couldn't keep from making guesses, but was glad Tyler shut him up, since the first answer to the riddle he'd thought of was crude. He chalked it up to his time in the Navy, where the men said "cunt" or "sleeve" as often as they said "fuck" or "shit."

Mike said, "Look, Tyler. Don't go off by yourself. Come on back with me. We'll give you a nice family supper, hang out with the girls, get Edmond and Evelyn over. Or is Bonnie still in the bungalow?"

"No," Tyler said. "Bonnie's not in the bungalow."

"Well, that's right," Mike said. "If you and Bonnie split up, I sure want it to be you who stays on in the bungalow."

Tyler looked pained. After a moment he said, "Right this minute, it's better if I'm off on my own."

Mike felt rebuffed. He said, "If that's what you think is best." Then he suddenly felt alarmed. He said, "Tyler. Listen to me, Tyler. You're not feeling . . . strange, are you? I mean, you're unhappy, but you're . . . okay, right?"

Tyler looked puzzled for a second, then said, "Oh." He shook his head. "No, that's not something I'd do. I may be crazy, but I'm not that crazy." He stopped. He looked past Mike. Mike turned and saw Bundy's painting of the Rivanna after a flood. Tyler said, "I'm sorry. I was just being emphatic so you wouldn't have any doubts."

"Okay. Look. What I meant is this—I was touched when I ran into Ezra after Bundy shot himself and Ezra asked me if I owned a gun."

Tyler said, "Yeah, I can see that."

"So you'll come by again, right?" Mike said. "Evelyn. You should talk to Evelyn too."

"Yeah," Tyler said. "You can call me at my office." He got up to go. "Oh yeah," he said. "The answer to the riddle is a post-office box."

◇

I haven't talked much about Tyler. I think I underestimated him, because his attentions were mostly toward the other grown-ups—Dad, Edmond and Evelyn, Bonnie One—and he was sometimes hard to understand. He said lots of bright things in a bright but obscure way.

When he went in to talk to Dad he was in a dilemma. The reason Tyler was guarded and standoffish with Dad is that Tyler knew everything. He wanted Dad to know and he didn't want Dad to know. He wanted Dad to know for lots of reasons. Tyler was furious at Bonnie One, furious at Mom, and he wanted vengeance. He also would have liked the comfort of Dad's being in the same boat. But Tyler made a distinction between Dad's situation and his, and Tyler decided that there was a chance that Dad and Nora and I might be saved. He figured it was just possible that he and Bonnie One would disappear, that he would somehow get her away, and that Mom, who'd been married for twelve years, who was the mother of two children, would return to normal without any cataclysm.

His whole script was riddled with misconceptions and misperceptions, but what is admirable to me now is that he felt himself being engulfed but kept himself from clutching at anyone else. As it turned out this stand of lonely sacrifice didn't do a bit of good. At least it had no effect on anyone else. It may have comforted *him,* may have helped him think that he was taking it like a man, and that taking it like a man was helping his adopted family . . . who might never know of his silent lonely burden. . . .

We're all suckers for certain effects.

Look at me. I meant to say something nice. Forget the mockery. Tyler was doing the right thing.

◇

Bonnie came to see Joss. When Joss saw her walking toward the house, she guessed. Joss opened the door and said, "So. The jig's up." Bonnie nodded. Joss shocked both of them by laughing. Joss took Bonnie by the hand and led her into the studio. Joss said, "The scene of the crime. At least one of the scenes of the crimes."

Bonnie said, "Joss . . ."

Joss said, "Yes, all right. I'll be . . ." She held her hands against her stomach.

"Tyler knows," Bonnie said. "That's all I know. That's all I know now."

"What happened? Did he see us someplace?"

"No," Bonnie said. "When I loaned him my car he took the whole key ring. So when he went to my office he found everything."

"Why?" Joss said. "Why would he—"

"That's the irony. That's the bitter irony. He found a postcard in my car. He wouldn't read someone's letter, but he found a postcard."

"I didn't write a postcard."

"No. It was from an old boyfriend. It wasn't anything. It was so not anything I just left it around. But Tyler thought it was something. So Tyler went into my office and got into my desk drawer, that side drawer. He was looking for an old boyfriend and he found us. Your notes to me. My letters to you we were keeping safe. I don't know where he is now. He made me drive away with him and we were way up in the mountains and he wouldn't drive me back."

"Are you all right?"

"Yes. He just talked and talked. At first he said he just wanted to understand. Then he ranted. Then he said he wanted to understand. Then he ranted. And so forth."

Joss said, "*Did* he understand?" and laughed again, two short barks.

"Joss, don't be strange."

Joss said, "Okay. What happened next?"

"Happened? I'm not through with the mountains yet. He said that I'd ruined his life. I told him that *I* wouldn't ever say anything like that—I have too much pride to say someone else could ruin my life."

"So I guess by then you weren't afraid he'd hit you or anything." Joss couldn't help her alien tone. She felt as if Bonnie One had dropped in from another planet, would make a few announcements about Mars, and then fly away in her flying saucer.

Bonnie said, "The question you should be wondering about is whether he's going to tell Mike."

"Okay, I'll bite," Joss said. "Is he going to tell Mike?" But then Joss sat down and felt her hands skittering off her lap. She said, "Oh boy. Ohhh boy," and wished her hands would get a grip on themselves. She moved them back onto her lap and entwined them.

Bonnie spoke with more authority now. "I don't think he will. I don't understand what he's up to, but I think he still has some hope, and that as long as he has hope he won't do anything that I would find unforgivable. He already did one terrible thing—he burned my diary and your letters."

Joss said, "So long as we still have the movie rights." She threw her hands up. "Just kidding. Don't worry. I'm fine now." She stood up and hugged Bonnie. She said, "Bonnie, Bonnie, you must be worn out." She stepped back and smoothed Bonnie's cheeks. She said, "You don't need my letters. You know my bones. So people burn everything up, so what?" Joss was suddenly angry. She said, "So what!" again, more fiercely. She felt her anger calm her. She took another step away from Bonnie and whirled toward the door. They'd tried to make her think her anger was a weakness. One of the seven deadly sins. But it was good. It was her shield and sword. And hey—this was just red heat. She could go to white heat anytime she felt like it. She said out loud, "They ain't seen nothin' yet." She thought, Let 'em show up with their law books and beards.

She could feel the sizzle from her elbow to her fingertips. She'd turn them to stone with her eyes. She'd breathe fire at them from their belt buckles to their button-down collars, melt their eardrums, boil their tongues in their own spit.

"Joss," Bonnie said. "Joss. Joss darlin'. We still don't know if Mike knows. This is what we've got to think about right now. He's going to come home soon."

"So when he shows up we'll know. He'll come trudging up the hill with his briefcase, and we'll see his face."

"Well, maybe. Maybe we should all be making a family meal—you, me, Edith and Nora. Maybe have Edmond and Evelyn over."

"Why?"

"If he does know, he won't be able to carry on, he won't be able to do anything. Then we could leave together. But if he doesn't know, then we'll know he doesn't know, and we'll have some time to analyze . . ."

Joss sat down. Maybe she should be calm the way Bonnie was. She found Bonnie's analyzing calming. Bonnie could sustain herself with plans. Joss found that hard to do. Perhaps it was a failing. It probably was a failing. It probably came from her not being able to be sure what she wanted. Her wishes didn't have the power that her anger did, her wishes could flicker out, be canceled by doubt or anxiety. And that was even before Mike got to them and started picking them apart with his on-the-one-hand, on-the-other-hand.

"I'll go get Evelyn and Edmond," Bonnie said. "Maybe you can get the girls to come down and help you with supper."

Joss didn't move from the studio. She heard Bonnie rousting the girls from the second floor, heard them clattering in the kitchen, heard Evelyn arrive and start laughing with them.

Joss saw Mike's head appear over the crest of the driveway. He stopped and took a comb from his pocket. He combed his hair with one swipe, then was more attentive to his beard. He was even more careful with his mustache, engaging the comb and then using it to bend the mustache hairs out to the side. This was not a man filled with fury. This was a small-town lawyer combing his mustache. Joss felt tender and forgiving, padded against harm by her own tenderness and forgiveness. She forgave everyone. She opened the front door as he arrived and said, "It'll have been worth being married to you just to have seen you comb your mustache."

Mike looked embarrassed. "The girls don't like it when it tickles," he said. "Oh. Did you hear Tyler and Bonnie are on the rocks?"

Joss turned toward the kitchen, toward the innermost part of the house. What had she been saying? What should she say? She nodded. She found her voice. "Just that. That's all I heard." She pointed at the kitchen. "Bonnie's here. And Evelyn. Better wait to talk."

They ate on the porch. Edmond wasn't back yet. Evelyn and the girls were having a fine time. Joss was floating in a bubble. Bonnie was amazing to Joss. Bonnie picked a winged seed out of Mike's wineglass with a completely steady thumb and forefinger. She said, "I may get a chance to go to Rome this summer." This was news to Joss. Joss shredded her napkin on her lap. Bonnie said, "I got my little summer grant. But it's not enough. If I can just find a cheap place to stay, then I'll have another look at all those churches you hate."

What could Bonnie be thinking of? Was she going to start teasing Mike?

Mike said, "You got me wrong. I don't hate them. It's just that some of them have strange associations for me. Take one of your specialties, the Gesù. I've been there. Checked out the main attraction. I put my two-hundred-lire piece in the slot and lit up that big silver altarpiece."

"It's the tomb of Sant' Ignazio."

"Is that right? Then old Saint Ignatius is in there spinning." He turned to Evelyn and Joss. "Anyway, this altarpiece is about two stories high, amazing. One of the amazing things is there are these two lifesize statues of angels floating around near the lower corners."

"They're not angels," Bonnie said, "they're allegorical figures. The one on the left is Faith winning over Idolatry; on the right it's Religion over Heresy."

"Better yet," Mike said. "Faith and Religion are babes. I mean knockouts. They're not nudes, but they might as well be. They're draped in some cloth that's clinging to them and trailing off about mid-thigh. Gorgeous bare legs."

"Honestly," Bonnie said. "You sound like that lecherous chairman."

"Wait a second, will you. Here's what occurred to me then. What those eighteenth-century Jesuits—"

"A little earlier."

"What those earlier Jesuits were doing to all those eighteenth-century—and earlier—Catholic guys is just what *Playboy* was doing to all us mid-twentieth-century American guys. They were floating these impossibly perfect babes in front of us. When I was looking at pictures of that stuff when I was younger—I mean that eighteenth-century art—I *used* to think it was the artists who were sneaking in their *vie-de-bohème* models and that the Jesuits were so dried out and lofty they barely noticed. I used to think maybe they just shrugged and thought, It's okay 'cause they're angels and saints. But this time in front of the tomb of my man Saint Ignatius, it occurred to me that the sly old Jebbies knew what they were up to. They were the Hugh Hefner of their century. Get the ordinary guys hooked on airbrushed babes and they'll stick around. Just like Hugh Hefner. I don't think that Hugh Hefner was all that interested in sex. I think what he really wanted was to be a big-time leader with a following. The Playmates and the Bunnies and the party girls were for the audience, like those floating angels with the most gorgeous legs in the world. The regular joe gets dazzled by gorgeous babes, better than anything he's seen in his humdrum life, and without really stopping to think about it, he gets this feeling—I mean a feeling beyond his turn-on—he gets this feeling that this must be a pretty nifty operation.

"He's ready for a new style of truth. The *old* style was grim—Saint Francis overcoming lust by throwing himself naked into a briar patch, Savonarola getting Botticelli to torch his paintings of naked women. Issue sackcloth and ashes to all enlisted men. And for us American Boy Scouts here in the 1950s it was cold showers, you'll go blind if you beat off, decent women are sisters, virgins, Mom. Don't even *think* sex. Life was an itching wool suit, might as well be sackcloth and ashes. But the new style is silk, the new style says you can have it all. That altarpiece is saying you can be rich, you can be hip, you can get turned on—hey, God made you *flesh,* we're the priests who understand *that.* Just join the club and we'll let you in on riches, babes, political power—we can make it part of the deal, we can make it all *ad majorem gloriam Dei.*"

Joss couldn't remember when she'd last heard Mike so vehement. His vehemence was almost like her anger. Almost, almost . . . But it was a banked fire, smoldering. Maybe there was a flame there, but trust Mike to get mad in Latin, for God's sake. And yet something was shaking him the way her anger shook her. If only he'd lose control, fill up his lungs and bellow, let his bones loose. It was as good as maniac dancing, as good as a third drink. Why couldn't he let it blow all the way open? When she blew it open, she didn't care about getting it right. She didn't care about defense. She didn't even care about winning. She wanted to empty until she was empty. The good stuff, the foul stuff—all gone.

She thought, Open your mouth. Wider. Louder. Show me a guy who'll jump up and down and yell back, and then we'll talk about fucking.

Bonnie put her hand on Mike's forearm. She said, "Well, that was all so fast and furious I may have missed part of it. So tell me—you're in favor of throwing yourself naked into the briar patch? You *want* Botticelli to burn his paintings? Is that it?"

"No," Mike said. "The point is that Saint Francis wasn't condescending. He wasn't manipulating. He wasn't figuring out what Joe Blow wanted and then serving it up. He was working it out for himself. The *Playboy* editors and corporate executives aren't working it out for themselves. They're figuring out what'll play to an audience they think is dumber than them. And that's what I think those Jesuits were up to."

"Well," Bonnie said. "So Faith and Religion are just centerfolds."

"They serve the same purpose. Speaking personally, I fell for the angels . . . for the allegorical figures. *Playboy* centerfolds don't do much for me, but that's another subject. The main similarity is this: men without a serious attachment to women—Jesuit hierarchy or Hugh Hefner—using female beauty to invite other men into a male group. They set some other hooks too—the buildings themselves—the Jesuits were putting up churches like crazy. And they cozied up to political bosses in helpful ways. They were working on the Emperor of China in the 1600s. It's not surprising to me that in that other Jesuit church a block or two away—"

"Sant' Ignazio."

"—with the painted ceiling—"

"The *trompe-l'oeil* by Pozzo."

"Before you get to that. The picture on the ceiling of the nave. It's all the continents, the wonders of the earth. The Jesuits had global ambition. You go in there and you get the message that they're offering you the world—all the splendors of the physical world."

"You don't think the physical world is splendid?"

"Sure I do, but not as bait. The way those angels with great legs are bait. Just remember the Hugh Hefner angel the next time you're hanging around inside the Gesù."

The next thing that happened took Joss by surprise. Mike and Bonnie One had wrangled a lot about the Jesuits, though who attacked them and who defended them switched. It was clear to Joss that they took whatever line led to the other's throat. Bonnie One knew the art encyclopedically and usually could tangle Mike up in coils of examples. Mike labored under ambivalent feelings about his own education. His biggest and bluntest weapon was that Bonnie didn't know enough history.

One time Bonnie was detailing the splendors of eighteenth-century Jesuit art when Edmond, somewhat surprisingly, said, "I remember from somewhere that the pope suppressed the Jesuits."

Bonnie One said, "Oh, there were all sorts of political rivalries and machinations. They don't really affect the artistic development. Pozzo was a Jesuit and he just—"

Edmond said, "But does 'suppressed' mean 'banned'? Or 'disbanded'? That would make it hard to go on working. When was it that they were suppressed anyway?"

Bonnie One said, "Look, I'm not a suppression historian."

Mike had laughed nastily. Then he said, "I didn't know your field was so specialized." But then he couldn't keep himself from running up the score. "Seventeen seventy-three," he said.

Bonnie opened her hand palm-up. "There," she said, "long after the work on the Gesù and Sant'Ignazio was complete. And of course the Jesuits got reinstated and so forth. But as far as the history of art is concerned, we needn't pursue all those little power plays."

Joss had been dispirited by that exchange. Usually she saw these Jesuit spats as taking place between Bonnie, who had a brilliant enthusiasm for the art and architecture, and Mike, who had a sullen resentment against how he'd been worked over and repressed at the hands of Jesuits but who was still proud of them, like a child bragging at school about the splendid punishments he got at home. But that particular time, though Mike had been his picky argumentative self, Bonnie One had been a fool.

This time Mike was being expansive, hot, and wholehearted. Joss didn't care whether his rant made sense, she just liked the burst. Joss was afraid that Bonnie would win by sniping, at this time of all times, when she wanted Bonnie to be straight and whole. So Joss was astonished when Mike finished, or wearily wound down, and Bonnie One said, "I like it. I really think you have an insight, I really do. There's always been a gentlemanly view—Kenneth Clark's view—that the late Baroque and Rococo were too preoccupied with illusion for illusion's sake and so forth. But this is a nice little twist—your Hugh Hefner–condescension theory. Of course everyone agrees the Church became more authoritarian starting with the Counter-Reformation and that the art became more luscious. I mean just look at Bernini's *Santa Teresa*. The real Santa Teresa was kind of a stumpy little thing with a plain everyday face, and Bernini made her not just ecstatic but a dreamboat in ecstasy. . . . And all this art with gorgeous women came at a time when the Northern iconoclastic Protestants were getting rid of Mary and all the glamorous saints. They were stuck with Saint Paul and other bleak males. So I was thinking, What a bad choice; boo, Protestants; good for you, Rome. But I really like your contribution—the notion that those withered Jesuits were *exploiting* the female image. . . ." Bonnie smiled approvingly. She said, "I like the way you look at all that art and take it personally. And talk about it in plain everyday phrases. I think it's just wonderful when someone's sensitive enough to get *wounded* by art."

Joss thought this was flattery on a tightrope. She could barely bring herself to look at Mike. But there he was, immobilized by it, like Miss Dudley stretched on her back to get her chest scratched.

◇

Nora and I have talked about Bonnie One's flattery. We agree on a description of the techniques. We disagree about the ratio of calculation to spontaneity.

Ganny once asked Mom, during one of the later hiatuses in the Bonnie-Mom relationship, what it was that Bonnie offered that was so compelling. Mom said, "Mush." When Ganny told this to me she told it sympathetically. Usually Ganny was merciless—Ganny didn't like Bonnie—the more so because Ganny *had* been charmed by her and then disillusioned. But Ganny did like Mom a lot, and although Mom's saying "Mush" exposed Bonnie's throat to attack, Ganny didn't sink her teeth in. The tender attentive way Ganny told me this so startled me that I nervously tried to make a joke—"How much mush could a mush-rat mush if a mush-rat . . ."

"Well, yes," Ganny said. "But your mother gave a difficult answer. She made fun of her being in love, but she told the truth about what was nice about it."

I was grateful to Ganny.

I told all this to Nora and she was touched too, so in a way I'm about to be unfair to Nora by remembering Nora's harshest analysis.

This is from a letter Nora wrote me.

Modern Witchcraft: Nine Spells

1. Disagree with the subject and then let the subject persuade you. If you have time, wait until the next day to announce your change of mind, thus showing how serious you are.
2. Tell the subject she/he appeared in your dreams. For additional potency go so far as to cast subject as a hero or mythic figure. (". . . I was listening to the most beautiful music—the conductor was Toscanini, then it was you.")
3. Ask subject's advice about a problem and take it. If advice works out, subject will be gratified. If not, subject will feel guiltily concerned.
4. Point out how undervalued the subject's efforts are. ("You really do a lot around here. This place would fall apart without you.")
5. Tell subject she/he has (A) a calming, (B) a stimulating, (C) a gladdening effect on you. (A) "I was just stupidly frantic all morning, then I thought of how you'd handle it." (B) "I couldn't get started, then I thought of that thing you told me the other day . . ." (C) When subject drops in, you drop everything and say, "I was just thinking I wanted to see you."
6. In the midst of one of those group conversations about self-improvement—we should read more, or be more concerned about the poor, or exercise more—say to the subject in a sudden aside, "You're lucky, you seem to *intuit* all of Sartre (or Proust, or the Romantic poets) . . ." Or ". . . you have a *natural* sympathy for

other people's suffering." Or "Of course some people don't need to exercise."

7. Do favors for subject, implying you're simply paying homage to subject's generally generous nature, to which you are especially sensitive. ("I'll drop it off for you, you're always doing things for other people. . . .")
8. After a large event—party, picnic, concert—say to subject you noticed her/him at a particular moment. ("I saw you when the little girl gave the flowers to the wrong person and everyone laughed. I was glad someone else saw how sad it was.")
9. Best of all: discover the subject's secret minor vanities and praise them. It is astonishing how modest most people are about their minor ones. Think of Dad's vanity about his singing voice. Think of Mom's about being able to throw a ball like a man. Think of Dad's and Tyler's about their cooking. (Of course in their case their secret minor vanities weren't all that secret.)

    As a last resort you can't go wrong praising people for their beautiful hands, feet, or voices. Praising the subject's vanity is as effective a way of gaining control as a voodoo witch doctor using someone's lock of hair or fingernail parings.

Nora didn't say she was talking about Bonnie One. She claimed later that she was talking about show-biz agents, producers, and directors, but she knew that I wouldn't be able to help noting about whom she first got this idea.

But it wasn't long after that that Nora mellowed. I remember thinking then that she had the good part of Mom's temper—that is, she could erupt and really get rid of her ill will.

I was afraid for a while that I had the worst of Mom's and Dad's tempers. Sometimes I'd erupt, but I'd never get it all out. Other times I'd spend days obsessively writing briefs in my head trying to line up authorities on my side.

I began to worry that all artists have a crazily explosive side that carries the good ones into an ecstatic visionary state and that all lawyers have an obsessive-compulsive control-freak side that carries the good ones into an analytical visionary state and that I just got stuck with the first bad half of both. And that was my inheritance.

So that was why Dad told me—preached and nagged at me—to be blithe.

And that was why, when I once asked Mom what I should be when I grew up, she said, "A scientist. I think we need a scientist in the family." It struck me at the time as a wacky answer. But I came to see it as her futile little hope, a puff of her breath against all the gusts that were going to blow me into being as turbulent as her.

It took me a long time on my own to be able to treat the contents of their wishes lightly, but to feel grateful for their wishing.

To get back to Bonnie's flattery. In my obliging older-daughter efforts to have everything be okay, it helped me to consider it from the perspective of natural history, a perspective I owe in part to Edmond's lessons. I view Bonnie One as a solitary organism using the only devices she had—she wasn't powerful, or armored, but able to change color, or squirt a cloud of ink, or perform favors. She found her niche, like those little birds that hop into a crocodile's mouth and clean its teeth. So it was just her nature to use all nine spells on Mom, and some of them on Dad. Even her specializing in Jesuit art was very much the bird cleaning the crocodile's teeth. She didn't get into the question of whether the Jesuits were right or not. She did research on their art, appreciated it, and glossed it, and they were glad to open their crocodile mouth for her. But it takes a high nerve and a high metabolism to be a clever organism.

Tyler's lessons were not as helpful as Edmond's. Tyler, for all his studies of modernism and postmodernism, really liked old-fashioned stories with a beginning, middle, and end. He loved Aristotle's helpful household hint: the beginning is that which has nothing necessarily before it but something necessarily after it; the middle is that which has something necessarily before it and something necessarily after it; the end is that which has something necessarily before it and nothing necessarily after it.

He loved the almost duh-duh simplicity, simplicity with a cleaver. Aristotle tutored Alexander the Great, who cut the Gordian knot.

Tyler was the first one of all of the grown-ups to wrap it all up.

Before a year was out he said to Edmond and Evelyn, "They fell in love. They fell in love and inflicted consequences and bore the consequences. That's what happened."

Evelyn told me this much later. She is very fond of Tyler, but she saw what he was doing. He was imposing an end on it, wrapping it all up, getting enthusiastic about it as a story. In this version Bonnie One is the protagonist. She struggles against this fate of hers—her "invert nature," to quote *The Well of Loneliness*, a book which Tyler had read when he cotaught a seminar with . . . guess who? The assistant professor who'd taped the chairman, who'd acted like a French Resistance heroine. And although Tyler couldn't pin the *croix de guerre* on her, he did put the Texas family heirloom on her ring finger.

They share a tenured slot. They had twins, a boy and a girl. Nora and I used to babysit them when we were in high school. Tyler and his wife coedited a book of children's stories and songs which, including the audio-cassette and videotape sales, earned them as much as if they were a two-income family. It just goes to show what solid forms Tyler could make with plain everyday know-how and energy.

What am I getting at with this arch tone of mine? Perhaps that literary criticism, even though distilled out of invisible and unverifiable notions, can provide a concrete and defined pattern of life.

Or am I just envying Tyler's temperament, his ability to sort out once and for all what he included in his life and what he excluded?

So many of the rest of us wander on, looking outside ourselves, praying that our missing element will be given to us when we get to Oz. Maybe Tyler simply has inside him the most crucial element of steadiness—a good digestion. The ability to take in whatever happens, consume it, and digest it—what's him is him; what isn't, isn't. Edmond once showed me an owl casting—a tiny ball made of mouse fur and specks of bone with a tiny mouse tooth poking out. The owl gulps down the whole mouse, then somehow in its crop it rolls together the indigestible and spits it out.

Happy, hungry Tyler at the top of the food chain.

But he is a nice man, and he is happy. So is it envy still that makes me slyly wonder whether being happy is the point of life? Am I just idolizing my own uncertain chemistry, the one I seem to have inherited from Mom? Having come this far, I can put down a strange thought. I remember, one time when I was babysitting Tyler's twins, Tyler came bouncing back in, boisterous and exuberant, beaming out rings of energy. I noticed that it felt like Mom coming in. And just then he even looked like Mom—his wild hair, his arms semaphoring as he talked, his sharp nose jutting independently between well-fleshed cheekbones. At age fifteen I tried not to dwell on it. I concentrated on picking up my schoolbooks and putting my shoes back on. But later I started considering all their faces. I began to see them as strangely similar, even though I knew their distinctnesses. I saw their faces suddenly as exposures of nerve endings. The grid of intricate flesh from ear to ear, from brow to chin, struck me as a horribly dangerous organ, as susceptible as an open wound—not to germs but to the feelings and ideas flashing from other faces. How could people walk around with bare faces? The faces themselves would always be in an overexcited state, wanting to feel other faces, wanting to absorb other faces, wanting to look like other faces, wanting to be all the other faces.

There must be a control deep inside people, right in the middle of whatever it is that keeps people being themselves. Otherwise the faces would pour out everything and suck in everything, and people would all be caught out of themselves in a state of bliss. Their thoughts and memories, their *boundaries*, would melt. Everyone would mix with everyone else.

What if I didn't have that control?

Okay, okay—you can chalk it up as just another adolescent-female sex fear after a flash of taboo interest. But it was very frightening. And it stuck with me for a long while as a problem, as a couple of problems. The first one is of course the fear of sex—not fear of pain but fear of being abducted. But it was also interwoven with pleasure, all that stuff I was finding out about how variously susceptible all these grown-ups had been. Maybe *they* didn't have the control. There was the notion that Bonnie One had been attracted to Tyler's face but then found something similar but more urgently attractive in Mom's face.

And there was a conversation I'd heard between Dad and Ganny. They were on the porch. Ganny was still comforting Dad, so I was no older than twelve, but I didn't get upset by what I heard until I had my face-vision at Tyler's house. Ganny said to Dad that she thought that Bonnie One could have gone in several directions. Bonnie One, according to Ganny, had eyes for Edmond and Dad. But Edmond was pretty much immune. Dad was less immune, but had a lot of fits of disapproval of Bonnie One along with his susceptibility to her flirting.

This line may just have been a smart idea of Ganny's—what better balm to apply to Dad's ego than to say that his wife's lover had a thing for him. But I heard it and felt it as another door opening into another strange dimension.

I don't know if at that time I'd learned that Mom had had a crush on Ganny, but I was certainly aware of Dad and Ganny sitting out on the porch in the dark, Ganny's voice low and humming into him. Nora and I had always thought Ganny was wonderful—she'd been as famous an athlete as Ezra but wasn't as aloof and scary. She was a lawyer like Dad, and just then, with Mom being away, she was paying a lot of attention to us. Her attention, which I now know was just because she liked us, was a little bit suspect then. Both Nora and I hated the goo-goo stuff that the women Dad had dates with in those days ladled out to us. We liked Ganny's attention, which wasn't goo-goo, but we couldn't help being suspicious of any woman Dad turned his face to. An odd thing was that we both liked it when Ganny bossed Dad around—made him clean the house, not smoke cigars, give up sweets, eat more vegetables. We hated it if one of his dates nagged or wheedled him. When Ganny did it, she reminded me of the way Grandma was with him.

In all there were only two and a half women in Dad's life who weren't in my face-vision—Grandma, Evelyn, and half of Ganny. On Mom's side three men—Edmond and Mom's two brothers. The rest of the world is full of these nightmare monsters who are both out to get you and are themselves horribly vulnerable—if you squeeze them, they break apart and want you to be part of their pulsing insides. Much scarier than the monsters that are just out to get you.

I put my shoes on and picked up my books, and Tyler drove me home, from his new house. He chatted the whole way, one of those conversationalists who happily ignore your silence. Like Dad. (Oh God, everyone *is* everyone else.)

Nora was home alone. She'd been nervous and was glad to see me. That calmed me a little. She'd made a pudding for Dad, who hadn't come home—his favorite: Pet milk, lemon juice and shredded lemon peel, and tons of sugar. It was a ghost of his *real* favorite that Mom used to make—lemon-almond torte.

Nora was thirteen, but I had to tell someone about the faces. I tried to make it mild—she didn't really know *everything* yet—but she sensed my panic.

I don't know if what she did next was masterful or lucky, selfless or self-centered. She began to talk about the terror *she* had when she was four or five. She'd ask Mom or Dad to go up any stairs first in case the monster was waiting. It was invisible, but very powerful. She called it The Whole Kiss. As far as the rest of us could figure out, it was a giant kiss—no face or lips or anything. Just a kiss. And maybe some invisible suction. She never made it altogether clear. But it was whole, and it kissed you right out of your shoes, the whole of you. Maybe she was mixing in "hole" along with "whole."

Mom and Dad unwittingly cured her of it by being proud of her invention. They adopted it, co-opted it, talked about it so much they wore it out. They even gave Nora a present of a big glossy red satin pillow shaped like a pair of lips.

By the time Nora got through going over how scary The Whole Kiss had been, we were both in a better mood.

Then the phone rang and it was Dad saying he was sorry he was late. Nora tore into him in a way I never could. She had an amazingly foul mouth at thirteen, and she could get on a roll that went on for a minute or two without repeating herself. She was already taller than me and stronger—so her red-faced rages were genuinely threatening. But even at thirteen she was already an actress, and in the midst of a tantrum she might suddenly find herself doing a Bette Davis or a Lucille Ball, or her school friend Tamika. ("I tol' you get out of my face, girl—next time I bust yo haid—yes, thass right, you keep on an' I be doin' some Afro-scopic surgery on yo skinny little ass.")

Nora would get into the part so far that she'd either burn up her own grievance, or would suddenly find herself funny even though she'd gone into it wholehearted.

Two years before, when we were due to spend Christmas with Dad, he'd announced that we were going to have a spiritual Christmas—gospel reading, midnight mass, meditation—and just one present apiece—he'd had it with commercial glut, etc., etc.

Nora jumped up on the bed and ranted at him for being unfair, miserly, mean, and not understanding kids. Then she yelled at the top of her lungs, "And you didn't even spoil us the year of the divorce!"

Dad and Nora both stood still for a second with their mouths open. Then all three of us cracked up—Dad, then me, then Nora.

So now Nora was on the phone with Dad, working through a few denunciations, getting louder and faster. I had no way of knowing whether she'd end up crying or laughing. Fifty-fifty. I became bitter that Nora stopped paying attention to me, that all the energy was now between Nora and Dad.

Why didn't I say something? Why was I the one with the cork? Was it because I was the one of the two of us who knew the big secret? And why was that? Did I *choose* to figure it out? Did I choose to be the older daughter? Did I choose to be the one who kept still, who kept calm, who kept the peace? Did I have a choice?

At the time it felt like it was the only job for me. Or that I was the only one for the job. So I sat there twisting my fingers while Nora and Dad went at each other. If Nora stayed mad, I couldn't talk to her anymore. If Dad came home mad at Nora, I couldn't talk to him. I wasn't scared of my face-vision for the moment, but it was still lurking, waiting for me to be alone in the wreck of another family quarrel.

I could have said to Nora, "Wait. Wait a second. If you're mad at Dad for being late, let's us go to the kitchen and eat all of his favorite dessert." I didn't say anything. I never took sides, and saying anything would put me on a side. I was sure there had to be someone not on a side or things would get worse. So all I could do was listen, feeling the good mood Nora and I had been in curdling while she screeched stuff like, "I was alone! At night! You've never heard of burglars? Rapists?"

Years later Nora said to me, Dad said to me, I said to myself, "You should have said something." A plain everyday phrase. The plain everyday response is of course, "You weren't listening."

But the truth is I *didn't* say anything. I thought I was keeping the peace, but I was just keeping still. Inside I wasn't still. I was as mad as the rest of them. Just quiet.

Yeah, too quiet.

◇

Mike went off to put the dishes in the dishwasher, Edith went to do her homework, Nora took Evelyn up to the girls' room to show her some drawings. Bonnie One checked the kitchen door with a glance, leaned over, and kissed the back of Joss' fingers.

Joss didn't move. It wasn't a conflict between fight or flight that immobilized her. It was everything. Everything against everything. All the freight of her life rolling loose, all the trains on downhill tracks headed for the same intersection. Was this *The Perils of Pauline*? A Technicolor cartoon?

She poured herself another glass of wine. She was going to have just one more. She filled it so full she couldn't pick it up, so she bent over and sucked out a half-inch. It wasn't a full glass anymore, so she filled it up again to the brim. She bent down and sucked up another half-inch. This filling to the brim and sucking required her full attention. She didn't count. She always lost track when she tried to count cards. She could keep track of the aces. An ace was the same as a whole glass. She would keep an eye out for an ace. Just one ace left, and it was right there on the table.

Bonnie One said, "Maybe we could take a little walk. Or maybe we could drive somewhere."

"Right," Joss said. She focused on the glass, carefully put her hand on it, raised the glass into the unfocused zone under her nose, and found her mouth. She closed her eyes and concentrated on the long trickle from her tongue to her tailbone.

Bonnie said, "Joss . . ."

Joss said, "Did I say 'right'? I meant wrong. Wrong-a-roonie. Because you don't have your car."

"We'll walk back to my car and take a little drive."

"*I've* got a car. I'll drive you to your car and then we'll have all the cars."

"I don't know," Bonnie said. "I've got a feeling that you shouldn't stay here."

Joss didn't say anything. Now that she knew she was getting drunk, she was perfectly happy. She couldn't remember the last time—a long time ago. So long ago she couldn't remember it, so long ago she'd forgotten how much fun it was. Getting drunk, just the pure act, no mixing it up with anything else. Not all this nonsense about taking a little walk or having a little talk or driving hither and yon.

She wished she was at her mother's. In a nice deck chair on the porch. Better yet in the middle of the lawn. Everyone else tucked into bed. Or wherever they wanted to be—she certainly wasn't going to tell them what to do.

Joss felt the skin on her arms become thicker but lighter. Her wrists felt particularly good, as if some nice person was wrapping them very delicately with invisible gauze.

Bonnie talked some more, but it didn't go very well with the skin-feeling or the gauze-feeling, so Joss moved to the porch. Not her mother's porch but a perfectly good porch. She sat on the deck chair and stretched her legs out on the long cushion. The gauze-feeling was just below her knee now, and felt even better, not just silky but puffed up with air, like a cozy blood-pressure cuff. What was pleasantly amazing now was that she didn't need to take another drink. She'd reached a stage she was fond of, in which she could produce sensations in herself without emptying the glass in her left hand or pulling her right thumb out of the neck of the bottle. Without moving her head to look, she very slowly moved her left fingers and then her right thumb, and they were right there where she thought they were. She felt like Stan Laurel, who could amuse himself for long periods of time discovering his fingers. She remembered him smoking his thumb like a pipe. Or he could blow through his thumb and inflate his shirt like a life vest. Actually she was better off than Stan Laurel, sweet as he was, because (A) she didn't have to put her thumb in her mouth to inflate herself and (B) poor old Stan always had Oliver Hardy showing up to bother him.

Joss did notice that Bonnie was sitting at the end of the deck chair, perched on the corner like a little rabbit, but she was one of the Stan Laurels of the world, not one of the Oliver Hardys. This Laurel and Hardy distinction was a truly good thought. A very good way to analyze *everybody,* and it was a shame she hadn't invented it until now. If everyone were Stan Laurel and there were no Oliver Hardy, what a wonderful world this would be.

The sky turned dark, the stars came out. Laurel and Hardy put her to bed and left her alone. She kept waking up, uncertain how she felt. No—she certainly didn't feel good. The least of which was that they'd uncorked her thumb from her bottle. She was pretty sure she'd promised she wouldn't drink anymore if they wouldn't take it away. Just like Hardy to slap her hand and get all hyper.

She discovered a wastebasket by the bed. That was just like Mike, expecting her to throw up. He used to hold her head; now he just left a wastebasket, a very noisy metal wastebasket. And smelly. In fact someone had thrown up in it already.

Then the things that were wrong started again. The houseboat was rolling. Something was wrong with it. Her mother's house was on fire. She got up to pack. She picked a big bag because there had to be room for the baby.

◇

Mike, sleeping uneasily on the sofa, woke up when he heard the noise. It was cloth tearing and then some bumping and thudding. He turned the light on and saw Joss sitting on the ladder stairs to the girls' room. She'd got her feet into the legs of one of the girls' pajama bottoms and was trying to put her arm into a pajama sleeve.

When she saw him she began talking in a soft but tense voice about a fire, the houseboat, a baby. When he pulled the pajama sleeve and legs free, she became docile. He put her back in their bed, near the wall. He got in on the open side. He immediately got up again to wash out the wastebasket. Joss was thrashing around some, but sound asleep. He lifted her head and slid a towel over her pillow.

He couldn't sleep with her tossing around, but he didn't want her getting up again.

He couldn't decide if he'd changed or if her drinking had changed. At first she'd just been fast-talking, raucous, sometimes sentimental, always funny. He'd often been half in the bag too. Then either she got worse or he minded more.

She still only got crazy drunk three or four times a year, but each time was a lulu. She'd get to her raucous-funny stage on a couple of drinks and then, sometimes with only one more, she'd be out of reach.

He was still her nurse—he did that part okay—but he'd also become her jailer. That was what she would mind. From her first drink to when she went down for the count. And the next day. Whether he said anything or nothing, she complained that she felt him hovering and reproachful.

At first Bonnie One had seemed to encourage Joss' drinking, but then she seemed to have helped Joss control it. But not tonight.

One time Joss had gone to a shrink on her own, but she came back furious. She'd told Mike that the psychiatrist just sat there waiting for her to say something. She'd outwaited him. The psychiatrist finally said, "What's making you so angry?"

Joss had said, "Your stone face. Your face is saying 'I'm calm, you're crazy.' It's saying, 'I'm Moses, you're the children of Israel.' I can get that at home."

Just before dawn it occurred to Mike that he could use his free counseling session with Bonnie Two. Joss certainly couldn't complain that Bonnie Two was a grim, controlling, guilt-inducing warden. Bonnie Two would be light as a feather, almost nothing.

Joss got up early. Mike overslept. By the time he got up, Joss had got the girls off to school. Mike called Bonnie Two and got an hour at the end of the day. Joss lifted her head off the dining-room table and listened.

She looked at him curiously. He hung up, shrugged, and said, "You want to go? I'm going anyway. I got a free session for doing some legal work for her."

"I thought you said she was a ditz."

Mike shrugged again. "Maybe, but she seems sympathetic in a way."

Joss said, "She's the one who said, 'America is just so violent,' when her drunk boyfriend tied you up with her."

"He didn't tie us up."

"But you bonded with her," Joss said. "You got into bondage with her." Mike squinted. Joss said, "'It's a joke, son,'" in her Senator Claghorn voice. She closed her eyes.

"Look," Mike said, "you want to come along? Maybe she'll let us hit a pillow with tennis rackets." Mike thought he had a plan: jolly Joss along into something that would turn into a family joke. But deep inside, in some little cartoon frame, he saw an imp. The next instant it was looking exactly like Joss twirling her wedding ring, rolling her eyes, crossing her legs, and jiggling her foot, her eyes seeing too many things, her ears crackling with too many sounds, her mouth filling with words that slid past her lips as relentlessly as if a magician were pulling out eggs, jokes, her real thoughts.

Mike looked at his hand. He opened it wide, palm-up. His fingers were trembling with a fine tremor, except for his ring finger, which was wagging independently in slow big twitches. The class clown.

He closed his hand. Was this what it felt like to be Joss? Was this the spurt of his sympathy that she'd been waiting for? Or was this just some spasm of his own? Or—the worst possibility—this could be a misshapen reflection of her in him, which, if she could see it, would confirm every one of her deepest complaints—you don't understand me, you have no idea what my life is like, you don't know me.

Last night's bottle of wine was still on the dining-room table, where Bonnie One had put it while Mike was walking Joss into the bedroom.

Mike decided that he *was* feeling the spurt of sympathy Joss was waiting for. No surprise that sympathy with Joss took the form of a furious little imp who could change mood as fast as turning over a card.

"I'm off to work," Mike said, and took a swig from the bottle.

Joss scowled at him. She said, "You think you're funny?"

The little imp did a backflip, cackled, and vanished.

"I meant something else," Mike said. "It came out wrong. I actually intended a sign of sympathy."

Joss closed her eyes. "Oh brother," she said. "I think I prefer your stony disapproval." Joss took her head in her hands, grabbed two fistfuls of her hair, and moaned.

Mike said, "I'm tired of being the one who disapproves."

Joss drowned him out with a louder noise. Mike stepped toward her, and she said, "Go away." She wasn't angry. She was tearing the words out of an emotion he didn't recognize. She said, "Oh God. Just go to work."

The first twenty minutes were pretty mild stuff.

Mike was pleased Joss had come, and surprised and pleased that she started in answering Bonnie Two's questions straightforwardly. Bonnie Two also surprised Mike by being comfortably assured in her script. And Mike surprised himself—he relaxed into his armchair and was lulled by the women's voices into a physical well-being he hadn't felt for days.

Bonnie Two was like a sweetly polite visitor being shown a family album. "Tell me more about your children." "How do you manage your working hours?" "There seems to always be a whole lot of people to supper at your house." "And you're friends with these people who live right next to you? They're both your friends, yours and Mike's?"

Joss responded amiably to Bonnie Two's promptings, which were almost murmurs. It was in the same low-pitched cooing tone that Bonnie Two started in on Joss herself. "Uh-huh. I can see how that could be a problem, all that confusion and noise. Tell me about how you feel about your drinking."

It was Joss' answer to that question that woke Mike up. Joss said, "Well, I like *it*, but it doesn't like me."

Bonnie Two nodded and said, "Uh-huh."

Mike said, "That's not a movie cliché, is it? You gave it a sort of good-sport Eve Arden–Our Miss Brooks reading."

Joss laughed.

Bonnie Two looked at Mike with a mixture of reproach and puzzlement. She said, "I think we're going to work on Joss' feelings just a little more. But did you say that thing about movies as a sort of challenge to Joss?"

"Yes," Mike said. "A sort of a little challenge. So that Joss wouldn't absent-mindedly get ironic."

Bonnie Two said, "Uh-huh."

"That's all," Mike said. "Just that. I'll be quiet."

" 'Cause sometimes it's real helpful to have a couple together. You can hear a different voice in this different setting. Later on maybe it would be good to see you separately. But just now . . . Is it hard for you to just be listening for a while?"

"No," Mike said. "In fact it's soothing."

But the germ of comedy was loose. Bonnie Two asked Joss, "Are you nervous a lot of the time? Or more nervous just now?"

Joss said, "This is about the way it goes."

"You're doing a lot with your hands," Bonnie Two said. "What are your hands saying?"

Joss made her hands into puppets. One hand said in a squeaky voice, "I thought she'd never ask. Shall I go first?" The other hand said, in a growly voice, "No. I'll go first." Squeaky voice: "You always go first." Growly voice with a Bogart twist: "That's right, sweetheart." Joss said to Bonnie, "I'm sorry. They don't get out much."

Bonnie Two said, "Do you do that a lot?" Mike was fascinated. He'd never tried being a dopey straight man to Joss.

"No," Joss said. "For the first time. Tonight. Right here on this stage. Making their TV debut. Let's give a . . ."

"Are you upset about your drinking? 'Cause sometimes being funny is sort of a defense. Sometimes it's good to be funny, but right now I think I feel you feeling bad."

Joss took a deep breath and blew it out. "Just letting off . . . something. I'll talk." Then she was off again. "Yeah. I'll talk. I'll tell everything, everything you want to know!" She put her hands over her mouth. She took them down and said, "Oops. No. Okay. I'll be fine. Drinking. Yes. Sometimes I have a little wine, no problem. Other times, kuhplow.

Heap big trouble. Paleface give firewater to Indian. . . . Oh shit. Just a second . . . Other times I just . . . get drunk. I like the first part. But then suddenly I'm in the second part."

"Uh-huh."

"That's it. Th-th-that's all folks."

"Well, alcohol is a poison. For some people sometimes more than for others. If you really want to work on yourself you'll have to detox. Especially if you're what's called an outbreak alcoholic. 'Cause it's harder to see that as a problem. 'Cause sometimes it's not, like you said. It kind of sounds to me like that's what you are, an outbreak alcoholic. I can maybe help you to see what kind of moods you're in when alcohol is likely to be real bad. But just doing that won't be enough. I think you'll have to have a program."

Bonnie Two raised the pitch of the last word of each of these declarative sentences so that they sounded like questions. But for all the tentativeness in her voice, the substance was no longer mild. Mike was afraid that Joss would erupt. He said to Bonnie Two, "Was your boyfriend an outbreak alcoholic?" Bonnie Two looked at him steadily without an expression. Mike said, "Perhaps it's not a proper question. I'll withdraw it."

Joss said, "A program? Like AA? With God and public confession and having to say to a crowd that you've been sober for *x* number of days? Hey—I thought being a drunk means never having to say you're sober."

Mike laughed.

Bonnie Two said, "There's a couple of other programs. I'll give you a list and you can call them and kind of hear a little bit about them. It seems like there's maybe a lot of other stuff bothering you, but you might not be able to work on it real well until you're less toxic?"

Mike felt alarmed for Joss and, simultaneously, triumphantly justified.

Joss took a breath, blew up her cheeks, and puffed out. She said, "Zowie."

Bonnie Two's wristwatch buzzed.

She turned off the alarm and said, "I'm sorry, Mike, maybe we can start with you next time. I've got this same hour free day after tomorrow."

Joss said, "We'll see if we can get a babysitter."

Outside Joss fished the car keys out of her bag and tossed them to Mike. She said, "So what do you think? You think she's right? I'm radioactive on Chardonnay?"

"I don't know. It wasn't what I expected, but it seemed . . . I don't know. . . ."

"Oh, come on. Tell me what you're feeling. What does your big toe say?"

Mike suddenly felt tired. Tired of being worried, of being angry, of being wary. He said, "Do you care? Do you care if I care? Maybe things would be easier if I just didn't give a damn."

"Ah," Joss said. " 'Frankly, my dear, I don't give a damn.' "

"Look. I'm not Clark Gable, you're not Scarlett O'Hara. We're not Nick and Nora Charles. We're not in the movies. Real life is slow. Not a laugh riot, not a lot of plot twists."

"That's all you know," Joss said, and looked down the street as if she were waiting for a bus. Then she shrugged and said, "You want me to go back and talk with your Bonnie Two? I'll go back. I'll go to AA. I'll do it."

"Fine. Maybe it is just a matter of taking care of things one at a time."

They got in the car. Mike said, "This morning I really was feeling sympathetic. I really was trying to imagine you. It used to be clearer. It used to be easier. Now it feels awkward. What I did was awkward. But for a second or two I felt . . . my hand moved the way your hand moves—taking a swig from the bottle was dumb, but my hand felt like your hand, my fingers moved the same way yours do. Is that anything? Maybe I should give up trying to figure things out and just let go and imagine. . . ."

"I don't think so," Joss said. "I really don't think so. I think you'd better go on being yourself."

"I thought you wanted me to be more imaginatively sympathetic."

"Yeah. Well, I want a lot of things. I don't know what I want. You'd better just keep your imaginary hands to yourself."

Mike laughed. Joss looked away.

After supper Joss took the car. Mike sat and watched the girls do their homework. Edith asked him who the Mongols were. He said, "Horse-riding, sky-worshipping warriors from way in the East who overran Russia about the same time as the Magna Carta in England."

Edith wrote down the sentence in her world-history workbook. He took a breath.

Edith said, "Dad, that's all I've got room for."

He said, "Pushkin said that, while Western Europe was learning algebra and Aristotle, Russia just got taxes and the knout. That's a whip."

Nora said to Edith, "Are you done?"

Edith nodded and went to brush her teeth.

Nora said, "Okay, Dad. I've got six more questions and I just want the answers. They're all about Fahrenheit and Centigrade. I don't have to show my work, just the answers, okay?"

Mike said, "Centigrade is easy. . . ."

Nora said, "No. Stop. I'll say the question. What is freezing in Fahrenheit?"

"Thirty-two degrees. You can write it faster—"

"Dad."

"—if instead of writing 'degrees' you put a tiny circle after the thirty-two and then put a big 'F' so you don't have to write 'Fahrenheit.'"

"Like that?" Nora held up the workbook.

Mike said, "No. That looks like a zero. You need a smaller circle farther up at the corner. Here." He erased the big circle and put in a smaller circle a little higher. He said, "You can do the same thing for Centigrade—a little circle after the number and then a big 'C.'"

Nora took the pencil back and rattled off the questions—freezing Big C? Boiling Big F? Boiling Big C? How many degrees between freezing and boiling in Big F? Big C?

Mike said, "So now we could figure out how to change Fahrenheit to Centigrade if you want."

"We're doing that in class tomorrow." Nora laughed. She said, "What if I go around saying Big C and Big F in class."

"I don't get it."

"Dad. The F word? The C word?"

"Oh. Well, say the whole thing."

Nora said, "The whole F word?"

"No, Nora, Fahrenheit."

Nora said, "Freezing is thirty-two Big F degrees."

"I'm sorry I brought it up."

"Miss Barnaby's Big C is boiling at—"

"That's enough."

"It's too late, Dad. What if Miss Barnaby writes on the chalkboard and asks what does Big C stand for? Someone's going to crack up."

"I'm sure Miss Barnaby has dealt with this problem before."

"You don't know her, Dad. She's such a dweeb."

"I'll tell you what. I'll give you a quarter if you're not the first person to laugh."

"A dollar."

"Fifty cents. But for fifty cents you can't be among the first three to laugh."

"How will I be able to tell? There may be people laughing way in back and I can't hear them."

"Easy. I'll ask Miss Barnaby at parent-teacher night."

Nora said, "Dad!" with more than just giggly embarrassment. In fact Mike was startled at how fast she'd skidded all the way across her own joke to the edge of alarm. But he was always slow to stop with Nora when she'd been poking him and he found a way to poke her back. He said, "Actually there's a better way. I'll just call her up right now and explain the problem. It's not too late. . . ."

"Dad!"

Mike looked at his watch.

Nora said, "Dad! Don't! She already hates me."

Mike heard the first harmonic of panic in Nora's voice. He said, "I'm joking, honey."

"It's not a joke! She really hates me! I made a joke at recess about her being divorced and I think she heard me. She probably heard me. I saw her look. If you call her up—"

"I'm not going to call her up."

"Why do you say things like that, then? Why do you do that?" Nora's voice now had a yip of anger in it, a puppy version of Joss' bark.

Mike said, "Honey, we were both kidding around. I didn't know about Miss Barnaby at recess. . . . Listen. It's okay. The truth is the whole thing probably won't come up."

Mike stopped. He was glad Joss wasn't there.

He said, "Listen," again, but for a while he had nothing to say after it.

"Listen," he said, "I wouldn't worry about Miss Barnaby hearing you. Nobody can hear anything at recess, it's just a hundred kids screaming. You can't hear anything two yards away. You probably looked at her and so she looked at you." He got up and put a hand on her back. He said what he usually said. "You're all squared away with your homework, right?" He felt a little black dizziness swim up through his eyes. Then he said what Joss said to the girls in her sweet mood. "You're a good kid, you're smart and you're pretty and you have a ton of friends. So go brush your teeth."

After he kissed the girls good night he couldn't sit still to read. He took a flashlight, left the porch door open so he could hear the girls or the phone, and walked down the path toward the river. He stopped halfway, not dizzy anymore but feeling his mind sliding sideways. It was as if he was caught in the aftereffect of Nora's swift lurch from laughing to embarrassment to alarm to anger. He still had the will and the affection to calm Nora, to put her little demons to sleep. But not Joss' larger demons. The old better-father-than-husband, better-mother-than-wife problem. He felt more weightless than ever. With Joss. With what else? He was surprised by how reassured he'd been by Bonnie Two, by how much he looked forward to settling into a chair and telling her everything, to listening to her murmur sympathetically. Bonnie Two—until today a straw-haired, small-faced, pale waif. Frail and soluble in her own milky life. Was his hopeful trust in her a measure of his increasing helplessness?

He moved closer to the river, onto a small knoll beside the canoe landing. It was an overcast night with no wind. There was a glow in the sky over the town, but the river was completely dark and silent. Not a sound from the full-leafed trees or the moving water. Not a movement of air against his bare cheeks or arms. He turned off the flashlight. He felt his hands holding it. Then it grew indistinct to his touch. And then the connecting lines of his thought to his senses loosened. At first it was a relief. No words, no thoughts, no senses, and without senses there were no things.

It was a relief to feel how much space there was in the midst of everything.

Then, in a panic, he wanted his senses back. He breathed hard through his mouth. Then through his nose and he smelled—what?—water? breath? the air from the river? the river breathing?

Not a sound, not a sound but his breathing, which dwindled to a whisper. No Bundy here, no Bundy voice in the dark. Just himself, the loosened parts of himself reassembling. Sense by sense. Now he felt the flashlight, knew what it was. Then he saw shades of lighter dark, maybe patches of river mist over the water. He turned the flashlight on and saw the slow brown water sliding in the sudden light, muddy coils twisting into each other, a liquid arm wrapping on a sunken tree limb, then slipping off. The river caught in the act.

He turned the light off. He blinked away a few afterimage dots.

What it meant. He knew what it meant. It didn't stop when he turned the light off. He kept seeing lips sliding across other lips the same way the river was sliding over itself.

They're in Joss' studio, printing their palms on pale skin. They're in the kitchen, swallowing each other's tongues, sliding their hands. They're in the woods, they're in the grass, staining their skirts, their bare feet sliding on their bare legs, slipping on wet ground. They're in the movie theater, they're in the car, still kissing—gobbling each other's face, panting and yelping. Joss is calling out. They're pulling their skirts up. They're slipping their hands into each other, Bonnie's skinny fingers first, then Joss' middle fingers right up to her wedding ring.

Mike sat on the ground holding the metal barrel of the flashlight to his forehead. He was working hard to see this vision as a nightmare fantasy, as a vicious attack his unconscious was making out of his dislike of Bonnie One and his anger at Joss. At the same time he couldn't help building the case for the prosecution from old clues. Bonnie One's seductive feathery touching of Polly Trueheart, instances of Bonnie One's setting Joss against him, Bonnie One's love of secrets, of other people's hidden sides . . . But Joss? There was her crush on Ganny, but that was a joke. An awfully long and elaborate joke . . . But he and Joss made love. . . . Perhaps not the way they used to, Joss did say Eros had waned, she did say . . .

Mike switched to doubting his shadow senses until he was settled enough to do something normal, something he had to do. Get back to the house, for one. Shake it off, just a bad dream. Load the dishwasher. Go over his appointment book, see if there was something else he should think about.

When he got back to the house he was glad to find Edmond and Evelyn at the dining-room table, contemplating a pie. It was a peach pie Evelyn had made and brought over for everyone. Edmond picked up a knife but Evelyn said it should cool just a tad more.

Edmond said, "Where is everyone?"

Evelyn took Mike's wrist in her fingers. "You all right, Mike?"

"Nothing dire," Mike said. "Just dire thoughts."

Edmond started talking about Tyler and Bonnie, about how oddly untalkative Tyler was being.

"And he's been gone for days," Evelyn said.

"He's come back a couple of times," Edmond said. "I saw the tire tracks. But I don't think either of them spends the night."

But then Edmond heard a screech owl, and they all went out on the porch while he called it in. He was very good at it—it was a mournful sound, a quavering fall, nothing like a screech. After three or four calls from the owl and Edmond, there was a slight whoof of air as the owl braked its glide with its flared wings, and then the rasp of its talons on the pine bark of a branch. Edmond pointed but Mike couldn't see it. Edmond had carried Mike's flashlight out, and he shone it at the tree, the top arc of the bright light picking up the talons and the pale belly. The owl tilted toward them for a second, then caught the air with a shrug of its wings, wheeled, and glided down toward the river out of the light, completely silently.

"They're so good at that," Edmond said. "They hunt by sound and they're the quietest flying bird. I've had one come in just over me from the back and the only way I knew was the puff of air on my neck when he flared his wings."

Mike imagined what that would be like—flying silently through the woods, ghosting over clearings, hearing everything, seeing everything. Maybe he wouldn't want to know all that.

They got up to go back to the pie. They sat at the dining table, and Evelyn asked him again if he was all right.

Mike said, "I'm glad you came over just now."

Edmond looked at Evelyn helplessly.

Evelyn took a deep breath and said, "I've got a new job. It's not all that far away. And it's not going to start until at least six months from now. It's over in the Valley and down the interstate some—a new veterinary center. It's got a whole lot going on there that's just what I'd like to get good at. They can do magnetic resonance imaging for horses, for example, so you can see what's going on in soft tissue. X-rays just show mostly bones."

"That's great," Mike said. "I mean, it sounds like a real big lab and hospital."

"Yes," Evelyn said. "But it does mean we'll have to move."

"No," Mike said. "Oh no."

"We've worried a lot about it," Evelyn said. "But with my having a better job it also means Edmond can finally quit Fish and Wildlife and get back to his own work. Virginia Tech has offered him a research appointment."

It took Mike a while to say he was glad for them. While he sat staring at the table waiting to say the right thing, he felt them grow as alert to him as if he were an animal. It was comforting that they were alert to his wordless signs of sorrow, which they could mark as plainly as if he moved his hand across the graph of the tiled tabletop—two tiles, three and a half, all the way to ten.

Mike said, "So this really is good for both of you."

Edmond said "Yes" and Evelyn said "Yes, it is," at the same time.

"Tell me more about it," Mike said. "Tell me this is going to fly you to the moon."

After a while they remembered the pie, and Mike got a pint of vanilla ice cream from the freezer.

"It's not that far," Evelyn said, "even in the truck it's only about two and a half hours."

"But it won't be daily life," Mike said. "It won't be Nora taking her cartoons to show you. It won't be . . ." Mike veered off. He said, "It won't be Edmond and me getting mad at you because we've finished our pie and you're only halfway through yours so we're going to have to have seconds and then only have iced tea and salad for lunch tomorrow."

"I like to let the ice cream get soft," Evelyn said. "If you all would just wait for your ice cream to get soft like civilized human beings . . ."

"It's not for six months," Edmond said. "Evelyn's got to find someone to take over for her."

"Sure," Mike said, "it's like a doctor selling a share in a practice. That's how we met our family doctor—I was the lawyer for Mary Ames. I could give you a hand with those details, a going-away present."

"That's nice of you," Evelyn said. "Although I'd rather see you planning how you're going to come visit." She laughed. "Now I know how Joss felt when you offered to help her with business advice."

The lawyerly questions were already threading themselves across the front of Mike's brain. The nature of her partnership agreement? Appraisal of good will? Should she ask for a percentage of the new vet's profits for a year or two?

"It's an anesthetic," Mike said. "I'm giving myself an anesthetic."

It was effective enough so that, when Edmond and Evelyn left, Mike made a few notes and then dozed off on the sofa. He woke up when he heard a car. He got out to the circle just as the headlights went off. He'd looked at his watch inside—just after midnight—and he was about to say, "Where have you been?" when, even in his night-blindness, something struck him as odd about the car. Double headlights.

It was Bonnie's car. Bonnie said, "Mike?" but stayed in her car. She rolled the window halfway down.

Mike said, "What is it?"

Bonnie wasn't very coherent, and he was still groggy, so it took a while for him to get the story.

Bonnie said, "She only had three glasses of wine, I'll swear to it. I can show them the bottle. She was just fine when she left. She was completely making sense. She said—"

"Where is she now?"

"Well, that's the thing. When she called me—"

"You mean on the phone?"

"Yes. When she called she sounded strange. I didn't understand all of it, but it sounds like she's in jail. I think she said for me to come—I mean I *know* she said for me to come, and I think she said I should bring a lawyer. So I guess that means you."

"How come you didn't just phone me? Never mind. Come inside while I call."

Bonnie said, "I thought I should just go there, but then—"

Mike put his hand on the car door to open it. It was locked. He pointed to the lock and said, "Open the door and come inside. I'll call."

The phone in the house rang. Mike jogged inside to get it. It was Joss' mother. She too had got a call from Joss, who wasn't very clear, so Mrs. Rogers had asked Joss to put someone else on the line. Mrs. Rogers said to Mike, "Joss isn't hurt. The policewoman was very nice—I've got her name here somewhere—here—Detective Sergeant Wiggins—and the number is—let me put my glasses on. . . ."

He said, "Did the sergeant say why they're holding her?"

"I'm sorry—I didn't ask. I just assumed it was drunk driving. But the policewoman was really perfectly nice and assured me that Joss was physically all right and that she—that's Sergeant Wiggins—would call you. Apparently Joss had some trouble remembering your number. So, dear boy, I'd better get off the horn and let you get started. I'm just relieved Joss is all right and I'm awfully glad you're there. So all my love and call me in the morning."

Bonnie was standing in the doorway, half in, half out. Mike said, "Come in and sit down, for God's sakes. I know where she is. I'll have to take your car and have you stay here. Oh. Don't tell the girls if they wake up. Just say . . . Think of something. Where are the car keys?"

"They're in the car."

The phone rang again. It was Ganny. Same story, except that Joss had told Detective Sergeant Wiggins that Ganny was her lawyer. Ganny said she'd meet him there.

Mike said, "Well, I'm on my way. No need for you to—"

"I might as well. If Joss said I was her lawyer . . . You know how they can be."

"Right."

Mike said to Bonnie, "Sit here by the phone, so you get it before it wakes up the girls. If it's Sergeant Wiggins, tell her that Ganny and I are on our way. Jesus. This is like a French farce."

"A French farce," Bonnie said, "I don't think I'd call it that." Before Mike could say anything, Bonnie One said, "I thought you only got one phone call."

Mike shrugged. "I guess that's in the movies."

Ganny was already talking to Sergeant Wiggins. Ganny took Mike aside and filled him in. The police had taken an alcohol-blood level and Joss was just below the legal definition of drunk. Wiggins had been surprised. Joss had driven up over a curb and onto someone's lawn, taken out part of a wood fence, and then stalled the car. When the police came she was wandering around the lawn, but she then got back in the car and drove it onto the street. The car had a flat front tire, and part of the fence was stuck between the wheel and the bumper. Joss had stopped the car and got out. She'd started wandering down the street. She'd wrestled herself free when Sergeant Wiggins took her arm. Detective Sergeant Wiggins hadn't written anything up yet. She'd backed off on the DUI, but she and Ganny were still talking about leaving the scene of an accident, resisting arrest, and reckless driving.

Ganny said, "I think if we agree to reckless driving Sergeant Wiggins will agree to let the rest go. Provided, unofficially, that you do the right thing by the house owner. He's still awake, if you want to call him. He just called in to ask why the police didn't take pictures of his fence and the ruts in his lawn."

"I'm going to see Joss first. Did you see her? What's she like?"

"She's okay. Pale and shaky. I told her to lie down and not do anything or say anything. They were starting to think she was wacko when she was on the phone—or that they'd fucked up the alcohol-blood level. If she just stays curled up for a while, I think we'll be able to take her home tonight."

Mike said, "It might do her more good to let her wake up in a cell."

Ganny put her arm around his shoulders. She said, "Mike, honey, you want to stay married? I'll call that homeowner. Then we'll see about driving. . . . How'd you get here?"

"Bonnie One's car. She drove out to our house. Joss called her first."

"Okay. You just sit tight for a minute."

It only took a half-hour for Ganny to spring Joss. While Mike was waiting, one of the Albemarle deputies brought in a prisoner with his hands cuffed behind him. The prisoner was a black man, a head taller than the deputy, who was white. The deputy gave a tug on the handcuffs, and the two men stopped in front of Mike. The deputy was the one who'd found Bundy's body. He said, "Good evening, counselor. Pardon me, but it's been on my mind to say how sorry I was about your friend. It didn't seem right to say it at the time, 'cause I'd tried to stop you going around the side of the house. I was just doing what they say to us to do. I hope you didn't take it as unfriendly."

"No," Mike said, "you were fine. Thank you."

The deputy said, "What brings you down here the middle of the night?" Mike took a breath, but before he could speak, the deputy said,

"Ezra Pritchett's not in trouble, is he? I sure am looking forward to his fight." The deputy said to the prisoner, "This here's the lawyer for Ezra Pritchett."

The prisoner turned his head and said, "Pleased to meet you, counselor. You got my vote."

The deputy laughed agreeably and said, "You won't be voting, son."

The prisoner said, "You think you got a felony? You so far away from a felony you need a rocket ship. You be lucky you get to serve me breakfast. Unless maybe I decide not to get my lawyer out of bed. What you got for breakfast anyway?"

The deputy laughed and said to Mike, "They start in talking law like that, it's a sign."

The prisoner said, "It wasn't me started talking about not voting."

The deputy said, "Let's go get started." He turned to Mike and said, "Nice talking to you. Tell Ezra I'll be at the fight rooting for him. We went to school together." He tapped his name tag. "Morrissey. T. J. Morrissey."

"Hey, tell him I'll be there too," the prisoner said. "He can count on it. My name's Clarence Bates. I did carpentry on his gym. I used to see you walking by there, carrying your briefcase."

"I remember the gym going up," Mike said. "Fast work."

"We didn't sit around."

The deputy said, "We got to get along now. Good evening, counselor."

The deputy and the prisoner went down the corridor as Ganny and Joss came up. The four of them passed each other under a group of fluorescent tubes, one of which was pulsing—brighter and bluer, then dimmer with a touch of orange. Watching them all pass under the fluorescent lighting, Mike thought he was losing the energy it took to know any of them.

Joss said to him, "Don't look, don't talk. I've decided. I'll go to your Bonnie Two program. I'll go. Just get me home. Just get me to tomorrow and I'll go. I'll be good. I was driving home. I was on my *way* home. Okay, I didn't get there. I acknowledge that. I acknowledge that I did not get home."

Joss had her arms crossed and her hands tucked in her armpits. Ganny had put her suit jacket around Joss and had her arm around her. Mike let Ganny lead her to Bonnie One's car. He took off his suit coat and handed Ganny hers. He fastened Joss' seat belt and gave her his coat, which she draped on her front like a blanket. He opened his hands and said, "Ganny. Thanks."

Joss said, "Ganny is wonderful. You should marry her."

Ganny laughed and said, "One thing at a time, Joss. Mike's going to take you home and put you in your own bed."

Joss said, "You come too."

Mike said to Ganny, "Where's Joss' car?"

Ganny said, "Oh yeah. Here's the keys. They say it's drivable. They parked it at the scene—Rosehill and Greenleaf. You can get it tomorrow. I'll drop off a copy of the police report with the insurance company in the morning. The homeowner's coming to the office at noon."

"Ganny," Joss said, "please come."

Ganny followed them back. Mike and Ganny walked Joss into the house. Joss put Mike's suit coat over her head like a cowl and walked straight to bed. Mike took her shoes off, and retrieved his suit coat. Ganny covered her with a cotton quilt. Mike put a towel over the pillow and another towel on the floor. Joss fell asleep.

Ganny and Mike went to the living room. Mike handed Bonnie her car keys. She handed them back and said, "You'll need the car to take the girls to the bus stop. If you just leave it here I'll walk over and pick it up tomorrow. That is if Ganny doesn't mind giving me a ride."

Ganny said, "Aren't you right here in the bungalow?"

"No. Tyler and I . . ." Bonnie put her fingertips together and then flicked them apart. "But my apartment's not far from yours. If you could . . ."

"No trouble. We're off, then. See you in the morning, Mike."

Mike nodded and then fixed on the back of Bonnie's head as she leaned over to put her shoes on. He had an urge to push her into the floor. He turned away and took a breath. He turned back and said, "She might have hurt herself. She might have killed herself. You shouldn't have let her leave after she was drinking."

Bonnie stood up. She looked down and said, "I know that. You don't know how I thought of that. And I would be as sorry as anyone." She raised her eyes and looked at him. "I told you that when she left I was positive that it wasn't one of those times. . . . When she called me I was terrified. I was terrified at what might have happened. You can't terrify me more."

"Is that right?" Mike said. "Is that right? I wonder if that's right."

"Your scary lawyer only scares Polly Trueheart."

"Cut it out," Ganny said, "stop pushing at each other. Mike has a right to be upset. You come on and get a ride with me."

"Well, you may be right," Bonnie said. "I'm sure Mike *is* upset. But now we can all be grateful that nothing really bad happened. If you'll just leave the keys in the car, Mike, it'll be fine. I'll just drop by tomorrow. I'll tell Joss I'm sorry"

Ganny held the door for her.

Mike listened to the car go down the gravel drive, whir across the bridge. He went to the kitchen, called Bonnie Two's office, and left a message on the machine asking for an appointment as soon as possible. He poured himself a drink from the one whiskey bottle, drank it, then poured the rest into the sink. He put all the bottles of wine into a grocery bag and walked down to the bridge and dropped them in two by two.

Back up the hill with the empty bag. Inside the door he listened for a minute. All squared away.

He stripped to his skivvies and lay down on the sofa. He closed his eyes and saw the owl gliding toward the river. He saw the river. He turned and put out the light. He still saw the river, its surface coils and swirls. He concentrated on dropping the bottles of wine off the bridge. He saw them fall, break the surface with dark splashes, then sinking, wobbling down, tumbling in the current, jostling each other, rolling on the riverbed, stirring the fine silt. Then they held fast in the deepest muck, a thick ooze that buried them.

An instant of fierce relief. Then he felt worse.

◇

Joss was sitting completely still, curled up sideways against the back of the armchair.

Bonnie Two asked Mike again how he felt about Joss' being taken to jail. He said again he was deeply concerned, worried about her state of mind. He looked at Joss, who was staring at the arm of the chair.

Bonnie Two persisted. "But how did you feel?"

"Okay. I felt tired. And I—I forgot to tell you this, Joss—I'd just learned that Edmond and Evelyn are going to move."

Joss nodded her head but didn't look at him.

Mike said, "So I was already sad."

Bonnie Two said, "But how did you feel about *Joss*?"

"I've already said. Concerned. I went and got her out. Then I felt grateful to Ganny. She's our associate, I think you met her at our office."

"Uh-huh," Bonnie Two said. "But what feelings—"

"Okay. Let me put it this way. It's hard to have feelings about Joss when something like that is going on. Joss isn't herself. She's not really there. So I just do the stuff that has to be done."

"Uh-huh. Do you feel angry?"

Mike sighed. "It wouldn't do any good. So I try to be hopeful. At the particular time you're asking about, my feelings were pretty worn out."

"Uh-huh. So do *you* feel worn out?"

"No. I'm tired. I'm not worn out. I can still get on with what I have to do."

"Uh-huh. So, Joss, how do you feel—"

"I feel like joining the witness-relocation program."

Mike laughed.

"That's funny," Bonnie Two said, "but I'm going to take it sort of seriously?"

Joss said, "Uh-huh?"

Bonnie Two said, "It'd be good that you're thinking of a new beginning. I mean, if you're thinking of some kind of detox . . . But I kind of get the feeling that there's another issue?"

"Suppose," Joss said with a sudden increase in volume, "suppose that there are times when alcohol isn't the only toxin. Suppose that there are times when everything is toxic. You—you talking on tippy-toe. Mike lumbering on in legal-speak. Me. Me turning everything into poison. The car. The jailhouse. The house-jail."

Mike turned sideways in his chair. He closed his eyes and said, "Jesus, Joss."

"Yeah," Joss said. "Jesus."

"You're feeling real bad," Bonnie Two said. "Do you think Mike said 'Jesus' 'cause he's feeling bad too?"

"Maybe he's saying his prayers. Maybe he's appalled at the sin of despair. Maybe he's wishing I'd driven off a cliff."

Mike shook his head and said, "Oh, for God's sakes."

Joss said, "The answer is—all of the above."

"Okay," Mike said. "Maybe you just have to say how bad everything is."

"Oh, neat," Joss said. "It's always darkest just before the dawn."

"Don't—" Mike said.

"What do you mean 'don't'? The two of you want feelings, so I'm doing feelings, I'm coming up with feelings. Then you make your meta-statement that I'm just saying bad stuff out of some need that you understand from on high. Oh, there goes Joss with her need to exaggerate. With her—"

"Okay," Mike said, "I'm—"

"Don't say 'okay.' It's not okay. You were better off saying 'Jesus.'" Joss turned to Bonnie Two. "And don't you say 'uh-huh.'"

Bonnie Two said, "Okay—if it bothers you . . ."

Joss slumped back in her armchair. "You two go ahead without me. I'm going to AA tonight. That's enough for one day."

"Okay," Bonnie Two said. "That's okay. We've got a few more minutes, Mike, so maybe you'd like to just talk a little?"

"Okay. About what?"

"Well, maybe about something different? Like has sex been all right for you?"

Joss laughed.

Mike said, "I'm always glad."

Joss sighed. Mike said, "What's that about?"

Joss said, "Well, it hasn't been exactly brimming with passion this last year or so."

"As long as that?" Mike said. "But the question is about how I feel, and I'm still glad. And eager. It may not be brimming with passion but it's not as though you've been . . . unsatisfied. I know you say, 'Eros has waned,' but I'm still hopeful that Eros can make a comeback."

Bonnie Two said, "You do stuff Joss likes?"

"I'm willing to make an effort if both of us aren't as interested as I am."

"Like what?" Bonnie Two said.

Joss said, "Oh brother."

Mike said, "Okay. Let's not talk about that. But what about this detox program? What I'd like to know is what there is that I can do."

Bonnie Two looked at Joss, who gave a single wave of her hand, palm-out, meaning "I pass." Bonnie Two then looked at Mike without saying anything. She opened her mouth slightly as if to speak but just breathed out. Finally she said, "You could go to Al-Anon. You know about Al-Anon?"

Mike sighed and said, "Yeah. I could do that. They're the ones who say 'Detach with love,' right? I could do that. It'd only be a problem if they meet at the same time as Joss' AA."

"It's a different night."

"Is it far? I don't like leaving Joss without a car."

"I could give you a ride."

"That's nice of you. I could certainly try it once. Anything else? That doesn't seem very direct."

"Well, right now it doesn't seem like there's much you can do for Joss. But maybe you could do some stuff just to help yourself." Bonnie Two looked at her watch. "Maybe next time we can talk a little about that." She pushed a button on her watch. "So, Joss, you're going to AA. I'll take Mike to Al-Anon. And then, later this week, I can talk to you, Joss, about your meeting, and then have a talk with Mike. And next week we can see how we feel about maybe all of us getting together."

They didn't talk on the way to the car. When they got to it Joss handed him the keys at arm's length, holding one key between her fingers and dangling the key ring. Before he started the car, Mike said, "This AA thing won't work if you think you've been railroaded into it."

"Don't worry," Joss said.

"I mean, you seem to have a certain amount of contempt for Bonnie Two."

"A certain amount."

Mike put the key in the ignition but didn't turn it. He said, "She sometimes seems foolish, but I think she's goodhearted, and she's providing . . . something . . . an arena. Oh. That reminds me. You think we should take Edith and Nora to Ezra's fight? I think Ezra would like it. He sent me four tickets. But it could be too much for the girls. Not just the fight, but the crowd. Some guy next to them yelling 'Kill the motherfucker!' "

Joss looked out her window. She said, "Ask them." Without turning she said, "No. Ask me later."

Mike started the car but didn't put it in gear. He said, "Would it help you if I gave up drinking too?"

"Suit yourself," Joss said. "I couldn't help noticing you detoxed the house."

"That's right. But I'll take the pledge too. Go on the wagon with you, if it would help."

"Take Bonnie Two's advice. Detach. Work on yourself. Take up golf. Don't become Carrie Nation breaking bottles with her ax."

Mike said, "I threw them in the river." And then he thought of the river. At first he thought he was thinking of the river burying the bottles in silt, but it was the river before that, before the owl flew down to it, it was the river caught in the act.

He squeezed the steering wheel. He didn't know if he was trying to speak or trying not to speak. He said, "You and Bonnie. Bonnie One. Last night it came to me that you and Bonnie One are lovers."

Joss said, "Yes."

He heard her shift her weight. He looked. She'd turned to face him. She said, "I have a passionate relationship with Bonnie."

He felt her sentence swimming inside him, about to find his bone marrow. He didn't know if it would freeze or scald.

Just before it darted all the way in, he had an instant of being dispassionately but keenly interested. He tried to hold on to it, to keep the toxin from entering his bloodstream. Didn't work. He held on to himself with steel hoops.

He put the car in gear. He looked carefully over his left shoulder and pulled away from the curb. He adjusted the rearview mirror. He drove home in second gear without saying anything.

When he turned onto their bridge, Joss said, "You're taking this calmly, are you?"

He said, "No."

He stopped the car on the bridge and looked at Joss. He was terrifying her, but he couldn't unclench his teeth or move his lips. He held up his hand so she would know he was about to speak. He breathed out through his mouth, breathed in, and on the next breath out said, "No, I'm not."

◇

Joss had imagined the conversations she and Mike would have. She had gone over them so often that she had to keep herself from hurrying him through the predictable parts.

She sometimes felt heartless—although the time she caught herself being the most detached was also the time she was—simultaneously—most terrified. They were sitting in her studio. Mike had already lost his temper once and banged on the table. There was a silence. Mike suddenly gritted his teeth, picked up his coffee mug, and threw it through the windowpane. Joss shrank into her chair. She heard herself bleat. At the same time she looked at the hole in the window, which for a moment appeared to be a perfect profile of the mug—the slightly narrowed waist and the big round handle.

Mike sank into his chair with his head in his hands. Joss studied him for a second, then looked back at the window. Too bad—it was just a big splattered hole. She thought it might be a nice moment in a film. The perfect coffee-mug hole. The mug sailing through the air, intact, upright, and full, passing through the glass, landing on the hood of a car at a stoplight, skidding across toward the open window of the next car and into the hand of the driver. A funny live-action short with cartoon physical laws. Explosions of human emotion would be magically rendered harmless, even sweetly helpful.

Been done? Jacques Tati? Buster Keaton?

She couldn't help it. The AA meetings. The sessions with Bonnie Two (who, when Mike said "Joss has someone else," nodded and said, "Uh-huh"). The formally scheduled conversations with Mike. All in all, a lot of hours of sitting still. She wasn't bored, but she felt as if seriousness was being poured over her—a warm liquid which then congealed. Not a physical torture—more like rubber than cement. It was only afterward, when she was alone, that she felt frantic. She felt like stripping naked and howling and swinging through the trees.

But in general her exasperated restlessness took a backseat to a new and strange sensation. It took her a while to figure out what it was. It was this: She was the center. She was the coherent one. She was the one who stepped back to be calm. It was Mike who now lost his temper, apologized, lost his temper again and left, and then came back in penitent. Well, semi-penitent, but certainly supplicant.

He was the one who spoke in long impassioned tumbling rants or pleas, and she was the one who said, "I'll think about it."

The sensation came to her completely one morning after she'd taken the girls to their bus stop and come back to find Mike lingering. He said, "Have you considered—"

"I'm sorry, I've really got to get to work. I'll see you at Bonnie Two's this afternoon." She touched his arm in a conciliatory way. He picked up his briefcase and hiked off down the hill. She went into her studio, thought of calling Bonnie One but didn't really have to. She breathed deeply and comfortably. It was that breath that caught her by surprise. She shook her head and laughed. She pulled out her index file of movie clichés and wrote, "Well, folks, it's a whole new ball game."

More seriously, she wondered how long it would be before Mike organized. He was still spinning, boxing the compass of his emotions.

How could you? . . . Don't worry, I'll never do anything to harm you.

Goddamn it, Joss! . . . Joss, I understand.

What about Edith and Nora—how could you do this to them? . . . Of course I know you love them, you've always been a terrific mother.

If this is what you really want, just go ahead now! . . . You can't really know what you want yet, I mean, after twelve years of marriage we need to take time to . . .

I can't stand it! . . . I can endure it.

She had no answers to his outrage, lament, and anger or to his flip sides of generosity, attentiveness, and hope. But she didn't have to answer.

She also felt whole and solid during this period, because for the moment she didn't see anything or anyone—besides Mike—being harmed. And even Mike wasn't falling apart, just having a terrible time.

On the whole she was well disposed toward this new unsettled Mike. Her good disposition didn't ever come near sliding into submission or even concession; it apparently wasn't subject to her old mood swings. At first she thought that was because Mike could be counted on to anger her at least once a day. He still worked up self-righteous attacks on her that relied on Natural Law and Western Civilization. That usually used up that day's ration of her benevolence.

And every time either one of them mentioned Bonnie One's name it was sure to lead to open anger. One time Joss was deploying a defensive argument about how women had always been forced into secrecy by men when Mike interrupted with a tone of contempt that startled her. He said, "I see you've been learning your feminist-guerrilla catechism from Bonnie One."

"You think she's the brains of this operation?" Joss said. "You think she's smarter than me, do you?"

"Sneakier. More self-justifying."

Joss said, "Forget about insulting her. Pay attention to your insult to me. You think I can't think up my own arguments? That I'm Trilby to her Svengali? Then you should go talk to *her* about all this. Why bother with me? Hey, I'm just the dummy. Go on. Call her up. You want her new number?"

Mike backed away. He said, "What I meant was that the argument isn't worthy of you." It was a limp pomposity that repelled her but made her lose interest in continuing the fight. Before, she'd never been able to lose interest in a fight.

Another time Joss was the one who brought up Bonnie One's name. She said, somewhat carelessly, "One of the things you probably haven't considered is that I feel *useful* to Bonnie."

"Oh? How's that?"

Joss immediately saw she didn't want to get into Bonnie One's emotional needs, so she steered into what she thought was a minor subject. She said, "Well, among other things, she grew up in very different circumstances from ours. She didn't have the advantages that you and I—"

Mike laughed an ugly laugh. He said, "So this is all part of the Fresh Air Fund? Send a deprived child to camp? Why do I find that not just dumb but disgusting? I mean, I know *she's* disgusting. If that's the line she's feeding you, next thing you know she'll be asking you to set her up with a trust fund. But why do I find *your* saying that so repulsive? Is it just the mushiness? Maybe it's your trying to whitewash sex with liberal guilt. Or is it your idea, your fatuous idea, that that vampire really needs your help? . . ."

Mike's tone was more poisonous than Joss had ever heard from him, and she was taken by surprise, but again she found herself easily stepping back out of range of his adjectives—"disgusting, repulsive, fatuous."

She felt no need to explain. Perhaps what she'd actually said *was* fatuous. What she'd had in mind was how pleasant it was to have something to give, how her love for Bonnie One was so much more than desire. It was amazing how neither of them spent time struggling for the upper hand, neither of them holding back her thoughts for fear of being criticized. At the same time, Bonnie One made Joss feel that Joss was the older one, the one whose family, upbringing, adolescent rebellions, first inspirations, old boyfriends, college years, marriage, and work Bonnie treated as a novel with whose heroine Bonnie sympathized admiringly.

Mike's attitude toward Joss' life had never been that of an absorbed novel-reader. For one thing, he often seemed to forget who the heroine was. In the early chapters, he was on her father's side half of the time. Or he was amused by what a handful she was for her mother. He was retroactively jealous of her old boyfriends, horrified by her old out-of-control escapades. He *was* sympathetic to her ideas, but with an eye to how they could be improved. He seemed to see his arrival in her life as the most significant event of the novel.

Joss remembered Edith and Nora's early games with their dolls. They'd make up fairy-tale dramas the climax of which was always the arrival of "the one true bridegroom." Where did they pick up that phrase? She hadn't taught it to them. Or if she had, it was when she was someone else altogether.

So now, as Mike was railing and making scenes, she felt an oblique and distant pity as if for an aging repertory actor who wasn't going to get the romantic lead anymore. Poor Mike, he didn't even realize they weren't going to be putting on that kind of play.

◇

What did Nora and I know then?

Nora was in tears because she'd learned that Evelyn was leaving. She was in a rage because she'd loved her third-grade homeroom teacher and both her prospective fourth-grade teachers were well-known meanies.

She was in a rage because Mom and Dad both talked about sending us to camp in late July or August. Nora said she'd go to theater-and-music camp, but only if I went. I said no way, I would only go to camp if it was real camp with camping out—hikes and tents and compasses and canoes. Dad liked that.

But Nora and I were thrilled that school was out. We were thrilled to be going to Grandma's. We talked about how the handsome tenant farmer's son would defend us against the littlest big cousin, who still terrorized us (the other two had begun to ignore us now that they were old enough to be interested in girls).

And then we had the family-packing-for-vacation scene—always comically horrible and wonderful. Dad lashing things to the roof rack, trying to teach me knots ("See—two half-hitches and it tightens this way, and it slides loose like this"), picking up stray objects and declaring them unnecessary. Mom arriving with armfuls of more stray objects—under one arm her marble slab for rolling out pastry, the hair dryer in her back pocket with the cord dangling, two straw hats on top of each other on her head, and in each hand a paper bag, one from the grocery store with jars of herbs and, to estop Dad from complaining, one bottle of Adolph's meat tenderizer; the other bag from the drugstore—sugarless gum, Oil of Olay, sunblock, and a plastic beach ball.

"The general store has all that stuff. We aren't going into the wilderness."

Mom fished out the Oil of Olay. "They don't have this."

Mom's theory was that the station wagon was a large suitcase. Dad's was that it was a boat and that loose objects were unshipshape menaces. One sea bag per sailor. So Mom always poured stuff in at the last minute, just when Dad was ready to cast off and too tired to argue any longer.

What strikes me now as extraordinary is that they played this scene with exactly the same lines and props as every other year. And naturally so did Nora and I. What neither Nora nor I saw were the two completely different invisible strategies. Dad hoped he was taking the intact family to a safe haven, presided over by Grandma, where Mom would come to her senses. Mom, on the other hand, hoped to park us there, and hook Dad up to a place he loved, to the roles he loved (dad, uncle, boatmaster, and fishing guide), and then she could get back to Charlottesville—to an emergency edit in her studio, to her chapter of AA, to some arranged necessity—to Bonnie One.

It was the last scene of normal family life. Nora and I imprinted it vividly. Maybe because we knew the outer husk of our communal life was disintegrating, both of us were more eager than usual to have our family life move to Grandma's, where uncles and cousins would replace Tyler and Bonnie and Edmond and Evelyn. Or maybe we'd picked up the Mom and Dad seismic quiverings. Whatever. We played all the car games as if our lives depended on it. Mom invented some of them—for example, who could be the first one to spell her name from the letters on license plates or roadside signs? Dad was a fiend at "I Packed My Grandmother's Suitcase." Nora and I were keyed up, but behaved very well. We answered Dad's quizzes about Civil War battles. Nora only sang "Tomorrow" once.

We quizzed Mom about what the big cousins had been up to all year. (We always hoped to hear bad stuff or at least embarrassing stuff that we could bring up if they teased us.)

Nora and I usually begged to stop at McDonald's. Dad always wanted to stop at a place farther along that served crab cakes and oysters. This time we gave in to him. We must have known something.

And then the last few miles, the last furlong on Grandma's farm road lined with daylilies and mint, then the tires crunching on the crushed-oyster-shell driveway up to the *porte cochère.* Everyone in the house coming out to meet us with hugs and kisses, laughing at the beat-up station wagon with the shiny canoe guyed fore and aft, the beat-up bicycle lashed to a rack on the back, the raggle-taggle gypsy branch of the family come for the summer.

That last trip and that last arrival have obliterated all the ones before.

Oh, there are small reasons for that last arrival's overshadowing our earlier ones—the biggest big cousin had brought his college girlfriend, and she was a development for Nora and me to contemplate with wonder. The middle big cousin had a new dirt bike propped on its kickstand at the end of the oyster shells, another object of wonder. The littlest big cousin came out in his bathing suit—and appeared almost deformed with muscles he'd built up in a single year of obsessive weight-lifting.

But the hugs and kisses and clamor were what we'd been waiting for. Chiefly of course Grandma—Grandma exclaiming over us, straightening our collars, lifting our hair, smoothing our cheeks with her fingers, and sending us off to the cool protection of our bedroom, which was like another caress of her hand. Then there was the easy stillness between Nora and me as we unpacked, pausing to take in the back lawn, the stone wall, the trees—all lit by the slow light of the summer afternoon.

But it's just then that the last scene of certain happiness becomes the first scene of uncertainty. It's then that beauty and happiness and love become separated. It's then that each acquires a shadow, and each shadow has the power to make me think that beauty, happiness, and love are only thoughts. Until then I thought they were something better—elements of the universe like light and gravity. I'd thought they were better than us. I must have known something, because that was the day I began to think that they're just us.

◇

Mike asked Joss to promise she wouldn't see Bonnie One when Joss went back to Charlottesville. Joss said she'd think about it. Mike said she owed him her undivided attention for a month, just a month.

Joss thought that was a dumb and desperate thing to ask. She also knew he would be tormented every minute she was gone if she said no. She said yes.

For the first half of the drive she thought she might keep her promise. For the second half of the drive she thought that she'd taken Mike's rules seriously enough by considering it for the first half of the drive.

She became more and more exuberant as she approached Charlottesville. She laughed at her own jokes.

She rang the bell of Bonnie's new apartment. She was surprised by how angry she was that Bonnie wasn't there. She thought of going home to see if there was a message on the answering machine. Of course there wouldn't be—Bonnie One had no idea whether Mike or Joss would go home first.

Joss drove to Bonnie's office. Not there. Walking back to her car, she saw Bonnie's car. She was surprised by the rush of affection she felt for Bonnie's car. She ran her hands along the left front fender, dizzily and voluptuously.

Maybe Bonnie was out for coffee, maybe buying a magazine. But most likely the library. She set off for the library, turned back, and left a note on the driver's seat in Bonnie's car. "Don't go anywhere. I'll be right back."

Joss jogged the quarter-mile to the library, jigging restlessly at the street corner waiting for the light to change. Just as she turned off the sidewalk onto the flagstone path to the library she saw Bonnie across the street by the university chapel. It was early twilight, gray but luminous, the grass around the incongruously rustic stone chapel glowing dark green. Bonnie was standing next to someone who looked like Nora's bouncy tap-dance teacher. But it wasn't Polly Trueheart. This one had the same springy curls, the same small waist and sudden shelf of hip and butt. What was different? She was shorter. And she had bigger shoulders, bigger arms, and an almost mannish vee to her back. She was wearing in fact a backless bathing suit that showed off her fine muscles. And violet spandex shorts that showed off her butt. And stubby hiking boots, little hard hooves to her legs. She and Bonnie were looking at the bell tower. Bonnie leaned her head closer to the springy curls to sight along the girl's bare arm pointing up.

Joss held her breath.

The girl began to climb the shadowed rock face of the bell tower. She went up nimbly about twice as high as Bonnie's upturned face. Bonnie moved closer. With one hand the girl plucked the end of a length of rope from around her waist. She reached up and ran it through a ring that was attached to the wall. The loose end dangled down to Bonnie, who took hold of it with both hands. The girl said something to Bonnie. Bonnie ran the end of the rope around her back. She put one hand on the end, the other on the length leading back up. The girl began to climb again, finding little edges of stone to grip with her fingers, then finding new footholds with the toes of her boots.

She stopped again to rig her safety rope higher. It only took her a few more moves to get within reach of the belfry. She snagged the top end of the wall with one hand. She swung to the right, her legs dangling, all her weight on one hand. Then she swung left and reached up with the other hand. She pulled herself straight up with both hands, got her stomach onto the top, and slithered out of sight into the belfry.

Her head reappeared. Bonnie let go of the rope. The girl pulled it up after her, then tossed it down. The girl had attached the end to a broad webbed belt which Bonnie now cinched around her waist. Bonnie began to climb, much more slowly than the girl and relying on the rope to get past the hard parts. Finally she was being mostly hauled up. When Bonnie got her chest onto the top she tried to swing her leg up, but it didn't quite clear the edge. The girl reached out and put one hand under Bonnie's thigh, the other hand holding the rope.

Joss reached out to brace herself against a tree, the bark rough on her palms. She was surprised to find that she'd crossed the street and drifted another hundred feet to the tree behind which she was now lurking.

Bonnie and the girl took a long time to get Bonnie over the top. In the pulling and scrabbling one of Bonnie's sneakers fell to the ground. Then Bonnie rolled over the top, and she and the girl disappeared behind the wall into the belfry.

Joss was aware of walking to the base of the bell tower and picking up the little white sneaker. But she was hazy about how she got back to her car. She was startled by her own voice, which said, "Well, this serves you right."

She argued with herself. She thought, This isn't anything. But, then, what's Bonnie up to? She isn't athletic or even outdoorsy. And how did she come to know this stumpy outdoor sexpot? You don't just go climb a bell tower with a stranger. And disappear behind a wall.

The sluice of jealousy opened all the way. She hated Bonnie One's little white tennis shoe.

She wanted a friend to comfort her. And then to explain to her that nothing was wrong after all, that she'd made it all up, including the girl's hand. Joss could see the hand clearly, a tough little knot of energy against Bonnie's pale underthigh. Joss wanted someone to erase that hand, to say persuasively that to an outside observer it meant nothing. Joss herself knew that if she shot the scene on film the hand would mean a lot. The whole scene would mean Eros climbing, Eros waxing, Eros sending sparks through every stubby finger of that hand.

Odd. Odd that she and Bonnie had never been jealous of the inevitable nights they spent with Tyler and Mike. It wasn't even a taboo subject. They might have even mentioned it along with going to a movie, making a meal. It wasn't making a meal, but they didn't worry about it. How on earth had they not? Because each of them had the power of pitying these two blind men?

But now. Now that she'd escaped the power struggle with Mike, now that she was on her own, she was falling into a new power struggle with Bonnie One.

Joss had thought that she and Bonnie were free of power's power to poison love.

She clutched the sneaker in her hand. She clutched it with both hands. She couldn't let it go. It weakened her. She couldn't even yell out loud. She exploded inside herself, but still trying to shield Bonnie. Fuck you, spandex butt! Fuck you with your thick back and tiny waist and thick thighs and tiny knees and thick calves and tiny feet.

She gave her own car a whack with the sneaker.

Oops. Wrong car.

She looked around. From far away, at the other end of the parking lot, someone was looking at her. She got into the right car and drove to a gas station. She still wanted someone else to help her. She thought of one good thing about Mike—he used to comfort her when she yelled at herself about how she was fucking up, when she cried in anger that she wasn't a genius. Now she was on her own.

Just to show herself how crazy she was, she got mad at Mike. If he hadn't turned to stone, she wouldn't be in this mess. If only he hadn't been so inert that he settled for putting up with her . . . What a meathead way of living—putting up with her.

And now she had to go to her AA meeting without any supper. She called Bonnie's office. No answer. She went to her meeting and sat through it with the sneaker in her hand. No one mentioned it. Why not? Because they had such weird good manners? She ate too many powdered doughnuts with her free hand and felt sick but still hungry.

She got back in the car. Home? Edmond and Evelyn's? Back to her mother's?—All the way back to the Northern Neck with confectioners' sugar all over her mouth?

All right. Driving away was too dumb, too quiet. She'd telephone Bonnie. If Bonnie was still out, she'd get the answering machine and she'd say . . . nothing. No message. If Bonnie was in, she'd . . . she'd hang up and go stuff the toe of the white sneaker in Bonnie's mail slot.

She got out and found the pay phone. She got the answering machine.

What was going on with the world? Robots had taken over. She was in a science-fiction movie. Even watching Bonnie watch the spandex girl with the beautiful back, and then watching Bonnie climb up after her—someone had turned that into a movie.

Joss wanted someone real. She'd forgive anything if she could find the real Bonnie. Not her car, not her answering machine, not her climbing a bell tower. She said out loud, "All right, I'll admit it, I'm desperate."

She drove to Bonnie's office. She saw Bonnie's car in the parking lot. She prayed that Bonnie was in her office. She didn't care if the violet-spandex-butt girl was with Bonnie. She didn't care if the girl's lavish ringlets were spread out on Bonnie's skin, if the girl's flat moon-pie face was hiding between her thick jumbled hair and Bonnie's bare skin. She didn't care if she had to kneel down and worship the violet spandex butt.

She'd blown up her life, and if she was going to be sailing through the air she'd better have someone with her who wasn't a robot. She held on to the sneaker, it was leading her to Bonnie.

The lights in the parking lot came on, changing the color of the air. She ran inside.

She was in the stairwell clomping upstairs to Bonnie's office. She put her right hand around the doorknob and leaned her cheek against the door. The white sneaker in her left hand jabbed into her stomach. The doorknob became warm in her hand. What was she waiting for? If she had a right to be anywhere it was here. What was she waiting for? She was waiting for either anger or desire to move her, and they'd both deserted her. She didn't exist in the world of rights. She'd left that world and slipped into a world of strange mechanisms. Robots moving her weightlessly around the town as if it were a planet without gravity.

This was no time for a vision or an anxiety attack. She held the sneaker up to her mouth and breathed into it, using it like a paper bag to stifle her hyperventilation. She took a deep breath and turned the knob.

The light from the desk lamp mixed queerly with the last light coming through the window. Bonnie's face was two colors. She gave a start that sent her chair backward on its little wheels.

In the sliver of time before Bonnie got over being startled and Joss started to think of what to say, Joss felt the floor tilt slightly, as if it were the deck of a ship. She held on to the doorknob. The light coming through the window was as strange as light on the surface of the sea. She was Columbus. She was Columbus when he'd just looked back and for the first time saw no land behind him.

So she was on her way. Out of sight of land. So long, Ferdinand. Adios, Isabella.

Joss closed the door behind her.

Joss pushed the button in the middle of the doorknob.

Bonnie stood up and said, "So there you are. You didn't say what day . . ."

"Here I am," Joss said. "Do you still kiss girls?"

§ 7

One of Mike's bits of practical wisdom was that the way to get through a troubled period is to set up a busy schedule. At first this seemed hard to do at his mother-in-law's, where he'd been used to letting go of time. He filled most of the lines of his appointment book, as if his vacation were a desperate week at work. Weed the vegetable garden (one hour), swim in creek (forty minutes), sunbathe (twenty minutes), rig five fishing rods (three nephews, one nephew's girlfriend, and self) (one hour). Lunch (confer with nephews about fishing expedition). Call Ganny at office (half-hour). Pick berries with Edith and Nora. Bicycle 4–4:30. Fish 5–7. Dinner 7:30–8:30. Smoke cigar on porch with Mrs. Rogers 8:30–9:30. Read to Nora 9:30–10. Read to self 10–12. And so to bed.

His youngest nephew-in-law persuaded him to start lifting weights—the boy had brought a barbell, two dumbbells, and a stack of ten- and twenty-pound plates. The boy also convinced him that aerobics would only produce endorphins if done vigorously for at least forty minutes. ("It's a real high, Uncle Mike. Those endorphins kick in and you'll feel good for hours. But you can't just swim that old-folks' breast stroke you do. You gotta get your pulse rate up.")

The boy was pleased to be an authority ("You might want to watch your sugar and animal-fat intake, Uncle Mike"). It occurred to Mike that the boy was in part revenging himself for many summers of Mike's instruction in boat and fishing lore, but Mike liked being put on a program. ("A good way to check your progress is to take your resting pulse in the morning. It should be lower in just a week or so. And you should start weighing yourself. Those first ten pounds oughta slide off pretty easy.")

It was while taking his pulse one morning that Mike found he couldn't multiply. He could count all right. He counted his pulse for fifteen seconds. Fourteen. He knew he should multiply by four. Four times fourteen.

He couldn't do it.

He thought he might be still sleepy. He counted for a whole minute and got fifty-six. That was good. According to his appointment book it was down from sixty-four the week before.

He went for his morning swim of forty-five minutes, up and down a hundred yards of the creek eighteen times. He could count perfectly well. He took his pulse at the end, while he was still breathing hard. He counted twenty-nine. He tried to multiply that by four. He couldn't do it in his head. He wrote it in the mud with his finger. Still couldn't do it.

He ate breakfast and went to his room with a notepad and pencil. He could remember numbers all right—the problem was four times twenty-nine. He still couldn't do it.

The mental block felt somewhat the same as not being able to remember someone's name—at first no more disconcerting than that.

He got a deck of cards and brought them back to his bedroom. According to his schedule, he was supposed to play Frisbee with Edith and Nora at 10:00 a.m. He had ten minutes. Good. He could still tell time.

He dealt out two hands of casino and tried to play. He couldn't. He put the face cards to one side and dealt out two cards at a time. Four and three. Four and three make . . .

He felt a little chill of panic. He held up four fingers on one hand and three on the other. He held his hands close together. He was able to count the fingers. Seven.

He repeated to himself, "Four and three make seven." He heard his voice, he understood the words, but he didn't understand . . . the idea of four and three. He said, "Four." He understood that. He held up four fingers. He said, "Three." He tapped his hand on his knee three times. He said, "Four and three make . . ."

He looked at his watch. Ten o'clock. That was clear. He went to the front hall, got the Frisbee, and went to the back lawn. Edith and Nora were in their room. He knew them. He knew their names.

They came out and began to play.

After a while he said, "Nora, how much is four and three?"

Nora said, "Dad. We're playing Frisbee."

"Yeah. But just go along with me for . . . Just tell me that one thing. Four and three."

Edith looked at Nora and then at Mike. Mike could see that Edith was puzzled, and also that Edith had made a small effort not to answer before Nora. Good—he could still see things like that.

He said, "Come on, Nora. Just tell me."

"Okay. Seven. And that's it. No more questions."

He felt okay physically.

Nora said, "We should get another dog. We could teach it to catch the

Frisbee." Nora held the Frisbee in front of her forehead, dropped it, and caught it in her teeth. She ran in circles saying, "Grrr, grrr."

Edith laughed. She called Nora. "Come! That's a good dog, come on. Here, girl!"

Nora ran around her, then got on all fours, opened her mouth, and panted over the Frisbee. When Edith tried to pick it up, Nora growled and planted her hand on it.

Edith said, "Bad dog! Now, sit. And stay."

Nora leaned forward with her tongue out and tried to lick Edith's hand. Edith jumped back and said, "Yuck!"

Mike wondered why he wasn't laughing. Were adding and multiplying in the same part of his brain as his sense of humor? Perhaps the mental block came from having a secret. Your mother and I . . .

Nora lifted her leg. Edith said, "That's Tyler's joke. Besides, you're a girl dog."

But what were he and Joss going to do?

Nora said, "I can be any dog I want."

Edith said, "Fine. Just stop hogging the Frisbee."

But he couldn't think about Joss and him anymore, not until he knew whether part of his brain had fallen out.

Edith was suddenly in a good mood. She said to Nora, "Fling the Frisbee! Fling the flying Frisbee flecked with foam!"

Nora said, "Flecked with foam?"

"Yeah. It's got your spit on it." Edith said this cheerily so Nora didn't get mad. "Fiercely fling the Frisbee farther."

Nora threw it to Mike. Mike said, "Float Frisbee, to the father." He started to throw it back to Nora.

Nora said, "Frisbee, follow through."

"Dad, wait," Edith said. "She has to say three 'f's to make you throw it."

Mike thought he should go somewhere safe and be alone until he felt better. When Joss got back, he could take the car and go to Charlottesville and find Evelyn and Edmond. Or Ganny.

Nora said, "Frow me the Frisbee first."

Mike threw her the Frisbee. Edith said, "Forward the falling Frisbee." Nora threw the Frisbee to her.

Nora said, "Feeble-minded family . . ."

Edith said, "That's two. You need—"

"Free."

Edith said, "You just thought of that because I said two. Like, one, two, free."

"So what?" Nora said, "Free the fucking Frisbee."

"Not at your grandmother's," Mike said, but his heart wasn't in it. He felt farther and farther away. He could see the grass, the trees, the water in the creek wrinkling under the wind, but it was a postcard of this place.

He thought perhaps he was having another sympathetic visitation of what it felt like to be Joss. No. He knew one thing about her—she could feel even stranger than this, even glassy-eyed and breathing hard with panic, but she didn't sink into self-pity.

Okay, then. Be practical. Could he drive? He walked a straight line, touched his finger to his nose, touched his two index fingers together.

He told the girls he was tired, Frisbee time was over.

He called the family doctor, Mary Ames, and her secretary made an appointment for him the next day. And, what the hell, why not Bonnie Two? Maybe she knew enough to tell him this symptom was normal.

If Joss got the car back by lunchtime, he could get to Charlottesville in time to catch Ganny at the office. No. He didn't want to go to the office and have to talk to his partners. He'd get to Charlottesville and call from the house.

He tried lying down but he was restless. He looked at the cards still laid out on the foot of the bed. He didn't want to experiment anymore. He didn't want to be here. He didn't want the girls to see something was wrong. Or Mrs. Rogers. Or anyone here in this place that was becoming stranger and stranger.

He decided he couldn't wait for Joss to bring the car back. Plenty of cars here. Joss' brothers' cars, even the oldest nephew had a car. Mrs. Rogers had two, her town car and the old Jeep.

He was surprised he didn't want to talk to Mrs. Rogers. Ordinarily he found her reassuring. Was it because she might ask him something to do with numbers? Was that crazy? Not necessarily, she might ask him when he'd get to Charlottesville and he'd have to add. . . .

He wrote a note to Mrs. Rogers. He wrote a perfectly coherent note. He checked to make sure he had his wallet.

Then he wrote a note to Ganny. That was in case he got to Charlottesville and couldn't explain to her what was going on. He wrote a sentence about not being able to multiply or add. He also drew a map. The map puzzled him. He put in a river and a mountain range, but he wasn't sure what they meant. He studied the map. There was a pass through the mountain range.

It became clear to him that the pass was where he was now in his mind. If he came back on his own, everything would be fine. If he went through the pass and couldn't find his way back, then the map would show Ganny where he'd got lost. She could wait for him there. He put an "X" by the pass. He put another "X" at the bottom of the page. He wrote, "X marks the spot where I went through."

He folded the paper and put it in his breast pocket. It made a crinkling noise when he touched his pocket. That was good, because that would show Ganny where the note was. And then she would know where he was.

He could see that the map would be hard to explain to someone else. But just because it was hard to explain, or even make sense of, that didn't mean it was crazy. In fact the map was not a crazy thing to do, because it made him feel much better.

When he got to the house in Charlottesville, he didn't call Ganny, because he felt mute. He didn't want to experiment with the phone and discover he'd lost the power of speech along with the power of multiplying and adding.

He could tell there were right things to do and wrong things to do, and, when he relaxed, his body led him to do the right thing. He changed into old clothes. A right thing. He got a shovel, went down to the river, and picked a spot for a willow. Right. He dug until he was pouring sweat. He took a shower. Right, right. He opened the icebox. Wrong. He shouldn't eat. He went to the bookshelf. Right. He took down two volumes of Kipling stories. He opened the icebox, looking for a beer. Wrong. There wasn't a beer anyway. Right. He lay down on the sofa and read story after story. Right. He fell asleep and woke up and read and fell asleep and woke up.

He finished one volume and picked up the second. He felt better. He was very pleased to have the second volume in his hand. He was grateful that Kipling knew so many stories about India—about soldiers, bridge builders, district commissioners, foresters, and the cleverest woman in Simla.

Kipling's appreciation of soldiers, bridge builders, engineers, district commissioners, and foresters was sentimental but robust and encouraging. It was the young subalterns who went to pieces. The older men kept on. It was a comfort to have this view spelled out. As for the cleverest woman in Simla, Mike was content that he was going to see Ganny and Dr. Ames, and even Bonnie Two. Ganny was as clever as the cleverest woman in Simla, and Dr. Ames and Bonnie Two certainly knew that two and two make four.

Mike looked at his watch. Five. The sky was getting bright. Five in the morning.

He said out loud, "Bonnie Two knows that two and two make four."

He laughed. He felt wonderfully rested. He must have slept . . . fifteen hours. No. He had to subtract the time he'd spent reading the first volume. About three hundred pages. Sixty pages an hour. TR = D, so T = D/R. Sixty into three hundred is five. So ten hours of sleep and five hours of reading and he was right as rain. Was it sleeping or Kipling? He thought of Joss' old joke. Question: "Do you like Kipling?" Answer: "I don't know, I've never kippled."

He was adding, multiplying, dividing, and telling jokes. Was he all right again? He decided to read more Kipling just in case he wasn't completely himself.

He'd gone under for a moment. No denying it. If this was a shipwreck, he'd gone under for a bit and hadn't known which way was up. Now he was back up, breathing air. He was still in the middle of the ocean, but clinging to the wreckage.

If Joss could read his mind now she'd laugh and say, "Just like you to start telling this as if it's a boys-at-sea adventure story." But he was alone, and he could put in as many boats as he pleased.

Later that day he abandoned his boys-at-sea. He ditched them as soon as he discovered another audience than himself.

When he saw Dr. Ames he told her the story of his odd mental block in three well-organized minutes.

She put the blood-pressure cuff on him and said, "Has anything been t-t-troubling you?"

He told her the whole Joss story in eight minutes. He didn't present it as if to a jury, but, rather, as if to a partners' meeting, that is, without any leaning one way or the other, just the facts and a few spare comments about what issues might prove to be the main areas of contention. No emotional adjectives, no metaphors of grief or loneliness. He said finally, "What is hard to assess is not just what Joss wants or doesn't want right now, but how changeable her wishes may turn out to be. So, at this stage, it's too early to tell Edith and Nora. There's still a remote chance that this is temporary. Of course I've got to watch out for wishful thinking."

Dr. Ames was very moved. Mike wasn't surprised that she was worried about Edith and Nora—she'd always been openly affectionate about them. What did surprise Mike was how awkwardly sweet she was with him. She put her palm on his cheek and said, "Oh, Mike, this is terrible." She didn't stutter, not even on the "t."

One part of him soaked up her sweet comforting. Another part of him registered with an alarmingly cool alertness that this sad story was more affecting when told with understatement, with a slight hint of the effort it cost him to be calmly objective. Was this part of a general principle of discourse—intimate stories are better when told leaning back rather than leaning forward?

Dr. Ames hugged him from the side and then went and sat on the corner of her desk. He had to remind her that the blood-pressure cuff was still puffed up tight on his arm. She deflated it, then remembered she hadn't taken his blood pressure. She puffed it back up and nestled the head of her stethoscope in the crook of his elbow, a gesture that now seemed to him affectionate.

"It's a little high," she said, "but that's not surprising. Are you getting enough sleep?"

He was about to say, in his old style, that her hugging him put his blood pressure up. He said instead, "So-so. Last night I slept a long time, but it was on and off. That little oddity of not being able to add or multiply—that seems to be better now. I suppose I should have canceled, I shouldn't have taken up your time. But I'm due for a checkup anyway, right?"

"Uh-huh. Lack of sleep can make your mind play tricks. And a whole lot of stress." Another sympathetic look, her fingers on his arm for an instant. Was this a law of physics—the more motionless he was, the more she was moved to touch him?

Dr. Ames said, "Are you seeing someone for counseling?"

"We were. I'm not sure we haven't sailed past that possibility. But at least Joss is going to AA."

"Uh-huh. But maybe you should see someone. This counselor, is he a psychologist?"

"She. Sort of. I'm going to ask her about a regular M.D. psychiatrist. I was a little scared by this blip in my brain, but on the whole I don't want to overdose on tea and sympathy." As soon as he uttered the last sentence he thought that it was an outright lie. Then he thought no—not entirely. He did want to go curl up in a cave. Then he thought that he was no better at saying what he really wanted than Joss.

And he contradicted that—he was positive about wanting everything the way it had been. But if everything was truly blown up, *then* what would he want?

Dr. Ames said, "Let me tell you an odd thing that a psychiatrist from Boston told me. The Irish—and that includes Irish-Americans—are the most difficult psychiatric patients he deals with."

"Why?"

"Because they deny pain."

"I would have thought that was more a Scottish trait—along with always wanting to set other people straight. Or maybe the English—all that stiff-upper-lip stuff."

"I'm just telling you what he told me. He said they'll talk your ear off, but they won't open up and talk about what's really making them feel bad—"

Mike said, "Or maybe the Swedes, brooding their way through sunless winters. And hey—talk about denying pain—what about Indians, American Indians? What about those braves who hang from a pole with hooks under their skin and twirl down until they pop loose? All that without uttering a sound."

"Mike. Mike. I'm just—"

"And anyway—what's so bad about denying pain? It used to be a virtue."

"Mike, listen. I'm just saying there's no point in your going to a psychiatrist if you talk about everything under the sun except what's going on with you."

"And what about the Mayans? They used to slice holes in their tongues and pull a string through the hole—and the string had thorns on it."

"Mike, stop going around the world. Anyway, there's a difference between deliberately bearing physical pain and pretending nothing's wrong with your psyche."

Mike stopped long enough to notice that she'd won a point, if not the argument. And why was he arguing? Maybe that was all he knew how to do. It was either argue or drown—was that right? His principal vital sign was arguing?

He said, "Okay, you win, I get it." Dr. Ames looked surprised and then very sweet again. Mike thought, if he slumped over and held his head in his hands, she would put her hand on the back of his neck. He decided not to, because it occurred to him his other bad habit/vital sign was flirting.

"I'll keep it in mind," he added.

"I'll get the nurse to come draw a little blood and so forth. If you'd like, I can ask a psychiatrist about your . . . multiplying-and-adding problem. Just to see if that might be something we should look into a little more. Will you be at your office?"

"I'll be in and out. I'll call back here before I leave town again." And then, before he knew what he was doing, he said, "I should use your office number for that, but to ask you out for supper I suppose your home number is better."

Mike was amazed at how swiftly Dr. Ames' face changed from benign to blank.

She said, "There are so many reasons why that isn't a guh, a guh, a g-good idea. . . ."

Mike felt his face squeeze up into a sympathetic grimace. "Not a good idea," he said. "I'll take your word for it." He sounded inane. He wanted to say something else but he was afraid he'd come out with a series of Joss jokes: That's easy for you to say, Dr. Ames.

Dr. Ames said, "I'll get the nuh-nuh-nurse."

And then Mike went giddy with imagining Dr. Ames' stuttering mouth pressed into the side of his neck; he imagined the sensation of her own stuttering changing under the spell of desire, every repetition of a hard consonant an erotic tic of her lips.

What was this? Mike took a huge breath, put his hands on his knees, and exhaled. Were his fantasies going to become as out of control as his arithmetic? Time to get hold of himself. Time to get stuck with a needle. Time to join a men's club.

But the next slot in his appointment book wasn't a men's club. It was Ganny. Mike poked his head in her office and said, "Got a minute?"

Ganny looked at him, looked at her watch, and said, "Okay—I'll eat an early lunch. When you say a minute, I know you mean an hour."

Mike decided to tell the arithmetic story first, and to tell it in a way that would be light enough and funny enough to keep Ganny in her slightly grumpy mood. Then break her goddamn heart by showing her the map he'd drawn just for her, his most trusted friend.

He got to the map part. Ganny hadn't said a word so far. He pulled out the map. Ganny looked at it. She looked up at him. "I don't get it," she said. "What is this a map of? The Northern Neck?"

"No. You don't get it."

"That's right. I just said I don't get it."

"It's a map of a mountain range. It's a symbolic mountain range. It's where I last was in my right mind. It's where you could look for me if I went crazy."

Ganny studied him for a moment. She said, "Is this something to do with Bundy? Bundy used to do stuff like this—leave me a note about where he was going when he went off to go camp out by himself. Leave a map."

Mike said crossly, "It has nothing to do with Bundy. I didn't know Bundy left you maps. This is completely different. I mean I now see that my map was a crazy idea, the sort of thing you write down when you think you've had a great idea in a dream and you wake up and make a note and in the morning it's just a scribble."

Ganny said, "So this is something you wrote down in the middle of the night?"

"No! That's the point. I did it when I couldn't add and I thought I was going crazy."

"But you feel okay now?"

"Well, yes. Sort of. I think so. But the point is it was *you* I thought of as the person who could save me."

Ganny said, "But you're feeling better now?"

"Yes, but that's not the point. The point is . . . I thought you'd get the point. It's not so good if I have to explain."

"It's not easy to see what this drawing is about."

"Ganny. Forget the map. The point is about you. I was whirling around and I thought, Who do I want to help me? *You*."

"Well, of course I'll help you, Mike. I mean if I can. But I don't see—"

"Okay. Never mind about the arithmetic and the map. That's all done with." He felt giddy again but this time with a whitening fear that, if Ganny didn't understand what he was trying to say, then nobody would. Everyone was falling into space away from everyone else, out of earshot, out of range of any signal.

He said again, "Okay. Let me try part two." He would do that story the way he'd told it to Dr. Ames, as fast and bright as a distress flare.

But Ganny said, "Wait a second. You're getting cross because part one didn't go just right. You snatch me up out of my office and start right in. I got to get my mind out of the office. I'm having a hard time with that client—the professor who's chair of Tyler's department. He was with me just before you showed up. He waltzed in and went through a dozen changes. Wanted to know if everything we said was covered by the attorney-client privilege, and when I said yes—unless he was planning a crime—he set out to tell me every last detail of every woman he'd been with. When I said, 'What's the point of all this?' he said, 'The point is that many of these women, I'm sure you'll agree, were not coerced. All of them are educated women, that is to say women who have seen something of life and who have read even more widely and who therefore can be reasonably expected to know their own minds. What's the point of learning literature if not to learn our minds? We are not dealing with foolish virgins, are we? I have never had a relationship with anyone who didn't have a Ph.D.—or at least an M.A. If I were to make advances toward you, you would have no problem deciding the matter as an equal. You might decline, you might accept, or you might choose to explore the possibility further. But it wouldn't occur to you to tape-record our private conversation and publish it. Isn't that a wrong? Isn't that a wrong that has been done me? Suppose this woman had said yes, or suppose you said yes, and I tape-recorded the ensuing encounter—every endearment, every sigh of pleasure. It would be outrageous. So I propose that we go on the offensive. And speaking of offensive, there's more to that tape than meets the ear. That's her pushing against my arm with her breast, to name but one tacit provocation.' "

Ganny had been imitating the man's elaborate wheedling voice. She stopped and scraped her tongue on her teeth as though she had a bad taste in her mouth.

Mike said, "Yeah, I knew he was going to be difficult."

"Don't say 'I told you so.' "

"But buried in all that, there is a point or two. I mean the covert taping, naturally. But the nonverbal context. Suppose she did rub up against him—"

"Oh, Mike! I'm not telling you this so you can spot the issues. I'm telling you this so you can imagine . . . Never mind."

"Wait. Don't stop. Say it. There's a lot of things to get. I'm just getting them one at a time. I mean how ridiculous he can sound, for one. That part about how he's never laid a hand on someone who doesn't have her Ph.D.—or at least an M.A. You're going to have to tell him how that'll go over at a hearing."

"That's *a* point. Not *the* point. The point is what it's like to have him in my office. If I were meeting him for any reason other than a hearing about his sexual misconduct, he'd be panting in my ear. He's doing it anyway, just from a safe distance. Listening to his voice is like being licked by . . . No, that's not it, that's too puppyish. It's more of a secretion. And it's deliberate. It may not be voluntary but it's deliberate."

Mike squinted and said, "How could something be involuntary but deliberate?"

Ganny said, "Yeah, well, maybe it's the way most men are. Maybe you can't help your general urge but you can help how you inflict it. This guy is circling and circling like some little sneaky dog trying to get behind you to take a bite. Or hump your leg. It's exhausting. I'll tell you, I didn't mind the way Bundy used to come on. He'd say those real dumb things, but he kind of knew he was being dumb, so all I had to do was give him a little shove and he'd laugh and settle down. Or Ezra. Ezra keeps it all in, acts cool. Then he'll say something, as if he's just that minute noticed you. He means, Hey, baby, this is it, this is your chance. If you shake your head no, he's right away back behind his cool eyes as if nothing happened. Both of them can't help coming on, but they don't go on inflicting it." Ganny sighed. "I mean Ezra doesn't, Bundy didn't."

Mike nodded but didn't say anything. He wasn't going to tell Ganny his news in this conversation. Not the way he'd meant to. He was annoyed with her and annoyed with himself for being annoyed.

Still, there was something bracing and astringent in this encounter. Gird up your loins like a man—another favorite Bundy Bible quotation. Just because Ganny wasn't available as a guardian angel this very minute was no reason to fall back into panic or gloom. What could he hope for from anyone? He couldn't imagine any useful advice or any comfort that would last more than a moment. All you could honestly ask for was distraction.

After Ganny and he finished lunch and were on the sidewalk outside the office, she said, "Oh—there's some people looking for you. One of them's Mr. Broome. I didn't recognize the other two, but they must be important, because Ritter gave them the VIP treatment. Maybe you should come in and find out."

Mike said, "Maybe tomorrow."

"Are you going back to the Northern Neck?"

"I don't know. Dr. Ames thought I should get someone else to . . . Look—I really don't want to come into the office. See if you can find out what those people want and I'll call you. Better yet, I'll buy you supper tonight."

"I'm sorry, Mike. I can't tonight. Give me a call. I'll be here till six. Say hi to Joss and the girls."

Mike walked a few steps away. "I don't know where Joss is. I think we're separating." Ganny took a step toward him. "I've got to get going," he said. "I'll call you later." He walked a few more steps, waved over his shoulder, and turned into the alley that went to the rear parking lot. He knew he was being petty, silly, and melodramatic. He had a license to be a jerk.

Even so, he should work out a rule. He'd only be a jerk once a day. And not to the same person twice. He'd apologize when he phoned this evening. He got out his appointment book and wrote down "5:40 call Ganny." He saw he had more than two hours to kill before his appointment with Bonnie Two. He also saw he hadn't done the exercises on his program. He walked to the downtown mall and bought socks, a jock, cheap sneakers, shorts, and a T-shirt that had "Virginia Is for Lovers" across the chest. He drove out to Ezra's gym and pedaled the exercise bike. After forty minutes, according to his nephew, the endorphins kicked in and made you feel euphoric. At forty-four minutes Mike felt horrible.

Physically not so bad but horribly depressed. It was all that pedaling without going anywhere, without seeing anything, without having anything to think about except himself and his sad story, which was beginning to bore him unless he was telling it to somebody else.

He put on a thin pair of gloves and socked the heavy bag.

Ezra came by and told him he needed to work on his left.

"A real good thing is double that left hook. Upstairs, downstairs. But they both got to be real. Not just arm punches. Get your body into it."

Mike hit the bag pretty hard. Ezra laughed and said, "You closed your eyes. You ain't going to kiss him, you know. And he ain't going to close his eyes and kiss you back. You better practice some punching with those eyes open."

"Okay, okay."

"Both eyes open."

"All right."

Mike was amazed how soon his arms got slow and heavy, how out of breath he was after a minute.

Ezra said, "Okay, you got the idea, you're making the effort."

Mike slipped off the light gloves and dried his face on a towel. Ezra said, "You do some more of that next time you're in. Relieve your frustrations."

Ezra was being surprisingly chatty. Mike said, "You feeling good?"

"I'm in shape," Ezra said, "I'm sharp. I just hate this last few days, when I'm tapering. No more weights. No hard sparring. Just a little skip-rope, a little dancing around the ring, a little roadwork. Last time I saw you I was complaining about three workouts a day. Now I'm missing it. Hard to sleep. I just don't feel tired at night. Got to watch out I don't eat too much. Got to watch out I don't drink any fizzy stuff, no beer, no soda pop. I go to the movies a lot. No buttered popcorn. It's amazing how dumb a lot of those movies turn out, no popcorn. I'd go dancing, but I don't want to get my mind on some female. What it's like, it's like I'm walking around vacuum-packed. I'm freeze-dried at the peak of perfection."

Mike laughed. "You know what this sounds like? It's the way I used to feel after going to confession on Saturday. I'd get through at five in the afternoon, do my penance, then I'd worry I'd do something bad before Sunday."

Ezra said, "Uh-huh," but he wasn't really paying attention.

Mike said, "See you at the fight. Good luck."

Mike looked at his watch. Still a while before he saw Bonnie Two. He showered and walked back downtown slowly. His skin felt good, but he was at a distance from it, a heavy inward distance.

Through a door he saw a TV over a bar. He never went to bars, but now he figured he'd be lucky to rise to the level of cliché: tell his story to the bartender.

The bartender was a handsome woman. So much the better. He ordered a beer. No one else at the bar. A few women at the tables. She looked at him for several seconds, looked at the clock on the wall. "Okay," she said.

Mike drank the top half fast, then nursed it. The bartender was watching a soap opera. Mike watched it too. He couldn't figure out what was going on, and at first this alarmed him. Then he saw that there weren't really scenes, but, rather, a succession of conversations between pairs of people, usually male-female, in which they exchanged information about the other pairs. What had thrown him off was that the actors gave oddly emotional readings to simple statements of fact. A woman said to a man, "I've got to go to the club now," in a way that made Mike think it was her doom. The man visibly struggled to get a grip on himself. He said, "Do you need a ride?" The woman stared at him with wide-eyed intensity. She said, "No. I've got my car."

Mike wondered if everything he'd said for the past two days had been like this soap opera—his voice filled with an emotion that was at odds with the simple meaning.

On the screen, another man and a woman spoke to each other inconclusively, and the program was over. It occurred to him that he was caught in the daily episodes of a soap opera that Joss wrote, that Joss and Bonnie One wrote. As in the soap opera he'd just seen, there was an underlying situation that everybody talked about without getting anywhere, without clarifying or resolving anything, without doing anything to move out of their semi-erotic miasma.

He had time for another beer, but he couldn't get the bartender's attention. There were more people now. The downtown offices must have let out. At last the bartender came over. She leaned her face so close to his it startled him. He drew back a little. Then he thought that it wasn't impossible that she was flirting, and he leaned forward again. She said softly, "You don't get it, do you?" He barely had time to look puzzled before she added, "You just wandered in, right?"

"Yeah," he said. "Just passing time till my appointment."

The bartender said, "Is it far?"

"No."

"If you left now, you'd be early?"

Mike looked at his watch. "A little."

"Okay. You know what Lord Nelson said? He said he owed all his success in life to arriving fifteen minutes early."

Mike sat up straight on his bar stool. He wondered if she thought he was drunk. He looked sideways the length of the bar. A row of women looked back at him. He turned and looked at the tables. All women. He looked back at the bartender. She said, "Your beer is on the house, okay?"

Mike said, "Thank you," but in his confusion took out his wallet. He'd heard of gay bars, but in New York or California. He'd never heard of this place, right here in Charlottesville. He put his wallet back, gathered up his bag and briefcase, and stood up. He kept his eyes on the bartender.

She tilted her head and pouted her lower lip as if she were going to say, "Poor baby."

Mike said "Good afternoon" to her. He nodded and said "Good afternoon" to all the faces which turned his way.

◇

Of course I feel sorry for him.

But of course I can't help laughing. One of his basic maxims about how to get along in the world was, Keep your eyes open, know where you are. We used to sail out of Grandma's creek, and about a mile into the big water when the shore began to flatten out and blur behind us, Dad would turn the boat and ask us, "So where's *our* creek?" Summer after summer it caught us by surprise, and Nora and I would go into an involuntary comic routine, pointing at wildly different spots. Always good for a laugh, this babes-at-sea routine.

I also have the suspicion that Dad, on some level, knew where he was. I mean in the bar, not in the bay.

There's one strand of feminist thought that maintains that language is male—phallic, patriarchal. I don't buy it. In most of the couples I know, the woman is the language master, the language juggler and comedian. Mom was certainly the lyricist, the stylist, the language dancer.

Dad had to have a plan before he spoke his words. He was good at the *architecture* of argument. I wonder if that's why guys are generally better playwrights. A play cranks along and cranks along, and all that teeing the ball up is just so that in the last act one of the characters can whack it a country mile. Three acts and one big payoff. Coherent, constructed, unitary, and simple. In like manner, I suspect, Dad wanted his day in Charlottesville to be a one-mood unit. Once he'd put himself in a position to have Dr. Ames blow him away, he went in for a whole day of being at a loss. He *could* have got Ganny to understand him. He could have appealed to her more openly instead of arguing his one prepared point about that pathetic crazy map.

And going to the gym and getting Ezra to show him how to throw a left hook was bound to make him feel like a klutz. So I wouldn't be surprised if his notion of coherent drama, his notion of constructing the rest of his day to make as much sense as a legal brief, was what led him into the only lesbian bar in the whole town.

Probably his big idea was: dig the hole deeper.

Even Jung says that women want to feel complete, whereas men tend to seek perfection outside themselves. That's what screws things up. To make something perfect outside yourself you have to go all the way, get rid of the ambiguities, the opposing forces. Dig the Panama Canal. Plow the field so there's not a weed left. You have to get it done. If you have motion, if you have thrust, you're going somewhere and you're the skipper. Even if it hurts.

So Dad built a what-a-rotten-day-this-is boat. He hoisted all sails. Damn the torpedoes, full speed ahead.

What he *wasn't* doing was considering Mom as a mystery, considering himself as a mystery. That would have required stillness. Not going anywhere, not doing anything.

It's not that Dad couldn't stand pain. He could stand lots of pain, so long as he was moving. That's what all that bicycling, swimming, weightlifting, digging the garden, driving to Charlottesville, reading a whole book of Kipling stories was—locomotion.

Of course he was in shock. Wacko with shock. That's why the course he was steering was so erratic.

What I don't know is if he was able to see any of this day as funny. Not so as he'd actually laugh, but just every once in a while feel a little comic bubble. I hope so. A sense of the sweet incongruity of himself as a big-suit lawyer with a jockstrap and Kipling in his briefcase watching a soap opera in a lesbian bar.

How do *you* spell relief, Dad?

◇

Joss and Bonnie One were lying on the floor of Bonnie's apartment. Each was propped on one elbow. They were eating Chinese food out of cartons. Bonnie was using chopsticks. Joss, who was holding up her head with her right hand, was eating with the fingers of her left hand. From time to time Bonnie fed her a morsel from the tip of her chopsticks. Also from time to time Bonnie licked Joss' fingers clean.

Joss was intensely happy.

Everything was better. She felt slightly guilty that she hadn't called her mother to tell her where she was or when she'd be back. She recited to herself, "'Ladybug, ladybug, fly away home. Your house is on fire and your children will burn. . . .'" She felt a quick pang of missing Edith and Nora, an impulse to jump in the car and fly away home. She'd drunk one glass of wine and felt a little bit bad about that and now was drinking grape juice and soda water and a squeeze of lemon, the very drink that she and Mike used to drink when she was pregnant with Edith on the houseboat and Mike had been nice. An even tinier catch of guilt by reason of nostalgia.

But every single one of these guilt tokens was weightless as a soap bubble. She could let them land on the surface of her skin and dissolve. Her skin was ready for anything. It was relaxed and taut, cool and warm; it was a million miles from her, it was clinging to her like alert silk.

The day before, she and Bonnie One had made love in Bonnie's office while Joss was still frantic with not finding her, with finding her with the moon-faced rock-climbing girl, with finding her by herself at last.

And then they'd made love again, soothingly and sweetly, on Bonnie's double bed, here in the apartment, in front of the chugging air conditioner. Later that night Joss had woken up each time the air conditioner had changed tune, and each time she'd felt a rush of comfort through her whole body as she curled herself against Bonnie, sometimes waking her so that they turned this way and that together, sometimes only waking herself to put her mouth and nose close to Bonnie's downy neck.

And then breakfast, with their bare feet touching. And then a slow walk around the lawn, through the gardens of the East Range, arm in arm but not kissing until they were back in Bonnie One's apartment. And suddenly it was evening again. And then they ordered Chinese food and made love with their clothes on, so that they were just finishing when the delivery boy rang the doorbell. Bonnie One had opened the door, smoothing her skirt down behind her with one hand, and the college boy, with their bag of Szechuan food tucked in his arm like a football, had opened his eyes wide at pretty Bonnie in her sleeveless shirtwaist, her throat and arms flushed. The boy almost fumbled the bag as he tried to hand it to her and take the money at the same time. Bonnie stood on one narrow bare foot, balancing herself with the toes of the other foot, swiveling her hips to take the bag and swiveling the other way to hand him the money. And a few more swivels, just a little swaying in the doorway to keep her balance as she held out a dollar tip. Every delivery boy's dream—every South Sea sailor's dream, her skirt tight at the hips but swinging loosely across her thighs, her long waist, and narrow rib cage like the upward sweep of a palm.

Joss had said, "You certainly had his tongue hanging out with your little hula there."

Bonnie had laughed, and then she'd sung prettily in a high dainty voice, "'Ain't gonna give him none of my jelly roll. . . .'"

Joss had laughed too, but in the middle of her brain she was a jiggle of quicksilver jealousy and desire.

Then Bonnie One had begun to feed her, and it was then that Joss started floating in her perfect skin.

Later that night she woke up completely and anxiously.

She no longer felt relieved that Mike knew. The secret had been an island. She and Bonnie One had been out of the way on their undiscovered island. Now it was even clearer to her that she was setting out, that she was already out of sight of land. She'd thought she was like Columbus, but she was less than Columbus. He'd had *some* idea. She was like one of those other explorers Mike talked about with admiration because they kept on going without a map, without a clue, no idea at all how big it all was. Somewhere halfway across an ocean or halfway down the Mississippi it dawned on them that they didn't know what the fuck they were doing. It wasn't being chased by pirates or caught in a storm. It wasn't the *forces.* It was big fat nothingness. It was looking with your eyes and seeing nothing. It was looking at your maps and books and realizing they had nothing to do with what you'd entered. It was imagining and imagining and not being able to imagine anything. In the face of nothingness, everything you knew would begin to shrink and fade. The boat, the people. How you began. How you began would become as unimaginable as the unimaginable end.

Joss found the bathroom in the dark and sat on the toilet seat.

Was that right?

Was she already at sea, about to go off the map? About to leave everything she knew? The safe shore of fathers and mothers, of fathers and daughters, of husbands and wives.

Mike hadn't got mad yet. Not fully and steadily. Not with full lawyer power and craft. Would he make her give up Edith and Nora?

Her mother would stop him. Could stop him. Or Ganny. Or Edmond and Evelyn.

But that was what she feared—that was the dimension of new nothingness that she now sensed—that she was leaving them, that she was leaving them farther and farther behind.

Was she brave? How could she tell? Mike had admired her nerve, her flair, even some of her blowups. But her bravery?

Scan the record quick. Daddy! Mummy! *Somebody* tell me.

She turned on the light and stood up. She was naked but didn't feel her skin at all now. It was inside her that all this turmoil spread and threatened to become a blank sea. She held on to the towel rack hard. She couldn't count on much—it wasn't even fair to count on Mike to be fair. She pursed her lips and thought she'd seen that clearly; she was being fair and brave about that at least.

And wait a second. Wait just a second there. Her inner turmoil, her panic—she'd been doing that for years! Even hyperventilating wasn't new. And Mike being a stone-faced lawyer—she'd been dealing with that for years too.

She felt better, or at least harder. Maybe being brave was just a matter of waiting for your mood to change. She could do *that*. She'd just done it. She could do that better than Mike, better than Bonnie One, better than anybody she knew.

◇

Mike was tired when he climbed the back stairs to Bonnie Two's office. He paused on the landing. It was where her boyfriend had shoved his feet between the banister posts. The whole town was becoming a map of spots where he'd made a fool of himself, been made a fool of. He could put a map on the wall and stick in little flagged pins—his campaign in central Virginia. He said to himself, "There are worse things." Plain everyday phrase. And another: "You'll get over it."

When he got to Bonnie Two's door he heard her singing. It was a country-and-western number. She had a surprisingly strong husky voice with a few yodeling breaks: "Oh I was dumb enough to fall for it / But I'm tough enough to take it. / You might just . . ." Then she stopped and said, "Shit. You might just *what*."

Mike knocked. Bonnie Two said, "Come on in. It ain't locked."

She was sitting on a stool hunched over a guitar. There was an open notebook and a pencil on the table in front of her. She said, "You might just da-di-dum-dee, just 'cause you're a man. I don't know. I give up."

She looked the same as always, but her voice was stuck in her country-and-western persona. Mike thought, Ganny with her head in her client problems, Ezra with his head in his pre-fight nerves, so why not Bonnie Two with her head in . . . what? A singing career?

She said, "So hey there. How're you? You want some iced tea?"

"Sure, thanks."

"Good, 'cause I need a little break about now, so if it's okay with you we'll just visit for a spell?"

"Sure."

"Then we can do a good hour working on yourself? Unless you're in a rush?"

"No. That's fine." Mike was fascinated by her voice in transition from down-home gritty to professionally soothing and tentative. He liked the down-home voice. He wondered if it was how she'd grown up talking, or if she was working at it. He said, "I like that line 'Dumb enough to fall for it, but tough enough to take it.'"

"Yeah. Well. That's where I'm stuck."

"Why talk about *him*? Why not go on with the *I*? Instead of 'You might just da-di-dum-dee,' go on with 'Just 'cause I ain't crying, don't mean I think you're true.' Or something like that. 'Don't mean I don't feel blue.'"

Bonnie Two laughed.

Mike said, "Well, okay, it's lame. I was just . . ."

"Oh no," Bonnie Two said. "What you made up is real good. I'm laughing 'cause you got right into it. Even wearing your nice summer suit and all." She got up, propped her guitar in the corner, brought back two glasses of iced tea, and perched back on her stool. She said, "I like those little rhymes of yours, but I'm going to have to fiddle around some more by myself. I'm after something kind of exact? It's supposed to be about a particular person. This man I knew. I might as well just blurt it right out. This married man I was having an affair with. And I knew from the get-go how it would end, but I just sort of shut my eyes and stopped my ears. I knew I was being dumb, so I didn't complain at all. I wouldn't hear from him for a whole week and he'd leave a message that he was coming to see me at some outrageous hour—I mean it could be ten in the morning or ten at night—and I'd just be there, ready and willing. It was like that was part of the mood of the affair? But it got to be part of the excitement for me, that I was just going to be this complete concubine. And what was odd was that by going at it like that I actually was in a stronger position than he was. That's the part about being tough enough to take it. Actually it was *beyond* being tough enough to take it. He was the one who'd lost track of how he felt about it, and I knew exactly what I was doing. I knew that one day I'd get a message that he was coming by and I'd just decide, nope, this act is over. Knowing that any day I could just not be there—that gave me the power to focus my fantasies in this real definite way? Like he'd be coming over and I could imagine that this was his last time. I could fantasize that he suddenly had to move to California, or that he was about to discover he had some medical condition, or—what was closer to the truth but still a fantasy—that I really had decided this really *was* the last time. And that gave me this surge of pity that was like this real powerful erotic stimulus?"

Mike said, "Uh-huh."

"It was helpful to me, because I'd kind of been trapped in this attitude that erotic encounters are only good at the beginning? Like that thing that Joss says—'Eros wanes'? But being with that particular man was different, it was the end that was good, and it went on for longer than most beginnings. That was because I was paying attention to my needs. Before then I used to be this complete extrovert—you know, the way Jung talks about it—where what's important to you depends on what's important to the other person? So you're just holding on to the other person?"

"Uh-huh."

"That doesn't mean I became a complete introvert. Like where you're just inward-looking, where all the urgency is inside *you*. I just needed to get a better balance is all. So I've been trying to figure out how to have that balance on purpose. But without being, you know, calculating? Without losing that kind of free fall? Where your mind is blacking out but everything else is real alert? When you're real aware of the other person but you don't have to suppress yourself one bit. You're incorporating the other person's space without taking it over in an aggressive way?"

"This fainting and awareness—are you talking about all the time, or are you talking about when you're, uh, embracing?"

"Uh-huh, that's good you asked that. All the time would be too much. But not just when you're actually making love either. Just some of the time, like you could be driving along in a car, just doing nothing but feel that feeling . . . I used to be real susceptible to someone else. I used to feel a stirring, and I'd think I had to turn myself over to it right away or it wouldn't be real? So I had to work on not being that susceptible. On being able to just feel my feeling for a while without having someone else validate it? Randy—that man you met? Here on the stairs? He wasn't a good experience for me in that regard. He didn't want me to have any of that introvert power. He liked it when I was extrovert, but extrovert just to him. He was jealous if I was having a good time just talking to somebody else. But he didn't want me to withdraw and be all alone. It's like he was jealous of me being with myself. Come to think of it, he was even jealous of me being with him."

Mike laughed.

Bonnie Two looked at him warily. Then she sighed and said, "Well, yeah. Okay. I should see when stuff is funny. I should do that a little more. I guess you're laughing because I'm not."

"No," Mike said. "That's not it at all. I saw this scene as a cartoon—the guy puts his hand on the woman's cheek, and she sighs with pleasure, and he jumps back staring at his hand as if it's someone else. . . . Maybe it's not as funny as I thought."

Bonnie Two said, "Uh-huh."

Mike said, "I bet I know the reason why you don't laugh at a lot of things. It's because you're so sympathetic. You have this power to sympathize. It's hard to laugh at a situation when you're sympathizing." Mike wasn't sure if this was bullshit. What the hell—some of it wasn't. He said, "It's a gift. To have such a vivid sense of other people."

Bonnie Two was hunched forward over her knees, her arms folded around them. Somewhere under her billowy skirt, her heels were on a rung of her stool. Mike was afraid she was going to put her feet down, look up, and say dryly, "Nice try, buster."

He thought of Bonnie Two as the last person in his day. Dr. Ames, Ganny, Ezra—and might as well throw in the bartender at the lesbian bar. He saw himself in an hour back at the house heating up a can of Campbell's Soup-for-One. He didn't even have a dog anymore.

He felt himself caught exactly between two impulses: a delicious self-pity that licensed him to be comforted, and a laughable view of himself as a lab rat frantically pushing levers to get a food pellet.

He said, "Of course maybe that's what you were getting at when you said, 'Extrovert—susceptible to another person.' I can imagine your sympathy being overwhelming sometimes. Maybe that's why you have a gift for music too."

Bonnie Two looked up. Her mouth opened. It was a little bit awry, as if she was about to say, "Oh brother!"

She closed her mouth, smiled, and looked away. She put her hand on her cheek. She said, "That's good, your saying that." She took her glasses off and squinted at them nearsightedly as she used a fold of her skirt to wipe them. "I mean it's making me feel real good."

The sun was now low enough so that it flooded the windows behind her. When Bonnie Two stood up from her stool the edges of her white skirt and loose sleeves and stray hair blurred in this backlighting. She held her skirt out to the sides and let it fall back. She looked like a luna moth fluttering against a windowpane.

She took a step. At first he wasn't certain where she was going—she turned toward the door, then back the other way, then a step closer to him so that her skirt brushed against the back of his hand. No uncertainty now. He'd called in this luna moth as surely as Edmond had called in the screech owl.

He leaned forward in his chair so that the next wing beat of her skirt brushed his cheek.

◇

I don't blame him. That is, I don't blame him for being desperate. But I'm going to avert my eyes. I suddenly find it hard to consider sex. Even in this lyrical, metaphorical way, just a couple of moths beating their wings. You may think, Hey—she's already sat through a few scenes of varied parental sexual activity, so what's the big deal?

I *could* say that this isn't love. No matter how prettily the light is shining, backlighting the luna moth. I'm not saying that being in love is a standard I would hold everyone to. I can't say that. But at least Mom and Bonnie One are in love.

I also find it easier to allow Mom to make mistakes. Her integrity never depended on her not making mistakes.

And Mom's crazy explosions, including Bonnie One, had some relation to Dad. What Dad is about to do is separate himself. He *thought* he was going over the hills and far away when he drew his map of going crazy (and isn't that just like him, to draw a map!), but this Bonnie Two frolic is where he really took off as an emotional vagabond.

When I was babysitting Tyler's babies I found a notebook of Tyler's poems and stories. I read it. It wasn't his *diary*, for God's sakes. There was a piece about his father taking him to a cathouse. I remember being shocked. I'd read a Maupassant story about a farmer's son, after his father's death, inheriting his father's mistress. That was chilling enough. But the Maupassant characters were presented as cold hard Norman peasants with more habits than sensibility (milk the cows, bury the father, feed the plow horse), so in a way the point of the story was that this was the nearest thing to expressing feelings that the son could do. Tyler's poem was the reverse. It was about his being a sixteen-year-old who worried he was strange and hoped he was brilliant but who thought at least he was living in a cozy settled household, when all of a sudden his father dragged him into this *truly* strange rite of passage as if it was just another part of a today-you-are-a-man celebration. Tyler's father took him to his office; then to his hat store, where he bought him a new Stetson; then to his men's club, where he bought him one shot of whiskey; then to his "social club." His father told him to hang his new hat on the peg labeled "Nancy" and then to go sit in the side parlor and Nancy would be along. Tyler wrote that at every stop he felt younger and more helpless. Office—fifteen. Hat store—fourteen. Men's club—thirteen. Whorehouse—twelve, eleven, ten . . . And then, when Nancy showed up and said, "You must be the birthday boy," his real self condensed into a little boy way down inside him, and his present self became counterfeit. Counterfeit—but spendable. A passable twenty. And Nancy was a good counterfeit too—she acted like a date. She said, "Let's just set here and visit a little." She asked him what sports he played, exclaimed at the calluses on his palm. She said, "Would you like to see my photo album? It's just upstairs in my room." And there she hung up his jacket and loosened his tie. She laughed at his jokes. She said she had a little crick in her neck and asked him to rub it. She sat on a low settee in front of a fireplace with an electric fire. Tyler stood behind her and massaged the back of her neck. She said, "Oh me oh my, that feels good." She opened some more buttons of her silk blouse and moved one of his hands onto her collarbone and said, "Oh my, that is even nicer."

Tyler wrote that he was reconciled to this simulation—in fact that he was well on his way to a willing suspension of disbelief. She was coaxing his hand with hers, inch by inch. She said, "That is so perfect, what you're doing. I feel like a cat by the fire. How're you feeling?"

Tyler felt a bubble of unease float up through him and then inexplicably pop out of his mouth. He said, "Well, I'm still as nervous as a whore in church."

He froze. He saw her turn. He saw her face. But in his paralyzed embarrassment he was sure that his father was about to burst through the door, grab him by the collar, and march him out in front of everyone. . . .

He said to her, "I didn't mean . . . It's just—"

She said, "Well, we ain't in church, sonny boy."

"Oh Lord," he said. "It wasn't what I meant to—"

She laughed. Not a counterfeit laugh. It riveted him. It wasn't angry or even bitter. It was resigned. Impersonally resigned. To what? A line of boys like him? Was she a specialist in boys? And only then it occurred to him that she might have done all this with his father. That she *very likely* had done all this with his father.

She stepped around the settee and stood close to him. He smelled face powder and breath mint. He said, "I'm sorry—it's just a thing Daddy says, and . . ."

She laughed again. She said, "Don't you fret about it," and set about the next part of the business at a brisker pace. For a minute it felt like being undressed for bed. She said, "Now, you're just going to love this," and slid to her knees.

He thought his head would burst. He was afraid his brain was being damaged. He held on to her head to keep from falling over. She stopped, stood up, and said, "Follow me," and he turned into a puppy scrabbling toward his food dish, awkward on the kitchen tiles. Tyler didn't dare look at himself, although there were lots of mirrors.

Then his skin became uncomfortably taut, prickly with woolly pleasures—pleasures he'd previously imagined as silky. Then he began to dissolve inside. He was split between pleasure and fear. The fear was that he was becoming insubstantial, that some of his inner self was being pulled out of him on a thread of pleasure.

Afterward he got a headache. He tried not to show it, he tried to beam appreciation and satisfaction. She said, "Now, don't you go doing this with your little girlfriends, except you wear a safe."

He thought his headache came from wanting but not daring to ask her if his father had been in this room, in this bed.

And ever since that headache—which he writes is a memory that always comes with any other memory of that day—he thought of his childhood as precarious, as a light-and-dark of fact and fiction.

I think he should have stopped there. His writing meandered on for a bit, but his heart wasn't in it. He wrote that he should have gone back to see Nancy and talked to her as a person, blah blah blah. His impulse to tell the story was childish, hurt, and lyrical, and that was coherent and pure. He should have stuck with that.

I say that now. When I was reading it—one ear listening to the crackle of the open baby-monitor, the other listening for Tyler and his wife's car—I was knocked over by every bit of it. For one thing it was a sex story, even if he tried to make it harrowing. It wasn't *Fanny Hill* (which I'd discovered on Tyler's bookshelf the month before), but still . . . And there was the queer satisfaction of seeing a sixteen-year-old boy—one of the very creatures making my life miserable at that time—taken down a peg in a sexual encounter. But of course there was fellow feeling too. Poor little Tyler face to face—in fact, body to body—with his father's stray sex life.

Last of all, and most lasting, there was a sinking feeling. If Tyler, one of the communal grown-ups, couldn't come up with anything better than lingering disequilibrium and anxiety, then I was going to be serving a longer sentence than I thought. I'd been hoping that I'd go to college, get smarter, and hike up out of the swamps and mists. But there was Tyler still floundering in the quicksand of his adolescence.

It wasn't until recently that it occurred to me that Tyler might have written it *long* before I read it. Maybe in college. Maybe in high school. The bit about wishing he'd gone back to talk to Nancy as a fellow human being has a high-school-senior solve-the-problems-of-the-world piety to it.

So. So, now that I've ranked on Tyler some, I'm calmer.

And I see what I'm doing. I'm bringing up old Guy de Maupassant and young Tyler to sidestep Dad and his luna-moth invasion. The same way Mom makes jokes to keep things at a distance, I'm making literary references, alluding to other fathers and their sex lives, and their children's view of them. Recollected in tranquillity?

Before I have another thought, I'm going to phone Nora.

Nora said, "Oh, *that*. Dad and Bonnie Two. I knew about that."

I called her at work and caught her between takes in her dressing room. I'd forgotten that when she's at the studio she's surrounded by cool professional attitudes. So I was annoyed. Then she was annoyed that I was annoyed. She said, "But look at what he's about to do next. It was sometime around then that he pulled himself together."

She knows I can't stand what comes next, what she presumes to call pulling himself together. No surprise about that, no secret, nothing private. Nora even has a scrapbook of press clippings. But Nora must know how I felt, how I still feel.

She said, "Got his act together and took it on the road."

I bit my tongue. But it came out anyway. I said, "And you became his wind-up Shirley Temple doll. You got to be such a perfect little trouper, you got to be the favorite daughter." I felt eleven years old. I said, "It wasn't getting his act together—it was just *another* crazy thing. And he probably did it because it was an old nightmare of Mom's and he knew it would've driven her bat-shit if she'd still been around. So you *chose* it. You *decided* to like it. Maybe you went along with him to get back at Mom. But it tortured *me*. *You* tortured me. You *knew* you were torturing me."

Nora waited. She didn't say a thing. Just like a psychiatrist. Her silence was driving me as around the bend as if she'd said something exasperating, like, "You should have rejoiced in your sister's good fortune." Or sighed and said, "Here we go again." She kept on saying nothing.

I finally said, "You have to say something—I'm paying for this call."

She laughed, but not meanly. She said, "If I say I'll call you right back, you'll say I'm throwing my money in your face."

She was right—not entirely right but right enough. I sometimes do get prickly about how much money she makes. When she complains about her director or producer I sometimes point out that they're no worse than my principal and Nora's making a zillion dollars for her trouble. When she was still writing scripts, I used to help her and then refuse to take the money she offered. That year she was making between five and ten thousand a month. I don't know what she's making now. I don't want to know. But I said, "You're rolling in dough, are you?"

"That's right," Nora said. "I just don't know what to do with it. Okay? Is that what you're waiting for?"

"All right, all right, all right," I said.

"Okay," Nora said. "Now, where were we? Oh yeah. Dad and Bonnie Two. How did I know? I don't know for sure, but when we were on the road, Dad and I slept in his campaign van. A couple of times Bonnie Two had singing gigs at the music tent at the same county fairs we went to. Usually he and I would turn in at the same time, but those times when Bonnie Two was around he'd tuck me in and come back late. She'd do regular performances at the music tent at night, but she also played and sang as part of the warm-up for Dad's speeches. She'd written this country-and-western campaign song, and she got me to learn it and sing it with her. Then she'd say, 'This here is Mike Reardon's daughter Nora. Ain't she somethin'?' That sort of corn. Cheese grits is more like it. She fixed it up one time so I clogged with the Buck Mountain Cloggers. That's that snapshot you hated—the one of me in my tap shoes and ankle socks and that short skirt with that crinoline puffing it out. And you're right—it was my start in show biz. Singing and dancing and saying my lines. Bonnie Two or some emcee would say, 'Say a few words to the folks, darlin',' and I'd beam and say, 'Hi! I cain't jes' come right out an' ask y'all to vote for my daddy, but I sure hope y'all stay around for his speech. It's real good!'" Nora laughed and said, "I know, I know. It was cotton candy. But I wasn't doing it to get ahead of you. I was just staying afloat. When I thought of you, it was to wish you'd have come along too. But I guess I knew you would've hated it. I got to like it. Here's a difference between you and me. I don't think you have to believe *all* of it to live it."

I said, "What's the 'it' here?"

"Whatever you're doing. Whatever gang you're living with. I'm not saying I close my eyes to what's bad or who's a creep or that I don't have an eye out for something better. Right now I'd love to move along and get some decent parts—a part in some really good film script or play. I know what's lousy and dumb about this series, but if I *despised* it, I wouldn't get any better. And I *am* getting better. Every time there's a passably good scene, I *do* it."

I said, "Uh-huh," in a fairly positive way. Somehow Nora had maneuvered my resentment about her running off to join Dad's political circus into my despising her present acting career. I didn't want to talk about that. There are days when I'll use my afternoon free period to watch her in her soap. Just to see her and hear her. But sometimes it saddens me to see the very thing she justifies herself with—a scene where she's really worked up and using a real part of herself. It saddens me and terrifies me. I've thought of reasons for this sadness and terror. My Nora throwing herself away. Not just that. I have to admit it's terror, not just an aesthetic judgment. It's terror that a single person is being watched by a crowd. All those faces looking at her, reaching for her with their attention, with their hunger. I remember Dad in front of crowds. It fills me with such terror that I say to myself, "It's just a bad dream."

It works for Alice in Wonderland. When she's in trouble near the end, she says, "You're nothing but a pack of cards," and she's right, the wicked Queen is blown away, Alice wakes up, she's on an English lawn, the tea tray is beside her.

But maybe Alice safely sleeping isn't true. Little Alice in her pretty pinafore with her limbs asprawl was just lucky that dodgy old Lewis Carroll was only watching, that being Victorian and British kept him reverential and maiden, kept him adoring Alice as the perfected bud of English civilization. Lucky Alice.

I tuned back in to Nora. She was talking about moving to L.A. She'd be near me. We could share a house. All she needed was to goose her agent into getting her a couple of parts.

"I don't live in L.A.," I said. "I'm more than an hour north."

"We could get a house halfway between. On top of a hill, we could see the ocean. We could grow figs and grapes. If I get two—no—just one good offer, I'll tell my producer to kill me off. Not a lingering disease—the last actress to leave us took three weeks to go. I think I'd like to go out in a blaze of glory—maybe saving a child—saving a child from a wild animal. No, animals are too expensive. A crazed killer. I shield this precious little body with my own and die in a hail of bullets. Then I pack my bags, you line up a real-estate agent—"

"You're always talking about this," I said. "But really—"

"Well, don't disdain it."

I said, "I'm not disdaining it."

"I talk about moving out there because I dream about it, and not just because of work. I dream about it because I miss you and I'd love to live with you. And you always bring up some tiny little practical obstacle, as though I'm hopelessly incompetent and couldn't manage to catch a crosstown bus, when in fact I've gone to four different continents in the last two years—"

I said, "Four?" I shouldn't have.

"Yes, four. We filmed in Switzerland, that's one, and *here,* that's two. And we did the part where I track down the man who swindled me on the oil deal, and that was in Morocco, which is Africa. And then we went to northern Canada—"

"That's still North America."

"We went north of the Arctic Circle and that's the North Pole."

"The North Pole isn't a continent."

"The South Pole is, so why not the North Pole? God, you sound just like Dad at his most boring."

"Okay, it was far away."

"I went to Aruba, and that's the same as South America."

"Okay, you travel a lot. That's not quitting your job and moving."

"I know what moving is. And you're pissing me off. I'm saying that we get stuck in our arrangements by accident and I'm saying I miss you and I'm trying to talk about doing something that would overcome the accidents and would take a lot of psychic energy and you're saying that you live north of L.A. and the North Pole isn't a continent and generally pushing me away. You want to know what your problem is?"

I said, "Not really," sounding as dully sullen as one of my students.

"Your problem is you anesthetize everything. You take out a needle and stick it in and squirt novocaine so you can poke around without feeling. . . . So here's what I want right now. I'm going to say, 'Hey, I'm thinking of moving to California,' and you're going to say, 'I hope so,' and I'm going to say, 'Maybe we could live together.' And then you'll say, 'That would be wonderful.'"

I couldn't say anything.

Nora laughed and said, "I don't care if you're lying. I just want you to gush. Gush affectionately. Here we go—just one take, because I've got a scene coming up."

I said, "Yes." For an instant I wanted to give Nora everything she wanted. I felt a present love that poured into me, that swept away all my wrangling. I said, "Yes." I said, "I hope you move here. It would be wonderful."

"There," Nora said. "Now, that didn't hurt. I've got to go, kiddo. They're calling me. I miss you."

I said, "Bye."

But the truth is, it does hurt. Nora may live in a world of make-believe where the language is darling-fabulous-fantastic-I-love-your-work, but she really pushed me and then pulled me out of being curled up against the cold, and my blood was zinging through me, stinging my frostbitten sense of things.

◇

Mike came out of a doze into a panic.

A cloudbank of cumulative panics. He'd been nuzzling into the back of Bonnie Two's frail neck, confusing her with someone else from long, long ago. Where was he? Who was he with? Was this dawn or twilight?

Okay—it was evening—that was the west that was still glowing. He was lying next to Bonnie Two. That produced the next pang. He was still wearing his shirt and tie, but that was all. Nope—socks too. He'd been hasty. And much too quick.

Bonnie Two had yodeled. Very loudly. First she'd sung out with a mezzo-soprano *oh,* then cracked her voice into a batlike *ee.* Mike had wondered if anyone from Broome and Havermeyer had been at their desks on the floor below.

RE: "too quick." Bonnie Two had been too sweetly reassuring. First she'd let out an interrogatory sigh—a rising tone like the endings of her declarative sentences. He'd said, "Gosh. Sorry."

"That's all right," she'd said. "Sometimes just holding each other is real nice."

Mike shied away from that mental replay only to bump into a lawyer-like idea: she was his client. And, more relevant to this appointment, he was *her* client.

In addition she—she and he—had violated the no-unusual-noise provision of the lease agreement he'd renegotiated with her landlord, the aforementioned Broome and Havermeyer.

On the other hand, his flesh and bones felt good. Hadn't felt so good for ages. He sank back down beside Bonnie Two. She was still wearing her gauzy white dress, the full loose skirt now drawn up and bunched between her arms as she lay curled on her side. They were on a pink comforter—Mike couldn't remember where that had come from. And he still couldn't remember who she smelled like, where or when he'd smelled that back-of-the-neck. Sometime when he was much younger and had no weight to his life.

He dozed off.

When he woke up again, Bonnie Two was on the telephone. She covered the mouthpiece and said to him, "Good, you're awake. I'm just starving. I'm ordering some Chinese food—they're faster than that old pizza parlor."

He thought he should make some telephone calls too. Mrs. Rogers—had he said anything about taking her Jeep? Ganny—wasn't he supposed to call Ganny about something? Edith and Nora—would they be worried? How strange had he been when he left? Had Joss got back there?

Bonnie Two said into the phone, "No MSG, all right? Yes, that's right, the very top door. Thank you."

She turned off the desk lamp. She was a blur of white in the dusk again. She knelt at the bottom of the comforter, sat back on her heels, and lifted his foot across her lap. It reminded him of her boyfriend picking up his foot and sticking it through the banister posts. He raised his head to say something. She said, "Hush," slid her fingers into the top of his sock, and inched it off. Then the other foot. Then the top button of his shirt.

He raised his head again to say he didn't think it would work just yet. Bonnie Two said, "Hush," and undid his tie. She laid it across his eyes. She undid two more buttons and pulled his shirt off his shoulders down to his elbows. She blew a puff of breath on his forehead. Then on his throat, then on his solar plexus. "You just hush," she said, "I'm energizing your chakras."

He heard her move. He brushed the necktie off his eyes. She was standing, lifting the loose skirt of her dress over her head. She looked small, pale, and indistinct. She let the dress fall on him. She lay down beside him and unbuttoned his shirt cuff. She said "Hush" once more and rolled against him, tucking his hand between her legs.

He felt the distances in his body disappear—between his mouth and his feet, between his hips and his chest.

He tugged his arms out of his shirt. Then Bonnie Two and he were batting away the dress between them, caught in weightless fumbling until his fingertips found her hips, her tiny iliac crests, her skin stretched thin. Even her kneecaps were small. His hands were now in some other dimension. They were in a diminutive zone of magnified time and fingertips. She was moving slightly—every breath she took only moved her the width of a fingertip.

Suddenly she sat up. She put her hands on his temples and guided his head onto her stomach. Then she touched the top of his head with her fingers, and immediately his head felt enormous. When she moved her legs, they too seemed larger. The pink comforter seemed to grow—the whole room expanded. Her voice came through a dark window. Her leg slid past his shoulder—she seemed to be growing by unhinging herself.

It was disconcerting to be shifted into this giant zone.

And then back into the miniature zone, his head floating, then guided lightly down by her fingertips as if it were on a counterbalanced machine arm.

When Bonnie Two began to hum and click her tongue and yodel, he became plain again. No longer envisioning miniature or giant zones, but feeling himself any old guy on his elbows and knees.

For a while he alternated between this dull state and an occasional reversion to the ecstatic. The reversion depended in part on what sounds Bonnie Two made. He was still startled by the yodels. He worried that her clicks and clucks might be disapproving. But the humming was just right. He wondered if he could mention it to her later, how disconcerting . . . No—be positive, say how he liked the humming.

She yodeled louder and higher. She put her fingertips on his head again, found the hinges of his jaw, and scooped him up face to face.

He was happy to find he was responding, but he found he was simultaneously engaged in thinking about who they were. A man in middle age in the middle of a fly-apart life. A woman, younger but with a longer loneliness. A woman with almost no bargaining position in ordinary life, at the mercy of landlords, car mechanics, drunk boyfriends, dubious clients; a woman with marginal licensing, without the protection of guild or union or institutional employer; a woman who spent her workday dealing with frantic people with whom she had no relationship that lasted longer than their trouble, with whom she spoke a language that was artificial to her but which was her only proof, her only assertion of her professional authority . . . A woman, therefore, who'd been happy to be discovered, had perhaps *planned* to be discovered strumming her guitar, singing her own hard luck ("I was dumb enough to fall for it, but I'm tough enough to take it") to the only person in the vicinity who (A) had been helpful to her, (B) had been a covictim of her drunk boyfriend's last outrage, and (C) was in enough emotional upheaval to be in a state of disrepair equivalent to—and therefore compatible with—her own . . .

This analysis flitted through his brain, not explicitly articulated but rousing a few left-brain cells into wisps of language. At the same time (simultaneous to his clambering forward) there was a kaleidoscope of picture fragments. They arranged themselves in various orders. As chronology. As causality (her gratitude, pictured as her hand smoothing her lease for him to read). As grounds for suspicion (her briefcase turning into her guitar). Pity (pictured as the floppy legs of her terrible floral-print pants suit). And then some not-so-clear arrangements where picture fragments were added, subtracted, altered. There was even a Joss view of Bonnie Two: Joss twisting her hands (what are your hands saying?), then Joss twisting her mouth in disdain; a Joss movie cliché in which the male lead removes secretary's glasses, secretary's hair tumbles free, and he says, "Why, Miss Jones . . . you're beautiful!" Cut to Joss' mouth forming a circle about to utter ha-ha-ha; but then Joss' face looming close to Bonnie Two's, about to kiss her too.

Mike gave a half-grunt, half-snarl, to make that picture go away. Bonnie Two answered with a fluttery cry—What? Had he scared her? pleased her? Didn't matter. They were squeezing together into a miniature zone, a giant zone, a magnified miniature zone. He tried to kiss her, got a mouthful of wispy hair. Didn't matter.

She said, "Wait," and he raised himself on his arms. She said, "Oh dear," and turned her head. She said, "Just a second," and she slid away. He sank into the pink comforter, into its still-warm bunches and folds. He hugged the top width of it into a pillow for his cheek and stretched his legs out with a last shudder.

Bonnie said again, "Just a second," and Mike now heard a knocking at the door. She turned a light on and burrowed upward into her dress. Mike rolled himself up in the pink comforter. Bonnie Two opened the door, and the delivery boy took a step forward with the bag of Chinese food.

Bonnie Two looked around for some money. She threw her hands up. "I can't find a thing around here." She looked down at Mike's head, the part of him still sticking out of the pink comforter. She said, "Mike, you got any money, honey?"

Mike said, "In my pants pocket."

Bonnie gathered up his pants, turned the legs right side out and fished out some bills.

The delivery boy said to Bonnie Two, "Don't you sing down at Dürty Nellie's? Thursdays?"

Bonnie Two smiled a huge smile. She put her fingertips on her chest as if to say, "Li'l ol' me." But when her fingertips touched bare skin, she realized that her dress front was unbuttoned in a massive deep vee. She gathered the edges together and said, "That's right."

The delivery boy said, "I thought that was you—you've got a real nice voice."

Bonnie Two smiled again. She said, "Why, thank you."

Then she said, "Oops! . . . I just dropped a . . . I just dropped a dollar bill down my front." She turned her back on the delivery boy, held her dress away from her, and then shimmied and twisted until the bill fell to the floor between her feet. She scooped it up and smoothed it out. She said, "It's not a dollar at all—it's a twenty! I guess I'm worth more than I thought I was."

She blushed and laughed. She held out the twenty.

The delivery boy said, "That's twelve thirty-seven out of twenty."

Bonnie Two stage-whispered to Mike. "How much do you want to tip?"

Mike couldn't do the figures in his head. He felt a trickle of alarm. Was he going nuts again? Ten percent of twelve? Fifteen percent of twelve? He said, "A couple of bucks?"

Bonnie Two said, "I'll make it three. All those stairs."

The boy thanked her, tilted his head, and waved a half-salute at Mike, saying, "You all have a nice night."

Bonnie Two closed the door after him.

Mike stared at the ceiling. He was too hot all rolled up in the pink comforter, but he had a feeling he should lie very still for just a minute.

Bonnie Two arranged the little cartons of food on a tray. She got a basin of warm water from the bathroom. She unwrapped him and wiped his face with a warm washcloth. She rinsed the washcloth in the basin and washed his chest and arms. In between his fingers. She dipped it again and washed his loins and legs. In between his toes.

A wire-service news bulletin from way inside his head: Sounds like fun. Was that a plain everyday phrase? A Joss movie cliché? There was no wry tone to it. It was just from very far away.

Bonnie Two patted him dry. She pulled off her dress and washed herself with the washcloth. Mike had thought she didn't wear any makeup, but now that she scrubbed herself he saw her eyebrows were so fine and pale as to be almost invisible. There were no tan lines on her body either. Now that she was cool again, her shoulders, small breasts, slender rib cage, hips, and legs were all one color. It wasn't a bad effect—in fact it made her look like a perfectly pale statue of a nymph in an Italian garden.

She set the tray by his head. She picked up a slice of bamboo shoot with her chopsticks and brought it to his mouth. He ate it and then started to get up. Bonnie Two put her hand on his brow. "You just lay there, sweetheart, till you get your strength back."

His body felt languid and drained, but there was a core of crazed energy in his head, synapses going off like Chinese firecrackers. Not a thought in his head, just this crackling in the dark. Maybe it wasn't anything new, maybe not anything he had to think about, he was just burning up the stray matter of the day, burning off all the embarrassments and frazzles.

She fed him and then washed his mustache and beard again. She said, "I guess I'm being your geisha girl." She hummed for a bit and then sang, "I want to be your red-neck geisha . . . treat you right when you treat me wrong . . . miss you a heap when you are gone. . . . Come on, baby, don't make me chase ya. . . . I'm gonna be your country geisha . . . yo-di-odle, oh-di-odle, ay."

While she was singing, she took hold of his hair with one hand, his beard with the other. When he started laughing, she gave him a yank, but he couldn't stop. He got the hiccups.

She said, "It's just meant to be kind of cute, not all *that* funny." She slid the tray away and curled up with her back to him. She said again, "Not all *that* funny." He put his hand on her back. She said, "If you're sorry, you should say something nice."

"It's kind of cute."

"You better say something nicer than that. Even that old delivery boy said something nicer."

"Well, he would've said more if I hadn't been here. He liked your little dance too."

Bonnie Two said, "I don't know why you bring that up. Maybe you like it when I get embarrassed."

Mike said, "No." He put his hand on her back. He fitted his fingertips between her distinct vertebrae.

She said, "You can do that a little harder. I'm still a little tense." She stretched out on her stomach. "Sometimes I like being touched real light, and sometimes kind of rough, but what I don't like is being laughed at."

Mike said, "No."

"I don't mind a lot of things, but I do mind someone being mean."

Mike said, "Yes." He was putting some weight into his hands now, spreading his fingers all the way across her back. He felt as if he were in a foreign country. He was only able to command a few words of the language. He should become more attentive to her tone and gesture. He should use this time abroad as a useful discipline, an exercise in alertness to other customs.

He knelt astride the backs of her legs, his weight on his knees and feet. He breathed out.

"I can feel that," Bonnie Two said. "That's good—when you do that cleansing-breath thing?" She was speaking in her tentative voice again. Was this an aspect of a verb of wishing?

When he took another deep breath and blew it out, she also took a deep breath and blew it out. But she didn't say anything. Perhaps he had mistaken the custom of the country. Perhaps polite custom prevented her from specifying a wish until he offered several choices. It had been a great while since he'd traveled abroad.

He rearranged himself. He stroked one of her calves and then the other and breathed deeply. She breathed deeply. He heard a hum in her exhale. He rubbed her calf and the back of her knee, and cocked his ear. Hum, hum. He ran his hands all the way up her spine. A single hum, but trailing off. Perhaps it was a tonal language.

Had he gone loopy again? As wacko as when he drew a map of going crazy? Or was he just getting a little strange in a strange situation? Maybe he was just being funny. Joss would think it was funny. He wondered if he'd lost his sense of humor—he'd had a good sense of humor once, it must be rattling around in there someplace.

He woke up in a dazzle of light. His back was stiff, his eyesight blurred, but he was having a vision. He was certain that this sunlight, this particular pattern of sunlight on the wall, was a message that meant that he was going to be all right. Not now, not just yet, but soon enough. If he kept on doing small things on his own behalf, larger things would come right.

He washed at the bathroom sink, scooping water into his armpits. He scrubbed his teeth with the corner of a hand towel, combed his hair and beard with his fingers. He shook out his shirt and suit coat, restored the crease in his trousers by pressing them between two volumes of Jung's *Transformations and Symbols.* He found his appointment book and made a list of people he should call. After only a moment, he remembered where he'd parked Mrs. Rogers' Jeep.

Bonnie Two woke up. He offered to buy her breakfast. She pulled the pink comforter over her head and said she needed a little more sleep.

He got his briefcase, and went down the outside stairs on tiptoe—past the windows of Broome and Havermeyer, past the back of his own office. At the Roasted Bean he had papaya juice and a mug of coffee, read the *Daily Progress,* the *Richmond Times-Dispatch,* and the *Washington Post.* No problem reading, no problem reading numbers.

He went to his office. He was glad to see that Ganny looked alarmed when he came in. He said, "I'm feeling much, much better."

Ganny said, "Those guys from the Democratic Party just called again. The summer temp put them through to me. They've called your house, they've called your mother-in-law. Where have you *been*?"

" 'Going to and fro upon the earth and up and down in it.' "

Ganny rolled her eyes and said, "Oh brother." Then she looked alarmed again.

Mike said, "I can read your mind. You're thinking about how Bundy used to quote scripture."

"No. Well, maybe. Mainly I was thinking you should go back to your mother-in-law's house. Get some more vacation. Duck these guys. They want something real bad, and that ain't good."

The summer temp came in. She said, "Excuse me. You *are* Mr. Reardon, aren't you?" Before Mike finished nodding, while he was still getting up from his chair, she said, "Good. There are two gentlemen to see you. Shall I show them in?"

Ganny shook her head. Mike said, "Sure."

They came in. Everyone smiled, shook hands, said names. Ganny got up to go. Mike asked her to stay. She offered her chair to the taller man, the tall man offered it to the short man, the short man held up his hand—"No, no"—and found another chair, then offered it to the tall man, who said, "No, no, you . . . I'll just . . ." But there wasn't a fourth chair, just a two-cushion sofa too far off in the corner. The temp came in with a straight-backed chair, which both men leapt to take from her.

During this Gaston-Alphonse interval, Mike felt a distinct calm occur in him. This calm space was in the region of his mind generally occupied by elegiac thoughts about either his father or his father-in-law. This time it was his father, who, without speaking or even taking shape, conveyed a message: Let them play the notes—you give full measure to the rests. Mike recognized this bit of instruction as coming from his father's volumes of lore concerning public demeanor. Item: Cardinal Spellman, who was very short, never looked up when carrying on a conversation with a taller man, thus inducing the taller man to bend. Item: Never argue in public with a woman or a priest. Item: If someone is being charming, be still and give your full attention. If you try to be charming back, they will be less charmed than if you sit still and take them in.

His father had uttered a thousand observations of this nature, footnotes to his narrations of conversations, conferences, caucuses, small public occasions. In tone they were a mixture: two parts straight Lord Chesterfield advice-to-his-son, one part Puck—that is, two parts praising a dignified demeanor, one part mocking it. Other times they were unalloyed admiration. Item: President Kennedy was amazingly efficient when being briefed. Most people being briefed can't resist asking long questions to show how much they already know or how much they care. Kennedy didn't do that. Saved at least two hours a day. Still other times, the observations were unalloyed amusement. Item: The Washington press corps once conducted a poll of reporters to see who was the dumbest man on the Hill. The congressman who came in first was outraged. He called a press conference to deny it.

The items this morning were all in favor of keeping your trap shut. No—more than that—keeping your trap shut while radiating a serene attention that hinted at deep reserves of energy and good judgment.

Mike felt as if these two men had been in his office for hours. He was surprised when the tall one cleared his throat and said to the short one, "Why don't I start off . . ."

Mike didn't move except to shift his gaze to whoever was speaking. The two men took a while to come to the point, which was that the Democratic candidate for the local congressional seat, now held by a six-term Republican, had withdrawn for reasons of health. The two men were interested in finding out if Mike was interested in running. They knew he'd been a legislative assistant to a Democratic congressman, who spoke highly of him. They had learned that Mike had a good Navy record, including a Purple Heart, that he'd served on the Charlottesville School Board, on a governor's special commission inquiring into the state taxation of retired federal employees' retirement benefits, that he was married, and had two children who attended public school.

Mike didn't say anything. The men cleared their throats. Ganny leaned forward. Both men turned their faces to her. Ganny frowned but didn't say anything either. The short man said, "You all probably have some questions."

The tall man said, "Anything at all."

Ganny said, "It's been a while, hasn't it? Since your man went to the hospital?"

"Well, Mr. Reardon here has been a hard man to find."

Ganny said, "I meant before that."

"The final decision to withdraw for health reasons took a long time. We realize there's not a whole lot of time left, but we'll get behind a new candidate real hard and real fast."

Ganny said, "Mmm," to show that he hadn't answered the question. She said, "Will all the campaign funds be transferable? I imagine some of the people who've pledged know your candidate personally. . . ."

The tall man nodded. "Uh-huh, I see your point. There might be a little bit of falling away, but for the most part we don't see people wanting their money back as a problem. There'll still be a fair amount of money to be raised. That's always a concern. It's money that makes the ponies trot."

Ganny said, "You don't mind if I ask a few more questions, do you?"

The tall man said, "Not at all," and the short man said, "That's what we're here for."

Mike turned back and forth as Ganny asked questions and the two men answered. His own principal thought was unspeakable. It was—I'm not sure I'm fit to practice law for a while, but I've seen some people run for Congress who couldn't find their own fingers and toes.

Ganny had by now asked several questions about the congressional district, and the short man laid out a map on Mike's desk along with some transparent overlays. The first overlay showed the areas in the district reached by the Washington, Richmond, and Charlottesville TV stations. "Forty percent, forty percent, and twenty percent," the tall man said, laying his palm on Washington, Richmond, and Charlottesville. The next overlay showed the coverage of those radio stations in the district that carried their own news.

Ganny said, "I guess you don't see this as door-to-door."

The tall one said, "You can't overlook direct voter contact."

The next overlay was of county fairs and the state fair near Richmond. Ganny said, "There you go, Mike. Mike Reardon, the farmers' friend."

The short man said, "Used to be there was a farmers' bloc. But our current surveys show there's only around one or two percent of the registered voters who list their occupation as farmer or agricultural worker. Lots of farm*land*, but hardly any farmers."

Mike was surprised. He was going to ask about all the apple growers, but the tall man spoke first. "A county fair'll still draw a crowd, so there is that press-the-flesh factor, but mainly it's where the media show up. It works best if you're doing something, like handing out a blue ribbon."

Mike noticed that these men, like Bonnie Two, had two styles of speech. The first was an educated version of good-old-boy, amiable and down-to-earth, like the talk of most of the native Virginian lawyers in town who could say "*subpoena duces tecum*" and "that dawg won't hunt" in one sentence. But these two men also spoke a semi-pro jargon. In the phrase "press-the-flesh factor" it was the word *factor* that turned the merely glib "press-the-flesh" into adman sleaze.

Whoops. Mike sat up straight. He felt the ghost of the pink comforter tickle his ears and the back of his head; he smelled sweet-and-sour pork.

The two men must have mistaken his sitting up for an expression of interest, because they now began to address themselves to him more than to Ganny. They opened up a looseleaf binder of sheets tabulating attitudes and income levels in the district.

The short man said, "On the face of it there are a lot of Republicans, but a lot of them are lukewarm. The registered Democrats are pretty much true-blue. The independents . . . Look at all those independents. Look at their issues. Education, environment, and the middle-class tax bulge. Vulnerable. This district is very vulnerable to a fresh face."

The tall man said, "So what do you think so far? You have any preliminary reaction?"

Mike said, "Cold biscuits."

Ganny laughed.

The tall man looked puzzled. The short man stiffened.

The tall man said, "I'm not sure I—"

The short man said, "He means the offer's been around the table. We're not passing him biscuits right out of the oven."

The tall man said, "Well, now. We're here to . . . *proceed*. . . . I'd like to think we're having a serious, good-faith discussion."

The short man said, "All right. You're not first choice. And it's a real long shot. But we think you'd be a good candidate, someone who could say things that need to be said. And we certainly don't want to just roll over and give up the district. It'd be hard to come back from that."

The tall man said, "The party would be very grateful for a good race here."

The short man stood and began to pick up the notebooks and map. He paused and said, "Tell you what. Why don't I leave these here, drop by in a day or two. If you have any questions, please call me." He gave Mike his card. Then they were all four on their feet, shaking hands—bow to your corner, bow to your partner. Mike managed to say "Thank you . . . I'm honored . . ." on the way past the receptionist.

Ganny followed him back to his office and closed the door behind her. She laughed and said, "So this is it? The inner workings of the white establishment?"

Mike said, "What did you expect? When I worked in Washington I heard less coherent conversations between congressmen."

Ganny said, "I heard a better pitch from the man who sold me my car."

"The short one was better later."

"Yeah, well. I liked your cold biscuits. Where'd you pick that up? That's real down-home."

"Family lore. It's what Alben Barkley said to my old man about Truman's offering Barkley the vice-presidential nomination."

"So there's some use to all that ancient history you got stuck in your head," Ganny said. "I was worried for a while about how long it was taking you to say no."

"I didn't say no. If I'd been saying no I would have been a lot nicer."

"Oh no, Mike. No, no. Not in a million years. It'd drive you crazy, you wouldn't have a minute to yourself."

"That's right," Mike said. "I'm looking forward to it."

◇

Meanwhile back at the ranch . . . Grandma was getting cross at Mom and Dad for being away, and at all three of the big cousins for being wild, but she was being a sweetheart to Nora and me. I don't know what she knew about Mom and Dad, but one of her great gifts was that she could tell beforehand when someone was about to come undone. Nora and I were acting completely differently from each other, but we were feeling the same thing. I had the feeling that the whole place—Grandma's house, the oyster-shell driveway, the raspberry bushes, the lawn, the boathouse—was beginning to go around like the start of a scary ride at an amusement park. The Spider. The Cobra. The Octopus. You got in one of the baskets and at first it was just the big flat circle that revolved. Very slowly. Then your particular basket spun a little, and then it flicked out on some jointed arm so you thought you were going to be thrown into the crowd. So you were going around in a big circle and spinning in a little circle and flicking in and out, faster and faster, and just when you couldn't stand another second, then the whole big circle suddenly jerked up on edge so the rim went way into the air, and you were going round and round and *up*. You opened your eyes and thought you were about to be thrown over the Ferris wheel, but then you were going down face-first into the ground.

Nora and I went on these rides every year at the Dogwood Festival. After the first year the scariest part was the slow part. It was when the machine began to hum and creak and was just barely moving, and it came back to you how awful it was. I would look at Nora and blame her, and she would look at me, and then we'd go slowly spinning way out, and I would feel the first pang of feeling sick, which wasn't from the motion but from knowing it was my own dumb fault. That's how it felt at Grandma's when Mom and Dad disappeared. I knew then that our family had been spinning slowly all year, and now it was getting faster and faster. And it wasn't built with wheels and hydraulic arms that finally brought you back to earth. It wasn't a three-minute ride with someone in a greasy ball cap to throw the switch to stop it. I looked at Nora and blamed her, but I was going to feel sick from knowing it was my own dumb fault.

◇

Joss went to old Mr. Broome of Broome and Havermeyer to talk about divorce. Her first impulse had been to go see Ganny, but when she'd said this out loud to Bonnie One, Bonnie One had looked stricken, then taken a deep breath and made the obvious objection in such cotton-candy language that Joss had felt her face grow hot. She'd come close to opening her mouth and sending out a blast. She'd decided to save it.

She'd heard Mike speak of old Mr. Broome as amiable, even courtly, fairly competent, slow, and honest. By contrast with the way Mike spoke of the majority of the Charlottesville bar, this was praise.

Bonnie One made some inquiries of her own and came up with Thibault.

Joss remembered Mike describing Thibault as a Jansenist. She'd asked what that was. "A Calvinist Catholic who mistakes grimness and misery for virtue, and therefore rejoices in punishing himself and others for their own good."

Bonnie One's information on Thibault was that he put errant husbands through the wringer. Really very satisfying alimony and child support. Joss pointed out that she was the errant wife. Bonnie One said that it was certain that Mike would soon be an errant husband and Thibault would be on her side. "A good defense is a good offense," Bonnie One said. "Or you could hire Harriet Varner. She's a real assertive feminist. She'd be sympathetic to us, and she's very sharp."

Joss remembered Mike on the subject of Harriet Varner. "She's a terrier. She's good at getting settlements from insurance companies by biting their ankles. But that's how she loses big cases. She yaps and nips but never manages to get a bite in higher than opposing counsel's big toe."

So Joss went to sweet old Mr. Broome. Mr. Broome ushered her into his office, held her chair, and said, "I don't suppose Mike was worried, but it could have been difficult. Personally I am delighted."

Joss said with surprise, "About what?"

"The caucus. I just got back this minute from the *ad-hoc* district caucus, and we made it unanimous. Mike is now our official Democratic candidate for Congress." Mr. Broome beamed at her until she said, "Jesus Christ."

This exclamation embarrassed and puzzled him, making him even slower than usual.

Joss herself was puzzled as to what Mike was up to. At first she took it personally—he must be doing this to *her.* Then she thought he'd gone nuts. Then she thought he might be simply feeling free. She had, in one of their stranger conversations—perhaps the one in which she'd advised him to marry Ganny—told him that he'd be happier without her, freer to do all the things he'd been wanting to do.

Mr. Broome was apologizing. He said, "I should have . . . I suppose Mike was planning to tell you himself. I am sorry. I guess I jumped the gun."

Joss felt one of her bubbles float her up. She hoped not into manic joking. She said, "Let me put all my cards on the table."

She thought, Good—no jokes, just movie clichés.

She said, "I want you to handle my divorce."

Mr. Broome's face moved several times but didn't resolve itself into an expression. Joss gave him what started to be a brisk chronology, but when she saw that she had his full attention—in fact, he began to nod his head of beautiful white hair in a very understanding way—she found she couldn't help enlarging on her state of mind.

She finished a little breathlessly, because she'd speeded up near the end, having to change the subject quickly when she found herself about to tell Mr. Broome Mike's description of him.

Mr. Broome sighed. He said, "Well, I can't say I understood everything. . . . Wait just a second here. Let me make a little note. I want to make sure this next quarter-hour isn't charged to you. . . ." He sighed again and said, "This puts me in a . . . somewhat awkward position. Now, you understand . . . that everything you say to me is completely confidential. Not a word of what we say ever leaves this office." Joss felt lulled by his beautiful voice—when he said "word" the "r" disappeared, but the vowel sound thickened and writhed into two syllables.

Mr. Broome said, "I have been a loyal Democrat in this district ever since I moved here, and I—"

"Oh," Joss said, "I thought you were born here."

"No, ma'am. I'm a South Carolinian."

"It's funny," Joss said. "I've lived here a long time and I still can't tell Southern accents apart." She was eager to veer into social chitchat, to postpone for a moment what she feared was going to be his refusal to take her case. She said, "So you must be from Charleston."

"I was born in Columbia," Mr. Broome said, "but I am received in Charleston."

She thought for a second he was making a joke. She looked hard at him, but there wasn't a ghost of a joke. Then she concentrated so hard on not laughing that she had to pee.

Mr. Broome returned to his subject. "As a Democratic district committeeman, I was overjoyed to get behind Mr. Reardon. Now, not but an hour later, I learn that his wife is about to leave him. So, on my own time here, I wonder if you'd mind satisfying my curiosity. . . ."

Joss said, "Sure."

"Are the facts of your situation widely known?"

"No," Joss said. "The love that dares not speak its name hasn't mentioned mine either."

Mr. Broome's expression didn't change but he said, "Well, good. And I'm glad to see that you have your sense of humor. Now, you say you and Mr. Reardon sought counseling about this. . . ."

"Well, when we first went to Bonnie Two—that's Bonnie Sproul—"

"Yes, that's Miss Sproul, our third-floor tenant."

"Yes. We talked about my drinking problem then—I told you about my little accident. And we did a session on this . . . other subject."

"Well, after being married so many years, do you think you might want to spend some time talking it over at greater length with a qualified counselor?" Joss sighed. Mr. Broome continued, "Before you answer, let me put my cards on the table too. If I'm to be your lawyer, my initial obligation is to explore the possibility of some sort of reconciliation. But you should be aware that I have another concern—"

How beautiful that was, Joss thought—"concern"—with its "r" changed into a double diphthong.

"—which is that it would be better for Mr. Reardon's chances—slim as they are—if this situation were not yet a matter of public record. Not until after the first Tuesday in November. After some thought on the matter, you may see this concern of mine as a conflict or a potential conflict of interest. It could be that I myself will feel I might be hindered by this conflict or potential conflict from representing your interests the way you might wish or the way I might wish. Each of us should consider the question."

Joss had two reactions. The first was that she liked being lulled by the cadence of his voice. It was the same careful lawyer-talk that she'd occasionally heard from Mike, but Mike's rhythm was much more staccato. Mr. Broome's sleepy-time-down-south voice made her feel as if there wasn't anything that couldn't wait until everyone had a nice afternoon nap.

But her other reaction was that she was lost in an underground cave. Try not to panic. Breathe slowly or you'll use up all the air.

Mr. Broome said, "There is another . . . opinion of mine you should consider. If you aim on going to court, that is. My very strong feeling is that, as far as family matters are concerned, a full legal battle is, in nine out of ten cases, a disaster for everyone concerned. I think two intelligent and decent people can usually—after a cooling-off period—work things out fairly. Especially where there are young children. Would you say Mr. Reardon has been a good father?"

Joss said, "Yes."

"Would Mr. Reardon say that you've been a good mother?"

Joss said, "Yes." But then her hand flew up to her face. She said, "I'm pretty sure he'd still say that."

"You should know, Mrs. Reardon, that courts in general and especially courts in Virginia are apt to grant custody to mothers in most cases unless the mother is shown to be unfit. Unfortunately, the courts tend to fit facts into simple categories without necessarily considering the subtler or more delicate aspects. . . . The only mothers I can recall being denied custody were either those mothers who were alcoholics or those mothers who were—if I may borrow your phrase—engaging in that love that dare not speak its name."

Joss said, "Yikes."

"Well, yes," Mr. Broome said. "Yikes indeed. But if Mr. Reardon is neither vengeful nor opposed to . . . sapphism on principle, there might be grounds for hoping that he would not play that card. Would you say that he is very angry?"

"Of course he is," Joss said. "I mean . . ."

"Well, yes, of course. Could you give some idea how angry? Can you remember anything he said?"

"He threw his coffee cup through the window."

"Through the window? Not at you?"

"Through the window."

Mr. Broome said, "Were you in fear of bodily harm?"

"Do you mean before he threw it, as he threw it, or just after he threw it? That's sort of like that Wallace Stevens poem, isn't it? 'I do not know which to prefer, . . . the blackbird whistling or just after . . . The beauty of inflections or the beauty of innuendoes.'"

Mr. Broome said, "That's a right pretty piece of poetry. But was your fear of bodily harm . . . a fear of inflections or innuendoes?"

"Actually, I thought it was like cartoon violence. And then he was so embarrassed I felt sorry for him."

"Cartoon violence?"

"Uh-huh—like when Wile E. Coyote gets blown up and burned to a crisp but next scene he's good as new, out chasing the Road Runner."

"Yes, I see," Mr. Broome said. "Well, maybe that'll be something to come back to." He sighed, pulled a little patch of silk from his watch pocket, and cleaned his glasses. He put his glasses back on and sighed again. "I've always enjoyed Mr. Reardon's Irish gift of the gab, but I think you might go him one better. I imagine you and he had quite a few entertaining conversations over the years."

"Not lately."

"Not lately," Mr. Broome said, his echo softer and longer. "Well, I'm sorry to hear that. As I get older, I rate the pleasures of conversation higher and higher."

Joss was touched by how mournful Mr. Broome sounded. She imagined how happy she could make him by inviting him to the Northern Neck to sit on the back terrace with her mother. She imagined Mike as white-haired as Mr. Broome, herself aging as elegantly as her mother. White-haired, white-bearded Mike, laughing at her jokes. The evening sun pouring light through the tulip poplars. Edith and Nora running toward them, dazzling Mike and her with their fast-footed eager love. Everything in that light was as it should be.

She wasn't blubbering, but she was crying visibly enough that Mr. Broome came round his desk and offered her his white handkerchief. She dabbed with it, gave it back, pulled out her own Kleenex, and blew her nose with a savage honk. What the hell had happened to Christopher Columbus? Where had de Soto and La Salle skipped off to? To hell with them. She could do it alone. Let Mike grow gray hairs. What was inscribed on that sundial he'd given her? "Grow old along with me! The best is yet to be." To hell with that.

"In case you were wondering," she said to Mr. Broome, "I'm not having second thoughts."

That evening Bonnie One expressed her disappointment in Joss' day by quoting Kierkegaard—"Purity of heart is to will one thing."

Joss said, "Mike used to say that." Bonnie One let her face fall slowly. Joss was in no mood for one of Bonnie One's silently-deeply-hurt facial displays. "He used to quote that to gear himself up for being ruthless in court." Bonnie One raised an eyebrow. Joss went on—"Or just to gear himself up to mow the lawn. I don't need a philosophical bumper sticker pasted on me now. I think Mr. Broome is just the lawyer I want. What would be the worst thing for me now is a go-for-the-jugular lawyer. In legal terms I abandoned Mike, if I don't get back to the Northern Neck it'll look like I'm abandoning my children. And anyway I'm an alcoholic lesbian. Not exactly solid ground to launch an attack from. It is just a big fat piece of luck that Mike is running for Congress and doesn't want a battle in open court either."

Bonnie One said, "But when he loses the election, he'll have nothing else to lose. In mid-November we'll have waited and waited just to please him, and he'll be twice as bad."

"Twice as bad as what? What's he done that's bad? Why not twice as good?" Joss hadn't had an argument in a long time and felt good, felt her lungs and throat warming up. "The only one with nothing to lose right now is you. *We're* not hiring a lawyer, *I'm* hiring a lawyer. And if my lawyer and I think mediation and negotiation and blah blah blah are better than going to trial, then that's that. And, yes, I'm going back to my mother's, and, yes, we're all going to Ezra's fight and look like a big happy family and get Mike feeling good, and get my mother to talk to him and Ganny to talk to him and persuade him that I'm not so bad in spite of everything—the daughter of his wonderful mother-in-law; the aunt of his nephews, who think he's neat; the mother of his daughters. Just not any use as a wife. Look—Mike wants to be Dudley Do Right. If he's in a melodrama, then he gets to be good by fighting a villain. But if he's involved in a natural disaster, which is just bad luck, then he gets to be good by helping everyone survive."

Bonnie One had moved to the end of the sofa. She crossed her arms, leaned forward, and stared at her feet. She said without looking up, "So I guess I'm the villain we have to keep out of sight. So I should just go ahead and go to Italy by myself."

Joss had several years of Nora using this tactic, so she gave the family answer, which was to chant, "'Nobody loves me, everybody hates me, I think I'll go eat some worms.'"

Bonnie One looked shocked. Before Bonnie One could utter a sound, Joss said, "And you got it wrong anyway. You're not *the* villain. You're only *one* of the villains. The villain I was talking about—the villain I want Mike to think of as shipwrecked by a natural disaster—is me."

"Are you sure you're not having second thoughts?" Bonnie One said. "Are you sure you don't want him to paddle out in his lifeboat and save you?"

Joss snorted.

Bonnie One sighed and put her fingertips on the tabletop. She said, "I know, I know. But can't you see how . . . how agonizing it is for me? Can't you feel the fear I have when you're over there on the Northern Neck with all that family, in that great big family house? Can't you . . ." She stopped, grabbed her head in both hands, and fell sideways on the sofa. She turned her face into a cushion and said, "I don't want to argue. I just love you so." She stood up, took a few unsteady steps. "I miss you. I miss you already, and you're still here." She smiled, took another step, and touched Joss' cheek with her fingertips, then the corner of Joss' lips.

As though she'd been pressing the backs of her hands against the door jambs, Joss felt her arms rise. She and Bonnie One touched each other's face and throat, caressed each other at arm's length.

Joss' irritation at Bonnie One's self-pity had pushed her upstream, each cross word she uttered had been a hard stroke against the current. Now, half seduced by Bonnie One's anguished "I just love you so," half by Bonnie One's long light fingers, Joss let go and drifted back into Bonnie's embrace. What would the world be like if men learned to lose a fight this winningly?

When Joss got to her mother's house, it was just before suppertime. As soon as she opened the car door, she heard a louder babble than usual from the back terrace. Not just louder—the pitch was higher, the rhythm faster. She held her breath for a second of alarm. Then she heard her older brother laughing, then Nora. She heard her mother's voice, trailing down from her upper register. So everything was as it should be.

Joss shut the car door and heard Mike's voice, gruff and abrupt, as if it were the echo of the car door slamming. She came around the corner. Edith was closest. She said, "Mom! Where have you been?" Joss' younger brother put a hand on Edith's head and said, "Don't fuss, kiddo." He kissed Joss and said, "Great news, huh?"

Joss was about to say, "About the divorce?" She pressed her lips shut and kissed Edith. Joss felt her cheeks getting hot. What the hell was Mike up to? Was this his pre-emptive raid to capture her family?

Joss' mother sailed across the terrace, Nora bobbing beside her, half hidden by the loose butterfly sleeve of her grandmother's dress. "Isn't it marvelous?"

Joss said to her mother, "'Everything was in confusion in the Oblonskys' house.'"

Nora said, "Mom, what are you talking about? Where have you been?"

Joss' mother said to Nora, "Never mind, dear. Just give her a big hug." To Joss she said, "I'm glad you got here. Do you want a quick bath? There's just time before dinner."

Joss was undone by Nora's face, which looked just like Joss felt—flushed red, wanting to be hugged and soothed but sullenly set against taking the first step. Joss said, "Orrie-Norrie, am I glad to see you," and put her own red face against Nora's.

Nora hugged her hard, and Joss was calmed.

Nora then whispered to her, "Edith doesn't want to go to the boxing match. Make her come."

"Why doesn't she want to go?"

"Because Dad told her he's going to sing 'The Star-Spangled Banner.' I think he's teasing her, so tell him to quit it and make Edith come. It's no fun if I have to go alone."

"I'm sure he's teasing," Joss said.

But it was true. Ganny told her. The arena was in the far-flung Richmond suburbs, on the Charlottesville side, and a sizable part of the audience would be from the Thirteenth District.

Joss turned to Mike. "I hope you know what you're doing."

"I was a choirboy. I used to sing solos. I even got paid once to sing 'Ave Maria' at a wedding."

"That was before your voice changed," Joss said. "But that's not what I meant." She turned to Ganny. "Do you know—"

"She knows," Mike said.

"That's not what I meant," Joss said, without turning from Ganny. "I meant do you know what kind of nightmare this is going to be?"

Ganny looked uneasy and sad.

Mike said, "Don't spoil the party just yet, okay? I would have told you, but I didn't know the number . . . the number where you were staying." He took a breath and said, "How did you hear? It's not in the papers yet."

"Mr. Broome told me."

"Oh yeah. He's on the committee. How'd you happen to run into him?"

"I hired him."

Mike stared at her, but just then the oldest nephew's girlfriend came up and said, "Mr. Reardon?"

Mike's face changed all at once and so fast it was like a magician's sleight-of-hand. Presto change-o.

Mike said, "Mike, call me Mike, or I'll think my hair is turning gray." His voice was suddenly musical.

This wasn't Mike flirting. He was working the room.

And what was this silly girl up to? She was volunteering for the campaign. She said, "Daddy's sort of a Republican, but he does want me to have a summer job."

Ganny said, "I don't know about a *job.* You can start as a volunteer, then we'll see."

So Ganny was in on this. Of course Ganny would be, that was okay. Still, Joss had had enough. She said to Mike, "There are one or two things we should talk about," and left to take her bath and change for dinner.

When Mike walked in, she said, "I didn't mean now." Mike turned to leave. She said, "As long as you're here."

For a moment it was odd to take her clothes off in front of him, but then it was the same as it had been all year. Mike sat on the closed toilet lid while she got in the tub.

He said, "You still going to your AA meetings?"

"Yes."

"See anyone you know?"

"I told you we can't talk about that."

Mike nodded and said, "Good. That's good."

Joss poured in some Vita-bath and stirred it with her foot. She changed her mind again—it wasn't quite the same after all, being naked like this. She poured in some more Vita-bath and slid under the bubbles.

She lifted one leg and ran a washcloth down it. *Now* what was she doing? Sally Rand, the fan dancer? Gypsy Rose Lee?

But Mike wasn't paying attention. His lips were pursed and he was staring blankly at the sink. Finally he said, "I appreciate your choice of lawyers. I mean, it could've been Thibault, in which case we'd all have had useless conflict. Anyway. I hope we can just have some reasonable interim agreement. A period of détente. Nothing definite—I mean, nothing rigidly defined. I mean, for example, you can live at the house in the fall. I'll hardly be there."

What the hell was this? He would allow her to stay in her own house?

He said, "And we could have some suppers together every so often, see how it goes."

"See how what goes?"

"Things," Mike said. "See how things go. See what you really want. I mean, for one thing, wait till you're well into your detox before you make any big decisions. You remember Bonnie Two talked about that?" Mike went on and on. He had points to make, even though he wasn't saying A,B,C, and ticking them off on his fingers as if he were pushing launch buttons for nuclear missiles. Quite the opposite. His voice had an agreeable casual tone, and he interjected agreeable phrases like "don't you think?" and "I know you may come up with a better idea." But he did have a program. Swaddled though it was in his soft hesitancies, camouflaged though it was as a casual chat, the plan was to tie her up with a web of

Lilliputian agreements. Then it occurred to Joss that he might not really be dealing with *her*; he was dealing with divorce as one of his campaign problems.

"Fine, fine, fine," she said. "Yes, yes, yes. Who cares?"

Now he looked at her.

"This isn't a boudoir," she said. "It's a smoke-filled back room."

He didn't say anything.

"Besides," she said, "this is as boring as President Carter's energy policy. Drone, drone, drone."

"Well, then, maybe *you'd* like to—"

"No. I don't feel like talking anymore."

Mike nodded and said, "Sure. You've had a long drive. That's okay."

What was this? Was he trying out his Alan Alda impression?

Mike put his hands on his knees and pushed himself to his feet.

Joss said, "I don't mean you have to leave."

He sat down and then stood up again. "Sorry. Watching you in the bath is turning me on."

Before she knew it she said, "What's wrong with that?"

At last he had an expression on his face she recognized. It was the same grimace he'd had when he'd just got his fingers unstuck from the top of the baby-wipes dispenser. Puzzled, angry, and sheepish all at once.

Now he ran his hand through his hair, took two steps, and bumped into the half-open door. He said, "Jesus!" with total rage. He ran his hand through his hair again and said agreeably, "You want me to leave this open?" He closed it. Then she heard him open and close the bedroom door, leaving her in her pine-green and now tepid bath wondering what strange spirits would possess her next. Was there some vulture in her that wanted to peck at him whenever he lay still and hurt? Seduce him and then tell him it didn't mean anything?

"Yes, yes, yes," she said out loud. "Who cares?"

As she climbed out of her bath she looked up at the large bull's-eye window set high in the southwest wall. The perfect summer day was still shooting fiery light across the sky, although the sun was down.

Everyone wanted her to make a deal. Everyone wanted a contract, conditions, guarantees. They all said she didn't know what she wanted. She wanted to be free. Free to be hot, free to be cold. Free to be corny and poochy. Free to be horrible.

§ 8

Dad was already in the parking lot when we got to the place where Ezra was fighting. Dad's new van was parked next to the Mount Zion Baptist bus, and Dad was shaking hands with the people as they got off. Ezra's uncle was introducing him. About half of the people were carrying purple choir robes on hangers with transparent plastic bags over them.

The arena was right next to a big amusement park. Nora asked Mom if she could go on the roller coaster. Mom laughed. She'd been nervous driving from the Northern Neck—she always had a hard time following directions. I'd been reading them to her, and sometimes I couldn't read her writing. Nora would poke herself up from the backseat and grab them, then Mom would grab them and squint at them. "East on . . . How the hell am I supposed to know where east is?"

But once she parked the car she was in a great mood. She started singing, "'Hit him with a left hand, a right! How were they to know it was the kid's last fight?'"

I felt terrible. The light was weird. The sky was still glowing, but the light in the parking lot was a mixture of sunset and those yellow-gray sodium lights that make women's lipstick look black. And there were flashing colored lights too, from the arena marquee and the amusement-park rides.

Mom loved it. She held her hands up to frame pictures. Nora asked her if she could get a Coca-Cola. Nora was getting into it too. She said, "Co'-Cola" like a little ol' Southern girl.

Ganny and another lady had come with Dad in his new van. Ganny ushered us all to the side of the van that said "Mike Reardon for Congress" and someone took a picture of Dad, Mom, Nora, and me. Nora got Dad to pick her up. I was between Dad and Mom. The photographer had us all hold hands.

Mom sang, "'Stan' up an' fight until you hear de bell . . . trade blow fer blow! . . .'" Mom hummed the rest of the bar. She could usually remember lyrics. Now I was suddenly sure that *Dad* would forget the words to "The Star-Spangled Banner." I didn't want to ask him if he knew them, because that would *make* him forget.

The photographer wanted a picture of Dad, Nora, and me holding hands underneath the marquee, where it had Ezra's name. But Nora posed with her fists up, and Dad thought that was great and got me to do it, and he did it too. "Hey—the fighting Reardons," he said. Then he scooped up both Nora and me, an arm under each of our butts. Nora put one hand in the air, so I had to too. I was sure I looked awful. I'd grown a lot that year, but just in the legs, these long spindly white things that just dangled down. Nora was still a cute butterball.

I thought we were going to our seats, so I relaxed a little when we went inside, but Dad led us all down some stairs to the dressing rooms. Ezra's uncle, Ganny, and the other lady all came along. Dad said to us, "Now, if Ezra's started his warm-up or if he's just concentrating, don't bother him."

"Taking a nap most likely," Ezra's uncle said.

"That goes for you too, Manuel," Dad said. "Don't break his concentration."

"Don't go telling me about his concentration," Ezra's uncle said. "I paid for a whole lot of that concentration."

Ganny said, "Have you helped Mike with his concentration yet?"

Ezra's uncle laughed. "You're a pistol, you are. How come Ezra don't ask you out?" Ganny gave him a hard look. Ezra's uncle said, "Maybe you like older men."

Ganny said, "Your whole church is here tonight—you think you can stop chasing around like a rooster?"

Ezra's uncle said, "Not with you egging me on." He looked down at Nora, who'd come up close so as not to miss anything. He repeated to Nora, "Egging me on." Nora laughed brightly.

Mom said, "Oh brother."

Our group kept milling on down the hall, Dad in front saying "Good evening" to anyone who passed by, while I tried to be invisible, or at least hide in the middle.

We got to the dressing-room door. It was open. A bright light shone into the hall. There was a bright smell too, peppermint mixed with dirty laundry. Dad held up his hand. Nora squeezed up past his hip and waved. Dad turned and whispered to Ganny and Ezra's uncle, "It's Sean O'Grady interviewing him. O'Grady used to be lightweight champion of the world."

The light on top of the TV camera went off, and Nora popped forward. "Hi, Ezra!"

Ezra was shaking hands with the man Dad said was Sean O'Grady. Ezra turned to Nora and said, "Hey, Nora."

Dad said in a booming voice, "Just dropped by to say we're rooting for you."

But Nora was stealing the scene in her pretty pinafore. Ezra said to Sean O'Grady, "Watch this," and held up his palm. Nora smacked it with two lefts and a right. Sean O'Grady flicked his eyes to the cameraman, who turned the light back on. He held the mike in front of Nora and said, "You come to see the fight?"

"Yes. Who are you? Are you the announcer?"

"I'm Sean O'Grady. I talk about boxing on TV. What's your name, sweetheart?"

"Nora Reardon. I'm a friend of Ezra's. He showed me how to punch."

"All right! And is Ezra going to win?"

"You bet," Nora said. "You're going to win, Ezra. I just feel it."

Mr. O'Grady said, "So that's a prediction from Ezra Pritchett's littlest biggest fan. Nora—can you show me your punch again?"

Ezra said, "Come on, honey."

Nora didn't need coaxing. Smack, smack, and then whack!

Dad and Ezra's uncle tried to sidle into the scene by saying, "All right! Atta girl!" and stuff like that, but the light went off.

As the TV guys were packing up, Dad got in a few words. "Mr. O'Grady—Mike Reardon. Longtime fan of yours, champ. Like your show too."

Dad was about to introduce him all around when a black man in a blue gym-suit began shooing us out. Dad said over the man's head, "Go get him, Ezra!" Even Mom joined in. "Knock him for a loop, Ezra."

Ezra's uncle wanted to stay, but Dad took him by the arm, saying to the man in the gym suit, "You've got Ezra in great shape. And he believes in you. You—"

"Uh-huh. Now I got to get him by hisself."

Dad said, "Right, right," as the man closed the door. Dad looked up and down the hall, caught up in his relentless alien energy.

Mom said to Nora, "You were great, pooch."

Nora said, "Now can we get a Coke?"

Dad gave Mom some money and the tickets. He said, "I should go warm up with the choir."

The woman who'd come with Ganny and Dad said, "You want me to come along?" But Dad was three strides down the hall.

I heard Ganny let out a deep breath. Ezra's uncle and Nora had calmed down. For a moment I felt relaxed.

The woman who'd come with Ganny said to Mom, "How're you feeling, Joss? Are things okay for you?"

Mom said, "I like that dress. It's a whole new style for you, isn't it? And the shoes—great shoes." The woman blushed. I would've too; Mom's eyes were large, bright, and intent. Mom said, "You don't know my daughters, Edith and Nora, do you? This is Bonnie Two—I mean Bonnie Sproul." Mom touched the woman's arm. "Sorry. Mike and I started calling you that when you were a client of his. I have a friend called Bonnie, Bonnie One—can't tell the players without a program. Speaking of which—do they have programs? Let's go find some programs."

"And some Coca-Colas," Nora said. "I'm dying of thirst."

Mom said to Bonnie Two, "Are you sitting with us?"

I said, "Can I go sit down? This hall is weird."

I wanted Mom to come with me, or Ganny, but they were both shifting their feet in a way that made me resign myself to more traipsing around, to more being stared at. Bonnie Two said, "Why don't I go with Edith? Would that be okay with you, Edith?"

I wasn't sure she was a competently protective grown-up, but what could I say? Mom was already peeling off two tickets.

Bonnie Two and I climbed back out of the dungeon. That was a relief, but now there was a small crowd in the lobby. Bonnie Two said, "Would it be okay if I held your hand? Just to get through these people here?"

The part of me that wanted to get to a seat and shrink in it thought that was fine, but another part of me began to record silently snarled sentences: Just do it, lady. Just get us to the seats. What is this? Mother May I?

Bonnie Two was okay with the usher. He didn't seem to believe his eyes when he read the tickets. Bonnie Two said, "I think it's way down there." She pointed to the ring. "Down there where Sean O'Grady is setting up the microphone."

On the way she bought two programs—five bucks apiece—and two cups of Coca-Cola—two bucks apiece. It made me laugh to think that Nora might not be doing so well.

And it was a relief to get in a seat and get the program in front of me. In fact I could have relaxed a little—there weren't many people in their seats yet—but this woman did want to talk.

She said, "I'm glad to be down here. Being bumped around in a crowd makes me kind of nervous. Is that how you feel?" I nodded. I wished she'd stop talking so I could organize things in my mind. Like, where the TV cameras were. And where was Dad going to sing? I hoped not standing up right beside us.

Bonnie Two said, "Are you nervous for Ezra?"

I hadn't thought of that yet. It made me go cold in my feet and stop breathing. Ezra was going to get up there and fight with some guy he didn't even know. Get hit in the face. How could Mom be singing songs about this? She liked Ezra.

I took a sip of Coke just to keep it from jiggling over the top of the cup.

"Ezra does this every day," Bonnie Two said. "He has a ring in his gym just like this one, and there are some people watching, and he boxes with someone. So he's real used to it. Your daddy goes to see him sometimes. Besides, Ezra and the other man . . ." She looked in the program. ". . . named Candeleras—they wear these huge gloves like pillows. It may look like they're kind of . . . violent, but at the end they just smile, and then they hug each other."

It hadn't looked like that on TV. I remembered hearing someone say on TV, "They're working on that cut, trying to stop the bleeding," while Dad got up to get a beer. When he got back, I asked him how they cut each other. Long boring explanation. But more believable than this goo-goo stuff Bonnie Two was spooning out.

Bonnie Two said, "I had a boyfriend used to watch boxing on the TV? Every Tuesday." She laughed. "Wherever he is now, he's probably going to turn it on this very night. I wonder if they show the audience at all. . . . He'll drop his jaw if he sees me."

Thinking about that quieted her for a bit. And the subject of boyfriends distracted me. I'd begun to be fascinated—as in the case of my cousin who now had a girlfriend—how did they decide to be boyfriend and girlfriend? I looked at Bonnie Two. She was pale and small, but pretty. She wore a red knit dress with little red cloth buttons down the front. Her knees were very small, the same size as mine.

She turned to me and said, "He actually met your daddy one time. I wonder if he'll recognize him when he gets up to sing."

I said, "Is that part going to be on TV too?"

"I reckon so. I know they show it at ball games. . . ."

That did it. This was worse than a scary ride at the Dogwood Festival. The ring—Why do they call it a ring? It's square—now looked like the top of an Aztec pyramid. I knew about the Aztecs because I wrote a report for school and Dad showed me a book of his—the priests cut out the hearts of people on top of the pyramid and then ate them. The priests cut the man's skin off and then got inside the skin. The crowd of Aztecs on the steps ate the rest of the body.

So I sat there with my program in front of me, not looking. After a while I could hear the crowd coming in.

Mom finally got there. She sat on the other side of me. She said, "Are you okay, pooch?"

Nora said, "Hey! She got a Coke!"

Mom said to her, "I told you I'm not paying two dollars—"

I handed my Coke past Mom to Nora. Mom said to Nora, "Leave a little for me, kiddo." She said to me, "Bonus points for you, pooch."

In fact, hearing Nora be her normal self reassured me some. But then the announcer—not Sean O'Grady but some guy in a tuxedo—climbed into the ring. The announcer drawled out some words so long it was like stretching gum out of your mouth to see if you could pull it to arm's length before it snapped.

Then he said, "Here to sing our na-a-ational anthem—accompanied by members of the Mount Zion Baptist Church choir—the contender for the Thirteenth Congressional Di-i-i-strict—Mike . . . Fighting Irish . . . Re-e-e-e-ardon!"

Dad waved cheerfully, even though there was no change in the noise level of the crowd.

Ganny, from Nora's far side, said to Mom, "That Fighting Irish bit has got to go."

The announcer said, "Please stand for our na-a-a-tional anthem!"

It took a while to begin, because some of the choir members were still bunching up their robes to get through the ropes. Others were unbunching their robes, shaking them out, and smoothing them.

Mom said to Ganny, "How'd he get a choir? I thought he was joking."

"Ezra's uncle. He's an elder."

The choir hummed a note. Dad suddenly looked terrified. He took a huge breath, but his "Oh" came out a weak moan. He gasped another breath and got out the "say," gasped again and sang "can you see." He put his fingertips to one ear, trying to hear himself, since the choir leader had gestured in alarm and the choir hummed louder. You could barely hear Dad's ". . . through the dawn's early light."

Dad stepped closer to the microphone. I closed my eyes. I was about to cover my ears after his "What," the "What" erupting as a mix of static and gargle, and the "t" as a brittle dot. But at last Dad got it—". . . so proudly we hailed, at the twilight's last gleaming . . ."—as if his Catholic choirboy self was suddenly brought back to him. Soft and a little thin, but clear. I opened my eyes.

The choir leader turned his palm down, and the choir hum diminished. Mom unclenched her hands. I saw a white half-moon in her palm from her one unbitten fingernail. She clenched up again for the escalating high notes—"rockets' red glare . . ."—but Dad was home free, an okay bel-canto head tone, his mouth wide open as he had demonstrated and explained to Nora and me in his habitual detail and at his habitual length.

He made one last mistake—he sang "home of the free and land of the brave"—but he didn't appear to notice.

There was some half-hearted clapping and other noise that might have been cheering or might have been all the people just sitting down and talking again.

I sank down too. I was exhausted. Mom, Nora, and Ganny—and Bonnie Two—stayed on their feet a little longer than the rest of the crowd, but they sat down when a bell rang, and the announcer took over to introduce some boxers in regular clothes who'd come to watch the fights. Dad held the ropes apart for the choir to leave, and then lingered in the ring to shake hands with the famous boxers after they had their moment. The same photographer who'd shot Dad and Mom and Nora and me took pictures of Dad with the boxers. But at last Dad climbed out of the ring, and came and sat down on Bonnie Two's right.

He said, "Jesus, Mary, and Joseph!" all in one breath.

Bonnie Two said, "Mike, you were just wonderful!" all in one breath.

I was amazed.

Having thought over the years about what Bonnie Two said and how she said it (and it was good that I didn't know what Nora was about to know about Dad and Bonnie Two—it kept the following reflections on public life and ego more abstract), I've realized several things. I'm right that the person appearing in public is about to be a sacrificial victim, that some part of their heart is bared. But the pros get right offstage into the hands of their entourage and get a first-aid patch over the wound. When Nora got her grown-up career going, she instructed me in green-room protocol: when you go backstage and meet any actor who's been on, you must say, "You were wonderful! Absolutely wonderful!" And I thought, Of course. They have egos that have grown coarse and thick-skinned. But there's that one wound into their spirit that's torn open again and again. They need it opened again and again. It is dangerous, but that wound is the only opening through which they can feed. Only that hyper-alimentation can reach their baby hearts beating deep inside their beautifully enameled public personalities.

Yeah, yeah, yeah—I've gone too far. Nora isn't enameled when she's with me. And some of her best friends, etc., etc., are actors, etc., etc. The process is not total or necessarily irreversible. One of Dad's favorite politicians, a very witty ex-senator, only finally dissolved his enamel through his children's making fun of him (and he himself having enough wit to get the joke). He was giving a speech—while still scaled—and the sound system was poor. Someone yelled from the back, "We can't hear you!"

"That's okay," he said, a reflex going off before he could stop it, "I can hear myself."

His daughter said to him afterward, "Now I know what to carve on your tombstone."

Years later Nora and I made fun of Dad's singing. Years later. But just then, at the arena, he'd grown his first layer of ego scales and laid his first piece of bare heart on the altar, and it was ditzy Bonnie Two who licked his wound.

The process had started.

I understand why congressmen are against the two-term limit. They're addicted. Most of them are only semi-attached to the job. What they're addicted to is campaigning. They say they hate it. And some of them honestly don't like it. So how can they be addicted? The answer is: an addiction is an obsessive craving for something you don't really like anymore. Problem is—it's the only way you can get your rush.

Much later Dad told me that Mom had been right about him in one way—he'd been unhappy without knowing it. He figured out (also later) that one of the reasons he'd been unhappy just being a good lawyer, a good taxpayer, a good etc., was that he was always either in his head or in his body. He didn't do both at the same time. Either he'd be this floating head, analyzing facts and issues, bobbing like a cork in the stream of some client's life, or he'd dig holes, paddle his canoe, get out of breath and blistered. His first rush from campaigning was that it was physical and mental at once.

I said, "What about trial work?"

He nodded and said, "Yeah, I could have done more trial work. But . . . there'd still be a client to worry about. Anyway, when that campaign fell into my lap, that was it. Zap. A lot more adrenaline than a judge, a jury, and a court reporter. I needed something big and crazy."

"Maybe you were taking the advice you used to give me," I said. "Be blithe, be carefree."

He considered for a bit. Then he said, "Maybe, kiddo. But the first impulse was more desperate than blithe. There was this high-pitched hum inside me. Kept me going all day. I depended on it. I got to like it. I thought it gave me good reflexes. Then, at night, it would suddenly stop, and I'd be wiped out. Never slept better in my life. Couldn't remember what I'd done all day. Didn't care."

I didn't bring up the night of the fight in that conversation. The "high-pitched hum" he said was inside him was close to a confession. No, not a confession. "Confession" is too grand. But it was an admission that he'd gone out of control, that he was as helpless as the rest of us.

What happened during Ezra's fight I've had to reconstruct, because part of the time I had my eyes closed. First off, there was another short fight before. Nobody had told me about that. The two boxers were huge, leaned on each other a lot, and didn't make a lot of noise. Neither did the crowd. In the lulls I could hear the boxers breathing hard. I was in a daze. But when Ezra's fight started I heard everything sharper, like when you've fallen asleep on a train and suddenly wake up.

The sounds were surprising. The crowd noise was like surf, but I heard the sounds Ezra and the Mexican made as they punched. The Mexican grunted noises like moans, torn out of his insides. Ezra grunted breathy little puffs. Very quick when he threw combinations—hah-hah-hah!—but not nearly as scary as the Mexican's.

I heard the punches too, a dozen different noises and tones, some of them sharp thwacks, others deeper, like Dad hitting wet earth with his mattock.

I couldn't tell who was winning. Anyway, I thought that one of them had to knock the other down or make him say uncle. (I hadn't taken in that the first fight had a winner even though nothing much happened.)

Ezra's fight went on and on. I turned my head toward Dad, who'd been yelling like crazy all along. I saw him stand up and start yelling, "Intentional! That was intentional! Hey, ref!" Dad smacked his hand on his forehead. "That was an intentional head butt!" Dad moved into the aisle. He was only a few steps from Ezra's corner. Ezra's uncle was there, next to the man in the blue gym-suit. Dad started talking to him like crazy. The man in the blue gym-suit turned his head and said something, then turned back to the fight. Ezra's uncle took Dad's arm and made him sit down.

When the bell rang, Ezra turned toward us to go to his corner. One side of his face was all blood. I turned my head and saw Dad stand up and start yelling again. The veins in his neck were popping out.

A man behind Dad—one of the boxers in regular clothes—started talking to him. This got Dad to sit down, but then he began to argue with the boxer. Dad said, "The ref's got to say now. He's got to give a ruling now. He can't just . . . If it's intentional, and the doctor stops the fight, then they go to the scorecards, right?"

The boxer said, "Man, if the ref didn't see it, then he didn't see it. Just see what happens, man."

The man in the blue gym-suit was up in the ring along with two other men, doing something to Ezra's eye. One of them wiped it with a towel, another dabbed it with a giant Q-tip, and then the manager picked up a thing that looked like a spoon and pressed it on the eye.

I looked away.

Dad started yelling again when they started fighting. He was yelling louder and louder. Ezra and the Mexican moved toward us, Ezra backing up.

Dad yelled, "Uppercut! Uppercut!"

Ezra didn't punch, but he pushed the Mexican's shoulder and slid away. When he faced me, I could see the blood. Not just on his face. It was all over his shoulder and chest.

Dad stopped yelling. He said, "Jesus."

Ezra backed away, wiping his eye with the side of his glove.

I have a fear of something sticking in my eye. Okay—who doesn't? But mine is a phobia. Some days I have to line up all the pencils and pens on my desk so that the points are headed away from me. I wear eyeglasses with clear lenses when I drive in case I go by a line of traffic cones. Yes, I know a traffic cone is too big to go in my eye, but they look pointed.

I can't remember when this phobia started. It must have been early. I didn't tell anyone about it. Nora was the first one to figure it out. When we had fights and I was about to smack her, she would stick all the fingers of one hand straight out and point them at my eyes. If it was one of my phobic days, I'd have to stop and put my hands over my face. I don't remember when she stopped doing this. Maybe it was when she got stuck in the eye with the umbrella spoke. Maybe it was later, when we stopped fighting because we guessed that Mom and Dad were breaking up. Or maybe it was when she noticed me at the fight having one of my phobic moments in sympathy with Ezra. I was covering my eyes with both hands, digging my fingers into my eyebrows. I may have been making whimpering noises, because Bonnie Two put her arm around me.

But I lifted my head to peek every once in a while, sometimes to see if Ezra was staying away from the Mexican, sometimes to see if Dad was getting up to make another scene. He was yelling again, nonstop, "Hey, ref! Get the doctor! Look at his eye! Get the doctor, for God's sake!"

The bell rang. When Ezra sat down on a stool in his corner, the ref did get the doctor. The doctor climbed into the ring, and now there were four heads and eight hands all hovering around Ezra's face.

Dad got up, went over, and leaned on the ring, looking up at the faces. Ezra's uncle took Dad by the arm, but Dad shook him off. Dad yelled at the ref, who was a few feet behind the doctor. Dad said, "Hey, ref! What do you say? Was that an intentional head butt? What's the ruling here?"

The man in the blue gym-suit looked at Dad and pointed to Dad's seat. Ezra had been completely still on his stool, leaning his back and head against the corner post, his arms along the middle ropes. So it was eerie when he slowly rolled his head to one side and said, "Mike. Shut the fuck up."

Ezra's left eye was huge. I mean the skin was huge. The actual eye was a little closed slit at the bottom of a sticky hole.

Dad didn't move for a bit. Then he took a few steps backward until he saw his seat. He put his hand out to touch the back edge and sat down, staring straight ahead.

At that time I thought good things happened because you were good, and bad things because you were bad. I thought all of us in our family had to be good for any one of us to be good. I didn't know that most of the time things are just happening. If you get mixed up in something just happening, you can get submerged or you can get raised up. With or without your being good. Sometimes your skill can help, but sometimes what's happening is just too big for your little dog-paddle efforts.

Does this sound depressing? It's not meant to be. Maybe I've overemphasized the negative. Here's the good part. What's happening—whatever force is operating—isn't out to get you. If you're in the way, too bad. But once it's gone by, that's it, it's over, it's not mad it missed you, it won't circle back, at least it won't circle back to make sure you're punished. It's just a force.

Some people think the "forces" are in "nature"—that the forces of nature are just the stuff you see on PBS nature shows—that they're not in, for example, an artificially lighted, air-conditioned, man-made arena in the middle of a ten-acre blacktop parking lot. But it's all nature. We're nature, Interstate 64 is nature, Aztec pyramids and priests are nature, the Thirteenth Congressional District is nature.

When Andy Warhol said that everyone gets to be famous for fifteen minutes, he might as well have said that everyone gets to be publicly humiliated for fifteen minutes. He was just looking on the bright side.

I wish I'd figured out by then that your being good or bad doesn't affect the forces. It would have helped at the time. I wouldn't have been so burned by the electric shock of Dad's humiliations. I wouldn't have flinched. I certainly wouldn't have felt that it was somehow my fault as much as his.

◇

Mike was in a frenzy that his case had failed.

The case had obvious merits. The head butt was intentional; the ref should have so ruled; the doctor should have stopped the fight; enough rounds had been fought so that the judges would go to their scorecards; Ezra had clearly won enough of the early rounds to be declared the winner. He'd thrown more punches, he'd initiated more of the action—three criteria that should substantially outweigh the only criterion by which Candeleras could be give any points, to wit, that his punches were heavier. That Candeleras could take a punch—that he in fact seemed indestructible—was not an issue proper for the judges to consider by any set of rules. . . .

If he'd had pen and paper, Mike would have written this up on the spot and submitted it to a member of the Virginia Boxing Commission.

These arguments sucked his attention inward during the entire three minutes of the next round.

He felt odd, as if he'd just walked in. He turned around and asked the man behind him what round it was.

The man said, "Ninth. Last round coming up."

"How'd Ezra do? You think he won that round?"

The man squinted at Mike. "What you talking about? Pritchett's on his bicycle." The man dipped his chin, looking at Mike curiously. "You own a piece of him?"

Mike was about to say, "I'm his lawyer," but the word "lawyer" suddenly seemed absurd. He said, "I'm a friend of his."

The man said, "I'm glad those Mexicans don't come any bigger. You can beat on 'em all day, they don't go down. But one fifty-five's about as big as they get." The man sighed. "Up till Pritchett started running, it was an okay fight."

This professional observation shocked Mike, not because of its complacent self-interest—the man was big, at least light-heavyweight, twenty pounds on the safe side of the Mexican menace—but because of its cold distance.

The man said, "Pritchett stays on his bicycle, he'll lose the last round for sure. Most likely the whole fight. So what's he going to do? Fight inside? Candeleras'll eat him alive. Pritchett got a sweet left hook, it ain't no mulekick, but, you know, sweet. Trouble is he can't see that side. Hard to hook with your eye shut."

Mike said, "Yeah. So what should he do?"

The man shrugged and said, "Except Pritchett lead with his right. He ain't tried that yet. Straight right and get lucky. But Pritchett gotta watch his head. Candeleras just head hunting now, Pritchett don't need to worry about the body, keep that left high. Fake that left hook. Just twitch that left shoulder and then pop the right. Real quick. Keep that boy off of him."

Mike was mesmerized. This was good counsel. Inside his own mind he tore up the draft of his brief, let the little yellow scraps flutter like butterflies. Mike felt himself deflate.

He looked down the row. Edith was sitting curled up under Bonnie Two's arm, her own arm across her face. Joss was cheering ferociously, calling over and over, "Ezra! Ezra!" Nora was kneeling backward on her seat, one hand on Joss' shoulder, the other on Ganny's, looking over the crowd, as if trying to put the noise together with the faces.

If each one of these females pulled in a separate direction, he would come apart. What did he think he was doing, wandering out into the world when he was so easily undone? Ezra had trained and trained, concentrated himself, and even he was in trouble.

Mike turned to look at Ezra. Ezra stood up, his seconds pulled away the bucket and stool. Mike thought, Joss is right to yell her head off for him. She's the one who's right now, cheering like crazy for Ezra.

Ezra took a deep breath, getting set in his lungs. He snorted out through his nose. Ezra was alone and coherent.

What did Joss admire? Perhaps she would like him again if he was solitary and coherent.

Joss was cheering even more intensely. Was she cheering for a solitary, coherent man? Or was she being like her mother now, reading with supernatural sympathy through Ezra's flesh into Ezra's deepest wish?

The crowd began to chant "Ez-ra! Ez-ra! Ezra!" The bell rang. Ezra tucked his chin in and glided forward, guided by his one good eye.

Even the man behind Mike got into it. In his right ear Mike heard the man say, "Smart! That's smart!" From the ring Mike heard Ezra's breath pop as he doubled up on his jab. Once there was a "Huh!" when he faked his left, followed by two right hooks. Then Ezra danced away, circled back in, and threw a straight right without a sound. And slid away fast, his swollen eye safe behind his left glove.

Candeleras kept coming. He was expressionless but intent, advancing carefully, moving to one side or the other in his attempt to cut off the ring, get Ezra into a corner.

For the first half of the round Ezra was able to keep from being clobbered by using his right and skipping away. By the second half of the round Candeleras was wise to the right lead. At first he'd been surprised, perhaps a little hurt. Now he picked off some of Ezra's rights, and the ones that landed didn't seem to slow Candeleras.

The man behind Mike said, "Uh-oh."

Ezra's back loomed in front of them, blotting out all of Candeleras except for his wide left jab, almost a hook. Ezra's back bounced against the ropes. Mike blinked as a spray of sweat from Ezra's head flew up bright against the lights. Then Ezra's back wasn't there anymore. Mike heard Ezra's "hah-hah-hah!" before he realized Ezra was wheeling so tight and fast Mike couldn't sort out whose legs were whose, he only saw a tangle of high-laced boots at eye level.

The man behind Mike said, "Sweet."

Ezra got in a third or fourth right—Mike lost count—which turned Candeleras' face sideways. Candeleras' left arm was under the top rope. For a fraction of a second it seemed stuck, as if he were trying to get it out of a shirtsleeve. Ezra threw a huge looping right toward Candeleras' head. Candeleras, with both feet set—Mike saw his calf muscles tighten—lunged forward, his left glove sliding free behind him. Ezra's right bounced off Candeleras' left ear, but the top of Candeleras' head, deflected only a couple of inches, caught Ezra in the face. Ezra staggered back. He was moving sideways and stumbled, but stayed on his feet by pushing off the canvas with his left hand.

Candeleras went charging after him. The ref got in his way, shouting in his face, bumping him chest to chest. The crowd was booing. Two rows back a man yelled, "Kill the motherfucker!"

Ezra came up behind the referee, his right cocked.

Ezra's manager bellowed, "EZRA!" so loud that Mike heard it over the crowd. The man behind Mike yelled, "Be cool!"

The ref pointed to a corner. "Go to a neutral corner. Go!" He looked at Candeleras' corner. "Tell him to go. I don't speak Spanish. Vamoose. *Vaya con Dios.* Go!" Finally he gave Candeleras a push. Candeleras' cornermen started yelling at the ref. The ref turned to Ezra and pointed for him to go to a corner. But then he took Ezra by the wrist, pulled him closer, and looked at Ezra's eye.

Mike heard Ezra say, "He didn't get my eye, my eye's fine, he didn't get the eye."

The ref, now that he'd started doing things, couldn't stop. He called for the doctor. While the doctor was climbing in, the ref bustled to each side of the ring, holding up a finger.

Mike said to no one in particular, "A point! He's taking away a point!"

The man behind Mike said, "The doctor must be just looking at the eye. It look to me like that head butt broke his nose."

Just as the ref said, "Box!" there was a thumping from Ezra's corner. Ten seconds. Ezra avoided the first rush, and even got in a jab as he backpedaled to his right. But Candeleras moved quick enough to corner him, and Ezra covered up again. Candeleras punched away, thumping wildly on Ezra's gloves, elbows, stomach, the top of his head.

Candeleras stopped to take a breath. Ezra peeked between his gloves and Candeleras drove his left in on Ezra's nose. The bell rang, the ref stepped in front of Candeleras. Candeleras threw his arms up in triumph, the usual end-of-fight display. Ezra clutched his temples, his face screwed up in pain. Then he managed to raise his left in the air and walk slowly to his corner, sliding his right hand along the top rope. Candeleras, having circled the ring, met Ezra there and hugged him. Ezra patted him politely on the shoulder, but his eyes were on his manager. The manager and one of the cornermen tipped Ezra's head back and went to work on his nose as he stood facing his corner, still holding the rope with his right hand. They swabbed it, packed it, and sprayed it.

Mike had breathed a sigh of relief when the bell rang, but he grew tense again watching Ezra's near hand squeeze the rope, his forearm muscles strung tight.

After a moment whatever they'd done seemed to be numbing Ezra's nose. After he got his gloves off he turned and walked to Candeleras' corner, his face drawn in stiff, even his good eye in a squint. But as he made his politenesses to Candeleras, the manager, and the two cornermen, he struck Mike as elegant. In pain, and perhaps anxious about the decision, he nevertheless moved gracefully, as if he'd willed away the beating he'd taken and realigned his body. Ezra's serenity was better than the fist-in-the-air bounciness of Candeleras. Had Ezra learned this or was he born with it? Mike heard himself beginning "The Star-Spangled Banner." He saw himself lurching up to Ezra's corner of the ring. . . . Was that what this campaign would do to him? Send him lurching toward people who hadn't asked for him?

Too late to stop. Better get better, dummy.

Bonnie Two turned from holding Edith and patted his hand. And bringing Bonnie Two, Mike thought, I'm leaking brains from both ears.

Edith looked at him. He couldn't tell what she was thinking. He said to her, "They're taking a long time with the scorecards. That means it's very close." Edith didn't say anything.

Bonnie Two said, "Edith honey, all this may have been a little too much. But it's over now."

Edith looked at Bonnie Two and then straight ahead. Mike saw Edith was pale from shock. So there was that too—bringing Edith to the fight.

He looked along the row at Nora and Joss. They were holding hands, leaning forward, their heads tipped back to watch the ref and the ring announcer, who were still hovering in front of the judges.

Mike thought, Good—Joss got into it, carried Nora along. He had a flicker of hope that Joss wouldn't leave their life after all—there were too many people in it, too many. . . .

He touched Edith's knee. She leaned back in her seat and closed her eyes.

The bell rang three times. The ring announcer crackled the mike. "Ladies and gentlemen. We have a split decision. Judge Antonio Tebaldi scores it 97–93—Candeleras. Judge Buster Bynum scores it 96–94—Pritchett. Judge Julia Romano scores it 96–94 for the winner, Ezra—Mulekick—Pritchett!"

Mike heard Joss cheer before anyone else. There were a few scattered boos. The man behind Mike said, "Could've gone either way." Mike was too relieved to say anything.

Ezra's uncle was in the ring with Ezra and his manager. Manuel clasped his hands together as if in prayer. Sean O'Grady and a cameraman were setting up in front of Ezra. Mike got to his feet. Edith leaned past Bonnie Two and grabbed the edge of his blazer. "Dad," she said. "Don't."

"I'm just—"

"Please."

Mike had a vision of his future, in which his grown daughters, backed up by their mother, lawyers, doctors, and family friends, hemmed him in, saying, "Don't. Please. Just don't."

But Joss and Nora were on their feet, followed by Ganny. Joss and Ganny hoisted Nora up through the ropes. She ran over to Ezra and held on to his hand with both of hers. Mike couldn't hear what she was saying. Ezra patted her head. Nora stood quietly, still holding Ezra's hand while Sean O'Grady held the mike up in front of Ezra, then in front of Ezra's manager.

Sean O'Grady and his partner stepped to one side to do their recap. Ezra's manager, the two cornermen, Ezra's uncle, and Nora led the way for Ezra out of the ring and up the aisle.

When Joss and Ganny went by, Edith and Mike tagged along.

When they got to the hall, Edith took Mike's hand. At first he thought she was herself again, but when he looked down at her she stopped walking and said, "I don't feel well."

He said, "Do you want me to carry you?"

"No. I just feel funny. Is there a bathroom?"

Mike looked up and down the hall. He said, "There's one in Ezra's dressing room."

"No."

He thought of how smelly the men's room would be. Maybe a ladies' room on the floor above. Edith solved the problem by taking two steps to the wall and throwing up.

He held her forehead for the second onset. He said her name and wiped her mouth with his handkerchief. Bonnie Two gave him a handful of Kleenex. Edith spat a couple of times and then moved sideways away from the puddle, sliding her hands along the wall. Mike took off his blazer and folded it for her to sit on. He helped her down and sat beside her. She tilted her head back against the wall and closed her eyes. He said, "Do you want some water?"

"Not yet."

"Do you want to hear about pine trees and a cool mountain breeze and a cold stream you can put your feet in?"

"Maybe later," Edith said. "In just a minute."

Bonnie Two was still standing there. Mike said, "You might as well go tell Joss."

Mike was relieved to see her go. It was bliss to be here with Edith leaning her head against his arm. He didn't think of anything else. She turned so that her forehead was against his shoulder, her eyes blinkered in his loose white shirtsleeve.

He said, "Do you want—"

"Dad, don't."

◇

Okay. Some of you amateur shrinks are probably thinking, She did it on purpose. Yeah, she was green with jealousy about Nora's showing off and did this classic passive-aggressive getting-sick stunt. Or maybe she was jealous of Bonnie Two. Or Bonnie One. Or . . .

You think what you want.

And I'll think what I want.

Which might be: Blow it out your ass, you fake-calm it's-okay-to-have-these-feelings nitwits.

Which might be (now that you're cowed and I've got my temper back): Of course I've thought of all that, but, hey—I was really, actually, empirically verifiably puking my guts out.

I know that's not a counterargument to the she-was-up-to-something-subconsciously argument. I'm just saying I felt terrible in that over-crowded, overheated creepy concrete dungeon. And then I felt better.

Not because I kept Dad out of a share of the triumphal scene in Ezra's dressing room, but because he always had a pretty good bedside manner. And I always liked him sitting down quietly. Nora liked him up on his feet. Mom might go either way. Come to think of it, his trying to deal with the three of us may have been good training for dealing with the diverse elements of the Thirteenth Congressional District.

Mom showed up. I heard her clickety-clacking down the concrete hallway, then slowing down in front of me and Dad. I felt his shoulder move as he lifted his head. Mom said, "Aw, pooch," and slid her hand onto my forehead.

The three of us stayed there a minute, Mom squatting down and stroking my head. Mom said, "Mike, maybe you could carry her to the car."

Dad said to me, "You feel okay enough to get carried, babe?"

I said, "In a minute."

"How's Ezra?" Dad said.

Mom said, "On cloud nine. Oh. He told me to tell you he's sorry he spoke sharply to you."

I felt Dad move his head.

Mom said, "Quite a night. He must be exhausted. I'm exhausted." She paused. Then she said, "You wouldn't like to drive us back? Tomorrow you could borrow Ma's Jeep to drive into Charlottesville."

I felt Dad's head lift. He said, "Sure"—very long, almost a purr.

Mom said, "Don't get your hopes up."

Dad breathed out a long breath. Then he laughed. He said, "Now, would that be a movie cliché or a plain everyday phrase?"

"Sorry."

Dad got to his knees and scooped me up. I felt better when we got outside, but I still got the front seat without an argument. Dad went off to give his van keys to Ganny, but when he came back he made a little face. He said, "I'm sorry, Joss. Ganny reminded me I've got a breakfast tomorrow. Crack of dawn. I could ask someone else. . . ."

Mom said, "Don't worry, I'll be fine."

Nora said, "How come you don't have a plane, Dad? Or a helicopter?"

"The van isn't even paid for, Orrie-Norrie."

"Well, when are you coming to Grandma's?" Nora said.

"Maybe you girls would like to come to some county fairs."

Mom said, "We'll have to talk about that. I don't want them just wandering around in a crowd while you're busy shaking hands with Miss Shenandoah Valley."

"No, of course not. There's Ganny and Bonnie Two. And Evelyn's going to come to one. And there's another woman—"

"Is your staff all women? You're going for the woman vote?"

"As a matter of fact, the polls show that women are where I'm making substantial progress."

Mom said, "What are you doing? Buying 'em all red dresses?" She started the engine. "Give me a call. We'll see what the girls want."

Nora said, "Maybe Grandma can take us."

"Keep your head down, Nora," Mom said. "I can't see to back up."

I was encouraged by Mom and Dad's tone—all that fast kidding around. But then I saw Dad in the headlights, his white shirt lit up, his jacket trailing from one hand while he waved with the other. Mom turned the car and he was gone, and I knew I wouldn't see him for a long time.

§ 9

Mike was seeing things that amazed and amused him. He wished he had time to savor his amazement or amusement. The first thing that amazed him was how many rich people there were in Albemarle County. As a member of the Charlottesville bar, he'd run into some rich people, worked on some of their tax problems, done title searches for several million-dollar country estates. But, stopping by big houses to raise money, he saw more than he'd thought possible. The campaign coordinator from Richmond gave him a list that was ten pages long, ten names and addresses to a page. And these were just the liberals.

He had a general phone solicitation working, but the hundred names on his list were to be visited in person, at their convenience. Just setting up appointments was time-consuming. A great many of the people on the list were away for the summer, but Ganny and her staff tracked them down (in Europe, in the Rockies, in Maine) and found a date when they'd be breezing back through town. Some made dates for after Labor Day, and some just didn't know when they would be back.

Evelyn went over her client list and added a dozen names of horse breeders and dealers. Mike asked her if she knew whether they were conservatives or liberals. Evelyn said that didn't matter, they were all mad as hell about practically everything and all he had to do was listen until he heard something he was mad about too.

Ganny said, "They must care about the environment."

Evelyn nodded. "Some of them care about that. But mainly the thing is some of them are just nice people who think politicians are scum, but I'll tell 'em you're a nice person." The media consultant rolled his eyes. His name was Jerry Medina. So far he hadn't said much, but he radiated impatience.

Mike spent two mornings with Evelyn zigzagging through the countryside of white fences, sometimes turning off a humpbacked dirt road onto a newly paved driveway that led a half-mile up to a handsome house with boxwood as high as the second story, sometimes turning off a paved road for a rutted driveway of red clay and parched weeds ending up at a barn shored up with tree trunks. Evelyn said, "You can't figure what they're worth by how it looks."

The first morning was pleasant enough, but slim pickings. The first man they met barely talked, in fact barely moved his features. His face was the same red color as the churned-up hard clay around the water trough. The longest phrase he uttered was to Evelyn. He said, "If you say so." He pulled out a fifty-dollar bill, and that was that.

Others were more talkative, and Evelyn was right that most of them were angry, though usually about things not solvable by any federal or even state action. The only thread binding the various complaints—the nonsense being taught at the university, the wrong people having too much money and buying up land they didn't know what to do with, the lack of skilled farm labor—was the underlying feeling that owning land wasn't what it used to be. Mike had heard this from a few clients in the past—the sense of betrayal that owning land was now just a legal matter like owning anything else—that nobody cared or even realized it should be a link as strong and sanctified as marriage. Their vehemence was like the vehemence of those who thought abortion was murder, or who thought that the system was stacked against blacks, women, or believers in God. Mike listened, took some pleasure in hearing a cry that would soon be as rare as the cry of a loon or the bugling of an Olympic elk. The large farms, Mike was learning, were owned by heads of corporations (including a handful of media tycoons on Mike's blue-chip list), actors and actresses (also on the list), or just plain rich folks without any occupation but their own money (not on the list). Some of the idle rich bought race-horses. One of them named his horse Tax Write Off (out of Right Stuff by Stands to Reason).

The man who told Mike about it said, "If I didn't hate the goddamn IRS, I'd call 'em up and tell 'em to audit the son of a bitch."

Evelyn said, "There must be a way to make those tax people see who's real and who's just being slick. You could do that, couldn't you, Mike?"

Mike said, "Yes."

Evelyn's endorsement was good for almost ten thousand dollars, ranging from the fifty dollars in cash to several checks for an even thousand apiece.

Mike felt fine physically, but he had the feeling that he was becoming a ghost. A very active ghost—he was putting in full days asking for money from individuals and small groups. In the evenings he'd written three speeches of his own on tax reform, national energy policy, and arms reduction. Jerry Medina read them and told Mike that they were well-written arguments. "Very well written, Mike. But we're still raising money and we don't want to paint ourselves into any corners. That's point number one. Point number two—political speeches are more like bumper stickers. What you've got is like a legal brief. Don't get me wrong, we can use all this good stuff later on. If we get Fenton to debate, you'll eat him for lunch. But just for now we're filling the old war chest."

Mike didn't say anything.

"I'll tell you a piece of your stuff I love, Mike, it's where you say, 'I've been a good lawyer for my clients, and I'd like to be a good lawyer for the voters of this district.' We can punch that up a little. It's a good finish."

Mike said, "I thought something more cadenced for the peroration." He meant to be difficult. If he was doomed, he'd rather sound like Adlai Stevenson.

Jerry was too intent to notice.

"Think more intimate, more close-up. Think Jimmy Stewart."

Mike laughed. "I can't do Jimmy Stewart. That croak in the voice is—"

"Mike, Mike. Don't be literal. Jimmy Stewart, Henry Fonda, Alan Alda, whatever. Not the voice, Mike, your voice is fine, it's a blessing. The manner. The manner is what I mean, Mike. I know you've got it. The way you talk to Ganny, the way you talk to your daughter."

"This manner is for the thirty-second TV ads?"

"I'm talking pretty much everywhere you're using a mike. Now, let's take a look at that good-lawyer line."

Mike said, "What about, 'I'd like to be the lawyer for all of you, and it ain't gonna cost you a dime'?"

"Don't get folksy, Mike."

Ganny said, "Give that 'ain't gonna cost you a dime' to Bonnie Sproul. It'd be real cute in one of her songs." She handed him a schedule. "Now, pay attention. Next stop is the Piedmont Environmental Coalition. That's a speech, no supper. Then you go to the Rivanna Rowing Club, there'll be about eighty people at their boathouse at eight-thirty. No speech, just shake hands, tell 'em you rowed for Georgetown. Tell 'em that story about when the German doctor put thermometers up your crew's butts."

"That was a four-man canoe."

"Whatever. Then Bonnie Two's going to take you to where she's singing—"

"I only rowed novice at Georgetown, and that was just for three months."

"You were only in Vietnam for three months," Ganny said. "But it counts. Oh. When you go with Bonnie Two, don't sing. She was talking about getting you to do a duet with her. Don't. All right? Just don't. I'll be in my car in the parking lot, so, after Bonnie Two does her first set, you slip away. I'll take you home. Tomorrow at dawn—at dawn, Mike—you're driving yourself to Brandy Station to talk to the Civil War re-enacters."

Jerry said, "I'll drive you. I arranged for you to inspect one of the companies. There'll be Richmond TV, we might get on for a few seconds."

Ganny said, "So you've got an hour to get ready for the Piedmont Environmental folks. That's the twenty-minute ecology speech. It's in the file cabinet."

Jerry said, "See if you can work in the I'll-be-your-good-lawyer line, it might get picked up. No TV, but there'll be local print. And I've got an account of the battle at Brandy Station in my car, so you can bone up on it."

"There were two actions at Brandy Station," Mike said.

"You know," Jerry said, "sometimes you remind me of Robert McNamara. I was at a Senate hearing, and someone asked McNamara how many tanks the Soviet bloc had. McNamara rattled it off by country. Right down to Bulgaria. The son of a bitch knew how many tanks Bulgaria had."

Mike said, "McNamara was secretary of defense."

Jerry said, "Nobody likes a whiz kid, Mike. You don't see college professors getting elected."

Ganny laughed. She said to Jerry, "You used to be in the big time, did you? So what are you doing here with us?"

"I fucked up," Jerry said. "But if I pull this off, I'll be back on top."

Ganny said, "After Brandy Station, you have a lunch in Culpeper, then you come back here. Then you and Nora go to the Nelson County Fair. Now go get ready for ecology."

After fifteen minutes Mike came back in. He said, "Tell me how you think this sounds." Ganny took him by the arm and led him back to his desk.

He said, "Ganny, can you just sit here for ten minutes?"

"Okay," she said. She held his hand. "Now, listen, Mike. Here's the deal. You get twenty minutes. Every day you get twenty minutes to tell me how bad you feel about Joss and everything. Then we get back to how much fun we're having."

Mike laughed.

"That's right," Ganny said. "That's part of the deal too."

◇

When Joss read in the *Richmond Times-Dispatch* that Mike was the "woman's candidate" she snorted and her knee jumped so that it hit the underside of the table.

Her mother, reading the Sunday *Washington Post* across from her, said, "I wish you wouldn't make that noise, dear. It rattled my coffee cup."

"That was my knee," Joss said. She was about to read aloud to her mother but held back. They'd had a minor tiff the night before. Her mother's initial reaction to Joss' complete confession—or at least account—of her situation had been sympathetic. Among other things, her mother had said, "You know how fond I am of Mike, but I assure you I'm on your side. No matter what. And I'll say the same thing to Mike."

Joss said, "You're going to say the same thing to Mike!"

"I mean, my dear, I'll tell him I'm on *your* side. You're my daughter."

That wasn't perfect, but okay. But when Joss had come in for supper wearing a denim smock and her Birkenstock sandals, her mother had said, "Where on earth did you find those what-do-you-call-'ems? Those—"

"Sandals."

"They're not sandals, darling. Sandals are things with thin little soles and thin little straps. Those are ground-grippers. They might be all right for gardening, but not at the dinner table. Please."

Joss' oldest nephew had said, "They're Birkenstocks, Grandma."

"Never mind," her mother said. "They make her look like a—"

"Like a what?" Joss said.

"Like a Bavarian farm girl digging beets."

Joss eyed her mother suspiciously for an instant, then decided she was innocent. Innocent at least of having been about to say "lesbian." But in her bedroom, as she squeezed her feet into espadrilles, Joss thought her mother might be unconsciously picking on her Birkenstocks as a symbol. It was true that her mother didn't let anyone, male or female, wear blue jeans or shorts to dinner, but citing Joss for a fashion violation had a whiff of ideology.

Joss calmed herself by thinking of her mother's loyalty oath. And, Joss thought, if her mother walked in and found her crying, her mother would wrap her right up in her arms. This thought sent an unexpected rocket of rage through Joss. What's the deal here? You have to go boo-hoo to get some affection?

So now, reading the Sunday papers with her mother, Joss wasn't sure if she could have the companionable conversation she wanted. Joss hated being at her own mercy, however, so she took a deep breath and started in. Slowly. "You don't mind if I chew some gum?"

"As long as you don't make that snapping noise, dear."

"It keeps me from smoking." That was tit-for-tat. Her mother still sneaked a cigarette now and then. "Listen to this—there's this puff piece in the paper—Mike Reardon, the woman's candidate. He isn't even for the ERA."

"Perhaps they simply mean he's attractive to women. Compared to Congressman Fenton, I mean. I sat next to *him* at dinner once, and he's hopelessly dull. A complete stick. He's quite old too. By the way, I thought it was awfully good of you to take the girls to that prizefight. I think a few gestures like that and you and Mike won't have any problem being sensible."

Joss sighed.

Her mother said, "Well, you know what I mean. Sensible—civil, forbearing. You're both capable of it, you're both perfectly nice people."

Joss sighed again, but this time her mother didn't guess what the sigh meant. It meant a good many things—fatigue at having to deal with the bureaucracy of civility, of being perfectly nice people. And a whiff of regret, a whiff of fear that her mother's love for her was based on her being a perfectly nice person (as her love for her mother was not). But it was chiefly a sigh of realization not only that it would take her mother a long, long time to stop thinking of her as part of the Mike-Joss couple, but also that her mother would never speak about Joss-and-Bonnie. Joss knew that her mother, no matter how many conventions she endorsed or put up with, was not conventional. She could float along comfortably and then suddenly be ruthlessly imaginative. Joss was never surprised at the people who turned out to be her mother's friends. And Joss recognized that in many ways her mother was a genius of affection—the way she loved, teased, quarreled with, bossed, and knew each of her children was vividly different.

Joss now measured the effort her mother would have to make to accommodate her. Joss was entering a zone into which her mother's sympathies, various and powerful though they were, couldn't follow. It was her mother's sensing this inability in herself that was making her touchy about Birkenstocks, nostalgic about Mike, decorous in her advice about being civil.

Joss said, "I'm a monster."

"No," her mother said. "No, dear, you most certainly are not."

Joss waited.

Her mother said, "Of course, there are things I don't understand, but I love you as much as ever."

"Well, in the muddle of my monster-heart I love you too."

"Perhaps you mean 'middle,' dear," her mother said, but put one hand on Joss', sniffed, and looked sweetly close to tears.

Not a minute after she'd got the comfort she'd wished for, Joss had a vision, dreary as a blueprint. She was a mechanical system. If she produced a unit of affection, she would produce a unit of anger. It was as sure as Pavlov's dog drooling. It was as sure as the clockwork laws of courtship: one of the two is always more in love; having someone more in love with you makes you retreat; being more in love makes you advance. Being advanced on makes you less in love; advancing on the retreating lover makes you more in love. It was physics.

She had been more in love with Mike at first. That only ended when she had children, with whom she was able to be more in love than with Mike. So then he got more in love with her. Too bad, because not only was she retreating from his advance, but she was also still mad at him for the time *she'd* been more in love.

She sighed again. Her mother patted her hand. Joss thought with relief that she wasn't going to be mad at her mom. She knew who was going to get her next unit of anger. Too bad, Mike. It's Newton's third law.

◇

The Brandy Station visit put Jerry Medina in a terrible mood. He couldn't find the person with whom he'd made his arrangements. He zigged and zagged through the crowd, grabbing one man after another by the elbow and asking more and more rudely for someone who knew what the hell was going on. Mike wandered off to a group of men in gray uniforms reclining in the shade near their horses. It turned out the main event wasn't that morning at all—they were just gathering, waiting for instructions, and then after lunch they'd all go to where they were going to bivouac for the night. The re-enactment was the next day.

Mike took off his coat and sat down. It was very hot even in the shade. One of the men gave him a drink of water from a wool-covered canteen. The man said, "That canteen there is the genuine article."

Mike stirred himself up to say, "That so? Is all your gear the real McCoy?"

"Most of it. Show him the flag."

Another of the men stepped into the trees and brought back a seven-foot flagstaff. He turned the staff slowly, unfurling a faded Stars and Bars. The men looked solemn enough so that Mike got to his feet.

"You can touch it."

Mike held a corner in his palm.

"That flag was with Lee's son, Fitzhugh Lee."

Mike sensed that they wouldn't have been displeased if he'd kissed it. He said, "Amazing. It's a real museum piece."

The man holding the flag said, "Better than that. When I'm dead and gone, it's going to the chapel at VMI."

So here was another piece of religion he hadn't encountered in his lawyer-life in a cosmopolitan college town.

He looked at the man with the flag. He said, "Well. Thank you. I was wondering . . . that is, I had some idea what this was all about, you all coming to these battle sites. I see it's more of a pilgrimage than I'd imagined. A pilgrimage and a meditation."

Like a gypsy fortune-teller, he'd groped his way to the fortune they wanted to hear.

After a while Jerry was back at the van, beeping the horn.

When Mike got there, Jerry said, "Hey. Don't wander off like that." He ground the gears, and the van lurched off the field.

Mike said, "Don't take it out on the car."

Jerry said, "Look. I finally got hold of this guy—"

"Don't take it out on the car because you fucked up. And don't take it out on me."

"Oh, for Christ's sake, Mike, don't make things harder than—"

"I don't mind if you fuck up. I do mind your being an asshole about it. So, if you can find somewhere I can give my five-minute speech, go there. I've got to add a phrase or two." Mike went to the table in the back of the van. He said—cheerfully, now that he'd bullied the guy back—"I'll bet you thought these guys were just playing soldier. Well it's a pilgrimage and a meditation. That's what it is. You remember that movie back in the sixties, *Black Like Me*? Well, this is *Gray Like Me*."

"Jesus," Jerry said. "You're not going to say all that, are you?"

"No," Mike said. "*Gray Like Me* is a joke to keep you and me having fun on the bus. Pilgrimage and meditation is what I'm actually sinking to."

Back at the campaign office Mike got a message to call Joss. "No time for that now," he said and sang, " 'Hi ho, we're off to the fair!' "

Ganny said, "You could call her on your car phone."

"I can't make personal calls on that phone," Mike said. "That's paid for with campaign funds."

Ganny rolled her eyes.

Bonnie Two ran her hands lightly down the flounces of Nora's dress. "You look just great, Nora."

Mike said, "That's right, babe. So let's climb aboard." These days he found it hard to read Nora—she loved her new dress, she was restrained but polite to Bonnie Two (who, on Mike's advice, had stopped calling Nora "sugar pie" or "sweet pea"). What puzzled him most was that Nora was so well behaved. All the time. He couldn't tell if she was keeping a lid on herself or if she'd suddenly changed. She appeared to enjoy her cameo appearances at fairs and malls, and she was very good at them. She also spent some time passing out campaign buttons and flyers, but there was still an awful lot of time when she was just parked somewhere waiting for Mike to be through with something that he'd said would take twenty minutes but that ended up taking an hour. And of course there were many nights she got left with a babysitter.

Now she climbed into the van first and took a back seat. Bonnie Two said, "Nora—you go ahead and sit up front with your daddy, darlin'."

Maybe Nora was behaving because she didn't have to compete with Edith for the front seat, the bigger dessert, the longer story at bedtime. Mike had always been so irritated by the girls' edging each other out that he hadn't been sympathetic to the strain of their sibling rivalry on them. This new state of peace made him think that childhood was as bad as a Hobbesian state of nature, the war of all against all.

He said, "Fasten your seat belt, babe," and patted her knee.

When he got into fourth gear on the highway, Nora held his hand.

Maybe this was the way to arrange child custody—Nora for a while, then Edith. Then both, for a spell of fragile family happiness. Maybe that's how Joss and he could work it out—time apart. Then he heard Joss' voice saying, "Don't get your hopes up." All right. Maybe the long intimacy of his life should be Edith and Nora—and of course friendship with Ganny and Evelyn and Edmond. Let romantic love be intermittent adventure, various and painless. . . .

Ten miles from the fairgrounds, he asked Bonnie Two to go over the schedule for him. She came forward and crouched between the two enormous bucket seats. She had it all by heart. Open-air awarding of prizes. Intro of Mike by chairman of fair. Mike's eleven-minute table-of-contents speech (here are the issues that I think are important; I'd like to hear from you all). Bonnie Two, Nora, and other volunteers pass out stamped postcards. Prize-committee members announce winners, Mike hands out ribbons, makes a few remarks about prize livestock, pies, flowers, jellies. Tours fairgrounds with Democratic county-committee member.

Mike said, "Wait. What's her name again?"

"Marsha Hawes. She's a widow who owns a hardware store. She's made a campaign contribution, so be sure and thank her. Then you eat supper at a picnic table with her, and she introduces you to some more folks. Then I'm singing with the band in the music tent. After the first set I introduce you to the crowd. You and Nora hang around, you maybe dance with Nora. Oh—here's something you might not know. There's another singer, and she does these bouncy songs, but they're religious? Well, don't dance then. It's not right to dance when someone's testifying. Okay? Then Nora and I do our little number and you and Nora can go home. Unless you want to do that little thing you and Nora did the other night? Where you say to Nora, 'It's your bedtime, honey—say good night to all these nice people.' "

Nora said, "I'll just say good night and wave."

Mike said, "Are you going to ride back with us?"

"I got to sing some more. The religious woman and I do a duet right at the end? I can maybe catch a ride back later on. If I get back before too late, I'll give you a call. Just to let you know how it went." Bonnie Two put her hand on Nora's head. "You got some dancing shoes, darlin'? I'll put 'em in my bag so we'll know right where they are." She smoothed Nora's hair and said, "You're going to have a ton of fun."

Nora said, "When do you and I eat? Maybe I can eat with Dad."

Mike said, "Let's see how it goes with Mrs. Hawes, babe. It might work. We'll certainly take you along when we go round the fair."

"Do they have rides?"

"I hope not. I've got to eat a plateful of pork barbecue. What's that ride Edith hates? The one at the Dogwood Festival. The Cobra?"

Nora said, "Yeah. You don't have to do the Cobra. Maybe just the Ferris wheel."

Mrs. Hawes took them on a tour. Nora stopped them at a midway event Mike had only seen in comic books. For a dollar you got a chance to swing a huge wooden maul. When you hit a flat metal target on the ground, a red ball shot upward. The red ball was threaded on a wire that ran from the back of the target to the top of an upright plank. The plank was marked with gradations. From bottom to top they read: Pantywaist.

Sewing Circle. Girl Scout. Not Eating Your Wheaties. Junior Lumberjack. Muscleman. Superhero.

At the very top there was a chrome gong. As Mike and Nora watched, a boy stepped up—or was pushed forward by his buddies. He was wearing a baseball shirt, which he peeled off. He wasn't a weight-lifter, but had a good wiry farm-boy build. He spat on his hands and started to pick up the maul. The carnie stepped forward and put his foot on the head of the maul so that the boy stumbled a little. Hoots of laughter. The carnie held out his hand, saying, "Gotta pay to play, sport."

The boy pulled out a dollar; the carnie took it and stepped back beside the plank. The boy swung the maul in a full arc and gave the target a solid whack. The red ball jumped, but stalled just above Muscleman.

Nora said, "Give it a go, Dad."

Bonnie Two put her hand on his arm and said, "Not yet."

They moved on. At the Wheel of Fortune, Nora asked for a dollar. Mike said, "There must be fifty pegs on that thing. That's worse odds than a roulette wheel."

Mrs. Hawes said, "You mind if I stake her?" She patted Nora's head and said, "Now, don't get your hopes up, honey."

"You've already made a very generous contribution," Mike said.

"Well, these odds are no worse than picking you to knock off old pickle-puss. That didn't stop me."

Mike laughed. He'd taken a liking to Mrs. Hawes, a solidly fat woman packed hard into a shiny blue dress. She slapped a dollar bill on the counter and said to Nora, "Pick a number, sweetheart."

"Thirteen."

"That's right, sugar," Mrs. Hawes said. "Mock those superstitions and you'll do fine." She said to the woman running the Wheel of Fortune, "Slow night? Don't you worry. When this little lady wins, I'll guarantee you a dozen. Round and round she goes, where she stops nobody knows. Lookee, sweetheart, it's slowing down. And you picked a winner, honey. What you going to pick as your prize?"

Nora pointed to a medium-sized black-and-white teddy bear.

"That li'l ol' bear? How about that great big one?"

Nora shook her head and said, "I really like the black-and-white one."

Mike was pleased. He himself found it hard to resist Mrs. Hawes when she was on a roll. As did the four men in her entourage, who ponied up their dollar bills for the next round. So did Mike. He looked around for Bonnie Two, thinking he'd put a dollar in for her, but she wasn't there.

Mrs. Hawes said, "Too bad, boys. Now let's go eat."

"I don't see Miss Sproul," Mike said. "She was going to take Nora to the music tent. Do you think Nora could eat with us?"

"My little good-luck girl! Now, why on earth not? You come right along, sweetheart." Mike tasted a bitterness on his tongue. It was one of the absurd arguments he'd had with Bonnie One during the last year. Bonnie One had gone on about how much nicer Italians are to children than Americans. What the hell, probably so, what did he know? He'd been depressed in Italy. Why did he argue? His lawyerly spirit of contradiction? Just a chance to snarl at her? Some part of him, some barking growling part, had sensed her as someone to drive away. So he argued, got tangled in arguments. And here he was, still tangled in arguments. Mrs. Hawes was his winning argument. He'd stack Mrs. Hawes and her "You come right along, sweetheart," against any cheek-pinching, child-spoiling Italian. . . . He wondered when he would stop keeping score in that game that hadn't been the real game.

Nora nudged him to show him her bear. She'd turned the plastic oval eyes so that the bear was cross-eyed. "Now it's like Edith's old bear," she said. "Remember Mom's joke? She called Edith's bear Gladly. Remember? Gladly, my cross-eyed bear."

"Oh yeah. I remember."

"Edith lost it."

"Oh yeah. At the Smithsonian."

"No. She left it on the train, and Mom got her a stuffed buffalo, because none of the bears at the store had eyes that would cross. Mom called the buffalo Bison-tennial because it was 1976."

"Yeah, I remember that. That was on the package."

"I thought Mom made it up."

"Well, it's just like one of her jokes," Mike said. "Why don't you try out your cross-eyed-bear joke on Mrs. Hawes?"

Bonnie Two popped up in front of them. She said, "Mike, you want to swing that maul now? You think you can hit that little old plate? You hit it smack-dab in the middle, you'll ring the gong. You want to try? Bring Nora along."

Nora said, "Do they give prizes?"

"Yes indeed," Bonnie Two said. "Come on, Mike. Won't take but a minute."

Mrs. Hawes, at the head of her group, turned back. "What's this? You want to try to ring the gong? You ever swing one of them things?"

"I split wood every so often."

"Well, why not, then? Come on, boys. One more sideshow before you get to eat. Give you boys an appetite."

Mrs. Hawes led the way into the circle of spectators. She went round her group and held all their suit coats. She said to Nora, "You hold your daddy's coat, honey. It'll bring him luck."

Mike took off his coat, loosened his tie, and rolled up his sleeves. Mrs. Hawes made her four go first. She said loudly, "Now, I don't want these good people to find out they got a bunch of pantywaists for their board of supervisors."

One of them came very close to ringing the gong; the other three were in the low range of Muscleman.

Mike spat on his hands and rubbed in a little dirt. The maul, although large, wasn't much heavier than his splitting maul. He hefted it to get the feel of it, then took a swing. On the downstroke there was a flash which made him blink, but he heard the gong. Bonnie Two gave a high-pitched yelp. He hadn't thought she could make that sound at will.

Mrs. Hawes moved Nora forward to collect the prize, which was a T-shirt with the words "I rang the gong" across the chest. Mrs. Hawes said, "Always used to be a kewpie doll."

Nora said, "I like the T-shirt."

Mrs. Hawes said, "That's right, sugar—you can wear it while you eat, keep that pretty dress of yours from getting barbecue on it." She led them off to her picnic table.

It wasn't until after supper, when she'd walked Mike and Nora to the music tent and Nora had gone to put on her dancing shoes, that she let Mike down gradually. "That's a darling girl you've got for a daughter."

Mike said, "Thank you. You've been very kind to her."

"And that Miss Sproul's a sharp little thing."

Mike cocked his head.

Mrs. Hawes said, "She must have spent some time around carnivals and the like."

"Ah."

"You know how you rang the gong? The carnie's got a way to tighten or loosen that wire. If it's tight, that ball shoots right up there. If it's loose, it don't go near so high."

Mike said "Ah" again.

Mrs. Hawes patted his shoulder. She said, "I think she slipped him ten dollars. But you cut a nice figure out there. I like the way you dirtied up your hands. I could see the boys not looking quite so mean."

"So for ten bucks I get to be Abe Lincoln splitting rails. Must be worth a vote or two."

"I'll tell you a little something about that. Last time there was a riot somewhere—maybe in New York City—we heard about it on the TV.

Next day a friend of mine named Mr. Yancey drives up to the gas pump front of my store. He says to the man pumping gas, 'Now, what set them coloreds off like that?' The man pumping gas tips his head back and says, 'Abraham Lincoln.' The two of them have a good old laugh."

"Is that how it is?" Mike said.

"That's the way it is. It's how Mr. Yancey gets to poke fun at all the news that's going on far away. When he's thinking about people he knows, he's decent enough. If he was on a jury, he'd be as fair as he could manage. He lives up a dirt road, a car goes by maybe every hour or so. He looks up every time and says, 'Who's that? What's he doing out here?' Last year at the school-board meeting he spoke against the bond issue. Well, he didn't really speak, he just said he was against it. The chairwoman said to him, 'But why, Mr. Yancey? Don't you want your son to have a better education than you had?' And Mr. Yancey said, 'I can't say as I do.'"

"Why are you telling me this?" Mike said. "I mean if Mr. Yancey isn't going to vote for me."

"He's a registered Democrat," Mrs. Hawes said. "He might vote for you. I'm not telling you this to suggest an issue that appeals to Mr. Yancey. All the Mr. Yanceys in Nelson and Greene and Madison might vote for you. They won't like your position on one thing or another, but you can't guess what Mr. Yancey thinks. I'll give you a for-instance. Years ago there was a hippie commune out here, and they used to swim naked in the creek. People wanted to pass a stricter ordinance. Mr. Yancey came to the meeting and said he goes skinny-dipping. A man's got a right to do what he wants on his own land, especially if it's natural. What's unnatural is for someone to go sneaking up on someone else to see what they're doing. Mr. Yancey'll come out like that sometimes. Other times he'll want the government to make a raid on the poultry-processing plant, make everyone do the right thing about clean food or clean water. You've probably got consultants telling you about the Bubba vote. It's what they say now instead of 'redneck.' I'm telling you about Mr. Yancey so you'll know it's not a question of Bubba or Bubba issues. What Mr. Yancey might like about you is you work hard, you got energy, and every once in a while you sound like a real person. You've probably got consultants telling you to be cool, calm, and collected, because that's good on TV. I'm telling you, if something takes you fierce, you'd do just as well to be fierce. You're a long shot, you've got nothing to lose. You just do the usual, folks around here will vote the usual."

◇

As it turned out, the first bit of fierce campaigning came from the Fenton side. They'd got hold of the photo of Mike at the McGuffey benefit, flat on his back, looking dazed, tangled up with Bundy and Ganny in her nun's costume. Ganny was holding her index finger up to check him for a concussion, but it looked as if she were saying, "Naughty boy!" The TV ad ran the picture with the caption: "Mike Reardon and associates." The screen went black. Then, in white letters, "Reardon?" Then, after a one-second pause, came more white print: "Get serious."

Sometimes that was the end of the spot. Other times it was followed by a full-color picture of Fenton in a business suit at his desk, behind him, stage right and stage left, the United States and Virginia flags on vertical flag stands, then a caption in red against a royal-blue background: "This is serious." New caption: "Congressman Howard G. Fenton."

Jerry Medina said to Mike, "Now, *that* is an attack ad." He couldn't keep the admiration out of his voice. "It doesn't seem vicious—I mean it's kind of entertaining—but pow!"

Mike, Ganny, Jerry Medina, and Bonnie Two watched a tape of the ad in the Reardon campaign office, a storefront on the Charlottesville downtown mall. They were in one of the windowless back rooms, the one that Jerry Medina used as his office.

Jerry Medina pushed the rewind button and said, "Hey, Mike—don't let it get to you. I know where this is coming from. Fenton's had a safe seat for so long the Republicans use his campaign as a training ground for their baby consultants. They get out of college, they intern for a year on the editorial page of *The Wall Street Journal,* then they go work for one of those right-wing foundations in a new skyscraper in Arlington. Tons of money, state-of-the-art video. There's probably three or four of those glib little pricks turning out this stuff for Fenton. But that's okay. They're new on the block. They're cocky and they'll get too cute."

"Too new, too cocky, too much money," Mike said. "That's what the Humphrey people said about the Kennedy people in the 1960 primary."

"Mike," Jerry said. "Don't be so goddamn historical. And stop arguing with me. Let's talk about right now. Let's get ready for our radio call-in show. The question is do we use any of that airtime to respond to this ad."

Ganny said, "Mike could work in something like this—if Fenton claims to be serious he should be serious enough to debate. The voters should get a chance to see the real Fenton, not just some staged photos."

Jerry said, "Okay, I like the staged-photos line. But we want to avoid echoing their 'serious' word. The point of this radio call-in is to show Mike's in touch, he's talking to folks, he's asking how he can help. The mood is 'I'm on the ball, I'm a nuts-and-bolts kind of guy.' We don't do a lot of ideology—this isn't a good year for ideology, and it's not a good district for it. We want to project energy. Project competence."

Mike said, "Okay, fine. What is it—two days to the radio show? What do I have today?"

Ganny said, "An antique-car rally. We've got a guy with an old Packard convertible taking you with him. No preparation—you just shake hands and tell everyone how great their car is. Then you've got supper at six with some hospital administrators. That's mainly to listen to them, but you can take a look at some notes on the way. One issue they're worried about is federal reimbursement for caring for indigents. There's a card in the folder."

"Who's driving me from the antique cars to supper?"

Bonnie Two said, "Me. But I can't pick you up, 'cause I've got to sing tonight."

"I'll pick you up," Ganny said. "I've got a meeting with some prospective volunteers here at eight. You can talk to them for a bit and then go home."

"Okay. So right now how much time do I have before the car show?"

"An hour and a half."

"Okay. I'll go think about the call-in. . . . Have you got something I should look at, Jerry?"

"On your desk. You want me to grill you?"

"Tomorrow. You and Ganny pick an hour for tomorrow."

After a half-hour Bonnie Two knocked and slipped inside his office door. She said, "I thought maybe you could come hear me sing tonight?"

"I don't know. I'm not sure what Nora—"

"Nora's spending the night with a friend."

"I can't say. I've got some work, I might be working late. Where is it?"

"At the bar at that new motel between Madison and Culpeper. I'm on between ten and midnight. Maybe you could just catch the last part. And then talk to me afterward—I'm always kind of keyed up."

"I'm not sure Jerry wants me making late-night appearances in bars."

"You don't need to worry about that. They're giving me a room and all, so I'll leave a key stuck up in the exhaust pipe of my car. You could stand in the back and catch the last song. Then you could just go to the room and we could just visit for a bit without all those people."

"I can't leave the campaign van sitting out in—"

"You've still got that little old Jeep belongs to your mother-in-law." Bonnie Two put her hand on the doorknob and looked at the floor. "Don't tell me now. I'll just do the last set and go to my room. It'll be dark and I'll just tiptoe in. I'll say, 'Mike?' And there's no answer. I'll turn on one little light and start undoing my hair. And then I feel you undoing my hair. . . ." Bonnie Two shifted her weight and looked at a corner of the office. "But maybe you're really not there. Maybe you're working extra late. And I go to bed all disappointed. But then maybe you decide to come after all, even though it's real late. And I'm in bed, all tangled up in the sheet, and I don't hear the key in the lock, 'cause I've got the pillow wrapped around my ears like I do when I'm alone and I don't want to hear scary noises. And I wake up 'cause there's this hand on me. And at first I'm confused and I say, 'Oh no, please.' And you don't say anything, so you don't know exactly when it is I know for sure it's you." Bonnie Two looked at him. She put her hands on her cheeks and closed her eyes. She said, "Now I've gone and made myself blush."

He was aroused, of course. And amazed that this small-boned woman (dressed for her day job in a crisp seersucker skirt and white blouse) could elaborate so many details in a single cartoon thought-bubble.

And then coldly appraising: The actuality of Bonnie Two's plan wouldn't be as good as the scenario. Not for either of them.

And then a reconsideration, half feeling sorry for her, half thinking that maybe after all . . .

To be fair, the luna-moth occasion had been a surprise and pleasure that he was still grateful for. The next several times had been mixed blessings. He'd felt furtive and impatient, holding her hand at first with dutiful tenderness, suppressing his annoyance as she ran her thumb up and down his in nonrhythm to her hesitant, upward-rising sentences. The unspoken arrangement seemed to be that he had to say something about a feeling before anything else could happen. To be fair (he found himself thinking "to be fair" more and more), Bonnie Two didn't require that the feeling have anything to do with the two of them. She even seemed content if he said that he missed Joss, or that he was angry at Joss, or that if he wasn't running for Congress he'd sue Bonnie One for alienation of affection. As soon as he brought up a feeling, Bonnie Two would give a little sigh. It was as if she'd burped the baby. And she would in fact leave the room—go to the bathroom or the kitchen. When she came back in she would stand squarely in front of him, rub her palms on her hips, and bite her lip. Then she would say, "I've just been thinking about something. . . ." Her rubbing her palms and biting her lips was a combination of self-stimulation and embarrassment, as was her standing at a distance and blurting out what she'd been thinking. The last time, she said, "I've just been thinking about something . . . about how it would be kind of exciting to make love with our clothes on?" She blushed but didn't look away, as if she was hypnotizing him or he was hypnotizing her, or (it finally occurred to him) as if his face were the shiny object a hypnotist dangled before her eyes. "It would be kind of like we're at the office? We're in your back room and it's late but maybe there's still someone out front and that's why we're just rumpling and mussing and finding our way through all those clothes."

Now, with Bonnie Two standing by the door offering him her version of their next scene—the setting, the lighting, the sound effects, and her single line of dialogue—he knew that late that night he would be tempted, that he would take a shower, brush his teeth, dress again, and even remember to bring a stick or—better yet—a straightened coat hanger to pull her room key out of her exhaust pipe. He knew that he would do all that with the full assent of his will. And he knew that, on the drive back, whatever pleasure he'd felt along his nerves would end up reminding him how tightly huddled and cold he was at the core.

◇

Mike sat in front of the microphone. Jerry stood behind him massaging his shoulders and giving him a pep talk. Jerry stopped while the sound engineer got a voice level from Mike. Jerry pointed at the engineer's booth and said, "I'll be in there. Keep an eye on me." Jerry gestured to Ganny in the booth. She held up a card. "Can you read that okay?" Mike nodded. Jerry put his hands back on Mike's shoulders. "The main thing today is we're getting in touch with the callers. We're reaching out to them. We're listening and we're saying we can help. If we get a hostile caller, we show patience, we show we're concerned. We are kindly, and when we make our points our whole tone is saying, 'We hear you and we're going to make it better.' Deep, calm voice. You've got the voice, Mike. You've kissed the Blarney stone. I'll be in the booth, and I'm going to love it."

There were many things about Jerry Medina that irritated Mike, but he found himself relying on him. Especially just before an appearance. Mike worried that Jerry's pats and massages and show-biz flattery were inscribing him, reshaping him in those moments when he felt himself most blank.

Mike answered the first several callers comfortably. He used variants of the Jerry Medina soft-response method: "What I hear you saying is . . ."

The first hostile question was one he'd rehearsed for. The caller said, "Congressman Fenton's been in for more than ten years now and I guess he knows his way around. Don't you think his experience counts for something?"

Mike said, "When I was first in the Navy I was impressed by anyone with years of service. Until one day I had to deal with an officer who just didn't get the point. But I saw all his stripes and I thought maybe he knew something I didn't. Afterward I said to my chief, 'He didn't go for it—but he's got ten years' experience.' The old chief said, 'Well, sir, maybe he's had ten years' experience, or maybe he's just had one year's experience ten times.'

"When I worked on the Hill I saw some congressmen who were doing nothing but filling a slot. Holding a congressional seat can be one of the most irresponsible jobs in the country. You don't actually have to do anything. It takes some individual will to keep on pushing."

Jerry held up a card: Education, environment, energy. Mike did the short version—Fenton dropped the ball on these key issues, time for fresh initiative. Jerry twirled his index finger—wind it up.

After a few more calls Mike found that he could hear his own voice, monitor it, and adjust it. His rehearsed answers to predictable questions began to feel more like singing than thinking. And then it occurred to him that the structure of this event was strangely similar to his recent dates with Bonnie Two. The caller was nervous, overcame nervousness to get into a situation that was both thrilling and defined. His appeal was that he had some trappings of a competent, ordered life but had come out of it for the moment—was now exposed, was possibly going to be publicly powerful but was now in some danger, and above all in need. And of course the caller could get what she asked for—if she was nice, he would be nice; if she got a little rough, he could get a little rough.

A caller came on with a breathy, hesitant "hello" that Mike took for a boy's shyness. "Hello there. Speak right up, son."

It was a grown-up man who said more loudly, "Mr. Reardon, you're a Roman Catholic, right?"

"That's right."

"Went to Jesuit schools, went to a Jesuit college—"

"I went to Georgetown University."

Jerry held up his hands, pressed his palms down several times. Meaning, "Keep it calm."

The caller said, "You believe in papal infallibility, right?"

Mike said, "We could fill up the rest of this program with questions—and they're interesting questions—about religion. But I'm not running for a religious office. No more than John Kennedy was. We're not living in the time of the Thirty Years' War—we're not back in the 1600s, when Protestant princes or Catholic princes imposed their religion on their subjects. When people killed each other over sometimes small differences. It was that experience of mixing politics and religion that the founding fathers remembered, that moved the framers of our Constitution to—"

"Do you know who Father Drinan is? Do you know that America now has a Jesuit priest sitting in Congress?"

"—to make sure that no one religion could get the upper hand. Americans won't put up with it. Would you like it if there was a religious test? If only people of a certain religion could practice medicine? Or could be admitted to the bar to practice law? I don't think most Americans pick their doctor or lawyer by what religion he is."

"Father Drinan—"

"Or she is." Mike saw Ganny roll her eyes and laugh.

The caller said, "Father Drinan is a Jesuit priest and as such he has to obey—"

"Look. Leave your name and address with the operator so I'll be able to talk with you some more, and swap stories about Jesuit priests we've had trouble with. Just for now, I think what you'd really like to know . . . Maybe you just need to be reassured that I'm not a Jesuit priest."

The caller said, "You say that. And I say this isn't Massachusetts."

The caller hung up. Mike said, "I'm not sure what that meant." He looked up at the booth. Jerry held up a card with the words "Among our volunteers we have . . ."

Mike said, "I should add something most of you would like to weigh in your judgment. Among our campaign volunteers we have a Presbyterian minister who's a chaplain at the university, we have an Episcopalian vestryman, we have an elder of the Mount Zion Baptist Church. One of the gratifications of this campaign is finding out just how much all of us in our community have in common." Mike took a breath, but Jerry gave him the cut-off sign.

The next caller worked at a poultry-processing plant in the Shenandoah Valley, complained fairly succinctly that her paycheck wasn't going as far as it used to, that when she went to the supermarket she couldn't even afford the turkey and chicken she carved up and packaged. Her boss said that, if all the workers got raises, then prices would just keep going on up and they'd all be worse off.

If this was Jerry's setup for the inflation question, he'd found a peach.

Mike said, "Well, your boss is giving you the hard Republican answer, the pat answer. Their idea is that this inflation is wage-driven. They've got hold of one end of the argument. According to their end of things, if you'd just tighten your belt and sacrifice some more, businesses wouldn't have to raise prices.

"The other end of the argument is that inflation is price-driven—companies scared of inflation have been raising prices on food and cars and soap and refrigerators. So who's right?"

The caller said, "I don't know. . . . The way things are going . . ."

"Can I tell you something I've found out? It's a fact that surprised me. American workers' paychecks have been cut by a third over the last fifteen years. That's in terms of what you can buy for your family. The dollar amount on your check is bigger, but your share of the pie is smaller. So it's not the workers who are driving inflation. You're right, you have tightened your belt enough.

"So is your boss the bad guy here? There's a lot of pressure on good solid companies whose costs are going up. Sooner or later they get pushed into raising prices. Of course it's usually sooner for their prices and later for your wages, and we ought to even that out some. That doesn't make your boss a villain. There are some villains, and it's not the workers, and it's not the government. It's speculators. There's log-rolling going on in real-estate speculation you wouldn't believe. One speculator gets a loan to get hold of a piece of land, sticks it in a corporation he sets up. He sells it high to another corporation that a pal has set up. The pal sells it back to him; now it looks like it's worth three times the original price. They use the inflated value to get a bigger loan—everything is inflating but they don't care, they're surfing on the wave of inflation. If things go bad, it's their fly-by-night corporation that gets wiped out, not them. They walk away, they've been paying themselves salaries. Their personal risk is minimal. Their chance to gain is huge. They say that their growth is our salvation, that a rising tide lifts all boats. But they're not a rising tide, they're a flash flood. That runaway speculative growth isn't doing good for anyone but them. Inflation is driven by speculators, by usurers. It's in Psalms—'Lord, who shall abide in thy tabernacle?' And the answer is, 'He that putteth not out his money to usury, nor taketh reward against the innocent.'"

Mike felt good. His breath felt good, his body felt good, he felt the surge of his own voice.

Jerry was waving. He was waving with one hand, holding the other to his forehead. When he saw Mike look at him, he opened both hands and pressed his palms down twice. Mike read his lips. "Calm down, for Chrissakes." Then Jerry began to scribble with a Magic Marker.

Mike said, "Of course we want enterprise, of course we want businesses to be productive. The difficulty is going to be how to rein in the rogue runaways without harming normal growth."

Jerry held up a card on which he'd written, "I'll come visit you."

"So," Mike said. "That's all in the long run, that's the hard legal job to undertake carefully and fairly. But right now what I'd like to do is come over to the Valley and visit with you. Maybe I could get to talk to your boss, see if there's some way to help out a small business—maybe some sources in the public sector, maybe some sources in the private sector. Do you think we could get together and give that a try?"

Now he was sounding like Bonnie Two in her therapeutic mode.

The poultry processor said, "Well, yes."

"Well, that's great—so if you leave your name and number with the operator, we'll get together on this."

Jerry had been writhing around in the booth. Now he leaned forward and spoke through his microphone into the studio. "Break. Sixty seconds. Look, Mikey—stick with the cards, okay? And don't overwhelm the caller, okay? Not too loud, not too long—your voice levels are way up, then way down. Keep it even, okay? Good energy, but K-I-S-S—'keep it simple, stupid.' Thirty seconds. Don't get me wrong, Mike, I don't mean you're stupid. I mean keep it simple and slow, okay? What else? Oh yeah, breathing. Breathe softer." Jerry was like an overzealous golf pro, telling him twenty things that were wrong with his swing and then saying, "Relax!"

The next caller was another woman. She said, "It's Psalms 5:15, young man. That psalm you just quoted."

Mike said, "Thank you. You must have an amazing memory."

"I used my concordance."

"Good for you. I wish more people had one in their homes. Next to the Bible . . ."

"How does it happen that you're quoting the King James Version? I believe I heard you say that you're a Roman Catholic. . . ."

"Yes, ma'am. But when I was a boy I sang in a choir, and our choirmaster was friends with an Episcopalian choirmaster who loved Gregorian chant. Both choirmasters loved it, so once in a while the Episcopalian had his choirboys come over and rehearse with us, show them the medieval notation we still used. And then we'd go over and rehearse with them, use the regular notation and the King James Version. For example,

'Lumen ad revelationem gentium' comes out 'A light to lighten the gentiles.' And *'Nunc dimittis servum tuum'* comes out 'Now lettest thou thy servant depart in peace.' So all of us—Protestants and Catholics—we were singing the same song. It's the part of my education I'm most grateful for."

"Then why can't we have that in our schools?"

Blindsided. Mike made his standard blocking move. "You mean in our public schools, ma'am? In our state schools?"

"Yes, I do. Instead of some of those things they teach about health, I don't mean health, I mean about things that are just about the physical aspects."

"I think I know what you mean. I've been concerned how they teach . . . I think we can refer to it as 'reproduction' without offending. . . . I've been very concerned about this concern of yours. I was concerned with the materials my little daughters brought home. Teaching about human reproduction without teaching about love."

"I hope you mean divine love. How can they teach anything at all without teaching God's plan of creation?"

"That is a hard question." Mike looked up at the booth. Jerry gave the wind-up sign. Mike said, "That is the hardest question of all, ma'am. And I can't . . . I can't give you the one answer that would completely satisfy all the students and all the parents of students. And that's because so many of them have different versions of God's plan of creation. In our private schools and in Sunday schools and Bible classes we can tell the next generation what we understand to be God's plan. Some of us may be right. Some of us may be like Job, who could say, 'I know that my Redeemer liveth and I shall see him—' "

" 'On the latter-day upon the earth.' "

"—yes. But some of us are likely to fall into being Job's comforters, who thought that they had God's plan all laid out for them like a contract. The comforters weren't bad guys—you remember how at first they sat with Job in silence for three days? But then they started pushing him around, and they were a little too sure of what they knew about God. And you remember what happened? When God spoke from the whirlwind it was to rebuke Job's comforters for not having said the right thing. You remember that part about the right thing, ma'am?"

"I do. 'For ye have not spoken of me the thing that is right, as my servant Job hath.' "

"And what the right thing is is this—Job felt the mystery of God, he felt the unknowableness of God. So one of the reasons we can't order up God's plan in state schools is that we risk being Job's comforters. We risk being too cut-and-dried, too humanly certain. We can't teach about God's plan the way we teach math or chemistry. We can hope that the order of science might lead students to the mystery of where all that order comes from, but that's too hard a thing to pigeonhole in a state lesson plan. It's such a mysterious thing. That's a reason we should let the state schools render unto Caesar. And hope that families and Sunday schools and keeping the Sabbath—we hope that all that will render unto God the things that are God's. So one thing I'd like to ask you, ma'am—do you teach Sunday school? It sounds as if you know—"

"The devil can quote scripture. Do you hear me? The devil can quote scripture."

Disconnect. Jerry Medina pointed his finger at his mouth and smiled exaggeratedly, meaning 'Say something nice.'

"That cuts both ways," Mike said. Jerry pushed the corners of his mouth up. Mike said, "Seriously, now. I thought we were getting somewhere, maybe working our way to an understanding."

He felt lightheaded. This was all too free-form. He knew well enough not to out-argue a witness—you could win the argument and lose the jury. But if you were dealing with a jury, you could stay in touch with them, take a look and see them tense up or look puzzled. Here in a studio he was alone, he was in the middle of nowhere. And who was who? He was in the middle of no who. He had a Joss pang. "No who" was a Joss joke. She would have rolled her eyes and snorted through his Bible commentary, but for no who she would have laughed.

He stuck to the cards for the next several calls. He felt more enclosed. Not because of Jerry Medina's little controlling prods and taps. Not because of the small acoustic-tiled room with double-plated glass giving only a view of an even smaller room. He was becoming enclosed in himself, his own bones softening, his public skin becoming thicker and harder. An exoskeleton. His only way out of it was his voice. His voice was the only tube out of his enclosure . . . a periscope, a clumsy remote-control arm that he operated blindly from his interior.

Welfare. Check flash card. Put it in perspective, 1 percent of budget. Welfare Cadillac an exaggeration. Corporate bailouts vastly greater. Not a permanent solution, a way station. Yes, should include job training, incentives to work. Welfare a debilitating circumstance. A phrase from an old speech his father had written for a Democratic congressman during the Great Depression—"We must save our people from the dry rot of dole."

Cut the tax in capital gains? Nothing so-so here. He stole a phrase from an old FDR speech. "Why should the economic royalists pay a lower tax on their unearned income than the rest of us pay on our working wages? The Republicans say it will encourage investment and business growth, and the benefits will trickle down. But let me ask this—what are people with extra money going to do with it other than invest? Why do they need encouragement? What else are rich people going to do? Hide it under their mattresses?"

The caller said, "Well, maybe investors will invest in foreign companies, and then we won't even get the trickle-down. Whole companies might just get up and leave."

"Well, if we let that happen, that would be a problem. But you know what? If you or I take ourselves overseas and enlist in a foreign army, you know what happens? We lose our citizenship. Do you or I get a gift for staying here? No we don't. We are prohibited from allegiance to a foreign government. We don't think of that very often, because there are so few of us who would even think of abandoning our country. We have individual consciences. Corporations don't. They aren't immoral, they're amoral. They're just institutions, they're just artificial entities chartered by the state. We give them their artificial citizenship and we can certainly decide that these artificial citizens should be as patriotic as the rest of us."

Then it was over. Mike couldn't wait to get out of the studio. His shirt was so wet he felt cold in the air-conditioned hallway. He went out onto the sidewalk before Jerry or Ganny left the booth. The sunlight was odd, he'd expected night—the same feeling as coming out of an afternoon movie.

Jerry and Ganny came out talking to each other. He didn't want to hear it. He dried his hand on the seat of his pants and went back in to thank the radio-station people.

When he came back out he said to Ganny, "What's next? I've got to change my shirt."

Jerry said, "You know what? We didn't get an abortion question. Probably just as well we didn't. I think we ought to—"

"Not now," Ganny said. "Let's just go eat and talk about something else."

Mike felt grateful to Ganny, but he couldn't bring her into focus. His mind did a back flip to the sound of his own voice. His last answer about serving in a foreign army didn't make sense to him. What would Mr. Yancey think? Stick to the flash cards. Jerry Medina had massaged that message in—"Voters don't give points for originality." But if he kept himself inside the boundaries of the rehearsed, he would lose his last live connection to other live people. He'd be locked in a windowless studio well papered with bumper stickers.

◇

Grandma sent me to summer camp.

I had become a too-quiet ghost in Grandma's house, shying away from the big cousins, silently but fiercely wanting all of Grandma all the time. For a while she was sympathetic. She taught me backgammon. She gave me books that she'd loved as a girl—the very books she'd written her name in, held in her eleven-year-old hands.

I would come into her bedroom along with her breakfast tray and get in bed with her. I would read her my/her book while she read the newspaper, occasionally commenting to herself. Once in a while she would stroke my hand or my hair. It was bliss, but I was miserable in a way that bliss couldn't reach. I knew that she knew, and that made me more desperately quiet and well behaved.

"I think you'd be happier . . ."

Now, there's a plain everyday phrase that almost always has a barb in it.

Nora was off with Dad. Mom was off to Italy with Bonnie One. Grandma never tried to get me to join Dad and Nora on the campaign trail. She knew somehow how terrible Ezra's fight had been for me. And she certainly didn't think it was a good move for me to go to Italy, although Mom had floated that idea by me on one of her shuttlings from Charlottesville to the Northern Neck. Grandma deflected it lightly, saying to me, "Such a short, hectic trip, dear girl. You'll get much more out of it later on."

I know now my going with Mom and Bonnie One would have created a battleground.

Fortunately, it was a battle Mom decided not to have. For all sorts of reasons of her own: It *was* a sort of honeymoon, after all. And taking me would have been expensive—an extra plane ticket, an extra room. I imagine Grandma also cautioned Mom that it wouldn't be wise to take me in case Dad got mad enough to have a custody battle. But Grandma knew that I was down a well and that she couldn't get me out by herself. "I think you'd be happier . . ." So off I went, distracted at first by a shopping trip to Fredericksburg, and then by the terror of being a new girl in the second half of summer camp, of failing at archery, tennis, or horseback riding. My exile wasn't all that far away—the Shenandoah Valley, right at the northwest fringe of the Thirteenth Congressional District. Grandma drove me. The camp director fussed over her and me. Wherever she went, Grandma always knew someone or someone knew her.

I was on the Red Team, because Mom had been a Red when she'd gone here. Mom's name was in the main lodge, on a varnished wood plaque listing old campers. Mom had been the under-twelve tennis champion, and she'd won the award for Campfire Spirit of Enthusiasm. So I threw myself into it too, from reveille to taps: braiding lanyards for Mom and Dad; whacking the hide off the softball, the tetherball, the tennis ball; churning away on the breast-stroke leg of the under-twelve medley relay—five points for the Red Team!

"Florida oranges, California cactus!
We use the Blue Team just for practice!"

Paddling in the under-twelve single-canoe event, a quarter-mile across the pond, leaning into it, keeping on course with a J-stroke flick. As furious, grim, and overheated as Dad. Five more points for the Red Team!

"Go back! Go back! Go back to the woods!
You haven't, you haven't, you haven't got the goods!
You haven't got the rhythm! You haven't got the jazz!
You haven't got the spirit that the Red Team has!"

I was Mom, I was Dad, I was the Campfire Spirit of making them stay in their places, trying to send them my goodness, paddling my canoe as if it were a Buddhist prayer wheel.

During the free period between supper and taps I walked to the stables and groomed my favorite pony. Back to the cabin on wobbly legs after hugging and kissing her on the nose. Sundays we had to write home. I wrote Grandma. Every sentence ended with an exclamation point. "I love Snickelfritz! She's a Welsh pony! They're bigger than Shetlands! Almost as big as a real horse!"

The camp summer session was cleverly plumped up to imitate the real year. Just before I got there they had a midsummer Halloween. After I got there they had a summer Thanksgiving—we decorated the dining hall with black construction-paper turkeys with orange crepe-paper wattles, and we ate a turkey dinner. Then we had a summer Christmas with a counselor dressed up as Santa Claus and the juniors dressed up as elves. I was too old to be an elf, but I wore a red party dress with a string of faux pearls that Grandma sent me. (Grandma even remembered the camp's fake Christmas!)

I think the camp would have had a fake Valentine's Day too, except that the place was a swarm of crushes—juniors on seniors, intermediates on junior counselors and horses, seniors on grown-up counselors. It would have been a certain occasion for tears before bedtime.

We campers saw through the fake holidays, but we were still effectively seduced by the special meals, dressing ourselves up, and getting presents. This made the fake holidays inadvertent training for our later experiences with boys and men. What was *advertent* on the part of the camp management—I'm almost positive—was that the fake holidays were divorce therapy. Without revealing anything about my own situation, I'd found out that five of the twelve girls in my cabin had divorced parents. I would have made it six. The daughters of older divorces told bragging horror stories about Thanksgivings and Christmases—getting sick on bumpy plane rides to Dad's new house, packing and unpacking and packing again. "And wait till you have to be nice to your dad's new girlfriend." What the camp did was to provide a bland simulacrum of family holidays—no big thrills but no anguish. A methadone program. Or maybe a couple of doses of lithium to level out the too-big hopes and too-big disappointments that come from having overexcitable parents.

The fake holidays, soothing letters from Grandma, and my own striving to be a good camper had stabilized me. So when Dad and Nora showed up I didn't know what to make of them.

They arrived in the campaign van that now had, in addition to the Purple Heart license plate, an American flag painted on the side and a "Reardon for Congress" glitter bumper sticker. Even if they hadn't brought the van, they were way too pumped up. On parents' visiting day the camp became slow Sunday lunch at a country club. Expensive station wagons, mothers in pretty summer dresses, fathers on their day off—no starch, but looking as if they might have been to church. Dad was *not* on his day off. He was a man with a mission. He even looked paramilitary—khaki pants, short-sleeved khaki shirt with shoulder tabs, canvas sand-colored hiking shoes. It was his notion of what to wear to politic at a truck-stop diner or fire-department softball game, which in fact was what he'd been doing. The theme was: Reardon—vigorous; Fenton—too old. And he did look vigorous. His hair was severely cropped, his beard was trimmed square and short, he was tan (I guessed it was from giving speeches outdoors, but he also used a sun lamp), and he'd been lifting dumbbells. Nora told me he kept a pair in the van, although he also went to gyms in Harrisonburg, Staunton, and Culpeper, and dropped in to use the weights at fire stations—a two-for-one deal, politicking and lifting in one twenty-minute visit. Ganny told me later that she'd advised him to do some exercise that would be good for his heart. Dad said to her, "That muscle doesn't show."

But the main thing was that he'd tapped into the energy of his anger, of his hurt feelings, of his craziness. He was using hustle and bustle, he was using adrenaline, he was using the whole campaign as a drug.

Nora was a little bit scared by his manic energy, but she was also drawn into it, hypnotized by the campaign, by people being nice to her, by the applause when she did her little side-show numbers.

When Dad showed up on parents' day, I had a moment of joy, then I shrank into terror and embarrassment. Terror sounds worse than embarrassment, but for me terror and embarrassment were equal. Perhaps for any eleven-year-old terror and embarrassment are hard to tell apart. But I think the epicenter of the terror was that Dad was changing and wouldn't be able to change back (so I would lose him), and that any change this drastic must be dangerous to him. The epicenter of the embarrassment was that he was still part of me—my father's face was me as much as mine was me—but now it was beyond control. I had had *some* control, Mom and Grandma had had some, his getting dressed in his gray suits to go to his everyday job had had some. Now he was in radioactive meltdown, now he was careering around exposing us to everyone at camp, to everyone in the whole state.

You think I'm exaggerating? Perhaps you think this is just oversensitive me? Here are plain facts:

Dad arrives. Parents and campers go on a tour of our activities. Dad naturally starts up a flirtatious conversation with the prettiest mother, parent of a nerdy junior named Bosie Fuller. Nerdy junior becomes visibly nervous. Nora and I are exasperated as usual. The pretty mother is amused, but as oddly amused as Bosie is oddly nervous. Dad is combining flirtation with campaigning and asks pretty mother where she lives. She says, "Culpeper." Delicate Virginia-gentry voice.

Dad says, "Oh, good, you vote in my district."

Pretty mother says, "I don't know why you assume that's good."

Dad laughs, a smug laugh that I could tell—that anyone could tell—means "Little lady, I like your spunk, but five more minutes of radiance and you'll be mine."

The pretty mother adds, "And I don't know why you refer to it as *your* district."

Dad laughs again, even more pleased with what he takes to be spunky teasing.

The pretty mother goes on, "It's Congressman Fenton's district. Has been for six terms."

"Up for grabs now," Dad says cheerily.

The pretty mother says, "And before that—"

"I can't believe you remember much before that," Dad says, "unless you were a very precocious child."

"Before that we had perfectly nice conservatives. Never a carpetbagger with a Yankee accent who's against school prayer—"

"I'm all for school prayer," Dad said with more careful cheerfulness, "just not *public* school prayer, just not state-imposed prayer. . . . You know, you have a truly beautiful voice. I'd love to hear you say, 'Reardon is right about tax reform.'"

"But then I'd be telling a story," the pretty mother said, "and my daddy told me never to tell stories."

"Well, good, I like a father who—"

"My father is Congressman Fenton," the pretty mother said, took her daughter by the hand and stepped briskly out of range.

Dad opened his mouth and took a step forward, but Nora took hold of his wrist.

So for the rest of camp I had to know that Bosie Fuller was Congressman Fenton's granddaughter. And she got to know that my father had made a fool of himself.

Dad didn't do anything unusually idiotic for a while. He was of course the first parent to volunteer to shoot a bow and arrow at the archery range, the first one to nibble a leaf of sheep sorrel that the counselor in charge of the nature walk said was edible. That sort of stuff. After lunch he went into the kitchen and thanked the cooks and kitchen staff, shook hands all around. He didn't make me go in with him. Standing by the double swinging doors, I could barely hear him over the clatter of silverware and lunch trays.

But at the parent-camper softball game he revved up again.

Mrs. Fuller was playing first base on the other team. Bosie was playing right field, safely out of the way, until she got her chance to pitch—all the campers got to take one turn at pitching. Dad's first time at bat, facing another father, he sliced the ball into right field, where it bounced once and spun sideways into the deep grass. Bosie couldn't find it for a while, so her mother ran out to help her. Dad trotted all the way around the bases, but the umpire (one of the counselors) said it was a ground-rule double. Dad stole third, but the umpire said there was no stealing, she'd explained that twice already.

When it was Bosie's turn to pitch it was Dad's second time at bat. Dad tapped his bat on the plate, pointed it at Mrs. Fuller, and smiled. But what he did was very carefully hit a little pop-up to Bosie. I could tell—anyone could tell—he did it on purpose. She was petrified, but it was right to her, and she caught it, smothering it against her chest with her glove and bare hand. That would have been okay, but just in case anyone had missed what a nice thing he'd done, he made a big deal out of it. "Atta girl!" he yelled. "Way to go! Nice catch!" He kept on down the base path toward first, where Bosie's mother was cheering too. Dad said to her in his remarks-to-be-overheard voice, "A vest-pocket catch! The trademark of Rabbit Maranville! On the old Boston Braves. Before your time, Mrs. Fuller . . ." Bosie, excited by her catch, and very likely flustered by Dad's continuing to trot to first, winged the ball toward her mother. Mrs. Fuller stepped forward to catch it, but it hit Dad on the back of his head. The bump made Dad hunch forward. Mrs. Fuller's glove curled around Dad's neck and her right hand clutched Dad's arm. Dad lurched and fell to his knees. She plopped backward onto her butt. Dad kept on falling forward. He put his hands on the ground to keep from crushing Mrs. Fuller, but he ended up on top of her, his knees between her splayed legs. Briefly but unmistakably in what the counselors later identified as the missionary position. They didn't tell us campers that, of course; that phrase reached us through the grapevine (counselors to junior counselors to campers).

One of the girls in my cabin filled us in after lights-out but before our junior counselor came to bed. The J.C.s spent this half-hour behind the boathouse gossiping and learning to smoke. The complete phrase reported by my cabinmate was "a three-point landing in the missionary position." Everyone laughed. I don't think most of the cabin knew what "missionary position" meant any more than I did. They laughed because just bringing up the subject of Dad on top of Mrs. Fuller was funny, even for the umpteenth time that day.

The girl telling the story wasn't satisfied. She asked the girl in the bunk next to her if she knew what it meant. The girl said, "Not exactly." The storyteller said, "Edith. *You* tell her." I could have said, "I don't want to talk about my father." Or I could have gone hog-wild and said, "The reason my father fell down is because he was wounded in Vietnam and talking about it reminds me of how he almost died, so it's not funny." I had no objection to lying. I just wasn't strong enough or quick enough. So I ended up desperately guessing. I said, "Well, it's like praying. You fall down on your knees and it looks like praying. Because that's what missionaries do, they're always praying."

The girl in the lower bunk of our double-decker bought it. I actually heard her say, "Oh." For a second I was home free. But then the storyteller laughed brilliantly. Some of the other girls joined in. She said, "*Praying.* Yeah, right. *Praying.* I guess you think they're praying when they . . . do it." Everyone laughed. The storyteller said, "Hey—no wonder your dad's against school prayer." And everyone kept on laughing, some because sex was always good for a laugh, others because they were glad they weren't me.

The problem with top girls is that they're often witty. They can be bitches who cut your heart out and serve the pieces to the rest of the gang, but every so often they're wickedly funny. And everyone laughs and laughs while you lie on top of your bed, lashed down by thick ropes of embarrassment.

Later, when I learned about the half-life of radioactivity, I had no trouble with the concept. I already had figured out that some embarrassing moments, however excruciating at the time, lose their power within a few years. But all the embarrassments that I felt for Dad that year, that I felt because of Dad, from Bundy's funeral to "The Star-Spangled Banner" at Ezra's fight to Dad's day at camp—they have the half-life of plutonium.

◇

In September Mike got hold of a stick to beat Fenton with.

One of Mike's volunteers, a young woman with the lavishly Celtic name of Fiona McCaig, had a former boyfriend who worked at the EPA. Fiona and he still went rock-climbing and camping together. The EPA worker told Fiona that Fenton's office had made a lot of calls on behalf of a waste-management company that was trying to get clearance for a dump site in Greene County. Ganny and Fiona started on the research. There was a maze of corporate name changes (Greene Waste Removal, Sani-Waste Inc., Clean-Up Corp., American Landfill Service Company) but a connecting thread of more or less the same people on the board of directors, all of whom were heavy contributors to Fenton. Nothing illegal so far, but a start. Not yet a newsflash—*Fenton Part of Plot to Poison Greene County*—but worth some digging.

Fiona McCaig took a hike to the property—a four-hundred-acre hollow—and snapped photographs of the excavation that had already begun. She got chased off by a rent-a-cop. She took a picture of him too. Also a picture of the signs on the chain-link fence: DANGER—KEEP OUT—HEALTH HAZARD.

Unfortunately, she also got such a severe case of poison ivy she had to go to the hospital. Mike stopped by to give her a mock Purple Heart that Nora cut out of a vinyl notebook cover. Fiona's duties included occasionally babysitting Nora, who'd taken a liking to her. Fiona was born in Scotland but was raised in the various countries where her father had worked as a bridge engineer—Indonesia, South Africa, New Zealand, and Canada. She appeared to be college age but had apparently got a degree from an English red-brick university while still in her teens. She'd been supporting herself in the United States for two or three years. She worked hard and was eerily self-assured and occasionally sly. When he asked her to get some government pamphlets for his visit to the poultry-processing plant, she came up with them the same afternoon. He said, "How'd you do that? The library said it would take a week through interlibrary loan. You couldn't have gone to Washington. . . ."

"No," she said. "I went to Fenton's local office. They're much better organized than you are." She'd made Xerox copies of the pamphlets, because the title pages had been stamped "Courtesy of Congressman Howard Fenton."

She had a peculiar accent, or, rather, a variety of accents. She could sound almost American when she was answering the phone at the office, but when she talked fast, some words and phrases had echoes of Scotland or northern England. She could also imitate accents. Mike had been enchanted with her reading the *Just So Stories* to Nora in a bubbling-soup Indian accent. But for all her far-flung voices and jack-of-all-trades bits of knowledge, she still surprised him by what she didn't know. When he handed her the Purple Heart she said, "What's this, then? A premature valentine?"

Mike explained. Fiona said, "Oh sure, it's that thing on your license plate that I'd been meaning to ask about. I guessed at first it was some Catholic-lodge sort of thing, the Sons of the Sacred Heart, but I knew that couldn't be right. I knew it was nothing so simple as your wearing your heart on your license plate."

Mike took a step back. He couldn't believe he was getting a zap from this kid, her eyes swollen half shut and her mouth puffed out like some coral-feeding tropical fish. The reason she was in the hospital was that the poison ivy had got into her throat, so she'd had a hard time breathing.

"Well, now you know," Mike said. "So how're you feeling?"

"Oh, fine, I'm ready to waltz right out of here, but they won't let me. Has Ganny found out anything more about the dump? They're total villains, you know. I wouldn't be surprised if they *planted* that poison ivy."

"Ganny's been tracking down something. I'll ask her to let you know. I just dropped by to . . . Oh yeah, don't worry about the hospital bill. Take it easy, okay?"

"If you don't mind, I won't. I can make some calls from this telephone. It's occurred to me that this company has some fiddle going on over stream classification. Most of the streams coming out of the Blue Ridge are classified what they call 'exceptional'—not that they're truly that—but I do remember a petition to downgrade a stream from 'exceptional' to 'high quality,' maybe even 'average.'" The Sierra Club sent someone to the hearing. If it's all the same to you, I'll make a telephone call or two to Richmond. I'm going mad just lying here."

"So you have boyfriends at the state level too?"

"Now, what kind of question is that?"

"I'm sorry. I withdraw the question."

"Here I am with my face swelled up like a baboon's arse and you're after me about boyfriends."

"I'm—"

"And then you go and sound like a barrister—'I withdraw the question.'"

Mike held up his hands.

She said, "I'm only teasing you. Say hello to Nora. And give us a call, will you? If you find out anything about the dump."

"Okay."

As he went through the door she said, "And thanks for the valentine."

As it turned out, Fiona was right about the connection between the stream hearing and the dump. She also found out that Fenton's law firm, in which he was still a nominal partner, had sent an associate to the stream-quality hearing, and the associate had overwhelmed the commission with a parade of expert witnesses and charts.

Ganny was happy with the dump issue. She'd lost an argument with Jerry Medina, who'd issued a press release saying Mike was a hunter, a gun-owner, and in favor of the right to bear arms. This was accompanied by a photo of Mike raising a double-barreled shotgun—his gaze and that of an open-mouthed retriever were focused upward on an invisible bird. Ganny's elaboration of Mike's position—against mail-order firearms, in favor of certain other limitations—had been edited by Jerry Medina to say only that Mike supported the Virginia Police Officers' Association recommendations and the National Rifle Association Gun Safety Program.

"It doesn't say NRA," Jerry had said. "Just their Gun Safety Program."

Ganny had said, "That won't fool any gun nuts, and it'll just piss off people like me who see it as sucking up to the NRA."

"The gun-control people," Jerry had said, "where are they going to go?"

So now Ganny cut Jerry out of the dump issue. Ganny and Fiona wrote a rough draft that came out seventeen single-spaced pages. Ganny gave it to him the evening before the press conference.

Mike was reading it when the phone rang. It was Bonnie Two, asking him if he felt tense.

"Yes. No. I've got to boil this thing of Ganny's down."

"Well, maybe when you get through. I'll be at home, you can call late."

"This'll take a long time. Look, I'm sorry, Ganny's waiting for this."

When Ganny came in, Mike said, "Seventeen pages. I can't read all this out loud tomorrow."

"I know. Here, look at my copy. The parts you read are where I've highlighted. Who was on the phone?"

"Bonnie Sproul."

Ganny laughed. "She sing you her new song? She had in mind to sing it at the press conference. That woman could make a cat laugh. 'He's a straight shooter and no polluter.' Saying no to her is the only thing Jerry and I agreed on all week."

Mike looked down and read a few of the highlighted paragraphs. He said, "No, it doesn't sound right. It's all supporting material—no statement. I need a *statement*. A statement that tells the story in a paragraph. A statement with some feeling, for God's sake."

Ganny turned away. She sighed and said, "Mike."

"No, listen—"

"Mike. Don't say no again. Read the damn thing. Don't just run your eyes over it and say no. I'm going home. You call me in an hour."

"Okay, okay. I'm—"

"And don't you go calling Jerry. You want the story, it's in there. We worked on that—"

"No, it's great. It's—"

"You don't know it's great. You don't know anything about it until you read it."

Mike slumped back in his chair. He stared blankly at Ganny. He knew he should say the right thing; he felt the silence thicken over his face. Ganny was standing still, but he could feel her anger, not just over the seventeen pages on his desk but over God knows what scattered disappointments.

He said, "Where's Nora? I have a feeling I'm supposed to—"

"She's at your house with Fiona. Maybe you should go on home, read it there. Get away from the office. Give me a call."

"Okay, right. I'm sorry. You're right. I got on edge. I'll just sit down and read. No rush. A lot of work, you did a lot of work. Mark, read, learn, and inwardly digest."

"Is that a Bible quote, Mike?"

"Probably. I don't know. Don't worry. 'Gird up your loins now like a man.' Now, there's a Bible quote."

"Mike. The trouble with the people I know who quote the Bible . . . You're not in that kind of hopeless thrashing around like Bundy got into. And you're not like Emmanuel Pritchett—quoting the Bible when he's up to something sly. But all of you are alike one way—when you all get too tense, those Bible quotes come squeezing out. It's a sign. So calm down. You ain't Job, honey. You ain't talking to God in the whirlwind. Nobody's done away with your camels and your she-asses, nobody's covered your skin with boils. You can gird up your loins all you want, but all you really got to do is go home and do a little homework."

So mild a rebuke after all. Such light correction. He was relieved.

Until he thought that he should have been like that with Bundy. Should have opposed him both more strongly and more gently. And he should have been like that with Joss. Way to go, Mike. Dead and divorced. You've got that magic touch.

"Mike, don't tune out on me. Fenton old, Reardon vigorous. Get up and go home. Call me in an hour."

When Mike drove the van up the driveway to his house, he was saddened to see Tyler's bungalow still dark and empty. Evelyn and Edmond's cottage showed a light, but there were cardboard boxes stacked on their front porch.

His own house was ablaze. Fiona and Nora had the stereo on full-blast and were singing along, belting it out face to face, stamping and prancing in place and semaphoring with their arms.

Fiona saw him and moved to turn the stereo off. Nora shouted, "Hi, Dad! Just another minute," and dragged Fiona away from the dial. Nora sang, "Let me in, let me in!" and Fiona joined back in "Wee-ooh! Wee-ooh!"

Mike dropped his briefcase and suit coat on the table, got a beer out of the fridge, decided not to have it, offered it to Fiona as the music ended. Nora begged for another song. Mike said no. She begged for a sip of

Fiona's beer, which Fiona was just tilting into her mouth. Fiona said, "Maybe it'll make her sleepy."

Mike said, "Anything for peace. I've got to get to work. I've got about one ounce of energy left."

Fiona applied the beer bottle to her forehead, to her flushed cheeks, then lifted her hair to apply it to the back of her neck. Mike's eye was caught by the sprays of ginger hair in her armpits, a shade lighter than the short-cropped copper hair on her head.

Nora said, "You think I'm going to drink out of that after you've rubbed it all over you?"

"Nora," Mike said. "That's enough. Up to your room."

"You said I could—"

"We'll save you a sip for when you get your nightgown on and brush your teeth."

"I don't like the way beer tastes after I brush my teeth."

Mike said, "My God, I've got a child barfly on my hands." He heard his father's voice in his.

Fiona laughed and poured a couple of fingers of beer into a coffee mug. Nora swallowed.

Mike said, "Fiona, you're no help."

Fiona said to Nora, "Go on up, now. I'll come read to you." She said to Mike, "Ganny called. She asked me to make sure you do your homework. I'll stay on for a bit in case you've some questions. Go on, now, read. I'll see to Nora."

Mike sat at the dinner table. He had got to the next-to-last page when Joss came through the front door.

Mike wasn't sure if either of them said hello. For a smudge of time there was a crackling in his senses like radio static. Then there was an odd sound in his head, halfway between a zing of feedback and a rasp of clearing his throat. And then he heard Joss say clearly, "Where's Nora?"

"Nora's in bed."

Joss shifted her weight from foot to foot and twirled her wedding ring with her thumb.

He said, "You're still wearing your ring. . . ."

"It's a help when I'm traveling."

Right. The quick retort, like "Don't get your hopes up." He looked at her stance, her face. A language he knew perfectly well—he was just a little rusty in it. Now he picked up something more—a point of serious anger on the agenda.

Joss said, "I assume you're familiar with the ads you're using in your campaign."

"Sure."

Joss pulled an eight-by-ten glossy from her shoulder bag and held it out at him, her arm straight, her fingers crinkling the top against the heel of her hand. It was a picture of Nora in the boxing ring. Nora was holding Ezra's taped hand in both of hers. She was looking up at his bruised face, her own face astonished, fearful, sympathetically elated.

Mike recognized the moment. He wasn't sure where he'd seen the picture. It came back to him—one of the leaflets Jerry Medina had put together. He'd told Jerry he liked it. Fold-out flyer for the black-voter mailing list. They'd also used a photo of himself with the Mount Zion Baptist choir.

Joss' arm drew back and jabbed forward again. Her fingers dug in, tilting the top of Ezra's head. Joss said, "Well?"

Mike said, "Well what? What am I supposed to say? I don't get it. Are you doing one of your movie clichés?—'Perhaps *this* will refresh your recollection.'"

Joss breathed hard, turned completely around once, and pulled her hair. She said, "Oh brother! You have no idea?"

"Look," Mike said. "Just tell me what's up."

"What's up is this—you're a goddamn pimp is what's up, what's up is you are using a nine-year-old, you are using your nine-year-old daughter, our daughter, my daughter. You are exploiting her. You told my lawyer you wouldn't permit Nora to stay in the same house with my Bonnie. Well, let me tell you, this campaigning, this exploiting Nora is a thousand times . . . *dirtier* than anything you imagined about Bonnie in your pig brain."

Mike said, "You're right—" Joss' auditory reflexes were so fast she looked surprised, about to be relieved. "You're right," he said, "I don't get it." He hadn't meant to throw her off balance. He said, "I'm really not . . . I don't mean to piss you off. Nora and I have been having a good time. Once in a while I feel bad leaving her with someone while I have to . . . but the campaign, especially the county fairs, going to softball games . . . it's not . . ." Mike stopped, began again. "Look. I assume you're not objecting to Nora climbing up in the ring with Ezra. Nora is crazy about Ezra, she was thrilled. *You* were thrilled. The only person I felt bad about that night was Edith—it was too much for her. But—"

"You are being a *moron*. It's not Nora, it's not Ezra. It's not Nora with Ezra. It's you *selling* her. It's you selling *them*. It's you using her affection for Ezra. It's *you* saying, 'Look, everybody. My cute little daughter loves a black boxer.'"

"Don't exaggerate, for Chrissake. And what's the big deal about race? Are you saying I shouldn't have black clients?"

"Oh, *pathetic.* Your trying to twist this around is pathetic!"

"Is this one of Bonnie One's ideas?"

"That's it. Nora's coming with me. Right now."

Mike forced himself not to say anything. Not because he was in the wrong, but because the one intimacy they had as strong as ever was that they could make each other crazier and crazier. He walked to the dining-room table and sat down. He squared up the typed paper. He breathed deeply and slowly. He said, "If that's what you want . . . if that's what you want to do, you should talk to Mr. Broome. I'm just making you madder. Mr. Broome will arrange what you want. I'll go along with anything reasonable. You've been away. Nora's missed you. But now she's gone to bed. You and Nora can have breakfast together tomorrow."

Joss busied herself putting away the photograph. She said, "And school starts next Tuesday. Have you given a thought—"

Mike said, "School . . ." He *hadn't* given it a thought. Jerry had said something about Nora and Mike going to the Price Club back-to-school sale. Before the press conference? "Look. We'll agree about school. Nothing to worry about . . . Tomorrow is Saturday, I'm jammed up. We can talk on Sunday, Sunday's an easier day. Are you staying with your mother? I'll drive over. I'll bring Nora. I'll see Edith. You can bring them back on Labor Day."

"I'll stay here in Charlottesville."

The door to Nora's room opened. Fiona came out, shut the door carefully, and came down the steps on tiptoe. She said to Mike, "Out for the night."

Mike turned to Joss, opened his mouth to introduce her to Fiona. Joss was staring at Fiona. Joss appeared to recognize Fiona, and to have some feeling—surprise? alarm? jealousy? Mike felt a bubble of pleasure at the idea of jealousy.

Joss said, "What are you doing here?"

Mike said, "Joss, this is Fiona McCaig—"

"Rock-climbing," Joss said. "You're Bonnie's rock-climber."

Both women looked at each other in complete stillness. It was only for a second, but Mike felt removed to a great distance.

"Yes," Fiona said. "Professor Campbell. The art historian. She had a brief interest in rock-climbing."

Joss lifted her chin an inch.

Fiona said, "Professor Campbell took the odd lesson. She never got all that far. Not a serious climber. I doubt she intended more than to give it a try."

"Tomorrow," Joss said to Mike. "I'll be here early to pick up Nora."

At the door she pivoted to face them again. She rocked one foot back on its heel and flipped her hand in a one-stroke goodbye. Her cockiness was a cover, but not for her straightforward anger at him. So what was it? He was reluctant to give up his pinch of hope that Joss was jealous of Fiona and him. He was also reluctant to think that Bonnie One buzzed around Fiona, perhaps because he wished Bonnie One as far from his life as possible—after all, that was one point of this new phase of his life. Or perhaps because he actually didn't want Joss to be upset, because then Joss was likely to take a poke at the wrong person. Or perhaps because . . . Enough.

He squared up the pages on the table again. Without looking up he said, "I suppose Ganny's filled you in? That my wife and I . . . that we've agreed to keep up appearances. For the campaign."

"Yes. Ganny told me about appearances."

"Good. So now we can get this press release boiled down."

Fiona said, "Your wife . . . your estranged wife . . . your apparent wife—has amazing eyes. Fierce blue."

"Okay. Let's get at these parts you highlighted."

"Without further ado," Fiona said.

"Without further anything," Mike said. "Now I've got about a half ounce of energy."

◇

Joss wanted a drink. When she got in her car she decided not to go back to Bonnie One's, because Bonnie One would give her one. (Joss had been very good in Italy—only soda water. But she hadn't really wanted a *drink* then, only the taste of wine.) And she didn't want to see Bonnie One right after seeing Bonnie One's rock-climber.

Joss really wanted to see Nora. That was why she didn't want to drive back to the Northern Neck, and that was how she would get over wanting a drink.

She drove down the driveway, unsure where she was going. Just as she reached the bridge, headlights appeared on the other side. Whoever it was waited for her to cross. As she pulled even, she recognized Edmond's pickup. She turned her car around at the first wide part of the road, went back up the driveway, and parked beside the pickup in front of Edmond and Evelyn's front porch.

As she reached to knock on the door she was astonished to see her hand tremble. What was this? Was she afraid they'd choose sides?

Evelyn opened the door. Joss hesitated. Evelyn cried out, "Joss!" and held out her arms. Joss stepped into her hug, faint and eager at the same time. Evelyn called, "Edmond! It's Joss!" Both Evelyn and Joss freed an arm to hug Edmond.

Evelyn said, "Have you eaten? Can you spend the night?"

This was what she needed.

"And Nora?" Evelyn said. "Why not bring Nora over first thing in the morning? It's been ages since we've had a big lazy breakfast."

But after this dizzy, sweet welcome, there was a muffled moment—Joss could plainly see both Evelyn and Edmond thinking of questions and then thinking better of them.

Joss looked around. The cottage was almost bare. No sofa, no chairs. Three open cardboard boxes of pots and pans. An unzipped duffel bag half full of sheets and blankets.

"Looks like it's hello and goodbye," Joss said. "Here today, Guatemala."

Evelyn didn't laugh, she looked grave. Edmond actually put his hand to his head and moaned.

Joss had forgotten how straightforwardly solemn they could be. The rehearsal dinner for their wedding had been at a country club near Evelyn's family's homeplace, bordered by a dark river that ran between cypresses. Edmond's father gave the first toast—"To the sovereign state of South Carolina." Evelyn's father rose, bowed, and said, "To the sovereign state of Georgia."

Joss whispered to Mike, "Yikes. We're not in Kansas, Toto. I'd better rewrite my toast. How's yours?"

"Underdressed for the occasion."

The next several toasts were as serious as a Japanese tea ceremony. Joss was used to the Northeastern style of toasting, in which feeling was veiled in ironic style. Perhaps there was a brief pretense of shyness to be standing in front of such an array of distinguished guests. Then some highly polished mock-heroic descriptions of escapades of the groom (har-har) or childhood foibles of the bride (her iron will or seductive caprice already evident in the nursery). And only at the last a swerve toward sentiment, spoken a tone lower to indicate awkward sincerity.

Fortunately for Joss, it turned out that, after the first un-ironic phase, Edmond's and Evelyn's cousins (first, second, and even third) and college friends came on with some roister-doister.

Joss was moved by this recollection of Evelyn and Edmond's nest of gentlefolk, and of how well Mike and she had once suited each other.

Evelyn and Edmond now fixed her a meal out of the carton of food they'd been about to deliver to Mike. They all sat on the floor, leaning against the bare walls.

Edmond said, "I feel as if we're sitting in a bombed ruin, somewhere in Germany, maybe Berlin in 1945. But I guess that means that things are about to get better."

Evelyn said, "It's real sad we're all being scattered, but there hasn't been a *war*."

"I just meant this moment," Edmond said. "Camping out in this house. Just the feeling of aftermath."

"I suppose you think I'm the one who dropped the bomb," Joss said. "That it's all my fault."

Evelyn said, "Oh, Joss! How on earth could that be so? *We're* going on account of my job. Why, this whole past year's had just a ton of sad things. I'm still sad about Miss Dudley. And Bundy . . . I'm sure Mike told you about how he hears Bundy's voice every now and again."

Joss felt a pang of her old jealousy of Evelyn. "No," she said. "He didn't tell me."

Edmond said, "It is odd, though—it does feel as if there has been some invisible turbulence. I've sometimes seen a herd of animals take off for no reason I could figure. Sometimes, if one member of the herd takes off, that'll set the others on edge, but then they'll calm back down. Other times, though, the whole herd'll jump at once."

"You and your animals," Joss said. "This isn't an animal story."

"Well, we haven't lost all our unconscious alertness. It's not extrasensory perception, it's just very acute sensory perception. I think about Mike hearing Bundy's voice, or his looking at the river and interpreting it, or his dreaming he was an owl—"

"I don't know about that either," Joss said. "I didn't know Mike was coming over here to tell all. I thought he was using Bonnie Two as his divorce counselor."

"I don't think you should get cross about it," Evelyn said. "He was in a daze, he didn't know what he was doing."

Edmond rubbed his hair forward, a sign that he was pondering. He said, "I remember how we all got so wild last spring, with all those games. And how close to hysteria Edith and Nora got every night. Edith particularly. She was sensing things that are out of the normal range."

"Nora too," Evelyn said. "I remember her drawings from then. I hope she's still doing them, I haven't seen her much since she's been traveling all over the place. I hope—"

Joss said, "All this acute sensing Edith and Nora were doing—I mean, you're talking about their sensing what *I* was doing. Let's call a spade a spade."

"I had in mind a number of things," Edmond said. "I remember Edith and Nora trailing around behind Mike after Bundy died, too timid to bleat, just wandering after him. . . . But, yes, I do have in mind their being nervous about you and Bonnie One."

"So I'm dropping bombs on my children."

"Oh, Joss," Evelyn said, "Edmond's just describing how people get wind of things. Edith and Nora are crazy about you, you're a wonderful mother. We're not finding fault."

"So you say. But you tell me, Edmond. Between Mike and me, you think it's more my fault. Is that right?"

Edmond pushed his hair onto his forehead and held it there with the palm of his hand.

Evelyn said, "Oh, Mike has all sorts of faults. He didn't appreciate how much you did, how much goes into taking care of two little girls."

Joss knew her relentlessness was unfair. She couldn't stop; Edmond couldn't stop himself from telling the truth. She also knew that she was using him for her own pain. Pain, not penance. She couldn't do this with Mike anymore. Mike was evasive. She couldn't hold Mike still and squeeze a drop of acid out of him. She watched Edmond as he leaned sideways against the wall, lowered his head, and ground his hair into it with the heel of his hand.

Evelyn said to Joss, "Why are you doing this?"

Edmond didn't pay any attention; perhaps he didn't even hear her.

Joss said, "Tell me."

Edmond looked up, nodded once, and said, "Yes."

Joss felt her face boil.

Evelyn said, "You knew he'd do that."

Joss felt her face, throat, and lungs grow hot. At the same time, a single cold drop of satisfaction slid through her.

They didn't talk much after that. Edmond blew up an air mattress for her and Evelyn got two sheets. Evelyn and Edmond went to their own bedroom. Edmond came back with an electric fan for her. He said, "You can be mad at me if you want. Evelyn and I are still your friends."

Joss lay awake. She didn't know exactly why she'd cornered Edmond this way, wounded him, wounded herself. Just for that one trickle of relief? It *was* relief. In Italy, once or twice a week she'd said jokingly to Bonnie One, "I'll burn in hell for this."

And last spring Mike had scourged her by remembering out loud to her—in all the detail he was capable of—how she and Bonnie One had shaved off Tyler's beard at the dinner table. Then she'd said, "Okay, okay, I'll burn in hell for it." Guilty, defiant, and joking.

She thought, "This is better. This is no joke."

The next morning, on the porch, just before crossing the yard to see Nora, Joss said to Evelyn, "I remember once when Edith was five . . . she was building a little cardboard dollhouse—some sort of kit where she had to cut out the pieces and then insert tab A into slot B. She was putting it together on the floor, in the front room, just outside my studio. Nora was playing outside. Then she came in. She saw Edith's tidy little construction, walked up to it, and planted her foot on it. Squashed it flat. Nora didn't even break stride, kept on walking to the kitchen. I heard her open the refrigerator. Edith didn't look up until then. I saw her little profile tip up. She said, 'Nora! Why did you do that for no reason?' "

Evelyn laughed, then stopped abruptly. "Well, actually, that's a real smart question. I miss Edith. And I've always loved Nora, but sometimes she is a terrible little devil. Of course I love that part too. . . ." Evelyn folded her arms across her chest and looked into Joss' face. "You don't need to tell me you're like Nora. Besides, last night you didn't do that for no reason. You wanted to find the hardest part of Edmond. Last night I thought you were reckless and mean with him. Now I think you were rough because you couldn't get what you wanted unless you put your head down and ran at him. You knew he wouldn't dodge you. But I guess you knew you'd get knocked over too. And you didn't know for sure that he'd get back up and bring you the fan. So now you'll go see Nora. And then please come back, and we'll all have breakfast together."

◇

I did get to campaign after all. Grandma arranged a fund-raising tea for Dad at a friend's house near Warrenton. She had lots of reasons, but I think her chief motive was to make Mom and Dad (and Nora and me) behave like a family. Once, when she was making one of the big cousins behave, he said to her, "Do you want me to *pretend* to be good?"

She said, "That's a start."

So Mom and Dad and Nora and I all got dressed up and drove to Warrenton—much smaller than Charlottesville, but even fancier horse country, even grander estates, and much closer to Washington and therefore more populated with rich people interested in politics and politicians interested in rich people. Grandma knew lots of both—no surprise—but she also knew a half-dozen newspaper people of an elder-statesman sort—Joe and Stewart Alsop, for example—as well as a couple of older women who in the old days had worked for the society page but who now wrote—much less frequently—for "Style."

Either Grandma or Dad banished Jerry Medina and Bonnie Two. And I actually heard Grandma say to Dad, "Mike, dear, one thing I insist on—you will not drive up in that campaign van of yours."

"Okay," Dad said. "Can I borrow your Jeep?"

"May," Grandma said. "No, you may not. Surely you can find some perfectly normal car this once."

Grandma was a benevolent despot to the rest of us too. Nora and I went shopping with her in Washington. She had a lot of stops to make, but the friend whose house she was using for the tea party sent a car and driver to pick us up on the Northern Neck, take us to Washington, go to three stores and a dozen houses. Sometimes we went in and sat still in living rooms too splendid to play in while Grandma got down to business. I'll say this for her, she knew how to keep it short. She would cry out, "Ella darling!," kiss and hug, introduce us, make her pitch for Ella darling to show up in Warrenton, and have us back in the car in ten minutes.

"You were angels," she said to us each time. Then on to another house.

At last she said, "You've been perfect angels, dear girls—just one more stop."

We drove to a building next to the Capitol and went in to some congressman's office. We waited a long time. Finally the congressman came out, much older than Dad. Grandma did the usual carrying on—"Peter, dear boy!," a hug and kiss, introduced us. But this time we got ditched in the anteroom with a secretary. She gave us Cokes, but I would have liked to see more of the congressman. I wanted to see what Dad might be like if he won.

The congressman came out again with Grandma. I was going to say something, but Nora got in first. She said, "I've been campaigning with my father. I sang his campaign song solo."

"Yes, dear," Grandma said, "but I'm afraid there's no time for that—"

Nora said, "Do you have a campaign song?"

Nora was playing about two years younger than her age, and I was glad to see the congressman wasn't buying it. He ignored Nora and said to Grandma, "I can't believe you have grandchildren." He kissed her on the cheek and was gone.

We got back in the car. Grandma took off her hat and rubbed her head. I could see she was exhausted. "I'm glad *that's* over," she said. "Now we'll all be very still and take a nap." She fell asleep before we were out of the city. Nora and I leaned forward and looked at each other across Grandma's lap. I was glad to see that Nora felt as strange and shy as I did. Nora carefully took Grandma's hat out of her hands and set it on the ledge by the rear window. What was strange was that Grandma had looked bright and strong all day, and then, just as we got to the car, she became old. She *looked* older—her hands seemed to have more veins and stringy tendons, her face looked grayer. She also *felt* older—the purr of energy that her body usually gave off stopped completely.

The Sunday of her tea party Grandma was powerful again. In the morning Mom and Nora and I rode to Warrenton with her in the same borrowed car with the same driver.

Grandma gave us a quiz just before the car got to Warrenton. "What is the name of your hostess, Edith? And what is the name of your host, Nora?" I thought Nora's question was unfairly easy—all Nora had to do was say Mr. instead of Mrs. But it was a trick question. He had been an ambassador, so you had to call him that—"How do you do, Mr. Ambassador?"

Nora said, "What's his real name?"

Grandma said, "Albert. But only your mother and I will call him that." Grandma turned to Mom. "You might start with 'Mr. Ambassador,' and then he'll insist you use his first name. You don't by any chance remember what he gave you for a wedding present?" Mom rolled her eyes. Grandma said to Nora, "And what do you call the congressman you met?"

Nora said, "Peter darling!," imitating Grandma's elegant croak.

Mom laughed. So did Grandma, who was nervous but in a good mood. Grandma tapped Nora on the knee with one finger and said, "He would be amused, but *I* would not."

The ambassador's house was on top of a hill, and the driveway was very long, because it looped back and forth. The house was a Georgian mansion with side wings, all in pale-red brick, with a white portico in the middle. I still see it from time to time in my dreams. The rhododendrons were past—a few blowzy flowers lagged behind, and there were heaps of white petals on the ground.

Grandma told Nora and me to play outside.

Through the large windows we could see Grandma and the ambassador's wife going from room to room. They would bustle along, then freeze just inside the doorway, each of them trailing a hand on a door jamb, each jutting her chin as the two of them scanned the room. Once Grandma said something to the ambassador's wife, who said something to the butler, who then told two maids what to do.

We were called in to change into our party dresses. The house was much more of a museum than Grandma's. It had more light in the big rooms, though it was darker in the narrow inner hallways. The windows were tall and long—almost up to the ceiling and all the way down to my knees. The glass was old and parts of it crinkled what you could see. Nora and I looked out over the circle of combed white pebbles in front of the house. When Dad pulled up in his strange (but normal) car, I didn't recognize him. I recognized Ganny first, as tall as Dad and shimmering in the windowpane in a red dress that blazed against her brown skin. Nora recognized the other woman. I thought it might be Bonnie Two, because she was wearing a red dress like the one Bonnie Two had worn to Ezra's fight. But Nora said it was someone new, Fiona, who was more fun and less goopy-syrupy.

Dad looked good in a crisp blue-and-white seersucker suit. I'd been afraid he'd be wearing something like he wore to parents' day, but of course this was Grandma's party. She was the one who waved her wand and got everyone to come to the ball looking just right.

She came in as Nora and I were about to run down to see Dad. She checked our dresses, put another hairpin in Nora's hair to hold her bow, told us we looked beautiful, and then let us go down the stairs.

We stopped cold at the edge of the living room. It was already filling with grown-ups in suits and dresses, moving nervously here and there across the rugs and shiny floors, blotting out the clusters of long-stalked flowers, looking quickly at themselves in the huge mirrors. Even Nora was shy, but less shy than I was. She moved quicker into enjoyment. She said to me, "This is better than Grandma's square dance. This is like a play. This is like the One True Bridegroom." That was the game Nora and I had played instead of Barbie and Ken (whom Mom and Dad had banned). We did use dolls, but the main attraction was dressing ourselves up. Grandma had given us some of her old gowns and finery. She put them in a trunk in her attic. It was the one game Nora and I played that we never fought over. We lined up rows of dolls and animals and took turns being the bride and the one true bridegroom, who got to use Grandpa's old uniform and sword. The one true bridegroom came in last and could be scary, using a red feather boa for a beard. Or he could be a victim—hiding in the attic to be found by flashlight. Then all the girl dolls and the animals jumped on him and undressed him to see if he had the mark of the one true bridegroom.

We must have mixed in pieces of "Cinderella," King Arthur, *Dracula,* and Mom and Dad's wedding album. Neither of us can remember which of us first said "one true bridegroom," but it came to mean the magic power that arranged grown-ups into parades, funerals, and weddings.

Nora was right. Grandma's tea party fit the category. It had more glamour than just a room full of grown-ups. And Dad fit the part of the bridegroom—he had the beard, which even looked a little bit red or at least ginger after the summer. He looked strong and handsome, but he'd looked strong and handsome at camp. Now he looked ceremonial, as if Grandma had passed her wand over him too. I knew enough to know that some of the people here would give him money if they thought he had the secret mark.

Nora and I went up to Dad, who hugged us both once, one arm for each of us. There was a camera click. Dad introduced us to the ambassador. I mutely held out my paw. Cutie-pie Nora said, "Mr. Ambassador," and made a curtsy. Click.

More men clustered around and talked. Energy policy. The yawning abyss, Mom called it. The ambassador said something and the clustered men stopped talking. Dad said to him—addressing him—"I see the ambassador is a secret scientist." It struck me as very odd. Was the ambassador so great and terrible that you couldn't say "you"? And Dad's charming tone—Dad was plumping pillows for him (Mom's phrase for sucking up), and he was (in Nora's later analysis) praising the ambassador for a minor and secret vanity, the witchcraft way to a person's heart.

The ambassador said, "If you want to understand Russia, you're better off knowing energy than Marxism."

Dad nodded. The ambassador went on, and Dad nodded some more. When the ambassador was done, Dad said, "Foreign policy and energy—I hope the ambassador is writing something on the subject."

The ambassador tilted his head back with pleasure. "Halfway through a book. Four hours first thing every morning. Hardest damn thing I've ever done. Chip Bohlen's doing his memoirs, told me to use a tape recorder. Tried it, couldn't do it. Dictated letters all my life, but fiddling with that machine drives me nuts."

Dad said, "Ambassador Bohlen is a famous raconteur. Perhaps what you're writing depends more on quantitative analysis. . . ."

"That may have something to do with it. And maps. I've got to put in lots of maps. Most people don't even know where Baku is. When I used to have to talk to congressional committees, I brought maps, because some of them . . . How's your geography?"

"Good," Dad said, and would have gone on, but Grandma, who was hovering nearby, said, "Maps. He's mad about maps." I couldn't tell if by "he" she meant Dad or the ambassador. It didn't matter, because all she really wanted was to take Dad away to meet the new people just coming in.

Nora got bored and went out to the flagstone terrace, where the buffet table and chairs and tables were set up. But I was horribly fascinated. I followed Dad around.

At home, if Mom or I started talking to him, he'd go on with whatever he was doing. Mom and I both used to ask, "Are you listening?" He was—usually—and could answer our questions while continuing to pot his plant or do his crossword puzzle. Here at Grandma's tea party, he was almost staring into the eyes of whoever he was talking to. He had a variety of attentive gazes. Years later, when Mom took me to see *Les Grands Manoeuvres* with Gérard Philipe, one scene in it crystallized for me that erotic quicksilver in political campaigns. In *Les Grands Manoeuvres,* Gérard Philipe is a cavalry officer whose regiment is sent to a provincial town. At a reception, Gérard Philipe is playing the piano. He looks up from the keyboard at least four times, each time fixing his exquisitely different gaze on a different woman.

When I said something about Dad and Gérard Philipe to Mom, she refused to get it at first. "Well, Gérard Philipe was so beautiful—and that was high romantic comedy. Dashing cavalry officers, plumes and sabers. Ladies all gaga. Your father put on a seersucker suit to ask some rich people for money. . . ." She gazed into her past and said, "When I first saw *Les Grands Manoeuvres,* I was enchanted. I was in college, on a date. Afterward I was gushing so much about this gorgeous French actor that my date told me—maybe he was jealous, maybe he was just mean—anyway this bozo told me Gérard Philipe was dead. I burst into tears. A real boohoo. Served him right—the bozo, I mean."

That was of interest, but I explained again about Dad's different attentive looks. I said, "And that room with all the flowers, and the light coming through all those windows. It was the same late-afternoon light as in the movie. And then Dad using these looks. And it was working. I could see it work. But of course in the long run it made things worse for him. There was this beautiful light in this beautiful house and for a moment he got to be the prince. That it was such a beautiful place and that it seemed to be part of Grandma's spell made it wonderful and then unbearable, because I saw that Dad was getting a magic wish, but he was using it up. He was using it on all those people he didn't know. And it was so short. Why do all that to yourself? Why, when it's all daylilies?" And then, the same as Mom after seeing that French movie, I went boo-hoo.

"Oh, pooch," Mom said. "I know, I know."

I boo-hooed some more, and then both of us thought it was funny, this genetically transmitted boo-hoo, along with being bad at math and having straight hair and soft teeth.

At Grandma's tea party Mom was agreeably doing her duty. She knew a lot of the people—Peter darling and most of the other darlings. So she didn't have a lapse until she went out onto the terrace. By then Dad had gone off for five minutes with one of the reporters, so I followed Mom out to get something to eat. Mom saw Nora and the short woman in the red dress standing by the rail fence at the far end of the lawn. Mom made the same mistake I had. She said, "What's Bonnie Two doing with Nora?"

I said, "It's not Bonnie Two, it's somebody else. Fiona something."

A small white horse came across the field and put its head over the fence. Nora patted its neck while it fumbled with its mouth at Fiona's collar, presumably looking for sugar lump. Nora climbed on top of the fence, and the horse turned to nuzzle her knees. It looked like fun. I was about to go to the fence when I looked at Mom. She had white splotches on her face. I looked back at Nora to see if she was getting her party dress dirty, although I knew perfectly well that Mom didn't care that much about dresses, and I also knew with a deeper sense that this was an invisible-force anger, that Mom was seeing something in Fiona's moon-face with its dumpling cheeks, in the way Fiona was laughing with Nora, in the way Fiona climbed the fence. I didn't want to sense what Mom was sensing. I couldn't help it. I knew, for example, that Fiona was aware of being watched, but that her awareness wasn't of Mom but of the little crowd on the terrace. I looked back and saw the people watching, the men with that hooded look, both predatory and wary. Fiona hovered for a second to say something to Nora. Fiona's hands were on the top rail, her feet on the next rail down. Her calf muscles swelled and her butt jutted out, waggling as she balanced so that the hem of her red dress flicked like a bullfighter's cape. Then she jumped over and down, one hand on the top rail. The horse snorted, took a step backward and whirled away. Fiona ran alongside and flung her arms around its neck. The horse stopped, dropped its head, then suddenly lifted it. Fiona seemed to be plucked up by it, but she'd jumped at the same time and swung her leg over its back. It looked scary and neat and pretty all at once. She grabbed a handful of mane with one hand, stroked its neck with the other, and slid her knees forward, hiking her red dress higher on her thighs. She walked the horse a bit and then went right to a canter, all the way across the field. She turned and came back in a big curve along the fence. One of the men yelled, "Wa-hoo!" and Fiona smiled but didn't turn. She walked the horse up to Nora and held out her hand. Nora was about to get on when Mom started running down the lawn. For some reason she grabbed my hand and hauled me along. Halfway to the fence, she yelled, "Oh no you don't!"

Nora said "Mo-om" in her whiniest voice.

Mom said, "I don't mean you, I mean this menace in a red dress. You!" She pointed at Fiona. "Go break your own neck if you like. Go gallop around like Lady Godiva. Do not go galloping off with my daughter."

Fiona blushed. It made her freckles stand out. But after she took a breath, she said, "We certainly weren't going to gallop. Or even trot, for that matter."

Nora said, "Mo-om."

Mom ignored her. "Don't contradict me. We've had enough of your careering around in your little red dress. . . ."

Mom's voice had lowered and become more deliberate. In fact her diction was oddly like Grandma's when Grandma had had enough of the big cousins' going over the edge. Mom took a step toward the fence. I was afraid she was going to smack the horse on the rump. But just then the ambassador, who either was slightly deaf or had very good manners, came ambling up. He said, "Capital, capital, Miss MacKenzie. What a good seat. Saw you change leads too. Just hitched your leg back, did you?"

Fiona said, "McCaig, sir, my name is Fiona McCaig."

"Of course it is. Go right ahead, Miss McCaig, you're fine. I was going to tell you he's got a soft mouth, wants soft hands, but what a damn fool I would've seemed." He turned to Mom. "No bit." He laughed. Mom didn't. He said, "No bit, Joss. Nothing in his mouth at all." Still nothing from Mom, so he went round her and patted his horse's shoulder. "Go right ahead," he said, patting Fiona's knee. "Off you go." He patted the horse again, and turned to Nora. "Here, young lady. I'll give you a ride."

I drew away from Mom, decided to slide back to being a kid, let myself think, "How come Nora gets all the rides?"

Nora attached herself to the ambassador's back like a monkey. He gave a grunt and started up the slope of lawn. "Don't know why I called her MacKenzie. Yes I do. Royal Navy officer, knew him during the war. Worked with your father, MacKenzie and I both. I was thinking of him. Wish he were here. Your father, I mean. Great treat to see your mother, though. I know how fond he was of that husband of yours."

The ambassador stopped to hoist Nora, who was slipping. He said to

Mom, "Your father worried when your husband got into a cul-de-sac in Washington. Seemed to lose his taste for the arena. But then your father had his stroke. Couldn't help. Not too late now. He seems eager. Your husband, I mean. I'm glad to help. It's time for you two to get back to Washington. Even if he doesn't win, he's making a good run. Ought to be able to hook up with something worthwhile. Get himself back in the arena." The ambassador stopped to let Nora down. He patted her on the head, but kept talking to Mom. "Washington's still interesting enough. You two shouldn't stay buried in Charlottesville. You know what I've liked about every job I've had? I had to read *The New York Times* every morning. Had to. Every morning."

"So *that's* it," Mom said. "The meaning of life."

"Now, Joss," the ambassador said. "You know what I mean. A benchmark. A symptom of whether a job is in the arena . . ."

"Yes, of course," Mom said. "Sorry. I just had a little fright about Nora, so I snapped at you. Seriously, you're a hero for doing this for Mom. It's great, you made her year. You're both heroes."

Even though I was alarmed by Mom's outburst at Fiona (which had an extra sharpness I didn't understand), I was more alarmed by how quickly Mom put a polite face back on. And I was still alarmed by Dad's courtier's charm, and by Grandma's suddenly being exhausted after our day in Washington. I feared this fairy-tale play with Grandma's darlings in this beautiful house with old-glass windows set on a soft lawn that was so much greener than the yellowing grass of the real world's end of summer. I feared the energy flickering all around, more powerful than Grandma's conjuring long-stemmed flowers or her darlings. I saw how wonderful it must feel too. I saw some people fill their lungs, brighten, and smile diffusely, whereas others contracted and pointed their keen faces specifically. All of them were fuzzed or striped with energy.

And what would happen to them? Would they be changed? What would happen to ordinary people? To Mom and Dad?

When Nora and I were in college—I deliberately far away at Berkeley and Nora at the university only a mile from Dad's chambers—we had a fight on the phone. It started with my remembering that Nora liked Grandma's party for Dad, that she'd risen to the occasion. I said, "Of course, you love parties, and you were the campaign poster-child. You wanted to sing for that darling old congressman, and you got the ambassador to give you a piggyback ride."

"Is that what you think? That you were the only unhappy one?"

"I forgot. You whined because Mom wouldn't let you be part of Fiona's bareback circus act. You liked Fiona, didn't you? You probably even liked Bonnie Two when she called you 'li'l darlin'.'"

Nora said, "At least I don't plump pillows for Bonnie One. I'm certainly not going to call her my stepmom."

"I only do that because—"

"Because you go to Berkeley. At *Berkeley* it's cool to call your mom's lover your stepmom. At *Berkeley* it's cool to have a lesbian mother. At *Berkeley* it would be cool to go to a cast party and find your father dancing with your drama teacher."

I had to admire Nora's rant. She had a gift. She could have written Grandpa Reardon's 1944 speech that Dad used to play for us—"*Hitler* knows . . . that if Dewey is elected . . . it will mean the crumbling of the Atlantic Alliance. *Hitler* knows . . . that if Dewey is elected . . ." Or even Roosevelt's "I . . . *hate* . . . war. Eleanor . . . *hates* . . . war. . . ."

I was about to ask Nora to do her Roosevelt imitation. I said, "Do you remember the speeches that Dad used to—"

"And besides," Nora said, "you were the one who drove off with Fiona and Dad that night. I was with Mom and Grandma."

"I didn't choose. We had to do whatever they said. You remember that part. We had to get in whatever car they said. We had to go to whichever house they said. And we always left the thing we wanted most at the other house."

"That's right," Nora said. "I'm glad you're saying *we*."

Nora was right. I did end up driving back to Charlottesville with Dad, Fiona, and Ganny. At least Dad remembered that I got carsick on country roads when I rode in the back. But he was overcharged every other way. He said to me, "What'd you think of that house?"

"It's beautiful," I said. "It's a mansion."

"I like your grandmother's house better," he said. "Don't you?"

He was trying to get me to be cheerful, to get me into his exuberant mood. Even before we got to the end of the driveway I could tell he was going to drive too fast.

"The world is full of terrific places," he said. "We can go anywhere. You and I can just ramble around. When this is over, that's what we'll do. We'll take the van, get rid of the stickers. We'll go to the mountains, camp out, catch trout for breakfast. We'll go to cities. We'll drop in on mansions. They'll be glad to see us. We'll live by our wits. We'll live like gypsies."

I put my hand on the dashboard and he slowed down a little. But he was still whirring inside with the idea of living like gypsies, catching at me and swooping me with his manic mood. I was tired and I wanted to go home and he was reminding me that home was now just another gypsy camp.

Here is what I liked about the summer before Dad campaigned. Grandma and Dad and I were at Grandma's walking on the path with the raspberries, mint, and daylilies. I said to Dad, "Why are they called daylilies?"

He said, "Because they only open up during the day, like morning glories."

Grandma said, "You're quite wrong, dear boy. They're called daylilies because they only last a day."

Dad picked ten blades of grass and tied them around the stems of ten open daylilies. The next day he took me out to look. The ten blossoms had either closed up or wilted. Dad opened his hand and gestured. "Now, *that* is the scientific method." I nodded. Dad began to laugh. He said, "Let's go tell your grandmother she's right."

I said, "She already knows she's right."

Dad looked at me. He was baffled for a second (I liked that), then pleased with me (even better). "Right," he said. "But still . . ."

I sort of knew why he'd laughed at himself. I sort of knew why he was pleased. What I liked was that I didn't need to know for sure, that we were at Grandma's, that we were floating together, happily not going anywhere.

§ 10

The day after the tea party, Mike came into the office still riding a wave of energy.

Jerry looked at him darkly, went into his office, and closed the door.

Mike looked at Ganny and Fiona. Fiona was wearing her red dress again. Ganny said, "Jerry's feeling left out. We had too much fun at the party and he spent Sunday in Richmond."

Fiona said, "Maybe you should buy him a red dress too."

Ganny said to Fiona, "Maybe you should go change. The party's over. You're going canvassing in the subdivisions." Ganny turned to Mike. "Bonnie Two's nose is out of joint too. When she saw Fiona this morning, it reminded her that she didn't get to go to the ball."

Or, it occurred to Mike, Bonnie Two might have seen Fiona's red dress as an indication of a *fait accompli*.

Ganny said to Fiona, "I want you to look the way they'd want their daughters to look. A nice blouse and skirt."

"That's just what I don't have," Fiona said. "There's a sale on summer clothes—"

"I want you to *look* like their daughters," Ganny said. "Not behave like them."

Fiona had been a great success canvassing the exotic communities around Charlottesville—Yogaville, Faber, the commune at Twin Oaks. She showed up in her hiking clothes carrying a natural-fiber backpack filled with campaign flyers and vegetarian recipes. In the same costume she was equally successful with the liberal bohemian enclaves in Batesville and Free Union. A lot of these people were old sixties marchers who'd retired to the hills to raise families, grow zucchini and arugula, and—as the bumper stickers on their Volvos said—think globally, act locally. With them Fiona discussed composting, organic gardening, and whether they should send their kids to Outward Bound (Fiona had been an assistant rock-climbing instructor at the Outward Bound school in North Carolina).

Then she pulled out the campaign literature. But Ganny was right about changing Fiona's look for the subdivisions with names like Camelot, Pook's Hill, and Stonehenge—symptoms of the Anglophilia which developers and real-estate agents used to package their Charlottesville product.

Ganny said, "Maybe you could borrow something from Bonnie Two."

"No," Mike said. "Here's my credit card."

"You better get your lunch at the grocery store, then," Ganny said. "No restaurants."

"Bananas," Fiona said, moving toward the door. "Nothing but bananas and water all day long."

Ganny turned to Mike. "Fenton's boys just issued a press release. Said your promise to interfere with IRS tax audits was unprofessional, unethical, and probably criminal." Mike said, "What? Did I say I'd interfere? I didn't say that."

"And they say your promise to attract a high-tech low-pollution industry to Greene County was a crude attempt to take credit for a deal Fenton's already made."

"What's that? That's bullshit."

Ganny said, "They say Fenton's the one with contacts in the business community, and you have none and won't ever have any, what with your wild-eyed antibusiness ranting. And so on. You want to think about a response? Oh. I found out Fenton's canceled a speech he was going to make at Hampden-Sydney. Some remarks at the convocation for the start of their school year. You want me to find out if they'd like you instead? I know someone down there. It's a rich boys' college. Students probably for Fenton, but they probably don't vote in our district. The faculty could be ours. And you could stop off at Longwood College. Work your way back through Dillwyn and Scottsville. Worth a shot?"

"Yes," Mike said. "Tell your pal there about my ferment-in-legal-education speech. I gave it to some U.Va. students last year, before all this. Maybe you could take a look at it. And could you find out . . . No, I'll get Jerry to find out. No, if you'll give me that Fenton release, I'll go write . . . What I want to know is did Fenton go on the air or is this just another press release from his office."

Ganny said, "Just a press release."

Jerry came out of his office. He said, "I've been doing the reports on what your mother-in-law raised. Not too shabby. For an amateur."

Mike said, "Maybe you should go back to the pros in Richmond, tell them the news. They're like banks, right? Only cough it up if you've already got it."

Jerry said to Ganny, "You girls have a good time at your party? Up there with the fox-hunting set?"

"Oh, for God's sake, Jerry," Mike said. "Not now. We're doing better. The better the team does, the better for you. Nobody else can deal with Richmond. You're on a team, you play a position."

Jerry laughed briefly. "I thought you and Ganny turned your noses up at football metaphors."

Mike said, "Not me. We're in the fourth quarter and we're not that far down."

Jerry said, "Where's Bonnie Sproul?"

"She went to the post office," Ganny said. "You need her?"

Jerry took Mike by the arm. "I need to have a word with you, Mike, if you can spare the time." He ushered Mike into his office and closed the door. Jerry took a step away from Mike and said, "Tell me, Mike. You got a zipper problem?"

"What?"

"Between men here, Mike. You got something going with Bonnie Sproul?"

"What brings this up?"

"I'll tell you what. I came back in here late Sunday afternoon, made some calls. Bonnie Sproul's minding the store, about to close it up. I'm on the phone, I hear her playing her guitar. I think, Not another damn campaign song. I get through with the call, hear her singing. She's singing, 'I used to rate with the candidate, but I don't rate no more.'" Jerry coughed into his fist. "So, goddamn it, Mike, I got to know. Like you say, it's the fourth quarter. But I can't go on working unless you tell me the goddamn score."

"I think I see the problem," Mike said. "I bought Fiona a red dress and that made Bonnie jealous."

"Oh Jesus. You got two of them? Oh, fucking brilliant. Chasing one skirt is dumb, but dumping her for another broad in the same office . . . Give me a fucking break!"

"No," Mike said. "Sit down and listen."

Jerry sat down in his desk chair and held his head in his hands.

Mike put a hand on the corner of the desk and said, "There's some history with Bonnie Sproul, back when she was doing marriage counseling. But if she's angry over the red dress, I can smooth that over. I have some reason to think Fiona's most recent experience is with a woman."

"What? What the hell is up around here? And how do you know? You put a move on her?"

"Never mind how I know. Bonnie knows about the woman. I'll tell her that part, she'll be fine. She'll treat that—and everything else—in confidence. She's a practicing psychological counselor, she has to."

"That ditz is a psychologist?"

"Yes. And she's actually pretty smart. She just—"

"Then what the hell was she doing singing that stuff all over the office?"

"She was stung. I don't know. It was just you—you were the only one here. She wanted . . . Look. She likes you. She knows I like you."

Jerry ran his hand through his hair. He said, "I don't know. . . ."

"Look," Mike said. "I may have a speech in a few days down in Farmville. I'll get Bonnie to drive me. I'll make sure everything's fine until then, then we'll have a nice long drive to Farmville. Completely settle things down."

"It's not an overnight trip, is it? No motel stops."

"No," Mike said. "Just one long day." He put his hand on the doorknob.

"One more thing," Jerry said. "Speaking of motels. I have a motel room here, and I keep one in Richmond. Don't you have an empty cottage out at your place? Ganny mentioned something about how your tenants are moving out. It would save campaign expenses."

Mike said, "Good idea. It's pretty bare. All I can do is lend you a cot."

"Just a place to crash."

Mike had been oiling the conversation so much that he didn't feel a scrape until he was out of the room. Let Jerry Medina live in Evelyn and Edmond's house? But of course they were gone.

Bonnie Two cried all the way to Keene. Mike asked her if she'd like him to drive. She shook her head.

Mike told her again that Fiona's red dress didn't mean anything, that he was working very hard and needed all the help he could get, that he put her, Bonnie, in charge of the office instead of taking her to the party because she was the most responsible, the best person for that job at that time, that Jerry had been sent to Richmond and he'd been sore but now he was okay.

It was all too defensive. He remembered he hadn't brought up a feeling yet. He said, "Of course, Jerry's kind of a coarse guy—he doesn't have your sensitivity. And I can see that campaigning may have coarsened me too. I feel bad."

She stopped crying but continued to sniffle from Keene to Scottsville.

When they crossed the James he said, "I haven't been canoeing for ages. I'd love to drift down the James with you."

"I can't swim."

"I'll buy you a life jacket."

"You buy a lot of things for a lot of people."

They entered the flatness of Southside Virginia. He said, "I have to do things for the campaign. You and I have been helping each other for longer than that."

"Yes. You went and talked about my lease. I'm sorry I couldn't pay you."

"No, you did. You were good with Joss. That was a help. I mean, it's not your fault she and I separated. That was beyond help. But you got her to go to AA. You gained her confidence. And she probably wouldn't have agreed to keep up appearances for the campaign without your help."

They came to an intersection. "You take Route 15 now."

"I know. And I know how you have to go on looking like you're married. And I'm sorry I got old Jerry Medina all dislocated. But I guess you may have missed the way he and Ganny and everyone treat me."

"I don't think you're reading them quite right."

"I know how I feel."

"That's a lot of it right there. You have more sensitive feelings. Jerry and everyone can be brusque. There's a kind of macho toughness in campaigning, and I've felt you providing a feminine element that no one else does. And I don't just mean you and me privately. Which has been important—"

"I get to be the dumb blonde."

"That's not how I feel. You remember Mrs. Hawes at the county fair? She said you're sharp as a tack."

"About that ring-the-gong thing? That's not much."

"And you explained to me about not dancing if someone was playing a religious song. But it's more than being smart. I've still got a lot of issues to work on, and I'll need your family counseling on how to talk about issues with Edith and Nora."

Saying the girls' names made him stop. He tasted bile in the back of his throat.

Bonnie Two leaned back from the steering wheel. She sighed and said, "That's right. There's a lot of . . ." She made a humming noise.

He remembered slipping into a motel room—into several motel rooms. She wouldn't speak as he came toward her but she would hum little notes to herself. She even embraced him at first so that her body only touched his lightly, now in one place, then another, fluttering touches that were an accompaniment to her humming. Later she would utter her fuller-voiced cries and yodels, which, depending on his mood, either alarmed or excited him.

The memory of her preliminary humming and light rustling aroused him. Her actual presence beside him in the car was close and stifling.

Bonnie Two said, "You're trying and that's good." She fumbled her hand onto his, keeping her eyes on the road.

He kept his hand in place as long as he could. He said, "I've got to go over my speech."

Not a bad speech, better than bumper stickers. It was a relief to read something he'd written without an ulterior motive. He'd written it a year ago for beginning law students. He described the shocks they would feel as they learned to think like lawyers—the shock to their intellectual balance and the shock to their moral balance. It was often hard to tell those two shocks apart. All the praise and rewards they would get would be for regaining their intellectual balance—for spotting issues, not for caring about them. Their reactions to cases would often be ridiculed. In many instances their reactions *should* be ridiculed as foolish, shallow, sentimental, or otherwise inept. But there would be some times when their sentiments and their fumblings toward an argument would be ignored, dismissed as "too metaphysical," or ridiculed when in fact they were making a morally intelligent point. And after that ridicule it would appear that the smartest thing to do was to get smart. Get smart in terms of the system.

Mike turned the page. The typeface was speech-size, extra-large, all uppercase. Ganny had highlighted the complicated parts in yellow (Okay—I'll go slow), and the vehement parts in pale purple (Very funny, Ganny).

> And you will get smarter in law school. Smarter in the way they want. Nothing wrong with that—it is valuable. But getting smarter in this analytical, mandarin way presents a temptation more subtle than the later temptations to make lots of money, to gain power, or generally to be an argumentative bully. This first temptation, as you become lawyerlike, is to beat up on the person you used to be. You'll be able to knock your old sense of things into a cocked hat.
>
> Here's a Cold War theory about the Soviet Union: the Soviets are digging their own graves by training so many technical scientists and engineers. All that technical training is bound to make them so smart they'll see through the communist system. But so far the biggest troublemakers are the poets and novelists. And that's because, although part of their education is systematic, they mainly rely on their own sense of things.
>
> It is possible for you to become smart as a whip in law school and

> abandon your sense of things. You can cut yourself loose from your unwieldy, inchoate naïve views. Or you can spend time criticizing them, reconstructing them, and improving them so that they are still part of you as you transform yourself. If you choose this second option of struggling, it won't help you get better grades—it will prolong your confusion, it will make you slower at a time when speed of thought is most highly rewarded.

Mike turned the page and saw he'd been haunted by a couple of his father's old speechwriting standbys—Yeats and Oscar Wilde.

> But you will have an inner dialogue of mind and soul. You won't enter your profession as a cynic—someone who knows the price of everything and the value of nothing.

A bit of rhetoric from the old man's bag of tricks. There was more, but trying to read in Bonnie Two's rattletrap of a car made him queasy. He loosened his tie. And he'd secreted something into his system by dealing with Bonnie Two, with Bonnie Two's singing about her hurt feelings to Jerry Medina. The first time with Bonnie Two—in her office, with her sashaying in her luna-moth dress—he'd lied a little. Flattered her, sympathized with her sympathy. It was a hot needy lie to get her to flutter closer. The way he'd lied to her just now was cold. He'd sealed her up with cold grease so she wouldn't make a fuss that might get in the way of his trawling for votes. It wasn't a favor to the Democratic Party anymore. Not just showing the flag. He wanted the job. And from "I want the job—I want to be your lawyer" he'd turned himself into a one-man traveling carnival, complete with fortune-telling booth. Today's fortune for the prelaw college boys was straight enough, the fortune for Bonnie Two a scam. How blithely he'd told Edith what fun it would be to live by their wits, live like gypsies. That had been yesterday's donkey bray of high spirits. Today he used his wits to scuttle. Why so frantic? For the first time in months, he looked inward and saw fear. Of what? That Bonnie Two would get mad and blab, then Jerry Medina quit, then the campaign falter and dissolve?

That wasn't enough to justify this height of fear. And it was *height*; the sensation of the fear, when he dared to consider it again, was vertigo.

He asked Bonnie Two to pull over for a minute. He got out and sat on the guardrail and looked across the flat Southside cornfield to the smudge of hills on the horizon. The edge of the guardrail cut into his buttocks, a small steadying pain, like that of a ridged *prie-dieu* in the school chapel.

Fear of heights? For God's sake, what *heights*? Preposterous.

As if "preposterous" were a code word opening up a file, a passage of his father's lore came to him. Your average bureaucrat, so the lore went, silently burrows deeper when alarmed. Your politician, when caught out, squawks louder and flies higher. Your bureaucrat is basically depressive. When trouble comes he'll stay in bed and pull the covers over his head. Your politician is manic. And delusional. One aspect of this delusion is that the politician imagines the people is a single wooable personage, particularly susceptible to him. She—for the male politician turns the public into an object of desire—is a fabulous winged creature, flying higher and higher, daring her suitor to fly as high, luring him higher with cries that only he can hear. And once he reaches her, he'll be the hero no ordinary harm can touch.

It was Mike's father's lore and his father's style of baroque mockery, so he wasn't surprised to hear his father's voice joining in to the rustle of green leaves on the standing corn.

"Am I not right, Joe?" His father sounded far more Irish than he had in life, but there he was, talking to his old pal ex-Congressman Joseph Delaney. They were in the locker room of the Burning Tree Golf Club, draped in togalike bath towels.

"You've got the gift." Joe neither confirmed nor denied.

"No love like it, is there, Joe? Aerial maneuvers with the plumed bird. The rapture of it all—' 'Tis better to have loved and lost than never to have loved at all.' "

"You should know, Bill. You tried it once."

"I did. And came within a feather's breadth of my delight."

"A feather, was it? More like seventeen thousand votes."

"You have a remarkably detailed memory, Joe, for the misfortunes of your friends."

Mike smelled the steam, the soap and hair tonic.

Joe said, "Well, maybe Mikey here will have a go. Pick up where your father left off, Mikey. You have a nice way with you in public. I saw you marching up the aisle at Saint Matthew's for your confirmation. I could see Archbishop O'Boyle taking note of you. Very manly and dignified."

"Oh yes, he's been praised enough for his solemn ecclesiastical bearing. . . ." And Mike waited for the other shoe to drop, the little sting. It didn't come, because both men stared at Roy Cohn walking by, naked except for the towel over his shoulder. After a moment Joe Delaney said, "Would you look at that little Jew strut? Normally it's the mouth on him you'd notice."

Mike's father sang, " 'Silent, O Moyle, be the roar of thy waters . . . ,' " and laughed.

Joe Delaney said, "Now, who the hell brought him here?"

"Someone with something to lose," Mike's father said. "But it won't do him any good, feeding that one a sop. The gang of them is 'all as hungry as the sea and can digest as much.'" (Mike knew it was Shakespeare; his father had memorized a lot of random Shakespeare when he was sitting in his law office circa 1929 untroubled by clients.)

Joe Delaney said, "I remember the days when it was a shocking thing for a fellow with a name like McCarthy to even vote Republican. I thought you could get excommunicated for it."

"And there you were a moment ago wishing Mike'd go into politics when it's all going to the dogs."

"McCarthy'll come down. Someone'll get something on him. It's just a matter of time."

"It's just a matter of time for anyone. What it's more a matter of is the turmoil now. If he'd stopped at a few oddballs in the State Department . . . Oh, I know, Joe, that Vincent fellow's a pal of yours. But what McCarthy's done that's more harmful is this—it's the end of sensible arrangements. Everyone in this city has at least one secret, and there's always someone else who knows it. But if you're the someone who discovers it, you don't go blurting it out all at once, for God's sake. You don't start all this hue and cry. That's like spending capital when you should be living on the interest. You let a fellow know quietly that he's got a problem, and you move him gently aside for a moment. You don't let things get out of hand. McCarthy has closed the shop. And there's a certain amount of actual business to get done, after all."

At first, hearing his father's voice again—and old Congressman Delaney's too summoned from the dead—Mike thought there might be some helpful hints, but all he got was the helplessness of being a baffled child. Sitting on this highway guardrail on his way to enlighten the future lawyers of America, he felt reduced. Not by his father's cynicism, which Mike had figured out early on came from yearning and was more jovial than bitter, but by his father's sharpness at spotting weakness or fumbling, even about the smallest things. "What are you up to with that? That's no way to lay a fire." Or the casual backhand swipe: Mike, shortly after his voice changed and he left the choir, answered the phone at home. The caller said, "Is that you, Bill?"

Mike said, "No, it's his son, Mike."

There was a click as his father picked up the extension in time to hear the caller say, "Well, God love you, boy, you've a voice just like your father's. There's no difference at all—"

His father said, "Unless you listen to the content."

And the major assessment, equally offhand. His father driving, Mike beside him. Mike halfway through college. The subject had been whether Mike should go to law school.

"Well, if you do go to law school, go to a good big one. I remember coming here and not knowing a soul." He sighed. "Washington still could be a good place to make your way, but I don't see you doing it on your own. . . . But you might make a good number-two man for somebody."

His father was peering ahead, intent on his driving—his hands in their fine gloves relaxed on the wheel. No malice, just an easy remark. Mike wasn't surprised when his father went on talking, sliding into another reminiscence. Perhaps the old man thought it was a compliment.

Bonnie Two leaned across the passenger seat and called through the open window, "You okay now, Mike?"

All right. He'd called down this assessment of his folly—flying high on delusion—wishing for a constituency to tell him he was more lovable and desirable at large than he was at home.

"Still fumbling the little moves, Mikey. What do you think you're up to with that? You don't go to bed with someone in the office, for God's sake. You need a roll in the hay, at least do it with someone whose life isn't more of a mess than your own. You still don't know a thing about women, do you? At least there's not a mother in the picture. God help you, you big-footed puppy, if you come up against a determined mother."

Mike thought he should reply to this direct address, but he stayed as mute as a child.

His father said, "The point Mikey doesn't get, Joe, is that he's a stray. He thinks it's his notions, that it's his speech-making. . . . But he hasn't a friend in the party, not one that counts. It's alliances that make a campaign. You know that. The boys are happy enough to let him have a go, they made that plain enough at the start. They plainly said, 'We don't expect much but a showing.' So it'll end up being what we used to call an educational campaign, meaning the poor bugger tried out a lot of issues and educated us . . . about what doesn't work."

"I see your point, Bill. Mikey might as well be running as an independent."

"You should know about that, Joe. Didn't you work for La Follette in 1924?"

"I did. It was an educational campaign."

"But you came round, and no one held your youthful fling against you. And didn't we help you then to eighteen good years? And then you weren't the voice crying in the wilderness, you were part of a sensible alliance. Mikey, on the other hand, hasn't been to see the Democratic governor of his state or the Democratic senator. He hasn't had so much as a breakfast with the Democratic congressmen, not even of the neighboring districts. He hasn't been up to see a national committeeman. And the only time two of his state committeemen came to see him—to ask him to make an orderly little effort—he wraps himself in the mantle of his dignity and says 'Cold biscuits.'"

"He got that story from you, Bill."

"He missed the point of it, then. Not just that Senator Barkley—Senator, mind—earned the right to a sharp reply, but that he knew I wouldn't repeat it—"

"At least not until—"

"A discreet interval had elapsed. But the real point of the story is that Senator Barkley, having had the satisfaction of his retort, was wise enough to amend it."

"But didn't Mikey say yes after all?"

"With ill grace. And the damage was done. It wasn't a confidential chat. It's no wonder they're leaving him hanging out to dry. And just now he sends that consultant to Richmond instead of going himself."

"He did well enough with that tea party, Bill."

"He should have cleared it first with Richmond. Not even a phone call. Someone's bound to say Mikey's got hold of money that could've been theirs."

"Well, God knows he's got enough to reproach himself with, then. I hope he won't lose heart."

"He's got plenty of heart. It's in the head department he's a bit short."

"Come on now, Bill. You never know how things'll turn out. And he seems to be enjoying the work."

"He can't stop. He's like the girl in the fairy tale with the red shoes, once she put them on she couldn't stop dancing."

"It's not like that at all. You're not remembering right. I did it nine times. Election day comes and you can't take another step. And when you lose, you leave your body. You see yourself, you hear yourself saying the lines, but really you've come to a stop. Everything is muffled. Your wife is biting her lip, your secretary's in tears, your campaign manager's angry—even people you hardly know are taking it hard. But for a while you're . . . dispersed. You see your body there, all its molecules doing the right thing, congratulating your opponent, thanking all the people to be thanked, but it's a newsreel picture. Just flickers, and something's wrong with the sound besides. So you say to yourself, If my molecules are there, then who the hell is this here? You don't remember that part?"

"Don't make a mystery of it, Joe. You were in shock."

"Well, I think it was the first time I knew I had a soul."

"You're sure it wasn't your guardian angel, now? Or maybe it was an intervention by Saint Jude, patron saint of lost causes. It's splendid how you've kept your childlike faith."

"*Pas devant les enfants,* Bill."

It was Mike's certain knowledge that Mr. Delaney didn't speak a word of French that made them go poof, back into the rustling of the gray-green leaves.

◇

Bonnie One said, "We just nuzzled a little, that's all."

Joss didn't say anything. She was puzzled about how she felt. Of course she was angry, but her anger wasn't coming up in any form she was familiar with.

Bonnie One said, "That's *all.* I swear."

Joss thought that if she asked Bonnie One another question she wouldn't be able to work. If she didn't ask another question it would only be as niggling as having a chipped tooth to explore with the tip of her tongue.

"It wasn't anything," Bonnie One said. "We didn't even—"

"Don't," Joss said. "I've got to go to work."

"You're the middle of my life. You're what matters to me more than anything."

"What matters right now is getting to work."

"All right," Bonnie One said. "You're torturing me. I can stand that if it gets us even."

"Don't," Joss said again. "I'm not torturing you—I'm doing what I do every day. I'm not doing anything but trying to get out the door without having to hear any more confessions or declarations or accusations."

"It breaks my heart when you—"

"No, it doesn't," Joss said and went out the door of Bonnie One's apartment. She could call Bonnie One at lunchtime and have a sweet reconciliation. Or perhaps at four.

. . .

Joss loved her new studio. It was on the downtown mall next to an old theater called the Movie Palace, which showed reruns, even some of her favorites—nostalgic double-features on Saturday afternoons. The only thing that was disconcerting about her studio was that from the front window she could see Mike's headquarters. She kept the curtains drawn on that side. From the back window she looked out on an alley, an arrangement of brick walls and wiring she found oddly encouraging.

She also loved her new apartment, a short walk from her studio. It was on the top floor of a five-story building on a hill. The living/dining room had a view of the Blue Ridge. Whenever she was home for lunch alone she sang, "I'm sitting on top of the world . . ."

Edith and Nora were going to spend most of their time with her until election day. The school bus dropped them in front of the apartment building along with the child of another divorced mother. The other mother took charge of them until the school bus was out of sight, and then Edith and Nora walked two blocks to Mike's headquarters for an hour. Joss always peeked out her studio window in time to see them walking up the mall. At four-thirty they came across the street and buzzed her.

Her life felt both compact and enlarged. She sometimes worried that she wasn't worried enough, that the pleasure of being alone in her studio, of being alone at lunch in her apartment, was a bubble. She worried that part of her everyday pleasure came from having had a program of her short films accepted by the film festival. She worried that Bonnie One worried that they didn't spend enough time together. She herself was content to sleep in Bonnie One's bed the one night a week the girls slept at Mike's. And she liked inviting Bonnie One over for the unexpected lunch—though she could dredge up a worry that part of her desire for Bonnie One came from having to be discreet—she still appeared in public with Mike—at a PTA meeting, at a fund-raising picnic.

But her worries were nothing compared with her steady surge of energy. She did have to remind herself to damp her mood at her weekly AA meetings. The gang was always happy to hear that she'd been sober for eighty-one, eighty-eight, ninety-five days, and that she was feeling better and better. But one night she'd added, "Hey—maybe these powdered doughnuts are undercover communion wafers." It got a laugh, but not from everyone. Her sponsor had pursed her lips.

But here in her studio she could draw the curtain on all of them. She could laugh at her own jokes, she could chomp on her gum and snap it as loudly as she pleased, she could pull her chair up to her old-fashioned Moviola and only care about the tiny world inside it. A few more days and this last bit of it went to the lab. Another week and her short films would all be on the screen at the Vinegar Hill Theater, only one show out of the fifty shows that went on during the film festival. She liked the idea of all these films—a dozen Hollywood blockbusters—dinosaurs with pea-sized brains—another dozen old black-and-white revivals, another dozen independent films of wildly varying quality—all swarming side by side at the scruffy Movie Palace, Vinegar Hill, and the university theater. She liked letting her little cage of household pets loose at the tail end of the stampede. Most of her audience would be in a daze after a week of movies. The few who weren't would be just the ones who would laugh at her short parodies. That was all she wanted—a few laughs from the kids in the peanut gallery, *les enfants du paradis.* She cocked her head and said out loud, "*Les enfants du* parody." She couldn't think of anyone but herself who would laugh at that. Time to put a fresh stick of gum in her mouth and get to work.

◇

Just before the festival Mom took us to her studio and showed us some of her short films.

Nora laughed out loud, even at the longer science-fiction one. She even laughed at the parts of it I didn't get. Later—much later—I called her on that. She said she got jokes by their rhythm, even when she was nine.

I liked that it was in black and white except for the green death rays which came out of the alien's flying saucer.

One thing that was hard for me to get used to was that the actors wore masks—not to fool other characters but to play the parts of famous real people. I recognized the Howard Cosell mask from when Dad used to watch Monday-night football and let me sit in his lap if I got up from a bad dream. Mom had to explain who Norman Mailer and William F. Buckley were. Both Nora and I recognized Muhammad Ali.

The alien inside the flying saucer was like a vampire except it sucked egos instead of blood. Its pale-green exploratory tendrils could reach out a mile and sniff out a big ego. Its emerald-green ego-sucking rays reached a hundred yards. The flying saucer landed in Washington, D.C. It sucked some egos from generals and admirals at the Pentagon, then took some time to digest them. It burped little green burps out a porthole. Then it flew to the Capitol steps and dipped into some senators. So the President, figuring he's next on the menu, asks a bunch of guys with particularly juicy egos to come to the White House. They're meant to distract the space creature from attacking him and Henry Kissinger. The four big egos (Ali, Cosell, Mailer, and Buckley) let themselves get probed by the tendrils. The men argue about who has the biggest ego. This increases their ego aura so much that the flying saucer lights up and begins to drool. Green light, green drool. But when it sends out its big emerald ego-eating rays, the men pull out mirrors and bounce the rays back. The saucer blows up in a bright-green explosion.

When the men are getting their medals for saving Earth, we notice that there are tinges of green in their eyes. They open their mouths, and tongues of green flame flick out. They've absorbed some ego fallout. They gobble up all the assembled egos, including foreign dignitaries and half the press corps. There is an aerial map of Washington showing a green firefight. Then a satellite photo of Earth which suddenly starts crackling with green lines. Earth is doomed! But it turns out that it's only men's egos that have been sucked out. The next and last thing we see is that women are in charge—they're behind all the big desks and they have really cute men secretaries.

When it was over, Nora said, "That is really neat, Mom. Can we see another one?"

Mom laughed with pleasure. She said, "Not today, pooch. I've still got some work to do." She looked at me, just a quick check. "You two run along back to the apartment."

I knew I should say something, but I was troubled by the obvious fakery—when the flying saucer flew you could see the blurriness around the edges, like in those old fifties movies with Sinbad the Sailor being carried in the claws of a giant bird. I said, "It has this old-fashioned look."

"Right," Mom said. "That's on purpose. It's part of the joke. Did you think it was funny?"

"Oh yes," I said. And then the next words just tumbled out. "It's funny, Mom. The way you get funny after a drink or two."

Her face froze. I couldn't take it back, I couldn't say anything.

Mom lifted her head and stared somewhere above me. She said slowly, "I see what you mean. . . . You probably don't know that I go to AA. That I don't drink anymore. At all. But I see what you mean. Wacky slapstick. On the edge, over the edge. I see what you mean."

I stayed dumb as a fish.

On the sidewalk Nora said, "I thought she was going to cry." She said this in an amazingly disinterested way.

I said, "Fuck you, Nora. You've spoiled enough Christmases to last a lifetime! I spoil one fucking thing and . . ."

I began to cry, the way I should have back in the studio, the way Nora would have, the way that would have got Mom crying along with me, saying, "I know, pooch. It's okay, pooch. I know what you meant."

Nora said to me, "We don't have to go straight home. We can hang out on the downtown mall. I've got a dollar."

Good, Nora. Good for you. But what I wanted—what used to help me in the old days if I got in trouble—was for Dad to explain me to Mom, or Mom to explain me to Dad. I wanted the sound their voices got when they explained how Nora or I hadn't meant *that*, maybe it was just *this*. It was an easy sound, but Nora and I couldn't make it for ourselves. It felt like Mom pulling my hair out of my collar, brushing it with her fingertips, and turning to Dad so that he looked at us. Or like Dad sitting on the corner of my bed making it sag so that my feet rolled against his hip. If he read aloud too long Mom would come in and say, "It's a school night." And Dad would explain that we were in the middle of a good part. And Mom would say, "Oh, a good part," and sit down with us.

◇

Jerry Medina stuck his head into Mike's office and said, "They're moving—the numbers are moving."

Mike said, "Which way?"

Jerry laughed. "Which way you think? Our way, champ."

"How much?"

"You're at forty-six percent. That's a jump."

"So what's doing it? The industrial waste? And who is it? Suburbs? Exurbs?"

"Can't tell. It's not an in-depth survey. But it's good, it's a good bump. I guess it's all over the lot. This is a goddamn impossible district. It sprawls. It's got pieces that don't make sense. We only paid for the numbers. I've been on the phone, trying to squeeze a little more out of the polling service."

"So is it worth the money to run another survey?"

"That's the question. They want three grand for another run with responses to issues. I've had everyone in the office do some spot-checking, and it's just too screwy. I don't think another poll will make it clearer. Like around Lake Anna? We thought those were nests of pissed-off independents: college, middle-class white-collar, forty grand a year. But one side of Lake Anna likes us, the other side doesn't. And then we have these little swings for us in odd places. Like in the part of our district sticks into

Southside? Keysville, Charlotte Courthouse. That's not issues, that's because the mayor of Keysville endorsed you. And maybe we called someone on the faculty from that college down there—where you made a speech. But what can we tell about an issue? We did good with a bunch of calls here in the city. And in these towns around here. No surprise, we worked them hard. Then there's another little hot spot where your pal Mrs. Hawes has been pushing for us. But what's the issue? So we could blow three grand, which we don't have to spare, and maybe find out one guy's moved by industrial waste, the next guy's pro-choice, the third guy's an idiot. While I was waiting around for a callback from my man with the polling service, I made a half-dozen calls myself just for the hell of it. Six different answers. One liked that you knew the Bible by heart. Another liked that you were going to vote against tax audits for your district. I asked if he heard the radio call-in show. He said that, no, he read an ad in the newspaper. So guess what? It was the Fenton ad. The one where Fenton blasts you for claiming to be able to intervene—"

"That's not what I said."

"That's the beauty part. Fenton's boys fiddled with what you said, and they ended up stepping on their own dicks."

"But that could mean that other people are hearing that crap and maybe buying it—'unprofessional, possibly criminal.'"

"That's right. But we got out our counterattack. Nothing else to do."

Mike said, "What about your other four calls?"

"Don't like you 'cause you're a Democrat. Don't like you 'cause you're a liberal Democrat. Don't like you. And one don't know. You could go over this stuff and make guesses till the cows come home. I'll stay on it, see if I can make any more sense of it. But look—it doesn't have to make sense. Columnists and talk-show guys—they can chew stuff like this over and over, contradict each other in smart-ass ways. Your job is to keep after it. Just do it."

"Yeah, fine. I'm doing it. But it worries me that you're throwing up your hands and saying such-and-such a reason is idiotic. That voters don't make sense. There may be a few idiots. But a lot of times you call a guy up, he gives an inarticulate response—that doesn't mean he doesn't have a rational response inside him."

Jerry rolled his eyes. "Mike, I know. I know all that. It's what I do. Believe me, for the little bit of money you're spending, you're getting damn good stuff." Jerry put his fingertips together. "Right now here's what I see. We're moving. So we keep on doing what we've been doing. But more. You're an articulate guy. So go out and articulate. It's the last round, champ. Lots of punches."

Mike said, "I think it's time for some kind of summation. But I need to know what the jury's taking in. See if there's a way to frame one big theme. The way you win a case is you go for the jugular."

"This isn't a lawsuit, Mike."

"You don't go looking for the jugular in the other guy's big toe."

"Mike, don't be so hard to live with. We've had good news. Go out and be the happy warrior." Jerry squinted. "That reminds me. One little detail. Remember the VFW meeting? There was that kind of hostile question about your Purple Heart. So you told it like a joke, got some laughs."

"Yeah. I decided it's the only way to go with it. I got hit with a splinter in my butt, and then tore my knee up falling off the bridge. Ended up on the deck tangled up in some camouflage netting. A Gerald Ford Purple Heart."

"If it comes up again, try modest understatement. And say 'a piece of shrapnel' instead of 'splinter.'"

"It was a splinter. I can't say shrapnel—shrapnel's a fragment of a round. This was a piece of our own armor. But I can say 'piece of metal' if you like."

"All right, all right. But look—when you say 'piece of metal' hold up your hands and show how big it was."

"That's like a guy telling a fish story—his hands get farther apart each time he tells it. I'll tell you what. I can hold up one hand, stretch my thumb and fingers apart."

"Okay. And then leave out the part about showing the scar—'If I were Lyndon Johnson I'd show you the scar, but . . .'"

"It was a bunch of guys there. They laughed."

"I'm not saying it wasn't funny then. I'm just saying next time it could go wrong. Be a little serious with it. You've got a radio interview tomorrow, and she's going to ask about—"

"Radio, huh. I'll be sure to hold up my hands."

Jerry sighed. "I'm being helpful and you're breaking my balls, pal."

"Piece of metal. You got it." He didn't say any more. There was something about Jerry's rhythm and diction that was annoying but also contagious.

He went to see Ganny for his afternoon and evening.

She said, "School for the deaf over near Staunton. They've got someone to sign, I sent him the speech already. Then Harrisonburg, meet some key people at that Greek restaurant. You got an hour to mingle, then two and a half hours to get to Richmond. I'll meet you at the Commonwealth Club—here's a map. No, I'll give it to Fiona, she's driving. Here's a list of who'll be at dinner. You know two of them, the other three you can read up on on the way. One of them's on the board of the Piedmont Environmental Coalition. Fiona knows him, so get her to brief you on him. These guys already gave a lot of money to environmental groups, but you're some new energy. You got a clean shirt? Be sure you wash up and change your shirt before you get to Richmond. And take a nap. Don't get talking to Fiona. It's time for you all to get going." Ganny went to the door and called Fiona.

Mike got up and put his arm around Ganny. "Tomorrow's easy, right?"

Ganny patted him on the back. "Some door-to-door. The fresh air'll do you good. Then a radio interview—she's a sweetheart, it'll be a puff piece. Then you and Joss go to the film-festival banquet."

Mike said, "Have you talked to her?"

"She's fine. She said she's rehearsing her 'This is Mrs. Norman Maine' speech."

"What?"

"It's the last line of *A Star Is Born*. Husband and wife, both movie actors. The wife gets an Oscar, and her husband doesn't, 'cause he's an over-the-hill lush. So the wife uses her married name in her acceptance speech."

Fiona came in. Ganny said, "Where's your clean shirt?"

"Home."

"No, hold on," Fiona said. "I put two clean ones in your desk drawer. The white one or the striped?"

"White," Ganny said.

"Good," Mike said. "I've got one extra thing. What the hell is it? I thought of it last night. Oh yeah—could you check and make absolutely sure we have drivers—"

"We've got drivers for election day. I've done that."

"Drivers for those vans with lifts. For the retirement homes."

"Mike, it's done. Stop worrying about my stuff."

"You're a genius." He turned to Fiona, who was back with the shirt. "You're both geniuses."

Fiona said, "Wait till you see me say 'Vote for Reardon' in sign language."

"Where'd you learn sign language?"

"When I was a bingo-caller on the Isle of Wight."

Mike was about to ask her to tie that together, but Ganny shooed them out. When they got in the van Mike decided not to ask. He climbed in the back to take a nap.

After a minute Fiona said, "You awake back there?"

"No."

"Are they good, your wife's films?"

"I don't know. I haven't seen them."

"Really? How very odd. Do you fancy her at all?"

"My wife?"

"No, Ganny."

"Ganny's wonderful. Now just let me—"

"Ganny *is* wonderful. Do you think she likes me?"

Mike said, "You're just doing this because I won't ask you about the Isle of Wight."

Fiona laughed and said, "True. All right, then—you can take your nap now. Oh. There is one more thing. Jerry tells me you have *two* cottages. It would be awfully convenient . . ."

"I'll have to ask Tyler. I don't know what's become of him. I'm pretty sure he doesn't want to live there anymore. I should call him anyway."

"Can you tell me why he wouldn't want to live there?"

"Not right now."

Fiona said, "Ganny told me you're a difficult child. Now take your nap or she'll be cross with you." She waited a second and said, "Chatterbox."

Mike turned over on the folded-down seat. He thought of a dozen things to worry about. He closed his eyes and imagined they were ducks. Ducks on the Yangtze River, swimming home to the wise-eyed boat. Except Ping, the littlest duck . . . Mike saw the book as clearly as if he were reading it to Edith or Nora. . . . He skipped to the last page. Ping's adventure is over, he walks up the gangplank, his uncles and aunts tuck their heads under their wings and fall asleep, Ping falls asleep. All the ducks, Edith and Nora.

Things were fine in Staunton—Fiona did indeed sign "Vote for Reardon" and got a friendly laugh and some applause. ("They were laughing at my accent," Fiona said.) Harrisonburg, fine. Dinner in Richmond with the rich and/or influential environmentalists, fine. (Fiona alternately flirted with the geezers and backed up Ganny and Mike in her earnest hard-facts mode.) Two good contributions and one pledge to get out the eco-vote with a membership phone tree.

Sunday morning he went door to door by himself on the hard side of Lake Anna. At the ninth house he fixed the rudder on a kid's sailboat. His mother asked Mike to eat lunch in their lakeside backyard. The wife phoned some friends to come by. Some of them phoned their friends. Mike followed Ganny's advice—take the "I'm here to listen to you" line. Went easy on the few combative questions—wrinkled his brow and said,

"I've wrestled with that one all right. Let me just see if I can line up the arguments. . . ." Talked fishing with some of the men, got invited back to go after lunker bass. He jotted down names and addresses, thanked his hostess, noticed in the rearview mirror that he'd sunburned his forehead and nose in spite of his tan, drove off dumbly satisfied and drowsy.

When he stopped in at the office Bonnie Two was there. Mike gave her the list of names. He said, "Could we write a few notes?"

"Aren't you supposed to be getting ready for the banquet? Fiona was in this morning asking Ganny for the key to your house so's she could get your tux cleaned." Bonnie Two stuck her chin out and added, "I didn't know she was going with you."

"She's not. I'm going with Joss. We're making an appearance. Here's the deal with the notes. They all live alongside each other, so make each one just a tad different." He wrote "fish" by two names. "That means write something like 'good luck with those big bass.' And then for that one—'Thanks a million for lunch.' For all the others some kind of nice-to-meet-you thing. Oh yeah—for that woman—'I'm still thinking about that question you asked.' You know how to work the pentograph? That signature machine?"

"It's broke. I thought you were going to dictate."

Mike said, "No, you can do it. It won't take you long."

Mike got some letterhead stationery and started signing his name just below the middle. "How many names there?"

Bonnie Two counted out loud, which irritated Mike. She said, "There's twenty-one."

He kept on signing. She rubbed his neck with one hand, then his shoulders with two.

"That felt good," he said, signing the last sheet. "So, if you'd just type in a line or two . . . I've got to run. You know, stuff like what a great neighborhood you live in, what a fun afternoon."

Bonnie Two said, "You got onions on your breath something awful."

Mike felt the squishy sullenness, Bonnie Two's version of Joss' blowtorch anger. He said, "Bonnie, I'm sorry—it's all in a flurry just now. Okay?"

"I'll have to stay late to do these. I don't come in tomorrow."

"You're a trouper. It's not just twenty votes. They'll talk about it."

"Your nose is red too. You better put some ointment on it or it'll peel."

His dinner jacket was at his house, hanging on the inside doorknob. He was singing again. It's keeping track of the little things, that's the secret. Twenty votes here, twenty votes there. The little things are what keep the big ones in place.

He met Joss on the front steps of the Rotunda. "Good outfit," he said.

"It's one of Mom's old ones," Joss said. "Thanks anyway."

Mike sensed a photographer and took her arm.

But once inside, Mike kept to the discipline he'd set himself for the event. As one of the official hostesses led Joss around to meet the movie stars and moguls, Mike stayed one step behind, one step to Joss' right. After Joss was introduced and the hostess turned to him, he stepped forward, shook hands, and stepped back. And then the hostess led them to another cluster of gowns and dinner jackets surrounding the next star. Among the bobbing heads he recognized a few whom he'd asked for money. He had an all-too-accurate memory of who gave what. One woman from his list of very rich liberals was in the next circle. He'd called on her himself. He'd made his pitch. She'd purred with enthusiasm—and written him a very small check. Now he couldn't help appraising her emerald necklace and emerald-spray earrings. Queen Isabella pawned her jewels to send Columbus on his way; this woman hadn't come up with the equivalent of one sprig of one earring—she hadn't even given up a trip to the beauty parlor, not if she'd had her hair dyed. . . .

At most cocktail parties Mike had a first moment of disliking all the faces—the idiotically smiling or the smugly aloof. Then one of them would say a polite word to him, and he'd think what a pleasure it was to meet all these nice people. But at this gala he was bottled up in his Trappist vow of silence. Since he was also bottling up his physical energy—his campaign habit of moving around with a bounce in his step and a swing to his gestures—his initial bad mood enlarged into a puritan contempt for the swagger of evening clothes, the jut of perfected faces, the hollow resonances of the big shots, the twittering of their idolaters—all the elaborations of vanity and vain event.

He shook hands and nodded and smiled at yet another group. Joss was drinking mineral water but was cracking a few jokes in her old style. At least he could be glad she was having a good time, partly out of generosity, partly out of self-interest. Courtly old Mr. Broome had called him saying Joss wanted Mike's permission to make an inventory of the pieces of furniture and other belongings she'd left behind. Mr. Broome had suggested that it would save time and lawyer's fees if Mike and Joss could work all that out by themselves. Mike had said, "I'll be on the road next week. It's fine with me if she just comes by and picks up what she thinks is hers."

"Well, that's most obliging. You're sure, now?"

"I'm sure. She'll be fair. When she's not angry, she's completely fair."

Since then he'd had a second thought—what if Bonnie One tagged along? Then he thought what the hell.

Now he had another second thought. Perhaps he wasn't acting out of pure blitheness. Perhaps he was slyly courting Joss with this gesture. Perhaps this was another case of campaign calculation seeping into every part of him.

This quick glance of self-observation wasn't much by itself, but it made him quit being pissed off at the vanity of vanities. Here he was in his dinner jacket, in his starched dress shirt with gray-pearl studs, in his patent-leather shoes. He was pleased that he'd had to take in an inch on his cummerbund; he'd admired his flat stomach in the mirror, had been sorry no one was there to admire him putting on the ritz. No Edith or Nora. He'd even peeked out the back window to see if Fiona had moved into the bungalow—he could have sauntered over to ask her any old question and she would have said something teasing but satisfying: "Oh my—aren't you the grandest tiger in the jungle!" All that was just high spirits, nothing wrong with high spirits.

So what was souring him here? Sure, there were some people preening themselves, some people flushing with silly excitement. There was even a laughably venal touch—Mike saw one of Charlottesville's pushier real-estate agents giving her business card to one of the moguls. So this folderol was not so different from most occasions of his new life—a county fair, a college convocation, a VFW meeting, Mrs. Rogers' party—except that on this occasion no one was going to tap a glass with a spoon and hand him a microphone.

The sensation of this thought made him jerk his head. It was obvious, as obvious as a hook to a fish once it swallowed the worm.

◇

Fiona showed up early at Mike's house. She drove the van into the circle between the cottage and the bungalow and pulled out an external-frame backpack that seemed almost as tall as she was. Mike was on the side deck doing his dumbbell exercises. Fiona pulled out a duffel bag, a bicycle, and two plastic shopping baskets filled with books. She left everything in a pile beside the van and ambled over. She said, "Don't stop. You'll lose the aerobic effect." She watched for a moment and added, "Keep your elbows closer to your body. And pull through higher. You want a full range of motion." She picked up the sheet of paper with his list of exercises and scanned it. "Good," she said. "You're on your last set, are you? Jerry wants to see you. Have you had breakfast? I'm famished."

Mike grunted, "No." He added two more dumbbell rows by way of showing off. He said, "There. Did Jerry say what's up?"

"No. Just be sure to stop by the office before you go see your wife's films. We haven't discussed the rent. I gather Jerry's staying in that cottage for free, but that's just until election day. I can't really afford much, not with what you and Ganny are paying me, but I imagine you could use a Handy Andy about the place. Your garden needs weeding. It's not too late to grow some greens. Perhaps some beetroots. And I could strip that horrible wallpaper in your front hall. It would look ever so much nicer painted white. Whether you win or lose, you'll want someone looking after things for a month or two. Those trees need pruning."

"You're doing what Nora does," Mike said. "She gets what she wants by inundation."

"So I'm getting what I want?" She smiled.

He said cautiously, "I have a lot of things on my mind."

"Exactly why you need me to take care of all bothersome details."

"I'm not thinking past election day."

"Nor am I really. We'll try it for a week, then, and see. I can come and go at a moment's notice. You'll scarcely notice me. Less than you do Jerry Medina. He's an awful man, isn't he? But I suppose that's a price you pay. I'll go make breakfast while you bathe. I brought some pears. I don't usually talk this much, I think it's something to do with you."

Jerry waved him into his office and closed the door. He said, "Fenton's boys are saying they want to talk about a debate."

"It's pretty late in the game—"

"I think it's bullshit. But I got an idea."

"Why do you think it's bullshit?"

"Because they're making impossible demands. Like total control of every detail. I said let someone neutral run it, like the League of Women Voters. That's the standard deal. Fenton's boys said no. They just want to be able to counter our line that Fenton refuses to debate. Hell, they wanted all the questions submitted in writing beforehand. They offered to videotape the two of you in some TV studio at their consultant's office building up in Arlington. Even if I agreed to something as dumb as that, my guess is they'd ask for something more. Tomorrow we'll see a press release of their saying we've refused their offer to debate. And I'll put out something saying how impossible their conditions are. But they'll have blurred the issue. So what we do—we just have time to do—is set up a couple of open forums. We'll get neutral moderators—somebody everybody'll recognize as impartial. Maybe even an honest Republican. We've got a hall in Staunton already. I'm working on something in Culpeper. You'll stand up there and you'll say, 'It's a shame Fenton won't show up, but here I am. And here you are—you the people—the ones who really matter.' The beauty part is that every announcement we run is an argument in itself. We can't make Fenton debate, but we're out in the open. We're saying, 'Folks, hit me with your best shot.' We'll call it 'A People's Forum.' Or maybe 'The Voters' Open Forum.' *Open.* 'Open' is the key word. 'Open Forum for the People.' We'll get in touch with all the civics teachers at the high schools, invite them to bring their classes."

"I don't know, Jerry. There's not a lot of time. And if I were a teacher, I'm not sure I'd like to get involved in—"

"Mike, the point is we *ask*. We are seen to be asking. It makes a nice last paragraph in the press release. 'The Reardon campaign committee has issued special invitations to . . .' And we put in the names of the teachers, the names of the schools. We're seen reaching out. We're seen to be doing the civic-minded open thing."

"So you don't care much about filling the hall. It's the stuff beforehand—"

"Mike—I know how to fill a hall, for Chrissakes. I know what to do beforehand. I'm doing what I know. I know what to do before, I know how to fill the goddamn seats, and I know what to do after. All you have to do is show up and talk to the people. That's what you know how to do. You're doing it, things are happening, I have a good feeling about this." Jerry clapped his hands on Mike's shoulders. "So look. We're already booked for Staunton on Friday. I'll set up the Culpeper thing for Sunday. I like that—right in Fenton's backyard."

"Daniel in the lion's den."

"That's good. You want to watch yourself with those Bible references, but that's good. Remind me—Daniel did what? He tamed them? He killed them?"

"An angel came and shut their mouths."

"That part I can't guarantee. So we do Culpeper on Sunday and then we're back here Monday for our election-eve rally. Right here on our downtown mall. I got you a brass band." Jerry hummed a few bars of "Anchors Aweigh."

The Vinegar Hill Theater was nearly full. Mike was about to take a seat in the back when he saw Nora in the second row with two empty seats on her right. To her left there were Joss, Edith, and Bonnie One. He sat down beside Nora just as the houselights dimmed.

He liked the little opening before the credits. Joss had used a still of Nora's drawing of the Admiral saying, "Do you know you're the first girl in the Navy?" She'd animated it so that the girl did a pirouette and said out loud, "So? So? So?"

The credits rolled. The last one was a dedication to Joss' mother, Edith, Nora . . . and Michael Francis Reardon. Stiffly formal but generous. Mike was trying to think of just how to say thanks when a woman swept into the aisle seat beside him.

Mike was alternately amused by the science-fiction parody and distracted by the woman beside him, who wouldn't keep still. She opened and closed her purse, put it under her seat. She fanned herself with her program.

Mike was admiring the imitation of Kissinger's voice when the woman crossed her legs, jostling his calf with her heel. During the meltdown of the flying saucer she uncrossed and recrossed her legs.

Mike was alarmed by the beginning of the next one. It was grainy black and white. A man and a woman entered a bedroom. There were black bars superimposed across their eyes. The music was a sidling, slinky shik-a-boom shik-a-boom. He sighed with relief when it became clear that this wasn't a late-fifties porn film, but a bizarre parody. The couple got into bed and picked up books. They reached up and shoved aside the superimposed black bars, which floated to the edges of the frame.

Mike became edgy again when the man turned out to be a pompous ass. The man corrected his wife's pronunciation of the title of the book he was reading. *Anna Karenina.* "AH-nah Kar-YEN-neen-ah." He made her repeat it. There was a shot in full color of the couple dancing at a ball. The husband was in uniform. He wore a Prussian helmet with a spike on top. He put his lips near her ear as they waltzed and said, *"EINS, zwei, drei—EINS, zwei, drei."*

Back in bed, the husband was in his flannel pajamas but still had the Prussian helmet on his head.

The woman beside Mike laughed. Mike felt unfairly criticized. If anyone had been going around correcting little details it was Bonnie One with her Jesuit churches.

The man in bed went through several other changes from the wife's point of view. When he finally fell asleep he had a great stone face like one of the monuments on Easter Island. The wife turned out her light and closed her eyes but lay rigid as the husband snored. A blue-tinted double—her ghost? her dreaming self?—rose out of her and floated across the room, her nightgown fluttering around her knees. The blue double drifted out the window. She lifted one hand and waved it across the night sky. It left a wake of light, as if the sky were a sea brimming with phosphorescent plankton. Her blue figure in fact seemed to be swimming in the air. She was joined by a dark shape, velvet black against the blue-black sky, its form distinct only as it blotted out stars or swam across the light-blue body of the dreaming wife. The two bodies spiraled around each other like dolphins courting.

There was a quick cut to a close-up of the wife in bed, her face softening. She murmured, "Ah."

Back to the blue and velvet-black figures swirling. Another close-up of the wife in bed, her head turning on the pillow as her mouth opened and closed, saying more distinctly, "Ah, nah." There was a flurry of phosphorescence in midair. The wife's head lifted off the pillow. She said, "Ah! Nah! Anna Karenina!"

The woman sitting next to Mike gave a shriek of laughter. She grabbed the arms of her seat, jostling Mike's elbow with hers. He turned and said, "Excuse me." He caught a whiff of her perfume.

On screen the wife's blue double melted back into her. In a voice-over the wife said, "That only happens in dreams." A different woman's voice said, "Sometimes in real life."

Mike was angry, but he was also confused. He recognized the dream/real-life exchange as something Joss and Bonnie One used to say to each other, but the perfume seemed familiar too. Was it Joss' perfume? Was it Bonnie One's? Was his memory failing? Or was his good memory not so good with smells? That wasn't true—he'd been haunted by the smell of Bundy's gun bluing, the taste of metal.

In his distraction Mike missed the beginning of the next one, and when he was just settling in to paying attention the woman next to him leaned forward, wiggled farther back into her seat, jangled her bracelet as she smoothed her skirt, and then recrossed her legs. "Excuse me," Mike said to her as quietly as he could. "I'm trying to watch this movie. I was watching a movie once with my wife and she kept crossing and uncrossing her legs, and I finally said to her, 'You're either trying to get me to leave or you're trying to arouse the man on the other side of you.'"

The woman sat up very straight.

"It's a joke," Mike said. "My wife laughed."

The woman put both her feet on the ground and her hands in her lap.

The last movie was titled *Mom's Scrapbook*. It began with three still photos: Mrs. Rogers, approximately age eleven, at summer camp on a horse; Joss, same age, same camp, on a horse; and Edith, same age, same camp, on a horse.

Mike said to Nora, "That's that camp where you and I went to see Edith. That's her favorite horse."

Edith heard him, leaned across Joss, and said, "It's a Welsh pony."

Old splotchy black-and-white film of Mrs. Rogers looking long-limbed and voluptuous, perhaps in her early twenties, stepping out for an afternoon stroll through the cherry blossoms with the Admiral (then a lieutenant j.g.) in his Navy whites.

Film of Lieutenant and Mrs. Rogers leaving church under arch of crossed swords.

Still photo of Mrs. Rogers with newborn first son. A few feet of an old newsreel of an FDR inauguration. Photo of Mrs. Rogers with newborn second son. Newsreel of Pearl Harbor. Photo of Mrs. Rogers with newborn Joss. Newsreel of the Admiral (then commander) being picked up from a life raft in mid-ocean.

Home movie of Mrs. Rogers and three children sailing into the creek on the Northern Neck, the Admiral (then captain) at the tiller of the gig.

Home movie (color, but low-quality) of water-pistol fight in backyard of Northern Neck house. Mrs. Rogers turns garden hose on her sons, their wives, and grandsons and Mike. The Admiral, with white hair on his head and bare chest, appears on second-story porch and tips a pail of water on Mrs. Rogers.

Voice-over of TV newsreel starts while family is still running around in wet clothes.

". . . served in the Navy and in the intelligence community under six presidents."

TV newsreel of Admiral's burial at Arlington Cemetery. The officer of the honor guard hands Mrs. Rogers the folded American flag. Pregnant Joss is next to her holding Edith's hand. Exterior. Night. View of house on Northern Neck from mouth of creek. A single window is lighted. The light gives a slight sheen to the dark water.

Exterior. Day. Same shot of creek and house. The camera lowers to show prow of the Admiral's gig nosing up to the wharf. Sons and grandsons clamber out. Sons turn to give a hand to Mrs. Rogers.

Interior. Night. Dinner table, gabble of grandchildren—a good-sized Nora now among them—sons, daughters-in-law, Mike.

Mrs. Rogers: Joss, darling, what *are* you doing? Put that camera away and sit down.

Later, some meal. Mike carries in hand-cranked ice-cream maker, puts it down beside Mrs. Rogers at the head of the table. She tastes ice cream with a long wooden spoon.

Mrs. Rogers: Dear boy, it tastes like tree bark.

Cut to kitchen, where Mrs. Rogers, her two sons, and Mike are playing Keep Away with a half-gallon container of store-bought ice cream, throwing it back and forth past the hands of the half-amused, half-outraged, very loud grandchildren.

Later same night. Mrs. Rogers in kitchen, filmed through doorway so that she is in a rectangle of light framed in darkness. She puts away a bowl in cupboard, then goes to the window, making a porthole of her hands against the glass so that she can see into the night. She drops her hands slowly, trailing them down the window, tilting her forehead against the windowpane. After a few seconds she lifts her left hand to the side of her head, and her shoulders curl forward. She is crying silently. After several seconds she stands up straight, lifts her head, and squares her shoulders. She says out loud to herself, "Well, that's enough of *that*!"

There is a blur as the camera sways away and moves down the dark hallway toward a dim source of light at the far end.

Exterior. Day. View of creek and wharf from second-story back porch. Mrs. Rogers walks out from under the porch with a pail. When she's gone twenty yards Edith and Nora come after her. Without turning around, Mrs. Rogers slides the wire handle of her empty pail up to her elbow and holds out her arms just as the girls arrive to put their hands in hers. After several steps Nora looks up at the sky and leans dizzily away, pulling on her grandmother's arm. She swings out and around and then jumps forward to catch up.

They all stop, drop their hands, and stand in a row. They march forward in step, dip at the knees, jump back with both feet, bob over at the waist, and then throw their hands up. All their pails are shining with smudges of late sunlight, and their long shadows slant off ahead of them, across the coarse grass all the way to the nearest raspberry bush.

Freeze-frame. Then the picture gradually darkened until only the deep-blue sky was still light. Mrs. Rogers, Edith, and Nora became shadows in the grass and bushes, signaled only by their bright pails.

Mike remembered the silly song-and-dance routine—"One, two, three, four . . . We . . . are . . . the *bloomer* girls!" He thought Joss was right that the scene was better without words, that without words the movements seemed to be a ritual, the childish but right way to approach the raspberry bushes.

And abruptly he hated the idea of ever going again to the house on the Northern Neck. He felt another rip in his sense of things: the point of Joss' piece was not only how much she loved the place, her mother, and Edith and Nora, but how fast the light changed and how queer and sad it was that the house, or even the captain's gig, outlasted flesh.

He thought, So get used to it, pal. A Bundy phrase, but not Bundy's voice. And then an echo of Mrs. Rogers' talking to herself in the kitchen, the same phrase she used to bring her family to order—"Well, that's enough of *that*."

There was applause. The houselights came up. Mike joined in the applause. He looked at the woman on his right, who was looking at him. He recognized her. She was Congressman Fenton's daughter.

Mike looked at the stage in front of the screen, where someone was setting up folding chairs. He turned and said, "Mrs. Fuller—"

She said, "It's Ms. Fenton. I'm using my maiden name."

"Ms. Fenton. I guess they're going to have some kind of question-and-answer thing." Ms. Fenton didn't say anything.

Joss and a professor with a bow tie took their seats onstage. Joss crossed her legs, wiggled her foot, and twirled her wedding ring with her thumb. The professor asked for questions. A long silence. Mike hoped that whoever was running this thing had had the sense to plant a question or two.

The professor frowned and straightened his bow tie, but then looked relieved and pointed his finger. "Yes?"

A woman in the middle of the audience said, "Ms. Rogers, in the Anna Karenina sketch—I mean Ah-nah Kar-YEN-ina"—laughter—"is that final sequence with the woman just a dream? Or is it about masturbation?"

Joss said, "Let me out of here." Laughter. Joss said, "No. I mean that's what her spirit is saying, isn't it? Let me out of here. Apart from that, your guess is as good as mine. It's really called *Eros Wanes*. One time my husband and I were at the movies and I was crossing my legs back and forth and my husband said, 'I can hear your nylon stockings scraping and you're either trying to get me to leave or you're trying to arouse the man on the other side of you." Laughter.

Ms. Fenton turned and looked at Mike. She said, "That's your wife? Ms. Rogers is your wife. . . ."

"Yes."

A man across the aisle from Ms. Fenton said, "That drawing in *Nora's Drawing*—that really looked like a child's drawing. How did you—"

"It *is* a child's drawing. My daughter Nora drew it when she was only six."

The man said, "Well, if I can follow up. I mean the film about your mother. That is your mother, isn't it?"

"That's my mom."

"Well, it's interesting that you're so—I mean this in the most complimentary way—Looney Tunes . . ." Laughter. "No. I'm a great fan. I mean, you have this cartoon quality but then a lot of your work is autobiographical."

Joss said, "Especially *It Came from Outer Space.* The ego-devouring monster? That's me."

Laughter.

"But what about the couple in bed, the Anna Karenina one? Is that some kind of feminist statement?"

"No. Anyone who waltzes with someone and says, *Eins, zwei, drei,'* is a lug."

The professor said, "Well, that sounds like you're saying that's what's wrong with men, they're lugs—"

"A lug is a lug is a lug. Maybe I mean *slug.* Slugs are asexual, aren't they?"

Ms. Fenton said to Mike, "Your wife has her own peculiar sort of wit. . . ."

Mike said, "A witty woman at her wits' end," and felt like a ventriloquist's dummy for Joss.

Ms. Fenton said, "But I have a great deal of sympathy for her."

◇

Joss couldn't remember what she'd just said onstage. She remembered Bonnie One's look of anxious pain. She remembered her intoxication at hearing the audience laugh at her remarks, and she feared that she'd played to the cheap seats. And then she worried that Edith might have hurt feelings because Nora's drawing played one of the leads. But her main worry now, as she slid past Bonnie One's narrow knees and sat back in her seat, was that her stuff wasn't right. It could have used another week of work, another month, year. She should have left it on a train, dropped it into a vat of acid, burned it.

The houselights dimmed again for the multimedia performance. A woman came onstage wearing a vest and a very short fringed cowgirl skirt. Perhaps it just looked short because her legs were so long. She started twirling a lasso, jumped through it, into it, and out of it. She dropped it and said, "This is really dumb." She put an apron on and strung the lasso across a corner of the stage as a laundry line. She put two clothespins in her mouth and started telling a story. On the screen a black-and-white silent movie started. A woman in a nightgown came out of a house. In a junk heap she found a dollhouse, obviously her long-lost dollhouse. And it was clear, now that her face was visible, the woman in the nightgown was the cowgirl hanging up laundry and telling a story about kissing an old geezer who'd given her a lift in his pickup. The woman in the nightgown was fondling the dollhouse, running one finger around the edges of the windows. She picked it up, hugged it, kissed it, and laid her cheek against it. Her face was intently lovely and dreamy. Just before the audience began to laugh, Joss saw how funny it was. She realized she was witnessing a basic principle of comic acting: your intentions must be absolutely, concentratedly serious.

Step by step the woman in the nightgown seduced the dollhouse, or perhaps the other way around.

While the cowgirl hanging out laundry was weighing out loud the pros and cons of kissing the old geezer in the parking lot of a gas station west of Fargo, North Dakota, the woman on screen had collapsed in the grass under the dollhouse, her arms around it, then her legs around it, her heels hooked onto the roof, the tendons in her neck taut as she lifted her head to kiss it again and again. Joss hadn't had such a roller-coaster ride of laughing for ages. She was delighted with this woman, bereft when the screen went dark, relieved to find her alive as the cowgirl hanging up the last shirt on the laundry line, winding up the story of the old geezer who was so pleased by how much she looked like his dead wife and so enchanted with his one kiss that he gave her his pocket Bible. Joss was transfixed by the cowgirl's mouth, by the unexpected sweetness of the old geezer's kiss which the words made palpable—the pressure, the dry lips, the brush of the smoky mustache hair, and the unexpected spark of pleasure in the middle of her sweet cowgirl mind. So what if everyone's in a whirl, flying away this way and that. She and the genius cowgirl would be happy wanderers, kissing old geezers and dollhouses. She imagined an old March of Time newsreel, the title flickering on the screen: "Gypsy Cowgirls Bring Relief to Farmers and Factory Workers Throughout Midwest." Then the sonorous baritone voice-over: "These zany beauties are on tour from the Dust Bowl to the Dakotas, answering the nation's desperate need for jokes, palm readings, sulfa drugs, and—for a few lucky old geezers—kisses. That's right, folks—kisses. So pucker up, pops, the gypsy cowgirls are headed your way!"

The show was over. Nora took Joss' hand and said, "Yours is better, Mom."

"Pooch."

"Hers is good, but yours is really, really better."

"We're both genius cowgirls, pooch. When you were campaigning, did it ever feel like that for you and your dad?"

"Mom, look. She wants you to go up there with her. Go on—while they're still clapping."

Joss hesitated, but Nora gave her a shove. Joss looked up and saw the gypsy cowgirl smiling at her and holding out her hand.

They took a bow together, holding hands. Out of the corner of her eye Joss saw Ganny crouching in the aisle, sending Nora up the steps with a bouquet of roses. That revived the dwindling applause. Nora flashed a sideways smile at the audience and gave the roses to Joss.

Nora whispered to Joss, "Give some to her."

Joss did as she was told. Nora took her hand and with her other hand waved to the audience. Nora then gave Joss' hand a gentle pull and led her off.

Joss said, "What a pro you are. You're a regular little show-biz pooch."

◇

Ganny came into Mike's office. She said, "Here's the printout of your schedule for the rest of the week." She looked at him, flicked the door shut with her heel, and said, "You feeling all right? I can tell you've been skipping your naps. Probably not eating right either."

Mike said, "Only a few more days. I can eat this schedule for breakfast." He picked it up, nibbled the corner, and laughed. Ganny didn't laugh. He said, "I'm making light of it, Ganny."

Ganny pulled a chair up to his, sat down, and held his hand. "You had a hard time with Joss' movies." She took his other hand. "I talked to Edith and Nora. They're doing fine. They're looking forward to your being around more. You've done a job with this campaign. I told you not to do it, but I was wrong. It's been good, no matter what. If you win, you'll be good. If you don't, then you and I'll get an office, we don't need to go back with your partners, you don't want them, I sure don't. You and the girls take a vacation. When you get back, either we go to Washington or we set up shop. Hell, we already got that chicken-plucking company wants to be a new client. And even that doesn't have to be the rest of your life. You've come up with something for yourself that's brand-new. Your speeches have been good. Well, all but two or three."

Mike lifted his head. Ganny said, "Don't interrupt me now." She squeezed his hands. "I'm sorry about that day you thought you were crazy and you kept trying to show me that map. But you got through that day. That was your worst day, and it's long gone. You're yourself now."

Mike nodded. He couldn't quite believe what she said, certainly not all of it, but he felt comforted. Enough so that he felt he could ask for more comfort. He said, "Things are still whirling around."

She said, "Of course things are whirling around. You just got to not whirl with them. I see where Bonnie Two is looking a little put out. That's all right. It must mean you're not sleeping with her anymore."

Mike blushed.

Ganny said, "Don't get all bothered about it. You weren't that conspicuous. Dumb, but . . ." Ganny slumped. "She knows as well as I do what you're coming out of. She may be fluttery enough to hope for something, but she's smart enough to see you can't be serious for a while yet. Just don't mess around with Fiona. She'll sting you so it really hurts. I like her a whole lot. Just don't get going with her."

"She's a kid. Besides—"

"She's a kid with an appetite. And she's sharp enough and quick enough to get a taste of someone's bone marrow. She wouldn't know she's doing any harm. She imagines everyone can slip away as free and easy as she can. You said yourself you got enough whirling around without that."

"Well, that's the thing. It's not just the whirling around. It's more that I've been enlarged, but not precisely enough. I'm enlarged in a clumsy puffed-up way. I can't pick up small-scale things. Talking to you now is the first time in a long while . . . No. It's funny. Joss and I went to the fancy party for the film festival. For a few minutes there we were talking the way we talked before. Five or six years ago. So that was the right scale, a lifesize scale, but it was in a time shift. Then I got thrown back into this dimension. Maybe I get inflated and fuzzy talking to all these strangers, talking into the air, into microphones. When I started out campaigning it was like watching a ghost of myself. Now that's the real me."

Ganny took her right hand away and cupped her chin in her palm. She shook her head and then started laughing. She squeezed his hand and said, "I'm sorry. I'm not laughing at . . . I was just thinking how it sounds like the truth about all this campaigning, but nobody better say it." She shook her head. "At least you got some idea about yourself." She squinted for a second and said, "The tricky part is this—you *have* got bigger, and some of it's real, some of it's hot air. Maybe it has to be both. But, now, you just make sure you know which is which. And then you can get rid of some of the hot air. Like that NRA kiss-ass. Like Mike Reardon, hunter; Mike Reardon with his long rifle. I'll help you on that one. Oh yeah. Getting back to details. Jerry's list of songs for the band. He put in 'Carry Me Back to Ol' Virginny.'"

Mike said, "It's the state song."

"But people know the lyrics and the lyrics say 'darkies.'"

Mike said, "I didn't know."

She patted his arm. "Well, that's why I'm here, honey. And now we got to get on with the rest of the day."

Staunton started okay. Mike found an old-fashioned rhythm answering a moderately aggressive but vague question about federal regulation. "Federal regulation? You bet. So the car you drive doesn't have a gas tank that explodes. So Interstate 81 is safe, so the planes, trains, and buses you ride are safe. Federal regulation? You bet. For the war against drugs and drug dealers and the arms profiteers who peddle them automatic weapons. Federal regulation? You bet." And on through OSHA, protective tariffs, a national energy policy, and winding up with the theme that the checks-and-balances system wasn't just between the executive, legislative, and judicial branches, but in this day and age the government should serve as a check and balance on big corporations. "I hope I don't offend any of you with cousins just across the state line in West Virginia, but there's an example of a state that was laid low by unregulated corporate interests." And the standard hedge. "Of course, if a federal regulation is old and tired and in the way—will I get rid of it? You bet."

Someone yelled, "Same for Fenton?"

The moderator said, "You'll have to wait your turn."

Mike said, "You bet."

But he almost blew the next one.

A woman came up to the mike and said, "Remember me?"

Mike drew a blank. He shaded his eyes and said, "I'm sorry, it's hard to see." He looked over at Ganny at the end of the front row, but she shrugged. At the other end of the front row he found Jerry, who mouthed something.

The woman said, "I called in to your radio show—"

"Yes, you did," Mike said. "And you're very kind to make the effort to get here tonight." He looked at Jerry and made out the word "chicken plucker." Mike said, "And how's it going in the chicken business?"

"Well, you said you'd come visit us and I just want to say you're as good as your word and God bless you."

The moderator said, "Did you have a question for the candidate?"

The woman looked at him and said, "When he says he wants to be a good lawyer for the district and it won't cost a dime, that's just about right."

To Mike's slight irritation the moderator cut in. "Your question, ma'am?"

"When's he going to come back?"

Some people laughed. Mike said, "Soon." A few people laughed. Mike said to the moderator, "May I just say a word here? The poultry-processing company where"—No name. Usually he was good with names—"this nice woman works was being squeezed just enough so they couldn't get ahead. When I take off on big corporations, I don't mean a company like that that's feeling the squeeze like anybody." Mike saw Jerry looking dubious about this aw-shucks line. What Joss used to call his faux populism.

Then a hard-to-figure question from a low, almost muffled voice: "A while back I went down to see a fight? Over to Richmond? A colored boy called Mulekick Pritchett and some Mexican?"

Mike said, "Candeleras."

"Yeah. So you were there. . . ."

"Yes."

"And you sang 'The Star-Spangled Banner'?"

"Yeah . . . Well, I learned my lesson about that. Leave the singing to the Statler Brothers." Ganny had told him on the ride over that the Statler Brothers lived in Staunton. The hometown reference got some laughter and a couple of whoops. Mike said, "So what would you like to know?"

"How's it come about you're mixed up with that kind of thing?"

Was this a lead-in to a black-white question? To a suggestion that boxing was an illegitimate enterprise? Mike said, "I'm his lawyer."

The man said, "You're his lawyer?"

Mike said, "Yes. I'm Mr. Pritchett's lawyer."

The man didn't say anything, just looked intent. But he stayed there, his head tilted toward the standing microphone.

Mike felt the dead air. He cleared his throat and said, "Boxers need legal advice, just like poultry-processing plants. And . . ." He felt his mouth go dry. He couldn't think of the next thing. He couldn't think of the category he was lost in. Examples of people who need legal advice? His other actual clients? Didn't matter—he couldn't remember anything.

Then, for an instant, he thought this might be the guy who had pressed charges against Ezra, the guy whom he'd cross-examined. No. Then what? Bonnie Two's old boyfriend? No. He was stuck on this nondescript guy with a nondescript suit of a nondescript brown hanging on him.

The moderator said, "I'm not sure I understand. Do you want to ask about—?"

"Just curious. Struck me as odd. Just curious." The man looked up at Mike without raising his head, and then went back up the aisle.

There were a couple more questions. Mike gave his answers without going dry, but he felt dull.

Jerry drove the van back to Charlottesville, Ganny up front beside him. Mike tried to sleep in the back. Couldn't shake the man but couldn't remember what he looked like. Just the suit. He felt as nondescript, as shapeless, as incoherent, and as pointless as the man standing there. Just better dressed.

He sat up. Ganny had her head against the window, maybe asleep. He said, "So, Jerry. Thanks for the chicken plucker. Was it obvious?"

"Nah. The shading-your-eyes thing? Covered it. And the I'm-glad-you-came thing. I used to work for a congressman, he would see constituents in his office. Their mom-and-pop tour of our nation's Capitol. He'd say, 'How was your trip?' and they'd go on and on and he could keep on working, looking through his bifocals at the speech on his desk. He'd say, 'See much of Washington?' and that'd give him another couple of minutes. Then he'd focus in for a minute, and it always turned out he knew someone in their hometown. He'd say, 'Now, you be sure you say a big hello to old Bob from me. I think the world of that guy.' Then I'd come in, take a picture of the congressman with the family. Give them some other memento—we had a deal on paperweights of the Capitol. During cherry-blossom season the congressman always had an hour a day for ordinary constituents. We booked ten families in that hour and he still could get thirty, forty minutes of reading done at the same time. And he was famous for being just folks."

This vignette made Mike see an anteroom full of brown suits. The congressman behind his desk in a brown suit.

Jerry said, "That was way back when. He's dead. Huge crowd at his funeral back in his home state."

Mike saw a churchyard full of brown suits, coffins full of brown suits.

He wished Ganny would wake up. She could dispel bitter visions. He said, in a voice that reminded him of his father's, "What did they put on his tombstone? 'He had the common touch'?"

Jerry heard his tone. He said, "Hey, Mike, don't make fun of him—he got elected as many times as Fenton. And *De mortuis*, pal."

Mike said, "*De mortuis nihil nisi* bogus."

"Hey, Mike. Lighten up back there. Smile and the world smiles with you."

Mike felt suddenly heavy as earth. He said, "I'm tired, Jerry. I'm right at the edge."

Jerry cocked an eye at the rearview mirror. He said, "Yeah, I hear it. But look at it this way—that means you're doing good. That means you're putting everything into it. A good night's sleep and you'll have enough for a big finish."

◇

Joss was grateful for Mike's sweet reasonableness about giving her a free hand in picking what she'd take from his house (she'd thought of it as his house in one way or another from the beginning—as strange a place to live as the houseboat had been). She also thought that she could give herself some credit for this treaty—after all, she'd kept their pact about appearing married during the question-and-answer period following her screening. She felt she'd been truthful with those earnest questioners about her little films, and at the same time she'd deflected their efforts to enlist her as an apologist for their ideological collective. The personal might be the political, but she'd always had doubts about how much was lost in the translation. When Mike had been in Washington, she'd been leery of the approximations, the compromises, and, above all, the enthusiasm-on-demand of public life.

She'd kept the peace with Mike, so she rented a small van and hired two U.Va. rowers to come along (they were renting themselves out to raise money for a new boat). So they rolled off along the road beside the Rivanna. The two preposterously tall, powerful, but puppyish rowers were in the back, stretched out on the quilted furniture padding.

She imagined the view from above: the truck, the road, the river, the bridge, the driveway, the house, the bungalow, the cottage. And in another dimension she saw the labyrinth of marriage that she and Mike had been frantically running around in—both of them baffled and in each other's way.

This was the third or fourth time she'd achieved this dispassionate lofty view. The first two times, she'd worried that being released from the maze would reduce her energy, that in the absence of friction she might grow cold. But there was still plenty of friction. She'd deal with that—it didn't scare her yet that she didn't know exactly what she wanted. For the moment it was reassuring to see the last twelve years from this remove—all the wheels and gears of their arguments, the valves and pistons of their rages whirring away in furious miniature.

She set the boys to moving a table and a sofa. She started packing books. That was easy enough—Mike always wrote his name in his. The boys were funny in an odd way. They were almost innocent of their strength as they grappled with getting the sofa out the door, turning it this way and that, one of them holding his end easily with one hand while he scratched his head and screwed up his face at the puzzle. The other one also held his end with one hand and used his free hand to illustrate his notion—"Turn it this way and stick this part through first."

She packed up some kitchen stuff. Plenty of pots and pans for both of them. Leave Mike the black cast-iron stuff, take the bright red and yellow enamel. Leave him one set of pretty plates, the ones her father gave them—Mike would like that, Mike had loved the Admiral. Leave the Waring blender, take the Mix-master, Mike didn't know what it was good for. It was all easy as pie. Speaking of which, take the marble slab and the heavy rolling pin, Mike didn't make pie crusts.

She had a little pang thinking of the narrow range of Mike's cooking—stews, soups, and hunks of meat. No more dainty dishes—he'd miss her brioches stuffed with veal kidneys, her lemon-almond tart. And what would he feed the girls? They didn't like Mike's cooking, except for hamburgers and Tater Tots. They only liked vegetables the way she made them. She'd send some of her recipes with them when they came to stay. Pin messages on each girl reminding him that Nora liked sweet red peppers, but only if they were scorched, peeled, and marinated in olive oil for a day—no garlic; Edith liked carrots, but only if they were boiled and mashed and mixed in with potatoes, with a pat of butter on top; and neither girl would eat grapes with seeds. Mike usually bought the big purple ones with seeds, and whatever he did to them—spit them out, swallow them whole, or crunch them—made the girls say, "Oooh, yuck."

After the kitchen, no more pangs, no hard decisions. The rugs were her mother's. She had the boys take them out to the porch and give them a good thumping. The pictures were easy too—Joss knew their provenances (Mom, Dad, Mike's inheritance from his parents' estates). She'd already moved the equipment from her old studio.

And soon enough the truck was loaded up. One of the boys asked about the tools. Joss said they were Mike's. The boy said that there were lots of duplicates and that she'd need a few basics. She said that it would be too hard to tell which ones Mike was sentimental about, he was odd about the oddest things, it would be easier to spend twenty dollars at the hardware store.

The boy said, "When I get divorced, I want to get divorced from someone like you."

She laughed but was pleased enough by the compliment that she let him drive. She sat in the passenger seat, and the other rower stretched out on the furled rugs.

They rolled down the long driveway. Joss was saying, "And thanks for . . . ," when she saw the two trash barrels on the far side of the bridge set out for the trashmen. The barrels were crammed so that the lids were askew. Trailing out of them were strips of yellowed blotchy wallpaper, but Joss recognized the pattern. Dark sailing ships on a dark sea. She yelled, "Wait! Stop! Here!"

She opened her door and swung down. The truck rolled another yard, dragging her feet through the gravel. She pushed herself away from the closing door and fell to one knee. She caught herself on her palms and was up in a second. She lifted the lid of the nearest barrel and fished out a squashed wad of wallpaper. She unwrapped it—she saw herself in early-fifties costume-drama Technicolor, bad King John unscrolling the Magna Carta at Runnymede—she even said, "How dare they!," possibly sympathizing with King John against his upstart barons, possibly measuring the dimensions of her hurt by making Mike plural. But at last getting to the most probable explanation: Mike as part of a couple. She heard his voice utter several statements in response to the other woman's question: *Negligent*: "Okay. Joss always hated that wallpaper. If you hate it too . . ." *Grossly negligent*: "Yeah, sure. Whatever you want." *Timidly malicious*: "I wonder if she'll notice." And that reminded her that she *hadn't* noticed, that she'd walked right past the walls, which were . . . what? White? Gray? Blue? That she hadn't noticed made her so mad she felt a white flash of a dizzy headache. And then imagined *malice aforethought*—the two of them laughing their heads off as they ran the steamer up and down the walls . . . the woman on the upper rungs of the stepladder scooping off ship after ship with a putty knife while Mike held the ladder steady . . . his left hand on the ladder, his right hand around her bare ankle.

Joss banged on the side of the truck with both fists. Then she turned and picked up the nearer trash can by the handles. She got it off the ground but dropped it back down. She dragged it onto the bridge, squatted, and put both arms around it. She heaved it up. It tottered in her arms and then tipped forward. The handle clanked on the bridge rail. The lid fell into the river. She pushed with her stomach against the bottom until she could get her hands under it. One more grunt and heave and the barrel went over, dumping half its load as it somersaulted in the air. She leaned over the rail in time to see it splash. She said, "Sink, you son of a bitch!," but it floated, bobbing more and more gently, turning in a slow waltz, a spill of wallpaper lapping over the rim like a tongue. Joss stared at it, couldn't think of anything else to yell but "Blah blah blah!"

When she turned around the two rowers were standing facing her, their heads both tilted to the same side.

The one who'd complimented her said, "Are you okay?"

The other one said, "Are you going to throw the other one in?"

Joss said, "Yes. No. I think I've said enough on this subject."

Her embarrassment in the face of the giant boys was, if not a blessing, a distraction. As was the jagged hole in her slacks and the scrape on her knee. When they got to her apartment they tried to make her sit down. She couldn't stay still. They did persuade her to put some Mercurochrome on her knee and change her slacks.

By the time she'd done that, the giant boys had got everything onto the sidewalk. All she had to do was carry odds and ends and tell them where the big stuff was to go. But when the boys set the sofa down, Joss suddenly found herself explaining—"See, there was this wallpaper, and for, oh, seven or eight years I begged my ex-husband to let me get rid of it. . . ."

The giant boys leaned—one against the wall, the other against the door jamb—letting their heads swing toward her on their long necks as she paced and they listened. When she finished they looked at each other.

One said, "Makes sense to me."

The other said, "Let me see if I get it. The wallpaper was bad. So your husband took it down. So that's good. So what got you mad is that he didn't listen to you. But maybe he finally did listen to you. Maybe he finally said to himself, 'You know, the old girl was right.'"

The first one said, "He doesn't mean *old*, like *old*. He means *old girl* like someone who used to be around."

The second one blushed. Joss could see his scalp turn pink between the bristles of his blond crew cut. He said, "Yeah. Like I might say, 'My old girlfriend.'"

Joss laughed and said, "Nice try, buster." She reminded herself of her mother flirting with young men, teasing them to the edge of their party manners and then giving them the verbal equivalent of a tap on the wrist with her folded fan.

But there was the question of who—she was sure there was a who. Mike would no more change wallpaper on his own than go shopping for clothes without being told. It had always been Ganny, with Joss' blessing, who made him go buy a new lawyerlike suit.

She had no right to be jealous. She had in fact practiced not being jealous of Mike and a new woman. She'd even achieved a fair-minded lightheartedness about Mike and a new woman. But not about old wallpaper.

◇

Mike liked the hall Jerry hired in Culpeper. The auction barn at one end of the fairgrounds. It was a hexagonal wooden building with a hexagonal cockpit lined with sawdust. There were six sets of bleachers rising steeply from the chest-high sides of the cockpit almost to the rafters. Two sawdust-strewn aisles made a V from the cockpit to two barn doors—one for leading the livestock in, the other for leading them out. Except for the sliced-out livestock aisles, a bird's-eye view of the bleachers would have looked like a spiderweb.

Mike liked that the bleachers were intimately close to the cockpit. Standing by the rail, he would be able to make eye contact with someone in the last row.

Ganny, Fiona, and Bonnie Two all had portable microphones they could carry up the flights of steps between the sections. Mike and the moderator were to sit at a table in the middle, though Mike pictured himself striding from edge to edge, perhaps ending up with his elbow cocked on the railing in a casually amiable posture.

Jerry told Mike he'd check the sound system while Mike had a short rest in the van. He'd send someone for him a half-hour before they began so that Mike could shake hands with the people coming in. He put a hand on Mike's shoulder and gave it a squeeze. He said, "Make like a welcoming host. Most people are embarrassed to be hostile to someone they just shook hands with." He turned to Ganny, Fiona, and Bonnie Two. "Flat heels, right? We don't want you ladies sinking into the sawdust. And hold your microphone in front of whoever's asking a question. Don't let some bozo grab it and start making a speech."

Bonnie Two said, "Mike, I brought my guitar—"

"Ask Jerry. I've got to go meditate."

The light outside the barn doors was a single overhead white floodlight augmented from time to time by the headlight beams of cars pulling in to park. Mike was seeing spots by the time Jerry brought him in to meet the moderator, a retired local judge with a narrow, impassive face and a slow, peculiarly penetrating tenor voice.

As soon as the judge and Mike sat down at the table, two men in the top row unwound a sheet and held it up. In foot-high letters made of duct tape it read "Yankee Go Home."

Since this was theater-in-the-round, most of the audience saw it at once. There were a few laughs behind Mike, and he saw people on the sides pointing, and then the people in front of him craning around to see what the fuss was about. Mike waved and said, "I used to see signs like that when I was in the Navy."

The judge pulled a gavel out of his briefcase and rapped it on the table. He said, "You'll have to put that away. I won't allow that in my court." The judge peered around the hall and gave another rap. "Raise your hand if you have a question and the chair will recognize you."

It didn't take long for Mike to realize that the most eager and therefore most called-on questioners were combative and well prepared, glancing at an index card for an exact quotation or a precise figure, but otherwise knowing their lines by heart. It crossed Mike's mind that the judge was in on the plan—he seemed to be calling only on the well-dressed young men with big red Fenton buttons who occupied most of the front-row seats. Then Mike thought that perhaps the judge was nearsighted.

Mike began to feel that he was like an over-the-hill prizefighter touring tank towns, prepared to take on all challengers. But these challengers weren't farm boys—they'd had a few lessons. One questioner began by saying, "I was talking to a Catholic priest who says you're pro-abortion—"

Mike said, "I'm not pro-abortion."

The judge said, "Let him finish."

The questioner said, "You're for federal funding for abortionists, and how can it be right for us to pay our taxes—"

"I'm for health care for poor people, so that everyone gets the same chance to consult a doctor and make up her mind. You don't know beforehand what a patient will choose—"

"That is Jesuitical. Don't deny what goes on."

"I'm not denying what goes on. I'm just not going to deny a woman free will in an area that is so morally uncertain for so many people—"

"You're morally uncertain, are you? It's no wonder that the priest I was talking to is going to vote for Congressman Fenton."

"Well, I won't deny him his free will either."

"And that priest said, 'I'd rather vote for a good Protestant than a bad Catholic.'"

Mike laughed. No one else did.

The judge said, "Next question. Yes sir, you—"

"The reason I'm laughing," Mike said, "is that that tactic, that good-Protestant/bad-Catholic tactic, was old when my father was—"

"Pass the microphone, miss," the judge said. "Mr. Reardon, there's a question over there."

Another young man in a spiffy suit. Where were all the hard brown suits when he needed them? This new spiffy suit chided Mike for making light of Congressman Fenton's twelve years of experience with "a sophomoric wisecrack."

Mike said, "Yes, I did make a joke. I said—"

"I know what you said."

"Mr. Reardon—" the judge said.

"I said Fenton didn't have twelve years' experience, he had one year's experience twelve times over."

The questioner said, "But is it not a fact that Congressman Fenton has sponsored over twenty major pieces of legislation—"

"Sponsored," Mike said. "Let me explain *sponsored* to you."

"It's a yes-or-no question."

"The congressman I worked for *sponsored* bills, every congressman is asked to *sponsor* bills. Every major bill has dozens and dozens of sponsors. All sponsoring means is that you sign your name because the party leadership asks you. It does not mean you had the idea, that you held hearings, that you wrote a draft, took it to the Rules Committee, or even spoke in favor of it on the floor of the House. Congressman Fenton hasn't *worked* on a major piece of legislation in years."

The next questioner asked, "Does your law firm represent a department chairman who tried to seduce an assistant professor by promising her a promotion?"

"I don't, but an associate in my old firm did. So what's your point? At the university there have been as many unproven accusations of that sort as there have been proven cases. Don't you think everyone should get a fair hearing?"

"Indeed I do, and that's why you're being grossly unfair to Congressman Fenton when you attack him because his law firm represents a trash-removal company. It's the same thing."

Slick. The little wise-ass out-maneuvered him. Only hope was to blow the bugle, fix bayonets, and go over the top. "The same thing? Boy, is it not the same thing. I have nothing to do with that professor. Fenton is up to his neck with those wheeler-dealers who want to put a toxic-waste dump—"

"Toxic? Who says it's toxic? There's not one shred of evidence in any of the hearings—"

"Who says it's toxic? I'll tell you who. The company itself says so. I have a photograph of their sign on their chain-link fence and it says 'Keep Out. Hazardous to Your Health.' That's who says it's toxic. That corporation had to close down a dump in New Jersey. New Jersey! And now they're putting a dump in our hills, a thousand feet up, so all those acids and carcinogenic PCBs come oozing down. And is Fenton alarmed? No. Fenton is helping them. And not just with his law office. It's his *congressional* office that has made calls to the EPA. And every single one of the board of directors has made a maximum campaign contribution to Fenton. That New Jersey corporation is buying its toxic-waste dump from the man who's supposed to be taking care of this district."

"That is a distortion, that is an outrageous accusation!"

Mike said to Fiona, who was holding the microphone in front of the man, "Miss McCaig, he's had his innings. Come on down."

The judge said, "Mr. Reardon, I won't have you—"

The questioner grabbed the microphone with both hands and Fiona said loudly into the mike, "Ow! You're hurting me!"

The judge said, "You, sir! Unhand her! And you, Mr. Reardon—I won't have you interfering with the chair's conduct of this meeting. I won't have a free-for-all."

"I agree, Judge. But I wonder if you could find a way to call on some people who actually live in our district. I have the feeling that we're being disrupted by people who've driven down here from some political institute in northern Virginia. Perhaps you'd ask the questioners to state their names and their hometowns. I have faith in an open forum, but I also believe in the virtue of local—"

"Virtue?" It was a woman's voice calling from the entryway. She said again, "Virtue?"

At first Mike couldn't see her, but then she walked out of the shadowed entryway onto the sawdust-covered pit. It was Ms. Fenton. She said again, "Virtue?" One of her heels sank into the sawdust and she tottered. A young man in a pearl-gray suit came from the entryway and supported her elbow. Ms. Fenton's hair had fallen across her face when she stumbled. She pulled it back with her left hand, raised her right hand, and pointed at Mike.

"I know about this man and his so-called virtue."

Mike said, "Good evening, Ms. Fenton. I'm glad you came. Can one of you find Ms. Fenton a seat?"

The judge said, "Good evening, Charlotte."

Ms. Fenton said, "Judge, this won't take but a minute."

The judge said, "In all fairness, I think we can spare a brief moment to hear the congressman's daughter. Especially since the congressman himself has other obligations which detain him elsewhere. If one of you ladies would pass along a microphone."

Bonnie Two took a step forward. Ms. Fenton looked her up and down but didn't move. The young man in the pearl-gray suit took Bonnie Two's microphone and held it for Ms. Fenton. She said, "Thank you, Judge. My father hasn't thought it necessary to answer the attacks this man has made. And I wouldn't stoop to answer him either, because most of you know the Honorable Howard Fenton and can tell a responsible public servant from this Johnny-come-lately."

Mike said, "Judge, this isn't a question."

"Oh, I have a question," Ms. Fenton said. "It's a question of character. And I ask for the chair's help in making sure I'm not interrupted. The question comes up because I went to the film festival in Charlottesville; I went in my father's place, since that's one of the many, many public projects he's supported over the years. And what did I find there? Oh, the regular movies were all right, but the so-called experimental films I saw were not ones you'd ever want to see in our movie theaters. Grotesque, perverse little films. There was one about a woman and a dollhouse. I can't describe it. I can only say perverse solitary vice." Ms. Fenton again pointed her finger at Mike and said, "And these unspeakable films were dedicated to Michael Reardon. It said so right on the screen. Dedicated to that man right there!"

In the section behind Mike a deep bass voice said, "Charlottesville is a city of the plain." Mike turned and saw a stout man holding his fists beside his face. The man repeated, "City of the plain," and unclenched his fists, spreading his fingers, which were the size of parsnips.

The judge rapped his gavel, pointed it at him, and said, "You'll wait to be recognized. The lady has the floor."

"No," Mike said. "I can't let that go by. I was sitting next to you and you were laughing. You weren't shocked, you were laughing your head off. Your saying you were shocked is what is perverse. You are perverting the truth."

The man in the pearl-gray suit said, "Are you calling this lady a liar?"

Mike said, "Who asked you, sonny?"

"I will not have a free-for-all," the moderator said. "Ms. Fenton has the floor."

"I'm asking *you*," the pearl-gray suit said.

"You're out of order," the moderator said.

"They're both out of order," Mike said. "Let's get on with something real."

"Mr. Reardon, I'll handle this."

"Well, handle it, then. I've had enough of these wackos."

"Excuse me, Judge," Ms. Fenton said. "That is an insulting thing for him to say. I don't think he should be allowed to use an abusive term."

"Mr. Reardon—"

"You think 'wacko' is abusive? I think it's descriptive. Now, can you get some order? We're supposed to be having a question-and-answer—"

"Mr. Reardon, you'll be in order. You, sir, in the gray suit, you'll be in order. Now, Ms. Fenton, if you have a question, I can permit you one question, and then we'll have to move on. Do you have a question, Ms. Fenton?"

"Yes, Judge, thank you, I do. How on earth does Mr. Reardon dare to stand up there and pretend—"

"Oh, for God's sake!" Mike said. "That isn't a question."

"Charlotte, that does sound highly rhetorical."

"I'm sorry. Does Mr. Reardon recall that, at that moving-picture show, in that darkened theater . . . does he recall leaning over and accosting me in an indecent way?"

Mike shouted: "Okay, that's it! That is nuts."

"Well, he did, Judge. He leaned into me and said something like I aroused him by crossing my legs—he said those words."

"No," Mike said. "The answer is no, nobody said anything indecent. There's your answer. Now, go find a seat like everyone else."

"Mr. Reardon," the judge said. "You may not—"

"Judge," Ms. Fenton said, "I've asked my question, so I'll leave it to you to establish that he said those words."

"Ms. Fenton, it's not my role to ask questions. I'm here to preside—"

"Then I won't take any more of your time, Judge. I just know I couldn't ever trust a man who accosted me in a darkened movie theater."

"In your dreams," Mike said before he could stop himself.

"Charlottesville," the fat man behind Mike said. "'It shall be more tolerable for Sodom and Gomorrah in the day of judgment than for that city.'" The half-dozen people around him clapped their hands once and bowed their heads.

Fiona said, "Oh, lighten up." Some of the people in the section behind her laughed.

The man in the pearl-gray suit said to Mike, "So what *did* you say to her?"

"Order," the judge said. "Mr. Reardon, is that all you wish to say? You have nothing further?"

Ms. Fenton shifted her feet in the sawdust, tottered slightly, and held on to the arm of the man in the pearl-gray suit.

Mike thought, If she totters out of here, it'll stick. He said, "Ms. Fenton, I think I see how you got your wrong idea. I'll go over the facts for you. I was watching my wife's movies. They're funny, they're nothing like your description. The film-festival committee saw them beforehand, they invited her to show them. My whole family was there, I was sitting with my wife and my mother-in-law, I was sitting beside my eleven-year-old daughter. I was concentrating on the movie. You came in late and took the seat on my right. Then you started fussing around with your coat and your handbag and crossing your legs and shifting around. I didn't want to say something rude, like 'Stop that noise.' So I told you a joke. I said that my wife and I were at the movies once and she was fidgeting and crossing and uncrossing her legs and I said to her, 'You're either trying to get me to leave or you're trying to arouse the man on the other side of you.'"

There was total silence. Mike took a breath. He looked sideways at the judge, whose expression didn't change.

Mike said, "My wife laughed at that. She said, 'That's marriage for you.'"

Mike looked at the section of the audience in front of him, twelve rows rising from eye level to the dimly lit tier just below the roof. It was brown suits. He saw dresses and sports coats and windbreakers and flannel shirts, but all the spaces between them, the motionless air and shadow, filled with hard brown gabardine. Maybe he'd spoken too fast. Maybe he'd left out part of it. Maybe he hadn't said anything yet, maybe his explanation was still bottled up inside him being smothered by this silence.

Jerry Medina coughed and managed to turn it into a labored chuckle. Far across the sawdust pit Fiona laughed a more plausible laugh, which her microphone picked up. She was probably laughing at Jerry Medina. It didn't matter, a few more people laughed, and Mike's hopes rose—it would only take a few more little laughs and maybe one heavy guffaw and soon there'd be a wave of laughter that would wash Ms. Fenton right out the door. But the laughter was not contagious.

Mike felt his reflexes slow. At first this slowness made him feel calmer, but when he tried to think of what to do next, he had to squeeze his will even to lift his microphone.

He managed to say, "Now that that's cleared up."

The man in the pearl-gray suit said, "What's clear is that the only person here who wasn't offended by that suggestive remark is that honky-tonk singer in the red dress over there." He was confusing Fiona with

Bonnie Two. "And she's on the Reardon payroll along with these other . . . I guess they're campaign workers."

Mike turned to the judge and said, "Could we—"

"Honky-tonk singer, is it?" Fiona was down the steps and onto the floor. "And who might you be, you great piece of window dressing? Suggestive remark? You're the one oozing suggestive remarks, the way you say 'campaign worker' with a suggestive sneer, the way you say 'red dress' with a dirty little smirk. I wouldn't be surprised to find out you're from a male-escort service. Now, give up that microphone and clear off."

The judge was rapping steadily with his gavel and saying "Order, order, order," but not making nearly enough noise to drown out Fiona, who was speaking right into her mike.

What did drown her out was the fat man and his clump of men and women rising to their feet and singing "I'd Rather Be an Old-Time Christian Than Anything I Know."

Mike sat down on the corner of the judge's table. Mike didn't think this group of singers was part of the Fenton ambush plan. Just an outbreak of old-time religion, just testifying. They weren't running out of breath, and the song kept coming back to the refrain in a Möbius-strip sort of way.

Mike considered walking out and letting Jerry deal with the aftermath, putting whatever spin on it he could. But Mike felt too tired even to make an exit. So why not just sit here in his hired hall? He felt empty of invention, and that emptiness was, if not soothing, at least physically restful.

Fiona gave her microphone to Bonnie Two and faced off again with the man in the pearl-gray suit. Ms. Fenton had backed up and edged halfway behind him, leaning her head out to keep an eye on Fiona. The man in the pearl-gray suit held the microphone behind him and pointed at the judge, who was still gaveling, though somewhat listlessly.

Bonnie Two said into her microphone, "I hope he doesn't get violent like that other one." She circled behind Fiona and kept on across the pit to the section where the people were singing. At the end of their next refrain she said, "Let's try 'Shall We Gather at the River?,'" and she launched into it.

Unlike the laughter, her singing *was* contagious. Some of the original singers took it up, and some of the other people in that section. By the time Bonnie Two got to the chorus ("Yes we'll gather at the river / the beautiful, beautiful river . . .") people in the neighboring sections joined in.

Was she brilliantly taking charge of the audience? Or could she just not pass up a chance to sing in public?

Bonnie Two finished "Shall We Gather at the River?" and started "Bringing in the Sheaves."

The judge said, "I won't allow a free-for-all."

Fiona and Mike both looked at him and laughed.

The man in the pearl-gray suit said into his microphone, "How come your girl in the red dress there is singing hymns? You don't even believe in school prayer."

The judge, still stony-faced, said, "Ms. Fenton, would you and your colleague approach the bench . . . the table here."

Ms. Fenton urged the man forward.

The judge said, "And you all over there, you'll have to stop singing now."

"The singing's okay," Mike said.

"Mr. Reardon, will you not interfere? Now, will you kindly ask that young lady to stop?"

Mike walked over to Bonnie Two, waited for the end of the verse—"We shall come rejoicing, bringing in the sheaves." He took her elbow in his hand. She said into her microphone, "Hey, you all are just great! Aren't they just fine, Mike?" She raised the microphone for him.

"Fine," he said. "Fine."

"Maybe we can do another," Bonnie Two said. "What do you say, Mike?"

Bonnie Two was pink in the face, and as she spoke, she gestured widely with one arm and turned her body one way and then the other. At first Mike thought this turning and twisting was show biz, making sure to play to the full width of the audience, but when she took his hand he felt a tremor and heat in her fingers. She swung his hand forward as she turned right, swung it backward as she turned left, and her turning now included a shudder of her whole body. She said into the mike, "All *right*! We didn't know there'd be so many of you folks who *sing*! We just love to sing, Mike here used to sing in a choir. A couple months ago he sang with a Baptist choir, they sang together just fine. I think you all can really reach out to one another when you sing. I know I felt the spirit moving."

The Young Republicans in the front rows were nonplussed. The people in the middle rows seemed to like her. Mike looked higher, to the top rows, at the original group of singers. Most of them stared blankly, but the stout man in the middle of them said in a bass voice so low it was a growl, "God is not mocked."

Mike stiffened and took a step back. Bonnie Two put both hands on her microphone and took a step forward, resting her forearms on the rail of the front row and bowing her head. Her voice was muffled but audible when she said, "That's right, brother. Amen to that."

She stood up straight and walked toward the moderator's table.

Halfway there she turned and said, "Brothers and sisters, we'll be right back with you."

Jerry Medina was out of his seat, bending over, and speaking earnestly to the Charlottesville correspondent of the *Richmond Times-Dispatch*. Poor Jerry—what face could he put on this? Whatever Jerry Medina whispered in his ear, the reporter would be gleeful. He wouldn't have to breathe life into another round of the same old slogans. He would have the rare joy of taking some whacks with a slapstick. Mike could see the fun of it. Hymns and honky-tonk highlight hee-haw at Culpeper. Religious right sings, Reardon campaign worker dances go-go to gospel. Congressman's daughter accuses opponent of indecency "in darkened movie theater." "In your dreams," says Democrat candidate.

The fat man rose to his feet and said, "I am here to ask about the things that are not yet answered."

Now that the man was on his feet Mike saw that he was large as well as fat.

"You have called on men with narrow disputations," the man said, "and you keep your back turned to me."

Mike covered the judge's microphone and said, "If you call on him, Judge, at least he won't start singing." Forgetting the dictum "The enemy you know is better than the enemy you don't know," Mike thought this preacher would take the play away from the Young Republicans and Charlotte Fenton.

The judge turned around and said to the man, "All right, sir. If you have a question, I'll have one of the ladies bring a microphone."

"I don't *need* a microphone. And I have a question . . . about what is happening . . . to our Christian nation." He was right, he didn't need a microphone. His voice rolled down from his high bleacher, across the pit, and up the other side. "I have *been* to *Charlottesville*. . . . I have *been* to the *university* . . . where the *Christian* word is scorned and *censored* . . . and where the money is heaped on those who study *Buddhism*. I have been to the towns in the shadow of Charlottesville . . . where Tibetans are honored . . . and Hindu *gurus* and *yogis* . . . Sufi *dervishes*. . . . And I have seen *farms* bought up and delivered freely to Vietnamese. . . ."

"Okay," Mike said. "I see what you're getting at, and let me just say one phrase for you to think about. *Refugees from communism*. In 1965, Congress reformed the old immigration act. I worked on that law as a legislative aide. One of the preferred categories for entry under the new law is refugees from communism. The Chinese communists are persecuting Tibetans for practicing religion. Tibetans and Vietnamese are coming to

America for the same reason the English Pilgrims and the French Huguenots came."

Mike heard his own voice as thin, hurried, and tight compared with the preacher's full, slow bass, but at least he was back on the platform. He was even getting to come out against the menace of Godless communism, a trump card a liberal Democrat usually didn't get to play.

In the middle of the floor Charlotte Fenton put her hand to her forehead and rolled her head. The judge said, "Charlotte, are you feeling all right?"

Charlotte Fenton said, "I'll be all right. Thank you, Judge. I'm just feeling the strain of . . . I'm sure you can imagine . . ."

"Perhaps you'd like to sit down," the judge said. He stood up and pulled out his chair.

The preacher said, "Refugees, but not pilgrims. These immigrants are not the children of Israel fleeing Pharaoh's army."

Charlotte Fenton said, "Thank you, Judge, but I'd prefer not."

The preacher said, "They come to Charlottesville. It is no coincidence that they come to Charlottesville. At Charlottesville they can worship the golden calf. At Charlottesville the university students hire women to dance naked at their fraternity orgies, to perform acts of *degradation.* I have *been* to Charlottesville on a *Sunday* morning. . . . I have seen the *gutters* of the streets filled with beer bottles and liquor bottles. . . . I have walked in the ornamental gardens there . . . and I have *seen* the torn wrappers of their fornication."

The judge was still attentive to Charlotte Fenton. He said, "Perhaps you'd like a glass of water." She nodded.

Mike said, "Okay, right, there are sinners. There are sinners everywhere, you don't have to go to Charlottesville—"

The preacher said, "It is a city where university doctors perform *operations* . . . to turn men into women . . . where public monies are given to the people of Sodom and Gomorrah . . . and the Christian students receive nothing. It is a city of the defilements I have named to you. . . . It is a city of the plain. . . . And those in it are blind to evil."

The men and women surrounding the preacher moaned. Several of them had been accompanying the preacher with single-syllable cries or hand claps, but this moaning was much louder and in unison.

Some of the Young Republicans in the front rows had appeared amused during the body of the speech, looking at each other with cocked eyebrows and squeezed little grins, but this moaning was eerie enough to make them draw in their bodies.

Charlotte Fenton stood at the corner of the table. She took a sip from the judge's glass and then dipped her handkerchief in it and touched her temples. She put the glass down, looked up at the preacher, and gave three little claps, barely touching her fingertips together.

Mike found this infuriating. He turned to the preacher and said into his microphone, "You don't feel sorry for many people, do you?" He spoke slowly now, for some reason as confident that no one would interrupt him as if he were speaking to a jury. "Just want to sit on sinners and crush them. . . . But why . . . why do you single out a few tortured souls in Charlottesville? And why just sins of the flesh? . . . There are seven deadly sins, not just one. And most of the seven are cold-blooded sins. There's pride. That's like the Pharisee praying in the temple who says, 'I thank thee, Lord, that I am not as other men.' And avarice—like these boys driving down here in foreign cars . . . that cost as much as most people's houses . . . and wearing suits that cost as much as most people's cars . . . just to make trouble for someone who wants a fair share for working people. And there's envy—which doesn't mean feeling bad you don't have all the good stuff someone else has. No . . . it means ill will. It means wishing pain on people. It means you're practically rejoicing in other people's sins so you can nail them. . . . It means *spite*."

When Mike stopped to take a breath, he could list his father's political precepts that he'd violated: (1) don't attack more than one person at a time; (2) never argue in public with a woman or a priest. Too bad. He wasn't stopping.

"So what's the point of all this preaching against sin? We're supposed to be talking about laws, about the federal government. We're all against sin, but there's very few of the seven deadly sins we make laws against . . . or even want to make laws against. For example, we wouldn't want to make a law against gluttony." Mike saw the preacher set his face. Mike knew he'd feel bad for the preacher's pain, but not yet. The preacher was just unlucky—Mike was taking out Charlotte Fenton on him.

And as for Charlotte Fenton . . . Mike wished for a way to undo her. Getting angry at her would win sympathy for her. Mocking her . . . Pitying her . . . Nothing. Even being visibly friendly could look bad. Okay, nothing. Just ask someone to give her a seat in the bleachers. If she left, she might look like a bad sport.

Mike said, "I'll be glad to answer more questions . . . so long as they deal with public policy." He approached Charlotte Fenton. "Ms. Fenton, I'm sure some gentleman in the front row here will give you a seat."

Charlotte Fenton looked at him blankly. She raised her hands to her cheeks. Her handkerchief fluttered to the ground. She blinked her eyes once, and then the pupils rolled up under the lids. She took a short step toward him and crumpled. He caught her as she sagged against his chest. There was a twinkling of camera flashes from the entryway. He scooped her up, one arm under her knees, the other under her shoulders. Ganny came up behind him and put a hand under her head. Ganny said, "There's a rescue-squad van out in the parking lot." Ganny tucked Charlotte Fenton's head into the crook of his elbow and said, "You got her?" Mike nodded and followed Ganny across the sawdust pit, into the dark entrance, where Ganny cleared a way through bystanders and photographers and out into the parking lot. A state trooper turned on his flashlight and started leading them to the rescue squad.

Charlotte Fenton came to in the cold air. She said, "Oh dear," and took a few deep breaths and held on to his shoulder. When they reached the pool of light at the back of the rescue-squad van she lifted her head. "Oh, it's you," she said. "Put me down."

The man in the pearl-gray suit came alongside and said, "Charlotte?" The rescue squad unlimbered the gurney. Mike sat her down on it, and a rescue-squad woman stretched her out. Charlotte said, "I'm perfectly all right now." She said to Mike, "I suppose you're thinking something."

Ganny took Mike's arm and led him off. Halfway back to the barn, she started laughing. "What?" Mike said. "What? I can't tell . . ."

Jerry came out the door. "Look, Mike, can you say a few words to a couple of reporters?"

"No," Mike said. "You talk to 'em, you'll think of something."

Fiona came out. "Bonnie's got her guitar."

"Oh, for Christ's sake," Jerry said. "Mike—"

"Let it go," Ganny said. "Fiona, you may as well drive Mike home. I'm going in and tell the folks that Ms. Fenton is all right, that Mike's making sure she gets medical attention. What do you say, Mike? I think we've pretty much covered Culpeper."

Over the sound system they heard the first chords from Bonnie Two's guitar and the faint rapping of the judge's gavel. Ganny and Fiona laughed. Mike saw what they thought was funny, but he was too tired to laugh.

§ 11

I remember election eve in two parts. Of course there was the hoopla, but even during that part I felt that Dad was in a huge slow-motion somersault in midair. When we were getting ready for the parade, the way he talked to Nora and me was light and wistful. It seemed to come from some Dad-part of him that was like a helium balloon he was tugging along on a string.

At his Charlottesville election-eve rally he gave a couple of short speeches, one at the beginning and one at the end. They were in his campaign style—his feet planted wide, his voice growly. But there was something melancholy about him when he was just sitting. Nora and I were beside him on the bandstand at one end of the downtown mall. We'd marched with him in the parade. We started at the county office building, where we all gathered. There were two bands, one in front with the flag carriers, one at the rear. Bonnie Two rode on a hay wagon with a bunch of teenage girls in white dresses. They looked like daisies stuck in a straw basket.

Grandma was with us. All five of us walked in a row—Grandma, me, Dad, Nora, and Mom. I'd been trying to get an idea of what a political campaign was. I knew I couldn't bear it, but I wanted to know. The way Dad explained it at first was that it was just like arguing before a jury. I knew that was wrong. I'd seen Dad do that and it was boring, which was fine. There were no gusts of wind, no crazy spirits blowing around the courtroom. Dad in court was like Dad explaining homework. Dad talking at Bundy's funeral was more like it. I felt the strangeness there, I felt the huge cave that we were huddled in front of, that no one was going to go into—not one step. So everyone dressed nicely and sat in church, and the priest and then Dad made a little campfire of words in front of the cave, a fire that was too small to give light or warmth, just big enough to fix our eyes on so we didn't have to look into the hole out of life.

But if you're the fire-maker, you get tempted to think you can make a fire anywhere, anytime. It's a little mistake, but you think you're a witch doctor.

And then there was campaigning as show biz. Dad singing "The Star-Spangled Banner." Nora putting on her square-dancing skirt and shiny Bell-tone tap shoes. Dad going into the kitchen at camp to say howdy to the cooks and dishwashers. Hi there! Let's fall in love. For ten seconds. A quick slick Don Juan. Both witch doctor and Don Juan can be human, but when you do them over and over and over, the script grows over your human self. You can't escape becoming a robot.

But on election eve, with Grandma there in a navy-blue suit, just right for the occasion and the weather (a mild fall night), I could imagine that politics was just another grown-up party, maybe even one that Grandma was giving. Lots of fuss, lots of exaggerated smiles and kisses, and lots of little rules, but basically controlled by a benign force. Grandma would make sure that the kids were entertained, that the old folks were comfortable, that the young men behaved themselves, that the interesting people met each other, and that everyone got enough to eat.

When we came onto the mall and saw the crowd, Grandma held my hand tighter and said, "Edith dear, this is such fun."

She meant this both as an encouragement and as a command.

There was a huge crowd. Some of them may have just been shopping or on their way to the movies or supper, but it's hard to ignore a parade. Some of them must have come on account of Dad, because they cheered. The storefront building that Dad had rented had a huge banner hanging from the second-story window. So did the two bookstores and three of the restaurants. In the display window of the women's dress shop there were three mannequins in red dresses with white over-the-shoulder sashes that said REARDON in blue sparkles. Just like Ganny, Fiona, and Bonnie Two in their red dresses with sashes, except all the mannequins had white skin.

Grandma bent over from time to time and pointed these details out to me, which kept me calm as we got to the end of the mall where the crowd was pressing more thickly. Grandma, Mom, Nora, and I had to sit in the front row of chairs on the platform. Nora waved at people she knew in the crowd.

The two bands were on either side of the platform, both playing the same thing now, so we couldn't hear each other.

A woman from the City Council introduced Dad, and after Dad spoke there were a half-dozen others. The only one who interested me was Ezra. The City Council woman introduced him as "the owner of our local Riverside Gym, the Virginia middleweight boxing champion, and the pride of Charlottesville." Both bands then played the theme from *Rocky* while

Ezra made his way to the microphone. I was interested because I knew he didn't like to talk much. I'd always considered this a bond between us. His uncle, who was in the second row on the platform just behind Grandma, called out, "You speak up, now, Ezra!"

I was pleased when Ezra turned halfway around and said, "Hush up, Uncle." There was some laughter. Then he said, "I'm not used to speaking to a crowd. The last time I seen a crowd like this, I had my hands taped and my face greased, and I was putting in my mouthpiece, fixing to throw some punches."

Someone in the crowd yelled, "That's right, Mulekick!"

"But I wouldn't have got there without my lawyer friend here. A while back I was a troublesome kind of young man. He helped me with all that. Then I wanted to set up a gym and he helped me with all that. And the way life is, there's always something new to come along, and I count on him to help with all that. If it's something you're doing wrong, he'll speak sharply. I've seen him throw his briefcase on the ground and stomp on it and say, 'Ezra, you dumb . . . so-and-so.' He said something like that." More laughter. "But if you got some trouble coming down on you, he'll work on it with you. Now, he can't sing too good—that's all right—and he still can't throw a left hook—and that's all right. But if you all want someone to work for you in Congress, then vote for this man right here."

What Ezra said struck me as a little bit fake. Not that the facts were wrong, or even that the tone was wildly different from something Ezra might have said in a normal conversation—at least not the part where he teased Dad about singing or punching. But I could tell, anyone could tell, that someone had put Ezra up to this.

Of course I was relieved that Ezra had acquired some ease and competence at public speaking. And of course I was glad for him that he was a local hero. So why did I feel so uneasy about it all? What did I want? All year long I'd felt emanations from Mom and Dad and the rest of the gang. I couldn't keep my eyes from zooming in on revealing close-ups of their bare faces. I wanted contradictory things—honest faces and shut-up faces. Everyone should wear a veil.

Dad got to his feet when Ezra finished. They shook hands and smacked each other's shoulders. Still holding on to each other, they turned downstage for a few flashbulb pops.

At least we didn't have to march anymore. A few more speakers, and then Dad finished up. The band played "Anchors Aweigh"; a bunch of balloons went up, scaring the starlings off the windowsills. Some pushcart vendors gave out free ice-cream cones. Some kids set off bottle rockets from rooftops (Dad hadn't been able to get a fireworks permit, but Fiona had given out petty cash to a half-dozen students in her rock-climbing class). Bonnie Two and her girls in white tried to get people to sing her lyrics to a thumping march tune that Dad said was "God Save Ireland," but that Bonnie Two told me later was "Jesus loves the little children, / all the children of the world." Bonnie Two's lyrics were "Vote, vote, vote for Michael Reardon / You'll be glad when he has won. / He's the natural candidate, / Get out and vote, it's not too late. / Vote, vote, vote for Michael Reardon." The united bands played the tune and fortunately drowned out the words. *Boom, boom, boom,* ta-ran-ta rah rah.

Grandma and Mom went back to Mom's apartment. Nora and I waited in Dad's storefront office for him to get through mingling with the crowd. We were supposed to stay at Dad's house that night. Finally Nora went out and tugged at his sleeve, saying, "Dad, come *on*. It's a school night." I know this because it was on the local TV news the next morning. What struck me about it (aside from Nora's charm—she was aware of the camera and yet gave her lines in only a slightly highlighted version of her true self) was that Dad had already sagged. He was unaware of the camera. Or aware of it but couldn't overcome his melancholy. He just nodded and let Nora lead him off.

Fiona drove the van back to our house. She asked Dad if she should help get us ready for bed. He shook his head. She said, "Well, give us a shout if you need anything. I'll be up for a while."

Instead of taking us into the house, Dad got us to sit outside on the side porch. I thought we might be in for one of his instructive talks, but we just sat around the table.

Nora finally asked him if he was all right.

He said, "We'll be fine here. This is a nice place." After a while he said, "Listen. You can just hear the river."

And after another while he did start talking, but it wasn't one of his lectures where the rhythm was always accelerating as he spun faster and faster, oblivious to us as he wove in more and more threads. This time he said, "Maybe your mother was right." Then he listened to some little noise in the woods. "One day your mother was pointing out all the things that are wrong with men. I was arguing with her, so I wasn't really considering. . . . But I remembered one of the things tonight. She said that men are always trying to get to a moment. Hitting a home run, getting to the mountaintop, landing a fish, killing the bull. '*Olé* moments,' she called them. Even little boys playing games in the backyard pretend there's a radio announcer, and the radio announcer almost always says, 'The crowd goes wild!' Little girls change their clothes and change their dolls' clothes and they make sure everyone gets a cup of tea. General contentment."

Dad stopped again when Mr. Medina turned out the lights in Edmond and Evelyn's cottage. He said, "I like it here in the dark." He held hands with Nora and me. He held our hands to his forehead and then let go. He leaned back in his chair. "What do you think? Let's have a little general contentment when the hurly-burly's done. You girls want to give me some hints?"

I wasn't sure of his tone. Part of it was tender, part of it was tired. I suspected part of it was angry. He wasn't mad at Nora and me, but he was having a hard time really settling down. He was like someone sitting on the ground and feeling a stone under him, and then a sharp stick, and then an ant on his ankle. I couldn't see him in the dark, but I could feel how jagged his mind was.

Nora said, "What do you mean? Why are you saying maybe Mom's right? Are you and Mom getting back together? Is that why you're saying she's right?"

I wouldn't have dared ask. I knew it was *no,* and I didn't want to hear *no.* I believed in grown-ups' decisions. Nora could go on asking a hundred times. And in fact did ask a hundred times over the next year. Casually, teasingly, angrily, hopefully, and desperately.

Dad said, "No." He shifted in his chair and said more softly, "No, that's not what I meant. I meant general contentment here, for us three. You know, you haven't lost—"

"A father or a mother," Nora said.

"Okay," Dad said. "I gather I can skip all the stuff about your mother and me being crazy about you."

"I don't mind," Nora said. "I mean, it's good. It's just that Grandma told me, and you and Mom told us, and when we went in for shots Dr. Ames told us. 'This is going to prick a little, dear, and remember your mom and dad are still your m-m-mom and d-d-dad.'"

Nora was winding up. I said, "Dr. Ames only stutters with grown-ups."

Nora said, "Well, she was talking *about* grown-ups. And I forgot Bonnie Two. She'd get me alone in the van and say, 'Nora darlin', your mama and papa are real special and they think you're real special too.' What is it with all these people? Everyone gets to go goo-goo and treat us like babies. I don't want them to even know, all right? If you want to know what would make me happy, just tell everyone you know to shut up. And make Evelyn come back. And get another dog. And get people to babysit who only like us and don't flirt with you and don't work for you and don't squirm around when you show up. Like Fiona does. When you came in that time she kept on dancing and singing, like she was saying, 'Tickle my freckles wi' your great hairy beard.'"

Nora was good at doing all their voices—Dr. Ames, Bonnie Two, and Fiona. Not just the accents, but the facial expressions too.

Dad laughed. This made Nora mad. She sometimes forgets how funny she is. In her own mind she was just making a point and couldn't help doing the voices.

Nora said, "I'm serious."

"Okay," Dad said, "seriously. I thought you got along with Bonnie Two and Fiona. I came home that night and you and Fiona were dancing and singing."

Nora said, "So? So? So?"

Dad said, "Well, then."

"She was going 'Oh, Mike,' in her tank top with no bra. It was like, Look at my boobs."

"I really don't like that word."

"Okay, okay. It was like, Look at my cute *bosom* and now I'll go put Nora to bed like I'm the mom."

Dad must have known that, if you pushed Nora down once, she'd bob up twice. If you wanted her to stop, you had to go along with her. The sure way to have her go on forever was to feed her with little bits of resistance. Sometimes it was fun. Sometimes I wasn't in the mood. What was driving me nuts this time was that Dad had been about to sit back and try to be nice and calm with us. This was the place where he used to go sit by himself and stare into the trees. Just sit still all by himself. And now he wanted us with him while he was sitting still and Nora started one of her talking jags, going off like a string of Chinese firecrackers.

Nora said, "So are you going to go on dates?"

Dad sighed. He said, "What if I do? Here's part of my theory of general contentment. You two are my family. I live here, and every week I can't wait for it to be my turn to have you live here. That'll be the main part of my life. I'm pretty sure you'd prefer that I have a few dates with different women rather than have one particular woman who—"

"If you have a lot of dates with one woman, I'll hate her," Nora said.

"Well, there you are."

"And if you have dates with lots of different women, I'll hate them all one by one."

I was afraid Dad was going to laugh again. He didn't, and for a moment he was almost as still as I could wish. Even then I knew that my wish for his calmness was more demanding than Nora's many wishes.

But then he said, "So basically you want me to take vows of chastity and obedience. You want poverty too?"

"No," Nora said. "You should try to be rich." Dad laughed. "You're still a lawyer, right? I mean, they don't make you stop being a lawyer? I mean because you're something else now. Did they pay you to do all these speeches?"

"No."

Nora was quiet for a bit. Dad lit a cigar. By the light of the match I saw his face. It looked tired. From far away he said, "Sometime last June I fell asleep out here in this chair. It's as though this campaign has been a dream from then till now." He was speaking slowly. I couldn't see him, but I could see the cigar smoke as it drifted up against a piece of night sky between trees.

"I haven't figured out all the things it's been. Well, tiring, of course. But one of the surprising things is that it pushed me back through almost every age I've been."

I said, "What do you mean?"

"I guess the youngest I felt was about your age. I had a dream about my father and a friend of his talking about me as if I was ten. Then, other times, I was baffled the way I was when I was a teenager. I had the feeling everyone else knew something I didn't. And then, other times, it was like first-year law school—I was nervous and angry and filled with great notions. And then it was like being in the Navy—I was an officer, so a lot of men had to salute—had to take me seriously in public, but God knows what they thought in private. But I was a young officer, and Jerry Medina was like the cynical old chief petty officer I had back then. I was his boss but he knew the ropes. And I've been moving around a lot, waking up in different places in different bunks. Join the Navy and see the world. This time it wasn't Italy or the South China Sea—it was the Greene County Fair, the Nelson County Fair, the chicken-processing plant in the Shenandoah Valley, the auction barn at Culpeper. But this time I got squeezed through all the different ages, all the different ways I've ever been."

I couldn't tell for sure what he was saying, what he wanted us to hear and feel. All I could see was wisps of his smoke. It wasn't just that he was speaking from so far away. I was scared that he was dissolving.

I said, "But what about that story you told Edmond? When you were in Rome and you stopped liking the Romans and Napoleon. Do you mean this campaign is like that? That it's made you so sad you're going to do something like go to Vietnam? Like volunteer to go to Afghanistan or Iran or anything . . ."

"No," he said. "No, I'm not going to do anything. That Rome stuff was a young guy getting disillusioned, getting into a frenzy over it. Now I've been through the mill. Kind of beat up but ground clean." Dad laughed. "Not purified." He drew on his cigar and said again, "Not purified. I've done some dumb things and some embarrassing things, and they're still rattling around. It's more that I feel simplified. This morning I thought, I'm just like everybody else. There was a time when, if someone had said, 'You're going to be like everybody else,' I would have thought, Oh no. Now I think it's a relief."

Nora said, "But what if you win?"

"That would be nice," Dad said. "But it won't be as big a deal as all the shouting. Another Democratic vote in Congress, that'll make me happy. But it won't make an extraordinary change. Most of life will roll along. People will work hard and it'll pay off, or they'll work hard and it won't pay off. Or they'll lay back and have good luck, or lay back and have bad luck. Politics now should be figuring out ways to even out the luck in the workaday world. It should be calm, even boring compromise. I don't know why there's all the razzle-dazzle. It's not as though this campaign is about Virginia seceding. Or deciding to fight Hitler. Or about the New Deal. It's about ants moving grains of sand. But this way of picking congressmen that we're somehow attached to—it's part mating dance, peacocks putting their tails up and making them shimmer. So I put up my peacock tail and made it go whir." He held up his hand and waggled it. "Nobody made me. I jumped in and did it the way everybody else does." He sighed and then said, "Did you have fun, Nora? At least once in a while?"

"I guess," Nora said. "I mean there were things that were fun. I liked the county fair where I won the bear. I liked the lady there, the fat one in the shiny dress. . . ."

"And getting to sing and dance?"

"Yeah, some of the time."

"Well, you're good at it. You come across well onstage. I know Bonnie Two drove you nuts sometimes, but when you and she were on together you really worked with her. A lot of people who perform well don't know how to perform with someone else. You got that right off—that zone of concentration."

I had a pang of jealousy, of course. I was about to turn twelve. But what struck me more was that he needed us for him to be himself. All that stuff I got to in college when I read Jung—Jung rattling on about God letting Job be put to the test so God could figure out who He was—all that was a piece of cake after that election eve. I saw Dad's cigar smoke and got a whiff of his fear, of his wondering what he was becoming, what parts of himself he might be forgetting. He hadn't just been squeezed through his little-boy self, his teenage self, his law-school self, his Navy self—in the process he'd lost them. They'd been shaken off him like withered berries from a vine. Sooner or later everyone either sheds or is stripped of parts of himself or herself, but Dad was discovering that he was still being stripped bare when he thought he was already stripped bare.

All this was beyond my vocabulary at the time. I felt him hovering in the dark, a very talkative but essentially shy boy, wishing to come closer to us. My pang of jealousy was overwhelmed. Nora devoured her compliment in silence, though I could tell she was going to ask for seconds.

For the first time I thought of the divorce as Dad being left. Of course I knew the facts as they'd been somewhat selectively and gently explained by Mom and Dad. But now I felt him drifting away in a thin stream of smoke, lightened too suddenly. I felt him realizing that being blithe and carefree and gypsy was the wrong thing. But I also saw that he could have reckoned his losses in a country-and-western song formula: I lost my dawg, I lost my friend, I lost my wife. So I saw why he'd run for Congress. But I thought it was a shame that he couldn't have made speeches as himself, just talked about wanting to be a good ant moving grains of sand. I forgave him for running for Congress. I also forgave Nora for chattering at him. I'd been afraid she was jarring him out of the way I wanted him to be, but it turned out that in her own bouncy way she coaxed him closer to both of us.

But even then I had a reservation. Why should it take a whole congressional campaign to press him into one hour of being tender and attentive?

◇

On election day Mike drove the girls to school, voted, and then stopped by the office. Jerry told him that their phone bank had been jammed the day before. He suspected the majority of the calls were Young Republicans from U.Va. with pockets full of quarters just tying up the lines.

Bonnie Two had found a Xeroxed list of questions left behind in the auction barn at Culpeper. "Look at that," Jerry said. " 'Have you sought psychological counseling in the last year?' They were loaded for bear. And they had the troops. That moderator never got to our friendly chicken plucker."

"You got her again?"

"I'm speaking generically, Mike. We did what we could at Culpeper—could have been worse. We made up for it last night. I got us some great coverage. Our rally is front page in Richmond and the local papers too. Some of them don't get to Fenton's statement till the jump."

"No returns yet?"

"No. Oh—Fiona just called. She needs the van to drive some people from the old-age home. We sent a van with a lift, but they could use another for the able-bodied."

"I'm going home anyway. I'll walk back here later—there won't be anything going on for a while."

"Well, you could be out strolling jauntily around, tipping your hat to all and sundry."

"Yeah, I'll do that. Now I'm going home, I haven't had a decent breakfast yet."

Jerry said, "The condemned man ate a hearty meal." He slapped Mike's shoulder. "Just kidding, champ. I got a feeling it's a horse race."

In the van Mike found a note Edith had left. "Dad, I hope you win. Love, Edith. P.S. I thought about what you said—the thing that Mom said about boys always wanting to win and girls being comforting. I know from camp that girls can be mean, and you were nice last night. So you don't have to worry." He put Edith's note in his appointment book so he'd see it again and not forget to say something when things got busier in the evening.

When he got home Fiona was sitting on the edge of the front porch of the bungalow in a wet bathing suit, drinking tea.

He gave her the keys and said, "Are you having breakfast or do you have to rush off to the old-age home?"

She said, "You mean *this* isn't the old-age home?"

"Ho-ho-ho."

"I'm due there at ten-thirty, it hasn't gone nine yet. I have a treat for you. We can celebrate the end of your campaign. What we *should* do is go for a long tramp in the hills, but that can wait. Come inside."

She sat him at a small table and brought him a cup of tea and a mango. She cut a slice and fed it to him. She stopped talking, and he felt the silence close around him. She put a hand on his shoulder and fed him another slice. He sat as still as he could, feeling so precarious that even moving his eyes might stop her. His left arm, flat on the table in front of him, gave a little hop.

She unstrapped his wristwatch. He felt weightless, touched only by her fingertips.

Somewhat later he was distantly aware of the bareness of her bedroom, only a straw mat and a folded blanket. Otherwise he was an unreliable witness. In fact he could remember only two instants clearly. The first, at the outset, was her single long sigh. The second, after an indeterminate time, was when he stopped and raised his head. She opened her eyes and said, "Oh dear." She took a breath that puffed out her cheeks. She squeezed her eyes shut, her cheeks grew bright red, and she fluttered against him, gulping one more breath that puffed her cheeks even rounder and brighter, until she blew out her breath with a pop. It was this puffed-cheek clown look, more than bliss, that made him fall for her completely, and, he knew even then, dangerously. He knew he should wonder who it was he was now kissing as shyly and softly as beforehand (or had they skipped that?). He knew she was too young and green to be wise or reliably kind; Ganny had warned him, he should listen to Ganny, he should listen to a recitation of skeptical lines on love from Shakespeare ("even so quickly can one catch the plague") or any author beyond adolescence—Stendhal, Voltaire. . . . No help. He alone knew that she was a blue spark, he'd known it a long time—he'd known it when she was in the hospital, her face swollen with poison ivy. He took that as a sign that this present bliss was a true beginning, only part of what she had in store.

He rolled onto his back and hummed.

"Oh, please don't sing," she said. "If you must do something, kiss the backs of my knees."

Fiona got up first. He lay in a daze listening to the sounds she made: her footsteps, the bathroom door squeaking open, the rustle of the shower curtain, the water, the odd sproing of the sheet-metal shower stall. These sounds seemed to be close to his ear but then to travel a great distance inside his head.

She came back in wearing a skirt and a blouse and sensible shoes.

"I'm off, then. Do I look right for the old folks? I was going to wait till tomorrow—I thought I'd kiss you once and let you think about it. Is that your phone ringing? Over in your house? I thought I heard . . . Maybe it was only an aftereffect of having it off on the floor. You wouldn't have a spare pillow, would you?"

Fiona's phone rang. She answered it in the front room and called to him, "It's Ganny. You're to come to the office right away. Something's come up."

Jerry and Ganny were waiting for him in his office. Mike sat down. Jerry pulled his chair close to the desk and leaned almost to the middle of it. He said, "Fenton's had a stroke. Fenton's people are sitting on the news. I have a feeling it's not his first one. That would explain a lot. Look—we need to get this out, get you on the radio saying you're sorry to hear about it, he's a worthy man, a great loss to his family—"

"Wait a second," Mike said. "You're talking as if he's dead."

"Well, he may be. I don't know. This kid reporter called me to ask if we had a statement. He happened to be at the Culpeper hospital when the ambulance came in, he was just hanging around covering the ER. Fenton's people wouldn't talk, they wouldn't even say it was Fenton. Then they pretty much hustled him out. I'd like to find out. I thought of going myself, but some of those guys know me."

"So we can't put out a statement until—"

"Sure we can. The reporter heard someone say stroke, he heard a doctor say stroke. He's pretty sure he heard a doctor say to call . . . Ganny—what's that name?"

"Dr. Vyborg."

"Yeah. Ganny recognized the name, big name in strokes at the U.Va. hospital. So I've got someone to stake out the U.Va. hospital in case they bring him here. Ganny says they might send a helicopter, so I've got someone watching the pad. But you've got to get something on the air right now. I'll work on the updates."

Mike said, "Jerry, I can't go on the air with what you've told me."

"Mike. You don't get it. It's ten o'clock. There's people going to vote during their lunch hour. I want them to know. We can say 'apparent stroke,' we can say, 'The outcome is uncertain and we're praying he'll pull through.' That's all true, for Chrissake!"

Jerry sat back in his chair and stared at the corner of the room.

Mike said, "Find out more."

Jerry said, "Ganny, talk to him. See what'll make him budge. I'm going to make some more calls."

Jerry got up and left. An instant later he opened the door and stuck his head in. "You know how come Bella Abzug lost an election? Her opponent was dying of cancer and everyone suspected it but they couldn't get it out. He won the election and died seventeen days later. She should have gone out on a limb and said he was dying. Her campaign manager should have. They dropped the ball on that one. Not me. I'm going after this one." He closed the door.

Ganny said, "Mike, maybe you should disappear for a while. He's likely to do stuff you might be better off not knowing."

"What can he do? If he calls the Culpeper hospital they won't tell him. Doctors don't talk about patients even under normal circumstances."

"Well, he's already got that woman coming in to see him, that private investigator with the ruffled skirts, the one that does surveillance on divorce cases. And he's pulled the Fenton family file. Maybe I shouldn't tell you any more."

"It's no good my disappearing. He works for me. If he's doing stuff I don't want him to, I'd rather know and stop him. That whole deniability maneuver is a crock. It's Nixon, it's Haig. So what else is he doing?"

Ganny said, "His line is that he was sent here by the Democratic committee. He works for them. On your behalf but for them. He's calling the Democratic committeeman in Richmond, he wants the committeeman to bring some pressure."

"How'd Jerry know I'd be a problem? He must be thinking of doing something he knows I wouldn't."

Ganny said, "Maybe he just wants to cover his ass. Anyway, he says he's just doing what any normal reporter would do."

"That's not much of a standard. What's he *doing*?"

"So far—besides lining up the private investigator—he's called the school Fenton's granddaughter goes to, to see if her mother took her out of school. They said she'd left for the day. Jerry figures that means Fenton's on his last legs. That's what he said to the reporter at the radio station."

"What! He said those exact words—"

"Not those exact words. I can't remember his exact words. He did say that Fenton's daughter had taken her child out of school, and then he was kind of cagey. He said something like, 'You work it out. What else could it be except Fenton's on his last legs?'" Ganny put her hand on Mike's forearm. "Let me argue the other side for a second. What's wrong with letting him thrash around? Calling the school's kind of unsavory, but isn't that why you keep someone like him around? Is this different from sending Fiona into the woods with a camera to take pictures of the dump site? She was trespassing."

"That was to get the goods on people who were putting something over on the public. They were doing a bad thing. If Fenton has had a stroke—if he's dying—then we shouldn't trespass on family grief. That's the distinction. . . ."

"Okay," Ganny said. "Let me make a further distinction, then. Let me distinguish between the family's grief and what Fenton's staff is doing. They're making a secret of the state of his health, which is something a voter would like to know to cast an informed vote. I'm talking about Fenton's staff—the ones who ran the 'get serious' ads. You remember how mad you were? And just two nights ago Ms. Charlotte Fenton claimed you made an indecent overture to her. She had that quivery little break in her voice when she said, *'in a darkened movie theater.'* She made herself part of the campaign with that move, she joined that team of Young Republican goons."

Mike sighed. He said, "How much of that argument is wholehearted?"

Ganny said, "As far as it goes, a lot. But there's a bigger question. It's about the proportions of all these things. I mean, if you think this whole campaign is no more than a basketball game, then it's not hard. Call off the game. But if you think you might really do some good up there in Washington, and you weigh that against your turning Jerry loose, against your being part of some sleaze, against your letting yourself think that Ms. Charlotte Fenton's behaved just bad enough so that you don't owe her any decency . . ." Ganny raised a hand and let it fall on the desk. "Then it's a tough call."

Mike said, "You remember how you and I felt when we went out and found Bundy."

"Yes," Ganny said. "Yes, I do."

Ganny took his hand. After a few seconds she said, "You told me once that you got into all this to take your mind off your personal problems. That sure didn't work."

"I'll tell you what I'm really worried about," Mike said. "It's that I'm getting addicted to crisis."

Ganny said, "That is a problem."

"I'm going to go find out what Jerry's up to."

Jerry had already left his office. Mike asked Bonnie Two which way he'd gone. She said, "Out the front. With some woman."

Mike went out onto the mall and looked. Clean getaway.

He went back through the office to the rear parking lot. Jerry's car was there. Didn't mean much—he could go off in the private investigator's car. He called her office, got the answering machine. He said, "Please tell Jerry Medina to call Mike Reardon before . . . before doing anything."

He got up from his desk and made himself walk around the room slowly. His mind kept sliding off the subject. Query: Was he opposed to Jerry just because he was fed up with Jerry? Was Ganny's position leaning toward letting Jerry do the dirty work, or was it completely neutral? And why had Jerry called him, argued so vehemently, if Jerry was planning to go off on his own? Mike suspected that Jerry had had misgivings, that if Mike had told Jerry plainly, "You're on your own," Jerry would have waffled. It was Mike's own lawyerly hedging that drove Jerry into rashness. Jerry had an experienced shrewdness, but very little trust in his own thought, very little patience with anyone's reflective thought.

Not that Mike himself was making much headway with his own reflective thought. He felt hungry. He hadn't eaten anything except mango slices. Now was not the time to go dreamy over Fiona. He needed to sink, to sink straight down into some part of himself that hadn't changed, some part of himself he still trusted.

He went out through the office onto the mall to find something to eat. Just as he got to the middle of the brick pavement the arguments tumbled through his mind again: Why not leave Jerry alone? Why not let it play itself out? What did he know that was better? And then he felt an instinct, perhaps only a fragment of an instinct, but it was better—as firm and sharp as if he touched it. There should be silence.

◇

Of course, now I see that Mr. Medina was in a manic state, that he thought everything he was doing was brilliant and inspired. What he was actually doing was crazy word association. He'd called Bosie Fuller's school, so school was on his mind. "School," he must have said to himself, "yeah, school—girl, Edith."

So I got called out of science class to go to the principal's office, and there was Mr. Medina and a lady in a flouncy skirt. Mr. Medina said, "Hi, Edith. We're just going to borrow you for a little while, do a little something for your dad on election day."

I must have shrunk back. And he must have heard from Dad or Ganny or maybe Nora how I felt about crowds, because he said, "Nothing in public, sweetheart. Just a little favor for your dad. We'll get you back in class pronto. Later on we'll watch TV, watch your dad become congressman." He said this last bit smiling at the principal.

When we got into the hall the lady in the skirt said, "There's one right there." She meant the pay phone.

Mr. Medina said to me, "Here's the deal. Easy as pie. I'm going to dial a number and you ask for Bosie Fenton. You know her from your summer camp, right? If a grown-up answers and asks who you are, you just say you're a friend of Bosie's from camp. If you get Bosie, you say, 'Hi, I'm sorry to hear about your grandfather. Is he okay?' I've got it written on this card right here—I'll be right beside you. If Bosie says something that sounds like bad news, you say you're sorry about it and say goodbye. This is just a little courtesy call, we have to make a dozen of them, and it's just a little thing, just a way to help out your dad on election day."

I said, "It's Bosie *Fuller* you mean. I don't really—"

"Hey, you're right. Her mom changed her name back. You're on the ball, Edith."

I said, "I don't really know Bosie Fuller. She was a junior and I'm an intermediate."

"Look, Edith. I've got to go do something important, and your dad and Ganny have their hands full at the office. We need you to do this. You don't have to worry how well you know her. It's just a thing that families in politics have to do."

"Bosie's mom will know who I am. She and Dad . . . they aren't really friends."

The lady said to Mr. Medina, "Maybe her sister knows Bosie." She turned to me. "Was your sister at camp too?"

I shook my head.

Mr. Medina said, "It's like a little play. You've been in a play at school, right? It's like that, except there's no audience. Just you and me. And you don't have to say who you are to the grown-up. Just say you're a friend from camp. Just say, 'I'm Edie from the cabin next door.'"

I said, "Nobody calls me Edie. And my cabin wasn't next door."

"Okay, that makes it better. Say 'Edie' just this one time. You're Edie from camp. I like that."

Mr. Medina dialed and then put in a bunch of quarters. He said to the lady, "Great. It's ringing. I was afraid they'd take it off the hook. Great, great, great." Then he put the phone next to my ear and put his head next to mine.

A woman said, "Ms. Fenton's residence."

Mr. Medina nudged me in the back.

I said, "Hello, hello, is Bosie there?"

The woman said, "Who is this? You one of her little friends from school, child?"

"I'm a friend of hers from summer camp."

"Uh-huh, she's around here somewheres. You wait just a minute."

Mr. Medina wiped his forehead.

Bosie said, "Hello?"

Mr. Medina held the card in front of me. I said, "Hi, Bosie. I'm sorry to hear about your grandfather. Is he okay?"

"No. Grandpa died. Is this Sylvia?"

Mr. Medina tapped the card in front of me.

I said, "This is Edie from camp. I'm sorry. I'm sorry about it. I'm really sorry about it. I'm sorry. I'm sorry."

Mr. Medina hung up. I started crying. Mr. Medina said, "Edie, you were terrific."

The woman in the skirt moved him aside and hugged me. She said,

"You're a real nice girl, I think you made her feel better, you were real sweet."

Mr. Medina walked up the hall, spun around, and walked back. He said to the lady, "We got to get going."

The lady said, "We can't send her back to class like this." She said to me, "Maybe you'd like to go be with your daddy. Is that a good idea?"

Mr. Medina said, "I can't go back to the office just yet."

I said, "Can I go to my mother's?"

Mr. Medina said, "Are you feeling better now, Edie?"

I said, "Edith."

Mr. Medina said, "She's feeling better."

The lady said, "You want to call your mama?" She fished out a quarter.

I called Mom's studio and asked if I could go there.

Mom said, "Are you sick? Do you want me to come get you?"

I was glad she asked two questions, so I could just say yes.

Mom said, "Okay. I'll be right there."

When I told Mr. Medina and the lady that Mom was coming, they were pleased, but they disagreed about whether they should wait for Mom to show up. The lady said, "It won't take but a minute or two. And one of us better go tell the principal Edith's going home with her mama."

Mr. Medina said, "Jeez Louise," but he went to the principal's office.

By the time Mom got there, I'd thrown up in the school parking lot. That was a relief, because it meant I hadn't lied to her.

◇

Joss' anger started consuming everything in sight.

At first she'd been pleased that her mother was having a soothing effect on Edith. Now she couldn't bear to hear it. Not jealous but enraged that her mother was making everything sound cozy and all right. Of course Joss wanted Edith soothed, but she also wanted the walls torn down.

She went to the kitchen. Her mother came in and said, "Joss dear, calm *down.* I'm just as upset for Edith as you are, but you don't know that Mike—"

"So whose campaign do you think it is? Who ordered up a brass band and a wagon load of virgins in white to sing 'Vote for Michael Reardon'? Who has an office full of bimbos in red dresses standing on tiptoe to comb his beard? That pseudo-psychologist with albino skin. That freckle-faced Scotch dwarf." Joss stuck a knife in the chopping board.

Her mother wasn't cowed. She said, "Scotch is a whiskey. Say 'Scots' or 'Scottish.' "

Joss said, "And that media consultant—he's living in our cottage. And that Scotch cliff-climber with those thick legs—she's in our bungalow. They're all part of it. This is every male command fantasy Mike has ever had. Except it's a Bosch painting and his little crew are monsters. She's out there stripping off the green wallpaper, and that media man sent out pictures of Nora and Ezra but just to black voters—"

"I don't see what *that's* got to do with *this*."

"It's all one thing, it's everything Mike's got up to, and I'm telling it to you all at once so you can grasp the whole thing. Mike is sacrificing his daughters. He's like that insane Greek king who chopped up a daughter on an altar so the gods would blow his ships to Troy so he could have a really glorious war."

"Joss, whoever got Edith to call poor old Congressman Fenton's daughter—"

"Granddaughter."

"All right, granddaughter. It was a perfectly nasty thing to do. But it's not *murdering* somebody. In any case the *point* is—"

"I know what your point is. It's that Mike is the kind of blustering workaholic man you'll forgive almost anything."

"The point is that Mike has been a perfectly good father and you'd do better—at least for the moment—to give him the benefit of the doubt."

"Jerry Medina and those women are Mike's employees, they're his agents, they're *his*! And they told Edith, they ordered Edith to do something so disgusting she threw up."

"I know, Joss, I'm sick about it too. But our going back and forth isn't getting us anywhere. My suggestion is that you talk to your friend Ganny. She's—"

"All right, fine. That's where I'm going."

"I meant use the telephone. Don't you think you should stay here with Edith?"

"No. You're doing fine. I can't tell her nothing's wrong."

"Well, at least comb your hair before you—"

The noise Joss made hurt her throat. She left the kitchen door open, the apartment door open, and the lobby door open, and before she knew it she was opening the glass door to Mike's storefront headquarters, opening the door to the back-office space, opening the door to Mike's office, knowing she was on fire and exploding.

Mike looked up.

She said, "This time you've gone too far."

He looked puzzled, then, without moving, he seemed to take a step back to a comfortable distance.

"What's up?"

"Don't tell me you don't know your man Jerry Medina and one of your girls went to Walker Middle School, took Edith out of class, and made her call Bosie Fuller, made *Edith* find out for *you* that he's dead."

"Jesus," Mike said. "So the poor old guy *is* dead. I never even met him." He stared blankly for a while. Then he said, "I think his daughter is going to take it hard."

"*His* daughter, you fucking totem pole, what about *your* daughter? She was in tears, she threw up, it's like child abuse, it's *violating* Edith, and you sent him and that Scotch bitch to do your dirty work—"

"Wait a goddamn second. Just shut up a second. I thought he was going to Culpeper." He got up and stuck his head out the door. "Ganny! Joss knows where Jerry went."

For a moment Joss suspected that Mike was putting this on to deceive her. But she trusted the relief she felt when he'd told her to shut up. He'd shoved back reflexively, the way he should have in all their fights, instead of putting on his stone mask.

Ganny came in and closed the door. Mike said, "Jerry got Edith to call Fenton's granddaughter. Fenton died."

Ganny said, "Lord Almighty. The poor man must have been just hanging on."

Mike said, "Look, Joss. Did Edith say that Jerry had a tape recorder?"

"No. Wait. She didn't say. She just said he listened in, that he was leaning down to listen in."

Ganny said, "He could have had one in his pocket. Or that private detective could have had one. . . ."

Mike said, "Look, Ganny—if he comes back here, keep him here. I don't care if you lock him up. I'm going to the radio station. Wait. Ganny, what's the law on this? If they taped a phone conversation."

"The radio station won't play the tape. Virginia law is funny—a reporter can use a tape for notes if one party is aware of the taping. That usually means the reporter taping it. But in this case it's Jerry, so . . . No, wait. One party to the conversation aware . . . If Jerry *said* anything, he's a party."

"Party," Joss said, "party of the first part. They're both kids. This is two little girls. This is like statutory rape or child pornography—"

"That's good," Mike said. "The conversation was *between* two girls. I don't know if it's how a ruling would go, but it could scare the radio station. Ganny, who's the lawyer for the station?"

"It's Mr. Broome."

"Okay. He's slow but he gets there. Let me get this in order. If Jerry shows up with the news that Fenton's dead, (A) he obtained it against my orders, (B) he obtained it by—what?—coercing an eleven-year-old girl to phone another little girl, or (C) if he has a tape—neither party was aware that the conversation was being taped. No awareness, no consent. Wait. Are we *sure* that Edith was unaware?"

Joss said, "You're not going to ask her. No one's going to talk to her. She's too upset."

Mike shut his mouth tight and stared at his desk.

Joss was horrified to hear two people she knew so well take this piece of life and grind it into legal hamburger.

"Wait," Mike said to Ganny. "If Jerry doesn't go right to the radio station, and I go to stop them, I'll be tipping them off earlier than he is."

Ganny said, "But your interest is . . . what? To keep Edith out of it? Or to kill the story?"

"I don't want Edith in it," Mike said. "And I don't want to be a ghoul. I don't want anyone from my office being a ghoul."

"So you want me to call Mr. Broome? Or shall I go to the radio station to head Jerry off?"

Mike said, "I'll go. Where's Fiona?"

Joss said, "I thought she was with Jerry Medina."

"No," Mike said. "He got hold of a private investigator. That's why we're thinking of a tape—she has all that equipment because most of her jobs are keeping tabs on errant spouses."

Joss wondered if this was a sly jab at her, the only officially identified errant spouse in the room. Probably not—Mike was in his plain straight-ahead mode, no detours for stray emotions.

Mike said to Ganny, "When you talk to Mr. Broome, see if you can clear up who Jerry thinks he answers to. As far as I'm concerned, I'm firing the son of a bitch." He stood up and started out the door. Joss said, "Don't you think you should pay some attention to Edith? At least call her up—"

Mike said, "I *am* paying attention to Edith. What I'm on my way to do is paying attention to Edith. I'm trying to bury her part of the story. Don't you or Edith talk to anyone. I'll call you at your apartment."

He left the office door open in his wake. The glass door onto the mall shut itself behind him. Ganny went to her office.

Joss watched people move back and forth across the front offices, more people walking up and down the mall past the glass storefront, some of them turning to peer in.

She looked around Mike's almost bare office. Then again at the campaign workers and passers-by. It suddenly seemed a strange little life he'd set up for himself, but one of frantic motion, like a man flapping the wings of an early flying machine which bobbed and skipped and fluttered but wouldn't soar.

She wasn't angry at him anymore, though still jangling with alarm for Edith. She mainly felt a befuddlement. She had lived in a world where everyone expected a gal like her to marry a guy like Mike. Why didn't more people see how crazy that was? Being married to a man was impossible—men led lives with such terrible plots—worse than the plots of action movies. Nobody told her. Mike pulled up in his car, held open the door, and said, "Hop in, sweetheart. Let's go for that ride down the highway of life," and she gathered her crinolines around her and hopped in. If he'd told the truth he would've said, "And now for the part of the action movie that's even more tedious than the plot—the car chase. And it's going to go on for twenty years."

But Mike hadn't known any more than she had. They'd both thought it was natural; everyone thought it was natural. What everyone thought was natural was as dumb as a movie cliché—"This plan of yours is crazy—so crazy that it just might work!"—but went on and on, way after the fun part was over.

And poor Mike. Here he was in the car chase of his life and it was wearing him out. All his energy, all his good nature burning up. She hadn't thought much about why he'd agreed to run for Congress. When he started she was still moving away from him and not looking back. Now she had enough sympathy to wonder. She was sure he had some civic-minded reasons, as crisp and stately as bonds in a bank vault. And he probably had some sporting impulses—Let's get in there and *win*! But Joss thought the chief and saddest reason was that he was looking for a new home. A new home, an old home, his Washington childhood home. For the first time Joss truly hoped he'd win. It wouldn't be so bad for the girls—he'd be back on weekends, Charlottesville was convenient enough to Washington. Maybe he'd get another houseboat—no, that would make him too sad for the few years he'd been happy with her, and she with him—when they were a rough-and-tumble young couple.

Maybe her mother would lend him the Admiral's gig—he could sail along the Potomac at sunset. A bit of nautical family fun would be nice for Edith and Nora when they went up for a weekend. Joss even saw herself stepping into the boat for a short sail—who could say what conversations they might have once they were comfortably apart and free?

Joss looked up when Fiona rapped on the open door. Fiona said, "Sorry—I just need to tuck this away." She was carrying a clean shirt. She opened the bottom drawer of Mike's desk, pulled out a crumpled white shirt, and slid in the clean one.

"Ah," Joss said, "iron that yourself? 'Mrs. Tiggy-Winkle was a very fine clear-starcher.'"

"I don't think I caught that," Fiona said.

"I said, 'Iron that yourself?'"

"I meant the Mrs. Tiggy-Winkle part."

Joss said, "I thought all you Brits grew up on Beatrix Potter. Jeremy Fisher? Peter Rabbit?"

"I see. Peter Rabbit. Of course. Not the more esoteric ones, I'm afraid. Of course, as a child I was more a nomad than what you'd call a Brit."

"And now that you're all grown up, what are you?"

"Oh, an undesirable alien most likely," Fiona said. "You mentioned starch. It occurs to me I never asked Mike about starch. Does he prefer starch?"

"I have no idea," Joss said. "He used to send his shirts out."

"Around here he goes through shirts too fast for that. Every time he gives a speech he needs a clean one."

Joss was now certain it was Fiona who stripped the green sailing-ship wallpaper. She could see her cocking her head to one side and saying to Mike, "Either that wallpaper goes or I do." Just like the little nuzzler to steal a line from Oscar Wilde.

Joss abruptly gave up her side of this obliquely hostile and brittle conversation—a wife-mistress scene from a late-thirties comedy in an Art Deco penthouse. Partly because they were actually in a depressing windowless office with linoleum tiles, a gray metal desk that looked like Navy surplus, and a scattering of metal folding chairs. Partly because she recognized that she herself was a frequent pilferer of Oscar Wilde and was pinning it on Fiona. Partly because she'd wrongly imagined Fiona as Jerry Medina's accomplice. And partly because she had no more right to wifely jealousy, over stripping wallpaper or ironing shirts or any other comfort Fiona might be offering.

Joss felt herself float to an advanced age, a time when she would have only a tender interest in Mike's well-being. She said, "What got you involved in this campaign anyway?"

Fiona shut the desk drawer with her foot and turned to look at Joss.

"Ecology," she said. "Even if Mike doesn't win—and I fear he won't—at least we put a stop to that waste dump, that one bit of villainy. Aside from that I've grown quite fond of Ganny and Mike. If Mike loses, what he and Ganny should do is environmental law. Get his friend Edmond to join him. Mike and Ganny in court, Edmond and I in the field."

"You know Edmond?"

"Oh yes. He was the one bright lad working for the Fish and Wildlife Service around here. There wouldn't be much money in it, but Mike's not a money-grubber. He'd be a good deal happier than if he were to go back to his old law firm."

Joss was stunned to hear this cozy, sensible plan. She was stunned by the ease with which Fiona chirped it out. Give this girl an inch—give this girl wallpaper and clean shirts—and she took a man's whole life, complete with his best friends.

Fiona said, "Of course he's tired now, all this campaigning has exhausted him, but I think it put him on to something, some new energy in himself."

Joss' eyes got up to one of their tricks—not the wiggly worms, but a sudden pinwheel effect, as if her irises gave a little spin. In case she was hyperventilating, she cupped her hands over her mouth and breathed out and in several times.

Fiona said, "Are you all right, Mrs. Reardon?"

She said, "I'm fine now. I sometimes have a little blurred vision."

Fiona said, "Would you like a glass of water?"

"Yes, thank you. And I'd like to use the phone. How do I get an outside line?"

"It's the last button on the right."

Joss called Edith. She said, "Look, pooch. I'm at your father's office, and we talked about Mr. Medina. We don't think you did anything wrong, and your father didn't send Mr. Medina. Mr. Medina got a little carried away. But there's nothing wrong with what you said. Your father and I talked about it, and you didn't do anything you have to worry about. Your father's gone off to see Mr. Medina and make him behave."

Edith said, "What's he going to do?"

"I don't know, pooch. Maybe he'll send him to his room without any supper."

"Mom . . ."

"Well, *I* thought it was funny. He'll do lawyer things, pooch. He can make it as if nothing happened, as if nobody did anything. Your father can explain it. He's not worried about it. I'll be back in a bit and we'll have lunch. Okay?"

"I guess. . . . Bye."

Maybe the way to live was to love your children and your friends. Maybe that should be the sure thing, and then the passions could come and go without giving your eyes wiggly worms or pinwheels, without wounding you, torturing you, or putting you in prison.

◇

On his way to the radio station Mike thought of Joss' opening line of reproach—"This time you've gone too far." He reminded himself to start on a softer note with Jerry.

He saw Jerry getting out of a car on a side street leading from Courthouse Square to the end of the mall where the radio station was. Mike waved cheerily. Jerry stuck his head back in the car to say something to the driver. Mike tried to put a pleasant expression on his face. He walked up to the driver's side, recognized the PI. She rolled the window down. Mike said, "Hi there. I thought you guys would be heading for Culpeper, check out the hospital."

The PI said, "I've got someone there."

Mike said, "So what's up? Did Jerry call that reporter back?"

Jerry said, "I got the word. We can get it out on the twelve-noon news. Fenton died."

Mike turned away. No face was all he could manage. He turned back and said, "When did he die?"

"We're not sure," Jerry said. "Ms. Fenton took her kid out of school probably a couple of hours ago."

Mike said, "You told me that. That doesn't mean he's dead."

"Oh, he's dead all right. We talked to the granddaughter. 'Grandpa died.' Look, we got to get cracking."

"Maybe you could play me the tape first." Jerry glanced at the PI but didn't deny it. Okay, there was a tape.

Jerry said, "Mike, there's no time to lose and you don't want to know. I'm on my own. Secret agent 007. Her Majesty's government denies knowing me."

Mike stepped around the hood to Jerry's side. He felt smooth, but as soon as he started talking he lost it. "I'm not Her Majesty's government and you're not fucking James Bond." He held his arms still at his sides to keep himself from grabbing Jerry's lapels. "*You* aren't running for Congress. I am. I don't care what big cheese you've talked to, I don't care what anyone in Richmond or Washington says. I'm saying you don't play a tape of Fenton's ten-year-old granddaughter on the air. Not in my campaign."

"Mike, for Chrissake, they won't air the tape. But they can *hear* the tape, they can *hear* the information."

"Not from my office."

"Get off your fucking high horse. We've been parading your ex-family around making like it was you and the missus and Grandma and the Brady bunch. And I've been covering up that you're shtupping every woman in this sacred office of yours. You're no Virgin Mary, pal. So let's get . . ."

Mike grabbed Jerry's suit coat high on the lapels and peeled it from his shoulders to his elbows.

Jerry cringed and tucked his chin to one side, but he came up talking. "Oh yeah," he said, "real smart move. Let's get this on video for the twelve o'clock news. Vote for street-fighting man." Jerry looked down the street toward the mall. "Come on, Mike. There's people watching. Let's get in the car, act reasonable."

With his fingertips Jerry managed to unbutton the middle button of his suit coat and pull an arm out. He got back in the passenger seat, closed the door, and pulled the suit coat all the way off.

Mike got in the backseat.

Jerry said, "You might as well pull a gun and go for the NRA vote."

Mike said, "You going to play me your tape?"

Jerry sighed. "Mike, I'm sitting here fifty feet away from the radio station. Fifty feet away from winning the election. The question isn't *if* the media gets the story, it's *when*. Sometime today someone's going to get it."

"Inevitability doesn't count. You're going to die, that doesn't mean I can murder you. And the question isn't *when*, it's *who*. And the who isn't going to be me or anyone connected—"

"Okay," Jerry said. "Let's be lawyers. Let's stipulate that Vera here"—he turned to the PI—"doesn't work for you. She works for me. Right, Vera?"

Vera said, "That's right."

"So, Mike, I'll tell you what. You and I will go back to the office, we'll let bygones be bygones, and we'll leave Vera on her own, nobody can make her say who her client is."

"Play me the tape."

"Mike, you are being one thick mick about this."

Mike didn't say anything. He sat in the middle of the backseat. He considered letting them go to the radio station. By now even courtly, slow Mr. Broome would have talked to whoever he had to talk to. But Mike wasn't sure that some eager newscaster wouldn't wriggle around Mr. Broome.

Mike considered why Jerry didn't just hop out and make a run for it. Probably because Vera had the tape. Her handbag was on the floor between her feet. Her motivation was considerably lower than Jerry's. Jerry wanted a win for his career, and from what Mike had seen in five months, his career was his life. But Vera—a lot of Vera's business was with Charlottesville lawyers, Mike's brothers at the bar. So Vera wasn't about to bolt on her own, though she might go with Jerry if Jerry told her to.

Jerry said, "Mike, I called you a thick mick—I'm a high-strung wop, what can I say?" Jerry gave a laugh, forced and nervous. So that was the other factor. Mike felt a little pump: he'd scared Jerry.

Mike said, "If you want to play your tape for anyone else, you have to play it for me first. So let's go back to the office—we'll have Ganny in to hear it too. She may go for it. She may get me to go for it. You know where the back entrance to the office is, Vera? You can use my parking spot."

Jerry considered this in silence for a moment, then said to Vera, "Can you play just the part where Bosie says her grandfather's dead?" He said to Mike, "Vera might have some material on this tape from some other case."

Vera said, "Yeah." Jerry nodded, and Vera started the car.

Mike held the back door to the office for the two of them, and ushered them along the hall. He called out to Ganny. He held open the door to his office. Vera went in first. Jerry stopped short in the door when he saw Joss sitting at Mike's desk, but Mike put a hand on his back and urged him in. Mike stepped aside to let Ganny in and pulled the door closed.

Joss sat up and grabbed the edge of the desk. Mike was afraid she was going to start an aria of denunciation. He said, "Joss, I think you know—"

Joss laughed. Mike could tell this bark of a laugh meant that she was still furious but struggling to keep a grip on her anger. He wasn't surprised when Joss tilted her head back and said down her straight nose, "You're wondering why I asked all of you here tonight." Ganny laughed. Joss said, "I can tell you this much—the murderer is one of you in this very room."

Mike said, "Okay, Joss. We're going to listen to what they've got." He moved three metal chairs closer to the desk.

There was a knock on the door, and Fiona came in carrying a glass of water. She set it on the desk; Joss raised it as if toasting her and said, "Thanks."

"This is getting to be an awful lot of people," Jerry said. "I mean you're the one trying to keep it under wraps."

Mike said, "Except for Vera, we're the people running the campaign." He put a fourth chair in front of the door and offered it to Fiona. Mike leaned against the wall. He said, "Go ahead. Play the tape."

Vera fished in her handbag and pulled out a tape recorder small enough to fit in the palm of her hand. It had two tiny jacks trailing wires the size of fine fishing line. One led to a microphone smaller than a thimble, the other to an earplug, which Vera put in her ear. She ran the tape forward and backward. Then she pulled the jacks out and pushed Play.

Bosie's voice came out very high and thin: "No. Grandpa died. Is this Sylvia?" There was a blurred crackling as Vera stopped the tape.

"Okay," Jerry said. "That was Fenton's granddaughter. We have some other indications, and we've got some other confirmations on their way. It's real simple, folks. If we get this to the media, Mike will win."

Fiona said, "Wait. I thought if one of your congressmen died in office the governor of the state *appointed* someone for the rest of the term. Fenton's term goes till January of next year."

"That's only for senators," Jerry said. "For the House it works like this—a guy dies, the governor has to call for an election. We got one going on. Today's election counts. If Mike wins, Mike wins. If Fenton wins, he's dead and the governor calls a special election. He can do it when he feels like it so long as it's within a reasonable time. In this case the Republican governor will probably call one around Christmas—catch half the professors and deans away on vacation. That's a lot of votes—a couple of thousand at U.Va. and the other colleges in the district—and throw in their wives. And then there's the schoolteachers; some of them can afford a vacation. These folks are seventy percent Democrat, plus we've pitched education very big. These are votes out of our pocket. The big plus, though, is this—if the news gets out now, a lot of Fenton voters won't go to the polls. Half of them don't know the law, a lot of the others won't make the effort just to throw it into a special election. I'd say it's a no-brainer. We've got to get the story out right now." Jerry looked at Ganny and said, "You've worked hard for this. Talk to him, Ganny. Last couple of days he's been down, he's overtired." Jerry put his hands on his knees and grabbed his pants legs in his fists. "God Almighty, this is crazy! It's like he's got the ball and he's running toward the wrong goddamn goal line." Jerry let go of his pants, grabbed his head, gritted his teeth, and moaned.

Joss turned to Vera and said, "I think he needs this glass of water." Joss handed the glass to Vera. Vera took it and held it out to Jerry, touching his arm. Joss picked up the tape recorder.

Joss stood and moved around the corner of the desk, squinting at the tiny buttons. Vera turned toward her when she heard the squeaking backward voices on the rewind. Vera said, "That's mine, that's my material."

Joss found the Play button. Jerry looked up as his voice came out, breathing and blurred: ". . . Edie from the cabin next door."

And then Edith's voice, thinner and farther away: "Nobody calls me Edie. And my cabin wasn't next door."

Joss held the tape recorder up and moved farther around the desk, until she was next to Ganny. The tape crackled on through the telephone call, all the way to Edith's voice saying, "I'm sorry. I'm sorry about it. I'm really sorry about it. I'm sorry. I'm sorry."

Then Jerry's voice saying, "Edie, you were terrific," was loud, almost loud enough to drown out the faint sounds Edith made.

Vera's voice came from a distance, across some rustling nearer the mike: "You're a real nice girl, I think you made her feel better, you were real sweet."

There were a few tapping sounds and their echoes, then the rush of blank tape. Joss turned her head to look at the tape recorder, as though surprised to find it in her hand. She twisted her wrist and peered at the buttons. Then she bent down, put it carefully on the floor, and stomped on it with her stacked heel.

Jerry said, "Jesus."

Joss picked it up, pushed at the hinge, and plucked out a loop of tape. She wrapped it around her hand as she unreeled it. When it snapped, she dropped the recorder and walked to the door, trailing a long single strand from her mitten of tape.

Fiona got up, opened the door for Joss, and closed it behind her.

◇

Mom was a wreck when she got back to the apartment. She'd walked all the way to the university trying to calm herself down. She had a blister when she got there, so she took a cab back, then discovered she had no money. Grandma and I next saw her standing at the door, her face wild and flushed, her shoes in her hand, asking Grandma to lend her three dollars.

I wouldn't have guessed in a million years she'd just been a brilliant mother.

Grandma made Mom sit down and went out to pay the cab herself. I think Grandma thought that something was wrong with Mom—that Mom was having one of her wobbly-eyed hyperventilating spells, or had maybe even gone off the wagon.

When Grandma got back, Mom started telling her the news, but she kept skipping around so much we couldn't make sense of it. In addition to being revved up into the red zone, she wasn't sure how much she wanted to say in front of me.

I knew my phone call to Bosie was a big deal, but I couldn't tell how it fit into the scheme of things. I now give Mom and Dad high marks for how they ended up dealing with Mr. Medina, even though there was a Keystone Kops flurry to it. I do like the part where Mom handed the detective a glass of water to distract her. It's what she used to do to Nora when Nora was three and had stolen one of my toys and both of us were in tears. Mom would give Nora something flashy to distract her and slip the disputed toy under her sweater. And then—still in rough parallel with how Mom dealt with the tape—nobody got to play with it.

But I didn't know that Dad had decided not to intrude on the Fenton family *before* he found out Mr. Medina got me to make the phone call. I thought I was the pivot, that my bursting into tears and throwing up were what made him decide, so that my weakness became his weakness. So one of my worries was that I'd made him stop his ship of state for a child overboard.

At the apartment Mom kept on walking from one corner to another and talking, but she was going too fast for me to get in a question. Grandma made me a child-soothing meal of mashed potatoes, canned baby peas, and a tiny hamburger.

After lunch Grandma tucked me in and I sank into a dozing nap, coming to the surface when Mom's voice became emphatic. She and Grandma weren't quarreling, but Grandma was alternating between two modes—let's-face-facts and there-there-it's-going-to-be-just-fine. Grandma said, "Joss dear, it's just asking too much—Mike isn't a monk. Men aren't saints, you can't send them off to a war or into a political campaign, especially when everything's up in the air at home, and not expect—"

"It's not about that. I have no right to be jealous about that. When Mike was fooling around with Bonnie Two, I thought it was funny. Half the time I thought it was funny. But this whey-faced Orphan Annie with her Scotch—"

"Scottish."

"—brogue—"

"Burr, darling. A brogue is Irish."

Mom said, "Are you doing this to remind me why I used to get mad at Mike?"

"I'm sorry, dear. What exactly is she doing?"

"Taking over. It's not just that she's living in the bungalow and stripping that wallpaper that I wanted stripped ten years ago. . . . I'm prepared to give up the material parts of our marriage, I'm prepared to do that. It's the invisible parts I mind. *I'm* leaving behind the invisible parts of me that were married. I think Mike should too. Let him make up some new jokes, new terms of affection. What I really can't bear is her waltzing into the middle of Mike's life and telling him what he should do next. She thinks she knows what kind of law he should practice. I would never have dreamed of stomping into him that way. She's pushing and pulling at his invisible inner self."

Grandma said, "Oh, darling, it *is* maddening. But—"

"At first I had this little home movie in my head of Mike taking her out in his canoe and his saying 'Cross-bow rudder' and her knowing exactly what to do. That was irritating."

"Of course it would be."

"No, wait. *Now* I see Mike taking her out in his canoe and saying 'Cross-bow rudder'—and she laughs and laughs and he blushes and gets embarrassed the way he did when he got his finger stuck in the baby-wipes holder, and then he laughs too, and then he never says 'cross-bow rudder' ever again."

"Yes," Grandma said, "that would be worse."

"She just shakes him and all his impossible pieces fall away."

"Joss, darling, it simply can't happen like that. Oh, Mike might stop shouting things when he's in a boat—perhaps he could change that one little thing. But not *everything*. He's just overexcited now and very vulnerable and perhaps he's kicking up his heels, but that's all. After all, he's been running for Congress practically every minute of the day. Everyone is astonished at how hard he's worked. . . . I wonder if there's any news yet."

Part of me was soothed by Grandma's voice. But Mom had conjured the dimension of invisible selves, and I began to fear that they could be lost, that they could be called away. How could you stop them? You couldn't see them or hear them. Mom's cross-bow-rudder nightmare was so real to me that I could picture Fiona's muscular back, the turn of her head, the flash of her teeth as she laughed. Her laugh-ray went through Dad's flesh and bone to his very center and rearranged it to suit her.

When Grandma and Mom turned the TV on, I was curled up tight around my pillow. For a while there was the drone of the newscaster giving a rundown of the races in different states. Grandma said things like, "My God, is he still around?" or "Now, there's a tough cookie."

And then either Mom or Grandma turned up the volume: ". . . House seats in Virginia. In the Thirteenth Congressional District, with less than ten percent of the vote in, incumbent Republican Howard Fenton holds a slim lead over Democratic challenger Michael Reardon."

"Democratic challenger" was one self Dad had become, and it was strange to hear it named on TV. But it was more haunting to hear "incumbent Republican Howard Fenton" when I knew that every wisp of every self Howard Fenton had ever been had left his dead body.

◇

At six o'clock both television and radio finally reported Congressman Fenton's death. Shortly after that a couple of cameramen and a gaggle of reporters showed up at Mike's headquarters. He read the letter of condolence he'd telegraphed to Charlotte Fenton.

A reporter asked, "Could you explain the situation—I mean what the law is concerning this?"

Mike had thought he wouldn't answer questions, but this one seemed objective and proper. He explained very slowly and abstractly. When he ended, another reporter said, "So, with nearly two hours till the polls close, are you urging—"

"I'm sorry," Mike said. "There's nothing more."

He went back to his office, turning his head at a last yelled question, half expecting it to be Jerry Medina jumping up and shouting—but Jerry was long gone. After Joss had left with the tape, Mike had said to Jerry, "I don't see . . . that there's anything left for you . . . to do. You'll probably be better off somewhere else."

That was when Mike had first noticed his speech was slowed, each phrase emerging like a turtle's egg. He worried a bit that something was wrong with his brain, something like his temporary loss of numbers at the beginning of the summer.

Ganny noticed it and asked if he was all right.

He said, "I'm okay. Maybe I'm turning Southern . . . now that it's too late to do any good."

Now, back in his office, he felt numb. There was no urgency in him. Ganny opened the door and said, "Bonnie Two's fixing to offer up a hymn for Fenton. You got about ten seconds to stop her."

"Oh, let her be," Mike said. "She actually has a sweet voice."

Ganny said, "Did you take a tranquilizer or something?"

Mike heard Bonnie Two tuning her guitar. He said, "Come and sit by me, Ganny. There isn't anything to do."

Ganny shook her head but sat down.

Bonnie Two sang, "Farther along, we'll know all about it. / Farther along we'll understand. / Why, cheer up, my brother, live in the sunshine. / We'll understand it all by and by."

"Well, there," Mike said. "Short and sweet. And it's . . . a very moderate proposition compared with . . . 'I'd rather be an old-time Christian than anything I know.'"

Ganny said, "Maybe you're right. Maybe all we can do is try to relax. There's no real numbers yet. What time are the girls coming?"

"After they have supper and do their homework."

"Maybe you should call them. Especially Edith."

Mike nodded but didn't reach for the phone. He said, "I'm glad I did this. I didn't do it right, but I'm still glad. For all the frantic rushing around to find ways to get after Fenton and ways for me to look good—underneath all that I had a feeling I was slowly uncovering something. Maybe I was just bumping into all the stuff I took in as a kid. Maybe for a child like me being a liberal Democrat was like being a Catholic. All that's left of that Catholicism in me is the architecture. It's beautiful, but uninhabited. But I found I liked the old politics buried in me. It's not soak-the-rich so much as share-the-luck. Share the good luck and share the bad luck—"

"You should make your phone call and then take a nap," Ganny said. "It may be a long night. Have you had supper?"

Mike said, "I don't think so. No. I remember going out for lunch, but—"

"And I'll bet you never ate breakfast."

"Fiona fed me mango slices."

Ganny looked at him. "Mike, you aren't a young buck. You may think you are, and you might get to carry on like one, but you aren't. And then, on top of *that,* you run around all day and don't eat. I should send you home and get someone to feed you."

Mike said, "Nobody's home."

"Okay," Ganny said. "No home, just the architecture. Never mind. I'll send somebody out to get something. You can call Edith later. The way you are, you couldn't cheer up your own dog."

Ganny left for a few minutes. When she came back she was dragging the mattress pad from the back of the van by one hand, and in the other she was carrying a lunch bag. She put a cup of soup and a sandwich on the desk and said, "Eat slowly." She laid the mattress in the corner and said, "I'll be back to turn out the light."

He ate, took off his coat and shoes, and stretched out on the makeshift bed.

When he woke up, Edith and Nora were sitting on the edge of the mattress. The light was off, but the door was ajar. The girls' faces looked mysteriously older in the shadow. He felt a fearful tenderness for each of them. He said, "So here you are. All dressed up?" He touched Nora's back. "It feels like a party dress."

"We saw you on TV," Nora said. "Before we came over. Just for a second."

Edith said, "It was about Mr. Fenton. And then they had Bonnie Two singing. Then some TV person explained the law. Then it was about someone else."

"You have forty-eight percent," Nora said. "So you're bound to win, right? 'Cause you only need fifty-one."

Mike said, "That's just forty-eight percent of what they've counted so far. But that's not bad. You remember Mrs. Hawes at the county fair?"

"Yeah, we talked about her just last night, Dad."

"I'm looking for something from her county. That's because she took a shine to you."

Nora lowered her chin, raised her eyebrows, and looked sideways at him.

Mike looked at his watch. Nine o'clock. Down 2 percent. Hanging in there. He reminded himself that the present participle wasn't right. The voters had voted. Nothing was going on now. The reports were an autopsy.

"We don't have to stay here," Mike said. "Maybe the ice-cream parlor's still open."

Edith said, "Will anybody take our picture?"

Mike felt a pang for Edith, who'd guarded herself as well as she could, only to get caught by a moving part of the machine at the last minute.

"We're back to normal now," he said. "Unless it turns out I win—then there'll be a little flurry. But we can go out the back. I'm sure there's no photographer covering the ice-cream parlor."

Edith said, "Maybe you could go and bring something back."

"Edith, listen. Nobody knows that the phone call was a way to find out that Congressman Fenton's dead. We didn't use it. Everybody—including Bosie Fuller and her mother—knows that we didn't say a word until after it was on the news. Mr. Medina and the woman with him came back here before they had a chance to talk to a soul. Your mother and Ganny and I stopped them. Mr. Medina's gone, the woman's gone back to some other job, and neither of them can talk about it, the same way doctors and priests can't talk. Mr. Medina made you think you had to do it and he was wrong and he knows he was wrong and now he's gone. *You* didn't do anything wrong. Everything is all right."

Edith was looking at her knees. Her expression didn't change. She said, "If I didn't cry and throw up, would you have told the reporters? And then would you be winning now?"

Mike was taken by surprise. Edith looked up, her eyes shining like Joss', the same hard brightness that came before an attack. But Edith was aiming at herself. His half-second pause before he said "No" was too long.

Edith shivered like a little horse and said, "Then why did Mr. Medina do it? Why did he do it if it wouldn't help?"

She was too quick, he was too slow. He said, "He was wrong. . . . He made a mistake."

Edith said, "You're just trying to make it all right. You and Mom and Grandma." She turned away and said, "I suppose you have to. But really I should have said no and not done it, or else I should have just done it. What I did was make Bosie feel worse and then ruin it for you."

Mike said, "No."

"Bosie Fuller," Nora said, and snorted like Joss. "Bosie Fuller's a whiny spoiled brat anyway."

Edith said, "You don't even know Bosie Fuller."

"I saw her at camp when Dad fell down on her mother," Nora said. "And, besides, you told me."

They were both swooping like swallows from child to grown-up to child.

"Maybe I'm being crazy," Edith said. "I'm afraid if I walk down the downtown mall Bosie's mother will see me and she'll point at me and tell everyone."

Nora put her hand on Edith's arm. "You remember what Grandma told you. You're just very sensitive." Nora turned to Mike. "Grandma goes, 'Edith, you're just very sensitive. Some people *say* they are. Salvador Dali *said* he was, but he was really a brute. Your grandfather and I used to see him lounging about in the lobby of the Saint Regis with those absurd mustaches of his. Your grandfather *loathed* him. But he adored Toscanini—he thought Toscanini was wonderful because he was a sensitive artist *and* he stood up to Mussolini. So, my dear, you can be terribly sensitive and strong too.'"

Edith laughed.

Mike was astonished at Nora's wickedly perfect mimicry. He'd heard her do her teachers and classmates, but never her grandmother and never such a sustained passage. And she'd got the names right, although he was sure she'd never heard of Salvador Dali or Arturo Toscanini or the Saint Regis. He was grateful for Nora's comic relief. He had his first peaceful thought about Joss since the separation—he was glad he and Joss had these children. Not for the credit of the children's goodness—no credit for that—but for their company.

Nora said, "Da-ad—come on—don't look that way. I'm not being mean, I love Grandma."

"I know you do. I'm just tired, honey."

The ice-cream parlor was still open, and even had black raspberry.

When they got back, Edith and Nora went to Mike's office and Mike went to the front room. There were three television sets, each tuned to a different channel, but no one was saying anything about Virginia. Ganny had jotted down the last numbers—still 2 percent with about a third of the vote in.

Ganny said, "I wonder what Jerry would have come up with now. All that stuff he'd pull out—all those marketing notebooks with ZIP-code profiles. And those maps of the district with ZIP-code overlays. Is that stuff bullshit? Or could he really tell us something?"

"Some of it is like Groundhog Day—'As Maine goes, so goes the nation.' If Ford sales are up in a district, it'll go Democratic. That's all Groundhog Day. . . . *Some* of his stuff was factual. Where he said don't buck the NRA, he really knew how many people in the district owned guns. But what good does it do us right now? We need an exit poll. . . . Fiona says the Republicans had a great big charter bus at the old-age homes. We had two vans. Their bus filled up first. But if it was me out there, I'd ride the luxury bus—that wouldn't mean I'd vote Republican. Most omens are nonomens. My father used to say—"

Ganny put her palm on his cheek. "I shouldn't have asked. Go back and hang out with your kids. I'll let you know if there's any news."

Edith and Nora found a TV channel that was showing an old movie. When it was over, he took the girls out the back and walked them to Joss' apartment. Joss' mother had gone to bed. Joss was drowsy. She shepherded the girls into the bathroom to brush their teeth and leaned against the door jamb. Mike once again was soothed by sounds—the clink of a glass, the running water, the click of the medicine-cabinet door. Joss looked back at him and said, "Should I stay up? Should I be standing by for my farewell appearance?"

Mike looked at the pile of sheets and blankets on the sofa.

Joss said, "I made Mom take my room."

"Go ahead and call it a night. It looks like it's going to drag on."

"Too bad. I made Ganny promise she'd introduce me by saying, 'And this is his lovely wife, Jocelyn.'"

"Still collecting clichés for your game, are you? What was it called?"

"Cliché Canasta . . . I may have to change the name. Nobody remembers canasta."

"We played it on our honeymoon."

"Oh dear."

Mike said, "I'll let you know the news."

The girls came out and kissed him good night. He walked back toward his office. It was almost midnight. The downtown mall was empty. His storefront looked like Hopper's all-night diner, a cube of mummified light.

He walked on by and kept walking. He tried not to notice things, not to make associations, not to think of time, not to feel anything but his body carried slowly by restlessness until his restlessness burned away.

He came to the end of a side street. There was a zebra-striped barrier. Beyond it was the river. He went down the bank. He took off his clothes and made a bundle of them, tying them up tight with his belt. He waded in and began to swim across, holding the bundle in one hand above his head.

He thought it would be too deliberate to cross the river. He turned and swam upstream, a few hard scissor kicks. Then he turned downstream, swimming slower, drifting faster. He rolled onto his back, put the soles of his shoes on his chest, his clothes on top of the shoes. The sky was starless. Low clouds held the glow that rose from the city.

All right—he had his sip of fantasy—if no high office, he could be a wandering boy.

He came ashore in a backyard. He dried himself with his shorts. He was cold enough so that he was clumsy putting his clothes back on. He had a particularly hard time with his shoe laces. He rolled his boxer shorts into a ball and stuffed them into the side pocket of his suit coat. He put his tie in the other pocket. He followed a chain-link fence past a boat trailer and found the graveled ruts of the driveway. The street he came to was strange to him. He fluffed his beard dry with his fingers. He was cold and tired out, but he'd washed off his restlessness.

He warmed himself up by walking fast. At last he came to East Market Street. He passed the old roller-skating rink, then the tombstone dealer's yard filled with blank stones leaning against each other. A few were at a high enough polish to reflect the blinking yellow light at the intersection. All this was familiar. And then the little slope up to City Hall, the main post office, the east end of the mall, the storefronts and second-story offices—all still, all in a mix of shadow and diminished light. Everything was familiar, but odd, as if he were seeing scrapbook photos of a place where he used to live.

◇

Mike was pleased to find a clean dry shirt in his desk drawer. Ganny came in as he was buttoning it. "Your friend from Nelson County called—Mrs. Hawes. She says, if it's real, real close, you should call her. She's looking into some voting high jinks."

"What sort of stuff? Dead people voting?"

"No. Some of her people are sure that some of your ballots got lost. They still count by hand out there, and in one of the schoolhouses there was kind of a lax situation. And the numbers seem funny to her, a lower total than usual by close to a hundred. They're voting for county supervisors, so Mrs. Hawes is on the ballot too—she's going to take a look into it. I got a list of other stuff. There's some late voting over in the Valley. They closed the entrance to the high-school gym, but a bunch of people came in the exit door and mixed in with the voters they'd already let in, so they went ahead and gave them ballots."

"This isn't Cook County," Mike said. "Last election the big story was someone raising a hue and cry about electioneering too close to the polls. I guess we can skip the small stuff. But keep in touch with Mrs. Hawes. A hundred votes isn't hay. But I don't know much about election disputes—what sort of evidence you need."

"Maybe we can get some help from the national committee."

"Maybe they'll just get in touch with their guy in Richmond, and he'll send us Jerry again."

Ganny laughed but persisted. "Tomorrow morning I'll get a couple of law-student volunteers to put together a memo. We're babes in the woods—I don't even know for sure how to go about demanding a recount."

Mike picked up his plate. "Let's go watch TV. See if we're even close enough to worry about it."

At three-thirty one network projected Fenton winning. The other two networks said it was still too close to call.

That was how the networks left it when they wrapped up for the night. All the big news was in.

Ganny and Mike were the only ones in the office. They turned off the television sets.

"Well, it could be worse," Ganny said.

"Not much worse," Mike said. "I'm not expecting miracles from the absentee ballots."

"I meant there's a Democratic Congress to offset that actor who got elected president."

"Let's go eat breakfast. Another half hour the Blue Moon Diner'll be open."

"Mike, honey, go to *bed*. And don't go eating mango slices. Get some rest. There may still be something to do. I'll give you a call if I need you."

"Where's the van?"

"I let Fiona take it. You take my car, I'll sleep in your office in case the phone rings."

When he turned on the light in his bedroom he saw Fiona curled up asleep. She stirred when he got in beside her. She said, "Don't wake me up. Whisper. Any news?"

"Not until morning."

"Good. Then hold me while I go back to sleep."

He slid an arm under her, and she shifted toward him, curving her back against his chest and straightening one leg to tuck her foot between his. He felt himself relax at her touch. Her head grazed his beard. He thought how wonderful it was that she could order her sensations to be his; how kind she was that, half asleep, she drew her contentment around them both. As he sank down to sleep he imagined a stream of bubbles floating out of him—his last small pocket of suspicion that he was making up wonders.

◇

By two o'clock the next afternoon the Republican governor, having in hand the certified tabulation of the votes in the Thirteenth District, called a special election for December 28. Mike, Ganny, and the two law students spent the day going back and forth between the office and the courthouse library. By Thursday evening they'd asked for a recount, and filed suits in the local circuit and Federal District courts as well as a petition with the Federal Election Commission.

On Friday the Republicans held a special caucus and announced that Charlotte Fenton was their candidate for the special election.

Mike got a phone call from the chairman of the Virginia Democratic Committee asking Mike for lunch at the Commonwealth Club on Sunday. The chairman asked if Ganny would come. He was boomingly jovial. "Lots of things to talk over. I hope you can plan on a nice leisurely lunch."

The chairman's joviality lasted all through the main course. They were eating in the same upstairs private dining room that Mike had been in to ask for money. The chairman told some fairly good stories about other political campaigns, interspersed with compliments for Mike's efforts. Mr. Broome was also there, and he also told stories and paid compliments. Mike was sufficiently charmed that he bridled but didn't boil over when Jerry Medina came in.

The chairman laid his hand on Mike's forearm and said, "Mr. Medina has kindly agreed to join us for dessert and coffee. I understand this may require some forbearance on your part, but I'd like to have him on hand for just a little bit of this." He patted Mike's forearm twice, then began to comment on the desserts, particularly recommending the apple brown Betty. Without a pause or a change in his tone he said, "And all these lawsuits, Mr. Reardon, all these motions, this whirlpool . . . Oh, I recognize it was a close election, but the effect on the voting public is that we're trying to get what was denied us in public through the back door of legal chicanery."

Mike said, "That's begging the question. We're trying to determine just what did happen in public."

"Of course, of course," the chairman said. "*I'm* not saying 'legal chicanery.' I'm simply reporting the popular view." The chairman looked at Jerry and said, "That is the popular view according to that little survey? . . ." Jerry nodded.

Mike said, "I'd like to know how the survey question was—"

"And another problem with going to law is that people wonder who in the Sam Hill you're suing when Congressman Fenton is dead and buried."

"I'm not suing him," Mike said, "I'm seeking—"

"*I* know that. I'm talking about what people will think. Now, the governor has called a special election."

Mike said, "I'm also seeking to enjoin him, pending the outcome of—"

"Well, there you go again."

"I'm also getting ready for the special election."

"Now, that's what we're here to talk about. You have built up substantial good will in the district, not surprisingly most of it in Charlottesville and Albemarle County. You have the good will of the liberal voters, and you achieved the highest turnout of your black community in years. Mr. Medina has the figures."

"Right," Jerry said. "Black voters remember your defending Ezra Pritchett five years ago."

"That factor," the chairman said, "plus the recommendation of the local bar make you an ideal person to fill a vacancy on the bench. We think you'd be an excellent and popular judge."

"The local circuit, I assume," Mike said.

"Circuit," the chairman said. "My gracious, our influence would have to be . . . A federal judge is a presidential appointment."

Mike had spoken absently, distracted by the memory that being a judge was what he'd blandly recommended as a way for Howard Fenton to spend his declining years.

"Consider this," the chairman said. "Let's suppose you keep winning your motions and lawsuits and appeals and that you even get a congressional subcommittee to consider the matter. And let's for the moment forget the bad taste it would leave in the voters' mouths. Why, by the time you get through with all that, it'll practically be time for another campaign. You'd be a congressman for a couple of months, and there's some circumstances coming up that will make it unlikely that you'd be a candidate for re-election."

"I've always wanted to be an ex-congressman."

Ganny laughed. The chairman said, "I see you're making a little joke."

Mike said, "Let's get back to these circumstances."

"I'm going to take you into our confidence now. By the next congressional election, we'll have substantially redistricted central Virginia. We're extending the Twelfth District to include Charlottesville, to make it solidly Democratic. Naturally we'd expect the Democratic incumbent in the Twelfth to be our candidate. So I'm afraid that that makes a series of court cases and administrative hearings something of a futile exercise. It makes the special election something less than a wise career choice, even if you were sure to win."

"Against Charlotte Fenton? Get serious."

"Get serious?" Jerry said. "'Get serious' is the Fenton campaign slogan."

Mike kept his eyes on the chairman and said, "Just how carved in stone is this redistricting plan? You can sit here and talk about lines on the map, but it takes some doing."

"We—and I mean all the Democratic leaders and some of the Republicans—have worked long and hard—"

"Long and hard," Mike said. "Then I'd say your telling me about it would have come with better grace when you sent your people to ask me to run."

"You don't go telling every Tom, Dick, and Harry before it's a done deal," Jerry said.

The chairman held up his hand and said, "I understand your point, Mr. Reardon. All I can say is that we had to approach the members of the legislature carefully, make each one feel that he was one of the few in on the planning. I'm entirely sympathetic to your sense that you were kept in the dark. But I have to add that it's my clear impression that we were frank with you, that we said right off that your campaign was conceived of as a holding action, a way of keeping the Republicans from having a free ride. You succeeded beyond all expectation, and our hats are off to you. But now it's a good time for us to recalibrate your position. It's of more moment to us to have a good judge, who also enjoys community support, than it is to have a one-term congressman. It seems to me to make more sense in your life too. . . ."

Mike said, "I should be grateful you're recalibrating my life so it makes sense, but that's an awful lot of recalibration to swallow on one cup of coffee."

The chairman turned to Mr. Broome and said, "You told me about how he's got that quick little twist. What do they call it? Blarney? I'm just now getting used to it, I'm getting to appreciate it." He turned back to Mike. "Perhaps you'd like something besides coffee."

Mike said, "Not for me, thanks."

"Well, then, let's not keep Mr. Medina any longer than necessary. Just a word or two, Mr. Medina, if you would, about the special election."

Mike pushed his chair back and crossed his legs. He vowed to keep his temper. This good-cop/bad-cop ploy was crude, but Mike saw no way to avoid it. The party chairman wanted to dump him. The chairman had control of campaign funds and he probably had control of the special caucus. For a special election Mike couldn't demand a primary. The things Mike had on his side were his lawsuits (although expensive and uncertain) and the possible outrage, or at least disgruntlement, of the people who'd voted for him. The chairman had the persuasive argument that the prize was so devalued by the redistricting that it wasn't worth the fight. Mike had the additional wild-card advantage of not knowing what he wanted. One thing he had learned from Joss was how ferocious she could be in a state of uncertainty.

Jerry sailed through some numbers—his old point about university professors and schoolteachers being on vacation, a new point about Charlotte Fenton's cutting into Mike's support from women voters. "Hey—you may figure you're a cute guy, Mike, but a quick sampling shows a lot of women are just going to vote for a woman."

"What's Ms. Fenton going to do with the abortion issue?"

"Waffle. But here's a funny thing—her riff about you making an indecent advance to her in a darkened movie theater? Most men voters tend to write it off, but the women . . . It's kind of a where-there's-smoke-there's-fire thing."

"How come that didn't make a difference five days ago?"

"We were mostly polling people who hadn't heard about it. I think the question was 'Have you heard that Charlotte Fenton said etc. etc.?' and the follow-up was 'If there is any substantiation, would that make a difference in your vote?' "

Mike said, "You know, you really are an asshole."

"Mr. Reardon, please," the chairman said. "Let's not have offensive language."

"The offensive language is in the wording of that question. It's a leading question, it's argumentative, and it's a hell of a stupid thing to do—spread it around to a hundred voters. At last count Fenton and I were less than three hundred votes apart."

"We didn't ask a hundred voters," Jerry said. "It was a much smaller sample. And look—if it's you against Charlotte Fenton she's sure going to use that line again."

Mike said to the chairman, "I hope you're not paying this bozo when he's working for the other side."

The chairman said, "Mr. Medina is just reporting. Don't kill the messenger."

Jerry said, "I got some private information on some things Charlotte Fenton said informally. She's plenty steamed up, but she doesn't come across as hysterical. She also said that she's outraged that you came to Culpeper while her father was ailing and made his last few days a trial with your cock-and-bull story about an ordinary landfill being toxic."

"Oh, I don't think they'll make that an issue," the chairman said. "I mean toxic waste. I expect her being a grieving daughter might appeal . . ."

Jerry said, "And she somehow got wind of the fact that you and your wife have separated."

"Charlotte Fenton's divorced," Mike said. "That's not an issue she can—"

"The issue is that you were covering it up."

"I never said anything one way or the other."

"Her point is you put on a charade . . . and that there's some peculiar circumstances. It all plays into her theme of Charlottesville as full of spoiled, rich, far-out liberals with artsy-fartsy cappuccino life-styles. I'm sort of paraphrasing here."

"I can deal with that," Mike said. "Regular hardworking lawyer who just wants to solve problems versus a fashion-plate country-club socialite with a mink coat and a real-estate license."

"Fine, that's fine," the chairman said. "But there's a point at the end of all this I'm eager to get to."

Jerry said, "And I should mention she's also pretty mad about the phone call your daughter made to her daughter."

Mike felt himself go still and cold. He said, "Well, we'll have to concede that point. We'll have to agree that that was bottom-of-the-barrel sleaze. In fact we may have to make a clean breast of the whole thing, get the whole story out. I told you to lay off. You didn't. You deceived and bullied a twelve-year-old girl. You taped the phone conversation. I stopped you on the way to the radio station. My wife destroyed the tape. I think we'll hang you out on this one. I think I'll come out just about even when I serve your head on a platter."

Mike hadn't raised his voice or moved while he was talking, but when he was done his right arm jumped up against his chest.

Jerry jerked back in his chair.

The chairman said, "I don't think that would be to anyone's advantage."

Mr. Broome cleared his throat and began to speak very slowly but steadily. "I've been worrying about this. And I know how upset Mr. and Mrs. Reardon have been. . . . But Mr. Reardon made a point when he called me on the telephone in the midst of this incident. He said that, if this underhandedness came out, it would give the Republicans a stick to beat us with throughout the commonwealth. So, however justifiable it would be for Mr. Reardon to pillory Mr. Medina, it would not . . . serve the interests of the party. Even if Mr. Reardon succeeds in distancing himself from Mr. Medina—and I know as a private matter that he was making every effort to do so—the fact remains that in the public mind Mr. Medina was working for the Democratic Party."

The chairman inclined his body toward Mr. Broome, a seated half-bow, and spoke almost as slowly as Mr. Broome. "That's very well said, Mr. Broome."

Mr. Broome said, "And yet I can't help but add . . . that it is Mr. Medina's good fortune that we are seeking a political accommodation here rather than attending to the rights and wrongs of the matter."

"Certainly," the chairman said, resuming his normal rate of speech. "So there we have the factor of not giving Ms. Fenton a chance to tar us with that brush. And there's the additional factor that Ms. Fenton appears to be somewhat obsessed with Mr. Reardon. All her energies are bent that way. So, if we don't run Mr. Reardon, she'll be thrown off balance for a brief period. And it's a short campaign. Now, we have also learned that our original candidate, for whom Mr. Reardon so generously substituted last spring, is now fully recovered. One term in Congress sits well with him, since in two years he'll very likely be running for lieutenant governor. That's just for us here in this room, you understand. But it would help all of us Democrats if he had a successful campaign as a warm-up."

Mike had felt swaddled by the tone of courtly old Mr. Broome's intervention. Now he tasted bitterness again. He said, "So you've got the pieces all lined up on your chessboard."

The chairman seemed to take this as a compliment. He said, "I try. If only the pawns didn't all want to be bishops . . ."

"So, to round it out before I take off," Jerry said. "The original candidate doesn't depend so much on the university vote, since he's from Orange and he scores high with Bubba." Jerry gathered the loose pages of his notes and stood up. He looked at Mike and said, "But the bottom line is—you ran against a dead man, and you lost."

After Jerry left, Mr. Broome said, "Was he of any use? This whole business of media consultants . . ."

Mike knew it was kind of Mr. Broome to ask him to speak, either to take a swipe at Jerry or to appear magnanimous, but all Mike could do was raise his hand and let it drop. It was only now that he was letting go and falling. He felt a part of himself tumble weightlessly down an inner space, while, as ex-Congressman Delaney had foretold, another part of himself watched with hard detachment.

Mr. Broome turned to Ganny and struck up a conversation about her future plans, the prospect of being counsel for the university. The chairman buzzed for the waiter and asked him to bring a box of cigars.

The chairman said to Ganny, "Would you mind if we smoke?" And then to Mike, "Upmanns. Not Cuban, but grown from Cuban seed that one of the Upmanns took to the Canary Islands."

It was a very good cigar.

The chairman told more stories and paid Mike more compliments. He asked Mr. Broome if he, as dean of the Charlottesville bar, saw any local obstructions to Mike's circuit judgeship. Mr. Broome thought there was none, he and Mike could talk it over back in Charlottesville.

The chairman asked Ganny and Mike if they would meet with the candidate after the special caucus. He said, "What would also be useful is if we don't tip our hand. Let Ms. Fenton keep sailing on her anti-Reardon tack for another week or two."

It was Ganny who roused Mike. She said, "I think Mike's *considering* going along with you chiefly because he doesn't want that telephone-call story kicked around in some way that would upset his daughter. So how do you keep Ms. Fenton thinking she's running against Mike and not have her bring it up?"

The chairman smoked his cigar delicately for a few pulls, letting the smoke drift out of his mouth. He said, "Maybe you should go see her, Mr. Reardon. Take her to lunch. You're there to apologize. You tell her the whole story. Ask her not to tell her version on account of your daughter's anguish. You've already said how sorry you are for *her* daughter's anguish. If she says she can't promise not to bring it up, ask her at least to hold off and consider the question. See if you can stretch it out, until we have our caucus." The chairman breathed some more smoke. "You might ask her to have another lunch, to which you each bring your daughters so that—"

"No."

"—so that you'll feel more of a pledge not to involve them—a parents' truce."

"No."

"All right. So we'll just have you and Ms. Fenton meet and reach some understanding. And, by the way, you must be curious as to how much of her account of your behavior she actually believes." The chairman knocked off some ash. "But on the main point—you could offer to drop your petitions and lawsuits if she'll not bring up the telephone call. It will appear to her to be a fair bargain."

"Suppose she asks me outright if I'm running? I'm not going to lie."

"I think that's unlikely. She is possessed by the idea. But just supposing she asks directly . . . I would say that as of right now you and I haven't finalized our agreement. You can truthfully say that our Democratic caucuses are unpredictable. If you have lunch with her tomorrow . . . I'm suggesting all this primarily so that, between now and our caucus, she doesn't tell that story involving your daughter. But of course I'd also like to hear your impressions of Charlotte Fenton, anything you might glean about her manner or substance."

The guy really loves this game, Mike thought. He's a connoisseur of situations, he savors them. Mike wanted to go home. He wasn't tired, but he was surfeited with the thick, sweet style of the chairman's speech. He said, "Lunch with Charlotte Fenton? Okay. I'll try. The whole deal? If Mr. Broome has a spare hour for me tomorrow morning I can call you in the afternoon."

Mr. Broome nodded. The chairman said, "One last word. If you do go on the bench, I hope you'll stay active. A handful of speeches a year would serve you well, along the lines of your address at Hampden-Sydney. While you're acquiring a certain *gravitas* from a few years on the bench, I hope that you won't neglect your interest in the public at large."

Mike felt himself being bottled, corked, and shelved for aging—drinkable now, but better in a few years.

He stood up. He stubbed out his last two inches of cigar. "Thanks for lunch. And for the Upmann—that's a grade above my drugstore brand."

The chairman held Mike's shoulder with one hand and slid another cigar in Mike's breast pocket. On the face of it a small kindness, but, like the whole afternoon, a braiding of geniality and dominance.

◇

Joss felt very odd sitting at the dining table alone with Mike. He put another one-page memo in front of her as though it were the next course of a long lunch.

"You keep the station wagon if you want," Mike said. "I looked up the blue book, it's not a lot, just over two thousand wholesale, and since we owned it jointly you only debit your side of the ledger a thousand."

Joss thought Mike had never looked better. He looked taut, but comfortable. His hair and beard were still a little wet, and there was a damp spot on the front of his wrinkled denim shirt. His old khaki pants looked loose, except at the waist, where the belt was drawn in tight to a new notch.

"If that's okay with you," he said. "It ought to be good for a few more years. Which is what Dr. Ames said about me."

Joss cocked her head, about to give him a compliment on how he looked, but Mike said, "And that reminds me—I've got you and the girls on my Blue Cross, which is good for another year." Mike looked out the window, showing a sharper, more complicated profile. He said, "I should have some sort of job by then."

Joss said, "Mr. Broome told me. Here come duh judge."

"He shouldn't be talking yet," Mike said, but so mildly that Joss didn't feel herself ruled out of order.

"All in the family," Joss said. "He's always reminding me that he's glad we're still conducting our lives"—Joss imitated Mr. Broome—"'under the penumbra of the marriage bonds.'"

Mike laughed, and Joss was as pleased as if a date was turning out to be fun.

For another half-hour Mike produced sheet after sheet of notes on things to be agreed upon, and Joss made small agreeable jokes and observed the patch of damp on his shirt fade into faded blue. She heard their voices as faded blue, a mild winter sky, quiet after a period of storms.

She felt her skin grow warm. At first she confused this warmth with an erotic feeling. There was some Eros, but it was a small rivulet that was diluted as it ran into a larger, more serene lake. Yet something was stirring in this picture: she was being charming, he was growing more charming by visibly feeling her little breezes of charm.

Mike said, "Mr. Broome can figure out what to do about that one. I'll be paying in the same amount either way, so you and Mr. Broome should weigh your tax consequences. Either of your brothers could be trustees—maybe one for Edith, the other for Nora."

"Uh-oh," Joss said. "I can hear it now—the girls bickering over who gets the better trustee."

Mike said, "I thought Edith and Nora liked both their uncles the same."

"Of course they do," Joss said, "but as soon as you get one thing, you want the other."

"They'll only have to talk about money with their uncles when we're old and gray," Mike said. "Or when we're dead. I hope that'll be when they've outgrown who gets the bigger dessert."

"I was just kidding," Joss said. "They won't worry about which uncle—they're getting along better and better. Don't you think so? I mean, we're all still walking on eggshells, but . . ."

"Walking on eggshells," Mike echoed. "Something has occurred to me about that. I haven't written a note, but I want to mention it. I think it's a good idea to limit not only our areas of disagreement but also our areas of apprehension."

Joss normally would have rolled her eyes at one of Mike's not-only-but-also legal sentences, but his tone was still wistful, still faded blue.

"Mr. Broome may have mentioned to you that in the Virginia courts alcoholism and lesbianism are, aside from actual criminal behavior, just about the only grounds for refusing custody to a mother. So, although I've never actually used this point as a lever to get you to agree to something, I do see that I've had the advantage of it hovering in the background as a Sword of Damocles."

Joss was saddened to hear his tone grow darker and denser, as unconversational as the sound of someone moving furniture.

Mike said, "I want to reassure you that I won't use that leverage, (A) because as a general matter I don't think that lesbianism *per se* is sufficient cause to deny custody, and (B) in the more specific instance of your relations to Edith and Nora, I don't think your romantic involvement interferes with your care for them, certainly no more than would a heterosexual involvement, had that been a factor in the case."

Joss felt her anger rising. She also felt restraining hands on her—probably her mother's, possibly Mr. Broome's. She shrugged them off. She was standing. She felt her throat squeeze and then open as sound rushed out. "Factor! What makes you the big factor-maker? You think you have all the factors? You think you have a key chain with all the factors on it? You think I'm in chains and you have all the keys? You're not the warden! You're just your own story!"

The phone rang.

Joss said, her voice still loud, "And you don't even know your own story."

"Just a second," Mike said. "I've got to get the phone."

The phone rang again. Joss said, "Get the phone."

Mike went to the counter and picked up the phone. Joss turned around and went into her old studio, which was completely empty except for a pail of water with a sponge floating half submerged. She picked up the sponge, squeezed it out, and made an "X" high on the bare white wall. It dried fast, faster than Mike's shirt, but it left distinct gray lines. Joss stood with her back to the wall and bit by bit traced herself, using the corner of the sponge.

She heard Mike giving directions.

". . . one-lane bridge, you can't miss it. Just keep on up the driveway, we're at the top."

What did he mean, "we"? She turned the sponge to a new corner. She pulled her dress tight and stood straight to make her waist long and small. She traced up to her armpit and a few inches of arm. She decided against tracing the full length of her arms. Let her ghost have one touch of Venus de Milo.

Mike said, "If it's no trouble for you . . ."

Joss finished the outside of her ankle. She hoisted her skirt and traced the inside of her legs.

When this was still her house she'd once stood in this spot, her skirt being gathered up by the inchworm motions of Bonnie One's fingertips. Which then went on to trace the inside of her legs. Bonnie One conveying admiration without a word from Bonnie One's lips, admiration for the line and texture of Joss' leg. And how had her skirt stayed up? Had it bunched and caught on her hips? Or had she herself clutched it at her waist like a gunslinger about to draw both six-shooters?

Where had Mike been? Oh yes. In his own story, in bed with his bruised ankles from being pinioned by Bonnie Two's one-legged drunk boyfriend. And in that story Bonnie Two's skirt had also been hoisted, furled right up to her waist as her boyfriend dragged her by the ankles, hauled her on her back so that her little pelvic rim clicked under Mike's chinny-chin-chin.

In that story Mike got another Boy Scout merit badge for defending the downtrodden. Another Purple Heart for his wounds in battle. He'd written chapter after chapter in his volume of Boys' Adventures, accidents in which he squandered his energy and good will in the world and came home expecting attention, comfort, and a hot supper.

No. That was too easy. He'd done something worse—he'd done *without* her attention and comfort. He'd made do by drawing himself into tight indifference, smoking his cigar in solitude on the porch. And coming to life for Evelyn and Edmond, brightening for Evelyn's peach pie, for Edmond's nature stories, for Tyler, Bundy, or Ezra. If he'd had the wit and nerve to speak his true state of mind about marriage he would have said, "I'm stuck here, but I can stand it."

Joss dropped the sponge in the bucket. She turned and looked at her outline on the wall. She wrote "wife #1" in the middle.

It occurred to her that Mike was behaving well with her so that she would be gone. That was the meaning of his soft blue shirt and the tender far-off look that had been charming her. That was the meaning of his cumbersome reassuring speech about not threatening her with the weight of the law.

Mike said goodbye to whoever was on the phone. Joss went back in. He was sorting the papers on the dining table, filing them in folders. Joss said, "Your hair is shorter. Your beard is even shorter. You've lost a lot of weight. Do you feel different?"

Mike shrugged. "I'm recovering from the campaign."

"The campaign," Joss said.

"It took more out of me than I thought it would."

"The *campaign* did," Joss said. "The campaign tried your soul. The campaign made you face yourself in new and difficult ways. But now you've begun to renew yourself."

Mike looked puzzled.

"Well, here's some advice in my own voice," Joss said. "Here's a bit of advice from your crazy, alcoholic, bisexual wife. Don't think it was the campaign. Don't think you're fine because the campaign is over. Don't think you're ready for your new life until you've figured out your divorce."

Mike opened his eyes wide and took a breath.

Joss spoke before he did. She said, "Oh, that. I've done that. Here's the story on that. My neurotic alcoholic bisexual wife fell in love with someone else. So I went back to work and got over it."

Mike let out his breath. "I don't want to argue, but I seem to remember your telling me to get on with my life. You told me that I'd be better off."

"I told you a lot of things," Joss said. "You can't just pick and choose."

"And, besides," Mike said, "what's wrong with that story? You did fall in love with someone else and leave."

"Did it ever occur to you"—Joss heard the crackle of flame in her voice—"that my so-called lesbianism might be another way of dealing with *you*?" She heard the *you* echo off the wall.

What did she mean? What was this she'd just torn out of herself? Was she actually trying to drag him back, grab one foot and keep him from getting out the door? Or was she trying to blow up his categories? At least that—smash his smug notion of what she was and make him think about who she was. And never get to the end.

He looked stunned. Then he looked baffled. All right. Then he relaxed, and for an instant Joss thought he would admit he should fight with her until he knew her, that he should learn much more from her before he could even begin to understand the last twelve years of their life.

But then he looked relieved. Joss read his look of relief clearly: I don't have to fight, I don't have to put on my asbestos suit. I don't have to put my head in your blast furnace ever again.

So his faded blue wistfulness wasn't just part of his tactic of being nice so he could get through the paperwork. His fleet was disengaging, his flagship sailing away toward the horizon. The faded blue wistfulness was real and was all the answer he was going to give her.

She might be grief-stricken later, but at the moment she was surprised to find the immediate motion of her heart was to be calmed by his calm. She came up with another joke. She put her forefinger on the pile of folders and said, "So this is the whole divorce package. What do I do with it? Climb on top, light a match, and commit suttee?"

Mike gave another hum of laughter. Then looked wistful again. "I wish you could have seen more of the campaign. You'd have been very funny about it." He squared the pile of folders. "These are in duplicate, one set for you, one for Mr. Broome." He stood up. "I've got to clear the table now. Charlotte Fenton's coming for lunch."

Joss said, "You do have a lot of women in your life." Mike looked wary, so Joss added, "That's not a criticism—I meant it sympathetically. Or maybe hopefully—maybe you'll learn—"

"This is business," Mike said. "This is just to make sure she doesn't use the story about Edith's phone call. We were supposed to meet at a restaurant near Madison, but she just called to say she'd rather come here."

"Ah." Joss was about to ask how he was going to make sure, but she didn't want to hear him explain anything else in his charts-and-diagrams voice. She was certain he would do whatever he had to do for Edith. At first that was a sweet thought—that, even if he didn't want to struggle with her about what their marriage had been, at least they would always be joined in caring for Edith and Nora. But then it occurred to her that they would most likely meet when either Edith or Nora was in trouble. She fended off thinking of Edith and Nora's future misfortunes.

She gathered up the pile of folders.

These days she was less at the mercy of her own thoughts—possibly because she was on the wagon, possibly because she wasn't dealing—at least not daily—with Mike's judgments tumbling down from his mountaintop to land on her already heavy conscience. She had plenty of judgments of her own, thank you.

Of course she and Mike would be together with Edith and Nora at moments of transit—at graduations and weddings. Perhaps even lesser moments—prom nights, middle-school Christmas pageants. All the rituals, the movie clichés of divorced parents getting dewy-eyed. But not plain everyday life.

"I'm sure you'll do fine," she said. "You'll have Charlotte Fenton eating out of your hand."

She stood up to go, to leave Mike to another hard day at the office. Did he have any idea *this* was a moment of transit? The band playing "Now Is the Hour," the steamship whistle blasting three notes, the stewards calling "All ashore that's going ashore," the passengers lining the rails, the debonair ones raising their champagne glasses, the sentimental ones tossing flowers that fluttered onto the black water as the ship backed out of her slip.

At the door she said, "And so, as the sun sinks into the Pacific, we say aloha to our island paradise." Mike gave another hum of a laugh.

Joss stopped on the bridge, rolled the window down, slid her wedding ring off, and tossed it over the rail into the Rivanna. She thought several small thoughts—Mike would like the ring in his river—she should tell him in case he wanted to throw his in too. She wondered if the girls would notice her ring was gone.

But then she was flooded in a rush that rose from her lungs to the full volume of her skull. She felt enormous. She was carrying away too much inside her. It didn't matter what it was made of—it was a solid mass, it had no categories of anger, sorrow, love—it was an amalgam of their whole life.

She'd done terrible things to him, and then she'd said terrible things to him, and he should be grateful because she'd torched her place in him, she'd burned it out clean and cauterized it. And now the dumb pig-brain in his faded blue shirt wouldn't do the same for her! He sat there being reasonable, actually being nice in his faded blue way, and then left the left-over marriage to her.

She felt a slow but steady panic blotting her out. She thought of her mother. She thought of her mother letting herself cry against the dark kitchen window on the Northern Neck. Joss almost rejected it as absurd, as a pathetically comic mechanism—getting a permission slip from Mom to have a good cry—but it was a relief. A few sobs and she felt less swollen with panic. A few more and she felt normally sad. She stopped when she heard Mike start the van at the top of the hill.

She started the car and drove off, hoping for no more of these mood-a-minute swoops. She thought of Mike's pig-iron will—she wouldn't have to fight against that anymore, that will of his alloyed with habits of church, boats, and law courts. Was that really her view? She was across the bridge now, she could let her guard down and be fair. He did have a gift of energy, and the flow of it had set off her own. For better or for worse. She wasn't going to tap into a boost like that soon. Not at Bonnie One's house, not at home—until the girls grew up. If she wanted to pick on someone her own size, she'd have to go out into the world on her own.

◇

Mike drove the van to get a suitable lunch for Charlotte Fenton, several small cartons of wispy delicacies from the Thai restaurant near his office. On his way back he was surprised to see Charlotte Fenton turning onto his bridge well ahead of schedule. Perhaps her friendship with the Madison judge made her immune to speeding tickets. She drove fast up the driveway. When he pulled up she was already out of her car. She shut the door with her foot, took off her black wide-brimmed hat and sunglasses, and tossed them through the open window. This gesture struck him as looser and freer than the way he'd been thinking of her.

She shook hands and started talking on a friendly note. She looked around and admired the trees, the river, the peace and quiet so close to town. She pointed to the side porch and said, "It's such a mild day, do you think we could sit out there?"

From the porch she admired the cottage and the bungalow. She said, "I suppose you get to know your tenants pretty well."

Mike said, "I used to. For years the tenants were good friends of mine. A veterinarian and a wildlife biologist and an English professor. It was wonderful."

"A regular boys' club."

"The vet is the wife of the wildlife biologist."

"Of course, silly me. And now?"

"Now everything's sort of up in the air," Mike said. "My media consultant was staying in the cottage until I fired him. I . . . I haven't had a chance to say how sorry I am about that phone call."

Charlotte Fenton put her hands on the picnic table and looked at them. She said, "Thank you. But perhaps we can wait until we've had our lunch before we . . ."

Mike put his hand to his forehead. "I left our lunch in the van." He got up. "Sorry, just a sec."

Charlotte Fenton said, "Where are all your ladies-in-waiting?"

But Mike was far enough away not to answer.

The exercise of making a tray for the two of them—"Wine? Beer? Iced tea?"—was ludicrously like a date. As was their conversation over lunch.

Mike said, "They put in chopsticks, but I can get you a fork."

"Oh, I can manage. We do have our Chinese restaurant in Culpeper, though we can't compare ourselves to Charlottesville in the exotic-food department."

"Actually this is Thai. . . ."

"Well, there you are."

Later on she said, "That was delicious. Don't tell me there was something in it I wouldn't dream of eating."

"I think you're safe—just shrimp and lemongrass and maybe a dab of something spicy. And the peanut sauce has ginger and garlic—"

Charlotte Fenton laughed. Mike raised his eyebrows. She said, "You're naming things so earnestly."

"You asked."

"I said, 'Don't tell me.'"

Mike put their plates on the tray. He said, "If we stay out here for our talk, do you mind if I smoke a cigar?"

"Not in the least. Here, let me carry some of those in. And if you could just show me where I can wash my hands."

Mike found the chairman's H. Upmann and slid it out of its tube.

Because of the oddity of Charlotte Fenton's being here, he felt more keenly how odd he himself felt in the house. When Joss had offered to sell him her half, he'd assumed he wanted it, assumed it would be a continuity for him and Edith and Nora. Now it struck him—especially on days like this, when the girls were with Joss—as a house he'd been asked to take care of while the real owners were away.

He also felt less human—human as he'd been—immediate, blurred, roly-poly, sensing others without alarm, and supposing them to be equally blurred and roly-poly until proved otherwise. His new sensation of wariness went beyond the way he'd been in court. That focus on a trial had been temporary, achieved by a deliberate effort, put on with his good suit. This new mode was like a mild amphetamine, like a nervous disorder with advantages of alertness. He wasn't sure he liked it. He wasn't sure where it all came from—surely the largest part of it was the speeded-up intuition of a politician, coming too late to help in the campaign, but not too late to deal with Charlotte Fenton.

She came out of the bathroom with her hair combed back. She was a very pretty woman. He sensed that she wasn't in love with her looks, but liked them as one of the several very nice things in her life.

She smiled. Mike looked earnest.

Out on the porch Mike sat downwind of her and lit his cigar. He looked at the river while he narrated the phone-call incident. He left out the fact that Jerry Medina had taped it, but emphasized that Joss and he had been united in opposition to Jerry Medina.

"It was a mean thing to do to your daughter," Mike said. "And it was a mean thing to do to my daughter. You have a right to be angry. I was furious, but then I had the satisfaction of getting rid of the guy." He turned toward her. "And then, of course, we didn't use the information. What I'd like to propose is that we leave children out of this altogether."

"When you say let's keep our children out of it," Charlotte Fenton said, "what you're really asking is for me not to talk about the dirty trick your campaign manager pulled."

"He was the media consultant," Mike said, "ex–media consultant. If there was a way to hang him out to dry without hurting my daughter, I wouldn't even try to stop you. I can understand your wanting satisfaction. The problem is that your satisfaction involves my daughter, who feels bad no matter how much her mother and I reassure her. I'm sure you don't count the pain she feels now as any satisfaction, and I can't imagine causing her even more pain would be satisfying to you."

Charlotte Fenton said, "Of course not."

Mike nodded slowly.

"Wait, now," Charlotte Fenton said. "Suppose I just say that your media consultant called my daughter."

"And . . . ?"

"And extracted the news of her grandfather's death from her by duplicitous means."

"Adding, in fairness, that he was fired . . ." Mike pursed his lips. "But that's the problem. I fired him. I have no control over him now. He might come back at you and say that's not the true story. And the whole thing would roll back and forth. Reporters interviewing our daughters. He might come back any number of ways. He might *want* some version of it to get around—he might say, 'So I had to con a couple of schoolgirls, that's hardball. And then my wimp of a candidate wouldn't let me use it.'"

"Perhaps you should think of some way to control him."

Mike got up. "I fired him!" Mike hit the porch railing with his hand. "Before he made that phone call I'd already told him to lay off. When I found out what he'd done, I grabbed him off the street. I grabbed the son of a bitch and dragged him back into my office and kept him there."

Mike walked away to the far corner of the porch. He ran his hand through his hair and said, "I'm sorry. I'm not yelling at you."

He turned around in time to see a ripple of alarm leave her.

He said, "I really just wanted you to know what went on at my end." He sat down in his chair and faced her. "I'm glad you agreed to come and listen." He settled back in his chair and looked at the river through the half-bare trees. He heard her stir in her chair. Before she spoke he said, "Would you like some coffee?"

"No, thank you."

Charlotte Fenton touched his sleeve. She said, "I'll have to have a little time to think about all this. You understand that I'm sympathetic."

Mike nodded slowly.

Charlotte Fenton said, "I'm making a speech tonight, but that's fairly general. I won't bring up the phone call. I can't say what will happen after your special caucus." She bit her lip. "My advisers may . . . But of course that's one of your points, isn't it? How someone on your staff can run amok. I'll think it over between now and your caucus. That will be the real start of . . . this campaign."

"One way or another," Mike said. "Our caucuses are generally less predictable than yours. Will you call me when you've thought it over? So that I could at least . . . Maybe I could send Edith to her grandmother's." Mike drew in a breath. "My wife saw the incident this way—a man taking Edith out of school, claiming I'd sent him, holding her, holding the phone to her ear—it was a grown man molesting a little girl. Afterward Edith vomited."

Charlotte Fenton's eyes widened. She said, "I'm sorry. I wish I could just say we'll never have to breathe another word about it."

Mike nodded.

She said, "May I change my mind about coffee?"

When he came back she tilted her head back and ran a hand through her hair. "I don't suppose we'll have another meeting like this anytime soon."

"Not for a while," Mike said. He held the tray while she took her cup and added sugar. "But this is a very short campaign. You're lucky in a way—I found five months of campaigning exhausting. But I started in the midst of some other troubles. I'm sorry—I shouldn't . . . I know you're in a more trying time."

"Thank you." After another moment she said, "But you were about to say something about . . ."

"About . . . ?"

"About the time before your campaign."

"Ah well. Not as heavy as your . . . But confusing and upsetting."

Charlotte Fenton said, "That sounds like my divorce."

Not just a shrewd guess. Mike knew that she knew. He said, "You know what they say about falling—it's not the fall that hurts, it's the landing. Is it true that divorce is the other way around? Finding out you're on the rocks is the worst part. By the time you get to the actual divorce . . ." Mike shrugged.

"You know, there's a very good book about that. It's called *Crazy Time.* I thought it was a great help. I could send it. . . ." Charlotte Fenton blushed. "I'm sorry. Maybe I'm jumping to a conclusion. It's just the way your house is so . . . bachelorlike."

"Is it?" Mike noted that Charlotte Fenton was lying, and, more interestingly, was embarrassed.

"Yes, very bachelorlike," she said, "very spare and masculine."

The old Southern-belle standby—tell a man he's manly.

Mike said, "It's okay, it's not surprising that you know I'm separated. In fact it's reassuring that you're embarrassed."

Charlotte Fenton frowned.

"I mean," Mike said, "that now we both know the other is more human than either of us thought." Mike sighed. "I'm wary of the dehumanizing effects of campaigning. It wasn't a charade—or at least not much more than the usual charade—when I paraded down Main Street with my wife and daughters and mother-in-law. I'm not divorced—we're about to sign an official separation agreement. And my mother-in-law, contrary to the cliché, is one of my best friends. But the whole situation—which you probably sensed when you saw my wife's films—is just too complicated. It's too odd, it's too human to fit it into political terms. It doesn't even fit into legal terms. I've seen divorces that go to court. It's like watching open-heart surgery done with pruning shears. As for family problems in terms of a campaign . . ."

Charlotte Fenton said, "Well, your wife, your ex-wife—"

"I suppose the technical term is 'estranged wife.'"

"She dedicated her movie to you."

"That was a nice surprise. In some ways we're on good terms. In other ways . . . Did you have a terrible divorce?"

"Oh, the usual. Maybe another time we can tell our stories."

"You're right," Mike said. "When it's all over, maybe you'll have time for another lunch."

Charlotte Fenton said, "That would be nice."

He turned to face her but didn't say anything. He had everything he wanted from her by way of a promise not to talk about the phone call until after the Democratic caucus. She seemed to assume his candidacy as completely as the chairman predicted, and Mike had been as equivocal as the chairman wished. Quick and charming though she was, he had no further pleasant notion, no warmer impulse. He hoped that, after the special caucus, a normal life that didn't require conniving would restore his good nature.

And yet, perhaps because this lunch with Charlotte Fenton had some of the trappings of a date, some of the texture of a prelude, he didn't want to let go quite yet.

While he'd been thinking, he'd put his fist against his mouth and gazed past her shoulder. She said, "My, you are deep in thought." She put her own fist to her mouth and furrowed her brow in an exaggerated imitation. He thought this particular gesture was that of a young girl at a dance fifteen or twenty years ago, and that fifteen or twenty years ago he would have been charmed.

He said, "Maybe you could tell me how you arrived at the exact phrasing—'accosted me in a darkened movie theater'?"

For an instant she looked desperate. He kept his eyes on hers. He was sure she'd prepared an answer, but she didn't come up with it right away.

Earlier he'd startled her by hitting the porch rail in a display of anger, then he'd moved her to pity for Edith, and then lulled her with some sighing truths about his marriage. Now he had a split-second advantage.

She tucked her chin to one side. She said, "That evening—"

"But your fainting was genuine," he said. "That part was real."

"Oh yes," she said. "Perhaps that's what makes it so hard to remember. . . ."

"But you recognize the phrase. Just now, when I said it, you had no trouble remembering. . . ."

"Oh, afterward I remembered I'd said *some*thing. Something about a suggestive remark I thought you made. I was very distraught that night. My father wasn't well. I was angry that you came to Culpeper. I hope you could tell I wasn't myself." She raised her head slightly, opened her eyes wider. If he didn't respond to her wide eyes, she would try offended dignity, but she wouldn't be able to make it quite stiff enough. He wasn't sure why he was doing this. He wasn't angry. Although his sentences were crowding hers, his tone was puzzled and mild.

She said, "Are you in the habit of cross-examining your—"

"But now that you're yourself again . . . Of course I realized later that you must have had a number of things upsetting you. But now that you're yourself, what do you think?"

"Well, I do remember we were *both* somewhat overheated. I believe you said that I was idiotic, that any forwardness of yours was in my dreams. . . . Some bits and pieces do come back to me, now that you've brought it all up. And then I believe you picked up your microphone and explained yourself quite fully."

"And that explanation—did it sound about right to you?"

"Well, I wouldn't be here if I thought otherwise." She cocked her head to one side and raised her hands palms-up. But then, sensing that she'd said either too much or too little, she closed her hands around each other and let them fall onto her lap. She said, "Really, it seems such a long time ago. I mean, that was before . . . everything else."

She was tiring. It occurred to him that the proper analogy for what he was doing wasn't Ezra's boxing, using his edge of quickness. This was more like playing a small fish on a fly rod. His mild tone was the soft touch necessary to keep the threadlike leader from snapping. If the trout tugged hard, he let her have some line to flutter and race this way and that. The tiny hook was just in her lips, the barb her slight sense of shame. She was as puzzled as a trout on a line. What was pulling her? Why wasn't her little fib dissolved in the good will and the good manners of their lunch, in the charm she'd displayed, in her recognition that the two of them were, after all, not so socially distant?

"Yes," he said. "And I imagine you were lashing out on your father's behalf. I suppose you felt protective more than anything else."

"Of course I felt protective."

"Yes." He nodded. He wished her to feel pain but to be confused about what was causing it, to know no more than a fish knew, only the barb in its lip, its own flailing and gradual weakening. For a moment he thought this was fair—payback for her foul-hooking him in the auction barn of Culpeper. Then he knew that he was enjoying it with a sly careful pleasure that should have rasped his sensibilities, had they not become harder and slicker.

But he didn't stop. He didn't want to stop this scanning of her wishes, inhibitions, and distress. And playing them. It was precise and intimate, but cold and, above all, unequal.

"And you'd been taking on as much of your father's work as you could. I believe you made some other appearances besides the one at the film festival. And then, of course, you had to manage all those bright young men who weren't sure you were the one to be giving them orders." Her head lifted just enough that he knew he was right. "And there I was making a big noise in Culpeper without a clue about the misery I was causing you. It's understandable that you did something desperate, that you blurted out—"

"You don't have to say it again."

"I say 'blurted' because I don't imagine you planned it."

"No." She looked away and said, "I believe I've explained that I just wasn't myself." He waited. She added, "So of course I apologize for that misunderstanding." She looked at him and looked away again. She said, "Oh, you lawyers have all the words for these things. Misconstrue." She waved her hand. "This—something or other."

Mike leaned forward and opened both hands. "I'm not trying to get you to apologize. All I want . . . I just want to be sure I understand you. If you tell me that I understand how it happened, we can let it go."

What alarmed her now wasn't that she was being shamed. What alarmed her was that she felt she couldn't move. Ordinarily she might have shaken loose and slipped away. Given her earlier impression of him, she'd certainly expected herself to be superior in enough ways to manage him. She was frustrated—and, because he'd veiled his pressing her with just enough of the clumsy earnestness she expected of him, she blamed her frustration on herself.

She said, "What more can I say? It was all so peculiar. . . ."

"Peculiar. I only meant that I hope I understand it in general." He lifted his head sharply. "You don't think I'm asking you to apologize in public, do you? That would be asking too much. I mean, at the very start of your campaign to say you want to correct a misstatement . . . This is just so there won't be any useless ill will between us. Oh, maybe somewhere down the road you might say something like, 'He's an able lawyer and likable enough, but far too liberal to represent this district. He might make a competent judge.'"

"That's what you said about my father—that he'd make a good judge."

"It was a way of disagreeing respectfully," Mike sighed. "The main thing is just this—you stung me. I admit I was stung. But later I saw more clearly how overwhelmed you were."

He watched her think. She couldn't settle on a thought. He watched her realize that her face was pinched in an unpleasant way. She stood up, said, "Excuse me for a moment," and went inside.

He put out the stub of the chairman's cigar. He'd done his imitation of the chairman's genial conniving. He'd done a bit more. It was here on this porch that Bonnie One had come out to soothe his bad temper, to dazzle and misdirect him. But she'd at least had the claim of being in a major love-plot. He'd just played with Charlotte Fenton's nerves for pleasure. He'd done more than his covert operation for the chairman; he'd been filled to the brim with his impersonation.

Charlotte Fenton came back out. He stood up. She said brightly, "Oh, don't get up." She'd washed her face and touched up her eyelashes. She sat down, crossed her legs, and smoothed her dress. "All those red books in your bookshelf," she said, "are they all in Latin?"

"They have facing-page translations. I need a page of English and then I can pretend I'm reading the Latin."

"Well, still," she said, "what a nice way to spend a winter evening—sitting by the fire reading Latin."

"Like an old woman with her knitting."

She laughed prettily. "You don't make a very convincing old woman."

Now that she was released, she was finding her balance again with flutters of charm. He looked at her—her sharp pretty face, the sleek fit of her black silk dress, her narrow knee, her long calf squeezed full. He saw her prettiness, but what he registered was only her sense of herself. He'd let a little connivance into himself, and it had taken over. It had taken over his normally warm-blooded response to a pretty woman, it had taken over his voice and gesture, it had taken over those sensitivities of his that were usually only alert to the uncanny. What if he stayed this way?

He saw that Charlotte Fenton didn't know what to make of it. She'd found him disconcertingly agreeable, but she'd also been seared by her other dim sense that he'd transformed something in himself—perhaps his anger at her, perhaps his anger at a broader target—into a slower but more powerful emotion. . . . But perhaps she was being too fearful? Perhaps her sense of being lesser was an accident—she'd slipped by chance.

He could see she was emerging from these thoughts, feeling a little giddy with relief now that she was over her unaccountable awkwardness.

He'd missed a sentence or two. She said, ". . . disagree respectfully. Although I may still have to say you're a reckless liberal and don't know a thing about money except how to spend it." She smiled. "I mean as a matter of public policy."

She did have a lovely voice, and he listened to it for a bit longer. She got up to go. He walked her to her car. They shook hands. She laughed and put her left hand on his forearm. "Now we'll have to put our public faces back on."

"Too bad," he said. She gave his hand an extra squeeze for that short gallantry and slid into her car.

He sat down on the porch steps. He thought, I won't have to do that again. Everything can be put back to normal. He could report to Mr. Broome and the chairman that the Jerry Medina problem was buried—not deep, but deep enough so that it wouldn't be an embarrassment to the party.

On to Edith. He'd taken care of it. And for good measure he'd got Charlotte Fenton turned around enough on her darkened-movie-theater remark that courtly old Mr. Broome could call her up and ask if she had any objection to his judgeship and she'd say no. Of course, for that to work, he'd have to go to the caucus and go through the motions. So the connivance wasn't quite over. But he could walk through that part—he didn't have to be possessed by that part of him that hooked and played Charlotte Fenton.

How odd it was to have sat at the dining-room table with Joss before lunch. Who was he then? An unmanned, decommissioned hull of himself as husband. And then, after a bite of lunch, his ship was suddenly lively again with a full pirate crew.

So he'd deceived and slyly bullied Charlotte Fenton. But that wasn't what alarmed him. What occurred to him now was that, in his attempt to avoid the pain and shock of the divorce, he'd hollowed himself out. And then he hadn't been careful about what he'd filled himself with.

He'd made himself quicker in every way. He'd done nothing to mend his good nature. He'd tried to make do with the remnants of schooling, institutional molding, fatherly advice, general orders—even plastered himself with slogans and bumper stickers. He hadn't dared to begin all over again. He'd gone back to his adolescent hope that his life was guided by good spirits, to his hope, when he was a nice young man, that he was part of the general progress of an ever-more-civilized America in which, fortunately, there was always room for bright, eager officers. . . . That shiny thought wasn't the dumb part. The dumb part was that he'd thought that chipping in here and there with good service to the commonwealth would take care of all the other parts of life. Including his own good nature. No wonder he'd slipped bit by bit until he was spending an afternoon with Charlotte Fenton being a con man. It wouldn't be hard to turn someone like him on to the con, someone who'd joined the ranks of the emotionally unemployed.

Mike had had enough for one day. He got up. He went to the toolshed, got his ax, and spent the afternoon splitting firewood, getting ready for winter like a sensible man, working up enough sweat to look like an honest one. He kept at it until he was tired and dulled.

◇

For the next five days he disappeared into a mist of Fiona. They did whatever she felt like doing. One day they built a root cellar into the side of the hill and lined it with five-foot logs. They got into the van to go buy hinges for the door but began kissing and went back to her bedroom. That night or another night they lay in front of the fire and fell asleep. That night or another night he read to her until she fell asleep on her straw mat. He went back to his house, fell asleep in his own bed, and woke up with her beside him. That morning or another morning he discovered that she could be made languorously helpless if he kissed the backs of her knees. For the first four days she was as enchanted as he was. On the fifth day they pulled up beets and turnips from the garden, stopping to embrace through their layers of wool. He emptied a basket of beets into the root cellar and told her he was going to be a judge.

She said, "Ah. There was some talk of environmental law."

"You mean work for the Southern Environmental Law Council?"

"No. Your own firm. You and Ganny."

"Ganny's got a job with the university. I need something steady for a few years. I have Edith and Nora."

"I thought you said you were going to do nothing for a month except take long walks and think about what to do."

"Well, this came up. I'll still have a month for long walks."

She went into her bungalow. After a while he went after her. He said, "Are you upset about this?"

"No."

"In fact, when you mentioned it, I think all I said was that the Southern Environmental Law firm is already—"

"Yes."

"Look. If you want to talk about what you're going to do—"

"No. You make your arrangements. I actually don't much like arranging things. I seem to do all right with whatever comes along."

"Well, take your time. You're all right here. If you want to go back to school, get some sort of graduate degree, we could work something out."

She said, "That sort of arrangement gives me the creeps."

He felt completely loathsome. He went back to his house. He couldn't remember whether he'd said anything after she said "creeps." Even during the next day he couldn't bring himself to remember the conversation, let alone think of defending himself.

The caucus was in the evening. Arriving at the high-school auditorium was familiar but without the familiar nerves. There was a lot of noise and movement to which he didn't have to pay attention. Only a few weeks earlier he would have been alert, he would have been flicking a snake's tongue of attention, tasting the mood of every cluster of people.

It all went as planned. The first vote was split three ways between the chairman's candidate, who was slightly ahead but without a majority; a woman from the former Citizen's Party, now on City Council, who was a respectable third; and Mike.

There was an interval of discussion and milling about. Before the chair called the caucus to order for another vote, Mr. Broome found Mike and put his hand on his arm. Mr. Broome said, "She's going to throw her support to the candidate." Mr. Broome made a slight motion with his head toward a knot of people around the city councilwoman. Mr. Broome added, "I think your announcement would be better if it preceded her."

"Okay."

"Very well," Mr. Broome said. "I'll put in a word to the chair that you wish to be recognized. Just stand up as soon as he asks for order."

Mike looked over the index card with his list of people to thank. His remarks were on the other side—a single sentence beginning, "In the interest of party unity . . ."

Mike spoke without a microphone. The only item of interest for him was a woman three rows in front of him who turned around to glare at him. As he wound up his party-unity sentence, she hissed loud enough for the chair to pick up his gavel. During the applause she couldn't be heard, but Mike saw her bare teeth, then a flick of tongue, and then her mouth in an O which she clamped shut. She repeated this several times. She was saying over and over, "Sellout." The woman next to her put a hand on her shoulder and she stopped and turned back to the front. Mike was oddly pleased by her gargoyle ill will, as if he were an old-time stage actor playing the villain who only knew he was on the job if people hissed.

The city councilwoman was recognized, made a somewhat longer speech than Mike's, and then the chair called for another vote, which the party chairman's candidate won handily. The chair asked if the caucus wished to make the vote unanimous, and there was enough of an uproar that he declared it unanimous by acclamation.

Apart from the gargoyle hiss, the only time Mike felt the needle jump out of the groove was at a phrase in the new candidate's acceptance speech. The new candidate, in praising Mike's campaign, said Mike had been "the voice of one crying in the wilderness." Mike grew alarmed for the man and wondered if he knew what he was saying. If he was comparing Mike to John the Baptist, was he comparing himself to Christ?

But there was no stir in the audience, and the speech went on in its energetic staleness. Mike couldn't get the phrase out of his head. It translated itself back into the Latin of his choirboy days—*vox clamantis in deserto.*

He congratulated the candidate, posed for a picture with him and the city councilwoman, everyone smiling. One of the reporters asked him how he felt. "Very pleased, very satisfied." He bit his tongue not to say that he did indeed feel like John the Baptist but somewhat later in his career—when his head was on a plate. He said instead, turning to the candidate, "He has picked up the fallen standard and now leads the charge." Mr. Broome inclined his head toward Mike. A hint of a reference to the War Between the States always went down well.

And then Mike was in the cold driver's seat of the van. He turned on the heat, the lights, the radio.

Along the Rivanna, across the bridge, up the driveway. Fiona's bungalow was dark.

Two days later the phone rang at six in the morning. It was Fiona. She said, "This isn't the Fiona you last spoke to. She was a terrible person. This one has to see you right away."

He couldn't say anything. She said, "Are you there? Get a pen and paper."

He said, "Okay."

She was about to start an eleven-day Outward Bound course in North Carolina. She was the assistant instructor for a group of twelve executives on a company team-building exercise. She had a free day—that is, she was free from lunch that afternoon until five the next morning. If Mike left right away he could reach the camp by noon. She gave him detailed instructions.

She said, "Bring warm clothes. I'll borrow a sleeping bag for you."

On the way there, sometimes he thought he was a fool. Other times he was filled with a nervous excitement that made him tremble. It was not the same thing as happiness.

On the last mile of the trip he was on a dirt road. He looked up from checking the odometer. Fiona was walking toward the van, dwarfed by an enormous backpack. She was carrying an extra, empty backpack in one hand. She laughed. He stopped the van and got out. She dropped the empty pack and held him by the back of his belt. He held on to the frame of her backpack. She kissed his mouth and then unbuttoned his shirt to kiss the top of his chest.

Later that afternoon they stopped to pitch her tent. It took a long time, since he kept holding her. He'd said very little while they walked, she leading the way but stopping from time to time to reach back and take his hand. Now she said, "Are you going to talk?"

He said, "I'm not sure."

She smiled across the top of the tent. She wrapped her arms around herself and said, "The effect I have on you has an effect on me." He was lightheaded. She came around the tent and took his hand. His head wobbled. She laughed, possibly thinking he was miming being helplessly smitten. Still holding his hand, she stopped and drew him after her into the tent.

The next morning she woke him up in the dark so that she would get back to camp at five.

He didn't have a thought until he was about halfway home. He stopped at a truck stop and ate a huge breakfast of bacon and eggs. Fiona and he had skipped supper. He thought how scalded he'd been by Fiona's saying, "That sort of arrangement gives me the creeps." How inert it made him. And then how enchanted he'd just been as they walked back downhill while the stars were still out, how beautiful the small leaves of the bushes were, all frost and starlight.

It would be painful for him to be in love with Fiona. She could scald him and enchant him at her will. But what would be hard for *her* was the weight of the other side of his life. His daughters, his work—and how being a judge would serve his being a father, serve his daughters' happiness.

Why not marry Fiona? There were reasons and reasons not to. She wouldn't wish to bear the weight. She was living for herself now. She couldn't bear the weight. He feared trusting her with the weight of any part of his life but his own selfish third.

Two days later Mike went to Richmond with Mr. Broome to meet the legislators whom Mr. Broome considered it a wise courtesy to visit. Mr. Broome collected their renewed assurances of support. During the car ride back to Charlottesville, Mr. Broome mused out loud about their worth. He considered them mostly secure, some on their word alone, some on their word plus a past favor, some on their word plus an imminent favor. Mike thanked Mr. Broome. Mr. Broome said, "*I* consider you a good appointment. The chairman wouldn't like people to think he leaves his wounded on the field."

Three days later Edith and Nora came for a week. He gave in to their demands more often than he thought was good. Twice they all went out for supper on school nights. Another night he took them to People's Drugstore to buy toothbrushes, hairbrushes, and combs so they wouldn't have to pack so much stuff going back and forth between houses. He ended up buying them lots of other things that caught their eye. They stayed up past their bedtime. He was surprised at how tiring it was. He thought he would have to organize home life better. Perhaps, when he started to work regularly, everything else would have more structure. But he missed the girls as soon as they got on the school bus. He could get weepy cleaning up their half-finished cereal.

Friday was their last full day. He promised to take them to the movies Friday night. They were to go back to their mother's Saturday morning. Before the girls got home from school, a strange car pulled up in front of Fiona's bungalow. Fiona got out and heaved her pack from the trunk onto the porch. The man driving the car got out, stretched, took off his sunglasses, and eyed the bungalow. Fiona and the man talked for a minute. She kissed him on the mouth. The man's hands moved across her back. He got in the car and drove away.

The girls came up the hill with their book bags while Mike was still standing at the window. It might have been two minutes later, or fifteen or twenty.

Before he and Edith and Nora left to eat pizza and then go to *The Black Stallion,* Mike went to the bungalow. He called in through the door, "I'm taking the girls to the movies. Maybe I'll see you later." Fiona opened the door. She had a cup in her hand. She smiled and said, "Just going to sneak off, are you?"

He said, "Who was that you were kissing?"

"Oh, brilliant," she said. "Go to the movies." She shut the door.

Not long into the movie there was a shipwreck. Edith was so afraid the Black Stallion was going to drown she had to leave. Nora was afraid too, but wanted to see what would happen. They all went to the lobby. Mike reassured Edith. Nora went back in and watched from the back of the theater, coming out from time to time with bulletins. Finally she said, "It's okay now."

In the van Edith said to Nora, "You could watch because you never really got to know a horse."

Mike said, "Nora didn't say anything."

"That wasn't a horse at your camp," Nora said. "That was a pony."

"No!" Mike said. He stopped the van and banged his hands on the steering wheel. He held on to it until his arms quivered. He lifted his hands, shook them, and said, "Don't do that." The girls were terrified. He felt terrible. He apologized. He blamed Fiona.

The next morning Joss showed up during breakfast. She left her station wagon running and stood outside the door. Mike carried the girls' bags to the car. Bonnie One waved to him from the passenger seat. The girls came out.

Edith said, "Are we going home or are we going someplace?"

"We're going to Crozet to pick apples."

Nora said, "That's really boring."

Fiona came around the house wearing an overcoat and hiking boots with no socks. She said hello to everyone. "I'm just on my way for a quick splash. Mike?"

"It's cold."

"Oh, Mike, I forgot to tell you how I got back from North Carolina. I got a ride with one of the executives and he's putting me in touch with a company that needs trek leaders. Piece of luck. Much more money than Outward Bound. Worldwide Adventure Tours."

Joss said, "Nora, Edith—get in the car." Joss drove away. Fiona walked toward the river.

When Fiona came into the kitchen her hair was wet. She dried it on a dish towel. She poured herself a cup of coffee. She said, "You see? Your wife jumped to the conclusion that I spent the night with you." She took a bite of Nora's leftover oatmeal. She said, "I must show you how to make proper porridge. It's a very good job. I mean Worldwide Adventure Tours. A month of work, a month off. If I do two months in a row I'll get three months off. Shall I show you exactly how I kissed him? Or did you jump to a more drastic conclusion?" She slipped off her boots and dried her feet. "I'm glad you're having a mood of your own. I was getting tired of having all the moods. But I think you've got all you can out of this one." She sighed. "What you *could* be cross about is my strolling into the midst of your difficult situation with your wife and children and your wife's lover and using that as a way to shut you up. And that means your wife may ask them in some subtle way whether I was in the house while they were here, and neither you nor I want them thinking along those lines. I really *was* on my way to the river, I wasn't lurking about. So I am sorry about that." She walked behind the chair he was in and put her hand on his forehead. "And I meant to give that man the briefest possible kiss, but then he lurched forward. My lips, which are small enough to start with, were pressed tight like this." She turned his head so he could see her mouth. She spoke through her squeezed-shut mouth—"See. No lips." She sounded like a kazoo. He laughed. "What a perverse man you are," she said. "You can't resist me when I make an ugly face."

There was no regularity to their ups and downs—they could be blissful for as long as five days and they could stay apart for a week. Fiona could always end a quarrel or a sulk, Mike only occasionally. In late December, Fiona went to the Florida Outward Bound School to fill in for another eleven-day course. In January she was back and began getting her shots for Worldwide Adventure Tours.

Mike was sworn in as a judge. Charlotte Fenton was sworn in as a member of Congress.

A week before she left, Fiona said, "I'm going to tell you this now so you'll have a bit of time to get over it and be nice to me when I leave. I'll be loyal to you but I won't promise to be faithful."

Three days later she said, "I'm not sorry I made us fall in love. I even considered marrying you. Then I thought I'd think about it in three years. When all the girls in your life are older."

The day after he drove her to Dulles Airport, he arranged to have a lot of work and then to have supper with Ganny.

But the next night, and of course many nights after that, he thought of Fiona. He imagined her coming back—unapologetic, laughing at his laughable resistance. He'd imagined a steady life with daughters and friends, with occasional passing fancies. He'd preached blitheness as a virtue. So he got what he wished for, with a twist.

The front log in the fire broke, flicking a handful of sparks against the screen.

Fiona might come back as a prodigal—I've been terrible, can you deal with it? Or in a strange mood—Can you find me in my maze? Or the old standard—I'm bad for you, you ought to get rid of me, but I see you're giving way. And so am I, because, after all, to tempt is to be tempted.

One half of the log twisted and slid between the andirons, the other half fell to the outside, setting its thick end in the ashes, flaring orange and blue out of a single long crack.

He'd been unconscious when he built his old life. He was more conscious now—or at least he was less surprised by himself. He hoped that he'd rid himself of his conniving part. Perhaps not for good. He could imagine the conniving part showing up again at the front door like an old schoolmate or cousin with far too much luggage for a weekend visit. He would deal with it.

So for his new life he had Edith and Nora. He had a job. He had the uncertainty of Fiona. Love and work, and a flickering he didn't know what to do with. It didn't all have to make sense. Two out of three. He wondered if Edith and Nora had understood him when he told them that at first he'd been disappointed at having to say halfway through his life, "I'm pretty much like everybody else," but the next time he said it, it had been a relief.

He wasn't sure if that was entirely true. What he was more hopeful about was that, by fits and starts, by the occasional satisfactions and graces at home, he was becoming better company for himself.

TWENTY YEARS AFTER

§ 12

Nora and I got a drive-away from L.A. to Charlottesville. Nora didn't know about drive-aways. The drive-away agency knows me. All you need is a clean driving record and some proof that you're a citizen with a job and seizable assets, and they give you the keys to a car belonging to someone (usually rich) who wants it someplace else (usually beautiful and fashionable). From L.A. I've gone to Santa Fe, Aspen, Bozeman, Vancouver, and Banff. Five free rides to my summer vacations. They allow plenty of time, so you can cruise for a couple of days. They pay for the gas and a car wash. Then you drive to the ranch house or the resort hotel and pull out your backpack. Usually there's enough of a tip to pay for part of your vacation—ten days' worth of trail food, say—and a bus ride back. In Bozeman, when I gave the keys to the owner he asked me my name, and when I said "Edith Reardon," he looked at me more carefully and asked if I was related to Nora Reardon. He drove me back to town, but no tip. He probably thought it would be unseemly. At the chalet near Banff, there was a party going on and the owner asked me in, but I caught a glimpse of someone on the side porch who I thought was Fiona. I split.

This time Nora and I had a drive-away to Charlottesville, still a favorite of the stars. Then on to Grandma's ninetieth-birthday party on the Northern Neck.

I asked Nora what she did with Dad when she went back to Charlottesville. She said, "Sometimes we just hang out. Sometimes he asks for advice."

I accidentally pressed on the accelerator. Nora flung her hands up and said, "Whoa!"

I slowed down and said, "Advice? Like what?"

"One time he asked me to sit in court for a while and then give him some notes on his performance. There was one thing he had to get over—when he was handing down a sentence he got this weird fixed grin on his face. He didn't know he was doing it. He was saying, 'I sentence you to three years,' and he leaned forward with his mouth twisted to one side and his teeth showing. He may have meant to express sympathy, but he looked like an evil Santa Claus."

"And what did Dad say?"

"He said, 'Really?' and he asked me to do the grin for him. Then he went and practiced different faces in his shaving mirror."

"What else?"

"Another time, a year or so ago, he was being roasted at a dinner of the local bar association. I wrote out some jokes for us to do. I played the part of a country lawyer appearing before Dad. I had Dad say, 'Counselor, surely your client has heard of the doctrine *volenti non fit injuria*.' And I said, 'Why, out in Nelson County we don't hardly talk 'bout nothing else.'"

I said, "Did the lawyer recognize you from TV?"

"Don't you think that's funny? It's an old lawyer joke but it fit in because Dad actually used to spout law-Latin."

I said, "Good. It sounds good."

"It was good advice," Nora said. "I mean for him to poke fun at himself. I found another one for him. See, they gave him this testimonial dinner on Saint Patrick's Day, so he said, 'You all know who Saint Patrick was—chased the snakes out of Ireland. But I'd like to propose a toast to the second-most-important man in Irish history—the man who invented the wheelbarrow and got the Irish up on their hind legs.'"

"Why do I find these jokes so depressing?"

Nora said, "Now you're slowing way down. Maybe you should put it on cruise control. Look—it got a big laugh. You probably can't stand the idea of a roomful of mostly male lawyers all dressed up in black tie with starched shirtfronts."

"Is it still mostly men?"

"Actually I couldn't tell, because it was couples, and of course some of the women were the lawyers and the husbands were just along for the ride. But there were definitely some housewives—they were the ones who recognized me from daytime TV. But it wasn't oppressive. Some of those old farts really like Dad. And it was good for him. The reason middle-aged men have those clubs is that they're so incompetent at arranging a real social life with friends. Most of Dad's social life is the gang of local lawyers, most of whom he has no interest in, and the ones he likes are workaholics, so they're not available for life. One or two banquets a year—that's about it for aging solitary males. You remember Edmond's story about the male orangutans?"

"Oh yes. But you're just talking about social life among the big suits. You're leaving out Dad's girlfriends. I don't suppose you help him organize that part of his life too."

Nora said, "You think you're the only one who has feelings about Dad and other women?"

We were still in New Mexico, so I certainly didn't want to start a fight. I said, "Sorry. Maybe I'm a little guilty that you take care of him more. And better. You're better at it. I admit it."

"Maybe if you just came home more it'd get easier. Dad would pay for your plane."

"I know. But I can't do that. He bought me a ticket once, and it started the whole visit off wrong. It infantilized me."

Nora laughed and then said she was sorry. "Certain words just do it to me. I know, it's this abstract concept, but when you say 'infantilize' I see you in diapers holding a bottle."

I didn't say anything, but Nora caught the flicker in my face. She said, "I'm not laughing at *you*."

I said, "Maybe in diapers is what I mean. Maybe that's what he wants."

"No," Nora said, "he doesn't want that. But he wants you back. You're his Cordelia. When we put you on the plane to go away to college, we went up to the observation deck, and Dad held on to the rail getting more and more tense. His face got stiffer and stiffer, and finally it crumpled up and he sobbed. He couldn't stop. He leaned over and bit the cuff of his jacket and he still couldn't stop. I had to lead him off to the end of the platform, because people were staring."

I was moved by this.

Nora said, "You're slowing down again. Do you want me to show you how to set the cruise control?"

I said, "I don't like cruise control. I can manage without cruise control. So what did you think? Were you jealous at all?"

"I'll tell you," Nora said. "But I'll get mad if you don't get it in the order I tell it. First I was alarmed and worried for Dad. Second—I was sad too that you were going away. And *third*—I'm saying third—way behind first and second—I thought, My God, he's using it all up."

"You thought there was only so much he could miss us, and that I was getting more than—"

"I knew you'd get it out of order."

"I'm only asking a question. And you can't threaten to get mad ahead of time just so you can be the boss."

Nora laughed. She said, "You know, Dad remembers all those things you and I used to say when we fought. We used to say, 'You're not the boss of this house.' He said life is easier for him now. He gets to smack his gavel and say, 'I won't have this bickering in my courtroom.'"

I said, "Okay. You can set the damn cruise control."

In the afternoon we were in the Texas Panhandle, speeding along at cruise-control seventy-five in our air-conditioned bubble. If we'd been outside we would have died from the heat—we might as well have been traveling on a hostile alien planet. Except that at the restaurant where we stopped for lunch the waitress recognized Nora even though Nora was wearing her sunglasses. The waitress said, "When you died, I just bawled my eyes out."

Back in the car I said, "Well, there. You've got millions of people crying because they miss you."

"I hope you noticed she only knew my character's name, not mine. I'm just a ghost to her. She won't go see me in a real movie."

I said, "Still. She bawled her eyes out."

"My agent had to fight for a lingering illness. They were going to have me die in a car wreck. So her tears at my Camille scene came from my being forced to burn my bridges to get out of my contract and then having my agent bargain our way out of sudden death."

"Doesn't matter," I said. "She bawled her eyes out. And I'll bet Dad bawled when he saw that episode."

It was Nora's turn to drive. She was accelerating back up to speed on the on-ramps. Nora said, "So? So? So?" She out-raced a truck hauling cattle onto the right lane.

"I suppose you think my brain has gone so soft from being in a soap that I'll settle for Dad going boo-hoo over make-believe?"

I wasn't going to start a fight while we were still in Texas. Maybe Tennessee. But certainly not with Nora driving.

I said, "No. I didn't mean anything like that. I was joking about Dad and TV."

Nora set the cruise control. In a minute I was as hypnotized by the open land rushing past as if we hadn't stopped for lunch. I had a sense of enormous speed and a sense of inching along. We were eating up Texas, we'd be in Texas forever.

I was considering moving back to Virginia, but I wanted to see it again first. All this empty space was making me feel too small to do anything. Dad would say, "You're terrific, Edith. Just be a little more blithe." Mom would say, "You're terrific, pooch. You can do anything."

That was what *they* had been bequeathed—this roly-poly optimism. It was what they tried to bequeath to us because it had been bequeathed to them. They were post-Depression babies. They were war bonds and victory gardens. Victory in Europe, victory over Japan. They were the UN, the Marshall Plan, and penicillin—and more victories, over McCarthyism, segregation, and polio. They came from bright benevolent America. It was no wonder they'd believed in throwing themselves into the current, no wonder they had sweet silly senses of humor, no wonder they said yes more often than no. Of course their psyches are particular, and I despise general notions like the ones that bombarded us about the turn of the century—God, what hooey about the year 2000—all those pretty TV faces blowing a soap-bubble cliché every time their slick lips pulled apart to pronounce "millennium."

As I was about to place Mom and Dad on their proper twentieth-century shelf, I went into meltdown. I think it was because I remembered Dad saying to me, his voice full of surprise and pleasure, "You know, I think you have a good sense of history." That compliment had lost none of its power to thrill me, but it still had the power to make me angry too: Who gave him the keys? Who gave him the power to bestow a benediction that would stay with me so long? But I do have enough sense of history to make me sad for Mom and Dad as startled, innocent parents. Dad once told me one of the things he'd liked about Mom was that she could restate the obvious so that it was zany. When Mom was pregnant with me, she and Dad were walking in downtown Washington. She suddenly grabbed his arm and said, "Look at all these people. Every one of them was *born*." The next week she put her hands on her stomach and said, "For all I know this is an invasion from Mars." It is the plight of every firstborn to be all humanity and to be an alien to her parents, but Mom and Dad were more susceptible than normal to this extravagant notion. To extravagant notions in general. There was an arrogance in their enjoyment of quick changes of notions, feelings, or situations. In those days they didn't feel the need to rein in anything in their lives. Living on a houseboat was only one symptom of their cockeyed sense that enthusiasm takes care of everything. Having a baby was another. They thought they could still work ten hours a day, frolic four hours, stay up late reading—they thought I'd fit right in on the houseboat along with Miss Dudley.

They became wrecks. Grandma told me about it later. Grandma made them think that she needed them down on the Northern Neck, but it was a relief for them. Mom relaxed in Grandma's well-run house; Dad liked spending four nights on the houseboat and three with us on the Neck. But my baby presence was the end of their free life. So, under Grandma's invisible influence, they settled for a narrower life. Their old Washington pals have told me Mom and Dad had always been manic workers, arguers, high-steppers. From the time Grandma took us in at her house on the Neck until Nora was born, Mom and Dad took that excess manic energy and beamed it on me. Talk about overstimulation.

Then Nora. I have two pictures of myself after Nora's birth. In the first I look dazed, a shell-shocked survivor of the change in my world. In the second Dad and I are a romantic couple wrapped in each other's arms on the wharf, each of us the other's consolation prize for the loss of Mom to the squalling Nora.

But that arrangement wasn't a stable solution. Mom and Dad still led a highly nervous life, overtalkative, overenergized, and overextended.

I feel sad for them then, and I feel sadder for them now. Now their bones and skin are frailer, but their terrible exuberances still shake them. They haven't ever quite done what they hoped. Oh, close enough. Nora's probably right that Dad has been a good judge. And Mom gets her movies in college film festivals and every once in a while on PBS. So they both keep climbing, shorter and shorter of breath.

Nora must have heard me sniffle. She looked over, and I poured it all out. After some comforting words at seventy-five miles per hour, she went into Nora-lore. "You want to know the difference between pathos and comedy? It's lighting and pace and distance. In the theater you take the pratfalls way upstage, so the audience doesn't hear the painful thud. You use bright lights. And you keep it moving quick enough so the audience sees how funny life can be."

"Did Dad ever tell you you have a great sense of theater? Never mind. I remember he did. So now you're preaching the theater version of 'be blithe.'"

"Look. I have just as many bad memories as you. You may be the family mind-reader, but you weren't the only one—"

"But you managed to slip out of it. I'm not being mean now. You were like a snake shedding its skin."

"Oh, great. Thanks a bunch. Edith the warm-blooded, Nora the reptile."

"That's not what I meant. I meant the shedding—"

"Nora the reptilian stripper."

"Okay—the absconding, if you prefer—"

Nora made a neighing sound, a Three Stooges stuttering falsetto of exasperation. She said, "I'll tell you what I didn't slither out of. After you went to college, I was still in high school for two years and then I was still in Charlottesville for college. Whenever you came home Dad wanted to have a long talk with you about the meaning of life. When he had long talks with me, he wanted to tell me about his love life. He wanted a *confidante.* All I can say is, it was lucky for me the Drama Department slotted me for comedy."

I said, "I thought he told you about the cases he heard, all that stuff you used when you started writing scripts."

"Yes, that too. But listen. You didn't have to hear about Fiona."

I said, "Did he ever ask your advice about Fiona?"

"Toward the end he moaned about her."

"Did she keep on with those yuppie adventure tours? I remember her bungalow being empty most of the time. Was she there more after I left?"

"Less. But Dad kept the bungalow empty for whenever she showed up. Sometimes she came because she had malaria or she'd broken her leg, other times she just needed a rest."

"What—Dad was her health plan?"

"Well, she liked him too. The problem wasn't that she got to be a houseguest. I don't think she really knew how disruptive she was."

"Why disruptive? If Dad wanted to be her rest cure . . . I assume he got to be more than her nurse."

"The problem was that she'd show up just when Dad was going out with someone sensible. Like Dr. Ames."

"No," I said. "*Our* Dr. Ames."

Nora said, "I know, I know. But really she would have been a good wife. I got a shock—no, I got a double shock when I saw them together. The first time was when Dr. Ames and Dad came backstage after a play I was in. It was my first play on the main stage at U.Va. I think they'd been going out for a while before he sprung her on me. So seeing her all dressed up for a date was a shock. The second shock was when she said to me, 'Nora, you were wuh——. You were wuh-wuhn . . . You were terrific.'"

I couldn't help laughing. I said, "So she was embarrassed too."

"Yes, but that alone didn't make her stutter," Nora said. "It was because I'd become a grown-up."

I said, "Oh, Orrie-Norrie, what a bad way to be certified grown-up."

"But two months later, Fiona flew in. And a month after that, Fiona was gone. But so was Dr. Ames."

"Because she found out?"

"Dad told her."

"Did he ask you if he should?"

"Not beforehand. But I'm not sure what I would have said. He told me he'd told her and that he was hoping that Dr. Ames would get over it. I had to explain to him that in the early stages nothing is forgivable."

"Wait. Is that true?"

"Maybe. I don't know."

I said, "So tell me more about Fiona. Did he go on and on being an idiot?"

"I have a feeling you're going to get mad at him about all this," Nora said. "I'll only tell you more if you promise to see it at a distance and light it for comedy."

I didn't say anything. I was pretty sure Nora wouldn't be able to stop. But Nora cleverly jumped sideways. She said, "I mean you and I can think about Mom pretty calmly—we're even willing to appreciate Bonnie One for making Mom's life better. We consider that weird period when Mom had a boyfriend and Bonnie One was tortured and we didn't like him either, and we can see all that as way-back-then. I can even see the comedy of it. The poor guy trying to figure out what to do about our sulky brooding and—whammo!—he gets blindsided by the return of Bonnie One."

I said, "That wasn't whammo. That was 'The fog comes / on little cat feet.'"

"Okay," Nora said. "High comedy, not slapstick."

"Why not romance?" I said.

"Okay, romantic comedy," Nora said. "A feminist romantic comedy, striking a blow for women everywhere."

"You were generous a minute ago," I said. "Don't spoil it."

Nora said, "Look, I'm not going to take sides. Nobody has to take sides. Mom and Bonnie One versus Dad and Fiona. I'm just talking about it. I'm not even sure how I feel about it. Just distant. Maybe, if you'd seen more of it, you might be easier with it. I mean there was a good side to Fiona. For one thing, when she showed up, she had an immediate good effect on Dad. He could get pretty far down on his own. I remember coming to see him one time and the whole house was a shambles. He was at the dining-room table reading the newspapers at arm's length. This was just before he got reading glasses. It was a hot summer night. It had been so hot that the unlit candles had drooped over like weeping-willow branches. The screens were ripped and he hadn't fixed them, so there were moths and damselflies and God knows what else hovering from one end of the house to the other. There were huge paw prints in the dust on the floor. I didn't know it was a cat until it ran out from behind the sofa, jumped in the air, and batted down a moth and ate it. It was an enormous animal, the size of a wildcat. It was like Dad's bad moods turned into a gargoyle. The reason the screens weren't fixed is that the cat could pry out a corner and peel it back. If you tried to shoo it away, the damn thing growled at you. All night long I heard it pattering around crunching bugs. When I tried to sweep up the next day, I found a dead rabbit in the corner. I tried to sweep it into the dustpan and the cat growled. I mean normally they just hiss, right? It was so big it didn't even crap like a cat, it left turds the size of Dad's cigar butts. There was a petrified one on the porch, and then it left one in my bedroom just to be mean. Speaking of cigar butts, there were three or four floating in the coffee mugs in the sink. It was like the house was the portrait of Dorian Gray. I mean Dad got up and went to the courthouse looking normal, but he was defeated at home. But the next time I came back Fiona had just been there for a month. The house was neat. Dad was in afterglow. He'd lost five pounds, he had some color. Fiona had put up heavy mesh over the screens and trained the cat to stay outdoors. She'd even made a cat house under the porch. And she made the cat act nicer."

"I never saw that cat."

"It killed too many birds and squirrels to suit Dad, so he gave it to Ezra's uncle to live in a barn that had rats."

"So what's your point?"

"That Fiona didn't just make him miserable. Her coming and going may have made his lows lower, but she made his highs higher. She *kept* him dazzled. I think he knew that was the deal. It wasn't as if he was her helpless victim. I don't know all the ins and outs, but every so often he was the one who said no."

"No to what?" I said. "To her asking for something more than a house, health care, and a Christmas bonus?"

"She didn't squeeze him. I asked Dad about that. It wasn't fifty-fifty in actual dollars, but for each time she stayed in the bungalow, she took him on a trip. For every time he took her to a restaurant, she cooked him a meal. She used to go hunting and fishing and bring him venison and trout. In that way she was like Bundy for Dad—a hunting-and-fishing pal. One winter Fiona and Dad went hiking on snowshoes near Cranberry Bog—that part of West Virginia that has freak cold weather. They got caught in a blizzard. So Fiona said they had to build an igloo. They got to the last block at the top and the whole thing collapsed. Fiona said, 'Oh well. Nome wasn't built in a day.'"

"That's not funny."

"That's not the point. The point is she had a spark. Listen. Another time they were in the Smokies and got caught in a rainstorm and Fiona had them build a little survival shelter made out of sticks and a pile of leaves. After they got back and Fiona had gone off again, Dad got this manila envelope in the mail. When he opened it up a single leaf fell out. There was a little white tag tied to the stem. The tag said, 'Survival-shelter starter kit.'"

I said, "She seems to have been plagued with bad weather."

"You're finding her not charming on purpose."

"Wait. Go back to the igloo that fell down. What did they do?"

"Dad told me he was just standing there in a daze watching the snow fall. He couldn't see five feet. Fiona took him over to the snowbank where they'd cut out the blocks for the igloo. There was a hole, and she laid sticks across the top and the snow piled up on them and that made a roof. So they had a little burrow. They might have frozen to death."

"He wouldn't have been out there except for her."

Nora rolled her eyes. She said, "You are being . . ." Then she exhaled and said, "Okay. I guess you can't help it, 'cause you're hearing it all at once. And maybe I shouldn't have just told about the times Fiona was in charge. Sometimes they went sailing, and then Dad got to say all his sailor stuff—'Ease her off, you're pointing too high.'"

"Oh yes," I said. "The basic principles of seamanship and navigation. I would've thought he'd learned from us that that's not the way to a girl's heart."

Nora laughed. She drove in silence for a while, and then she suddenly put her hand on her forehead. She said, "I said Fiona was his female Bundy. I should have said Dad missed Cordelia."

I said, "You mean Fiona gets to be his third daughter? The one who's nicer than us? So we get to be Goneril and Regan?"

"No, dummy. You're Dad's Cordelia. You're the one he tried to teach sailing to. You're the one he yearns for."

"Oh, come on. He tortured both of us in that sailboat. And you got to be his campaign sweetheart."

"Leaving aside the fact that he wanted *you* to campaign," Nora said, "leaving aside that I was just filling in—who would you rather be, Shirley Temple or Cordelia?"

"Wait," I said. "Wait, wait, wait. Leaving aside the fact that Cordelia ends up dead . . . Wait. Are you trying to say that Fiona is my Cordelia substitute, so Fiona is my fault?"

We weren't really fighting, we weren't really joking. I didn't know where we were. Nora kept driving. After a while she said, "One time when you and I were staying at Dad's house—we were still in middle school—I was sick or faking being sick. Dad came home to have lunch with me. I was watching a soap and I made him watch it with me. One of the story lines was this: A young wife is sick with a fatal blood disease. The doctor tells the husband that she will die unless they circulate her blood through someone else and back into her. But here's the catch. That someone then has a fifty-fifty chance of catching the disease and dying. The doctor asks the husband if he'll take that chance. Break for commercial.

Dad said to me, 'I'd do that for you.' I said, 'Who else would you do it for?' Dad said, 'Edith.' He paused a beat and said, 'And your mother.' I said, 'What about Ganny?' Dad said, 'I love Ganny, but I can't do it for her until you and Edith are grown-up.' What's odd is that I wasn't thrilled. It just seemed a pleasantly normal answer. Dad and I were sitting on the sofa watching that ridiculous nine-inch black-and-white TV of his. I may have even asked him when he was going to get a real TV like the one at Mom's house. But I was happy. It was winter and rainy and gray and Dad always kept his house too cold, but we had that purple crocheted afghan across our laps. Remember that? I used to stick my fingers through the holes. It felt like having rings on all my fingers."

We drove for a while.

I said, "It's a gift. You have a gift of letting things make you happy."

"But listen," Nora said. "Whenever I think of—"

"I always envied how you could make Dad do dumb things with you. Like watch TV. And I remember how you used to make him read catalogues and magazine ads for women's clothes and he had to make a list of the best dresses. When he and I sat around together I always felt he wanted me to do something like read the Bible or learn to play chess. I remember you getting cross with him because you thought he was picking how pretty the women were instead of the dresses. I always wondered how you got him to do stuff like that."

"Listen," Nora said. "Here's the other thing I always think of when I remember the purple afghan. I was in high school. You'd left for college, so I was fifteen. Dad and I were driving somewhere. Remember how we used to have to make deals with him about the car radio? I had to check the NPR station before he let me get a rock station. And if it was news we had to listen. And Dad would drive me nuts because he always repeated the foreign names out loud. He was still doing it ten years ago. The news guy would say '. . . fighting in Srebenica' and Dad would say 'Srebenica.' Sometimes twice, so he got it right. Anyway, this one time Dad was driving me home from my lacrosse game. I turned to NPR and there was a panel about women in the arts, three or four women talking and then one woman reading something. So Dad said, 'Okay. You can switch.' And I said, 'Dad, listen.' And he said, 'It's okay, take your turn.' And I said, 'Dad, don't you recognize her? It's Mom.'"

After a few seconds Nora said, "It took me a while. . . . I mean at first I was just surprised. Later on that night was when I gave up imagining that they'd get back together." Nora was speaking calmly but she was crying.

She said, "I know I'm crying, but it's not that bad. I used to use that for sense memory in acting class. Not for reacting to bad news, but for reaching out to find something and there's nothing. And you feel worse because you should have guessed. After all, everything vanishes—why should your particular hope have a longer half-life?"

I'd been about to feel sorry for Nora, but I became both curious and irritated. I said, "So, when you use something up for your acting, are you through with it?"

"Use *up*?" Nora said. "I know what you're thinking. You think I've spilled myself all over, sold everything cheap to a lot of strangers."

"No."

Nora said, "Well, your memories are locked up in a museum."

"No."

Nora said, "Your problem is that you think everything happens only once."

One of the things that fascinates me about Nora is that she doesn't bother with defense.

Nora said, "Wait. Now I know what I meant."

I said, "It's okay, I just got it."

"Okay," Nora said. "I'm saying some feelings *are* like other feelings and you think each feeling is particular."

"Okay," I said. "So we're having an argument about everything."

Nora said, "Well, we can get back to that. So where was I? So I got over Dad not recognizing Mom's voice on the radio. Well, maybe not over it, but by it. So then there was Dad by himself in his house trying to have this theory that his children would be the main intimacy of his life. And next there'd be his friends—he thought he'd zip over to the Valley every other week and hang out with Evelyn and Edmond. We would be the cities of his life. But when it came to falling in love he'd be a gypsy. Hi ho for the open road. That was his theory. Even I could see that it wouldn't work, that he was whistling in the dark, that he was just getting over Mom and trying to feel as free and easy as Fiona zooming in and zooming out. What he wasn't figuring was that his job was what gave him a life and took up most of his life. And he wasn't figuring that, after he was fifty and then fifty-five, he didn't have as much energy. It was hard for him to see that. He could work harder than ever, he still walked to work, he still went to Ezra's gym three times a week. All his *habits* were still there. He just didn't have energy to spare. Whenever he felt out of gas, he chalked it up to Fiona breaking his heart. He managed to ignore all the little things running down. Having to get reading glasses, having to get bridgework for his teeth, going a little deaf, going a little bald. One time he said to Fiona, 'I sometimes worry that our feelings are too physical.' Before she could stop herself she laughed. And then made it worse by saying, 'I'm sorry, I'm sorry,' and clapping her hands over her mouth to keep from laughing."

"That cold bitch," I said. But I also felt some satisfaction that Dad got his just deserts.

"I know what you mean," Nora said. "But wait. It wasn't easy for her. He came into her life so early, and she really cared for him. It made it hard for her to feel free. She *acted* free, but Dad was part of her life. You can think of her as spoiled—roaming the world and at the same time having this geezer who's so sweet on her that she can bring him round whenever she feels like it. But having an arrangement like that hobbled her. Almost everyone who has an unconventional life gets caught between not being able to give it up and wishing she could just start over normally. And then Fiona turned thirty and then thirty-five. Dad had already had a family, and he had a career and he had a hometown and a home. What Fiona had was a lot of free-lancing around the world and an old geezer and a place to stay. Half a home. Because she came and went, she kept him dazzled, but his being dazzled kept her dazzled too. But dazzle is only half of love, so she only got half of that too."

I said, "But Dad only had half of *her*."

"Yes. But the other half of *his* life was more settled and satisfying. I'm not trying to stick up for her—I'm just trying to . . ."

I said, "Well, you're not exactly lighting it for comedy."

Nora ignored me. She said, "Dad misses talking to her. She didn't let him get away with anything. She used to say, 'Do you *know* that or are you just *formulating*?'"

I said, "I hope she told him he had a good sense of history."

"I know," Nora said. "I know, I know. Where does she get off having that power? I was jealous too."

"Is it about sex? Is it just because he gets to squeeze between her stumpy legs? All right, all right—her amazingly muscular mountain-climbing legs. And then he fucking *worships* her? And she gets to torture him or thrill him, whichever she feels like. And he dumps Dr. Ames, who is a goddamn saint compared to that . . . to that . . . to that mountain goat!"

"Okay, okay," Nora said. "Maybe I came around about it like this—remember how Dad was when you were in high school and we all thought Dad didn't want boys to come near you and he'd go around muttering about what louts boys are, but it turned out he was mad because they *weren't* calling you—"

"I had dates."

"—weren't calling you *more*."

That little bit of balm made me laugh. Nora said, "So eventually I was grateful that Fiona made Dad eat his vegetables and cut down on fat and take long hikes. And she saved him from the occupational hazard of lawyers."

"Saying 'A' and 'B' all the time?"

"Thinking in X-rays."

I said, "*You* could've kept him from doing that."

Nora sighed. She said, "Sure. Maybe. But not until I was grown-up. I mean not until Dad thought I was grown-up. Which was a long time after Dr. Ames stuttered at me."

"So now he listens to you?"

"He'd listen to you too . . . although maybe you should start out dealing with small things. You and Dad always get into fights about the way the world should work."

I said, "So I should stay off major issues and just tell him what color tie to wear?"

Nora let that go by.

"Okay," I said, "but he starts it."

Nora laughed.

"Let me rephrase that," I said. "When Dad and I disagree, I can hear in his voice that he's putting on his judicial robes."

"Tell him," Nora said. "Tease him about it. He told me once that one of the happiest times of his life was when he was driving you and me to Grandma's—I think we were twelve and fourteen—and we didn't fight with each other the whole way. We teased him instead. We ganged up on him and teased him about how he'd go to the general store and smoke a corncob pipe instead of a cigar and try to be folksy. You pretended to be Dad puffing away—you said, 'I reckon you're aiming to just go set a spell with the old-timers.' And Dad laughed. Do you remember? He was laughing the whole way from Fredericksburg to Kinsale. He even forgot to tell us anything about the Civil War."

"I remember," I said. "Actually it began before Fredericksburg, somewhere around the Wilderness."

"That's right, the Wilderness," Nora said. "We must have been funny."

Oklahoma looked like Texas. I didn't mind. The light was softer now that the sun was sliding down behind us. I didn't know if Nora was managing me or if I was simply relieved to feel her heft the past with such strength and good cheer.

We stopped for supper while we were still in Oklahoma. Another waitress recognized Nora. But this time it wasn't for her soap character but for a small movie part as a televangelist. Nora was very pleased. The waitress said, "I thought that was your real voice in that movie, but now I hear you, I'm just amazed. Do you think you could talk like that lady preacher for me? Just a word or two?"

Nora said, "We're driving from California and we're real tired." Nora was halfway into character.

"Of course you are, honey."

Nora intoned, "When you are aching and empty"—she took the waitress by the hand—"fill yourself, my child, fill your whole being with the Holy Spirit." And then she gave a little moan.

The waitress stared at Nora. I thought the waitress might be embarrassed, but I was projecting. "That is just scary," the waitress said. "You could do that for real and no one would know."

Nora smiled and said, "Thank you."

How nice and even Nora can be. I think these easy little exchanges, at least with her women admirers, steady her.

My turn to drive. Nora said, "Could you tell that was a little bit of Bonnie Two? The way my character was written, she was kind of a crude caricature of a hypocrite. A made-for-TV Tartuffe. I thought it would be better if she had her genuine moments, so I went to one of Bonnie Two's revival meetings."

"Bonnie Two was genuine?"

"Oh yes. She loves to love. She wavers and changes, and for her a wisp of a feeling is a belief, but she genuinely wants to be filled with love, and she had such bad luck with men that she was ready to try the Holy Spirit."

Nora insisted on driving late into the night, so when we finally went to bed in a motel we would sleep in till eleven and eat a leisurely breakfast, and then the sun wouldn't be in our eyes. This struck me as Dad-like, not so much for the idea itself but for the earnest attention to planning, as if our driving along the interstate in this air-conditioned, cruise-controlled jumbo car with a stereo CD player and a makeup mirror was somehow like sailing across the Atlantic in an open Viking boat with Leif the Lucky—we had to keep a sharp lookout or we'd miss Greenland.

But my giving in to Nora put her in a good mood the next morning. I let her talk me into doing her exercise routine with her first thing out of bed—twenty minutes of prancing and writhing around to an Annie Lennox oldie—"You've Got to Keep Young and Beautiful, If You Want to Be Loved"—and then twenty minutes of paddling around in the motel pool to the ogling of three teenage boys who couldn't take their eyes off Nora as she breast-stroked and back-stroked to and fro in her silver lamé swimsuit. When Nora was done, she climbed the ladder into their midst and said in her Mae West voice, "Hello there, boys." The boys looked at each other, then back at Nora for a blink, then away. Nora said, "You want to watch out how you stare, boys—you're liable to sunburn your eyeballs."

A wrinkly old guy sitting under an umbrella clapped his hands twice and said, "Mae West. I thought nobody remembered Mae West. How come you know how to do Mae West?"

Nora rolled her shoulder and said, "I learned it at my daddy's knee . . . and other low joints."

The old guy said, "Whoo-ee," and wanted to say more, but we slipped on by.

"That's Dad's joke," I said.

"It's Dad's father's," Nora said.

"Why is it," I said, "that in this ancestor worship we're stuck with you get to remember the corny jokes and I get the 1924 Democratic Convention?"

After breakfast Nora made me drive, because she wanted to make an audiovisual presentation. "You think it's just corny jokes?" she said and pulled out a folder.

She said, "This is what Mom was reading aloud on the radio when Dad didn't recognize her voice. It's not by her, it's from a nineteenth-century woman's diary. It's about living alone in middle age.

> "I have suffered for the whole winter a sort of mental paralysis, and at times I have feared the disease extended to my affections. It is difficult for one who began life as I did, the primary object of affection to many, to come by degrees to be first to none, and still to have my love remain in its entire strength, and craving such returns as have no substitute."

I said, "Whoever she is, she's asking for the moon."

"It's not about asking. It's what she felt, and the reason Mom picked it to read is because she felt that way too. That was when Bonnie One moved away when she didn't get tenure, and she and Mom sort of broke up, and Mom stayed in town so she could be with us even though we were in high school and getting ready to light out on our own."

"All right," I said. "It is sad. I'm abashed. Why are you abashing me?" I thought I sounded lighthearted.

Nora said, "Because you're a hard-ass puritan. You believe in work and love, and that's okay, but you want people to work at work that has no corruption in it and you want people to love with love that has no corruption in it. . . ."

I said carefully, "I've been understanding about Mom, I've been sympathetic to Mom. I wouldn't say I'm a puritan about people's loves. And not about yours either. And not about anybody's work."

"Even if you don't say anything, you're a living reproach. You're always doing something good—you teach, you make house calls to your poor students. Even your boyfriends are always doing good. And the way you were understanding about Mom and Bonnie One was good—"

"Don't you dare say I was being politically correct."

Nora said even louder than me, "Don't you dare say that that's what I'm saying." She took a breath and said in a much lower voice, "I'm just worried that you're being too good. That you're too concerned about fucking up—not just your fucking up but other people's. You think people wanting the wrong things makes them unclean. And when you think that, it makes you draw back. And when you draw back like that, it makes people afraid of your judgment."

"I'm not a puritan. You're really exaggerating when you call me a puritan. It's mean." Nora settled back in her seat and sighed. I said, "Who are we really talking about here? Is it you and me, or is it Dad and me? If you're afraid of my puny little judgment, then I'm sorry. I don't think you're perfect, but I don't sit around condemning you. Or even the times you fuck up. On the whole I'm thinking of the good things about you. I'd say something nicer but I'm pissed off. If you could hear the things I've been thinking about you lately, you'd feel terrible." Nora laughed. I didn't. I said, "You know what I mean. You'd be the one feeling abashed."

Nora wasn't a bit abashed. She said, "Well, you're hard to please. You want people to be as good as they imagine they are. Don't make the mistake Mom made about Dad—she thought she either had to believe his version of himself or blow it up. Let people have a few little vanities, a few follies."

I said, "I don't want it to be that easy."

Nora said, "I'm just making it *sound* easy. You always think I'm being shallow when I'm just being cheerful."

I didn't answer her. After a while I told Nora that of course I don't think she's shallow, that I can tell when she's being funny and offhand. But all the way across the rest of Arkansas I wondered if I'd been too desperately disappointed in Dad. Maybe it's because I'm afraid, if I give up my disappointment, then I'll have to give up the blind absolute love I once felt.

Crossing the Mississippi, I thought it was odd that of the two of us it had been Nora who had first felt that it is terrible that everyone dies. I remember Evelyn carrying small frantic Nora back to our house, cooing at her and kissing her forehead. Nora wasn't crying. She was in a rage. I knew the same fact she knew, but it was in the large clutter of grown-up facts that I had quickly absorbed and about which I'd had no immediate passionate reaction. I envied her ferocity (and Evelyn's attention), but I also could take pleasure in feeling above her tantrums when they weren't aimed at me. I still can't judge whether she was a precocious genius, taking after Mom in her talent for restating the obvious ("You mean I'll die and then I won't be here!"), or whether she was having a six-year-old howl on the order of her other six-year-old howls. It doesn't matter. She got it right.

I thought about Grandma.

I feel the same way about seeing Grandma as I do about coming back to Virginia, into the Great Valley from Tennessee, seeing the first of the Blue Ridge Mountains that I can name, the first towns that I've actually been in (Nora will be better at this when we get up into the old Thirteenth Congressional District). I'll be thrilled and weepy, but I'm afraid that coming back won't reach as deep into me as I wish. And I'm afraid that it will.

The next time Nora was in the passenger seat, she brought out her folder of papers. I asked, "Have you been planning this Dad reconstruction for a long time?"

Nora gave a single laugh that turned into a "hmm." Then she said, "Reconstruction? It's not a reconstruction in the sense of a vindication. It's just reconstruction."

I said, "Of course it could end up being reconstruction in the sense of what the Yankees did to the South after the Civil War."

"You're certainly the one with a sense of history."

"But are you trying to get me to get along better with Dad?"

"Not really," Nora said. "I'm just thinking out loud. Here's part of a poem Fiona copied out and sent to Dad." Nora pulled out an index card and read aloud.

> *"I do not pity the old men, fumbling after*
> *The golden bird of love, the purple grapes of laughter;*
> *They drank honey once, they fingered the falcon's hood.*
> *I do not pity the old, with ash in their veins for blood.*
> *It is the young whom I pity, the young who are lovely and cruel,*
> *The young whose lips and limbs are time's quick-colored fuel."*

It took me a while to be able to say anything. "Cruel," I said finally. "And fucking arrogant. Who says she's the golden bird of love? Who says she's lovely? Where does she get off writing that?"

"She didn't write it," Nora said. "She found it and copied it onto a postcard."

For an instant I saw Fiona as Nora wanted me to—afflicted by Dad, packed into a corner, feeling half kept in the bungalow that was only half a house of her own, feeling her freedom half haunted by being half attached to Dad.

I said, "Did she really mean it?"

"I'm not sure. Part of Dad's lament for himself about Fiona was that she would be horrible one day and a sweetheart the next. I heard more about the horriblenesses, because horriblenesses are more quotable. And she enjoyed being drastic. Dad told me that she said to him, 'If I moved in with you, then I'd have to care for you during your terminal illness.' But when he told me this, he laughed. I think he was saying that it was a joke as well as a smack in the mouth. . . . He didn't want me to feel sorry for him. He wanted me to say, 'Wow! You guys sure play rough.' The thing that bothered him more was that she'd send him photos of herself on top of a mountain in New Zealand or skinny-dipping under a waterfall on some South Sea island. And of course he'd wonder—who took the picture?"

Now we were in Virginia, on a long swooping curve into a river valley, and I was sympathizing—if not with Dad at least with Nora's sympathy for him.

I said, "Did they ever think of getting married?"

"Yes. But whenever one thought of it, the other didn't. Fiona wasn't sure, and Dad still had a Catholic hangover about divorce. He told me that at one point he looked into an annulment. Apparently it's pretty easy when it's a case of one spouse taking off with a same-sex lover. There are lots of cases like that, and with a little metaphysics you show that the gay spouse couldn't have taken the marriage vows with a complete assent of her will, and—presto!—the marriage vanishes."

"So what kept Dad from doing that? Would it have made us bastards?"

"No, it wouldn't. Don't ask me how that works." Nora breathed out through her nose. "Dad said that, when it came right down to it, one of the few things he's sure of is that he and Mom were really married."

"So, if he doesn't go for that hocus-pocus about annulment, why doesn't he check the rest of his medieval boyhood?"

"I don't know."

"Maybe it's a convenient way to stay a bachelor."

"Could be a little of that," Nora said agreeably. "But from time to time he's tried to clarify himself, maybe even purify himself. It never quite works, but he does wrestle with himself. That little struggle with the annulment question may have been one of the few he won. But here's one he never got on top of. He tried giving up being attracted to women. Complete asceticism. He did the whole bit—cold showers, more exercise, no red meat or spicy food. He avoided going to movies or watching TV—too many babes. He tried to have a social life just with men."

"And?"

"It caved in like his igloo."

"Fiona showed up?"

"No. When he was trying this she was away for six months. I saw him just before the cave-in. He came to New York. I didn't know what he'd been putting himself through. I showed him around the studio, and then we went out for dinner. I sensed that there was something odd going on. I should have picked it up on the set, but halfway through dinner—we were at a restaurant in midtown—I realized what it was. He wasn't looking at women."

"Dad?"

"I finally got it because this fairly attractive woman walked by our table and Dad actually averted his eyes. He must have caught a glimpse—and he certainly got a whiff of her perfume. He turned his head away until she was gone and then did alternate-nostril breathing and then a cleansing breath."

I laughed, and Nora started laughing too.

"I know," she said. "But he was trying."

Nora was distracted by the sight of a Howard Johnson's. She had a craving for a club sandwich that kept her busy nagging me about how to get on the off-ramp and under the overpass. It wasn't until after lunch (during which no one recognized her), when she had started driving, that I asked her what Dad tried after that.

Nora said, "'Tried' isn't the right word. I can tell you one thing that happened without his trying—and it explains why Fiona kept showing up. Sometime in his fifties Dad got nicer. I don't mean charming. I mean . . . You know that old Mr. Broome and Dad became friends? Here's what Dad said about him at his funeral. Dad said, 'He was active in politics in the best way—in fact he was active in life in the best way—he gave up the anxiety of ambition without giving up any of his enthusiasm.'"

I was touched. I knew that Mom had been sad when courtly old Mr. Broome died. I think she was the one who pinned that tag on him. And then I was reminded of Dad at Bundy's funeral. I think I may have been afraid of being more than touched—afraid of being pierced—so I said, "Dad can be very nice to his dead men friends."

Nora gasped. And then I felt her make one of her swoops of intuition. She didn't say anything back.

After a while she said mildly, "Dad has women friends. There's Ganny, there's Evelyn. Ganny's in Washington for now, but he still sees her. It's a shame Evelyn and Ganny aren't in Charlottesville—they might have introduced him to some women as nice as them. Have you ever figured out why it is men are so bad at finding nice women for their men friends? Most of the time they just *don't*." Nora laughed. "Ganny would have stopped him from going out with Charlotte Fenton."

"Wait. You should remember that the subject of Charlotte Fenton and Bosie—"

"I don't think anything came of it. They were both in Richmond on a governor's committee, something to do with prison reform. Dad was the token liberal, and Charlotte Fenton and he argued all day, and then she asked him to have dinner with her. I think it was fascination with the enemy. The political scene in Richmond is a fishbowl, and they may have liked the idea of being seen arm in arm—a little comic shock-effect."

"The problem I'm having with your lighting all these news flashes for comedy is that I haven't had time . . . I mean, you must have spent a while arranging all this so that it doesn't horrify you. I keep falling out of your sprightly narratives into stuff like—this is the Dad who was telling us to snap our wrists when we throw a baseball, to leave our campsite cleaner than we found it, and in his late middle age he was another American male with no second act. I think it's terrible he never managed to have a wholehearted . . . a whole mature relationship with a whole mature woman."

Nora said, "He's wholehearted with us, he's wholehearted with friends, and he's wholehearted with his work."

"I know you're being open-minded and fair. Well, good for you."

Nora drove for a while without saying anything. A couple of times she took a breath as if she was about to speak. She looked over at me once, but not for long. She knows I don't like it when she takes her eyes off the road.

"Okay," Nora said. "Okay. You can smell out every bit of corruption and then what? So you've got the goods on him. So? So you've still got to decide whether you love him or not."

"Of course I love him. And I can be disapproving. And I can be angry. Don't try to tell me whether I love him or not."

Another few miles in silence. We went down to cross another river. When we came up again there was a long line of mimosa trees in the median strip, all in bloom. They remind me of crested cranes with their frilly plumes.

"Anyway," I said. "You seem to be the one reducing him to a buffoon with all these reports of yours."

"That's not what I'm doing. I'm—"

"Then what *are* you doing? Are you tearing him down or sticking up for him?"

"Yes," Nora said.

"Yes what?"

"Yes both." Nora breathed out through her nose. "And, besides, I'm getting tired of being the only one who knows this stuff. I want you to get used to the way he is now. Not just that his beard is gray and his hair is white and when he gets up in the morning his face looks like a wrinkled sheet. . . . I mean everything. All the ups and downs. Look, if I visit him by myself, I have to be nice. If you're with me, one of us can be nice and the other can tell him he's a silly old coot who ought to sneck up."

"Sneck up?"

"It's from *Twelfth Night*. I think it means 'get your shit together.'"

It was clever of Nora not to oppose my little rush at her with her full weight but, rather, to make me join hands with her and to twirl me around in her dance: be nice to the graybeard, then call him an old coot.

And there was something else. I once told my brightest student about plot. First I made fun of her infatuation with Hollywood high-concept plots—nothing more than assaults on our nervous systems, and most of the characters nothing more than test-crash dummies. I told her that the proper use of a plot is to apply pressure to a fully human character until she cracks open, and we get a savor of her inmost psyche. When I said this I surprised myself. What I had in the back of my mind was a clear memory of Dad and me gathering kindling. I was four. Dad picked up a stick of red cedar, which looked more or less like all the other sticks. He broke it on his knee and showed me the inner vein of red. He held it up to my nose. I had no words for how it smelled—better than Mom's brown bread in the oven, better than Dad's cigars, which I liked, more piercing than our balsam Christmas wreath, more wonderfully bitter than Dad's roses, and, best of all, many different notions all in one breath.

I found this sort of surprising pleasure again in certain stories and poems when some piece of business would break the plain brown stick of words open to the inner red.

I hoped that Nora was trying to do this for me, that she was telling me all these things so that one of them might break open the thick old stick, and, underneath the knots and fungus, the gray old wood, she would show me that Dad's fumblings, obsessions, blindnesses, and disgraces were all absorbed and filtered into one red center.

Nora said, "Dad's going to be at Grandma's. He still goes to see her pretty regularly. But this is the first time he'll be there when Mom's there. I hope Grandma doesn't get confused. She's been drifting into the past lately. When she comes back to the present, she makes fun of herself, she says, 'Have I been gone long?' and laughs, but you can tell it upsets her."

"I know," I said. "I saw her last year."

"Well, she does it more now. And it takes her longer to focus on who you are."

"I know," I said. "I talk to her on the phone."

"Really? She has a really hard time on the phone. Maybe not every time."

"No," I said. "Not every time."

"But she was really sharp when Mom and I took her to Washington to the National Gallery."

"I know," I said. "Mom told me about it." I couldn't help adding, "And she told me about your producer's stretch limo."

"Look," Nora said. "It was just sitting around in Washington while the producer went back to L.A. Those guys love to do good deeds. And Grandma loved it. The way you say 'your producer's stretch limo,' you make it sound like I was exposing Grandma to some Hollywood sleaze virus, like there were ghosts of socially unacceptable people crowding her off the backseat."

I said, "Did I say that?" but it was feeble. Nora and I were speeding on too much coffee, interstate hypnosis, and going home. Our glassed-in time-and-space module was filling with combustible vapors.

Nora said, "I can hear your tone."

I said, "Okay, you did a good deed. Okay, I had a possessive pang about Grandma. I should be happy Grandma had a good time. And I should rejoice in my sister's good fortune."

Nora sighed.

"Okay," I said. "So I can't help being a little too arch."

"It's not that," Nora said. "It's that I can't remember when Dad first said, 'Rejoice in your sister's good fortune.' I remember his *quoting* himself saying it. And we all seem to know he said it once and meant it, but I can't remember when. And then I wondered where all that family vocabulary will end up. Probably the same place where good stage performances go."

We didn't talk as we stopped heading north and turned east—across the rising edge of the Valley for a bit and then a sharp climb into the gap through the Blue Ridge. We looked down toward Charlottesville twenty miles away, held still in the summer afternoon that poured over the mountain.

My heart clenched as it hadn't before, perhaps because I'd been fearing that I wouldn't feel enough, perhaps because we were dazed from four days on the road, perhaps because Nora had been kneading me, letting me rise, punching me down, letting me rise. There was enough.

◇

Nora didn't say anything until we were down the mountain. My ears popped. I laughed at myself for remembering a corn-dog oldie from my Charlottesville years—"High on a Mountain of Love." I already knew that the bliss part of anything is a bubble. If something else stays longer, you're lucky.

We rolled up and down the foothills, and Nora thought out loud about whether we should stop in Charlottesville, drop off the drive-away and rent a cheapie, or push on—which meant one of us would have to drive the drive-away back from Grandma's to Charlottesville. Then Nora said decisively, "We can get to Grandma's before supper. We're allowed four more days on the drive-away. I'll bring it back. I have to see some people in Charlottesville."

That was fine with me. I might get another shot at my sense of the volume of our lives at Grandma's.

We retraced our old summer-at-Grandma's route—in less than an hour we were passing the battlefields from Wilderness to Fredericksburg, onto the Northern Neck, past the signs to the birthplaces of George Washington and Robert E. Lee—all the drowsy heat-bleached detours of Dad's wishing us to have a sense of history.

Just past Stratford Hall, the Lee home place, I remembered one of Nora's wilder defiances. I said to Nora, "Was it Stratford Hall where you said, 'Dad, get a clue. I don't care about anything that happened before I was born'?"

Even in profile Nora's face showed lightning flashes. She stopped the car on the shoulder and started several different sentences. "That is . . . Why do you remember . . . You're as bad as . . . You and Dad have goddamn tape recorders for brains. You remember stuff ruthlessly. You remember stuff and don't care what, so long as you can give yourself a gold star for memory. I think it's a terrible thing to remember that all these years. Here. You drive."

"No," I said. "It was good. You were great. It was a great thing to say."

"So what did *you* say, Miss Charlottesville High School History Prize? You probably named all the presidents."

"I didn't say anything. You were right. It was funny."

"I remember it, and it wasn't funny. I *hated* being the one who didn't know stuff. I said what I said because I was hating myself. I wasn't being funny. And I missed Mom, who would have stuck up for me. And it was too weird that Dad was still going to Grandma's."

I said, "Dad and Grandma always liked each other."

"Yeah, fine. Now I know. But back then I thought it was another act, like putting out milk and cookies for Santa Claus, another act to make us think we were a functional family. You think you were the one who took it all harder! You think it was easy for me because I got to have outbursts!" Nora flung her arms open. Her left hand was stopped short by the closed window. She looked at it. She turned and looked at me over her right hand and said, "You probably think I'm being funny now."

Nora's timing was too precise. I squinted and squeezed my mouth shut not to laugh, but my head looked as if I were holding in a sneeze. Nora said, "Don't you dare laugh!"

I bit the inside of my cheek.

Nora said, "I don't laugh at you."

"We're fifteen miles from going coast to coast. Let's not fight now."

"We're not having a fight. We won't have a fight if you don't laugh. I don't laugh at your little strangenesses. Like that thing with your eyes." Just the way she used to when she was a furious seven-year-old, she pointed the fingers of both hands at my eyes. I drew back. Nora wiggled her fingers and said "Booga booga booga!" I laughed. Nora fluffed her hair up and said "Booga booga booga!" again. I couldn't stop. I said, "Don't. I'm going to pee. Say something to make me stop."

Nora said, "Really? You really want me to?"

"Yes."

Nora said, "Maybe we should be serious. We're about there."

I stopped laughing. I said, "I really do have to pee." I got out and went behind a bush. When I got back in Nora said, "That reminds me. One of the things Dad told me about Fiona was that, when they used to go hiking and they'd stop to pee, she could take two steps off the trail, pee, and be back hiking before he was done."

"Are you telling me that to stop me laughing? I don't want to know—"

"No," Nora said. "I meant to tell you something else before but I was afraid you'd think I was making it too pathetic and I didn't think you were ready to—"

"What?" I said. "Just say it."

"Fiona got married to some New Zealander."

"Dad's better off," I said.

"Maybe. I guess they always knew it was impossible. But she was certainly in love with him, and he may still be in love with her. It was on-again-off-again for so long." Nora sighed. "Have you ever thought how strange some of this is? Dad said in one of his campaign speeches that Fenton wasn't a bad old guy, why not make him a judge? And bingo, Dad's a judge. And Dad barely got over Mom dumping him and he could have ended up with any one of a number of perfectly nice women who were eager to settle down, but he fell for Fiona and he must have known she'd be in a permanent state of infidelity. . . ."

"Well, so was he."

"Yeah. But I think he wasn't as tough as she was. Whenever she left he had to take a Xanax to get to sleep."

I said, "How do you know that?"

"I found the pills and I was worried he was getting a habit. He said, 'No. I only take one whenever Fiona goes away. If she's gone for more than three months and I have an intuition she's with someone, I allow myself one more.'"

"So what did he do when he found out she was gone for good?"

"He'd given up Xanax by then, if that's what you're worried about."

"No," I said. "That's not what I'm worried about. I can feel sorry for him. . . . When did she get married?"

"Last winter. He was stoic about it, but I think that's what turned his hair white."

I said, "Don't exaggerate." As soon as I said that I regretted it. Nora shrugged and started the car. I said, "I just meant that a few years ago he already had gray hair."

Nora said, "Maybe you're cross about Dad with Fiona because he wouldn't stop getting hurt. It got to me too. I'd feel pity for him and then I'd get mad at her for getting so much of his attention by hurting him and then healing him, and then I'd get mad at *him* for making me feel that pity on account of Fiona, who was Dad's choice in the first place."

That was a good offer on Nora's part. How could I refuse her breathless swirl of anger and sympathy, into which she welcomed me? It was volume in its own way—not the large vision of it I'd had for an instant from the Blue Ridge, but elbow room for the two of us.

It made it easier for us to come to Grandma's together. Nora slowed down when we made the turn from the hardtop onto Grandma's oyster-shell driveway. I saw the raspberry bushes, the mint, the daylilies. There was a jumble of cars parked like thorns along the turnaround. A small boy ran around the corner of the house. A woman came after him with long stooped strides and lifted him onto her hip.

"Who are they?" I said.

"She's the wife of one of the big cousins. All three of them are married."

The woman saw our car, shielded her eyes, and then waved her hand, not a welcome, just "Ahoy there."

Nora pulled up just before the *porte cochère.* The woman came to Nora's window, lit up with recognition, and said, "Nora!"

I guessed she recognized Nora from Nora's soap, but maybe Nora had gone to her wedding and was in her album.

"We're here for Grandma's birthday party. We can just go on in, right? I mean it's not a surprise party, is it?"

The woman said, "Everything's likely to be a surprise for her." I hated her quicker than she could apologize. "Oh God," she said. "That just came out wrong. . . . You must be Edith." She jounced her son higher on her hip and said, "This is Jeremy. Say hello to your big cousins, Jeremy."

I said, "A big cousin is who you married. We're still the little cousins." I looked at Jeremy, who was staring at Nora's rings. "So, Jeremy, that makes you another big boy cousin."

"And I'm Belle," the woman said.

"Of course," Nora said. Nora turned to me. "Belle married John. Antoinette married Christopher. Mimi married Tom. And they all have children, but I can't do them." She turned back. "Except you, Jeremy." She wiggled Jeremy's small foot. "You're a handsome devil, Jeremy."

I said, "Let's go find Grandma."

Belle leaned down more to look at me. I realized how tall she was, which, along with how pretty she looked in her pretty green dress, was annoying. But then I figured that she was taller than John, the shortest and youngest of the big cousins. I've always admired tall women who marry short men, so that was in her favor. Belle said, "She's resting up for supper. Your mother's around somewhere. Your father's out in a boat with John. I guess your mother'll know what room you're in."

We found Mom in the kitchen. She shook off her cooking mitten, spread her arms, and folded us in, crooning our pet names. She was making supper along with a cook, whom we didn't know, and a teenage girl, who was the oldest of the new batch of cousins.

Mom said, "I'm sorry, pooches, you don't have your old room. We're packed tight. You can go up on the third floor with the two babysitters; it's a little hot, but you two have the corner room with four windows. Your father's camping out in the boathouse, so I suppose you could go there too if you'd like."

I'd wanted to be eleven again, but that room was taken. I was glad Mom was cooking. It helped splice in our strand. The hired cook was a lean young guy with a blue stud in his ear, maybe a sapphire. He'd come down from Washington with Mom and Bonnie One. When Mom introduced us, he said to Nora, "I love your work," in a way that made Nora smile with professional courtesy and ask if he was an actor too. He said, "Yes, but I've still got my day job," and flourished the whisk he was holding.

Nora and I went up to the third floor. One of the babysitters was in the shower, so Nora and I decided to go for a swim in the salt creek. Nora knocked on the bathroom door as we left and said, "There's four of us up here now, so save some hot water, okay?"

We floated on our backs and watched the gang of kids playing on the lawn. Uncle Jonathan was there with assorted grand-nephews. His son, the biggest of the big cousins, was the father of the teenage girl in the kitchen. She was as tall as me.

Nora had started out swimming seriously. She'd breast-stroked down the creek to the boathouse, her head high to keep her hair dry. When she got back she said, "To hell with that," ducked under, and floated on her back beside me. I was glad she was sticking with me. After four days on the road you might think we'd had enough of each other, but I wanted her by me. For a moment I thought it might be that there were so many swooping females who weren't kin but who'd birthed their way here. And then so many of the blood relatives were boys, dragon's-teeth replacements to the boisterous big cousins.

In time I'd come to love some of them, but I was trying to keep my balance in the precarious present.

Nora saw the boat first. She waved and Dad waved back. He stood up, portly and gray, wearing baggy red swim trunks. He spoke to Cousin John, who steered the boat into the mouth of the salt creek. Dad let the sail down and then pulled one of the small boys from under it. The other boy held up a fish and yelled at the gang on the lawn. Dad clambered onto the boathouse wharf and came galumphing up the bank of the creek. When he got near Nora and me he sat down and slid into the chest-high water. He shoved his eyeglasses back into place, took two steps, and hugged us both, just the way Mom had. However, his first words were, "Wait a second, my feet are stuck in the mud." He turned around, grabbed the edge of the bank, and pulled himself up a little. Even the back of his hair was white. He could have been Santa Claus trying to go back up the chimney. He lowered himself into the water again, this time careful to float. Then, deliberately, as if overcoming a shyness, he reached out and held my hand. He could only hold it for a second, since we needed both hands to keep our feet off the muddy bottom.

The small cousin with the fish started up the lawn from the boathouse. "Ask him to hold up his fish," Dad said. "Tell him what a big fish he caught."

Nora laughed and said, "Are you running for office here, Dad? Trying to get the kid's vote for uncle?"

"No, *you* say it. Come on, Nora. It's a big deal for the kid."

"What's his name?"

Dad said, "That's Christopher Junior. He's called Toph."

Nora called Toph over, and we all admired his fish, which was as long as the boy's arm. Nora said, "What is it?"

Toph said, "Judge Reardon says it's a rockfish."

"He's our dad," Nora said. That didn't appear to interest Toph. Nora said, "And *your* dad is our cousin."

Toph, who'd been holding the fish up high, lowered it so the tail bent on the ground. He said to Dad, "Uncle John says I should get you to clean it."

"All right. Go show it to your mother and then bring it back to the boathouse. Bring a piece of string, and we'll catch a crab with the guts." Toph left, dragging the fish. Dad said to us, "You come too. We'll have a beer on the dock before supper. There's still time before the mosquitoes come out."

Nora said she had to dry her hair. I went with Dad. He got two beers from a plastic cooler just inside the small door, and we sat on the edge of the dock, just keeping our feet and ankles wet. He looked across the dazzling water for a while. One of the nice things about being on this side of the Neck was that the sun set across the Rappahannock, a wide estuary this far down. I said, "So you're teaching the next generation the basic principles of seamanship."

Still looking out across the water, he said, "Your uncles and your mother will probably have to sell this place."

"Why?"

"Your uncle Jonathan can give you the details. Among other things they'll need the money to take care of your grandmother. Pretty soon she'll need round-the-clock nurses."

"What if we all chipped in? All three of the big cousins and Nora and me. And you. And Mom and Bonnie One. And don't some of the big cousins' wives work? They could do something. They have full-time babysitters and that fleet of cars out there. . . ."

Dad said, "You'll have a chance to talk to Jonathan."

"I could come stay with Grandma."

Dad moved closer to me and put his hand on my shoulder. He cleared his throat but didn't say anything.

Toph stepped onto the dock with his fish. Dad got a knife, a spoon, and a crab net from the boathouse. He slit the fish up the belly and pointed out the stomach and the heart to Toph. He showed Toph how to rub the edge of the spoon on the fish to scale it. He rigged a crab line, tying the string around the stomach and guts, and lowered them into the water. He gave Toph the end of the line. He finished scaling the fish, stuck it in the water, and washed it. He said, "It is wonderful here. . . . Look, he's got something. Can you get a pail, something to put a crab in?"

When I came back, I said, "You could buy the boathouse. And the boat. You always loved the boat."

"Slowly," Dad said to Toph, "very slowly pull it in." He said to me, "You remember how to come up from underneath with the net? I think he's got two of them on. Make sure you get the big one."

I said, "Maybe you should do it."

"You used to love this. Quick. They're tearing the bait off."

I slid the net way under the crabs and lifted it.

"Look at that, Toph," Dad said. "Your aunt Edith hasn't lost her touch. See if you can get 'em loose from the net and into the pail. If you grab him right there, he can't—"

"I know," Toph said. "My dad showed me."

"And guess who showed him," Dad said.

Toph put the crabs in the pail and started back to the house.

"Dad," I said. "Stop owning everything." Dad lifted his eyebrows. "I'm sorry," I said, "but you're getting into your Barnacle Bill routine."

"Okay."

"And I'm not his aunt. I'm some sort of cousin. I don't even know these kids."

"First cousin once removed."

"Whatever. It's pretty abstract."

Dad said, "You'll be seeing more of them. Your two uncles will have the big family parties. They're crazy about you and Nora. If you come back east . . ."

"I don't think this is going to help, Dad. I don't want the long view."

"Okay."

I was about to be nice to him when something else occurred to me. I said, "Wait. Are they selling because something's wrong with Grandma? You should have told me that first. If they're selling to get some legal deal done before Grandma . . ."

"No. There's nothing wrong. Nothing you don't know. Your grandmother's very old. . . . Look, your uncles—her sons—love her. They care about her, they care about everything you care about. Your grandmother kept this place going for a long time."

"You keep saying 'uncles.' Isn't Mom part of this? Or is it that everything to do with more money than a grocery bill is men's work?"

"Your uncle Jonathan has your grandmother's power of attorney, so he's doing a lot of the paperwork, but he doesn't do anything without consulting your mother. And he talked to your grandmother some time ago. . . . Look. Talk to your mother about it. And talk to Jonathan." He said this carefully enough so that I was about to say I was sorry, but he added, "Be sure you let him lay it all out before you start your questioning."

I said, "Don't worry. I'll be a good little girl."

"Okay," Dad said. "Let's not . . ." He sighed. "I love this place too." He was quiet for a while. He said, "Your grandmother . . ." He squeezed his mouth shut and pressed his knuckles into his cheeks. His back and shoulders rose and fell once. I'd forgotten how big he was, still large-muscled under his loosening skin. Then, like a little boy, he wiped his nose with the back of his hand. He leaned over and scooped a handful of water onto his face.

He said, "Your grandmother's been asking for you. I know she'd like to see you alone. You and Nora. Separately, I mean. You might speak to the nurse after supper. She's more or less keeping track of your grandmother's energy."

"You've been coming here all along, haven't you?"

"Once or twice a year. Your mother's fine about it. She liked my bringing you here. Then she wasn't crazy about my coming by myself. Then she liked it. She liked my taking care of the boat. It took two or three days to put the boat in and a day in the fall to take her out. It's nice sailing here in the fall."

"Did you bring your girlfriend?" I said this without any hardness.

Dad stirred the water with his foot. He said, "A long time ago." When he said, "It's nice sailing here in fall," I'd seen the two of them in the boat, eager-faced and bright-skinned in the wind and so proud of themselves. There is that about being in love—those few days you feel that it is an adventure for heroes and that you are heroic.

Now he stirred the water with his foot again and stayed quiet. The sun, touching the horizon, grew wider at the bottom and showed a streak of red, the color under your fingertips when you pull loose a section of blood orange.

Dad slapped a mosquito on the point of his shoulder and got to his feet. He said, "Once the first one comes . . ." He took my hand to help me up. We scuttled inside the screen door of the boathouse. He picked up his old terry-cloth bathrobe with a hood and said, "You want to wear this to get back to the house? And I've got some bug repellent somewhere." His canvas tote bag was hanging on a peg. Tilting back his head to look through the bottom of his bifocals, he pulled out his vitamins, his melatonin, his cigar case, his Swiss Army knife, which still had its ivory toothpick. He shelved all these items on his forearm, which he held against his chest. He said, "Ah," and handed me a bottle of mosquito repellent. One by one he began to put the things on his forearm back into the bag, and I saw him not exactly through Fiona's eyes but over her shoulder. Over her shoulder but halfway in her mind as he rummaged to find one last thing to give her before she left. His mumbling slowness no longer exasperated her. Perhaps I had it wrong in an unimportant way, perhaps he was putting away the one last thing that she gave him. She didn't need to call on her patience—she was saying goodbye, her arms and legs were already giving in to a day of droning across the Pacific. I sensed other secrets in her out of my reach. But I sensed her sense of the two of them. Before, I'd only thought of Dad playing his solo airs; now I thought of their two voices—with words, without words—and their long attentive silences. I didn't hear anything they ever said, but I sensed the years. It was clear she'd loved him in spite of her sharp tongue and waywardness and that she still felt some inextinguishable tenderness up to the last. I let her go.

Dad was holding the hooded bathrobe for me. I put it on. I dabbed my legs and face with mosquito repellent. Dad said, "Take it with you. Maybe you'll need it. Maybe you'll come back down here for a late-night chat."

"What'll you do about the mosquitoes?"

Dad opened his bag and pulled out a fishing hat with an attached drapery of mosquito netting. He put it on, fluffed the netting around his face. "Maybe I'll wear it at supper. The veiled prophet." He took it off. He said, "We used to make you and Nora laugh a lot. Your mother and I. When you were little. So—how was it driving across the country together? You and Nora."

"Good," I said. "Really good. See you at the party."

◇

There were two big tables for the grown-ups and a small one for the children. The two babysitters sat at the small table. Grandma's nurse had a place next to her. It was a shock to see the nurse wheel Grandma in in a wheelchair, but when I bent to kiss her, she held my shoulders with strong hands and said, "Edith, dear girl."

Nora and I and Mom and Bonnie One were at Grandma's table, along with our two uncles and two of the big cousins. Dad was at the other table, next to Belle, Cousin John's pretty wife.

Mom came in from the kitchen—she and the actor-cook and the teenage daughter of the biggest big cousin were going to serve dinner.

I hadn't realized that one of the big cousins' wives was an Episcopalian priest. I poured myself a glass of wine and had it halfway to my lips when she stood up to say grace. Everyone stood up except Grandma. Everyone except Dad, Nora, Bonnie One, and me had gone to Episcopalian schools, the kind that have crew and compulsory chapel, so, when this priest in an evening gown said, "Bless, O Lord, this food to our use," they chimed right in with "And us to thy service. Amen." Before anyone sat down, Bonnie One cleared her throat and said, "And we ask a blessing for this wonderful family—and a special blessing for this wonderful woman, this mother and grandmother and great-grandmother. . . ."

Grandma said, "We needn't go into all *that.*"

Dad laughed, but so did Uncle Jonathan. And then three or four others. Mom and I said, "Shh."

There was a ragged group amen. Mom brought in a leg of lamb on a platter and put it in front of Uncle Jonathan with a vehement thud.

The actor-cook brought in another leg of lamb and put it in front of

Dad. Dad whetted the edge of the carving knife against a tine of the fork several times and said, "Look how crisp that is. Joss has a trick—half an hour before it's done, she takes a cup of coffee with cream and sugar in it and pours it right on top. Makes the skin sweet and crackly." He poised the knife to carve and then stopped. He said in his speech-making voice, "You know, the best grace I ever heard of comes from Borneo. There's this tribe there, and before every feast they say, 'O Lord, we thank you for making food taste good—you could have made it taste like parrot droppings.'"

Belle tilted her head, clutched Dad's arm, and laughed. Uncle Jonathan, who'd tipped his chair back to be sure to hear Dad, laughed too. Grandma put her hand on her nurse's arm and said, "What did he say?" The nurse leaned toward her and told her. When the nurse finished, Grandma said, "Well, I suppose that's funny, but someone should tell him to just calm down. You too, Jonathan."

Uncle Jonathan turned to Nora, pointed to Dad, and said, "But he started it." All the younger grown-ups and the kids laughed at the senior men being rowdy bad boys. I saw it more harshly. After all these years, Dad was reverting to his yard-dog reaction to Bonnie One. I heard that whole Borneo-tribe prayer as a stiff-legged, bristling woof-woof. I imagined someone giving Dad a description of some other woman in Bonnie One's situation here—a woman at a gathering of her lover's family, known and accepted by half of them, uncertain about the other half, tripped up in the middle of a saccharine but well-intentioned attempt to join in, and then laughed at. . . . If Dad heard all that as a stranger, I believe he would be sensibly sympathetic. Nora says he's a good judge. So where does his judicial temperament go when he's seized by bristling and woof-woofing?

I was angry for a while—after all, down at the boathouse I'd managed to drink a cup of kindness for Dad and his auld-lang-syne Fiona. But then, after the lamb course, Grandma sent her nurse to me to change places. When I sat down next to Grandma she clasped my hand and held it on the arm of her wheelchair. She said, "It's all right, Edith dear," and closed her eyes. Her hand was ancient. It was light and dry and fragile.

I softened toward Dad. I also felt how much of the volume of our life Grandma had framed. I wondered if it would hold in place as she was fading. Mom has Grandma's largeness of spirit. Her nephews adore her. I watched her teasing Cousin John halfway down the table from Grandma and me. Mom is a great appreciator of bad boys. I admire her, but she can't be the spirit of a settled place.

I studied Grandma's hand lying on mine, both our hands on that grooved aluminum arm of her wheelchair. The wheelchair was an intrusion in the large room, which floated tablecloths and candle flames and related faces. (I included Bonnie One, whom I call my stepmother, my small contribution, I suppose, to our volume.) The grooves in the aluminum pressed lightly on the back of my hand. Every other part of me was floating in the same weightless field as the tablecloths, flames, and faces. For a moment I imagined my hand was keeping Grandma afloat, peacefully apart from the gravity of time.

Mom got up and began to clear the table, rousting her two brothers to help. Grandma opened her eyes and said, "I've been away, haven't I?"

Cousin John came over and knelt on the other side of Grandma's wheelchair. Nora came and stood beside him, leaning down toward Grandma. Grandma said, "What are you—"

"I'm John," Cousin John said.

"I know who *you* are," Grandma said. "You're trouble." Grandma hooked a little finger around John's little finger and wiggled their hands, a flirtatious gesture she'd always used on the men in the house. She'd done it to Dad in the old days. Grandma said, "*What* are you two up to is what I want to know. I'll bet it's trouble."

Cousin John said, "I've come to move you back a little. I have to make room for your birthday cake. It's enormous."

Grandma said, "You watch out for him, Norrie. He's trouble."

Nora laughed, and that made Grandma laugh. She began to cough, and Nora held her water glass to her lips. Grandma waved it away with the back of her hand. She took a few breaths and said, "All right. Now." She used both hands to guide the glass to her mouth.

Everyone sang "Happy Birthday." Grandma's breath didn't reach the candles on the far side of the cake, which was two feet wide. Nora and Cousin John turned it around, but it still took Grandma three tries.

After supper Mom and Nora and I wheeled Grandma back to her bedroom. Grandma said, "Now you all go dance. I'll take a little nap, then maybe I'll come out again."

Mom said, "You gave a terrific party. Everyone's having a good time."

"I'm just sorry all your brothers didn't come," Grandma said.

"They're both here."

"No," Grandma said. "That other one. I'm sure he said he was coming."

Mom said firmly, "You're having a little delusion. You have two sons and they're both here."

Grandma stared straight ahead for a moment. Then she looked at me and said, "Is that right?"

I said, "Yes."

Grandma said to Mom, "Thank you. They don't always tell me these things." She closed her eyes. "I go away every now and then, and sometimes I bring back a funny idea." She opened her eyes and took Mom's hand. "Joss, be a dear and help me get ready for bed. I'll see you two girls later."

I kissed Grandma good night and stepped back. Grandma held Mom's hand on one side and Nora's on the other, smiled, and looked at me. She said, "You came such a long way, Edith dear. I'm so glad. Now take your sister to the dance. You two come and have breakfast with me tomorrow."

Nora and I stood in the hall. The nurse came past us and started to go in. Nora stopped her and said, "Our mother's with her. Could you give them another minute?"

The nurse said, "She's pretty excited by all this."

"Mom's getting her ready for bed," Nora said. "Grandma had a little delusional material but she handled it. Does she usually deal with it fairly quickly?"

"It depends."

"Well, does it happen more when she gets out of breath? I mean, would that affect her blood gases?"

The nurse said, "I suppose it might. Her doctor will be here tomorrow, and you can ask him. I'll just go in now and make sure everything's cozy."

After the nurse closed the door, Nora said to me, "Don't look at me like that. I was just giving Mom a little more time."

"Where'd you get that stuff about blood gases?"

Nora laughed and said, "'I'm not a doctor, but I play one on TV.' Let's go find Dad."

The big cousins were all dancing with each other's wives, Uncle Jonathan with his teenage granddaughter. Bonnie One was in the kitchen helping the actor-cook clean up.

I said, "He's probably gone down to the boathouse to smoke a cigar."

"Probably," Nora said.

"I hope he doesn't go wandering off in the boat."

"There's no wind."

"He might row. He likes to go off in the dark and get that little whiff of risk. It cheers him up, makes him feel like an adventurous boy."

Nora sighed. "I know. What's he going to do when he's as old as Grandma?"

I said, "What are *we* going to do?" I didn't mean it selfishly. I really wondered what we could do to make Dad happier. I thought of another knack of Grandma's that Dad had spoken of with wistful admiration. He'd said, "When she comes to visit she always leaves a day before you want her to.

And, come to think of it, conversations with her tend to be over a little sooner than I'd like."

I mentioned this to Nora as we slathered mosquito repellent on ourselves. Nora thought a moment and said, "Well, at least it's a knack he *admires*." Halfway to the boathouse she said, "And he's easier to tease off his long set-pieces these days. Grandma could always do that. I remember one time she swooped down on him and took hold of his beard." Nora did her Grandma voice—" 'Mike, dear boy—this is all so positively gripping, it's exhausting!' "

The water was only visible where stray light glistened on it. The boathouse door opened. Dad turned on the porch light. The yellow bulb lit up the inside of the screened-in cube, a tiny corner of the stage. Dad lit his cigar, sat in one of the Adirondack chairs, reached back, and turned off the light. Now there was just the glow through the dusty windowpanes and the red speck of Dad's cigar. I thought it was certainly not lit for comedy. But then Dad gave a raucous squawk. Nora laughed. She called out, "Dad! What was that? What are you doing? Remembering an embarrassing moment?"

Dad cleared his throat and said, "I'm practicing my green-heron call."

Nora laughed again, her laughter the equivalent of a brighter light.

When we came up to the screen door, Dad opened it halfway and blew smoke at the crack. He said, "Quick, quick. The mosquitoes are following you."

Nora patted his head and laughed again. We found two more chairs in the gloom. I said, "We were afraid you might have gone for a row."

"We could do that," Dad said. "There aren't any mosquitoes once you get out a ways on the water."

Nora and I both said, "No."

Dad was leaning forward. He said, "How's your grandmother? Did you get a chance to be with her? She was talking about you both all day long."

"She got tired," I said. "She'll see us for breakfast." I willed him to lean back in his chair.

He rested his elbows on his knees and ran a hand through his hair. "Well, it's good you're both here."

I said, "Dad. Do me a favor and sit back. I think you're about to jump up and do something."

Dad said, "What?" and grunted but settled back.

Nora and I both said, "Ahh . . ."

Dad said, "What is this?" and then laughed.

Nora said, "It's different being here now. All these new children. All these pretty wives. I don't feel as if I've grown up so much as grown out."

"Do you dream about this place?" Dad said.

"More often about just getting here than being here," Nora said. "Just turning into the driveway."

"Yes," I said. "Except I dream about those times when Grandma would send the big cousins off and take us to pick raspberries. Floating along with her in her mood . . . But it was our mood."

"Maybe we can take her raspberry-picking tomorrow," Nora said. "We can wheel her wheelchair along the driveway."

"I think your new cousins have pretty much cleaned out those raspberries," Dad said. "There might be some on the other side of the creek. I don't know how you'd get her wheelchair over there, though."

I said, "We could just pick flowers."

"Well, see how she feels."

Nora said, "She had a little delusion tonight, but Mom brought her right back. She started asking about her third son."

Dad said, "Maybe she was thinking about me."

I said, "You egomaniac!"

Dad said, "I only meant . . . ," and then his face sagged. He lifted his head, but it sank back.

Everything was still. With two words I'd pushed him all the way back into himself. He couldn't speak.

Inside my silence there was a swirl. It was as hot as Dad's was cold. I was horrified and sorry, and I felt pity, but the pity kept curling at the edges. I felt amazement at how powerfully he'd been knocked back, and with it a breeze of thrill. I hated it. Hating it didn't stop it.

Then I wondered in what tone I had said "You egomaniac!" Hissed it? Yelled it? Said it as slowly as a thumb pressing the plunger on a syringe? Or said it fast, sticking out my dagger to stop him before he took another step?

Dad and I were holding our breath. Then we breathed out at the same time. Dad said, "I only meant . . ."

I said, "I understand. You didn't mean—"

"No. I only meant . . . I only meant to make her mind wandering . . . seem less strange to you."

"Then I'm sorry."

How strange it felt to be the one who helped him when he lost his balance.

Perhaps all aging single fathers, once their capacities for vagabond adventures diminish, inevitably turn into captive Merlins, waiting spellbound in their solitary caves for their daughters' visits, sending out promissory bulletins of quiet behavior, of repentance for past blunderings, of newfound attentiveness and appreciations for their daughters, who are now the ones who can appear at will, or vanish.

◇

Nora and I talked about all the summers we could remember. Dad was subdued but attentive, the occasional brightening of his cigar tip signaling that he was anchored nearby.

Nora told him she'd come stay with him in August, after she finished a job at the movie studio in Wilmington, North Carolina.

Dad said, "You can stay in the bungalow. You'll have a little more elbow room."

Nora and I made a sympathetic noise; that was as close as we cared to come to saying we were sorry Fiona was gone for good.

"In fact," Dad said, "it makes tax sense for you to *own* the bungalow. I'll give it to both of you. It'll take a couple of years to keep it a nontaxable gift. If you rent it out, I'd like to have a say in who lives there, but you'd get the rent. We'll do the same thing with Edmond and Evelyn's cottage. And of course if *you* want to just stay a while . . ."

I said, "Don't you want to have a guest house? Who knows? You might have guests. Maybe you should give us the cottage, and you keep the bungalow."

"I use your mother's old studio as a guest room. Each of you should have a place of your own in your hometown."

I said, "Before supper you were telling me real estate is just real estate."

"Did I say that?"

"You were trying to get me to feel better about Mom and the uncles selling this place."

"Yes—but I don't think I said *that*. Anyway, I just thought you might like a little piece of the old homestead."

Nora and I said, "Of course."

Nora said, "That's great, Dad."

"It is," I said. "Thank you."

"Well, good."

Nora laughed and said, "At least we didn't have to make speeches about how much we love you to get our third of the kingdom."

There it was on the table—*King Lear* lit for comedy.

"Yeah, well," Dad said. "There ain't much kingdom to divvy up. You just better hope my pension'll cover an old-age home."

Nora said, "Oh, cut it out, Dad. You have years to go—you're thirty years younger than Grandma."

I said, "And you might still marry a rich widow."

"You shouldn't give your old-age-pensioner speech so often," Nora said. "You might slip into the part prematurely."

"I'm not sure I know that speech," I said.

"Sure you do."

"Remind me," I said.

"It's the one about his organs," Nora said.

"Oh, the old-age-pensioner *organs* speech."

"All right, all right," Dad said. "What a shame vaudeville is dead. You two could've replaced Gallagher and Sheen."

"Dad," I said. "You never saw Gallagher and Sheen. That was your *father.* What is this? You aren't satisfied with *old*? You're trying for *ancient*? You think that'll give you a leg up on *eternal*?

Dad laughed hard enough that his hand holding the cigar made a semaphore motion to the side. Nora laughed too, and I heard for the first time how completely she'd inherited Mom's laugh.

After that we got even sillier—single phrases, even single words set us off. Just to name a subject that one of us might conceivably make a joke about was joke enough.

And after that we drifted into a pleasant calm.

I thought of Mom's bending toward Grandma in a soft rush, of how Mom's love for Grandma comes out as boisterous tenderness, the way it did for us when we were young.

I could tell Dad was happy. When he spoke his voice was easy, no more insistent than the creek moving into the river. Nora bubbled up again. She asked Dad to do another heron squawk, but she started laughing before he made a sound.

"There's an interesting footnote to herons," Dad said. "There's an island in the Chesapeake called Wop Island, spelled W-O-P—it's on the navigational chart. It's called that because it's a rookery for black-crowned night herons, and black-crowned night herons go 'wop.' That's what the local watermen say. It's nothing to do with insulting Italians, it's because black-crowned night herons go 'wop.' Now, the great blue heron—"

Nora and I said "Dad . . ." and started laughing again.

"—gives a longer call. And that's all you two are going to get out of me. One day you'll want to know," Dad said, "and you'll feel this terrible gap in your education."

"Oh, all right," I said, "just one blue-heron squawk."

"Rawk," Dad said. "Rawk-rawk-rah-awk."

"You're such a pushover," Nora said, and I was reminded that Nora was right—it was easier with both of us there. For a while we'd suspended the weight of children leaving, of parents declining. On that small screened-in porch of the boathouse, Dad gave in to us and was playing with us as pleasantly as he had when we were very young, before Nora and I came into our first real alarms and sadnesses, the ones that couldn't be coaxed away. Now we found we could buoy him up too. Perhaps that was because we'd learned that by the time you get past the alarms and sadnesses of childhood there is, even in a life without catastrophe, only a short interval before you feel the first squeeze of perspective toward your vanishing point. Luckily it's possible, every now and then, to forget that you are moving toward it. It's possible to feel an intimacy that makes a still moment within its rush, creates a chamber out of shared memory and love in which someone else holds your attention and attends to you. In that fragile chamber you can keep the ghosts you love, not just their rights and wrongs, but the savor of their lives.

Nora and Dad started laughing again.

Acknowledgments

I wish to thank: Carol Brown Janeway, editor; Michael Carlisle, agent; Anthony Winner, Duncan Kennedy, Maud Innis Casey, and Eleanor Dudley Casey, readers and critics; Peter Spain, Katie Floyd, Anna Small, Susan Williamson, and Deborah Sussman Susser, typists, readers, and retypists; the American Academy in Rome for a residency in 1990–91; the Ingram Merrill Foundation for a fellowship in 1990–91; the American Academy of Arts and Letters for the Harold and Mildred Strauss Living Award (1992–97); the University of Virginia and the Sewanee Writers' Conference; and the harbor of my life, my family, especially Rosamond, Maud, Nell, Clare, and Julia Casey.

Permissions Acknowledgments

Grateful acknowledgment is made to the following for permission to reprint previously published material:

Alfred A. Knopf, Inc.: Excerpt from "Thirteen Ways of Looking at a Blackbird" from *Collected Poems* by Wallace Stevens, copyright 1923, copyright renewed 1951 by Wallace Stevens. Reprinted by permission of Alfred A. Knopf, Inc

Paramount Music Corporation and *Four Jays Music Publishing Co.:* Excerpt from "That's Amore" by Jack Brooks and Harry Warren, copyright 1953, copyright renewed 1981 by Paramount Music Corporation Reprinted by permission of Paramount Music Corporation and Four Jays Music Publishing Co , on behalf of the catalog of Harry Warren.

PolyGram International Publishing, Inc.: Excerpt from "Make Believe" by Jerome Kern and Oscar Hammerstein II, copyright 1927 by PolyGram International Publishing, Inc , copyright renewed. All rights reserved. Reprinted by permission of PolyGram International Publishing, Inc

Warner Bros. Publications U.S. Inc.: Excerpt from "Brush Up Your Shakespeare" by Cole Porter, copyright 1949 by Cole Porter, copyright renewed, assigned to John F. Wharton, Trustee of the Cole Porter Music & Literary Property Trusts. Chappell & Co. owner of publication and allied rights throughout the world. All rights reserved. Reprinted by permission of Warner Bros Publications U.S. Inc., Miami, Florida, 33014.

Williamson Music: Excerpts from "Stan' Up an' Fight" by Oscar Hammerstein II and Georges Bizet, copyright 1943 by Williamson Music, copyright renewed. International copyright secured. All rights reserved. Reprinted by permission of Williamson Music, a division of the Rodgers & Hammerstein Organization.

Adam Yarmolinsky: Excerpt from "Pity" by Babette Deutsch. Reprinted by permission of Adam Yarmolinsky, Literary Executor of the Babette Deutsch Estate.

ALSO BY JOHN CASEY

SPARTINA

A classic tale of a man, a boat, and a storm, *Spartina* is the story of Dick Pierce, a commercial fisherman along the shores of Rhode Island's Narragansett Bay. A kind, sensitive family man, he is also prone to irascible outbursts against the people he must work for now that he can no longer make his living from the sea.

Pierce's one great passion, a fifty-foot fishing boat called *Spartina*, lies unfinished in his yard. Determined to get the funds to buy her engine, he takes a foolish risk. But his real test comes when he must weather a storm at sea in order to keep his dream alive.

National Book Award Winner

Fiction/Literature/0-375-70268-7